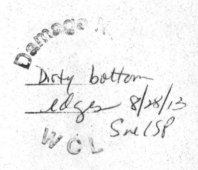

Imager's Battalion

Tor Books by L. E. Modesitt, Jr.

Imager's Battalion

The Sixth Book of the
Imager Portfolio

L. E. MODESITT, JR.

TOR®

A Tom Doherty Associates Book

NEW YORK

This is a work of fiction. All of the characters, organizations, and events portrayed in this novel are either products of the author's imagination or are used fictitiously.

IMAGER'S BATTALION: THE SIXTH BOOK OF THE IMAGER PORTFOLIO

Copyright © 2013 by L. E. Modesitt, Jr.

Map by Jon Lansberg

A Tor Book
Published by Tom Doherty Associates, LLC
175 Fifth Avenue
New York, NY 10010

www.tor-forge.com

Tor® is a registered trademark of Tom Doherty Associates, LLC.

ISBN 978-0-7653-3283-7 (hardcover)
ISBN 978-1-4299-6548-4 (e-book)

First Edition: January 2013

Printed in the United States of America

0 9 8 7 6 5 4 3 2 1

For Logan Elizabeth

CHARACTERS

Bhayar	Lord of Telaryn
Aelina	Wife of Bhayar
Kharst	Rex of Bovaria
Aliaro	Autarch of Antiago
Quaeryt	Subcommander Fifth Battalion, Imager, and friend of Bhayar
Vaelora	Wife of Quaeryt and youngest sister of Bhayar
Deucalon	Marshal of Telaryn
Myskyl	Submarshal of Telaryn
Skarpa	Commander, Third Regiment
Meinyt	Subcommander, Fifth Regiment
Khaern	Subcommander, Eleventh Regiment
Zhelan	Major, Fifth Battalion
Calkoran	Major, Second Company, Fifth Battalion
Zhael	Major, Third Company, Fifth Battalion
Arion	Major, Fourth Company, Fifth Battalion
Voltyr	Imager Undercaptain
Shaelyt	Imager Undercaptain, Pharsi
Threkhyl	Imager Undercaptain
Desyrk	Imager Undercaptain
Akoryt	Imager Undercaptain
Baelthm	Imager Undercaptain
Khalis	Imager Undercaptain, Pharsi
Lhandor	Imager Undercaptain, Pharsi
Horan	Imager Undercaptain
Smaethyl	Imager Undercaptain

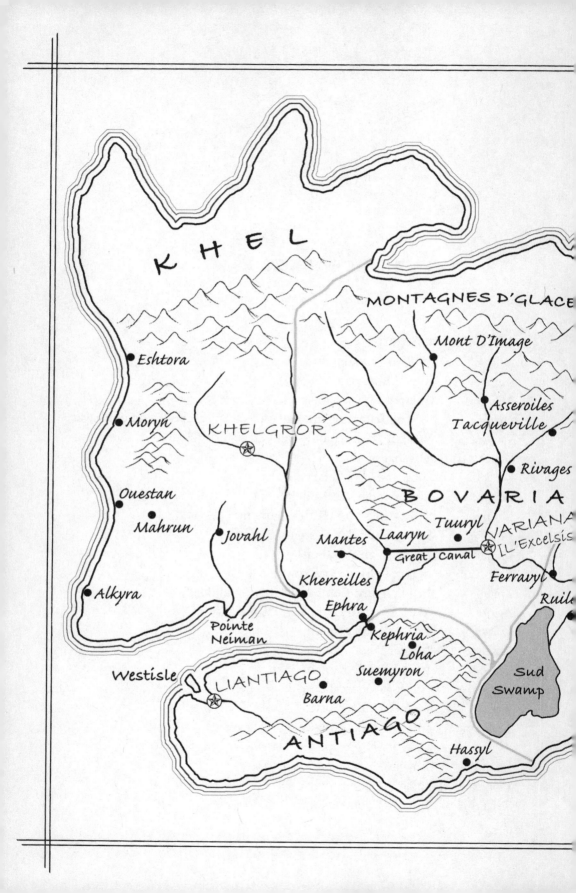

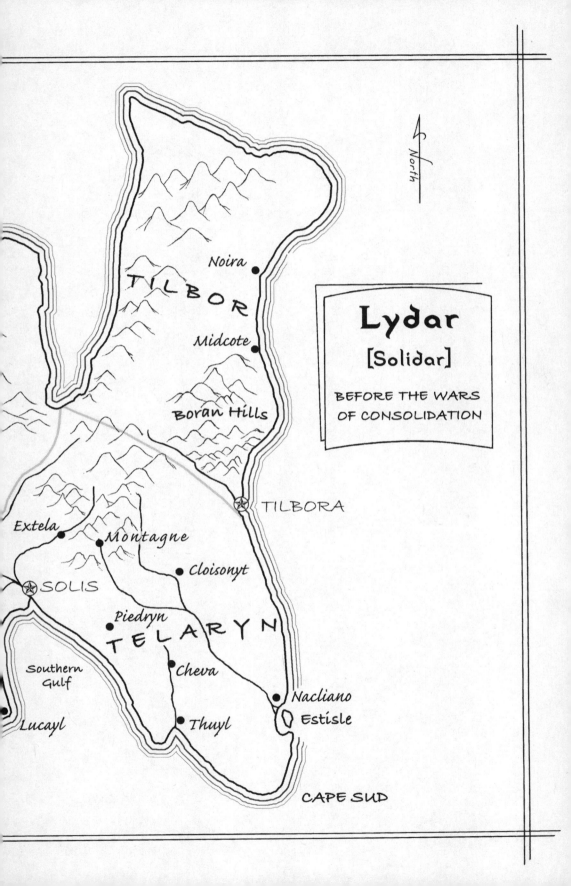

North

Lydar
[Solidar]

**BEFORE THE WARS
OF CONSOLIDATION**

Noira

TILBOR

Midcote

Boran Hills

⊛ TILBORA

Extela

Montagne

Cloisonyt

⊛ SOLIS

Piedryn

TELARYN

Southern
Gulf

Cheva

Nacliano

Estisle

Lucayl

Thuyl

CAPE SUD

Imager's Battalion

In the early summer afternoon, Quaeryt paced back and forth across the narrow stone stoop outside the main entrance to the hold house at Nordruil, occasionally blotting the sweat off his forehead, and glancing up at the worn and graying limestone walls and the single square tower that was likely centuries old. The grounds had received indifferent care, and it was clear that the hold house had been cleaned quickly and received new linens just before he had arrived, along with a few rankers and others to assist the hold staff.

Just for Vaelora and me? That was only one of the things that worried Quaeryt about what Bhayar had in mind.

Quaeryt had been waiting for Vaelora for well over a week. He had mostly recovered from the efforts that had changed the battle over Ferravyl from what would have likely been a bloody standoff into an overwhelming victory for Lord Bhayar and Telaryn—but at the uncounted cost of revealing to Bhayar the scope of his imaging abilities . . . and the other cost he had not even imagined. He shook his head, not wanting to think about it, or about the icy dreams, along with the bruises and strained muscles, that had kept him from sleeping on several nights.

Before all that long, he'd be recalled to duty on the forthcoming campaign into Bovaria . . . and yet Bhayar had insisted that Quaeryt recover at one of Bhayar's less imposing estates and wait for the arrival of Vaelora.

Is that to keep me away from the commanders and the imagers? Why? So he and Myskyl or Deucalon can see if they can do without me? Somehow, Quaeryt had strong doubts that Bhayar's protestations of concern about him were the only reasons why he had been recuperating in the comparative luxury available at Nordruil, even awaiting Vaelora. Especially since he likely would only be able to spend a few days with her.

He paced back across the stones once again. A courier had galloped up less than a glass before, saying that his wife was some three milles away. Since then, every moment of that Mardi afternoon had felt like a quint, every quint like a glass. He'd even asked the kitchen staff to have a light afternoon meal ready; not that he felt like eating, but she might well after the long ride.

What is taking her so long? He glanced toward the long winding drive once again, then stopped as he saw riders. He forced himself to stand still and wait while they rode up the narrow worn and graveled way. When they were more than a hundred yards away, he could see Vaelora, with Captain Eleryt riding beside her, and a full company following them.

Once more, he was amazed at the grace with which she rode and what a striking figure she was in the saddle. *But then, you've always found her so.*

Their eyes held each other's as soon as she turned her mount around the overgrown garden that the approach drive circled, although neither spoke as she rode toward him and then reined up.

"My thanks to you, Captain." Quaeryt inclined his head to Eleryt, then stepped down to the mounting block.

"My pleasure, sir."

Quaeryt was already looking into Vaelora's light brown eyes, even before she dismounted and stepped into his arms. For several moments he just held her before murmuring, in Bovarian, as they did when alone, "I missed you."

"I missed you, too." Her arms tightened about him.

"I worried about you."

"Worried about me? When I heard you'd been injured . . ." Vaelora eased back. "I didn't hurt you?"

"It wasn't that kind of injury. I got caught in the ice storm." He lowered his voice. "I'll explain later."

"You'd better," she whispered as her arms went around him again, if but for a long moment before she stepped back. "It's been a long ride, and I was so worried."

"Would you like something to eat?"

"If you wouldn't mind, dearest." Her smile was impish. "If it doesn't take too long to prepare . . ."

"Those should have been my words," he replied with a soft laugh.

"I said them for you . . . but I am hungry."

"I thought you might be. I asked the kitchen to have a light meal ready." Quaeryt turned to Eleryt, who remained waiting. "I do apologize, Captain, for my preoccupation. There are refreshments for you and your men and quarters as well. Lord Bhayar has requested that you remain here until further notice. I trust that will not inconvenience you and them."

Eleryt smiled. "Sir . . . that is not a problem."

Quaeryt understood that, since Eleryt's company would have better quarters and fare. "We will talk later."

"Yes, sir."

As two of the rankers assigned to Nordruil hurried out to unload Vaelora's gear, Quaeryt took his wife's arm and led her through an ancient square arch into the hold house, guiding her toward the shaded rear terrace beside the fountains, far cooler than any chamber inside.

"I've never been here before," said Vaelora, her eyes taking in the stone walls of the main corridor as they passed through the receiving hall.

"Until last week, I don't think Bhayar had been, either," replied Quaeryt. The thought that Bhayar had so many properties that he'd never even visited one as large as Nordruil—and that Bhayar thought it small—still amazed Quaeryt, although he understood how that could be as they walked past the matching parlors, and then the main dining hall and the grand salon, and finally into the study, with its single wall of books, and out through the double doors and onto the terrace, where a table for two awaited them.

"What would you like to drink?" asked Quaeryt after he seated her.

"A pale or amber lager, please." Vaelora looked to the serving woman.

"Two, please," added Quaeryt.

The one serving woman eased away, and another placed melon slices before each of them, graced on the side with lime wedges. The first returned with two beakers of a pale golden lager.

"Thank you," said Quaeryt quietly.

Vaelora immediately took a lime wedge and squeezed it over the melon, then began to devour the melon—if gracefully, Quaeryt noted.

He ate his own melon not quite so quickly, but asked as he finished, "How was your journey?"

"I can't believe I ate that so quickly." Vaelora blotted her lips with the pale cream linen napkin. "The ride was long and hard. I'm a bit sore in places. I was so worried about you. Yet I had the feeling that you would be all right. Then I worried I was deceiving myself."

"I worried about you . . ."

"You need to worry about yourself, dearest."

"I usually don't have time for that, and when I do, it doesn't matter, and I worry about you."

"Keep saying things like that." Vaelora took a sip of the lager. "This isn't bad."

"For the south, you mean?" Quaeryt grinned.

Vaelora returned the expression.

In the momentary silence he could hear the raucous call of a bird, most likely a redjay, coming from the gardens to beyond the lawn behind the terrace.

The first serving woman removed the melon platters, and the second replaced them with strips of chilled seasoned fowl, accompanied by sliced early peaches drizzled with thick cream.

Quaeryt was surprised to find that he was actually hungry, and neither of them spoke for a time.

"Are you going to tell me what happened?" asked Vaelora. After a moment she went on. "Bhayar met me in Ferravyl. He told me about the ice storm, and how the imagers exploded the Bovarian barges."

Quaeryt couldn't help but frown.

"Dearest . . . he is my brother, and we spoke for less than a glass. He was very earnest in not wanting to delay my reaching you."

"I'm certain he was earnest about that."

"We can talk about him later. I want to know about you."

Quaeryt glanced to the side of the terrace where the two servers stood, then back to Vaelora.

She nodded in understanding. "Just what happened, although they may not speak Bovarian that well."

"The ice came down in sheets. Most of it covered the Bovarians. Bhayar said that we lost almost a battalion. They lost close to eight regiments. It was truly awful." He paused. "Yet . . . we were so evenly matched that . . . without the storm . . . we both might have lost even more." He shook his head.

"What about you? When I heard . . . That was why I rode from first light into the night every day."

"I was caught close to the ice. They told me I didn't wake for three days, and they weren't sure I would. They piled quilts over me . . ." He shook his head wryly. "I finally woke up sweating."

"You did too much."

"Anything less wouldn't have worked." His eyes again flicked toward the serving women.

"You can tell me more . . . later." Vaelora took a last swallow from her beaker. As she set it down, her eyes met his again.

Quaeryt blushed.

"Would you mind . . . dearest . . . if I bathed?"

"Of course not."

"You could . . . keep me company . . ." Her smile and eyes were more than inviting as she glanced to the upper levels of the hold house and then back to Quaeryt.

As he rose and guided her from her chair, Quaeryt doubted he would recall what he ate.

Later—much later, in the orangish glow of twilight—Vaelora sat up in the ancient goldenwood bed. "You're looking at me as if you've never seen me this way before."

I haven't . . . not exactly like this . . . not understanding what I might have lost. "I told you. I missed you. There were times when I didn't know if I'd see you again."

"You got my letters?"

"I got the note you left in my saddlebag, and the one you wrote about the warm rain . . . that was what made it all possible. I don't know that I would have thought it out without your letter."

"I'm glad. I think you would have, but I wanted to make sure . . . or try to." After a moment she went on. "I told you that Bhayar did not wish to delay my reaching you. After seeing your bruises and . . . everything . . . I can see why." She reached out and let her fingers run down the side of his face, along his jawline, before leaning forward and kissing him. Then she straightened, slightly disentangling herself from his arms. "I'm not going anywhere. Nor are you. Not in the next few days, anyway."

Quaeryt couldn't help but frown. "He told you that?"

"He told me more than that. He was proud of what you did. He won't tell you." She paused. "How did you do it?"

"I told you—"

"Dearest . . . it had to be more than warm rain, did it not?"

"It was mostly warm rain . . ." He paused, yet . . . who else could he tell? "Imaging takes heat . . . or something like it. Everyone thinks that the rain froze the Bovarians." He shook his head slowly. "I'm not certain, but I think the imaging froze them first, and the ice rain coated them afterward."

"The imaging . . . it sucked the warmth out of them?"

He nodded. "I fear so."

"Have you told Bhayar?"

"I've told no one but you."

"Good. Never tell anyone else."

"I dare not tell Bhayar. Not the way he is playing us both."

"Of course he is. What else would you expect? You've proved to be a great weapon, and you love me, and I love you. He'll use both of us to become the ruler of all Lydar . . . or destroy us all in trying."

Quaeryt was still astounded at the matter-of-fact way in which she regarded her brother and how she could balance sisterly affection with cold calculation in assessing Bhayar. *Then again, it could just be that women are better at that than men.* Quaeryt didn't know. He only knew that Vaelora was adept at seeing the undercurrents between people, but he'd never really known another woman, except in a casual sense, and he'd never talked as honestly to anyone as he did to her. "I don't see destroying him, first or later, as a good idea, either."

"No, someone has to unite Lydar, and we'll all be better off under him . . . especially with you at his side."

"That's not exactly a foregone conclusion," Quaeryt pointed out.

"It's anything but," Vaelora replied, "except the alternatives would be less happy for both of us."

Quaeryt nodded slowly. History indicated that the relatives of unsuccessful conquerors seldom survived, and an imager who served such a ruler certainly wouldn't—unless they fled in obscurity, and that wasn't a path Quaeryt wanted to take . . . and doubted Vaelora did, either.

He laughed, not quite bitterly. "That appears to be settled."

"There's another complication, dearest." Vaelora smiled.

"Complication?"

"It's early . . . but women in our family know almost immediately."

Women in your family? Quaeryt swallowed. "You're not . . ."

She nodded. "I feel that she'll be a girl."

"Does Bhayar know?"

"No. And he won't, not until long after you and he leave Ferravyl."

Quaeryt didn't know what to say.

"I . . . decided . . . on those last days in Tresrives. I knew you'd be safe. But . . . I still couldn't let you go . . . not without . . . I just couldn't." Her eyes were bright.

Quaeryt leaned forward and folded his arms around her. "I love you. I love you both . . ." He could feel his own eyes tearing up.

As Quaeryt and Vaelora finished breakfast on Meredi, a meal taken somewhat later than was usual for them, Quaeryt lifted the small volume. "This is the book I was telling you about."

"The one about Rholan?"

He nodded as he handed it to her, after opening it to the title page, which held only the title *Rholan and the Nameless* and the words "Cloisonyt, Tela."

"The title is ironic, you know?" observed Vaelora, taking the small volume.

"More like a double meaning." He paused, then rose from the table on the terrace and walked to stand at her shoulder. "There's one page I thought you might find especially interesting. That's where I put the bookmark." He watched as she turned to the marked page, reading over her shoulder as she scanned the text.

> Rholan spoke at many times and in many places about the vanity of attempting to achieve greatness, most notably at Gahenyara before his last trip to Cloisonyt, but it is interesting to note that he never spoke of the cost of actually accomplishing great deeds . . .

"He spoke in Gahenyara? There are no family stories about him, and you'd think there would be," mused Vaelora.

"Read on," suggested Quaeryt.

> Many have suggested that Rholan was a giant of a man, a great warrior, with shoulders a yard across and thews like the trunk of an oak, green-eyed and black-haired with a full black beard, others that he was small and slender, almost frail, with fine red hair and piercing blue eyes. Neither description is accurate. In his prime, he was a man slightly larger than most other men, but by no more than a few digits in height. His eyes were black and his hair white-blond, and his left arm was shorter than his right, and crooked, as

a result of breaking it while trying to chop down a young oak tree
as a youth . . .

"A lost one?" asked Vaelora.

"The author never says . . . not in what I've read so far, anyway."

"And you haven't read it all while you were waiting for me?" teased
Vaelora. "You just pined for me?"

"I did indeed pine for you, as you should be able to tell . . ."

Vaelora blushed, then closed the book and looked up at him. "Tell me
you have not read every page of this volume."

"I should have said that I have read nothing that names a lost one, or
singles out Rholan as one of any such group." Even as he spoke, Quaeryt
frowned. *Someone* had said something like that . . . somewhere. When had
that been . . . ?

At the sound of boots on the terrace stone, Quaeryt turned to face the
ranker who had hurried out through the double doors from the study.
"Yes? What is it?"

"Lord Bhayar is riding up the drive, sir."

Quaeryt turned to Vaelora. "We will have to discuss my reading later,
my lady. Shall we go greet your brother?"

"We should." Vaelora rose. "He would be disappointed otherwise."

Left unsaid, as they reentered the hold house and walked toward the
main entrance, was that neither intended to disappoint Bhayar—at present.

The Lord of Telaryn had not yet reached the largely neglected circular
garden around which the entry drive curved to the main entrance when
Quaeryt and Vaelora took positions on the wide stone stoop. They watched
the company of Telaryn troopers follow Bhayar and then rein up around
the drive as Bhayar rode forward to the entry, followed by a single ranker,
and halted the large gray gelding.

"You both look far happier than when I last saw either of you," announced Bhayar as he dismounted and handed the gelding's reins to the
trooper behind him. He walked up the steps briskly and stopped, survey-
ing the couple. "I had hoped that would be the case."

"Dear brother, you did more than hope," said Vaelora. "You made it
possible."

"One still hopes. Not everyone knows what is in their best interests,
even those to whom one is related."

"You have always held our interests dear," replied Quaeryt.

"As I should, for those who are related and who hold a ruler's interests as dearly as their own are few indeed." Bhayar smiled, and for an instant even his dark blue eyes smiled as well. "But, alas, I am here to inform you of your increased responsibilities." His eyes turned to his sister. "You should join us in the study as well, so that you may tell Aelina all that is planned when you return to Solis. You will return with my personal guard this time, because your husband will need every company under his command and that of Subcommander Meinyt."

Subcommander Meinyt? Quaeryt didn't like the sound of Meinyt's promotion at all; not that Meinyt didn't deserve it, but because it signified that Bhayar had something in mind that was potentially dangerous to Quaeryt and the imagers. Still, Quaeryt merely nodded as he and Vaelora followed Bhayar into the hold house.

Behind them the company of troopers rode slowly to the side courtyard.

When the three entered the study, Vaelora nodded to Quaeryt, then closed the door from the corridor before walking to the double doors and closing them.

Bhayar pulled a chair up to the small circular table, but waited for Quaeryt and Vaelora to move to the other chairs before seating himself.

The Lord of Telaryn looked to his sister. "I think this marriage has been good for you."

"I don't know that marriage has been good to me, but Quaeryt has been," replied Vaelora.

"Good. Keep it that way . . . both of you." After a pause, he went on. "Much as your domestic happiness pleases me, that is obviously not why I am here."

"You're here to tell us what our roles are in the coming campaign." Vaelora smiled sweetly. "I am to provide you and Quaeryt with my thoughts and observations and then retire to Solis and console Aelina while you and Quaeryt begin the long and arduous conquest of Bovaria."

"Not exactly, sister dearest. You and Aelina know the internal and court politics as well as anyone. You also have seen Quaeryt struggle with balancing the finances of a province, as Aelina has seen me do with all Telaryn. You will return to Solis with a document of financial regency which places you and Aelina in command of the finances of Telaryn until my return to Solis, with full access to all ledgers and accounts. In practice, what this means is that you two jointly have the power to stop any uses of tariff revenues that do not directly support the war against Bovaria. There is also a letter to Finance Minister Haaraxes that declares that any attempt on his part to thwart or oppose your exercise of that power will be regarded as treason. He may appeal a decision you make to me, but he must abide by it, until I decide."

"In short, matters proceed as they always have unless we act, and in all likelihood, we will be limited in what we do."

"Exactly. Except . . . except . . . it allows me to summarily execute Haaraxes if he indulges in more than petty thievery, with no complaints by the High Holders or other ministers. The document will make that most clear." Bhayar turned to Quaeryt. "While you have been recovering, we have developed a plan of attack and restructured our forces to accomplish that attack. We have formed armies of the south and of the north. The army of the north will advance westward along the north river road of the Aluse directly to Variana. Because most of the population in the area is on the north side, this will be the larger force."

Quaeryt had a good idea with which force he and his imagers would be placed, but he just listened.

"The initial force that will travel the south river road, or what passes for it, will be commanded by Commander Skarpa and will consist of two regiments and a full battalion. Those will be Skarpa's Third Tilboran Regiment, the newly constituted Fifth Tilboran Regiment under Subcommander Meinyt, and the Fifth Montagne Battalion under you. That title is largely for effect and because you were governor of Montagne."

Worse and worse . . . if interesting. Quaeryt nodded again.

"Marshal Deucalon, Submarshal Myskyl, and I were not at all pleased with the performance of the Second Ryntaran Regiment from Piedryn. So we have implemented a certain amount of reorganization. Two battalions from Second Ryntaran have been transferred to First Tilboran under Submarshal Myskyl. That allowed us to transfer two battalions from First Tilboran to Third, which in turn allowed Third and Fourth Battalion of Third Tilboran to be moved and become the core of the new Fifth Tilboran, along with the remaining two battalions from Second Ryntaran . . ."

That made sense to Quaeryt. Skarpa, Myskyl, and Meinyt were all good officers, and especially good at training and improving troopers, although Quaeryt trusted Myskyl not at all.

"You and Major Zhelan face a challenge and an opportunity." Bhayar did not smile as he spoke, for which Quaeryt was grateful. "Your first company will remain as it has. Your second, third, and fourth companies are not properly from Montagne. They actually consist largely of Khellan cavalry that spent nearly two years making their way through the Montagnes D'Glace after the battle of Khelgror. There were originally close to two regiments, but the mountains and the winters were hard on them . . ."

Khellan cavalry . . . riding for two years . . . Quaeryt had heard about the Bovarian savagery reputed to have followed the fall of Khel, but to cross the continent by way of the northern mountains?

"For reasons we all know," Bhayar continued, "they wish to be part of the campaign against the Bovarians. They know of the background of our family, and they asked if there happened to be a Pharsi officer under whom they could serve. I told them that the best I could do was a Telaryn officer who was of Pharsi descent and married to my sister." Bhayar did smile, if faintly. "I felt that was an accurate representation . . . was it not?"

More accurate even than you know, it appears. "That was accurate, sir," replied Quaeryt.

Vaelora nodded.

"That will provide a full battalion under you, but Marshal Deucalon thought it might be best if Major Zhelan remained as your second in command. Major Zhelan expressed pleasure at remaining as well."

"Zhelan is an accomplished and practical officer," said Quaeryt.

"As are you, from all reports." Bhayar leaned back slightly in the wooden armchair. "We have had to wait some for additional forces, and there are others that will join us as they can. Kharst has likely only received reports of what occurred at Ferravyl in the last week, and there will be no reports on what we plan to do. He will doubtless pull troops from the border with Antiago, but those will likely withdraw directly to the area around Variana. He will be using conscripts, perhaps heavily. We will move decisively, and it is likely that we will not face great resistance until we near Variana . . ."

As Bhayar continued to summarize the situation, Quaeryt and Vaelora listened.

". . . unlikely Kharst has many imagers, if any, and they will be held in reserve. I would prefer that you not strain yourself or your imagers any more than necessary." Bhayar stopped and cleared his throat. "And now, I must take my leave. I expect you to spend Vendrei and Samedi in Ferravyl with your forces. You may take Solayi off, as will all forces, and we will set out on Lundi, we for the west, sister dear, and you for Solis." Bhayar rose from the table.

Quaeryt stood, as did Vaelora, although Vaelora did so in a deliberate if graceful way, almost as if grudgingly. Both accompanied Bhayar to the main door and outside.

There, Bhayar turned and inclined his head. "My personal guard will be here for you, Vaelora dear, by seventh glass on Lundi. There will be a leather folder with my authorization for you and Aelina."

"You think of everything, brother dear."

"I do attempt such, but dealing with you, as your husband will discover, if he has not already, can be a challenge." With a broad smile, Bhayar mounted the gray.

Quaeryt and Vaelora watched as he rode down the drive and joined the waiting troopers.

"How much does he know?" asked Quaeryt.

"About you . . . being a lost one? Or as strong an imager as you are?" Vaelora paused. "I could not say. I doubt he actually knows everything, but one of Bhayar's strengths has always been a feel for what is so, even when he does not know."

"He also has no illusions about people."

"Dearest . . . no successful ruler does."

Quaeryt laughed, then took Vaelora's hand as they turned and stepped back into the hold house.

On Jeudi morning, while Vaelora finished dressing, Quaeryt picked up the small book that appeared to be both a biography and a commentary on the life of Rholan, and as seemed often to be the case, he found himself rereading a section with particular interest.

No deity, should one exist, needs a name. Those who worship such a deity need that name, for otherwise how can they be certain that their prayers, their hopes, and their plaints go to whom they are meant to be addressed. Gods do not need worshippers, but most people need gods. Rholan addressed the paradox of names by calling the almighty "the Nameless," a stratagem far more clever than either his contemporaries or those claiming scholarly insight have seemed able to recognize.

As Vaelora stepped from the dressing chamber, Quaeryt closed the small book, smiling in spite of himself.

"Is that smile for what I'm wearing?" asked Vaelora, her voice mock-stern.

"Hardly, dear. I'd smile were you wearing nothing."

"You'd smile far more than that. You always do."

"Can I help the fact that I find you beautiful?"

"Lust can make any woman beautiful."

Quaeryt had strong doubts about that, because one of the aspects of Vaelora he found so appealing was her intelligence. After all, her letters had captured him even when he'd had no thought of anything more. "You will write me . . . as you did before?"

Vaelora blinked, as if what he'd said had no relation to what they'd been discussing. "What . . . ?"

"I was thinking about your letters, that I found what you wrote so entrancing . . ."

She laughed softly. "You still surprise me."

"I hope I always will . . . in a good fashion."

From the bedchamber, with its antique stone walls, walls softened somewhat by the not quite so ancient cloth hangings, they made their way down the stone steps barely wide enough for two abreast and then to the small breakfast room, rather than the terrace, since the night had brought rain and drizzle.

Again, as he ate the near-perfect omelet that the serving woman placed on his platter, he thought about the days ahead with hard rations, or worse. He smiled wryly.

"What are you finding so amusing?" Vaelora's tone was openly curious.

"How life changes. A year ago, I wouldn't have dreamed of having so much good food, when even decent meals strained my purse, and there were times when regimental rations would have seemed a luxury. Now . . ." He shrugged.

"Dearest . . . it comes with a price. Have you not noticed? Did not our stay in Extela . . . ?"

He nodded. "Part of that price was because I chose accomplishment over popularity when I had not time to achieve both."

"Dearest . . . there is always that choice."

Quaeryt smiled. "Not if the one who seeks accomplishment is not the one who needs popularity . . . or one to whom little attention is paid. We talked of this before. Perhaps as a mere subcommander . . ."

"Even that is dangerous . . ."

"Perhaps," Quaeryt replied, "but my idea of costs and prices may not be what you have in mind. What are yours?"

"Little more than a year ago, you could have walked away from danger, or handled it quietly, with no one being the wiser. In fact, I'd wager you did. Can you do that now? A year ago, the only one whom you hazarded by your acts was you. Now . . . tell me what might have happened had you failed in the warm rain."

"I would have died," he replied dryly, "but that wasn't what you meant. Thousands of troopers would have died as well."

"And . . . ?"

"Your point is taken, dearest." Of course, Quaeryt had known what she meant. He still didn't like thinking about matters in those terms.

"You don't like admitting that you have hostages to fortune. You also do not wish to admit that your sense of responsibility makes you a captive of others and of fate." Vaelora sipped her hot tea.

"Does any man with any sense wish to admit that?" Quaeryt lifted a beaker of lager and took a swallow. In the summer, at least in the hot

midlands, tea was too warm for him even at breakfast, even when breakfast was early, not that this morning it was anywhere close to early.

"There is a difference between admitting it publicly and admitting it
to one's self."

"You're all too right, dear, but there are those who publicly profess to
have hostages to fortune, and who in the end act as if those hostages have
no worth to them at all. More than a few rulers—or those who wish to
rule—have been such."

"Are you saying Bhayar is?" Vaelora raised her eyebrows.

"I suspect he is of the other type, who denies that those who are close
to him have any value, while quietly valuing them."

"Why do you say that?"

"Think upon our marriage. Ostensibly, he punished you for your apparent willfulness by marrying you to someone beneath your station. Yet . . ."
Quaeryt shrugged.

"Yet what, dearest?"

Quaeryt grinned and ignored the slight edge in her voice. "He did not
go against your wishes and marry you to someone you could not stand."

"There are times," she responded, her voice holding a hint of playful-
ness.

Quaeryt was about to respond when he heard bootsteps. He waited.

"Sir . . . there's a Commander Skarpa who just arrived from Ferravyl to
see you . . ." offered one of the rankers from the door to the breakfast room.

"Escort him to the study. I'll meet him there."

"Do you think . . . ?" asked Vaelora.

"I don't think so. I'd judge he wants to see me before I return to talk
over how he'd like us to work together.' Quaeryt stood and smiled wryly.
"But you never know."

He reached the center hall at the same time as did Skarpa. The ranker
escorting the senior officer stepped back in deference to Quaeryt. The
commander had obviously worn an oilcloth waterproof, since his uniform
shirt and tunic were dry, while his trousers beneath the knees were wet.

"I hope the ride wasn't too difficult," offered Quaeryt, gesturing down
a corridor made gloomy by the heavy clouds outside.

"Wet, and long, but not hard."

"You could have sent word for me to see you early tomorrow."

"Then I'd have gotten a courier soaked and made tomorrow even longer for both of us."

Quaeryt reached the study and motioned for Skarpa to enter, then followed, closing the door behind himself. Skarpa stopped and extended a visor cap, an officer's cap with the insignia of the double moons. "I thought you might like a replacement. I heard yours fell apart . . . in the ice. You'll need it here in the south."

"Oh . . . thank you." Quaeryt almost flushed as he took the visor cap. He'd never thought about the cap. Half the time, he forgot he was wearing it. Sometimes, he'd just forgotten it. He stepped toward the circular table, where he seated himself, as did Skarpa.

"I wanted to talk with you where we wouldn't be interrupted before you returned to Ferravyl," said Skarpa.

"That suggests problems or matters of which I'm unaware . . . if not both."

"There are always problems. Sometimes, we just don't recognize them. Sometimes, they're people who shouldn't be problems, and sometimes we hope, against hope, that they'll disappear." Skarpa laughed. "I learned a long time ago that it's best not to rely on hope if there are other paths. I'd rather save my hoping for times when there is no other way."

"What are the people problems?" asked Quaeryt.

Skarpa shook his head. "I don't know, except it takes Deucalon far too long to decide. That happens most often when a subordinate raises too many questions that don't matter."

"You don't have any idea?"

"No. Even if I did, what difference would it make? He won't listen to the most junior commander about subcommanders and majors he's worked with for months or years. Especially not about more senior commanders."

Quaeryt could see that.

After a moment of silence Skarpa said, "I understand Lord Bhayar visited you yesterday. I presume he did discuss more than family."

"I understand Zhelan and I will have to deal with three Khellan companies . . ."

"It's worse than that. Each company is led by a Pharsi officer who used to be the equivalent of a major or a subcommander, with another officer below him, and most of the troopers don't speak either Tellan or Bovarian. The officers speak both Bovarian and Pharsi. That was another reason for putting them under you."

"Another reason?" inquired Quaeryt lightly. "Besides the fact that he can claim I'm of Pharsi descent?"

Skarpa nodded, then said slowly, "There's also the fact that people around you who aren't loyal to Lord Bhayar . . . don't . . . prosper. And that you seem to know quickly who they are."

"How many officers besides you have come to those conclusions?"

"Myskyl, of course, and he told Deucalon. Every officer in all the Tilboran regiments." Skarpa grinned. "So by now . . . just about every officer."

On top of everything else . . . Quaeryt shook his head.

"Could any of your imager undercaptains handle his own company?" asked Skarpa. "Not now, of course. We don't have the troopers. I'd like to start, when you think it possible, by giving each a squad, with a senior squad leader at their elbow."

"I wouldn't put any of them in command yet . . . even of a squad." *They know far less than I did, and I knew almost nothing.* "Desyrk's got the most common sense, but he's not that strong an imager. Voltyr has sense, and he and Shaelyt are stronger, but they have a lot to learn. In time, it might work if the squad leader were in charge of the squad's movements to begin with, and those three were told they were being trained to take over greater leadership. But I wouldn't do it now, or anytime soon." Quaeryt grinned ruefully. "I'm barely effective with a company, and that's with Zhelan to keep me from making too many mistakes. But that's why he's there."

"You're better than that, but unlike some officers, you understand what you can do."

"You think this is going to be a much longer war, don't you?"

"Don't you?" returned Skarpa.

"I don't think that fighting large battles will take all that long. What comes before may take months, and what comes after will take years."

"That's why I wanted to know about your undercaptains. Who's the strongest imager . . . among them?"

Quaeryt didn't care for the way the question had been phrased, intentionally, because Skarpa was effectively pointing out that Quaeryt was the strongest imager, without saying so. "That would be Threkhyl, but he's like an ax with a greasewood shaft."

"Good to keep in mind, but that's not what we need right now."

"I didn't think so."

"There's another question I had. An observation. It looked to me that you and the imagers created that bridge."

"I'm just their subcommander."

Skarpa raised both eyebrows.

"I might have helped some," added Quaeryt.

"I'm not the only one with doubts about that statement."

"It's true."

"I'm certain it is. Rescalyn, Myskyl, and Governor Straesyr all agreed on one thing. Nothing you say is untrue. It's just not always the entire truth, or it has nothing to do with what the question was, although it may seem that it does. Myskyl said you and your imagers built the bridge and Third and Fifth Regiments will be the first to use it."

"So we're assigned to the south side of the river because we created the bridge?"

"Can you think of a better reason?" asked Skarpa. "Besides the fact that we're the three most effective regiments they have?"

"Three? I heard that you'd have two regiments and a battalion, and that half of each regiment was composed of Piedran rejects."

"Any regiment under Meinyt will be effective, and a battalion under you and Zhelan is as good as a regiment."

"I do marvel at your optimism."

"Realism. We've had more actual fighting than any other regiments, and we've killed and captured more than any others, and we've had fewer casualties. Bhayar knows that."

"I'm certain he does."

"He also knows one other thing."

"Which is?"

"You are absolutely loyal to him." After a moment Skarpa asked, "Why? You can't have liked the way he treated you after all you did in Extela."

"He did what was necessary. I made a choice between doing what was politically wise and what was best for the people. It wasn't necessarily the best for the High Holders. I knew there were risks. You even told me so. I made a mistake. I thought I'd have more time than two months. But . . . unlike many rulers, Bhayar does not discard those who support him."

"No . . . he uses everyone to their advantage . . . and his."

An astute observation. "He's been known for that. It's one of his strengths."

"And yours, if I do say so, is to use others' needs for your own ends while overfulfilling their wants."

"You grant me too much capability," protested Quaeryt.

"No. I do not. You are fortunate that Bhayar does not see what I do."

But he does . . . and wishes to use me to help him gain the rule of all Lydar. "He sees enough that I must be cautious." That, too, was true. Quaeryt smiled. "What else need I know before tomorrow?"

Skarpa smiled in return. "That is all for now. Enjoy the day . . . and your wife. When we leave on Lundi, it will be months, if not longer, before you see her again."

Quaeryt rose from the table, sensing that Skarpa would not be the first to stand, even though he should have been, given that he was Quaeryt's superior. "I intend to." *More than you can imagine.*

"Good."

They walked from the study together toward the front entry and the cold rain that awaited the commander on his ride back to Ferravyl.

4

Quaeryt rode out of Nordruil just after dawn with only half a squad as an escort. He would have preferred even fewer men, so that more would remain at the holding to protect Vaelora. She had pointed out that taking fewer men would have suggested to anyone who was watching that he was either foolhardy or a powerful imager. Needless to say, Quaeryt heeded her advice. He also carried full imaging shields the entire ride, the first time he had done so since the last battle. He'd only been able to hold partial shields on the ride to Nordruil, and not even all the way. Even though he was feeling much better, when he reached the fortified bridge over the Aluse, a quint before sixth glass, he felt tired from the strain of holding the shields.

After he crossed the bridge, now largely repaired, he noticed a small stone tower, three yards tall, on the east side of the approach. He couldn't help but frown. He hadn't seen that before, had he? Fretting that he was short of time, although he had no reason for such feelings, he urged the mare forward and then westward and into the courtyard, where he reined up behind the north wall before the chimes had announced the glass.

Zhelan was waiting for him. "Good morning, Subcommander."

"Good morning, Major." Quaeryt dismounted.

"The senior officers' meeting is in the conference room on the second level. In moments."

"Thank you. I'd like to meet with you after that."

"Yes, sir. I'll meet you in the corridor outside afterward."

Quaeryt handed the mare's reins to one of the rankers and hurried through the closest door and then up a back staircase. As he took off the visor cap and tucked it under his arm, he was obviously the last officer to enter the room, given the looks he received, but at least Bhayar wasn't there yet. Meinyt and Quaeryt, as the only subcommanders, sat at the foot of the long table, below some fourteen commanders, although Quaeryt was seated beside Skarpa, who was clearly the junior regimental commander at the table.

As Quaeryt slipped into the chair, he murmured, "You didn't mention the meeting."

"It was announced at ninth glass last night," Skarpa replied in a low voice. "By Deucalon's adjutant."

The one raising unnecessary questions . . . or just one of several? After a momentary hesitation Quaeryt nodded. Skarpa hadn't been about to send a courier—or several couriers—through a driving rain in the middle of the night to make sure that Quaeryt arrived on time for a meeting where the only thing desired of him was his presence and his silence. *Still . . .*

The meeting-room door opened.

"Lord Bhayar!"

All the officers rose.

"As you were." Bhayar's voice was dry as he approached the end of the table, where he stopped and remained standing. "As Marshal Deucalon and some of you already know"—Bhayar drew out the silence before continuing—"we have seen no sign of Bovarian forces near Ferrravyl. It's most likely that Kharst has pulled back his forces, possibly as far as Villerive, or at least to positions where the terrain is more favorable. I would prefer beginning this campaign tomorrow, but the first two regiments from Ruile will not be ready until Lundi. Unhappily." Bhayar turned to Deucalon. "If you would." He seated himself and looked politely at the marshal.

Deucalon did not stand, but his deep voice carried the length of the long table easily. "The best roads lie on the north side of the Aluse. So do most of the larger towns. So does most of the population of those that span the river, particularly Nordeau and Villerive. Variana is also largely on the north side. The northern army will advance along the north. Beginning at sixth glass on Lundi, we will begin barging men, mounts, and horses and wagons, unless, of course, the imagers can create another bridge from Ferravyl to Cleblois . . ." Deaucalon looked down the table.

"I fear not, Marshal," replied Quaeryt. "Not unless you can create another massive warm rainstorm." *And be willing to sacrifice thousands of men and mounts. Or others.* At that thought, he managed to keep from shuddering.

"I thought as much, but it was worth inquiring." Deucalon cleared his throat in a fashion that strongly suggested disappointment. "So we will have to rely on barges and guidelines to cross the Ferrean. In the meantime, the southern army under Commander Skarpa will take the bridges and advance along the south. The southern army is not to proceed more than a day in advance of the northern army . . ."

Quaeryt listened as Deucalon described the general plan of attack, in essence to take both sides of the Aluse and all the towns while heading directly to Variana. What Quaeryt worried most about wasn't the attack along the river, or even taking the Bovarian capital, although the campaign leading to Variana could not be anything but bloody. What followed might well be worse, since even if the initial campaign were a complete success, at the end Bhayar would hold little more than a tenth of Bovaria. Then what?

The people in what had once been Khel might well flock to Bhayar, but that would still leave a large part of Bovaria unconquered.

"... now that you all have been briefed on the overall strategy of the campaign, you need to inform your officers and continue with your preparations. That is all I have." Deucalon turned in his chair. "Lord Bhayar?"

"I have nothing else. You all know what to do better than I could tell you." With a warm smile, Bhayar rose.

So did all the officers.

"Good day."

Quaeryt watched as the Lord of Telaryn departed, followed by Deucalon.

That none of the commanders or the submarshal said a word as they filed out of the chamber did surprise Quaeryt, if only for a moment. *No one wants to reveal anything.* It also saddened him, after a fashion.

Once outside in the corridor, he started to turn to Skarpa, then paused. The commander was looking at the three officers who had met Submarshal Myskyl—two majors and a subcommander.

The black-haired major had a face even more forbidding than Bhayar's seneschal in Solis, and his eyes flicked across Quaeryt and Skarpa, taking them in and instantly dismissing them. The slightly older-looking major, with longish sandy brown hair and a brush mustache, concentrated on Myskyl with what Quaeryt felt was a fawning intensity. The subcommander offered a warm smile, clearly directed at Skarpa, and inclined his head as well before returning his attention to Myskyl.

"Are those three part of Deucalon's staff?" asked Quaeryt.

"Subcommander Ernyld is his chief of staff. I don't know the majors," replied Skarpa quietly, turning back toward Quaeryt.

"Is there anything else for now?"

"No. You and I and Meinyt should meet outside the senior officers' mess two quints before dinner."

"I'll be there."

Skarpa just nodded, then headed for the main staircase.

Quaeryt looked around for several moments before he saw Zhelan waiting at the end of the corridor and made his way to the major. "Sir?"

"Can you gather all the officers of the battalion for a quick meeting?"

"Yes, sir. I'd thought you might wish to talk to them after the senior officers met, and I told them to stand by. The best I could find was an empty storeroom off a tack room—"

"That will be fine. Lead the way." After a moment Quaeryt asked, "I understand first company received reinforcements and replacements. How do they look to be?"

"Half of them have some experience, and I've had the squad leaders working the others hard."

Quaeryt nodded.

"You know, sir . . . about the other three companies?"

"I know that they're Khellan, and that few of the troopers speak either Tellan or Bovarian, and that each is commanded by an officer who was once a major or even a subcommander. What else have you found out?"

"They're all pretty much Pharsi. Each company has two officers. One is a major, and the other a captain. They don't like us much, but they hate the Bovarians."

"You're worried that if we're too effective, they'll try to massacre the survivors?"

"The way they were talking, I wouldn't be surprised."

"How long have you spent with them?"

"Four or five glasses over the past few days. Commander Skarpa didn't tell me until Mardi." Zhelan handed Quaeryt a single sheet of paper.

Quaeryt scanned it.

2nd Co.   Major Calkoran D'Kors
          Captain Eslym D'Kors

3rd Co.   Major Zhael D'Kors
          Captain Wharyn D'Kors

4th Co.   Major Arion D'Kors
          Captain Stemsed D'Kors

D'Kors . . . they can't all be related . . . He almost shook his head. That was the Bovarian naming custom. D'Kors just meant they were cavalry officers. He folded the paper and slipped it inside his jacket, a jacket that was too warm even before eighth glass. "Thank you. I appreciate it." He image-projected a gentle sense of appreciation.

"Those are matters I can help with, sir."

Quaeryt understood all too well what Zhelan wasn't saying—that the major knew full well that Quaeryt was more than anyone, including Quaeryt, was admitting.

When they reached the stable storeroom, Zhelan stepped in first, announcing, "Subcommander Quaeryt."

Quaeryt followed him into the storeroom, where all the officers stood waiting. "As you were." Realizing the Khellans hadn't understood, he repeated himself in Bovarian. After that, he said nothing for several moments, running his eyes across the battalion officers before him, some seven command officers, and the six imagers. All of the Khellan officers had brown or black hair, although two were old enough to have streaks of gray in it, and five of the six had the pale honey-colored Pharsi complexion.

Several of them were close to staring at him.

"Yes," he said in Bovarian, "I am Pharsi by blood, but I was orphaned young and only know a few phrases in Pharsi." Quaeryt could tell that most of the imagers hadn't understood a word, but then they weren't regular Telaryn officers, although he suspected the Bovarian of many Telaryn officers was marginal at best, at least given the reaction to the few homilies he'd given in Bovarian over the past year. He continued in Bovarian. "After this meeting, I will meet with the officers of each company in Fifth Battalion separately, beginning with first company. Fifth Battalion is part of the southern army, led by Commander Skarpa. Our task is to clear the southern side of the Aluse River . . ." He went on to summarize what Deucalon had passed on at the earlier meeting. When he finished, he looked to the Khellan officers. "If you have any questions, you can ask me personally when I meet with you. Is that clear?"

They all nodded.

"Now, if you please, I will meet with Major Zhelan and with the first company officer. I'll meet with the undercaptains after I meet with the command officers. Those I'm not meeting with may wait in the tack room." Quaeryt waited until the storeroom emptied and he was left with Zhelan and an older undercaptain, with a narrow face under brown hair. An old scar ran across his right jaw.

"I don't believe you've officially met Undercaptain Ghaelyn," said Zhelan, "recently promoted from senior squad leader."

"I have not. It's good to see you here, Undercaptain. We'll be relying on you a great deal because we'll have to use extra care with the other companies to begin with."

"Yes, sir. The major made that clear."

"Do you have any questions that the major hasn't answered?"

"No, sir."

"I wouldn't think so. The major is very thorough, but it's good to meet you officially." Quaeryt refrained from smiling. The whole point of that meeting had been for Quaeryt to see Ghaelyn's face . . . and little more.

After the undercaptain left, Quaeryt motioned to Zhelan. "I think it might be best . . ."

"For you to meet the Khellan officers alone? Yes, sir. I thought so. I've already talked to them. Major Calkoran is the most senior."

"You ordered their companies by their seniority?"

"Yes, sir. It seemed the best way."

"Remind me not to argue with you about procedures, Major." Quaeryt smiled warmly.

Zhelan looked taken aback, and Quaeryt realized that he'd given Zhelan a statement that a good officer couldn't really answer. Quaeryt laughed softly. "That wasn't a fair order. Thank you."

"Yes, sir."

In moments, both second company officers returned to the storeroom. Major Calkoran was stern-faced, with silver streaks in his black hair. Captain Eslym had short wavy brown hair and was probably about Quaeryt's age. Both sets of dark eyes fixed on Quaeryt.

"You are young for a subcommander," offered Calkoran. "The major says that you are brave and that you are experienced. You are a scholar and from the Pharsi. Is that not so?"

"I doubt I am any braver than you who have crossed the Montagnes D'Glace after fighting against the Bovarians for years. I am a scholar, and my parents were Pharsi. My wife has many Pharsi forbears as well."

"You bear the marks of a lost one."

"I have been called that more than once," Quaeryt admitted. "I will not claim that . . . or disavow it. My acts define who I am."

Calkoran smiled wryly. "You talk as one as well."

"As we both know, acts define the man . . . or woman."

"What would you have of us?"

"To be good officers. To follow orders." Quaeryt paused, then added, "And to remember that your enemies are not the Bovarian people. Nor are your enemies the Bovarian troopers once they are defeated. Your true enemy is Rex Kharst and the senior officers and High Holders who support him."

Calkoran fingered his chin, almost as if he had once had a beard that he had stroked. "The Bovarians fought as demons of the Namer, and they killed when they had no need."

"I do not doubt that. But . . . would you be of the Namer? Lord Bhayar seeks to unite all Lydar and to create a land where all are equal, whether Bovarian, Telaryn, or Pharsi."

"Even Pharsi?"

"You may ask any of the troopers in the southern army about how Lord Bhayar has punished those who attempted to defile Pharsi women or attack Pharsi men."

"I have done so. They do not speak ill of Lord Bhayar. They say that you were a governor, and that you stood up for the Pharsi. We will follow you, and trust your judgment of Lord Bhayar."

Quaeryt could sense the unspoken words—*and hope that judgment is accurate.* "I could ask no more." He inclined his head just slightly.

Major Calkoran inclined his head more deeply. "Subcommander . . . sir."

The captain inclined his head as well.

"I look forward to our working together to make Lydar a better place for all."

"As do we." Both officers bowed again "By your leave, sir."

Quaeryt nodded.

While Quaeryt would have liked to have learned more from the Khellan officers, he understood that the present wasn't the time to do so. He did plan to spend part of each day riding with each of them.

His meetings with Major Zhael and his captain, Wharyn, and with Major Arion and Captain Stensed were as short, as formal, and as satisfactory as the one with Calkoran had been, that is, acceptable and the beginning of a working relationship.

Quaeryt took a deep breath before Undercaptain Threkhyl appeared, then squared his shoulders and waited.

"Good morning, sir," offered Threkhyl, pleasantly enough.

"Good morning. How are you feeling?"

"Don't know as I've felt any better. Have felt worse."

"Do you have any questions or thoughts about the campaign ahead?"

The ginger-haired imager frowned for a moment, then asked, "Is it going to be like the last battle, sir?"

"I would judge it will be more like the first skirmishes on the south of the Vyl. That's until we get close to Variana. Then I'd think we'd see more fighting in larger groups. Have you been practicing your imaging?"

"Yes, sir." After another pause the undercaptain added, "I never knew I could do some things."

"Such as?"

"I built a stone tower, all neat like, like the one in Piedryn, in the square. Except mine was only three yards high." He laughed. "It's still there, on this side of the bridge, by the approach."

That answered one question.

"I offered to help the masons on the bridge, but the engineering major . . . I don't think he trusted me. I did image some cut stones for the side walls, and they used those. Had a bit of a headache when I finished on Meredi, but I didn't have as much trouble yesterday."

"Good." While Quaeryt was pleased, he hoped the other imagers had worked at improving their skills as well. He still didn't want to have to rely on just a few, especially if one of the few happened to be Threkhyl.

"Sir . . . there is one thing . . ."

"Yes?"

"I don't like having to listen to that Undercaptain Ghaelyn. He used to be a squad leader."

Quaeryt repressed a sigh. "He won't be giving you many commands. If he does, listen to him. He'll only be doing it to save your skin. He knows far more than you do about staying alive in a fight. That's especially true if you're where you can't image."

"I'll listen, sir."

Quaeryt again could guess the unspoken words—*but I don't have to like it.*

"Good. You might also start asking why various orders and formations are used."

Threkhyl frowned.

"It could just happen that you might end up in charge of a squad if the squad leader is hurt. The more you know, the better."

Threkhyl looked as if he hadn't ever considered that.

"That sort of thing was what got me into being a command officer," explained Quaeryt. "During the Tilboran Revolt."

"I don't know that I'd planned to lead troops, sir."

"There are many things we don't plan for. With some fortune, you won't have to, but it's better to be prepared for . . . everything that you can." Quaeryt had almost said, "prepared for the worst." He smiled. "If you'd send in Shaelyt . . ."

"Oh . . . yes, sir."

As Threkhyl left, Quaeryt considered. The ginger-bearded imager was acting more like an undercaptain, but Quaeryt still wondered how far he could trust the man.

Shaelyt arrived, stiffened, and said, "Good morning, sir."

"Good morning. How are you feeling?"

"Very well, sir. I've been accompanying Major Zhelan and watching him conduct training and maneuvers. Well . . . Voltyr came with me." Shaelyt flushed slightly. "Actually, it was his idea."

"His idea or not, you were wise to follow it."

"Thank you, sir." Shaelyt looked down for a moment, then back at Quaeryt. "Sir . . . begging your pardon, but I have been practicing imaging ever since I recovered—"

"I suspect you're much, much better, are you not?" interjected Quaeryt smoothly.

"Yes, sir. I can create holes even in iron plate at over a hundred yards. That's if I don't have to do it over water, and I can image a handful of arrows out of the sky."

"That's excellent!" Quaeryt didn't have to counterfeit the enthusiasm in his voice.

"But . . . begging your pardon, sir, even working together, Voltyr and I couldn't create a bridge. The best we could do was a piece of stone wall maybe four yards long and two yards high. Neither one of us could see much for a day. Our heads split for two."

"That might well be because you weren't facing eight regiments of Bovarians. That sort of threat can concentrate your effort more than one might realize. You also weren't doing it with others."

"Sir . . ." Shaelyt looked down. "It's said that some of the lost ones . . . well . . . they looked like you."

"I've been called a lost one by more than one Pharsi," Quaeryt admitted. "It's pretty clear that I'm from Pharsi blood, but as for being a lost one . . ." He shook his head, then asked quickly, "What else? Did you understand what the Khellan officers were saying?"

"Mostly. They speak a little differently from the way we do at home.

They'll do what you say, sir. Some of them think you're a lost one. Some of the younger ones think . . . well . . . that you're not."

"They think I'm a fraud, and that Bhayar's having me pretend to be something I'm not?"

"Something like that."

Quaeryt nodded. *If you show you're not, you'll likely reveal for certain that you're an imager, and if you don't . . .* Once again, no matter what he did, there were negative consequences. Then he laughed, softly, but ironically. "I don't pretend well or convincingly, Undercaptain." *Misdirect fairly well, yes, but out and out pretending isn't exactly your strength.*

This time Shaelyt nodded. "If you'll pardon me, sir. They worry that you are less than you seem. I can see that you are more than you wish anyone to know."

"Time will show whether you're right, Shaelyt. Until then, I'd appreciate it if you'd keep that thought to yourself."

"Yes, sir." Shaelyt's response was warm and cheerful. "I'd thought to, sir."

"Do you have any other thoughts or questions?"

"No, sir. Not now."

"Then you may go. Send in Voltyr, please."

"Yes, sir."

Almost as soon as Shaelyt had stepped out through the storeroom door, Voltyr entered quickly, closed the door behind himself, and looked directly at Quaeryt. "You're an imager . . . sir. Isn't that what being a lost one means?"

Quaeryt shook his head. "Being a lost one means being favored of Erion and also being slightly physically flawed. Blond Pharsi with dark eyes are considered as possible lost ones. I look like a lost one, and I limp like one. Being an imager would be a possible mark of favor, but it's not the only mark." *Not that anyone ever let you know what any of the marks of favor are.*

"You didn't answer my question, sir."

"You didn't ask one, Undercaptain. Do you really want an answer? If I don't answer, you won't have to lie.'

"Why should I . . . ?" Abruptly Voltyr broke off his words. "I think I understand."

"The less anyone knows about what you undercaptains—and I—can do, the greater the advantage we possess. I was telling you the absolute truth about my goals when I said I wanted to make Telaryn—and all Lydar, if it comes to that—safe for both scholars and imagers. A secret shared between two people can usually be kept. One between three usually can't. Shaelyt suspects. He may even know. We have not discussed that. I'd ask you not to discuss whatever you believe me able to do. You can certainly speculate about what the rest of you can do. You can even suggest, if pressed, that there might be something about an obdurate multiplying the effect of imaging." Quaeryt smiled ruefully. "Is that acceptable?"

"Even being married to Lord Bhayar's sister, sir, you tread a dangerous path."

"No more dangerous than yours. Mine is just different."

Voltyr nodded. "Given all you risk, you have my word, sir."

"Thank you. Do you have any other questions or observations?"

"Only that you should never trust Threkhyl, however useful he may be."

"I've worried about him."

"I would keep worrying."

"Anything else?"

"Nothing else that cannot be discussed before all the officers."

"Then . . . if you would send in Desyrk."

"That I will." Voltyr smiled, almost sympathetically, and turned.

As Quaeryt waited for Desyrk to come in, he just hoped that he didn't have to deal with too many more questions and that he could get on with more imager training, including getting them more practice with sabres, as well as having Meinyt or one of the other officers give them some instruction in mounted unit maneuvers . . . and if and when that took place, he'd be there as well.

5

The remainder of Vendrei went as Quaeryt had planned it, even to the point of getting Meinyt to spend more than a glass detailing the basics of mounted unit commands and maneuvers to the undercaptains . . . and to Quaeryt, who listened more intently than did some of the imagers.

Much of Vendrei afternoon Quaeryt spent in observing the Khellan companies in maneuvers. So far as their horsemanship and discipline went, he had to admit he was impressed. More to the point, so was Zhelan. Yet it made sense. Those who were not burning for revenge would have long since slipped away.

And no matter what the Khellan majors say . . . that is going to be a problem, one you need to be prepared for when the time comes.

Late in the day, Quaeryt gathered the imager undercaptains once more, this time for a demonstration of their abilities. All showed considerable improvement, even Baelthm, who could now actually image half-size daggers at a hundred yards. Quaeryt couldn't help but wonder what they, and others, could do if educated and trained from a young age. *None of that matters, not unless you make certain Bhayar is successful and you're part of that success.*

Their progress also raised another set of issues. *When will any of them be strong enough to learn about shields, and whom can you trust enough to instruct about them?* As with too many things, he didn't have answers, but he knew he needed to work that out in a way that kept the shield ability from being noticed by any commanders, and especially by Myskyl or Deucalon. The last thing the imagers needed was to be used to shield troopers. That much effort, Quaeryt knew, would render any of them, including himself, unable to do anything else, and eventually end up getting them killed because the commanders would use them up to protect their troops, and Quaeryt was going to need every imager he could find, both for their sake . . . and his.

The meeting with Meinyt and Skarpa was short, since Skarpa only wanted to hear their views on their companies and troopers.

Meinyt was not quite dismissive of the Piedryn troopers. "They know which end of the sabre's sharp, and they can ride and understand orders. They do their best to obey."

"That's a considerable improvement from last week," Skarpa said dryly "Keep working them."

"I've scheduled drills tomorrow and Solayi morning as well. They don't like it, but they're getting the idea that it's preferable to dying."

"You do get your point across," replied Skarpa with a laugh.

Dinner at the senior officers' mess was quiet, and Quaeryt ate with Meinyt and Skarpa and said little.

Samedi dawned misty and foggy, but the summer sun burned off the fog by ninth glass, long before Fifth Battalion's practice in maneuvers was over. By the time Quaeryt returned to the bridge fortifications, where he and his first company were quartered, his uniform was soaked inside and out.

Damp uniform or not, he and Meinyt had to meet with Skarpa at third glass, and still blotting his forehead, he made his way toward the small study that Skarpa had found to use.

"Has he said anything to you?" he asked Meinyt as they walked down the stone corridor that was only slightly cooler than outside.

"Not a thing, except that we should have easy going at first."

Skarpa was waiting for them, standing beside a small table desk. He did not seat himself, but said, "This won't take long. I was hoping for more information from the scouts, but nothing's changed. The latest reports say that there aren't any large bodies of troopers nearby on the south side. The locals farther upriver say that they've seen Bovarians in uniform in the last few days, but not in the twenty milles or so west of the new bridge. We should be able to make good time because we don't have to ferry the supply wagons over either river."

"We'll be almost a day ahead of the northern army by Mardi afternoon," Meinyt said.

"Most likely." Skarpa nodded. "The nearest bridge over the Aluse in Bovaria is at Villerive, but there's a cable ferry at Rivecote. It joins Rivecote Sud and Nord."

"That's what . . . sixty milles upriver?" asked Quaeryt.

"If the maps and the millestones are accurate, and I wouldn't wager on that."

Neither would Quaeryt.

"I'd like to reach Rivecote Sud well before Deucalon nears Rivecote Nord. It will be even more important that we reach Villerive before Deucalon does. The Bovarians don't expect an army, even a small one, to advance on the south side of the Aluse. If we hold the ferry and the bridge, then we cut off their retreat . . . or we can attack their rear. Either way, that will put us in a stronger position."

"Then we'll be more than a day ahead of the northern forces," said Meinyt evenly.

"What the marshal had in mind, I am certain," said Skarpa, "was that we should never be far enough ahead of his forces that we could not support him. I intend to be able to support him where and when it is possible. There are sections of the southern side of the river where there is no road, only a path. Preparing to be able to support him will require our getting an early start."

Meinyt nodded, not bothering to hide a smile.

"Can your imagers smooth out things or remove rocks if necessary?" asked Skarpa.

"If they're not too large," replied Quaeryt.

"That could prove most helpful. We're short of engineers."

Quaeryt glanced to Meinyt, then back to Skarpa.

"Myskyl said that the northern army needed them in case the Bovarians tried to destroy more bridges, the way they did over the Myal River when we were riding to Ferravyl. So Deucalon took the engineers from Third Regiment and left us with those from the Piedryn regiment. Meinyt never got any engineers for Fifth Regiment." Skarpa shrugged. "Myskyl did say that if your imagers could build bridges, they ought to be able to repair them."

"It's not that easy," Quaeryt said. "I'm also not certain anyone wants to risk freezing the regiments to build a bridge. He seems to have forgotten that we killed almost an entire battalion of our own troopers."

"He didn't forget. He's never forgotten anything," Skarpa said in a matter-of-fact fashion. "Though there are times when I'm not certain he's learned anything from what happens. It doesn't matter. We don't have good engineers. We'll do the best we can." He looked to Meinyt. "We'll be sending our own scouts out. Do you think we'll need a recon in force?"

"Not on Lundi. Perhaps not on Mardi. After that, if we see more than a few tracks, I'd recommend half squads. Full squads as we near Rivecote."

That brought another nod from Skarpa. "Quaeryt . . . I'd like to keep the imagers near the front. Do you have any problem riding with me and keeping them close?"

"No, sir. I'd recommend that for the first few days. After that, it would depend on what's ahead."

Skarpa continued to ask questions and seek observations for another half glass, then abruptly said, "That's all." He turned to Quaeryt. "You might as well leave for Nordruil now, or whenever you're finished with your battalion. I'd like you back tomorrow evening."

Quaeryt understood that all too well. Lundi morning would come all too early. "I'll be here."

6

On Samedi evening, when Quaeryt reached Nordruil, Vaelora was waiting at the front entrance for him, dressed in a flattering, and clinging, green cotton dress that somehow made her light brown eyes look almost luminously amber. Even before he dismounted, he wanted to wrap his arms around her, to lose himself in her. Instead, he permitted himself a long embrace and a tender, but passionate kiss, far more than was proper in public, he knew.

As he lifted his lips from hers, she said, "You're only here for tonight and tomorrow, aren't you?"

He nodded. "We leave before dawn on Lundi."

"Then we should make the most of the time. Dinner will be ready in less than a glass." She smiled. "You need your uniform washed, and you need to bathe." After a moment she added, blushing, "Just bathe. Be patient. The evening will be long enough."

Quaeryt looked at her again.

"That is not a scholarly look."

"It wasn't meant to be." He grinned. "I take it you have already made preparations for my bath?"

"Of course. I don't want to waste time . . . either."

Quaeryt laughed.

Then they walked into the hold house and up the stairs.

Quaeryt had to admit that he felt better after bathing, but he didn't luxuriate in the porcelain tub, because Vaelora had left him there to make certain dinner would be ready. He had his doubts that her absence was totally for that reason, but, he reminded himself, *you're far more fortunate in having her than you ever thought, and there are times when it's best to let things be as she wishes.*

He dressed quickly, and as he was pulling on a clean shirt, not a uniform, she entered the dressing chamber.

"They're washing all your uniforms so they'll have enough time to dry. Are you hungry?"

"Yes." *In more ways than one.* But dinner would come first.

They walked down the narrow stairs together. Quaeryt did hold her hand, firmly, but not too lightly.

She looked at him. "I'm glad you miss me."

"I wish I didn't have to."

Vaelora shook her head. "If you don't do what you must, then you'd come to blame me. I would not have that." She smiled faintly. "Do not tell me you wish it were otherwise. I would not love you so much were you not striving to change things for the better. I have not told you this, but I would not change one thing you did as governor now that I have thought about it. I told Bhayar that also."

"Thank you." Quaeryt squeezed her hand again. "What did he say? Or did he just look at you with those dark blue eyes?"

"That doesn't work with me. He tried it too often when we were young. He laughed. Then he said that I was getting to be as dangerous as you, and that he would have to watch both of us." She shook her head, then smiled. "I told him I'd learned it all from him and Aelina. He said that he was surrounded by dangerous people, and that was the price of using those who were most able."

"He's right about that. Anyone who can carry out tasks well can turn that ability against one."

"So a ruler has the choice between faithful incompetence or dangerous competence?"

"All too often, don't you think?"

"I do."

"Still . . ." mused Quaeryt, "there is one aspect that many overlook. Often those who are most able can see that they can accomplish more by working with a ruler than against him. It is usually to their interests to do so."

"Unless the ruler is not trustworthy."

"A ruler should always keep his word . . . that is, if he wishes to remain a ruler."

"Has my brother?"

"So far as I know. Do you know otherwise?"

"He did not as a youth. Our father whipped him once for breaking his word."

That was something Quaeryt had not heard.

"Father told him that lesser men could break their word, but not rulers. He also said that treachery and lying was a shortcut to ruin." Vaelora smiled ironically. "He also said that there was little need to deceive men, because most men would deceive themselves." She stopped as they reached the table on the terrace, placed so that the trees beyond the terrace shaded it from the last rays of the sun.

Once they were seated, Vaelora looked across at him. "You are tired."

"I'm not that tired . . . but the last two days have been long."

"How did it go with the Phars officers?"

"They will obey and follow my orders." He laughed softly, not quite bitterly. "At least until I prove I'm not one of the lost ones."

"And what if you are?"

"They may find that they do not want what they have wished for."

"Oh . . . dearest . . ." Vaelora reached across the table and took his hands in hers for a moment, then released them as the serving woman approached, setting a pale lager in a beaker before each of them.

Quaeryt took a long swallow. He hadn't realized just how thirsty he still was. "I do like good lager."

"You like most things that are good."

"So do you," he said with a smile.

"Don't most people?" She took a sip from her beaker, then set it down and waited as the serving woman placed a small platter of sliced peaches and cherries before her, and then another before Quaeryt. "I thought fruit, and then fowl, would be good."

"It all sounds good." He ate one of the cherries, careful not to bite on the pit, then another, before going on. "I'm not sure that most people like what is truly good. I think most of us want to think that what we like or what we wish to do is good. Just think about what happened in Extela. The grain and flour merchants wanted higher prices for flour, even though the price they wanted would have beggared many people. When I kept the price from going too high for just a few weeks, while restoring order, they all condemned me and complained to your brother. When I questioned High Holder Wystgahl about his motives and about the fact that he'd supplied weevil-ridden flour to the post, he got so upset that he died, and his son and everyone condemned me. No one said a word about the nature of the flour, or that his actions were a theft of so many golds that a poor man would have been beheaded for taking that much. Yet all of them believed that they represented what was good." Quaeryt doubted he'd ever forget what he'd learned from his short time as governor of Montagne.

"You're very right, dearest, and we can correspond about it. We should enjoy dinner . . . and the little time we have left together at present."

Quaeryt was glad for the last two words she spoke, even as he knew she was right. He would have more than enough time without her to think over how people defined what was good and what was not. He smiled and lifted his beaker. "To your wisdom, to us, and to the evening."

Vaelora raised her beaker as well, extending it so that it touched his with the faintest clink. "To us."

They drank, eyes locked.

7

Quaeryt found himself once more in the saddle, looking out through the rain at the massed Bovarians as the horns began to sound. The mournful penetrating call shivered through his bones. As one the Bovarians began to advance toward the Telaryn forces on the low ridge south of the River Aluse, closing in from the north, the south, and even the west.

Quaeryt cleared his throat, extended his shields to encompass Desyrk and Shaelyt, then concentrated on imaging the bridge he visualized, with high slight arches to a central pier, a massive structure necessary for what must come.

Nothing happened, and the Bovarians kept advancing.

Could he do it again? Draw power from the warm rain, from the warmth of the Bovarian troopers and their mounts? From the river itself? Could he again slaughter tens of thousands?

Yet if he did not . . .

He reached out for that warmth—and from everywhere came lances of pain, strikes like cold lightning Overhead, the clouds darkened into masses blacker than a moonless night without even the thinnest crescent of either Erion or Artiema, and liquid ice poured down like sheets in an arc around him, slashing through his shields as if they did not exist, sucking all the warmth within him away.

From somewhere came a mocking whisper. "Should you not suffer what you wrought?"

He wanted to protest that he hadn't been the one who had begun the war, but the chill froze his tongue in his mouth. Brilliant lines of white ice-lightning flared through his skull, and the tears caused by that pain froze instantly on his cheeks. White fog billowed below him . . . and icy whiteness froze him into stillness. He struggled to escape, to move somehow, but he could not, chill as he was. He tried to blink, but failed, as if they were frozen open watching thousands freeze around him, even as ice built around him. Somewhere, he could hear rain, icy droplets . . . falling, coating him with yet more ice.

He shuddered, trying to escape the endless ice and chill.

Suddenly there was light all around him, light so bright he could hardly see, but he was cold, so cold he was shivering, even with all the sunlight.

Before he could say anything, Vaelora's arms were around him. "It's all right, dearest. It's all right."

Her words did not register with him, not for several moments, because they were in Bovarian. "What . . . ?" he murmured, half mumbling because his lips were so cold they felt numb.

"It's all right. I'm here. I'm right here."

She'll freeze, too. ". . . chill you . . . the way . . ."

"I'm warm enough. Just hold on to me. Talk to me. Tell me what happened." With her arms wrapped around him, slowly the cold deep within him began to melt away.

Later, when they finally moved apart, at least enough for Vaelora to look at him, worry in her eyes, she asked, "What was it? The ice storm? You were so cold." She swallowed. "The walls . . ."

"What is it?" Quaeryt could see the concern on her face.

"You started shivering in your sleep, and then there was frost. It was all over the walls."

He glanced around the bedchamber.

"It's all melted now." She laughed uneasily. "It is full summer. But can't you feel how cool everything is?"

Quaeryt managed not to shudder again. *Did you image in your sleep? Enough to cause frost to form?*

"Were you dreaming? About the ice storm you caused?"

He nodded. "It was worse than that. I was fighting the battle again, and I didn't want to image and kill thousands again, but they kept coming . . . and coming." He shuddered in spite of himself.

"What you've been doing with the regiment isn't the only reason you're tired, is it?"

"No . . ." he admitted warily.

"Tell me about it. All about it." Her words, gently as they were spoken, were not a request.

"This wasn't the first time. I dream about getting caught in the rain, being frozen in place, along with the . . . thousands of others . . . the Bovarians . . . some of ours . . . I try to escape . . . but I can't." He finally shook his head. "I struggle with the ice until I wake up."

"Does where you sleep feel cold to you when you finally wake up?"

"How could I tell? I always wake up cold and shivering, no matter how hot it was the night before.' After a moment he added, "I never saw frost . . . but I never looked for it, either."

Vaelora offered a smile.

Quaeryt suspected she'd forced the expression, but he smiled back.

"You do make the bedchamber more comfortable in summer," she said quickly. "It was rather warm . . . until . . ."

He looked at her, pale in the morning light. "How long have you been awake?"

"A glass, I'd guess. You were so tired, and I didn't want to wake you, then . . ."

"You're hungry, enough to feel faint, aren't you?"

"That seems to be happening more, now that . . ."

Quaeryt sat up in the wide bed. "We need to get you something to eat."

"You're not doing much better than I am."

Quaeryt laughed. "Then we need breakfast." As he put his feet on the floor a moment of light-headedness swept over him, suggesting he had indeed been imaging as he dreamed. *How had that happened?* He managed not to frown, not wanting to worry Vaelora any more than he already had.

They washed and dressed quickly. Even so, by the time they reached the terrace, the hold house servers had moved the table closer to the study so that it still rested in the morning shadows. Tea and lager were waiting for them, and two platters appeared almost immediately, with biscuits, omelets, and strips of fried ham.

Neither said much until they had each eaten several mouthfuls. Then Quaeryt looked to his wife and said, "We were hungry."

"*We* were." Her words and smile warmed him through, if in a different way. "All three of us."

"Are you feeling better?"

"Much. You?"

He nodded, since he'd taken another mouthful of the omelet. Then he had a swallow of the lager . . . and more omelet, and bread with berry preserves.

"I've been thinking," Vaelora said carefully. "Do you remember the story the old Pharsi woman told us in Extela, after you rescued her from the mob?"

Quaeryt glanced toward the serving woman who stood on the terrace beside the study door.

"They don't speak Bovarian well, remember," murmured Vaelora, "only the common terms spoken slowly."

Quaeryt nodded, then replied, "You noticed the old woman. I just followed your suggestion. You really rescued her."

"All right. After we rescued her."

"I remember. The story was about four Pharsi, three men and a woman. The woman and her distant cousin who was courting her were lost ones. The brothers were seeking easy fortune."

"Do you remember the refrain of the young woman?"

" 'Do not argue over what is not and may never be,' or something like that."

"Dearest . . . what sort of story was it?"

"It was a parable. The two brothers kept finding things and wanting more and arguing over what they'd found until they lost everything because of their quarrels." Quaeryt grinned. "The only one with any sense was the woman."

"Not quite. The cousin who was a lost one and, according to the old woman, looked like you, also had some sense." She smiled sweetly. "He had enough sense to listen to her."

"Your point is taken, dear."

"Why did she tell the story to us?"

"I don't know," he admitted. "I've wondered about that."

"She made a point of telling us. Not anyone else. I don't think it was to please us or to entertain us."

"No. It was to warn us. That was clear enough. We are young and carry Pharsi blood. She saw we had some power and position, and she wanted to warn us about wanting what we could never have."

Vaelora nodded. "How did she know that? She'd never seen us before."

"You're suggesting . . . ?" *Farsight?*

"I don't know. It's just . . . it's bothered me on and off ever since."

"Why did you bring that up now?"

"In a way . . . in a way, you need to look at the ice storm like that. You've said that no matter what you did, thousands would die. You had no choice about whether troopers died. Your only choice was which thousands died."

"If I could have found another way . . ." *Like you did with Rescalyn.*

"The only choice we have is to do the best we can when we can. You're thinking about Rescalyn, aren't you?"

"How did you know?"

"How could I not know? You've talked about it before. It's bothered you as well, but by killing him in a way that made him a hero, you stopped a bloody revolt that would have slaughtered more thousands than you did at Ferravyl. Don't you think that if Rescalyn had provoked a rebellion, whether he had been successful or not, it would have weakened Telaryn? That Kharst would have attacked even sooner? Then, how many more thousands would have perished?"

Quaeryt did not answer that. He knew the answer, and so did she. "Still . . . it doesn't help that I've had to act as a chorister of the Nameless, giving homilies about virtue . . . mercy . . . and then . . ."

"You acted in accord with what you said, dearest."

"That doesn't help as much as I'd like."

She let the silence grow for a moment, then repeated, " 'Do not argue over what is not and may never be.' That includes arguing with yourself, dearest."

"It's hard not to think about the consequences when you're the one who causes the deaths of so many."

"Kharst decided to attack. His actions determined that thousands would die. Your actions merely determined which thousands."

"Merely?" said Quaeryt dryly.

"You know what I meant. Are you determined to take on totally a responsibility that is only partly yours at best?"

"My dreams are suggesting it's more than that."

"You need to inform your dreams otherwise." Vaelora's voice was almost tart.

That's easy enough for her to say. She wasn't there when thousands froze because of what you did.

"Dearest . . . do you want Lydar to be a better place? Or do you want rulers like Kharst killing all the Pharsi, and Aliaro enslaving all the imagers?"

Quaeryt sighed. "I understand your words. I understand your logic. My head agrees with you. My heart, my feelings . . . they only comprehend all the deaths."

"I thought that scholars were ruled by their minds." A faint, almost mischievous smile lurked at the corners of Vaelora's mouth.

"It's easier to declare the mind superior when you're in a scholarium," replied Quaeryt. "It's harder when you see the results of what your mind declares is the best course."

"That was one reason why Bhayar was trained as a common trooper and went to Tilbor at the end of the conquest. He was twenty, then."

"He went to Tilbor? I didn't know that. He's never mentioned it."

"He wouldn't. Everyone would assume he was either boasting or that he'd been protected by a full battalion. He wasn't. He did have a pair of experienced troopers with him. Father worried the whole time. He said that was the hardest part."

From what Quaeryt had heard about Lord Chayar, that seemed improbable. But then, he never would have guessed that Bhayar had served as an ordinary trooper, even in a somewhat protected position.

After a moment of silence, Vaelora spoke. "How are your imagers doing?"

"They've all improved, especially Threkhyl, Voltyr, and Shaelyt." Quaeryt snorted. "I wouldn't trust Threkhyl as far as I could throw my mare."

"Believe in your feelings on that."

"But not about the ice storm?" He raised his eyebrows.

"You have to learn when to trust your feelings and when not to."

"Oh?"

"Women should take care in trusting their feelings with regard to men. Men should take care in trusting their feelings when it comes to battles and fighting, especially for power and glory. Both should take care in dealing with golds. Especially those of us raised without having to count them."

Quaeryt smiled at the dryness of her last words.

"What about the others?" asked Vaelora. "Can you trust Voltyr and Shaelyt?"

"As much as one can trust anyone. They both have much to lose should anything happen to me."

"As do I, dearest." Vaelora pursed her lips. "You must take care . . . but not too much, for that is worse than no care at all."

Quaeryt could see the brightness in her eyes. He stood and walked around the table, putting his hands on her shoulders, as comfortingly as he could. "I will balance heart and mind as best I can."

Vaelora slipped from his grasp and stood, facing him. "We have a little time. Would you walk with me through the gardens?"

"There are gardens?"

"There are. They have been neglected, but there are remnants of their beauty."

Quaeryt rose from the table and extended a hand. "I would be pleased to walk with you."

Her fingers twined around his as they set forth from the terrace, not looking back.

"You see here . . . they planted matching birches on each side," said Vaelora as she stepped onto the path that had once been white gravel, but now held gray and white pebbles, with patches of bare earth covered with moss in between the gray stones set unevenly into the ground. "There is also a gray cat, but it is fearful, and it is as still as a stone when it hears footsteps."

Quaeryt glanced around. He saw no cat, but a flash of blue and gold as a southern finch darted into a pine. "What else?"

"The housekeeper says that there's a black coney deep in the garden, but that when it appears it's a sign of ill fortune to come."

Quaeryt almost laughed. *A black rabbit a sign of misfortune?* Abruptly he realized he'd never seen a black hare, not wild or domestic. "Then we'd best not look for it." He pointed. "Those stone squares—there once were two stone pillars on this side of the birches."

"Sometimes, nature does outlast the works of men."

In the end, always. Quaeryt squeezed her hand.

"You can smell the wild roses. They're so much more fragrant than the ones cultivated for gardens. Over there . . ."

As he walked with Vaelora, Quaeryt knew the day would be far too short, and that he would have to leave all too soon.

Before he knew it, fourth glass had arrived, and he had changed into a clean uniform and was leading the mare into the courtyard. Vaelora walked beside him, and they made their way to the drive in front of the hold house.

As he stood beside the mare, ready to mount, she turned to him. "Remember, with your thoughts and your heart, that you did not bring this war to pass. All you can do is your best for everyone . . . and for us, the three of us." With her words came tears.

He held her for a long time, murmuring his love for her, before she released him and stepped back.

He mounted, and then looked at her. Neither spoke. *What more can we say?*

Her smile was unsteady.

He touched his fingers to his lips, then blew a last kiss to her before he turned the mare and rode to join his escorts waiting farther out on the drive.

Halfway down the drive, as he glanced back one last time toward Nordruil, he wondered how long it would be before he saw her again.

His lips quirked into a wry smile. *And to think, a year ago, you had met her but for a few moments, and had received one very scholarly letter.*

A year had changed everything. He just hoped the year ahead did not undo all that the previous year had brought. He pushed that thought away and looked at the road ahead, leading to Ferravyl.

8

Quaeryt did not dream of ice on Solayi evening, nor did he wake before
dawn on Lundi morning to frost coating the walls of the small stone chamber he rated as a subcommander. He dressed and hurried to the senior officers' mess in the north side of the bridge fortification. Once there he
quickly ate a breakfast of overcooked scrambled eggs and chopped mutton.
He washed down his food with poor ale—which reminded him to image
better lager into his water bottle when he reached the stables and saddled
his mare.

Major Zhelan had Fifth Battalion largely formed up in position north
of the bridge over the Aluse River when Quaeryt and the six imager undercaptains rode up. Quaeryt eased the mare over beside Zhelan's chestnut
gelding.

"Good morning, Subcommander."

"Good morning, Major. Any difficulties?"

"No, sir. Not yet, anyway."

"Have you learned anything more about or from the Khellan officers?"

"No, sir."

"Once we're over both bridges, I'll spend a glass or so riding with
each one of them, starting with Major Calkoran. Tonight we'll talk over
what I discover." *Or what you don't, if you fail to learn anything of importance or
interest.*

After his initial meeting with the three majors, Quaeryt had decided
that he'd learn little or nothing in any formal meeting, at least not until
the Khellans were more comfortable with him, and he thought the only
way to do that would be to ride with them for periods of time during the
advance on Variana.

"Fifth Battalion stands ready, sir," announced Zhelan formally.

"Thank you, Major. I'll report that to the commander. I will be riding
with him for a time. As always, you are in command in my absence."
Zhelan knew that, but Quaeryt made the statement to reinforce that fact
to the imager undercaptains, and he was leaving them with Zhelan at the
moment. Although Skarpa half requested, half ordered the imagers to ride

in the van, Quaeryt didn't think he'd mind at least until they had crossed the second bridge into Bovarian territory.

"Yes, sir."

Quaeryt turned in the saddle. "Undercaptain Voltyr, you are in command of the imager undercaptains, but you answer to the major in my absence."

"Yes, sir."

Quaeryt turned the mare and rode toward the head of the column to meet with Skarpa, arriving just before Meinyt reined up.

"Good morning, Subcommanders," said Skarpa.

"Good morning," replied Quaeryt. "Fifth Battalion stands ready."

"Fifth Tilboran is ready," added Meinyt.

"Then we should proceed." After a moment Skarpa added, "Whoever would have thought a major, a captain, and a scholar would have ended up where we are?" He grinned at Quaeryt. "Except for the scholar, and he didn't expect to become a subcommander. I told him he ought to be an officer."

"Everyone's allowed some doubts," replied Quaeryt with a laugh.

"Any last moment news about the Bovarians?" asked Meinyt.

"There's no sign of any troopers within fifteen milles," said Skarpa. "The scouts haven't covered the area west of that except along the river, but there's no indication of Bovarian forces."

"First indication is when we lose someone or they attack," said Meinyt.

"They won't attack soon. They don't have many men close enough to attack in force. They've barely had enough time to get a messenger to Variana and to ride back here."

"Archers or crossbowmen and destroying bridges?" suggested Quaeryt.

"We'll have to keep alert for those sorts of things," said Skarpa. "I think Marshal Deucalon will face more of that, though. His force is larger, and the roads on the north side of the river are better." He raised his arm and nodded to the hornist.

The call for the advance echoed across the north end of the river, and the outriders started forward. Meinyt nodded, then turned and rode back to Fifth Regiment, which brought up the rear and guarded the supply wagons.

"If you wouldn't mind my riding with you, sir, for a bit?" asked Quaeryt. "It's acceptable that the imagers remain with the battalion for a time?"

"For the morning, perhaps longer, depending on what the scouts report." Skarpa urged his mount forward, and Quaeryt eased the mare in alongside him. "What do you have in mind?"

"I'm not certain I have anything in mind. I was more interested in anything you might have considered."

"I'm sure you've noticed that we have all the elements of the Telaryn forces that might be considered suspect or different."

"Piedryn forces that are less well trained, Khellan rebels, and imagers, you mean? Not to mention Tilbcran regiments commanded by officers considered possibly less . . . traditional. With far fewer archers and engineers, as well. Have I missed anything?"

"You didn't mention a subcommander married to the sister of the Lord of Telaryn. He is an officer with a habit of not respecting the privileged excesses of certain High Holders."

"Has it been said like that?"

"Not quite. It might as well have been, though. Why do you think the forces were split that way?"

"The most obvious reason was because the forces on the north side of the Aluse will face greater opposition. A careful commander would place his strongest forces where he expects the greatest opposition."

"That is certainly what Marshal Deucalon has said."

"You don't believe him?"

Skarpa smiled. "Do you think that Lord Bhayar is a gambler?"

Quaeryt shook his head. "He calculates, but he is anything but a gambler. He will let others take risks, but only so long as he will not be the one to pay if they lose."

"That is why we were ordered not to get too far ahead of the northern force."

"Because we have to be forward in order to be successful, more than a day, and if we fail, that failure falls on us?"

"I thought you would understand."

As they reached the midsection of the fortified bridge, Quaeryt glanced to the western wall. It was difficult to tell the section that had been damaged by the Bovarian barge when it had exploded against the bridge pier below at the beginning of the battle for Ferravyl. Several of the replacement stones looked identical. *Those Threkhyl imaged?* "They repaired the bridge so well you can't tell it was damaged."

"The roadbed was hardly touched in the center. You and the imagers preserved it more than any would have believed possible."

"They still have a lot to learn."

"It's interesting that you know so much about what they need to know."

"Scholars need to know a great deal, and I've always enjoyed learning."

Skarpa might well suspect, or even be convinced, that Quaeryt was an imager, but he wasn't about to admit it yet. And not in public.

"You do know quite a bit. Everything from imaging to rulers, even to
the Nameless." Skarpa grinned at Quaeryt. "You know we still don't have
a chorister in the southern army . . ."

Quaeryt groaned.

"I can't really insist that a subcommander . . . but . . . the officers and
men . . ."

"All right . . . but no offerings and no blessings."

"I thought you might see it that way."

"Did I have a choice?"

"No. That's because you're an honest man, and you worry about your
officers and men."

"And you're a persuasive scoundrel," countered Quaeryt.

"Of course. That's why I'm a commander. In wartime, anyway."

As he rode down the south half of the bridge, Quaeryt looked out at
the triangle of land between the Aluse River and the Vyl River, and then at
the stone bridge that he and the imagers had created. Two weeks before, the
ground had been covered with ice and frozen bodies. Despite the comparative pleasantness of the morning, he shivered for a moment.

Two long mounded berms of freshly packed earth now crossed the
triangle comprising the bluff above where the rivers met. The mounds
were the final resting place of more than twelve thousand Bovarians. A
smaller pyramidal mound with a stone before it was located to the north
and east. For the Telaryn dead.

"You'd never believe what this looked like two weeks ago." Quaeryt
felt he had to say something.

"Lord Bhayar ordered every man in every regiment to spend time dealing with the dead," replied Skarpa.

That was another thing Quaeryt hadn't known, although he had seen
hundreds toiling when, barely able to ride, he had been escorted to Nordruil. "How did they take it?"

"They complained when they thought no officers were listening. What
else? Of course, many of them ended up with better weapons or a few more
coins. But it was better than letting them just strip the dead and leave them.
Had to do something, and do it quickly. That's the problem with fighting in
summer near a city."

Quaeryt nodded.

As they rode along the road beside the berms and neared the imager-built bridge, Quaeryt could see wagon ruts in the still-soft ground. "The locals haven't wasted much time in using the bridge."

"Not at all." Skarpa snorted. "Except the local ferryman wrote a complaint to the marshal. Said the bridge had destroyed his livelihood."

There's always someone. "All he has to do is move ten milles upriver. There aren't any bridges there, and most people won't travel ten milles downstream and then back to take a bridge if there's a ferry." Quaeryt paused, as a thought struck him. "But there's likely already a ferryman there."

"The same thing would have happened sooner or later. If Bhayar wins, he'd have built a bridge. Same thing if Kharst had won. Just would have taken longer."

As the mare carried Quaeryt onto the bridge, he could see that it was not quite as large as he had thought from a distance, although it was wide enough for two farm wagons side by side—if with little space to spare. The side walls were low, only a little more than a yard high, but the paving stones were smooth and well fitted.

Skarpa looked to Quaeryt. "We'd best win this war, or this bridge will work against us."

"We could explode it," joked Quaeryt.

"After all the death around it, I'd hate to do that. Better just to conquer Bovaria. Might even be better for the Bovarians."

"I've never heard much good about Rex Kharst."

"Has anyone?" countered Skarpa. "He keeps everyone in line by killing anyone who disagrees. It works, but . . ."

"How does he keep the High Holders in line?"

"That's what he used his troopers for . . . and his imagers. Among other things, I've heard."

"Oh . . ."

Skarpa nodded. "That's another problem you might have to face. If it comes to that, and after what you did at Ferravyl, it probably will."

As if you needed another one. "At least, if that's true, his imagers were killing High Holders and not merchants and the common people."

Skarpa frowned. "That's better?"

"How many High Holders who support Kharst is Bhayar likely to allow to retain their lands? You can't punish every factor and merchant in Bovaria, but you could . . ." Quaeryt paused, then shut his mouth.

"Could what?"

"I was going to say that Bhayar could replace most of the High Holders, but he can't. Not unless he wants chaos."

This time, Skarpa was the one to shake his head—again.

Once the entire column was clear of the bridge, Quaeryt cleared his throat. "Sir . . . if you don't mind . . ."

Skarpa smiled. "Go."

After a nod, Quaeryt turned the mare and rode down the shoulder of the narrow dirt road that was barely wide enough for a single wagon. He finally eased the mare in beside Major Calkoran.

"Sir?" The Khellan officer did not conceal his surprise at Quaeryt's presence.

"It will be some time before we encounter any Bovarians. You fought them for a long time." Quaeryt kept his Bovarian as precise as he could.

"On the borders for years. Almost a year after they invaded. We almost broke them at Khelgror. There were too many of them."

"You have seen how they fight. You know what they do well . . . and what they do not. I have fought the Tilborans, but not the Bovarians. I would like to hear what you can tell me about the Bovarians."

"You know we do not trust any of the rulers in Lydar."

"I do." Quaeryt laughed softly. "One must take care with all rulers, but I believe Lord Bhayar to be the best of those who remain."

"So it is said." Calkoran shrugged. "Why do you think so?"

"His father punished those who attacked Pharsi women in Tilbor. The son upheld the same values in Extela."

"The word is that you upheld those values and were removed." Calkoran fixed his dark eyes on the subcommander.

Quaeryt shook his head. "I was removed because I angered the merchants and the High Holders. I would not let them charge too much for flour after the eruption in Extela. I supported the Pharsi who stopped a soldier from violating a girl, and Lord Bhayar supported me in that." That was close enough to the truth, although the reality had been more complex.

"Did you take any golds?"

"No."

"Not a one?"

"Only what I was paid as governor."

"That is what the major who is paymaster said." Calkoran laughed. "You must be the only governor who did not fill his purse."

Quaeryt shrugged.

"Why?"

Quaeryt decided to tell the truth behind it all. "I would not be content with golds. My dreams are larger I want a land where Pharsi, scholars, and imagers can all be what they will, under the same laws as everyone else."

Calkoran looked at him, then said quietly, "You are either mad . . . or a lost one."

"Is there any difference?"

The major smiled and shook his head. "Let me tell you what I know about the Bovarians. They follow their officers, but most follow like they are sheep . . . They attack in mass formations . . ."

That was what they did at Ferravyl . . .

". . . they try to split your forces and then butcher any who are cut off . . . They ask for surrender. If one does not surrender, they show no mercy . . . not to men or women ."

Quaeryt continued to listen as he rode beside the major under a clear sky and a morning sun that was already hot and threatened to be sweltering by midday and intolerable by midafternoon.

9

Meredi morning dawned early and warm, promising to be even hotter and damper than the previous two days. The south river road had not narrowed, but it had become more and more rutted with each mille traveled toward Rivecote. The local people were mostly croppers and peasants, from what Quaeryt saw of their fields and cots, for not a person was visible when the regiments rode by dwellings or through hamlets. Nor was any livestock, and while he saw a few dogs, they were at a distance. He couldn't blame the locals.

Although there were no signs of Bovarians, Quaeryt continued to carry full imaging shields, rather than the lighter shields that triggered full shields, as part of his efforts to rebuild his imaging endurance. Just before eighth glass, Quaeryt was riding with Major Zhael, who had obviously talked with Calkoran, since Zhael asked no questions about Quaeryt's background.

"What did the Bovarians do that you did not expect them to do?" asked Quaeryt.

"We thought they would do their worst, and they did."

"What sorts of things?"

Zhael offered a sour smile. "They burned the grasslands so the forage for our horses was less. They burned every dwelling beside any road they traveled. When they could not burn crops they rode their horses through the fields and broke the plants."

"Did they offer any reasons?"

"They did. They told those who survived that the destruction was because they had not accepted the merciful offers of Rex Kharst." Zhael spat away from Quaeryt. "We know the mercy of the Bovarians. A generation ago all the Pharsi in Kherseilles had their shops and their lands taken after the Rex invaded. They were marched into the barrens north of Mantes and told to rebuild there. Many fled to Khel. Rex Kharst's father demanded their return. Our High Council refused. The rex did not want them back. He wanted a reason to attack us. He did. We defeated his best, and sent them back to Variana with their tails between their legs, those that even had tails remaining, and we re-took Kherseilles."

"What was different this time?"

"The Red Death. Some say that Kharst loosed sick rodents from merchant ships he had hired. Others say he worked the pus from victims into cheap woolens. The plague started in Eshtora, Ouestan, and Pointe Neiman. Almost half the young men in Khelgror died . . . and many of the young women."

Quaeryt had known of the plague that had ravaged the west of Lydar five years previously, and Vaelora had mentioned the deaths in Khelgror. But half the young men?

"I see your doubt. Most great illnesses take the old and the children. This one did not. It took all ages, but mostly the young and hale."

"Why do you think Kharst was to blame?"

"He had his armies ready in the spring after the cold of winter. We almost threw them back, but we had too few troopers. Even the women fought. They suffered horribly if they were captured. Most would not let themselves be taken."

"I'm sorry to hear that." Quaeryt didn't know what else to say.

"You could not have known." Zhael shrugged fatalistically. "Few who were not there would believe."

Quaeryt understood more why the Khellans were so determined to fight against Kharst. But can you keep their rage limited to the Bovarian fighting men?

They rode quietly for a time, Quaeryt blotting his forehead now and again, continually readjusting his visor cap, wondering how much hotter it would get, and knowing that it would.

Then, more than a mille ahead, above the trees on the south side of the road, Quaeryt saw smoke, more than was likely from a hamlet's chimneys in summer. "Excuse me, Major, I need to see what the scouts have reported."

"The smoke?" Zhael shook his head. "It may be crops burning. Kharst would not hesitate to burn his own people's yields."

"I hope you're wrong."

Zhael lifted his eyebrows.

Quaeryt guided the mare onto the shoulder of the road and urged her into a faster pace. Even so, more than half a quint passed before he reached Skarpa at the head of the column.

"What is it?" he asked as he eased the mare beside the commander.

"Crops burning. Winter wheat corn."

"Where?"

"To the south of the river road. The road's clear."

"The Bovarians aren't even trying to stop us, but burning the crops of their own people? What's the point of that?" Quaeryt shook his head. "We can't harvest it yet, and all that does is beggar the people."

"That's Kharst for you. If he can't have it, neither will we." Skarpa looked at Quaeryt. "Do you have something in mind?"

"I'd like to look into it. It might not hurt if we could get rid of the Bovarians firing the fields."

"They may be counting on that," Skarpa pointed out. "Just don't hazard your troops unnecessarily, and don't pursue for very long."

"I'll just take first company."

Skarpa nodded.

Quaeryt rode back to Fifth Battalion where he explained the situation to Zhelan. Then he went on, gesturing to the southwest. "The fields are there. The Bovarians won't come this way, and they probably won't take the river road back west. That means that they have to move south or hole up. Let's see if we can find them. Just first company. I'll accompany them, but the imagers will stay with you and the rest of the battalion."

Zhelan offered a concerned look, but said nothing.

"The Bovarians can't have that many troopers here, not after Ferravyl and not on this side of the river, and you've told me that Undercaptain Ghaelyn is very experienced."

"That's true, sir."

"The entire battalion can't move that quickly."

"Yes, sir."

Quaeryt smiled. "We'll be all right. We might not even find anyone."

"I'm not certain the Bovarians have enough sense to flee. When there's a fight, there's always a chance . . ."

"I know. I will be careful." *Just not in the way you think.*

Zhelan gestured behind him, and Ghaelyn rode forward.

"Undercaptain, the subcommander has a mission for first company. He'll direct you."

"Yes, sir."

"Undercaptain," said Quaeryt. "We need to keep the Bovarians from burning crops. More crops. That means we need to get about two milles to the southwest, and not by the river road, so that we can get behind the Bovarian raiders who seem to be firing the fields of the local peasants."

"Well, sir . . . there was a clear track south a few hundred yards back."

"We might as well try it," replied Quaeryt.

Almost half a quint later, Ghaelyn and Quaeryt followed the scouts and three outriders down a dusty dirt track that headed south. After less than a mille, the track curved to the southeast around a pond surrounded by rushes and cattails. On the far side of the pond was a meadow or pasture, with a cot and a large shed, not quite big enough to be a barn, set farther back on a low rise. Behind the buildings was a stand of trees, possibly a woodlot.

Beyond the trees, Quaeryt thought he saw another smoke trail, and he gestured to Ghaelyn. "See that?"

"It looks like they might be burning another field or two."

"Can we swing south and then west?" Quaeryt stood in the stirrups and looked for a path or a trail.

"There looks to be a narrow way over there." Ghaelyn pointed.

"Call in the scouts," ordered Quaeryt. "Until they're just fifty yards or so ahead. Then have them lead the way."

The undercaptain frowned.

"Go ahead. I don't want to give the Bovarians much warning."

Quaeryt waited until the outriders and scouts repositioned themselves, then nodded to Ghaelyn. "Quiet riding from here on."

"Quiet riding. Pass it back."

Quaeryt extended a concealment across the company, including the scouts. He could feel a definite strain, and dropped his personal shields to the lightest of triggered shields. He'd promised Vaelora never to ride without shields. *You didn't say how strong a shield.* Still, he hated the idea that he wasn't following exactly what she'd meant.

The narrow path barely allowed two mounts abreast, and riders' trousers and boots continually brushed the bushes and vegetation.

Abruptly the path came out of the brush and trees and passed between a gap in a low stone wall that marked the eastern edge of two wheat fields split by the continuation of the path. A line of fire was burning across the field to the north.

Quaeryt glanced to the southern field, where three men with torches were on foot, trying to ignite the golden winter wheat close to harvest. Four others were mounted, three of them holding the reins of the mounts of the men on foot. All wore the gray-blue uniforms of Bovarian troopers.

"They haven't seen us," murmured Ghaelyn. "Again." He looked quizzically at Quaeryt.

"Get ready to order a charge with first squad," said Quaeryt.

After several moments, when first squad was clear of the woods, he turned to the undercaptain. "Now!"

"First squad! Ready arms! Charge!"

Quaeryt held the concealment until the troopers reached the outriders, then dropped it and raised his own full shields.

The Bovarians looked up, startled at the muted thunder of hooves. The three men with torches started to run. One stopped and thrust his torch at the nearest Telaryn trooper, who avoided the flaming brand and then back-cut with his sabre. A second trooper cut down the Bovarian. The other two tried to mount the horses left for them.

Two of the Bovarians tried to fight from horseback but were run down. The other two wheeled their mounts and spurred them across the field to the west of the one just beginning to burn.

"We don't want to chase them, sir," said Ghaelyn quietly, just so Quaeryt could hear him.

"No, we don't."

Quaeryt imaged away the saddle girths of the closer of the two fleeing Bovarians. The Bovarian tried to grab his mount's mane as the saddle slipped under him, but after several moments, with his boots dragging the side of the path, he lost his grip and tumbled to the dirt.

"Second squad! Bring him in!" ordered the undercaptain.

While the troopers rode toward the dazed Bovarian in his ripped and soiled uniform, Quaeryt glanced to his right, where the fire continued to race across the golden stalks of wheat corn. *No clouds in the sky . . . nothing you can do.*

Then he looked to where first squad had run down the others. Three Bovarians were facedown on the ground. Another remained mounted, but blood stained his right sleeve, and he was cradling his injured arm. Another was still fighting, but as Quaeryt watched, one of the troopers clouted him on the back of the head with the flat of a sabre, and he slumped in the saddle.

Quaeryt counted. Besides the one who had fled immediately, another Bovarian had to have escaped. Quaeryt shook his head and waited for the troopers to bring back the Bovarian he'd unhorsed with his imaging.

"Only eight of them," said Ghaelyn.

"Only eight here. I hate to think how many others there are torching other fields." Quaeryt pointed to the smoke rising into the sky farther west, adding to the summer heat haze.

"Wouldn't think they'd have too many."

"Neither would I, but it doesn't take many."

Both watched as first squad returned.

"Here's the one who tried to get away," announced the squad leader.

Two of the rankers had dismounted and held the Bovarian, whose hands were tied behind his back.

Quaeryt looked down at the sullen-faced man, older than he had expected. "Where were you supposed to meet when you finished torching the fields?" asked Quaeryt in Bovarian.

The ranker's eyes widened slightly, presumably at being addressed in his own tongue, but he remained silent.

"Once more, where were you supposed to meet?"

Quaeryt image-projected authority and the sense that if the man didn't answer, he'd be staked out on the ground and burned, slowly, limb by limb.

The Bovarian ranker shuddered, turned white, and crumpled in the arms of the two Telaryn rankers holding him, both of whom also paled.

"Throw water on his face," Quaeryt said dryly.

When the Bovarian regained his senses, Quaeryt just looked at him. "Where were you supposed to meet?"

The man swallowed . . . finally stuttering. "West . . . a mille, by the tumbledown barn . . . in back."

"Tie him up and leave him for the locals to deal with."

The captive turned pale again.

"They're your people," Quaeryt pointed out. He turned to Ghaelyn. "Tie him up to that small tree over there. Quickly. Do the same with the others who are alive. Then we'll see if the remaining Bovarians try to meet at the barn."

Quaeryt could sense Ghaelyn's disapproval, but he said nothing until the company was riding westward again.

"Undercaptain . . . I'd rather not be fighting, but they started this war. I don't believe in violence against people who aren't fighting. Burning these poor people's fields wouldn't help the Bovarians. Those crops wouldn't help us anyway. We don't have time to wait for harvest. All it does is harm people who have nothing to do with the fighting. And I won't have that— whether it's by our men or theirs. You can pass that on. If someone lifts a weapon, even a pitchfork against a trooper, then he's an enemy, and they can cut him down. But we're not here to destroy people's lives, just to prove we can. Do you understand?" Quaeryt looked sidewise at Ghaelyn. He thought the undercaptain understood. "Besides, I don't think the peasants and small growers really care who wins so long as they aren't hurt. They'll be a lot easier to govern if they aren't starving and angry." *You hope so, anyway.*

"Yes, sir."

The ride to the tumbled-down barn was fruitless. Although there were tracks around the collapsed structure, the Bovarians had hurried off.

Quaeryt studied the horizon in all directions. He didn't see any more smoke, but all that meant was that they'd stopped some burning for at least a while. Still, there couldn't be that many Bovarians around, could there?

Two glasses later, with first company returned to the main body, Quaeryt rode to report to Skarpa.

"I see the locals didn't come out to thank you," observed the commander dryly as Quaeryt rode up beside him.

"I didn't think they would."

"How many did you capture?"

"We didn't," Quaeryt said. "Some fled. Of the rest, those we didn't kill outright in the fighting were all wounded, and I left them with the locals."

"They may not fare well . . ."

"That's their problem. I don't like troopers who burn the crops of their own people, and it's only fair that I left them with their own people."

Skarpa's mouth opened, then closed.

"You might talk to the Pharsi officers about how Kharst took Khel. Or think about the fact that as soon as Kharst found out that Extela had been devastated by an eruption he was massing troops for an attack on Ferravyl."

"Aren't you acting like him?" asked Skarpa.

"No. I kept my troopers from touching or hurting the locals, and I did my best to save their crops. But when troopers don't even care for their own people, and when they kill anyone who doesn't immediately surrender, I tend to lose patience."

"Do you think the Bovarian people will understand that difference?"

Quaeryt smiled tiredly. "I think it will become clear before long." *At least you hope so.* But he was all too conscious that such might well not be the case.

10

The two regiments and Quaeryt's battalion made good progress on the rest of Meredi, despite the narrow rough road. They ran across only one other area where the crops had been torched—apparently even before the fires Quaeryt had attempted to prevent, because the fields farther west were black, without a trace of smoke or embers. Other than that, they saw no more signs of Bovarians.

Jeudi morning was cooler, and thick clouds rolled out of the north. By late afternoon a cold deluge poured down, with no sign of letting up anytime soon. The regiments took what shelter they could, split between three hamlets each some five milles apart along the river. Quaeryt and Fifth Battalion made an encampment in the smallest hamlet, making do with several sheds, and a few tents and waterproofs used as slanted awnings.

Once he had inspected all the shelters, and checked once more with Zhelan and all the company officers he went back and found Major Arion, where he had last seen him, standing by the doorway to a shed, looking out into the rain.

Although the Pharsi officer was the youngest of the Khellan majors, he was likely several years older than Quaeryt. "Sir?"

"Major Zhael mentioned the High Council. Khel was the only land in Lydar that was not governed by a hereditary ruler. How did the Council come to be? Do you know?"

Arion smiled. "I have heard the tales. Does anyone know how true they are?"

"Tales are better than ignorance. Tell me about the Council. Then tell me the tales. Besides, what else are we going to do right now?"

"Why do you wish to know?"

"There are many reasons. One is simply that it may be part of my heritage, and I know little about Khel, and nothing about the High Council."

Arion looked out into the rain again, but began to speak. "Once, every city in Khel was governed by a clan, and the elders of the clan met and made decisions. Unlike Bovaria, many of the elders were women . . ."

From what he'd seen so far of Pharsi women, that scarcely surprised Quaeryt.

"But the cities and even the towns grew. There were soon two or three or four clans in a town, and some clans were of herders, and others of crafters, and still others of growers, and each clan wanted its needs to come first. So the elders in Khelgror, for it was the first, formed a council for the city and the lands around it, and each year, the head of a different clan headed the local council. Then came a time when one region felt its needs were more important than another. The head councilors of each region decided that they would form a council from all the chief councilors in Khel. Each year the councilor from a different region would head that council. They called it the High Council. The High Councils lasted longer than there has been a rex in Bovaria or a lord in Telaryn." Arion shrugged, but did not look at Quaeryt.

"Weren't there struggles in all that time?"

"There were arguments. Some of them lasted years. And there are stories. Some even say that the lost ones come from a clan in the western part of the Montagnes D'Glace, and that they were lost when they went to take up arms against those below the mountains. Erion threw a mountain from the sky and sealed the way from their valley. Only those wise enough to know when to use arms were able to leave the valley. The price for leaving was to bear the mark of Erion."

"The mark of Erion?" prompted Quaeryt, suspecting all too well what Arion would say.

"You bear it, though you do not flaunt it. Hair almost as white as the ice, and a reminder that the worship of physical perfection is vanity." An ironic smile crossed the major's lips. "A form of Naming, if you will, for those who follow the Nameless."

"You follow Erion and Artiema?" asked Quaeryt.

"I would say that we believe that they are manifestations of the one who cannot be named. Calling that one the Nameless is another way of Naming."

Quaeryt nodded. "I've often pondered that."

"That does not surprise me, Subcommander." Arion paused. "Why did you turn the Bovarians over to the growers?"

"Because the Bovarian troopers destroyed the crops of those people. I thought they should decide."

"What if they fear Rex Kharst so much that they release them?"

"That is their choice. To do otherwise would tell the local people that Lord Bhayar would merely be another ruler like Kharst."

"How do you know he will not?"

"I think I know him well enough to say that he will not."

"How well does he know you?"

"Well enough to allow his sister to wed me."

Arion smiled softly. "He thinks to bind you. In the end you will bind him because you cannot escape who you are. He is trapped, and he knows it not. He cannot conquer Lydar without you . . ."

"You give me far too much credit."

The Pharsi officer shook his head. "You are a lost one, and the hand of Erion. If Lord Bhayar rejects or destroys you, he destroys himself. He may not know that, but it is so. Did not his sister seek you out?"

"She wrote me," Quaeryt admitted. "How did you know that?"

"I saw her." Arion smiled. "Actually, I heard she rode to find you when you had fallen, and I made certain I saw her. She did not see me. She has the sight."

Quaeryt frowned. *How can he know that?*

"My grandmere had the sight, and there is a way, a certain . . . I cannot describe it, but your wife is the only woman beside my grandmere I have ever seen who is like that." The major sighed softly. "Grandmere saw the Red Death. She warned the High Council against trade with Bovarian merchanters, but the coastal clans sought the Bovarian golds. Golds always speak louder than sight or wisdom."

"I've seen that more than once."

"That is good that you have. You will see it again . . . and again."

"Then how does wisdom prevail?" countered Quaeryt.

"Only when those who are wise know when to use force and what force to use."

Does it always come down to that? Brute force? Except . . . did it have to be brute force? Was there a way to apply force without the devastation of a battle such as that at Ferravyl?

He was still pondering that when he realized that Arion had slipped away, back into the gloom of the shed.

As Quaeryt stood in the dimness of a rainy twilight fading into a cold, wet, and dark night, he couldn't help but wonder: *For all your unbelief in the Nameless, in any deity, how can you know whether you chart your own course? And, for all your thought, whether it is truly the right course.*

11

Quaeryt did not sleep well on Jeudi night, and not because of the damp and the crowded conditions in the shed he shared with others. The conversation with Major Arion had disturbed him more than he would have believed.

It wasn't that Arion had predicted victory. He hadn't. He'd as much as said that Bhayar would fail without Quaeryt, but that didn't mean Bhayar would succeed, either. By implication, Arion's words declared that Quaeryt was a tool and would not accomplish what he wanted by himself. Quaeryt had known that. It was the major's preternatural *knowing* that had disconcerted Quaeryt. And yet, from the bearing and the reactions of the other two Khellan majors, it seemed clear to Quaeryt that Arion had not told them. *Why not?*

Quaeryt didn't have an answer for that question. Nor did he feel comfortable asking Arion, although he could not have said why, and he didn't want to press the matter until he could figure out the reason for his own unease.

While the skies were clearing on Vendrei morning, mud was everywhere, and getting the wagons on the road took an extra glass. The air was cooler than the day before, but Quaeryt had no doubts that by afternoon it would be even steamier than on Jeudi.

Because Fifth Battalion had no engineers and needed fewer supplies than a regiment, it had fewer wagons, and those wagons carried little beside spare sabres and food. Before long Quaeryt and Zhelan were at the head of the slow-moving column, behind the outriders and a vanguard of one company from Third Regiment. Quaeryt rode on one side of Skarpa, Zhelan on the other, with the imager undercaptains directly behind them.

They had covered two milles, and the road looked to be getting firmer when a scout came riding around the curve in the road ahead, making straight for Skarpa.

Even before he reached the commander, he called out, "Sir, there's a barge coming downriver. It looks to be filled with Bovarian troopers."

"How many?"

"Two squads of foot, it looks like, sir. They're packed in tight." The trooper pulled up beside Zhelan and looked across at Skarpa.

"Do they look to be seeking a landing nearby?"

"I wouldn't think so, sir They're keeping well to the middle of the river."

Skarpa turned to Quaeryt. "They want to land a force behind us to cause trouble and force us to leave men behind . . . or slow us down."

"We'll see what we can do." Quaeryt glanced to his right, but the road had turned southward around a low hill covered with trees and brush, and immediately behind them was a wide stretch of swampy ground between the road and the river. "We'll have to ride back east to get closer to the water." Quaeryt turned in the saddle. "Imagers! On me. Single file. We're riding back east." He guided the mare onto the shoulder of the road. While her hooves sank somewhat into the wet ground, the shoulder wasn't as sloppy as the road itself, although it certainly would have been had the entire battalion been riding there.

As he rode, he glanced back and spoke. "There's a barge filled with Bovarian troops. We need to get to where we can sink it. Pass it back."

"Yes, sir," replied Voltyr, riding directly behind Quaeryt as they headed back past the companies of Fifth Battalion.

"We're headed to sink a barge filled with Bovarian troopers . . ."

The grassy slope that Quaeryt recalled was farther east than he'd thought, because he rode for close to a quint before he saw it, and another half quint before he reined up, moving past the troopers of Fifth Regiment, headed westward, who glanced curiously at the imagers who joined Quaeryt on the grassy and muddy patch barely large enough for all seven of them.

Quaeryt scanned the river for several moments before he caught sight of the craft, still upstream of where he was, but by only a hundred yards, if that. The river stretched perhaps seventy yards from shore to shore, and the single craft near the middle wasn't a barge, but more like a flatboat, except that what would have been the stem on a ship was flat across the front, but angled forward like a ship's prow. *For grounding where there aren't wharves?* It also had a pilothouse in the rear with a long sweep rudder extending from the stern.

"Threkhyl! Forward!" Quaeryt ordered.

The ginger-haired undercaptain pulled his mount up beside Quaeryt. "We need some holes in the front hull of the barge. Now."

"Front hull?"

"It's got a flat front. More water will go in a hole there."

Threkhyl concentrated.

"Shaelyt, Voltytr! Holes in the side hull! Desyrk, Akoryt! You two as well."

Quaeryt also imaged what he hoped was a large gap in the front of the boat, then watched.

For several moments nothing happened, then a man in gray, likely a crewman rather than a trooper, threw a bucket toward the troopers packed in the forward part of the barge. The tillerman leaned forward through the opening in the pilothouse and yelled something, pointing toward the imagers.

Quaeryt held his shields ready, but none of the troopers lifted a bow. Instead, the flatboat-like craft slowly turned toward the north bank of the river, if sluggishly.

The closer the barge got to the bank, the lower and lower in the water it appeared to be. Then . . . some fifteen yards from the swampy area that formed the bank, it lurched to a stop.

"What was that?" asked one of the imagers.

Quaeryt didn't immediately recognize the voice, but thought it might have been Akoryt. "Sandbank or mud bar. It didn't hit that hard, and that's going to be a problem for them."

"Sir?" asked Shaelyt.

"It hit at an angle. It's still sinking, but the current's going to swing the stern downstream and back toward the deeper water. It might pull it off the sandbar, and then they'll be sinking in deeper water."

Bovarians began to scramble out of the barge as the stern swung outward and toward the middle of the river. Those closest to the swampy area moved a yard or two, their feet on the bar, then stepped into deeper water, most of them flailing and not expecting the sudden change in water depth. Quaeryt couldn't help but wince as he saw that most of the troopers could not swim.

Then the current pulled the flatboat, now totally awash, back toward the center of the Aluse River. More troopers jumped off the apparently sinking craft.

Quaeryt wanted to shake his head. If they had just hung on to the boat, awash as it was, they likely could have lasted until it eventually grounded. Belatedly, he realized that there were too many troopers for all of them to do that, but even the last ones ignored the pilot who was clearly trying to tell them to stay with the boat.

Quaeryt turned away. "Form up. We need to catch up with the battalion."

"You're going to let them drown, sir?" asked Baelthm.

"What would you suggest?" asked Quaeryt. "We can't do anything from here. What's left of the boat is floating downstream faster than we can ride. Even if we could help, should we? They wanted to attack us from the rear. If they had, we would have had to stop them, and that would have meant killing some, if not all of them. For now, some can swim and will survive."

"It seems . . . wrong . . . sir."

"What is the difference between killing Bovarians directly by imaging ice rain and sinking their boat?"

Baelthm was silent.

"We are at war, Undercaptain, and they attacked us. They even burned the crops of their own people."

"Yes, sir."

Quaeryt could tell that Baelthm was not convinced, but he only said, "I'd like you to think about it. If you still have questions, we'll talk later."

"Yes, sir."

Quaeryt turned the mare. "Forward!"

12

For another three days, Skarpa led the southern army westward. At one point, the river road ended at a swamp, and it took most of Samedi for Fifth Battalion and the regiments to make their way through marshy ground, fields, and along paths barely wide enough for a single rider before they reached another section of road . . . that lasted for ten milles before they had to detour yet again, a delay made longer by the need to replace the axle of a wagon that collapsed at the narrowest part of the path they followed when they tried to get around a section of the road washed out years before and never repaired.

The imagers were of little help, because none of them had any experience with wagons, and imaging, Quaeryt was reminded, required a knowledge of what needed to be imaged . . . or a great deal of time and experimentation. In a bitter sort of way, Quaeryt realized that he knew far more about how bridges were constructed than he did about wagons and axles.

Unfortunately, there was enough of the clayey soil in the rugged area they crossed on Samedi and Solayi to create mud, so that his boots and his trousers below the knees were mud-spattered, as were the lower quarters of all the horses.

Given the sorry state of men and mounts, Skarpa did not call on Quaeryt to conduct services for the Nameless on Solayi evening, but after locating a rocky and sandy area on the edge of the river, he had the regiments and Quaeryt's battalion clean up themselves, their mounts, and their equipment.

Lundi dawned slightly cooler and drier, and the condition of the south river road improved as well, so that there were only occasional patches of mud.

"The road's better because we're nearing Rivecote Sud," said Skarpa, riding beside Quaeryt.

"I still wonder why Kharst let the roads get so bad."

Skarpa shrugged.

"Do you think they'll use the cable ferry to send troopers across to stop us?"

"Your guess is as good as mine. They might not even know we're here, but I don't think we'll be that fortunate." Skarpa laughed. "I'm not even sure how we managed to get here."

"We haven't seen any new signs of Bovarians or their scouts," Quaeryt said.

"That only means they haven't left tracks where we could see them. Even if they didn't send out scouts, some of the locals might have passed on word."

"Or some of the troopers who survived the flatboat sinking."

"Someone did. One way or another. We'll likely run into some opposition before long."

Quaeryt glanced at the fields on the south side of the road. While the cots and outbuildings were less ramshackle than those he'd seen on the two previous days, they were still placed comparatively far apart, and there were places where the only thing that seemed to grow was a big-leafed ground cover that swallowed everything. Or was the plant so hardy that it was the biggest problem for the locals? "It should be a while yet. The cots are so far apart that I can't believe we're that close to even a village of any size."

"I wouldn't think so . . . but, with Bovarians, how would we know?"

Are people that different? Quaeryt did not voice the thought.

By the time they had ridden another glass, the cots and barns were larger and closer together, and looked more prosperous, some even with brick and mortar walls and slate roofs. The scouts returned and reported that the outskirts of the town were less than two milles away. They also had observed a force blocking the road just outside the town.

Skarpa called a halt and ordered the troopers to arms, then sent out more scouts in all directions. "Doesn't make sense to put a small force on the road outside of the town."

"Are they trying to delay us?"

"Might be. They also might be trying to use the cable ferry to bring over more troops."

"Or destroying it to keep us from using it," suggested Quaeryt. "Could we advance slowly, while you have Fifth Regiment circle the town and move in from the southwest?"

"That was my thought. I'm waiting for Meinyt."

Scarcely had Skarpa finished speaking than Meinyt rode up the shoulder of the still-narrow road and reined up facing the commander. "Sir?"

"I have a mission for you."

"You want us to circle and attack from the west?"

"See if you can take the cable ferry. Before they cut the cables, if you can."

"Yes, sir. Is there anything else?"

"Try not to make a mess of the town or the people, but don't hazard your troops."

"We'll do what we can." Meinyt nodded. "Anything else?"

"No. You know what to do." As Meinyt rode off, Skarpa turned to Quaeryt. "Let's start our deliberate advance."

A half mille later, after rounding a curve in the river road, Quaeryt and Skarpa were at the end of a gentle slope. Three-fifths of the way up a slope covered in low bushes, grass, and patches of dirt were the Bovarians, a ragtag force arrayed behind a makeshift line of pikes embedded in the small earthen berms that had to have been hastily piled up across the road and for some fifty yards on either side—until they reached stands of trees and brush. In the center was a company or so of regular Bovarian troopers, or at least men wearing those uniforms. On either side were men and even youths in gray shirts with bows and spears. Quaeryt even saw several ancient halberds. Another fifth of a mille behind them were several houses, and a row of shops.

"This could be a slaughter," said Skarpa, "unless they've got another force hidden."

"What do the scouts say?"

"They've circled the town. They can't find any sign of any other forces."

"There have to be other tricks that they have in mind," offered Quaeryt.

"My thought as well. They want us to attack. There's straw all across the ground, and most likely pits with stakes concealed there." Skarpa smiled ironically. "Or they want us to think that there are."

"What if we don't attack? What if we stand off and shoot arrows into them?"

"We've only got one squad of archers," said Skarpa. "Almost all of Bhayar's archers are on the other side of the river. Can you and the imagers do something?"

Quaeryt studied the berms and the pikes embedded in them. There was nothing there that could burn, and he really didn't want to fire the buildings behind the defenders. "We could probably kill a few at a distance, but not enough to make a difference."

"Could you do anything to make them less able to fight?"

Quaeryt frowned. He'd put oil under the boots of slam-thieves, imaged bread into mouths and throats, and used imaging in a variety of lethal ways, but except for the ice rain, most of his imaging had dealt with only a single person at once, or at most a few.

In the momentary silence, from behind him, someone sneezed—loudly.

Sneezing . . . of course . . . if we can do it. He concentrated, trying to image pepper flakes on the back of his hand that held the reins.

The fine black pepper appeared in a small circle.

Then he turned to Skarpa. "We might be able to do something." He turned in the saddle. "Shaelyt, how long can you deflect arrows?"

"For a time, sir."

"Threkhyl . . . you're one of the stronger imagers. How far away could you image something that doesn't weigh too much, say . . . a chunk of wood the size of a dagger?"

"A hundred yards, maybe two."

"All right . . . now can you image pepper, just a small amount . . . ground fine, into your hand?"

A puzzled expression crossed Threkhyl's face.

Shaelyt tried to hide a grin.

"Go ahead. I need to see if you can."

"Ah . . . I might be better with the red peppercorns."

"You might, but I want the kind that cause people to sneeze."

"I could do both." Threkhyl frowned.

A cloud of fine red and black flakes appeared above Threkhyl's hand.

"Good," said Quaeryt. "Now, get rid of it, gently."

Threkhyl wiped his hand on his trousers, and even though most of the pepper was well below his face, he sneezed several times, once violently. "What . . . ?"

"We're going to move forward, slowly, until we're close enough to image a cloud of pepper dust over the Bovarians."

"Why not just charge them?" demanded Threkhyl.

"Because we're still a long ways from Variana, and Commander Skarpa and I would like to arrive to fight the important battles with as many of our troopers as possible. Besides, most of the men in that group are locals, graybeards, and youths." Quaeryt was guessing about the graybeards, but he'd seen the locals and youths. "If we charge them directly, most of them will die, and we'll still lose men, and the Bovarians won't lose any of their seasoned troopers."

Skarpa cleared his throat, then said quietly, "You'll still need troopers. They'll attack you and the imagers immediately if you ride up alone."

Nothing.

"I know," replied Quaeryt in a low voice, then raised it. "Major Zhelan, Undercaptain Ghaelyn, forward!"

Both Zhelan and Ghaelyn rode up beside Quaeryt as if they'd been expecting the command, and they probably had, Quaeryt thought.

"Sir?" asked Zhelan.

"I need first company to escort the imager undercaptains up that slope. We're planning a surprise, and if it works, there may not be much fighting. If it doesn't, Major, you'll have to charge the locals. I think there are staked pits across the slope, but if first company and the imagers can advance slowly, we may be able to see and avoid them."

"They have a pike line, sir," said Zhelan.

"If you have to charge, leave first company with me and the imagers on the slope and cut to the north side and try to circle back behind the pike line."

Both Zhelan and Ghaelyn nodded. "Yes, sir."

Quaeryt looked to Skarpa.

"We'll support you as necessary, Subcommander."

Quaeryt understood what Skarpa hadn't said—that any failure was on Quaeryt's head, if only between the two of them, because commanders always got the credit . . . and the blame. Quaeryt also knew that Skarpa really didn't want a slaughter on his hands.

Almost half a quint passed before Quaeryt got the word that Fifth Battalion was in position and ready, time that he had used to offer detailed instructions to the imagers. He turned to the undercaptains. "Keep a line abreast behind the first ranks of first squad." That meant right behind him, although he didn't say that. Then he nodded to Ghaelyn.

"First company . . . forward."

The troopers rode forward at a walk.

First company and the imagers were within two hundred yards before a handful of arrows arched out from behind the berms, falling short by a good thirty yards.

"Shaelyt, don't try for any arrows until we reach where those fell."

"Yes, sir."

"Imagers, except for Shaelyt, no imaging until my command."

"Yes, sir."

As soon as the front rank crossed the ground where the arrows lay, another flight of shafts arched toward them. No more than a score, but all of them vanished.

That impressed Quaeryt.

A second volley followed, and those vanished as well as first company and the imagers continued forward. Quaeryt prepared to extend his own shields across the width of the front rank, not that he wanted to unless it was necessary.

"Threkhyl, image pepper."

Quaeryt added some pepper of his own, and a fine cloud drifted down on the waiting Bovarians.

Another volley of arrows arced toward the company, loosed just before the imaging, and Quaeryt extended his shields, which was just as well, because only half the shafts vanished from the sky. The others dropped harmlessly onto the dirt and grass in front of the company. Quaeryt could feel some strain, but he wasn't light-headed . . . not yet.

"All imagers, more pepper!" he ordered, imaging a second cloud of finely mixed red and black pepper across the middle of the uniformed Bovarians. "First company! Forward! At my pace!" He didn't know a command for the deliberate pace he wanted.

For a moment the fog of pepper was so thick that it appeared like a cloud.

As he led the company toward the sneezing, coughing mass of defenders, Quaeryt could see a line of pits, not covered well, but obvious enough to a rider moving slowly. "Beware the pits!"

As first company moved forward, a handful of uniformed Bovarian troopers realized that the pepper was mostly where they were and dashed forward into clearer air, their blades out. Some of the uniformed troopers lifted blades, and a few of the locals waved and thrust a few pikes and spears wildly, but it was obvious that few could even see or react. Then, most of the locals in gray threw down whatever weapons they had and ran for the stand of brush and trees to the south side of their line.

"Fifth Battalion! . . ." came the order from Zhelan.

"Forward!" Quaeryt heard Skarpa's command. "Deliberate pace. Beware the pits!"

As he continued to ride forward, imaging yet more pepper, Quaeryt could see the confusion, blindness, and sneezing among the defenders, and when first company neared the line of pits, he called to Ghaelyn, "Have them hold, arms ready!"

"First company!"

Within a quint, the skirmish was all over. The defenders, those who were able and had not already fled, found themselves attacked from behind and pushed toward their own staked pits. Only a handful even tried to fight.

Quaeryt hoped too many of those had not been killed or badly wounded, because he doubted most had really been true Bovarian troopers. Nonetheless, he held the imagers and first company in readiness just in case.

After a time, Skarpa rode over, and Quaeryt rode from his position to join him.

"You know that pepper trick won't work against regular troopers?" said Skarpa.

"I know. They'll have too many archers, and they won't let us get close enough." Quaeryt smiled. "But it might work in close combat when matters are not going well."

"You have a nasty turn of mind, Subcommander. It was a good tactic for this."

"I hoped it would be."

While the troopers of Third Regiment continued to round up the uniformed Bovarians, who looked to Quaeryt to be more of a militia or a local guard of some sort, Quaeryt studied the edge of the town, far too neat to have been supported by the gaggle of cots and small holders to the east. That suggested that they would find more prosperous lands along the south side of the river farther to the west, because the cable ferry wouldn't have been developed or used without trade and people going back and forth.

A courier rode toward Skarpa from the center of the town, reining up beside the commander. "Sir . . . Subcommander Meinyt has captured the cable ferry tower. There was little resistance."

"What else?" asked Skarpa.

"Even before we reached the tower, sir, the Bovarians had cut the cables."

"Thank you. Tell the subcommander we will join him shortly."

"Yes, sir." The courier turned his mount and rode back up the brick-paved street.

"The Bovarians were watching from the north bank," said Skarpa. "They don't want us to be able to reinforce Deucalon."

"They couldn't even see the fighting," said Quaeryt. "They must have cut the cables when they saw Meinyt's men reach the cable tower."

"We're likely at least two days ahead of Deucalon," said Skarpa.

"How do you figure that?"

"We had a day on them to begin with, and I know how Deucalon moves. That means we can take a day here and rest the men and the mounts."

"You don't think he'll try to send a messenger across the river?"

"He knows the terrain. There's no way to get a messenger and a mount across from where he likely is so that the messenger could catch us until we're both west of Rivecote. That's another reason to wait."

"Orders?"

"He suggested it before we left. Besides, we need to get the town in order." Skarpa grinned. "You have much more experience with that than anyone else."

Quaeryt offered a mock-groan. "You would remember that."

"So . . . what do you suggest to begin?"

"Patrols on all the streets, half squad size. No violence against people unless they start it. Name-calling isn't violence, but inciting others to violence is . . . We need to get that word out to the people immediately as well . . ."

Skarpa nodded and listened.

13

By late on Mardi, Quaeryt had trooper patrols riding the streets of Rivecote Sud, with already experienced and effective troopers because, with Skarpa's approval, he used those companies from Third Regiment who'd served the same function in restoring order to Extela after the eruption—and Rivecote Sud was a far smaller place. Then he, Skarpa, and Meinyt had to obtain what passed for quarters for more than three thousand troopers and their officers, although Skarpa did take over the largest inn for the senior officers and the imager undercaptains.

By Meredi morning, the militia or local reserves that Skarpa's force had captured were working hard and removing the earthen berms, filling in the staked pits, and burying the handfuls of Bovarians killed the day before.

Quaeryt and Skarpa had ridden out to see the progress of that work under a slightly cooler sun and a silver hazed sky that promised a far hotter afternoon.

"Just four deaths?" asked Quaeryt.

"So far. There might be one or two more from wounds." Skarpa shook his head. "Pepper. Who would have thought it?"

"I was fortunate." Quaeryt sensed that the limited number of deaths, given what could have happened, was a relief to Skarpa. It was certainly a relief to him, because, for what he still wanted to do, the more the casualties could be limited to troopers and those seen to rule, the better.

"I've heard that from you before, all too many times," replied Skarpa. "You need another phrase to disguise what you don't want to explain."

"How about the fact that it really was chance? I heard someone sneeze . . . and that led me to think about what caused sneezing."

"What if no one had sneezed?"

"We might have had more casualties."

"I'm glad you said *might*," replied Skarpa with a jesting tone that suggested he had trouble believing Quaeryt. "Have you seen the cable ferry?"

"Ah . . . no," replied Quaeryt. "There was the business of setting up patrols and a few other matters."

"You should, and I need to see how our few engineers are coming in restoring it to use."

"When Deucalon reaches Rivecote Nord?"

"When Deucalon and Lord Bhayar reach the other tower. It might be good to have communications, but that will mean I'll have to leave at least half a company here to keep matters in order—if you think that is sufficient."

"A full company might be better, but let me think about that." Quaeryt understood Skarpa's reluctance to leave too many troopers behind because each garrison left behind reduced the men available for the next battle.

Skarpa turned his mount uphill toward the river and the center of the small town, and Quaeryt followed, still holding full shields.

As they rode down the brick-paved main street, Quaeryt noted that most of the dwellings and virtually all the shops had brick walls and slate roofs. Was that because brick was better in the damp climate . . . or because there was a brickworks nearby, or both? He also couldn't help but note that the majority of dwellings and shops, especially the larger dwellings, were set on what amounted to a long rise that ran an angle from the northeast to the southwest. For a moment he wondered why, then nodded. The ground was higher and less likely to be inundated during times of high water, such as floods or the spring runoff.

In less than a half quint, they reined up in the south courtyard that surrounded the ferry tower. After dismounting and tying the mare to one of the hitching rings, Quaeryt followed Skarpa up the outside brick staircase to the second level of the tower, girded on all sides by a railed open balcony. Skarpa walked to the river side of the balcony. "What do you think?"

Rather than answer immediately, Quaeryt studied the tower and its surroundings. The cable ferry was far less elaborate than he had pictured. On the south side of the Aluse River was the stone tower where he stood and from where he could look out across the river, located on a bluff that rose some ten yards above the surface of the water. The top of the tower was about five yards above the base of the paved courtyard, and three above the low stone wall enclosing the courtyard. Two thick braided cables ran from a square timber framework secured in an open gallery facing the river down to the sheltered water downstream of the bluff where a single oblong flatboat was tied up to a dock, beside a large winch powered by an ox-driven capstan. The cut ends of the cable were draped across the flatboat.

From what Quaeryt could determine, the ferry was linked by shorter cables to a set of sliding pulleys that had run on one of the two main cables, with another set of cables linked to the winches on each side of the river. There were two slips below, suggesting two ferryboats were used to cross the sixty yards of water separating the two towers.

Quaeryt looked across the river at the gallery area of the north tower, where he could see three men in blue-gray Bovarian uniforms. While it wouldn't be difficult to send another boat across the river, although it would have to start much farther upstream and carry light line that could lead to rope and then cable, there wasn't any point in trying so long as the Bovarians held Rivecote Nord. And that was assuming that there were spare cables available in Rivecote Sud.

"Effective, but less impressive than I'd pictured," he finally replied to Skarpa's question.

"Effective is what matters."

Quaeryt couldn't disagree with that.

A Telaryn captain, an engineer, hurried toward them, then stopped and inclined his head. "Commander, Subcommander."

"Have you found the spare cables?" asked Skarpa.

"There are several sets, sir, but . . ."

"There's no point in trying to reattach them until we hold both towers? Or is there another problem?"

"Someone smashed the gears in the winch. We haven't been able to find any spare gears. We can rig a way to use the capstan once we can reattach new cables, but it will be slower."

"Do that for now," said Skarpa. "They might have spare gears on the other side."

Or the Bovarians might end up smashing the winches on both sides. Quaeryt frowned. "Could I take a look at the winch?"

"Yes, sir. Now?"

"Why not?"

"This way, sir."

Quaeryt followed the engineer down the staircase he'd just climbed, across the courtyard to a small gate, and then down another narrow set of stone steps cut into the bluff leading to the ferry slips. The winch was located on the wide center wharf between the two slips.

There the engineer pointed to the uncovered mechanism. "Looks like they smashed those three gears there. Be a bitch to replace them, even if we can find spares."

Quaeryt studied the winch's workings for several moments. "The imagers might be able to help. If you could send someone to summon them . . . they're all at the inn—the Grande Sud."

"Yes, sir. We can do that." The engineer captain hurried off.

While Quaeryt waited for the imagers to arrive, he studied the winch in greater detail, slowly imaging away a loose chunk of gearing in one place and then in another, just enough to see if he could do it. Then he concentrated on rebuilding just one gear tooth on a large gear.

It appeared . . . and it looked solid, but was it? He waited half a quint before he tapped it with a mallet from a tool kit. It sounded solid, but again, the proof would be in the operation.

After that, he walked back and forth along the slips, waiting.

It took almost three quints for the rankers Quaeryt sent out to locate and return with all the imager undercaptains. All of them had puzzled expressions as, one by one, they joined Quaeryt on the wharf. He waited to explain until they were all there before the damaged winch.

"The reason I summoned you is that we have a problem here. The Bovarian troopers, or the cable ferry operators, smashed this winch. You can see the damaged gears there. It would be most helpful to Lord Bhayar and his forces if we could get this winch in working condition again so that once Marshal Deucalon takes Rivecote Nord, we can get the ferry operating as quickly as possible. We need to accomplish two things. First, we need to remove the broken pieces of gears. Then we need to image the gears as if they were new."

Quaeryt looked over the undercaptains. "Has anyone had any experience imaging parts of things?"

"Ah . . . I have," said Baelthm, "but much, much smaller parts, no bigger than a finger."

"Anyone else?"

No one spoke.

"All right, the first thing we need to do is to image out the broken pieces, one at a time. Threkhyl, you're first. Do you see that chunk of iron gearing there?"

"Yes, sir."

"I'd like you to remove it, image it away. Just it. Nothing else."

The ginger-bearded undercaptain concentrated, and in a moment the broken gear section was gone.

"Good. Voltyr, this other piece . . ."

It took almost a quint and two efforts by each undercaptain to remove

the broken metal, and Quaeryt had to give a little hidden assistance to
Baelthm.

"Now . . . the next part is harder. The gears are iron, and we need to
replace the broken teeth, and they have to meld with the others . . ."

Imaging the sections of gears back in place took almost two glasses,
and left all the imagers exhausted, because Quaeryt was effectively making them match gears by eye and that required both imaging and un-
imaging and smoothing . . . and doing some of them over two and three
times. More than a few times, he ended up doing some of the work, although it appeared that none of the undercaptains noticed.

Finally, Quaeryt motioned to the engineer captain, who had been
watching from a distance. The captain walked swiftly toward him, then
halted a yard away.

"Captain, while it appears as though we may have fixed this winch, I
honestly cannot tell if the repairs the imagers have made will stand the
strain of operation. Can you turn it without any load just to see if the
gears mesh properly? And do so very slowly?"

"We can, sir."

Once again, Quaeryt waited, as did the imagers.

*Everything about war is a flurry of action, then a lot of waiting, or slow traveling, fol-
lowed by action, and more waiting.* At least, that was the impression he'd gotten
in the Tilboran Revolt, and the war against Bovaria looked to be following
the same pattern.

Finally, a crew of rankers appeared and took the capstan bars, rather
than the ox, which also appeared to be missing, but then the engineers
might have removed the animal to work on the equipment.

"Forward, slowly . . ." called the captain. "So far . . . so good."

"A little faster, now . . ."

After a time the engineer called out, "Stop . . . that will do." He turned
to Quaeryt. "It seems to work. Thank you, sir . . . imagers."

"This isn't something we normally do," Quaeryt said. "We just hope
the repairs will hold."

"Well . . . you cleaned out all the smashed pieces, and that alone was
a help."

Quaeryt turned to the undercaptains. "Thank you. Now, you can return to the inn, or you can walk through the town, but you need to do so
in pairs. We'll meet at the inn a quint before mess . . . dinner."

"Yes, sir."

Desyrk and Baelthm were the first to leave, followed by Akoryt and Threkhyl. Voltyr and Shaelyt remained, then eased toward Quaeryt as he headed to the stone steps up to the tower.

"Sir . . . ?" offered Voltyr.

"Yes . . . ?"

"The winch . . . how did you know . . . ?"

"All that iron," added Shaelyt.

Quaeryt smiled. "I didn't, not for certain, but there are winches and capstans on every merchant ship, and I spent six years at sea. This wasn't that different. It's a bit heavier and simpler, that's all."

"Sir . . . it seemed like—"

"It was a great deal of work for all of you, but the engineers appreciate it, and so do I, a great deal, and I think it probably improved all of your imaging skills and controls. Don't you?" Quaeryt smiled warmly.

Voltyr looked to Shaelyt.

The Pharsi nodded, then smiled. "Thank you, sir."

"I'll see you both later at the inn."

"Yes, sir."

The pair nodded respectfully, then stepped back and turned.

Quaeryt knew very well what that had all been about, but he hadn't even wanted to let them ask the question, especially not in public and with the engineer not all that far away. He stood for a moment, watching as the two undercaptains walked off the wharf toward the main street, talking quietly. Then he turned and headed for the stone steps.

Skarpa, surprisingly, was waiting when Quaeryt returned to the tower courtyard, breathing heavily from the climb back up the steep steps from the ferry slips.

"Did you repair that winch?"

"It's no longer jammed. Whether the repairs the imagers made will hold under strain, I can't tell. Neither can the engineers." Quaeryt paused, then added, "We did manage to image out all the broken pieces."

"By the time this war is over, you and those imagers will be worth a regiment."

Quaeryt hoped so . . . if he were ever to make the position of scholars and imagers more secure, but he only said, "I'm trying to get them to do what they can and to improve their abilities as much as possible." *And before long, when they're better imagers, I'll have to decide whether to teach them about shields . . . or whom to teach and how.*

"That's becoming clear. I'll see you later," said Skarpa, mounting and then riding out of the courtyard.

Quaeryt mounted. He needed to ride through the town and see how orderly things were, and how the patrols were working out.

14

Although it was close to ninth glass when Quaeryt returned to his small room in the inn on Mardi night, he was anything but sleepy after checking the patrols of the town's streets. Some of that might also have been the aftereffect of imaging. So . . . although he knew it might be days, if not weeks, before he could send a letter to Valeora, he sat on the edge of the bed and used the small table there to write. Part of his reason, he had to admit, was also knowing that if he did have a chance to send something, he might not have time to compose it. The words did not come easily, but finally he had written all that he could.

> My dear,
> We are now in Rivecote Sud, where there is a cable ferry across the Aluse, or was until the Bovarians cut the cables, and we must wait for our forces advancing along the north side of the river to catch up to us.
> Several days ago we came across a small Bovarian force that was setting fields of winter wheat corn afire. We managed to stop the worst of the damage and tied up the men we caught and left them for the locals. The wheat wasn't quite ready for harvest. Even if it had been, we couldn't have taken the time to harvest it. But Kharst was sending men to destroy his own people's crops, as if torching the land would help. We'll either hold Variana before winter or we'll have withdrawn. Either way, all that sort of act does is hurt the people.

Quaeryt had stopped writing there because he wasn't certain of his conclusion. He wasn't even sure about Bhayar withdrawing if the Telaryn forces couldn't take Variana. He thought Bhayar wouldn't be foolish enough to continue an indeterminate or losing war . . . but he couldn't be certain. The only thing Quaeryt was certain about was that so long as fighting continued, no matter how matters appeared, nothing was truly certain.

Probable . . . but not certain.

He still was anything but sleepy.

> Reading the book about Rholan might put you to sleep . . .

With that thought, he took out the small volume and leafed through the pages, trying to see if he could find something the ancient writer had put down that might, in some way, be applicable to what had happened in Rivecote Sud. A word struck him, and he stopped turning pages and began to read from the top of the page.

. . . Self-created mythologies are a form of Naming. On that point, Rholan and I agree, not that he ever deigned to acknowledge when others were right, except in noting that they agreed with him. Rulers and would-be conquerors create their own mythologies. Rex Caldor has just claimed that he has unified Bovaria, but what he means is that he has merely reduced the total independence of the High Holders and entered into an arrangement of mutual distrust based on the realization that he can destroy any one of them, or even several, who displease him, but not the High Holders as a body. Khel remains fiercely aloof, and Caldor is not enough of a fool to enter war with either Khel or his own High Holders. Yet, if Caldor's words triumph over his actions, he will be remembered as the unifier of Bovaria, until another "great" conqueror appears . . .

Will Bhayar be that conqueror? wondered Quaeryt.

. . . because, of course, all such conquerors, or would-be conquerors, style themselves as "great." Rholan understood this and observed that when a man instructed others to refer to him as "great," it was absolute evidence that he had become an apostle of the Namer. More interesting is the fact that this is already one of his few observations that has lapsed into oblivion, and only in a few short years.

Hengyst is now claiming that Ryntar and Tela must unite . . .

Quaeryt paused. *This was written in the time of Hengyst, but before the unification. So who is the writer, if he knows Caldor—or about him?* Because he had no answers, he continued to read.

. . . in order to avoid being swept into Bovaria. It remains to be seen how much of that is because Tilbor offers little in the way of men, gold, and resources, and a will to resist to the last hill holder, and Tela is scarcely more than a patchwork of high holdings agreeing to accept Ofryk as Lord of Tela so long as he does not impose unduly

on their privileges. Tela will fall, as have all lands whose local interests supersede those of the greater good, and even Rholan's efforts to
unite the people under the Nameless have fallen short.

It could not have been otherwise, for those who have listened to
his words have little power, and those who have power have not
listened. So it often is with the words of those who proffer wisdom.
That may be because so few can tell the difference between what is
wisdom and what they wish to believe as wisdom . . .

Quaeryt stifled a yawn. Fascinating as the small volume was in its odd
way, and with its puzzles about who the writer was and how accurate his
depiction of Rholan was, he was getting sleepy . . . and tomorrow would
come all too soon.

He closed the book, snuffed the oil lamp, and partially disrobed for
bed, yawning once more.

15

Even after his reading and writing, or perhaps because of it, Quaeryt still did not sleep well, with dreams he could not remember, but which left an after-sense of unease, and he found it difficult to rouse himself. Even though he did manage to struggle awake and washed and dressed quickly, he didn't get down to the public room of the Grande Sud for breakfast until two quints before seventh glass. Skarpa, Meinyt, and most of the other officers had already left when Quaeryt sat down at a small table near the wall. Several junior engineers were seated at another table, but were rising to leave, and there were no other officers remaining in the public room.

A server stepped up to the table, a woman neither girlish nor matronly in appearance, but with the demeanor of someone not quite worn out by life, but well on the way. "We've got cheese and eggs and biscuits with milk gravy."

"That will be fine. Do you have lager?"

"Amber, not pale."

"Good."

"The commander fellow said we got to charge three coppers plus two for the lager. No more, no less."

Quaeryt eased five coppers onto the table.

The server scooped up the coins, then paused as her eyes took in the silver crescent moon insignia. "You got the same emblem on your collars as him, except yours are silver. You a commander, too?"

"A subcommander."

She nodded, then hurried toward the kitchen, returning immediately with a beaker of lager. "Be a bit for the eggs and biscuits. You got a different uniform from the others. Different color anyway. That mean anything?"

"I was a scholar before I was an officer. That's why it's shaded brown."

"Never seen a scholar before. Heard tell of 'em. Not much more. What do scholars do?" Her voice suggested she felt she had to say something, rather than that she was truly interested.

"Some do the same things as other people. Some teach children. Others write books. Some advise rulers or High Holders."

"What about you?"

Quaeryt laughed softly. "A little of all that, before I ended up as an officer, anyway."

"How did that happen?"

"That's a long story. Just say that I asked the wrong question, and I ended up in the middle of the Tilboran Revolt, and it turned out that I managed to lead some troops and we all survived." That was a gross over-simplification, but he didn't want to explain.

"You must have been pretty good, then."

He took a swallow of the lager, not to be impolite, but because his mouth and throat were dry. Then he shrugged and smiled wryly. "There's no way to answer that. I was good enough to survive and keep too many men from being killed."

Still standing there, she glanced toward the archway into the kitchen, then spoke in a lower voice. "Some of the old fellows said that you Telar-yns have imagers and you didn't fight fair. You imaged them with pepper dust."

Quaeryt looked directly at her. "Would you rather have them all dead? That was what would have happened otherwise. They weren't that well trained, and most of them would have died. Our fight isn't with you or the people here. It's with Rex Kharst. Right after thousands of people were killed in an eruption, he massed his troopers and tried to invade Telaryn. And right after the Red Death struck Khel, he did the same thing. It wasn't our idea to fight. It was his, and we're going after him so we don't have to keep worrying about him."

The server looked at him without speaking.

Quaeryt smiled softly. "Do you know why all those soldiers are riding patrols down your streets? It's to keep order, so that no one gets hurt. Last week, we found Bovarian soldiers firing the fields of growers. We stopped as much as we could. We couldn't have used that wheat, but Rex Kharst ordered it destroyed. The only people who will suffer are those poor growers."

"I'd best get your food." Abruptly she turned and walked away.

Quaeryt almost sighed. He shouldn't have tried to explain. No one wanted explanations, and most people didn't care. The writer of the old book had that correct in his observations about wisdom. *If you believed him, then why did you bother?*

He took another swallow of the amber lager. It wasn't bad, but it wasn't great, either.

16

Quaeryt, Meinyt, and Skarpa sat at a circular table in the public room of
the Grande Sud just before eighth glass on Meredi.

"I've sent out scouts along the river in both directions," announced
Skarpa. "The ones to the east will look to see how far Deucalon has advanced. The ones to the west"—he shrugged—"you both know what
they're looking for." He looked to Quaeryt. "We need more supplies. The
marshal told me to obtain them with as little cost as possible. What do
you suggest?"

"Do we have the golds to pay for them?"

"We have some golds, but not enough to take us all the way to Variana."

"Then we find the least popular High Holder around and persuade him
to supply us at a very reasonable cost," said Quaeryt.

"That might cost us more troops than taking Rivecote Sud," said Meinyt.

"Not if we take imagers out with us," suggested Quaeryt.

Skarpa nodded.

Quaeryt rose and beckoned to the serving woman—the same one
who had been rather cool that morning—and waited for her to approach.
As she did, given her earlier diffidence, he image-projected reasonableness and unquestioned authority. "We need to know some things."

Her eyes flicked to the other two officers and then back to Quaeryt.
"There'd be others who'd know more than me."

"There are always others." He smiled. "I doubt they'd know more.
Everyone talks in a public room. Who are the High Holders on this side of
the river? Nearby."

For a moment a puzzled expression appeared on the server's face.
"There's only two. High Holder Cassyon and High Holder Rheyam."

"One's to the south and one to the west?"

"Yes, sir. Rheyam's a few milles south on the road off the west end of
town."

"And Cassyon?"

"To the west. Don't know how far. Never been there. Folks say some
eight–ten milles. Really closer to Deauvyl."

"What do folks think of Rheyam?"

The woman frowned.

"Is he fair and honest?"

"I couldn't say, sir."

"What about Cassyon?" pressed Quaeryt.

"He's really the High Holder for Deauvyl, but some folks here'll do work for him."

"Do many folk here do work for Rheyam?"

"I wouldn't know any, sir.'

"Is there a town council here, or someone who's in charge?"

"Only councilor I know is Fleigyl. He's got the chandlery three doors up."

"Thank you." Quaeryt returned to the table, sitting and easing three coppers from his purse onto the table. "I suggest we talk to the good councilor Fleigyl."

"It's a start," said Skarpa, rising.

Quaeryt stood, and the three left the public room and the inn. They followed the wooden sidewalk to the chandlery, accompanied by three troopers. Quaeryt couldn't help but notice that the few men nearby immediately found other destinations that left a wide empty area around the three officers. When they reached the chandlery, the three troopers entered first. A moment later one reappeared and held the door open. Quaeryt, Meinyt, and Skarpa stepped inside.

A short-bearded man with a soiled apron stood beside a table containing little but leather goods. "Sirs . . . I have but little . . ."

"We're not here for your goods," said Quaeryt. "You're one of the town councilors?"

"I'm only a councilor. The newest and youngest one. The head councilor is Yurmyn."

If Fleigyl, who looked to be twenty years older than Quaeryt, was the youngest, thought Quaeryt, the others truly had to be graybeards. "Where might we find Yurmyn?"

"Ah . . . he departed when he heard you were . . . coming this way."

"Then I guess you're head councilor in his absence," said Skarpa.

Fleigyl swallowed.

"Don't worry. We just have a few questions. There don't happen to be a few High Holders around here, do there?"

After a moment the chandler sighed. "The only ones close are Rheyam and, I guess, Cassyon, except he's really nearer Deauvyl."

"Tell us about Rheyam."

"He's a High Holder. He's got a place south of here. We don't see much of him. They say he lives most of the year in Variana."

"Who runs the holding, then?" asked Quaeryt.

"He's got a steward."

"His name?" asked Skarpa.

"Clukyn."

After another half quint of questions, the three left the chandlery, but it was almost a glass later before Quaeryt's first company, with the imager undercaptains, Skarpa, and four empty supply wagons, rode out of Rivecote Sud toward Rheyam's holding.

Finding the holding was not difficult, because the road that began on the west end of the town heading south was the best maintained Quaeryt had seen since they had left Ferravyl. The long straight drive from the brick pillars off the road was paved in a reddish stone, stone soft enough that years of carriage, coach, and wagon wheels had worn slight channels in it. The drive was flanked by tall oaks, set far enough back from the stone that the roots had not disrupted the stone and close enough that the trees would provide shade throughout the hottest periods of the day. Beyond the oaks on each side was an area of grass some fifty yards wide, and beyond the grass were woods, although Quaeryt saw little undergrowth, a sign of a private park of some sort.

At the end of the drive was a circular paved area. A set of wide stone steps rose some five yards to a two-story redbrick structure, more the size of a small palace, dominating a low rise that was so regular that it had to have been created for the building. The holding house looked to be a hollow oblong, with perhaps a courtyard garden in the center. A trimmed hedge separated the house and immediate grounds and low gardens from the outbuildings on each side.

As the company drew up, a white-haired man in a cream jacket and dark trousers stepped out of the front door and walked past the white pillars and down the steps.

Quaeryt rode forward and reined up. "Commander Skarpa of the southern army of Telaryn is seeking High Holder Rheyam," he announced, projecting pure authority.

"Beggin' your pardon, mightiness, but he's not here, hasn't been since mid-Avryl. Doesn't like to spend the hot months here."

"Then Steward Clukyn will do."

"Ah . . . he left with all the valuables soon as he heard you Telaryns were coming. All the pretty maids, too."

"So . . . you're in charge?"

"You might say so, your mightiness. I'm Exbael, assistant to the steward."

"Good. We're here to purchase some supplies."

"Sirs . . . I can't do that . . ."

Quaeryt smiled. "Of course you can. You can explain to Steward Clukyn that in his absence you were faced with the choice of selling the supplies or having all of them burned."

"Lord Rheyam . . . he'd flay me alive, if Clukyn didn't first. Anyways, they're all locked up. Clukyn took the keys."

"Let's have a look."

"The warehouse has thick walls and iron bars . . ."

"We still need a look. After we inquire with others in the hold house that you are who you say you are."

Exbael gave Quaeryt a despairing look followed by a deep sigh. "Most are hiding in the cellar, except for the cook."

Quaeryt turned in the saddle. "Major, if you'd provide a squad to accompany Undercaptain Desyrk to verify matters?"

"Yes, sir."

Desyrk rode forward and dismounted, frowning momentarily as he looked to Quaeryt.

"You understand what your task is?"

"Yes, sir. I'm to make certain this man is who he says he is."

Quaeryt nodded, then watched the troopers escort Exbael and Desyrk into the hold house.

Almost a quint later the group returned, with Desyrk in the lead.

"It's like he said, sir," said the undercaptain. "I talked to all of them. They all say pretty much the same thing."

"Mount up, then." Quaeryt turned to Exbael. "To the warehouse."

"This way, your mightiness." Exbael began to walk, dejectedly, to the right, toward the paved lane that led to the outbuildings on the north side of the hold house.

"Undercaptains, and first squad, with me," ordered Quaeryt.

Exbael took his time, and it was close to half a quint later when Quaeryt, Skarpa, and the imagers reined up before a large oblong structure, the outbuilding farthest from the hold house. The walls were brick and windowless. The heavy, iron-bound, oak-timbered double doors were secured with eight iron bars that were slid into iron-lined circular holes in the oak-timbered lintels, and held in place by iron hoops on the doors. Each bar ended in the middle with a heavy iron circlet, with an equally heavy iron lock joining the two tightly mated circlets.

"You see, your mightiness?" Exbael gestured to the doors.

"I do see," replied Quaeryt. "You'd best go and get some writing materials. You do write, don't you?"

"Yes, sir." The assistant steward's voice was worried.

"You're going to need to write out two copies of what we purchase and what we'll be paying High Holder Rheyam."

"Sir . . ."

"Don't complain, and just fetch the writing materials."

"Yes, sir." Exbael turned and began to trudge back toward the palatial hold house.

"Imagers forward." Quaeryt dismounted and handed the mare's reins to the nearest ranker. "Thank you." Then he walked to the warehouse door and waited.

Once they were gathered, he gestured to the door. "You're going to take turns imaging out just enough pieces of the lock shackle so that we can remove the locks and bars. When we're finished loading the wagons, we'll replace the bars and locks, and you'll image the shackles back together. We'd like to leave things as we found them—with the exception of what we're purchasing." He gestured to Akoryt. "Why don't you start with the shackle on the top lock?"

"Yes, sir." As usual, the undercaptain's flat brown eyes revealed little, but he imaged away two small chunks of iron, and the heavy lock dropped. He barely managed to catch it.

"That's right," said Quaeryt. "Try not to let the locks get broken." He motioned to Baelthm. "You work on the next lock."

In less than half a glass, the locks and bars had all been removed, and the heavy warehouse doors opened. Even after Exbael returned and offered some assistance, it took time to find a lantern and light it, then to study the contents, to check the dates marked on each barrel, and then to open several barrels to inspect the contents. Finally, Skarpa sent for the wagons.

While Quaeryt waited for their arrival, he turned to Skarpa. "You've seen what's there. He's got barrels of salted mutton, salted pork, a fair number of barrels of flour, and even a few barrels of rice. Don't see any potatoes or root vegetables. They'd like to be in a separate root cellar. How much do you want?"

"As much as the wagons will hold. Who knows when we'll have another chance to resupply with this little difficulty."

"The difficulty will come later," Quaeryt said dryly, "when the High Holders of Bovaria protest. There are too many of them for Bhayar to replace them."

"You're assuming he'll conquer Bovaria."

"He'll at least hold the eastern part. He won't let that go, and I can't see Kharst taking it back anytime soon."

Skarpa only nodded at that.

With a company of troopers, and four wagons, it still took over a glass to pull out the barrels, and then roll them up planks onto the wagons, and wedge and stack them in place. Quaeryt had Baelthm make certain that every barrel was counted and entered on the manifest that Exbael was writing up.

When the loading was finished, with every wagon loaded to its limit, and the two copies of the manifest completed, Quaeryt turned back to Skarpa. "That's sixty barrels of flour, twenty of salt pork, and ten of dried salted mutton, a total of ninety barrels. The going rate is around eight silvers a barrel for flour. Since we're doing the transporting and this is war, we shouldn't pay that much. What if we give High Holder Rheyam four silvers a barrel? That's thirty-six golds."

Skarpa frowned. "I'll give him twenty-five. Tell the assistant steward that we'll post that amount in the town so that everyone will know . . . and so that he can't make off with it."

"I will have to flee anyway," said Exbael despondently.

Quaeryt smiled. "Let's do this another way."

The steward offered a puzzled look.

"Let's leave the golds and the manifest and payment statement inside the warehouse, right on top of a barrel behind the doors. We'll close the doors and replace the locks." He grinned at Exbael. "How could you have anything to do with it? You don't have the keys, do you?"

"No, sir."

Quaeryt could see Skarpa smiling behind the assistant's back.

"Roll one of the barrels we've left over there right in the space behind where the doors close and set it upright." Once the barrel was in place, Quaeryt took the manifest, the payment statement, and the golds and weighted down the two papers on the upper barrel butt with the coins, then stepped out of the warehouse. "Close the doors, and replace the bars." Quaeryt waited until that happened. "Undercaptains forward." He nodded to Ghaelyn. "If you'd take the steward over behind the wagons."

"Yes, sir."

When the steward was where he couldn't see the doors, Quaeryt nodded to Voltyr. "If you'd repair the first lock."

"Yes, sir."

Voltyr gingerly held the lock up to the shackle and concentrated. The first attempt left the shackle crooked, but when he could remove his hands from the lock and study the lock and shackle, the second attempt resulted in a joining so smooth that none could have told the shackle had been severed.

"Threkhyl . . . you do the second."

The ginger-bearded imager managed to repair lock and shackle in one attempt. So did Shaelyt with the next lock. Desyrk took two attempts with the last one.

"Exbael, you can return."

The steward walked from behind the wagons and looked at the iron-bound and locked doors. His mouth opened, then closed. Then he stepped forward and inspected and pulled on the locks one after another.

"The High Holder's goods are safe," said Quaeryt. "The golds and the manifest are inside."

Exbael looked at the locked door and murmured something.

"What did you say?" asked Quaeryt.

The assistant to the steward swallowed, then finally spoke. "Just that I might as well have chanced on a black hare, sir."

"It could have been worse, Exbael, much worse." *Do all the southerners have this worry about black rabbits?* Quaeryt didn't say anything, though, as he mounted.

They left Exbael standing forlornly by the warehouse and rode back toward the front drive, the wagons creaking. There, the rest of the company joined them for the trip back to Rivecote Sud.

As they turned from the paved drive onto the packed earth and gravel road that headed north, Skarpa looked to Quaeryt. "He'll still have to flee, you know."

"I know. There's no help for it with a holder and a steward like that. But we didn't hurt anyone or damage his property. Removed a bit of it without full compensation, but that's not unreasonable in a war."

"I will post a statement in Rivecote Sud, saying that we bought goods from the holding of High Holder Rheyam and damaged nothing."

"Oh?"

"That way the steward will have to explain . . . if he can."

Quaeryt did not smile . . . quite.

The ride back to the town took a good glass, and Quaeryt couldn't help but puzzle over the fact that the road to the holding looked to be better than the main road westward along the river. Reloading the barrels across all the supply wagons took even longer than the return to Rivecote Sud, although Quaeryt did not remain to watch that, but spent a good glass checking the patrols, and then briefing Captain Shaask from Skarpa's Second Battalion, since he'd been chosen to garrison the town and keep order.

The remainder of Meredi was uneventful. Most of the locals stayed off the streets, and the scouts discovered no signs or tracks of Bovarian forces, although Quaeryt had no doubt that there were at least some Bovarian scouts watching Skarpa's force from a distance. The Bovarians continued to hold Rivecote Nord, as evidenced by the presence of uniformed troopers or officers on the north cable ferry tower.

Skarpa's scouts from the east reported back in late afternoon that they had spotted Telaryn troops on the north side of the river some fifteen milles east of Rivecote Nord. With that information in hand, Skarpa summoned Meinyt and Quaeryt to discuss preparations for the regiments and Quaeryt's battalion to depart on Jeudi morning. That meeting took another glass, and Quaeryt's guts were growling by the time he walked into the public room for what passed for the evening mess.

The skeptical serving woman looked at him, neither warmly nor coldly, then turned away. But when he sat down at the table with Skarpa and Meinyt, she reappeared and set a beaker of pale lager in front of him.

"Thank you."

"No thanks, not for now." She nodded and stepped away.

"What was that about?" asked Meinyt.

"I think it's a reminder and a suggestion that things might not be too bad if we leave the townspeople to their lives." Quaeryt took a sip of the lager. It was far better than what he'd been served for breakfast. "It also might be a quiet thank you."

He thought so, but in war, how could he ever know for certain?

As the southern army moved out of Rivecote Sud early on Jeudi morning under a hazy sky that promised more hot and damp weather, Skarpa, Meinyt, and Quaeryt rode side by side behind the vanguard.

"If we make good time, we'll reach Villerive before the first of Agostas," said Skarpa.

"That's without trouble, and there's always trouble," countered Meinyt.

"What sort of trouble do you see?" Skarpa's voice held an amused tone. "Besides more merchants and holders happy to take the troopers' coins? Or do you think our troopers will be enticed by the charms of the local women?"

"Not on this side of the Aluse." Meinyt snorted. "At Villerive, we'll all have trouble. They say it's the bawdiest city on the Aluse. It's got more taverns and taprooms than even Estisle. Myskyl thought he had trouble with Rescalyn's vale? He didn't know trouble."

Skarpa looked toward Quaeryt. "What sort of trouble do you see?"

Quaeryt thought. "I'd be surprised to see Bovarian troopers or raiders trying to burn crops until we get close to Villerive. That's more likely on the north side of the river. The lands are better there. So are the roads, and there should be more High Holders." He added, "I think we should pay a visit to High Holder Cassyon. Or his holding."

Skarpa raised his eyebrows.

"We already visited Rheyam. It also won't hurt if Lord Bhayar has a better idea about as many High Holders as possible. Or if they get the idea he keeps a close watch."

"Won't he just replace them all?" asked Meinyt.

"He could, but that wouldn't be wise," said Skarpa. "The only people he could use that would be trustworthy and able to keep the holding in line are officers, and they'd have to be at least majors. That would take more majors than we have. If he brings in the junior sons of Telaryn High Holders, that will mean we'll end up fighting more . . ."

Quaeryt nodded.

"We all don't need to see each holder," said Skarpa. "That will just slow us up. You should. You're the one with ties to Bhayar, and he'll listen to you."

"I wouldn't take the whole battalion, just a company, and an imager or two. First company, this time."

"First company until you've worked more with the Khellan officers," said Skarpa mildly.

"That was my thought. Is there anything else I need to know now?"

"I'll send a courier if the scouts discover anything."

"Yes, sir." Quaeryt eased his mount onto the shoulder and rode back to Fifth Battalion, assigned to follow Meinyt's Fifth Tilboran.

Once back in formation, beside Zhelan, he turned in the saddle. "Major, we'll be making visits to High Holders along the way to Villerive. The first will be at High Holder Cassyon's. His holding is this side of Deauvyl. I'll be taking first company and two of the undercaptains, Shaelyt and Akoryt. Undercaptain Voltyr will be in charge of the remaining undercaptains." Quaeryt could sense Zhelan's curiosity and added, "I'm gathering information about the High Holders for Lord Bhayar. The more information he has, the happier he'll be about that."

Zhelan nodded. "I can see why you were picked for that, sir."

Quaeryt didn't quibble. He'd picked himself, and Skarpa had agreed, and that almost amounted to the same thing in practice. *Almost.*

After riding a glass or so with the battalion, but also riding out and making several inquiries from local growers—through closed and barred doors, and at more than a few times getting no answers at all—Quaeryt and first company finally came to a pair of brick and redstone pillars flanking a graveled drive that angled up a low rise to the south of the river road.

Ghaelyn and Quaeryt followed the outriders up the drive, with the company behind them, and onto a hilltop that had been flattened, decades before, if not longer, judging by the size of the oaks that surrounded and shaded the hold house. With two stories, plain yellow brick walls, and a length of less than forty yards, the hold house was positively modest—for a High Holder.

As Quaeryt rode toward the front entry, a brick-paved area with a roof extending over the drive and supported on the far side of the drive by two brick pillars, he saw a tall, dark-haired man, flanked by two others, standing on the brick stoop in front of the double goldenwood doors.

"First company, halt!" Quaeryt turned in the saddle and looked to

Shaelyt, Akoryt, and Ghaelyn. "Hold here." Maintaining full shields, Quaeryt rode forward and reined up short of the stoop. "Greetings," he offered in Bovarian.

"Greetings to you, officer," returned the tall man.

"Are you High Holder Cassyon?"

"Why might you suggest that?"

"Your reputation," replied Quaeryt.

The man laughed, if with a slight nervousness. "I'm Cassyon, but what is it about my reputation?"

"Some people in Rivecote Sud would rather deal with you than with the nearer High Holder. I surmised that a holder with that reputation might be one to greet an invader's forces."

"Invader? Most would style themselves liberators or something more flattering."

"Such as unifiers?" Quaeryt offered a wry smile as he thought of the small volume. "I won't claim that for Lord Bhayar. Rex Kharst invaded Telaryn. We destroyed his forces, and Lord Bhayar determined that there would be no peace in Lydar until either Telaryn or Bovaria triumphed." Quaeryt smiled ironically. "You might say that we're invading to procure peace since the alternative was to be invaded."

"What do you wish from me . . . is it commander?"

"Subcommander."

"You're young even for a subcommander . . . or are all Bhayar's senior officers young?"

Quaeryt smiled. "I'm by far the youngest subcommander."

"If I may observe, then you are either very good or very well connected, if not both."

"I've had the fortune to accomplish what Lord Bhayar required."

"As do all officers who survive." Cassyon moistened his lips. "I understand that your army has the power to take or destroy all that I have, but I would prefer that it not come to that."

"I have no intentions of such . . . unless you attempt something foolish. Right now, all I require of you is your pledge not to take up arms against Telaryn so long as we control the lands east of Deauvyl, and to sell any goods we deem necessary at a price we set."

"Oh?"

"We purchased flour and other goods from Rheyam at about one-third of the market price. I'd prefer to pay more, but at the moment, that's not possible."

"What did you do with Rheyam's goods you did not purchase?"

"Replaced the locks and left them."

"Might I ask why, assuming you're telling the truth, you are so comparatively generous?"

"That's very simple. Lord Bhayar would prefer to rule than to destroy. As for the truth, you can send someone to Rivecote and to Rheyam's hold and have them see for themselves."

Cassyon nodded. "And if I do not so pledge? What will you do?"

"For the moment .. nothing, unless you immediately raise arms. Once the fighting is over, however, you risk losing everything."

"If I pledge to Bhayar, when the fighting is over and Kharst has won, then I will lose everything."

"I am not asking you pledge to Lord Bhayar. I am asking that you pledge not to raise arms against him so long as his armies control these lands."

"I could pledge and lie."

"You could," said Quaeryt. "That would be foolish." As he spoke the last words, he image-projected absolute authority and the sense that Cassyon's lands would be in ruin and all on them would be dead.

Cassyon took a half step backward. Then he looked at Quaeryt, even more closely. "Who . . . what . . are you?"

"Subcommander Quaeryt, sometime scholar, former governor of the province of Montagne, and brother by marriage to Lord Bhayar."

"And you are a *mere* subcommander?"

"That is what I have earned, High Holder Cassyon."

"I will pledge not to raise arms so long as your lord holds these lands and to sell to him or his commanders what he may require. I do so because you are not a subcommander, or not just a subcommander." Cassyon shook his head. "I am not a coward, but a man would be a fool to stand against death upon a horse." He paused. "Do you require goods now?"

"No. We may never require goods of you. Then, we may." Quaeryt nodded. "Good day." He flicked the reins gently, then guided the mare back to where first company waited.

As they headed back down the drive, Shaelyt eased his mount up beside Quaeryt's mare.

"Sir . . . what did you do?"

"I talked to him, Undercaptain I asked him to pledge not to raise arms against us and to sell goods to us, if required. That's all I said."

"Sir . . . even I could sense death and destruction rise around you and flow over the High Holder."

"Even you, Shaelyt?" Quaeryt smiled. "You're Pharsi. You're one of those who can sense what is not said or spoken. Perhaps Cassyon could as well. I did attempt to convey, without words, that failing to pledge would lead to death and destruction. But I said nothing of the sort."

"You are like the ancient lost ones . . ." Shaelyt's voice was low.

"That . . . I couldn't say, not having known any of them. I don't even know who my parents were, save that they had to have been Pharsi, because I look that way and because I remember a few words and phrases."

"No, sir, you are Pharsi, and you are a lost one. You may even be the lost one."

"Shaelyt . . ." Quaeryt let a little exasperation show in his voice. He'd been called that several times, but never where he could follow up on what it meant. "Would you mind telling me exactly who 'the lost one' is supposed to be. If you're going to insist that I might be something, it would be helpful to know what it might be."

Shaelyt said nothing for several moments as they neared the pillars at the end of the drive.

Quaeryt could see that Third Regiment had caught up and was passing the gate. He reined up and signaled the company to halt. It would be easier to let the regiment pass and then cross behind the supply wagons and catch up to Fifth Battalion going single file and using the wider shoulder on the river side of the road. He turned to the Pharsi undercaptain. "Go ahead."

"Sir . . ."

Quaeryt waited.

"The first lost ones were those imprisoned in a valley in the Montagnes D'Glace by Erion. He sent shafts from his mighty bow into the pass that led to the northern valleys of Khel and brought down the cliffs on each side on the warriors who were about to attack the Eshtorans. He said that while the descendants of those warriors might escape, their past desire to slaughter innocents would always mark them as lost ones, and that they would not be truly saved until the time of the last lost one—the lost one who would change everything across all Lydar. He also said that the lost one would come as one truly lost to his heritage and from afar, and that he would have a voice that few could resist and that he would triumph not by force of arms, although few would ever be able to withstand him, but because he sought justice and mercy for Pharsi and non-Pharsi alike." Shaelyt paused, then added, "My father told me that most Pharsi forget to mention the last part. They don't like it that the lost one would seek mercy for both the Pharsi and for those who have persecuted us for generations."

"Does this . . . legend say anything about what justice is supposed to be?"

"Not that I heard, sir."

Quaeryt shook his head. "I'm a scholar who's gotten tolerably good with a half-staff out of necessity"—*and imaging*—"and I'll admit I'd like to see justice and mercy for those who've been denied it, such as scholars, imagers, Pharsi, and anyone else who's been deprived. But . . . I don't think that qualifies me as the lost one. There have been men before me, and there are those today, and there will be others in the future who seek those ends. Certainly, Rholan did. In his own way, so does Lord Bhayar, and that is one reason why I'm here." *Not the only one, but I wouldn't be here if I didn't believe that.* Even as he thought that, another thought crossed his mind. *If you hadn't believed that, you wouldn't have Vaelora.*

He managed to stifle a bemused smile.

"Sir . . . ah . . ." Shaelyt edged his mount almost stirrup to stirrup with Quaeryt.

"Yes?"

"None of them called down ice torrents and slew thousands." Shaelyt's voice was firm, but barely above a murmur.

"We all did that," replied Quaeryt quietly. *Even if I probably did most of it.*

Shaelyt's eyes fixed on his. "Sir . . . I have no illusions about what I can do. I have watched and watched. You have hidden behind a cloak of light or something like it an entire regiment so that no one saw us approach. You have known exactly what exercises will improve us as imagers. I have seen men and mounts fly away from you in battle without your ever touching them . . ."

"And you've also seen me almost die," countered Quaeryt.

"Yes, sir. You have not been afraid to risk your own life to save those around you." The young undercaptain smiled softly. "Tell me honestly, that you are not an imager and not a lost one."

What do you say to that? Quaeryt looked back into the other's dark eyes and smiled ironically. "You know I cannot say that. But I also cannot affirm it, not now, and not if we are to succeed. But . . . please, do not insist that I am the lost one."

"You do not want what you are known because the marshal and the vice-marshal do not want it said that an imager is a subcommander?"

"Let us just say that Lord Bhayar knows what I am, although we have never spoken of it, and he would prefer matters remain as they are."

Shaelyt nodded. "Then . . . that is how it shall be. If anyone asks, I will say that is a question that they should pose to you, and not to me."

"Thank you, Undercaptain."

Shaelyt nodded solemnly.

"What else can you tell me about the lost ones?"

"I've told you what I know . . . what I remember. My parents didn't talk much about the lost ones or the old ways, only when my father drank too much on holidays." Shaelyt grinned. "Then he talked too much, my mother said."

"I do appreciate what you have told me. Thank you."

"Thank you, sir."

As they waited for the last riders of Third Battalion to pass, Quaeryt felt that he'd handled the questions Shaelyt had raised as well as he could in the situation in which he found himself. Sooner or later, it would all come out, but it would be best if it came out somewhat later.

When the regiment finished passing, Quaeryt signaled, and first company rode quickly across the road and onto the shoulder. Less than a quint after Quaeryt and first company returned to the main force, Skarpa called a halt, in order to rest and water mounts and men.

While Fifth Battalion was waiting for access to the river, Threkhyl walked his mount over beside Quaeryt and the mare. "Sir?"

Quaeryt turned. "Yes?"

"I'm the strongest of the imager undercaptains, am I not?"

Quaeryt was happy with the way Threkhyl had phrased the question, if less than happy with its thrust. "You are, at least at present."

"Then why don't you ever put me in charge when you leave?"

"Because you don't have the experience that Voltyr does in dealing with superiors who aren't imagers. And I don't take you with me because I want to leave the strongest imager with the battalion in case strong imaging is needed."

"It sounds like you want a strong back . . . except it's an imager's back."

Despite the truculence barely concealed behind Threkhyl's almost pleasant tone, Quaeryt managed an even smile. "Voltyr has had years of experience in dealing with people with more power and less patience. You have a temper, and you haven't had much practice in holding it in. What you do reflects on all imagers . . . and to some degree, on all scholars as well. At present, scholars and imagers are held as untrustworthy and temperamental. Everything we do must refute that belief. You need to watch and learn more, both in terms of your imaging and your understanding of how regiments and battalions work. If you do, there will come a time when you're given more authority and more responsibility."

"What about you, sir? Did you start out as an undercaptain lackey? Or were you a captain or a major?"

"No. I started out riding patrols with ordinary troopers, and I took a crossbow bolt in the chest. You can ask Subcommander Meinyt. He was in charge of the company I was riding with."

Threkhyl opened his mouth . . . then shut it.

Quaeryt caught the signal from Major Zhelan and nodded to the undercaptain. "It's our turn to water mounts." He raised his voice. "Fifth Battalion! Single file . . ."

Threkhyl eased his mount back toward those of the other undercaptains.

If it isn't one thing, it's another. Quaeryt smiled wryly as he led the mare down the packed trail to the river.

18

Early on Solayi morning, Quaeryt woke in a tiny room of the White Ox, one of the two inns in Roule, a town that was barely that, even if larger than any of the hamlets that dotted the south side of the River Aluse, but certainly the largest place through which the Telaryn southern army had passed in the twenty-odd milles since leaving Deauvyl. In that whole length, they had passed but one high holding—or rather the abandoned remains of one that looked as though it had been burned more than a few years in the past. The innkeeper at the White Ox had reluctantly admitted the evening before that Roule did have another such personage west of Roule, but that others had said the High Holder was personally absent from the holding.

Although it was barely light, and the single lamp in the room barely shed enough light on the wash table—from which he removed pitcher and basin in order to use it as a desk of sorts—Quaeryt decided that since he was wide awake, he might as well write more on his letter to Vaelora. *But what can you tell her that is interesting and yet will reveal nothing if it falls into the wrong hands?*

Finally, he began to write.

. . . We are now north and west of Rivecote Sud, having traveled a most uneven river road. Outside of the less than effectual resistance to our taking the cable ferry at Rivecote Sud, the local people, while taking great care to keep their distance as much as possible, seem strangely indifferent, as if it matters little to them who governs them, so long as that governance is largely at a distance and does not fall too heavily upon their shoulders. They appear far more concerned about the vices and virtues of the High Holders around them than about who rules in Variana, although they are careful in the manner in which they discuss local matters. They will mention favorable traits of people, but when asked questions that might require a negative reply, the response is almost invariably, "I wouldn't know about that." That response does provide some information, if not all that one might desire. We've seen no boats to speak of on the River Aluse and no Bovarian troops on this side of the river since Rivecote Sud. This suggests that Rex Kharst is likely gathering and massing troops farther upriver, possibly at Villerive or closer to Variana.

I would that I were speaking to you across a table or elsewhere, but such talks, which I have always enjoyed and appreciated, will have to wait until the conclusion of the entire campaign . . . and perhaps beyond that. I have asked one of the Pharsi officers about the myth of the lost ones, and discovered that, according to the old stories, the original lost ones were . . .

Quaeryt went on to recount what Shaelyt had told him, ending with

. . . so it would seem that revealing such characteristics might well subject whoever did so to considerable speculation as to his origins, his motives, and his goals, and, as we both know, speculation about unusual characteristics almost always leads to misunderstanding. Yet there always comes a time when events will conspire to require acts where the truth must out, or the speculations will be more unpleasant and the consequences more dire than the effects of the revelation of the most unpalatable of truths. In this, as in all matters, timing and judgment are paramount.

He added that sheet to those in his leather folder and slipped the folder into his kit bag. After returning the table to its usual function, he washed and dressed quickly, then hurried down the wooden steps to the small public room to eat with Skarpa and Meinyt. He could feel the ancient wooden steps flexing under his boots, and wondered just how old the structure might be.

Less than a half a score of steps from the bottom of the stairs, along a narrow hall was the archway leading into the public room. Quaeryt stepped through, immediately catching sight of Meinyt, seated alone at a corner table. Quaeryt made his way past tables filled with majors and captains and sat down at the table opposite the other subcommander. "Have you seen the commander?"

"Not yet. I asked for two lagers and an ale." Meinyt glanced around, his eyes passing over the overgenerous figure and gray hair of the innkeeper's wife. "They must be keeping the young servers out of sight."

"Wouldn't you?"

"Can't blame them, but . . ." Meinyt shook his head, then said in a lower voice, "Does it seem to you that the folks here don't much care who rules?"

"I wouldn't be surprised if that were so in most towns and hamlets, so long as the ruler leaves their lands and their daughters alone."

"Or pays well and treats the daughters tolerably well." Meinyt snorted.

"You're more cynical than I am."

"Not much. I've known men who'd, if you will, lend out their wife for enough golds or other rewards. As for daughters . . ." He shook his head. "Heard tell that Rescalyn's mistress found him a gentleman compared to Kharst and his crew."

Quaeryt nodded. "She never said much, but the few times I intimated such, she didn't disagree, and she fled Variana after her sister's death in rather sordid circumstances involving Kharst. She confided in Vaelora, but Vaelora had to promise not to tell me anything, except that where women were concerned, Kharst was far worse than any of the stories about him."

"The stories tell of a man who's little more than a beast."

"I can only tell you what I've heard, but Vaelora doesn't exaggerate, and I don't think Mistress Eluisa does, either." Absently, he hoped that Eluisa D'Taelmyn was still at the Telaryn Palace in Tilbora. Then he almost smiled as he recalled that Vaelora had never finished learning the clavecin pieces from Eluisa. There were always loose ends, in personal and professional sides of life.

Skarpa slid into the seat between the other two officers. "We just got a dispatch from Deucalon."

Quaeryt decided to say nothing.

Meinyt snorted.

"Neither of you looks pleased." Skarpa took the ale that the serving woman had left and took a swallow. "Can't say that you're wrong." He set down the mug. "They're still in Rivecote Nord. Their casualties were few, since the battalion stationed there decided to withdraw after initial contact rather than face destruction. They've got the cable ferry working. The rest of the dispatch is politely worded. We're not to advance precipitously. He wants better descriptions of where we are, since the places we've been aren't on the maps he has."

"Did he say anything about our taking Rivecote Sud?" asked Quaeryt.

"Not a word. I wrote a dispatch before we left to be sent to him once they got the cable ferry back. Told him your imagers had made our capture of Rivecote Sud almost without casualties." Skarpa grinned momentarily. "I also mentioned the winch repair. His dispatch said it was still holding up after they replaced the cables and restored the ferry service."

"I'm glad to hear that," replied Quaeryt.

Skarpa took another swallow of the ale, then looked up toward the gray-haired woman.

She hurried over. "Yes, sir?"

"Appreciate your serving the three of us."

"Yes, sir." She scurried off.

"I'll have to reply, right after we eat," Skarpa went on, "since the marshal requested that I confirm his orders, and commanded the dispatch rider to wait for my response.'

"Worries about your initiative, does he?" said Meinyt.

"All marshals worry about their commanders' initiative, whether they have too much or too little. Just as commanders worry about that in their subcommanders."

"Some commanders," suggested Quaeryt, "are less uncomfortable with initiative in subordinates."

"Only when they trust them," said Skarpa dryly, "and I can trust you two to overextend yourselves and your men . . . and somehow make it work." Before either subcommander could say more, he added, "Is there anything you haven't told me that the marshal should know?"

Meinyt shook his head.

"The locals don't seem to have any great affection for Rex Kharst," Quaeryt said. "The marshal might see if that's so on his side of the river, or just here because it's more isolated."

"I'll mention that. Anything else?"

"Not that we haven't told you.'

"Good. We might as well eat hearty." Skarpa glanced at the server approaching with three platters.

19

Later on Solayi, Quaeryt and first company rode out to the local high holding, only to find that the dwelling was shuttered and secured, as were all
the outbuildings, with no sign of retainers or tenants. That, Quaeryt suspected, was likely true for many holdings as they neared Villerive. They
left everything untouched and returned to Roule where, thankfully, Skarpa
did not require services, perhaps because he had the men readying themselves to set out on Lundi morning. Quaeryt did notice that Skarpa sent a
dispatch to Deucalon announcing his actions just as they left Roule.

By Meredi evening, a dispatch courier caught up with them, bearing
orders for Skarpa to stop in the next sizable town and to inform the marshal of their location, and not to advance unless attacked or required to
deal with Bovarian forces . . . or unless he received orders.

Skarpa made no comment, but only passed the dispatch to Meinyt and
Quaeryt.

"Does he want to take until winter to reach Variana?" groused Meinyt.

"Marshal Deucalon is very cautious," suggested Quaeryt.

Skarpa raised his eyebrows, then said, "We'd best find a good sizable
town, then."

That took another three days, because the commander deemed all
those through which they passed as hamlets or "little better than hamlets,"
although several were almost as large as Roule or Rivecote Sud. Skarpa did
send off dispatch riders every day, reporting on each of the hamlets or
small towns, and their locations, while observing the lack of sizable towns
on the south side of the river that met Deucalon's criteria.

Finally, just before ninth glass on Solayi morning, the scouts reported
a millestone stating that Caernyn was six milles ahead.

"That's even on the map," observed Skarpa.

Both subcommanders, riding on each side of him, laughed.

The scout looked puzzled, but set off once more to investigate the town.

Two glasses later, the scouts returned, riding hard before they reined up.
"Sir . . . they've got troops. More than we've seen since Ferravyl. They're

dug in behind stone walls, not really exactly forts, on the slopes south of the town. There's a long swamp on the south."

Skarpa looked to the subcommanders "Had to happen sooner or later." Then he asked the scout, "What about the troops? How many?"

"It's hard to tell, sir. They look to have more than a regiment, and some are wearing maroon uniforms."

"Maroon uniforms? Are you sure?"

"Yes, sir. I couldn't say that they all are, but most of those we saw were."

"What else? Did you see any catapults? Or cannon?"

"There weren't any cannon ports in the walls, sir, but we couldn't rightly see what was behind them. We had to ride hard to escape one of their patrols."

"How does the river road approach the town and those slopes . . . ?" Skarpa asked questions for almost a quint before he sent the scout off to discover what else he could. Then he ordered the regiments forward once more.

"Maroon uniforms," offered Meinyt. "They wouldn't be Antiagon troops, would they?"

"Who else would be in maroon? But why would they be here? It's more than five hundred milles to the nearest part of Antiago."

"The Autarch did wed Kharst's niece," offered Quaeryt. "It just could be that Aliaro fears that if Bhayar takes even the eastern half of Bovaria, he'll turn his sights to taking Antiago."

"That's more likely, except that regiment had to be in Bovaria before we even set out from Ferravyl," said Skarpa.

"Maybe the Autarch thought Kharst would defeat us, and he wanted his share of the spoils," suggested Meinyt.

"We need to give him his fair share," said Skarpa sarcastically. "If we can."

"If we can?" asked Meinyt. "They've only got a regiment."

"They're using stone walls," said Quaeryt. "Do you think they might have imagers and Antiagon Fire? Was that why you asked about catapults?"

"With Antiagons, that's possible." He frowned. "They probably won't have imagers, not in Bovarian territory. Antiagon Fire—that's more likely. If they do, we'll need your imagers."

Quaeryt frowned. "I'll have to think about what they can do." He glanced to the hazy but clear sky. *No chance of rain. Not soon, anyway.*

"One of them can deflect arrows. Why not a fireball thrown from a catapult?"

"Arrows don't weigh nearly as much."

"And a bridge doesn't weigh anything?" asked Skarpa.

"They weren't trying to stop it or move it," Quaeryt pointed out. "They've never dealt with Antiagon Fire. Neither have I." *You've only watched it being fired from a cannon in a strange shell . . . and only once at that.*

"None of us have," Skarpa said, "but we're likely to find out sooner or later."

"I need to talk to the imagers." Quaeryt guided the mare back along the narrow shoulder of the road until he reached Fifth Battalion. As he eased in beside Major Zhelan, he called out, "Undercaptain Voltyr, forward."

Voltyr rode forward.

"Do you know anything about Antiagon Fire?"

"Sir?"

"We're likely about to face an Antiagon regiment that's positioned behind stone walls. Would you like to wager that they don't have at least some weapons that employ Antiagon Fire?"

"No, sir. But I don't know much about it."

"It has to be created by imagers, it's said."

"Yes, sir, but I don't know how. No imager I know ever knew how."

"What do you know about it?"

"It's supposed to be a sticky liquid that's dark, like bitumen, and it has resins mixed in it, and some say brimstone, and then there's a yellow-white powder that's mixed with that, but it has to be coated with hot wax or it will burn, even on top of water."

"It burns on top of water?" asked Zhelan.

"I've read about that," replied Quaeryt. "Do you know why it takes an imager to make it?"

Voltyr shrugged. "No, sir, except I heard that only an imager could create the powder."

Quaeryt looked to Zhelan. "Have you ever encountered it?"

"No, sir. Aren't the Antiagons the only ones who have it?"

"At least one High Holder from Nacliano has it," replied Quaeryt. "His ships have special cannon and shells they use against pirates."

"I wouldn't know, sir."

"Voltyr . . . ask the others if they know anything about Antiagon Fire, then ride back and ask the Khellan majors."

"Yes, sir."

In little less than a quint Voltyr returned with the information that none of the imagers or Khellan officers knew more than he and Quaeryt had already discussed.

As he rode on, Quaeryt continued to think. Given the way Captain Shuld had handled the shells on the *Diamond Naclia*, it had been clear they could easily explode. That meant a regiment likely wouldn't carry large amounts . . . *But what if they kept them in small containers, like miniature cannonballs that would fit in small catapults? He* tried to recall what had happened to the pirate ship. *The flames hadn't appeared until after the shell struck* . . . Yet it couldn't have been the impact that created them—or they didn't need much of an impact because there were too many reports of Antiagon Fire being used against troops in situations where the impact of a shell or globe grenade could not have been that forceful.

When, a glass later, just after midday, Skarpa called a halt more than a mille from the stone emplacements, Quaeryt still had no answers. For all his questions, he had come up with only one possible way of dealing with the Antiagon Fire. And it was a way he really didn't want to try, especially after he rode forward to join Skarpa and Meinyt and surveyed what lay before them.

The approach to Caernyn was suited far more to defense than attack. The river road followed a tongue of land, likely man-made, through a marshy lowland before leaving the swamp and rising along the right side of a slope that extended a half mille or so before flattening out. The marsh continued around the base of the slope as far as the eye could see, turning into a lake at some point. The far left end of the slope was heavily wooded, and the woods angled westward away from the marsh. The river road rose from the swampy lowland into a gradual slope that bordered a bluff overlooking the River Aluse. Near the top of the slope a waist-high brick wall some five yards from the right shoulder of the road marked the edge of a steep drop-off down to the River Aluse. Between the road and the woods was an expanse of meadow that held grass and a few low scrub bushes. At the top of the slope, between the road and the woods, was a pair of long walls rising two yards above the matted grass that grew right up to the ancient stones.

At the river end of the wall flew a banner bearing the emblem of a chateau in the center of a yellow sunburst against a vivid blue background. At the southwestern end of the walls was a second banner, bearing a jagged lightning bolt of green and yellow crossed with a stylized halberd, all against a bright maroon background.

So . . . Kharst . . . or those who ruled before him . . . believes he is the sun whose light illuminates Bovaria? Do all rulers believe they are at the center of everything? Quaeryt was afraid he knew the answer to his question.

"Subcommanders, do you have any suggestions as to how we might best attack?" Skarpa raised his eyebrows.

"Go around them if we can, and attack from the rear," suggested Meinyt.

"It's twenty-five milles around the southern end of that swamp and lake," replied Skarpa. "Might be farther than that, and it looks like the approach from the west isn't much better."

"Why'd they build a town here, then?" asked Meinyt.

"Just for that reason," said Quaeryt. "In the early years it was probably hard for river reavers to get to flatboats who tied up here."

Skarpa nodded. "It's a good spot to stop on the river, and the higher ground along the river goes for maybe eight milles. The map shows the marsh and the lake as just one long lake. Could be the place was an island in the river a long time back. Anyway, it's here, and we can't just go around it and leave an Antiagon regiment sitting here."

"They were sent here to stop us," suggested Quaeryt. "They'll have Antiagon Fire and who knows what else. They might even know that you've got imagers."

"That thought had occurred to me," said Skarpa. "Do you have something in mind?"

"Just that I'd rather not lose a lot of troopers this far from Variana." Quaeryt paused. "Is there any way to get to those woods over there?"

Skarpa smiled crookedly. "The marsh is filled with swamp lizards, some of them three, four yards in length, with teeth as long as a man's hand. If you stay away from the water, you'll be exposed, but it's a bit far for their archers."

"Can you send scouts to see what the woods are like?"

"I already have, but none of them have come back . . . and they should have by now. That means I'll need to send a squad, because we don't want to mount an attack and discover another regiment on our flank."

Left unsaid was the fact that the casualties would likely be high for a recon squad.

A quint later, Quaeryt watched as a squad from Third Battalion rode across the lower part of the grassy slope, some fifteen or twenty yards above the reeds that marked the edge of the marsh. A few shafts flew from the stone ramparts, but fell short. Then, when the scouting squad was less than a hundred yards from the woods, scores of shafts flew out, and four riders slumped in their saddles immediately, and several others were hit. The squad turned and withdrew, not quite at a gallop, and not quickly enough to avoid having three other troopers take shafts.

"I'd say that they've got two companies of archers there, maybe more," observed Meinyt.

"There is one way," mused Skarpa. "We could do exactly what they want. Just do it at a time and in a way that they won't expect."

"A night attack?" Meinyt frowned.

"That or an attack well before dawn," said Skarpa. "We'd have to make certain that there aren't any pits in the road or on the shoulder or in the grass beside the road." He looked to Quaeryt. "Could your imagers put smoke and pepper behind the stoneworks just before we attack. With that and in the dark . . ."

"I'd have to get them within a few hundred yards. First company would need to be one of the lead companies."

"Why not all Fifth Battalion?" asked Meinyt. "The Khellans need to do their share."

"That might be best," agreed Quaeryt.

Skarpa nodded. "Once it's dark, I'll have men walk the road. They should be able to get within a few hundred yards before the Bovarians—or the Antiagons—start lofting shafts. They can mark any pits or traps with reeds."

"Getting the reeds might be a problem," said Quaeryt.

"There are enough along the part of the road we just traveled away from the swamp lizards," replied Skarpa. "Once the pits are marked, we'll wait a time, then form up silently—or as quietly as the troopers can—just out of range of bows and catapults . . ."

After another half glass or so, Quaeryt returned to Fifth Battalion. First, he briefed Zhelan, Ghaelyn, and the imager undercaptains on what they could expect, with possible tactics with which they could respond. Then he summoned all the Khellan officers. Once they had gathered, he surveyed them, then began, in Bovarian.

"There are likely two regiments at the top of the slope. One is Bovarian, the other Antiagon. The Antiagons may have their fire. They also have filled the woods to the west with archers. The idea behind their defense is to force us to take the road, and then pin us against the wall and the cliff . . . or to require us to make a direct attack on stone ramparts. It would take two to three days to withdraw and then make our way around the swamp and lake . . . and the western approach is almost as bad. The marsh and the lake to the west are filled with swamp lizards, and we don't have boats."

Six pairs of dark eyes studied Quaeryt, along with those of Zhelan and the undercaptains.

With a smile Quaeryt wasn't certain he felt, he went on. "So we're going to do what they expect in a way they don't expect, and Fifth Battalion will be among the lead forces. After dark, scouts will walk and creep up the road and mark any pits or traps . . ." He went on to explain the details of the planned attack.

When he finished he asked, "Is that clear?"

Major Calkoran nodded politely, then asked, "Do you wish us to give quarter?"

Quaeryt responded, "If someone has fallen or is too badly wounded to fight, leave them. Do not pursue those who flee—unless Major Zhelan or I give the order to do so. Our task is to defeat those who oppose us and take the town, not to slaughter the helpless." He smiled. "This is not kindness on my part, or that of the commander. Slaughtering those wounded who cannot defend themselves wastes strength and takes time. We need to defeat and scatter them so they cannot re-form those who might delay us on our way to take Variana and to destroy Rex Kharst."

"Then we must make every blow count," replied Calkoran.

Quaeryt understood what he meant, but there was little help for that. Still, with the Khellan companies attacking first, he doubted they would find many of the enemy helpless or already wounded. "Any other questions?"

Calkoran looked to the Khellan majors and captains and said something in Pharsi. They all nodded. Then he turned back to Quaeryt. "No, sir."

"Then rest your men. We will not attack until shortly after eighth glass."

Once the Khellans had left, Quaeryt motioned to Shaelyt, then waited until the undercaptain stepped up to him. "What did he say to them?"

Shaelyt smiled. "His Pharsi is a little different, but I think he said, 'Do not waste your efforts on the cowards and the weak. To avenge Khel, we must first destroy the strong.'"

Quaeryt couldn't disagree with that.

20

For Quaeryt, the glasses between the time he briefed his officers and sunset seemed to drag by endlessly. The local forces remained behind their stoneworks, barely glimpsed so that it was not obvious how many troops there might be, and after the use of archers, Skarpa, Meinyt, and Quaeryt had to assume that they were well trained.

Skarpa did not send out the scouts with reeds until full dark, close to eighth glass. By then, Quaeryt had slipped away from Fifth Battalion and raised a personal concealment shield to walk up along the side of the road, just far enough so that he could watch the scouts. If the Bovarians saw the scouts, their sentries or lookouts gave no indication, or none that he could see or hear.

That bothered Quaeryt. *What if they've already anticipated a night attack? What would they do?*

Unfortunately, he had too many ideas of what might come. So he watched the scouts and where they placed the reeds. That placement confirmed his suspicions, because there were no reeds closer than four yards to the road, and none at all on the river side. That indicated, as Skarpa had surmised, the defense strategy was to funnel attackers onto the road, with a possible bombardment of Antiagon Fire . . . and there was no way to tell if the attacks, countermeasures, and defenses Quaeryt had planned for the imagers would work.

Once the scouts moved beyond what he could see in the dim light, Quaeryt walked back to where Fifth Battalion waited, lifting the concealment before he was close enough so that anyone might see him reappear, and waited with Zhelan and the imagers.

Another glass passed before the scouts returned, and Quaeryt formed up Fifth company, as silently as possible. First company led the way for Fifth Battalion, with the imagers riding the right flank of the company, on the shoulder of the road, escorted by half a squad from first company. Quaeryt led the imagers, riding almost even with the front rank of first company. The plan of attack was simple enough—to get enough riders high enough on the slope to be above the stone walls so that they could swing and ride down from behind, trapping the defenders between their walls and their other defenses.

In the stillness of the night, with both Artiema and Erion less than a quarter full, the sound of hooves on the road echoed like thunder in Quaeryt's ears, although he kept telling himself that the mounts were walking slowly and that the sound was nowhere near that loud. It couldn't have been, because first company reached a point on the road less than three hundred yards below the walls, without any outcry or action from the defenders.

Then, Quaeryt thought he heard . . . something. Out of caution—and fear—he extended his shields across the front rank of first company. Barely had he done so when he felt an impact, followed by a wave of heat and flame as a fire grenade flared across the shields. As he watched, some of the crimson-greenish-yellow fire splashed over the top of his shields and spilled onto riders in the third rank, turning several into instant torches, even as the other riders moved away, helpless to do anything.

"Charge!" ordered Quaeryt, and Zhelan immediately echoed the order.

"Watch the walls!" Quaeryt urged the mare forward, trying to hold his shields to protect the front rank for at least a time. "Image pepper and smoke!" Since he could not see much except the outline of the walls, not with the Antiagon Fire burning a few yards away and the darkness beyond, he could only hope that the undercaptains' imaging would have some effect.

A fire grenade burst into flame just short of the charging riders. One mount reared, and several others piled into it, but most of the squad managed to avoid the column of fire.

Another grenade rebounded from Quaeryt's shields, flaring into flame as it slid toward the left shoulder of the road, where it ignited grass and brush. Quaeryt felt as though that fire had burned his face.

Still another grenade arched overhead, heading farther downslope, trailing flames, then exploded above the lead company of Fifth Regiment, with lines of fire falling across the troopers. A second, and a third followed, with more globs of sticky fire raining down on the troopers. Despite the screams of horses being burned, and the jostling to avoid the patches of Antiagon Fire, both regiments moved up the road swiftly.

Quaeryt reined up near the top of the rise, bringing the imagers to a halt against the stone wall at the edge of the bluff and letting first company and the rest of the battalion swing toward the stone walls. As they thundered past, he stood in the stirrups, looking to the walls and trying to locate the catapults, but he could see no frameworks or timber structures, suggesting the catapults were comparatively small.

A handful of defenders rushed forward with pikes. Quaeryt glanced back, then concentrated on imaging the contents of the last grenade back against the defenders. Only about half flared up, but that was enough to unsettle the others. But as they fell back, more pikemen rushed forward to try to halt the oncoming troopers.

Then, in the light of the Antiagon Fire that he had imaged against the pikemen, behind them he saw a figure with a framework and a sling-pouch—what he thought was a one-man trebuchet, or something like it. As the sling-catapult arm went back, Quaeryt imaged away part of the wooden arm, and the sling-pouch swung sideways, and Antiagon Fire flared along the wide trench behind the stone wall, and toward the pikemen.

"More pepper and smoke!" ordered Quaeryt.

Even he spoke, he heard the muffled *thwump* even before he saw a larger dark globe arc from a larger catapult through the air and strike the shoulder of the road more than a hundred yards downhill from where he watched, then explode into a ball of mixed crimson and yellow-green flames, an incandescence whose heat he could feel from more than a hundred yards away.

What can you do to stop that?

Almost without thinking, he imaged that mass of fire back onto the pikemen—except a good half of it vanished as he did, and there was a loud sizzling and a welter of steam rose around the remaining pikemen.

Why—He didn't bother to complete the thought. He knew why. All the effort it had taken to image the Antiagon Fire back uphill had created ice around it and the ice had dropped on the edges of the fire.

Another fire grenade slammed against Quaeryt's shields, and he could feel his control slipping. He contracted them to protect himself, feeling guilty as he did, glancing back in the direction of the sloping meadow and stone walls.

One trooper, trying to escape another fireball, rode off the road and across the grass toward the stone wall. His mount appeared to stumble, and then a gout of flame rose from the concealed pit, immersing man and mount in greenish yellow flames with crimson overshades.

From somewhere in the direction of the town, he heard a horn, and then several squads of men, perhaps a company of cavalry, plunged down the road toward Quaeryt and the troopers of Third Regiment who were pressing past him and toward the stone walls.

"Fourth company! On me! To the right!"

Quaeryt didn't recognize the officer's voice, but appreciated the speed and decisiveness of his action.

Even so, close to a squad of Bovarian riders broke past fourth company and rode down the narrow strip between the road and the wall, galloping toward the imagers at full speed.

Although some of the rankers in Third Regiment saw them, Quaeryt realized they wouldn't react in time. "Imagers! Attack from the town. Image pepper!"

He hoped that they would react quickly, but suspected most wouldn't be able to change their focus fast enough, and that some were probably already exhausted. He urged the mare forward, widening his shields slightly.

The three leading Bovarians raised blades, markedly longer than Telaryn sabres, and spurred toward him.

Quaeryt aimed the mare between two of them, then let the shields knock them aside. One mount veered into the one closest to the stone wall and that horse crashed into the stone. The remaining Bovarians slashed at Quaeryt, and while he could feel the impact of every blow on his shields, they held. Then he found himself in a small open space short of Third Regiment's fourth company, in the process of cutting down and routing the Bovarians.

He turned the mare back toward the imager undercaptains, then reined up. The Telaryn troopers had followed him—or enough had—that the Bovarians who had charged the imagers were either wounded or dead. From what he could tell, the Telaryn forces had overrun the stone walls, at least to the extent that no more fireballs had appeared.

After a time, he eased the mare along the wall back toward the undercaptains. Once he returned, he stopped and studied them. Akoryt was slumped over the neck of his mount. But the others were more upright in their saddles, although Shaelyt looked to be shivering . . . or shuddering.

Sweat dripped from under the visor cap, through his hair, and down Quaeryt's brow, while tiny flashes of light flickered across his vision. After another glance around, he pulled out his water bottle and took several swallows of watered lager. Several swallows later, the light flashes subsided, but did not entirely vanish.

Should you have continued the charge with the battalion? Even though he knew he'd been able to do more from where he placed the imagers, letting

Zhelan lead them had bothered him, much as he knew that the major was far better trained in that than he was, and that he'd survived by imaging skill and not skill in leadership or arms. He was also aware that he was getting tired, and that any more imaging might not be possible.

His eyes scanned the slope and stone walls once more.

The night had taken on a muted lurid light, with patches of Antiagon Fire still burning here and there, and other fires that had spread through the drier vegetation. The various kinds of smoke billowed and swirled in an unpleasant and acrid mixture.

Quaeryt's head ached so much that he could barely see. His eyes burned from the smoke, and his guts were churning from the odor of burned flesh. Through tearing eyes, he tried to make out the walls, but in the gloom from all the dying embers, he could make out little, except that it was clear that the Bovarians and Antiagons had broken and were fleeing . . . and that there was little more that he could do for the moment.

Several defenders fled downhill. In the dim light, Quaeryt saw one man flail and then disappear into a hidden pit. With all the sound of horses, riders, and weapons, he couldn't hear if the Bovarian cried out.

"Sir?" asked Voltyr, moving his mount up past the leading rank of the squad protecting the imagers. "Do we need to do anything more?"

Can any of you? Quaeryt didn't ask that. He turned. "Not now. I hope not. We'll see." He glanced at the fires and the smoke and stifled a cough. Was there any way he could project small shields away from him—to stop the fire grenades right after they were launched, so that they would explode then and shower fire on the Antiagons? Should he have thought of that earlier?

It wouldn't have mattered. You'd have to see them much earlier than you could in the dark. He shook his head. *You need to teach some of the imagers about shields. At least, Voltyr and Shaelyt . . . and the others later.* Some of them might have noticed the way the fire hadn't struck him, but in the darkness, they couldn't have been certain, and he doubted that they'd been looking at him all the time, not in a battle. Still . . . that was another problem.

He took a deep breath.

He was still watching the last of what appeared to have degenerated into a slaughter two quints later when Zhelan rode back out of the heavier smoke that surrounded the stone walls.

The major reined up. "Sir . . . the area is ours. Those defenders who remain are dead or in no way able to fight."

"What did it cost?" asked Quaeryt. "Do you know yet?"

"No, sir, but it looks worse than it was. Ghaelyn reports he lost ten men and has five wounded. The Khellans . . . they don't know yet."

"You did better than I hoped, leading the attack." Ghaelyn's casualties didn't sound too bad, not when he'd been the first to reach the defenders, but Quaeryt worried about exactly why the Khellans didn't know. *Hunting down fleeing Bovarians?*

"They were bunched in too tight, and got in each other's way. The smoke and pepper helped. At first, they couldn't see much." Zhelan paused. "If there's nothing else, sir?"

Quaeryt managed a laugh. "Trying to gather up the Khellans?"

"Yes, sir."

"Go . . ."

Less than half a quint after Zhelan vanished into the lurid gloom and smoke, Skarpa rode over to Quaeryt and reined up. "A good third of the survivors, it looks, have run down into those woods. Those who are left."

"You don't want to send troopers in there in the dark?"

"Would you?"

Quaeryt wouldn't. "Are there any of their catapults intact? Or any fire grenades left? That's about the only thing you might do. You might see if you could use their catapults and drop the Antiagon Fire grenades into the woods. There's enough open ground between where the trees end and the town proper. Then have the men wait for them to come out."

"The fire could still spread to the town, and we might lose men trying to figure out how to use them."

"It could," said Quaeryt. "And you could lose more men in the woods. Or you could post men around the woods and wait."

"And we could wait for days or weeks."

Quaeryt nodded. "Or you could just let them hide and slip away. Just post a company or two between the woods and the town."

"Your imagers can't do anything?"

"They're spent."

"I'd rather not endanger the town. We may be here for a while. And I'd rather not burn the survivors out. Would you?"

"No. It's one thing in battle, another afterward." Quaeryt snorted. "Not that Kharst would see the difference or care." The wind swirled around him, blowing past him from the northeast. He glanced at the meadow and the fires still burning in front of the stone walls, then said, "You may not have a choice if the wind continues."

Skarpa shook his head. "Rather not have that happen. If they surrender, we'll have a few days to work out something." He paused, then said, "Even in the dark, you look like something the Namer dragged in."

Quaeryt laughed hoarsely, then blotted his eyes with his sleeve.

"Once you've got your battalion back together, why don't you see if you can find quarters or the like for them." Skarpa's last words were not a question.

"Yes, sir."

Quaeryt couldn't disagree. Every moment was an effort. He watched as the commander rode toward the slightly higher ground behind the devastation around the stone walls. He just hoped the Khellans hadn't gotten too out of hand, but in the smoke and darkness there was no way he was going to be able to track them down.

He could only deal with it later—if they had exceeded his orders—after the fact, because he was in no shape to do anything else.

That bothered him as well.

21

Somehow, in the seeming chaos that followed the battle, if it could be called that, Quaeryt and Zhelan managed to muster Fifth Battalion, but it was well after the first glass past midnight by then, because while only some of the woods had burned, that had been enough to force out many of those defenders who had fled, and dealing with them had taken more time. Second glass had almost passed before they located a livery stable and adjoining sheds on the southeast side of Caernyn. The quarters, if they could be called such, were cramped, but he hadn't wanted to try to roust out locals in the middle of the night, not with the potential chaos and additional deaths such an effort might have caused. What with one thing and another, it had been after third glass before Quaeryt had collapsed on a pile of hay in the livery stable, his legs shaking so much he could barely stand, and his head pounding.

When he struggled awake in the grayness of Lundi morning, his lungs burned. He felt as though the smoke from the previous day had all settled in his nose, throat, and chest. He slowly rose and then staggered as much as walked, because his bad leg was giving him trouble, as it often did when he was overly tired, to the door of the stable where a pair of troopers stood guard.

"Good morning, sir."

"Good morning." Looking out over the trampled mud of what passed for a courtyard, all he could see was gray. A grayish sky, with haze and smoke still everywhere . . . and the stench of burned wood and flesh. He had to swallow the bile that rose in his throat.

"Sir . . ." A junior squad leader hurried toward Quaeryt. "The commander would like you to meet him for breakfast at the River Inn. It's three blocks that way." He pointed.

"What about the men?"

The squad leader looked puzzled.

"I need to make sure they're fed, first." Quaeryt tried to sound calm and pleasant, even though his head still throbbed, and the burning sensation in his throat and lungs had not completely subsided.

"Ah . . . sir."

Quaeryt turned at the source of Zhelan's voice.

"As you suggested, sir, we've taken over the stable owner's kitchen and spaces," said Zhelan. "It will take a bit longer to feed everyone, but . . ."

Quaeryt had suggested no such thing, but he appreciated, again, Zhelan's tact. "Thank you. I'm glad you were able to work that out." *You shouldn't have said anything until you knew what was happening.* But then he wasn't thinking well, not on as little sleep as he'd had. That was just another reason he had no business being a subcommander. He should have been up earlier to take care of things, but he didn't have the years of training and experience to be able to know what to do without having to think about it. And . . . he'd forgotten how much imaging took out of him. He turned back to the squad leader. "If you would let the commander know I'll be there shortly."

"Yes, sir."

Once the squad leader had left, Quaeryt turned to Zhelan and gestured for the major to follow him along the dried mud beside the stable for several yards, until they were well away from the troopers. "Thank you."

"Sir . . . that's what I'm here for."

To Quaeryt's ears, Zhelan didn't sound condescending, patronizing, but just matter-of-fact, and not in the resigned way he'd heard too often in Bhayar's court. "That may be, but I appreciate it."

"Thank you, sir." Zhelan paused. "We lost four more men this morning. I think the rest of the wounded stand a good chance of pulling through."

"What's the town like? And the Khellans?"

"They followed your orders. There were even wounded Bovarians where they fought."

Thank the Nameless. Even as that thought came to mind, Quaeryt almost smiled at the incongruity of his offering thanks, however inadvertently, to a deity he wasn't even certain existed. "That's good. Very good."

"Sir . . . the commander . . ."

"Oh . . . thank you."

Quaeryt pulled himself together, then headed in the direction that the squad leader had pointed, finding himself accompanied by a pair of troopers. Smiling wryly at that, he also checked his shields, holding only the lighter trigger shields, which weren't any effort to speak of, as he walked northward.

The River Inn was actually a solid three-story building, with a half squad of troopers stationed on the covered front porch.

"Good morning, sir," offered the squad leader as Quaeryt stepped onto the solid planks of the porch. "The commander is in the public room, the first arch on the right."

"Good morning, and thank you." He had just stepped through the doorway when he couldn't help but hear a few words behind him.

". . . must have taken out half score himself with that staff of his . . . protecting the imagers . . ."

Had he? Did everyone watch him? Not many did, only those who weren't preoccupied with their own survival, but a few had, and they'd seen the overt physical things. That would change as the other imagers became more able and there were more imagers to watch. He pushed those thoughts aside and made his way into the public room where Skarpa sat alone at a circular table. In fact, except for a serving woman standing by the door to the kitchen, he was the only one in the room.

Quaeryt slid into the chair across from the commander. "I overslept this morning . . ."

"It's not quite seventh glass," replied Skarpa mildly. "That's not all that late."

"For a subcommander of a battalion? I told you I wasn't meant to be an officer . . . and after that mess last night . . ." Quaeryt started to shake his head, but even beginning the gesture hurt. Instead, he reached for the mug of lager than Skarpa had waiting for him. After a swallow, he went on. "Zhelan kept me from making a fool out of myself this morning."

"There are times when everyone has to do that. You've done it for me, whether you know it or not."

When? Quaeryt couldn't think of a time when he could have done that.

Skarpa motioned to the server. "Breakfast for the subcommander."

The woman nodded and hurried into the kitchen.

"Zhelan understands something you don't," Skarpa said.

Quaeryt took another swallow of the lager, then waited for the other boot to come down.

"You can't do everything. Last night, what you and the imagers did saved hundreds of our troopers. I told him to make sure you weren't disturbed."

"But then I shouldn't be a subcommander."

"You have to be, or you won't have the authority to do what you need to do." Skarpa snorted. "There's not a man in your first company that doesn't know you'll put your life on the line to do what needs to be done. If you don't lead every charge, they all know it's because you're doing something else, and it's usually something that saves their ass. If the Khellans don't know it already, they will before long." He stopped as the server returned and set down a platter heaped with a mixture of rice fries and scrambled cheesed eggs, with a small loaf of dark bread.

Once the server moved back to the kitchen door, Skarpa went on. "Now . . . eat and stop worrying. I need you with a clear head so that you can get to work making sure that the patrols I set up are doing what they should. I told them to do what they did in Rivecote Sud. We also need to go over supplies." The commander shook his head. "I'm afraid we'll be here for a time."

"Have you heard from the marshal?" Quaeryt took a bite of the warm rice fries, surprisingly good, but that might have been because he was indeed hungry.

"No, but he's not likely to be able to move as fast as we have."

"Do they have a ferry here?"

"They've got slips, but no boats. Not exactly surprising, when you think about it."

"What have you learned from the Antiagons?"

"They were sent to join the attack on Ferravyl, but Aliaro sent them by way of Variana." Skarpa laughed softly.

"What? That sounds like he was stalling."

"My thought as well. Then, on the way down the Aluse, their commander found that the Bovarians weren't too friendly on the north side of the river, and they took the bridge at Villerive. They were told to wait here for a Bovarian regiment from someplace called Asseroiles. By the time that regiment arrived, they'd learned of the defeat at Ferravyl, so they were ordered to hold Caernyn against any attackers."

"What did their commander say?"

"He didn't. He was killed when you and your imagers exploded that Antiagon Fire in their trench. One of his majors—the only one who survived—told me. He's got a broken leg. He was very upset. Apparently, when they use Antiagon Fire, everyone flees, and they just mop up the survivors. He can't understand what happened."

"We still lost too many."

"We always lose too many. That's war. We can only make sure the Bovarians lose a lot more. Now get back to eating so that we can get on with the day. Oh . . . and by the way, we're making better arrangements for all the troopers and officers while we're here in Caernyn. The officers will all be billeted here, and we've taken all the inns and the like for the regiments and your battalion."

"Thank you, sir."

"Don't thank me. Thank you for keeping the damage from that Anti-agon Fire to a minimum."

"I've got some ideas for handling it better. After we get the patrolling settled, I'm going to work with the imagers."

"Good. Eat," ordered Skarpa.

Quaeryt took another swallow of lager, a mouthful of cheesed eggs and more rice fries.

After finishing with Skarpa, Quaeryt then had to deal with Meinyt and the companies from his regiment assigned to patrol duty in Caernyn. In the end, it was early afternoon before Quaeryt gathered the imager undercaptains and several engineer rankers together, and they walked toward the battlefield. Quaeryt had earlier sent one of the engineer rankers to confirm that at least one of the Antiagon catapults looked to be in working order. The other rankers carried baskets holding various empty fired-clay containers. One carried a small spade.

As they reached the top of the hill above the stone walls, Quaeryt could see that below the walls, Bovarian and Antiagon prisoners were still digging graves and carrying bodies to them, although a number of the formerly trapped and staked pits on the slope were already being used as communal graves. He recognized the mounted undercaptain overseeing the work on the northeast side of the slope—Sengh, from Skarpa's first battalion.

"Undercaptain . . . we need to use one of the catapults for training. Will that be a problem?"

"I wouldn't think so, sir. We've already cleared out the area behind the walls. I'll just send word over to Captain Moragh. He's in charge of the other side. That's where the catapults are."

"I'd appreciate it. How are the prisoners taking it?"

"They're not happy, especially the Antiagons. They think we should have at least given their dead a common pyre. The commander said that if they wanted to burn they should have used their own fire when they had the chance." Sengh smiled wryly. "Funny how folks don't like the idea of taking their own poison."

"That's true of most of us." Quaeryt nodded. "Thank you. If you'd have your man tell Captain Moragh that we'll be flinging things toward the woods . . ."

"Yes, sir."

As Quaeryt led the way across the top of the hill toward the southwestern end of the walls, he couldn't help but think about the Antiagon attitude toward burial. *Does it really matter whether your corpse is buried or burned after you're dead?* While Quaeryt frankly thought it more sanitary to be burned, he knew that there had been great debates over death and the dead. According to some choristers, Rholan had claimed that excessive attention to the body was a form of Naming. Although Quaeryt didn't recall anything offhand, he wondered, absently, if there were any passages in the little book about what Rholan had really thought about burial or burning, not that Quaeryt had had time or energy or light in which to read in the past days. If he ever got a chance, it might be interesting to see.

When they reached the end of the walls, beyond the area where the worst of the deflected Antiagon Fire had seared men and earth and everything else, the odor of burned vegetation and even burned flesh remained, if not so overpoweringly as it had been the night before.

Quaeryt swallowed, then turned to the engineer rankers. "Undercaptain Vaelt said you could operate the catapults."

"Yes, sir," replied the hard-faced older trooper. "Might take a bit to make sure we get it right." After a brief pause, he added, "You just want us to throw these pots?"

"We'll start with them empty. Then I'd like them filled with dirt or sand. That's why the spade."

"Yes, sir."

"Go to it, and let me know when you're ready." Quaeryt turned to the imagers. "You all did the best you could last night, and Commander Skarpa was pleased that you were able to keep the damage from the fire grenades to as little as it was. So was I." He paused. "I'd still like you to be able to do better in the future. If we encounter more than one Antiagon regiment, or one that's better equipped, you'll be overwhelmed. Given how you did last night, with a little practice, all of you can do better."

Quaeryt could sense the silent protest that they were all tired. He smiled and went on. "I know you're tired, but one of the things that makes you better and stronger is trying things when you're rested, but still tired. If you'll recall, every one of you has gotten more accomplished each time you've stretched yourself. Now . . . once the engineers have the catapult working, they're going to fling pots toward the woods over there. We'll walk downhill before they start. Each of you, in turn, will image something into one of those pots with enough force to break it. The idea is to break it before it passes over the wall." He paused and studied the faces. "Tell me why, Undercaptain Threkhyl."

"So it won't get to our troops."

"That's half right. What's the other half, Shaelyt?"

"If we do it quick enough, it might explode on their own men?"

"Exactly. And if we can do that, they might not be so eager to try using it. Either way . . ." His words got nods from Desyrk, Voltyr, and Shaelyt, and he turned back to the engineer rankers. "How long before you'll be ready to start?"

"Half a quint, sir, if nothing breaks. Might be a bit longer."

"We'll be walking down the slope, but we'll be away from the trees. Give me a hail when you're ready. When I tell you to start, I want you to send off six, but not in regular intervals. Vary the time between each."

"Yes, sir. We might have to try a few first."

"That's fine."

Quaeryt motioned to the undercaptains, then walked to the end of the stone wall, around the still warmish pile of charred wood and other items that had been pushed or shoved there, then past a matted and trampled area of grass and brush, and around a long earthen mound that had likely been a staked pit dug to protect the corner of the stonework, but which had clearly been turned into a burial mound. Something rustled, and he turned to see what he thought was a rat, scurrying into deeper grass. *Scavengers always are quick to show up, even among the animals.* He kept walking.

Fifty yards below the end of the stone wall and some twenty yards from where the woods began, Quaeryt stopped and waited for the undercaptains to join him. "We'll start here. Once the engineers signal they're ready, I'll call out which of you I want to try to destroy the pot coming off the catapult. Try to get it before it crosses the wall, but don't stop trying until you do."

"Yes, sir."

Not all the imagers murmured affirmation, but Quaeryt ignored that.

Almost a full quint passed, along with several objects flung toward the woods, before one of the rankers peered over the wall and called down, "We're ready, sir!"

"Begin launching!"

Quaeryt pointed. "Akoryt!"

He'd barely gotten the name out when a dark pot flew over the wall toward the woods.

Akoryt never did manage to image anything into it.

"Shaelyt!"

The youngest undercaptain managed to hit the pot some thirty yards from the wall.

"Baelthm!"

Surprisingly, Baelthm imaged something into the jar almost when it crossed the stone rampart, but whatever it was happened to be so small that the jar just broke in two and both halves flew into the woods.

"Good aim," called Quaeryt, "but you'll need something a little bigger. Desyrk!"

Desyrk exploded his pot just before it reached the woods.

"Threkhyl!"

Not surprisingly, Threkhyl destroyed a larger pot less than five yards from the ramparts, with little more than small fragments remaining and cascading down.

"Good!"

"Voltyr!"

Voltyr was almost as accurate as Baelthm, but more forceful, so that some of the shards actually dropped onto the stone of the rampart.

"Excellent!" Quaeryt paused, then said, "We'll try another round here, and then we'll move downhill."

During the second round, Quaeryt imaged a rough shard of hot iron into the pot meant for Akoryt when it was almost over the trees, so that it looked like it had hit a tree. That was because he wanted to see if he could do it himself.

Then they walked downhill another fifty yards and repeated the exercise. After that, they retreated another fifty yards. All in all, by the time Quaeryt had finished with the exercises, he and the undercaptains were exhausted and dripping sweat. He'd had to remove his cap several times and blot his forehead to keep the sweat out of his eyes. He was as tired as they were because he'd imaged objects into the pots the imagers had been unable to destroy at the moment they were about to strike the trees. At the end, when they were more than three hundred yards downhill, that meant he was imaging three times as often as Threkhyl, Shaelyt, and Voltyr. Although he'd had to send one of the engineer rankers back for more crockery and other objects, Quaeryt wasn't displeased with the results. Even Baelthm had managed to destroy pots up to a distance of a hundred yards.

The sun hung low over the buildings on the west side of Caernyn by the time Quaeryt and the imagers started back up the hill toward the town.

As they neared the edge of Caernyn, Quaeryt could hear Desyrk whispering to Shaelyt.

"How does he know all this . . . must be more than an imager . . ."

"You'd have to ask him." replied Shaelyt in a low voice, "but the lost ones always know things that no others know."

". . . these lost ones so powerful . . ." added Threkhyl in a louder voice, ". . . why aren't they the lords and rulers?"

". . . part of the curse Erion laid on them . . . to be powerful and wise enough to rule . . . and never be able to do so . . ."

Quaeryt almost stumbled as he heard those words. *Why hadn't Shaelyt told him that?* After a moment he smiled. The young undercaptain just had, because he'd spoken more clearly and loud enough for Quaeryt to hear. Then Quaeryt frowned. Had Shaelyt created that myth on the spot . . . and if he hadn't, why hadn't he told Quaeryt earlier?

At the moment it didn't matter, but he did need to talk to Shaelyt about it. He also needed to work in some sort of training about shields for Shaelyt and Voltyr.

Quaeryt knew that he needed to visit the High Holders in the area, but after working with the imager undercaptains on Lundi afternoon, it was far too late to set out. Instead, he arranged for fourth company to accompany him and the imagers on Mardi. Then he made inquiries of shopkeepers and others along the main street of Caernyn to find out more about the local holders, discovering that there was only one located close to the town itself, three milles west on the higher ground that he still thought might have once been an island in the River Aluse.

High Holder Haeryn owned and controlled the river docks below the town, situated at the south end of comparatively deep waters that amounted to a bay of sorts, sheltered by two points of higher ground that did not look entirely natural to Quaeryt, much as the locals assured him that the river harbor had not changed much in generations. Haeryn also owned the taproom and the two inns nearest to the river docks, as well as two large warehouses on the higher ground above the docks. Quaeryt suspected the High Holder owned far more than that, but more indirectly.

Although Quaeryt had planned to leave comparatively early on Mardi morning to visit Haeryn, at breakfast Skarpa asked Meinyt and Quaeryt to meet with him at eighth glass. Quaeryt made arrangements for fourth company to stand down until further notice, and then talked with each of the company commanders in turn while he was waiting to meet with Skarpa.

Both Meinyt and Quaeryt were at the near-empty public room of the River Inn a half quint before eighth glass. Skarpa arrived just after they did.

"I didn't have a chance to read through the dispatch and orders from Marshal Deucalon. I'd received them just before breakfast." Skarpa shook his head. "He sent ten pages of instructions and cautions." Then he motioned to a circular table in the middle of the room. Once the three were seated, he continued. "They're barely past a point opposite Roule. I don't know what's taking them so long, because they haven't fought anything much. Just a few companies here and there, but they've been trying to stop crop-burning. That can take time, according to Deucalon, because he doesn't have imagers."

Quaeryt didn't hide the wince.

"You disagree, Subcommander?"

"The troopers did more than the imagers to stop the burning we encountered. Imagers can't do everything he thinks they can."

"I don't think I'll mention that to the marshal. They're also having problems getting supplies. Apparently, there aren't that many large factors or High Holders near the river on the north side, and most of the factors already sold their stores to the Bovarian forces who attacked Ferravyl. That means we're supposed to stay here until we get further word. We're also to report our supply situation in the next few days."

Skarpa turned to Quaeryt. "Didn't you tell me your imagers can remove locks?"

"If the iron of the hasps isn't too thick," replied Quaeryt cautiously.

"Good. We've got all these warehouses along the river, and some of them might have supplies we can use. No one seems to know where the owners are." Skarpa snorted. "I'd rather not break down the doors because then we can't secure them. I'll have a squad of quartermasters ready for you after we finish, and you and your imagers can open the warehouses."

"I'd thought to visit the nearest High Holder, to see about supplies there as well."

"Let's see what we've got here in town first."

Quaeryt nodded.

"Here are our instructions and I've been told to read the first part word for word to you two." Skarpa smiled. "It appears that Marshal Deucalon is aware that you both have creative ways of interpreting general orders."

Meinyt did not roll his eyes, but he might as well have, given the brief expression that crossed his face.

Skarpa ignored it and cleared his throat. "'The mission of this campaign is to bring Bovaria into a union with Telaryn. The mission is not to ravage, pillage, or otherwise destroy the lands, the buildings, or the people of these lands, except when and where they offer armed resistance. Force against those not wearing the uniforms of either Bovaria or Antiago should be used only as a last resort, and such use should be appropriate to the situation at hand . . .'"

Reading the remaining three pages of "instructions" took another quint, most of it wasted, Quaeryt thought, since the message was what he'd already told his officers and men.

After that, Quaeryt and the imager undercaptains followed the quartermaster squad to the warehouses. The two warehouses belonging to Haeryn

were locked—and empty. So was the one belonging to the river factors'
guild. A smaller warehouse, belonging to a factor from Nordeau, held not
quite a hundred barrels of flour, dried meats, and some dried fruit.

By the time Quaeryt and the imagers finished with the locks at the four
warehouses on the river, it was close to two quints before the first glass of
the afternoon. Another quint passed before Quaeryt rode out along the road
west of Caernyn accompanied by Shaelyt, Akoryt, Baelthm . . . and Major
Arion and fourth company.

"This High Holder . . . he will not be at his holding," offered Arion in
accented Bovarian.

"It's likely he won't be," agreed Quaeryt.

"Then will you take what we need for supplies?"

"We will have to see," replied Quaeryt. "It might be that there is nothing to purchase or take. I can't imagine he has vast lands, or that they pro-
duce much."

"The High Holders of Bovaria always have much."

"True . . . but the battalion can't eat golds or silvers."

At the dryness of Quaeryt's tone, Arion laughed.

Before that long, the battalion reined up short of the pair of stone pillars that marked the entrance to Haeryn's holding. Each pillar supported
an iron gate, chained shut in the middle. A stone wall, less than two yards
high, ran some fifteen yards from each gate pillar, parallel to the road,
ending just short of a hedgerow.

Quaeryt turned in the saddle. "Akoryt, if you'd come forward and image away the hasp of that ugly lock . . ."

"Yes, sir."

Quaeryt thought he saw a flash of . . . something . . . in the undercaptain's normally flat brown eyes, but he just watched as Akoryt eased his
mount to a halt just short of the gates. After several moments, while the
undercaptain concentrated, the body of the lock dropped away from the
hasp.

"Are we to replace the lock once we leave, sir?"

"That would be best," replied Quaeryt.

Akoryt dismounted and lifted the hasp clear of the chains, then unwound the chains and picked up the lower part of the lock. By the time
he'd finished, two Khellan rankers had dismounted and began to open
the gates.

"Forward!" ordered Quaeryt.

The outriders led the way along the white gravel drive running straight from the gates to the columned portico in the center of the white stone structure that dominated a low rise surrounded on all sides by lawns and gardens. When Quaeryt reached the portico, less than half a mille from the gates, he could see that every window was shuttered. Two decorative iron outer doors were locked across the entry to the hold house whose two wings each stretched some fifty yards from the center of the building, not quite a miniature palace, but far more than a mere mansion.

Quaeryt hadn't seen any recent tracks on the drive, and the stone steps up to the covered portico were dusty and without any trace of footprints. While he suspected the outbuildings would be locked—and empty, based on what they had found in Caernyn, he turned the mare and led the company along the drive on the west side of the hold house. Every building was locked and shuttered, even the stable, and the two other dwellings on the property were also locked and shuttered.

The almost-eroded deep ruts outside the structure that looked to be a storehouse suggested that it had been emptied weeks earlier. Even so, Quaeryt had Baelthm sever the storehouse lock, but a search of the building revealed only a few barrels of odd provisions—pickles, and several spoiled—from the odor—barrels of dried fruit.

Investigation of the other buildings and the hold house confirmed that there were no supplies to be had anywhere on the holding.

While Shaelyt repaired the lock on the main door of the hold house, Quaeryt considered. The next nearest High Holder was Fauxyn, reputedly ten milles farther west along the river. Quaeryt thought about heading out directly from Haeryn's holding, then shook his head. Fauxyn's lands lay far enough away that he needed to discuss that with Skarpa, especially since he had no idea what the scouts might have discovered, and it would be close to dark, if not later, before they returned to Caernyn.

"We'll head back to town," he announced to Arion and the undercaptains.

Once they were on the road, after Akoryt repaired the lock on the main gate, Arion looked from his mount to Quaeryt. "You did not wish to inspect the main house with greater care? There might have been much of value there."

"Lord Bhayar would prefer the allegiance of the High Holders, rather than their enmity," replied Quaeryt. "Also, if you destroy all they have, you lose leverage. A holder who has much to lose is much more easily persuaded. Besides, we saw nothing of obvious great value. I imagine such items had already been removed."

"You truly believe Lord Bhayar will prevail?" asked Arion.

"I don't know that I could explain why," said Quaeryt with a slight laugh, "but I feel that is the way in which it will end."

"Will he be so generous with the High Holders in Khel . . . those who took our lands?"

How do you answer that? Quaeryt managed a wry smile. "We have not talked about that, but much of his family is Pharsi, and I would doubt that he would regard seizure of lands by Bovarians without cause as rightful ownership. I certainly would not."

"You say 'without cause' . . ."

"I'm trying to be careful. I'm quite certain that when Bhayar defeats Kharst, he will consider Kharst's actions cause enough to take Kharst's personal lands. There are times when seizure is necessary . . . but those of you who serve with us have a claim for restoration of your lands." *And Bhayar should honor it . . .* Quaeryt wasn't about to voice the last thought because Bhayar would do what he would do, although he was usually fair. *But not always.*

Arion laughed, a shade bitterly. "Claim? What about a right?"

"Right is always determined by power and who rules. For me to say anything is a right is meaningless because I do not have that power."

"You have other powers. Will you back our claim?"

"As I can and based on what I see of you and your men."

Arion nodded abruptly. "I can ask no more." After a moment he said, "Do you know anything of your parents?"

"Beyond a few memories and a handful of words and phrases in Pharsi?" Quaeryt shook his head. "No one even thought I was Pharsi because of my hair. Not until I met a Pharsi woman in Bhoreal. She was the first to insist I was a lost one. I didn't even know what that meant. I suppose that shows how truly lost I was." Quaeryt made the statement just slightly ironic, hoping that Arion would pick up on it, wondering if Arion would, and if what he said was similar to what Shaelyt had revealed.

Arion smiled. "My grandmere told me about the lost ones, but there were none in Khel. It is said that they were forced to leave because of their pride, and that Erion requires even the highest of the lost ones to serve another in recompense . . ."

Quaeryt mostly listened to the major on the ride back to Caernyn.

Once the company had returned and the mounts were stabled, Quaeryt dismissed fourth company and Akoryt and Baelthm. He sent Shaelyt to find Voltyr.

While he waited outside the stable for the two to return, in his mind he went over the steps by which he had created his own shields. *Will it work for them?* He had no idea, but he needed to have them develop shields, because, in the bigger battles certain to come, he couldn't protect them, and he would need to send at least the more able imagers out alone with other companies, perhaps even the other regiments.

He still worried about giving the ability to use shields to Threkhyl, but he'd decide on that after he taught Shaelyt and Voltyr to develop their own shields. *If you can . . . and they can.*

When the two returned, Quaeryt was standing by the stable door, still pondering the best approach.

"Sir? You wanted us?"

"I did." Quaeryt glanced around the area, but there were troopers everywhere, if not especially close. "We'll need to take a walk."

The two exchanged glances.

"This way." Quaeryt turned and headed for the street in front of the stable. He said nothing until they were well away from the main street and standing on a small bluff overlooking the river in an overgrown area between a tinsmith's and a cooperage. There he turned, with his back to the river, and said, "You two need to learn another imaging skill."

"Sir?" Voltyr's forehead furrowed.

"You may have seen that not all blows meant for me struck or impacted me fully?"

Voltyr grinned and looked at Shaelyt, who stifled a grin, then nodded.

"Every imager may have to find his own means of doing this, but . . ." Quaeryt paused, "according to what I know, if you think of the air around us as if it were like a colorless cloud . . . and images tiny hooks holding a piece of it together like an invisible wall . . . well . . . it could form a barrier, depending on the imager. You'll have to find out if you can do something like that, the results are more than worth the effort."

"But . . . the air . . . it's nothing," said Voltyr.

"You might recall that the air turned cold enough to freeze eight regiments. How did that happen if the air is nothing? The wind blows. Sometimes it can push people over. If there's nothing there, how can it do that?" He paused. "You might think about the air as being tiny bits of invisible smoke . . . but if you hook them together with imaging . . . they become stronger. If you can image links strong enough, they might stop or slow arrows or blades."

Once more the two exchanged glances. This time the expressions were knowing.

Quaeryt waited.

"If . . . any imager," began Shaelyt, "could do this, wouldn't he be most powerful?"

"I think creating and holding such a shield takes much practice to learn how to do it, and much effort to hold it for long." Quaeryt offered a wry smile. "Why don't troopers carry big heavy shields anymore?"

"You're saying they get too heavy."

"Could any of you have done any more imaging at the end of the battle the other night?" asked Quaeryt.

"Maybe a little," said Voltyr.

"Could you have if you'd been carrying a shield weighing a half stone for the entire battle? Do you think that holding an imaging shield is any less work?"

"The best troopers could, sir . . . I mean, carry shields and blades in the old days," said Shaelyt.

"The very best could. You're right. How many years of training did it take them? You're both better imagers than you were when you were made undercaptains. How much have you improved, and how long has it taken? I've been training you and trying to get you to strengthen and improve your abilities the whole time." *Mostly, anyway.*

"How do you know we can do this?" asked Voltyr.

"I don't," replied Quaeryt. "I do know it can be done. I also suspect that not all imagers can, but I thought you two were the most able and likely, and that you should know that it's possible." He paused. "If you can create such shields, there may be ways to use them more effectively, but . . . first you have to see if you can. I'd also appreciate your not talking about it with the other imagers for now."

"You're just going to tell us it can be done . . . and that's it?" asked Voltyr, not quite plaintively.

"Voltyr . . . can you explain how to image to anyone else, even another imager?"

"Of course."

"Fine. Explain it to me. What do you do?"

"You create a picture in your mind and think about making it real."

"How do you make it real?"

"You . . . just think about . . ." After a pause Voltyr stopped. "I see what you mean."

"Description only goes so far. You both know, if you think about it, that some forms of imaging shields are possible. Knowing something can be done is the first step. Figuring out how to do it on your own is the second. In a way, it's like many things. A child has to learn to walk on his own. Once he can walk and is older, a teacher can show him how to run better and faster . . ."

Voltyr nodded once more. So did Shaelyt.

"I'd like to hear how you progress on this, but I understand that it may take some time. Remember . . . we will be going into larger and larger fights and battles . . . and the better you can protect yourself . . ."

"Yes, sir," said Shaelyt. "We understand."

Quaeryt smiled. "Good. See what you can do. I suggest you practice where it's not obvious." With that, he turned and started back to the River Inn.

Behind him, he caught a few words.

". . . told you . . ."

As he walked back toward the inn, he began to think about what he could do to improve his own skills.

When he reached the River Inn, looking for Skarpa, he discovered that the commander was meeting with the officers of Third Regiment in the public room of the inn. So he waited half a glass and then slipped into the public room as the officers were leaving.

Skarpa caught sight of Quaeryt and motioned to him.

"Did you find any supplies at the High Holder's place?"

"No, sir. Everything was locked and shuttered, and there were no recent tracks or signs of anyone being there recently. The imagers undid the locks on the storerooms and all the buildings. They were empty. Just like his warehouses here in town. We replaced the locks and left the grounds and buildings untouched."

Skarpa nodded. "No sense in ransacking if there's nothing we need."

"I thought I'd take some men to the next nearest High Holder tomorrow . . . if you didn't have any reason I shouldn't. His place is something like ten or twelve milles west."

"How much of the battalion do you plan on taking?" asked Skarpa.

"I'd thought one of the Khellan companies would be sufficient."

"Take two. The scouts haven't seen signs of more Bovarians, but I'd feel better if you took two. And tell the officers the dispatch riders on Jeudi will also carry personal missives—for the usual considerations." Skarpa smiled. "I imagine you might be using their services."

"I just might," Quaeryt agreed.

Skarpa nodded, effectively a dismissal, and Quaeryt left to check with Zhelan and the company commanders before the evening meal.

That night, after eating and handling other duties, Quaeryt settled into his chamber in the River Inn and wrote down his recollections of the high holdings and holders he had visited since he had left Ferravyl, while he could still remember details. Then he wrote a few more lines on his growing letter to Vaelora. Finally, he opened *Rholan and the Nameless* and began to page through it, trying to see if the unknown author had ever commented on death and the ceremonies surrounding it. He was about to turn past a chapter that seemed to deal with justice and mercy when a phrase caught his eye, and he went back and read through it once more.

Rholan spoke often of justice and mercy. While he deserves credit for addressing them both and for expounding the distinctions between them, he was even more astute in recognizing the fundamental difference between justice and law, perhaps because he had suffered from that difference as the bastard son of a High Holder. Rholan was far more competent than his younger half brother, who in fact inherited the lands of Niasaen upon the death of their father and who squandered it all before his early death in a drunken stupor in his hunting lodge, leaving his young widow no choice but to marry the second son of their father's greatest rival . . .

It could not but have galled Rholan to be the one Thierysa requested to return Nial's body to the hold house, for he had pled suit to her, and despite her affection for him, she rejected his suit in order to save her own family's fortune . . . and in the end, she had to marry another she did not love to save herself.

It may well be that Rholan's later views on funeral ceremonies took root after the death of his half brother, because in accepting the charge by his brother's widow, he had to deal with a corpse that had putrefied greatly in the summer heat and doubtless sit through a lengthy memorial before Nial was quickly placed in the elaborate stone mausoleum that still dominates Niasaen Hold. All of that celebration of a younger half brother who was a wastrel likely had great impact, because Rholan held forth on more than one occasion upon the vanity of glorifying the body both in life and in death, and of the total emptiness of the gesture of elaborate tombs, claiming that a man's worth lay in his deeds, not in the exaltation of his name after his death . . and that the body might well be burned for all the good the cost of such funeral arrangements did a man, his family, or his reputation.

Quaeryt nodded slowly. What the writer had put down made sense, but it also raised another mystery, again. *Who was the writer, that he knew so much about Rholan, and why had he chosen to remain nameless?*

24

Quaeryt and third and fourth company left Caernyn promptly at seventh glass on Meredi morning, heading westward toward Fauxyn's holding under a sky filled with puffy white clouds. From what he and the scouts could tell, almost no one had used the road as far as Haeryn's gates since he and fourth company had ridden back the afternoon before—just one rider and a single cart pulled by an ox. That didn't count any scouts, either Bovarian or Telaryn, of course, because they likely would have ridden on the harder parts of the road or on the shoulder to minimize their tracks.

Some three milles beyond Haeryn's gates, the road dipped down into another marsh, the western end of the lake that had swamps at both ends. Quaeryt caught sight of one swamp lizard, more than three yards long, before it slipped under the murky water. The levee-like road across the swamp was more than half a mille long before it again rose onto the higher ground bordering the River Aluse. While it widened once above the marsh, the roadbed was more rutted and not all that well traveled.

Both Major Zhael and Major Arion rode near the front, one with Quaeryt and the other with Captain Wharyn, Zhael's second in command, alternating occasionally. All six imager subcaptains rode behind Wharyn.

The first thing that Quaeryt noticed as they neared where Fauxyn's holding was supposed to be was the high and thick hedgerow along the river side of the road, and the fact that the road ran along the south side of what appeared to be a long ridge whose crest had been flattened years, if not decades, before. There were no breaks in the hedgerow, and the top ranged from three to five yards above the shoulder of the road.

When they reached the holding entrance, Quaeryt blotted his damp forehead. He was mildly surprised at the plain gray stone and the dull iron gates and the fact that there were no tracks or wheel ruts from the gate onto the river road. He was less surprised at the chains and double locks.

At Quaeryt's command, Shaelyt removed the locks, and two troopers swung open the gates to reveal a stone-paved lane that led directly to the rear of a two-story structure situated on a low rise less than half a mille from the gates. The lane bore no tracks at all, as if it had been swept recently. As Quaeryt, led by the scouts and followed by the two companies, neared the hold house, he could see that it was far more than a hold house, with wide covered porches, a walled garden off the rear verandah, and a small garden off each wing of the small palace, not to mention a pair of hedge mazes flanking the side gardens.

A thin wisp of smoke rose from a chimney, possibly the one serving the kitchen. That, and the fact that none of the windows were shuttered, suggested the hold had not been locked and abandoned . . . and that it was occupied with the holder either absent or most confident.

"They do not expect us?" murmured Zhael in Bovarian, from where he rode beside Quaeryt. "How could they not know?"

"Perhaps no one told them," replied Quaeryt. "Did you see any other access to the grounds? I didn't."

"There must be another entrance."

Quaeryt nodded, but he was convinced that they had not passed anything that would have afforded access to the grounds. Part of that mystery was resolved when they followed the lane up the rise and to a point where the ground leveled out just east of the holding buildings. From there, Quaeryt looked down a long gradual slope to the river, where an elaborate dock, with an elegant boathouse, jutted out into the water. From the foot of the pier a wide lane wound up the slope through elaborate gardens in sweeping turns, ending at a paved circle under a roofed portico supported by fluted stone columns. A row of statues, sea-sprites, crowned the low wall between the columns on the river end of the portico. The leaded glass windows overlooking the river were wide and tall.

"Access is largely from the river," said Quaeryt.

"It looks more like a summer palace for the rex," observed Arion from behind Quaeryt.

"It displays more taste than that," countered Zhael.

Quaeryt noted that no boats were tied at the dock, but it was possible that the large boathouse held some craft, since one end extended well out into the river. His eyes turned to the small palace. Several windows on the upper level were open. As he studied the portico once more, two figures in livery stepped out and took positions on the wide white marble steps.

A smile crossed Quaeryt's face. High Holder Fauxyn had style. Whether he had any sort of power was another question, but Quaeryt wasn't about to leave himself open to attack. He strengthened his shields as he directed the scouts to follow the stone lane to where it joined the wider lane leading up from the dock.

Quaeryt ordered the two companies to draw up in formation well back from the portico, then turned to the officers, nodding at Zhael. "Arion will accompany me. You're in command."

"Yes, sir."

"Undercaptain Voltyr, you're in charge of the imagers. I don't expect any difficulty, but if something should happen to us, you're to bring down this entire confectionery structure."

"Yes, sir."

Quaeryt nodded to Arion, and the two rode forward, reining up just short of the wide white marble steps.

"Honored sirs," announced the taller dark-haired man in the white and peach colored livery. "High Holder and Lady Fauxyn bid you welcome to Fauxheld."

"Are they present?" asked Quaeryt.

"They are indeed, sir." The functionary's eyes went from Quaeryt to Arion and back to Quaeryt. "How might I announce you, sir?"

"Subcommander Quaeryt and Major Arion." Quaeryt noted that the functionary had a military bearing, not to mention a scar across his forehead above his left eye.

"Yes, sir."

Quaeryt eased the mare to the side of the steps where there was an ornate gilded hitching ring. There he dismounted.

"Allow me, sir," said the shorter retainer, stepping forward and extending a hand for the mare's reins.

"Thank you." Quaeryt let him take the reins . . . and waited while he also took those of Arion's mount.

"If you would follow me, sirs . . ." suggested the taller retainer.

"Stay close to me," Quaeryt murmured to Arion.

The dark-haired retainer turned, opened the right-hand, gilded-iron outer door, and then the inner door, ornately carved with hunting scenes. He stepped back until the two officers stood in a vaulted receiving hall, then closed the inner door, but not the outer one. "This way. I am requested to escort you to the parlor."

"Don't most visitors come by river?" Quaeryt glanced around the receiving hall, its walls covered in a peach damask above the darker golden-wood wainscoting. Two full-length portraits, one on each side, each of a man in formal attire of some time in the past that Quaeryt didn't recognize, were the only decoration. He did note that both men portrayed, one blond and one brown-haired possessed eyes of a color that partook of both blue and violet—an odd shade.

"They do, sir." The retainer walked through the archway into another chamber, from which corridors extended directly ahead and to the right and left. He turned to the left. "Only certain goods from the local area come through the rear gates, and that is by prior arrangement."

"How long has the hold been in the family?"

"I could not say, sir. No one can recall the memory of a time when there was not a High Holder Fauxyn." He stepped into the first archway on the left and bowed.

Quaeryt repressed a frown at the way the retainer had replied.

The individual waiting in the parlor, if a chamber some ten yards by five could be called a parlor, was not High Holder Fauxyn, but a blond woman who looked to be about Quaeryt's age. Her eyes were a shade that was neither blue nor purple, but somewhere between—and intense—much like the color of the eyes of the two men in the receiving hall portraits. Her skin was a flawless creamy peach, and her form was exquisitely female, accentuated by the not quite sheer and clinging pale green gown she wore. The shade of her shoes matched the gown, but the stone in the pendant attached to the golden rope chain around her neck was the same color as her eyes.

"Lady Fauxyn, Subcommander Quaeryt and Major Arion." The retainer bowed, then retreated to the wide hallway outside the archway into the parlor.

"Officers." Lady Fauxyn smiled warmly, even with her eyes.

That she could project that warmth in such a situation chilled Quaeryt through. "Lady Fauxyn," he replied, inclining his head slightly.

"My husband will be here shortly, but I thought it would be best if I made you welcome." Another smile, warmer than the first, followed her words in Bovarian.

"Shortly?" asked Quaeryt politely in Bovarian. "As in within a quint . . . or within several days?" He glanced around the parlor, noting another doorway at the end of the chamber, the door half open, revealing beyond the doorway a bookcase filled with richly colored leather-bound volumes . . . and little more.

"Certainly within the glass, if not sooner. Might I assume you are here to assert some sovereignty or control over Fauxheld on behalf of Lord Bhayar . . . temporary as that may be?" A light but not mocking laugh followed her words.

Quaeryt smiled in return. "Time will tell whether that sovereignty is temporary, but since Rex Kharst lost more than eight regiments down to the last man at Ferravyl, I rather doubt that Lord Bhayar's sovereignty along this part of the Aluse will be transient."

"You speak Bovarian better than most in Kharst's court, and far more eloquently. What rank is a subcommander?"

"Subcommanders command large battalions or regiments."

"Your uniform differs, Subcommander, as if you are half scholar and half commander."

"You are most perceptive, Lady, for that is indeed what I am."

"And have you been in battle?"

Arion cleared his throat. "Sir . . . ?"

"Just the basics, please, Major," said Quaeryt.

"The subcommander is modest, Lady. He is the most effective and most accomplished commander in Telaryn, and one of the few who has led his men from the front, both against the rebel holders of Tilbor and against Rex Kharst's regiments."

"Your man is most loyal, Subcommander. Are his comments accurate?"

Quaeryt laughed. "He's not my man. He's a Khellan officer who joined the Telaryn forces. From what I've seen, the Khellans are far too proud to stoop to lying."

For just a moment Lady Fauxyn was silent, as if his words had struck somewhere, but so short was her hesitation that it was barely noticeable. "My name is Ghretana. I'd prefer you call me that. When you address me as 'Lady Fauxyn,' I expect to turn and see my mother at my shoulder."

Quaeryt was about to send Arion back to the companies outside, suspecting that Ghretana's delaying was for a purpose that would scarcely please him, when the doorway to the library or study opened more widely, and a slender, but muscular man stepped through it and into the parlor. He was attired in white breeches, rather than trousers, with pale peach hose above white shoes, and a brilliant white shirt, over which he wore a sleeveless vest of a rich and darker peach. His smooth-shaven face was gently tanned, and his light brown hair was cut short in tight ringlets against his skull, ringlets that Quaeryt suspected were anything but natural. Fauxyn's nose was straight, and neither too long nor too short.

He walked with his shoulders back and square, his head up, more like a dancing or fencing master than any High Holder Quaeryt had ever met, and at his side was a blade that was narrower than a sabre or rapier, but more substantial than a foil. From his gait, his body carriage, and Ghretana's welcome, Quaeryt had a very good idea of what Fauxyn was—and was not . . . and more important confirmation of who Ghretana was.

"Greetings, Officers. What brings you to Fauxyn? Do tell me that it is something more substantial than the hope of plunder and pillage, not that Ghretana dear might not enjoy certain aspects of the pillaging, especially if it preserved Fauxyn."

"She married you to save the hold?" Quaeryt was half probing, half guessing, based on what he knew of inheritances and what he had observed since entering the hold house.

"Rather an impudent question, don't you think, Major?"

"Subcommander," corrected Arion.

"You don't resemble any of the portraits in the hallway. She does."

"That matters little. I remain High Holder."

"Only at Lord Bhayar's sufferance," Quaeryt said mildly.

"Perhaps for a brief time, until Kharst sweeps you all away. Kharst always has what he wishes." Fauxyn glanced meaningfully, if briefly, toward Ghretana. "I do not believe you ever stated the reason for your unannounced visit."

"There were two reasons for our visit. One was to meet the High Holder, if he happened to be present, and the other was to obtain supplies."

"You have met him, and we have little enough in the way of supplies to feed an army."

"I'm certain that you can spare some," suggested Quaeryt.

"Who are you to say what can be spared, Major?"

"I'm the subcommander with two companies outside your front entry, and a battalion within a few milles, not to mention two full regiments at Caernyn."

"Fauxyn . . ." said Ghretana mildly.

The High Holder turned toward his wife. "You are determined to have it your way, aren't you? You always are, not that it has afforded you the least success."

"As if you have not?" Her voice was velvet and cool.

Abruptly, for no reason that Quaeryt could discern, Fauxyn's hand went to his waist and then back toward Quaeryt. Gold coins scattered across the thick pile of the carpet.

"Take those. Take whatever you will. You're the type that thinks you're honorable. Here's what I think of you and your lord . . ."

Quaeryt laughed. "Pick them up and put them back in your wallet."

"You can't make me. Not unless you're willing to kill me." Fauxyn sneered. "You aren't good enough to kill me yourself. You don't even carry a blade, and that means you're lowborn. So you can't afford to do that. Besides, you'd have to explain to your lord why you killed me when he'll need the cooperation of all the High Holders to rule. That is, if he even manages to keep what he's taken."

"Major Arion," said Quaeryt quietly, still in Bovarian, "if you'd have one of your men bring me my weapon."

"With pleasure, sir." Arion stepped back, then turned and hurried from the study.

Fauxyn offered a cold smile. "What weapon might that be?"

"One designed to teach arrogant High Holders a lesson."

"Killing me will only make matters worse . . . for you . . . and for your lord."

"Who said anything about killing? One doesn't kill willful children. One disciplines them."

Fauxyn couldn't quite conceal the puzzlement behind his smile.

As Arion hurried out through the archway, Ghretana's face remained pleasantly impassive, but Quaeryt suspected she was pleased.

"I could kill you now, you know?" said Fauxyn.

"You could try," admitted Quaeryt. "But if you succeeded, you'd only have killed an unarmed man, and neither Kharst nor Bhayar would find that either honorable or acceptable. Nor would you find much satisfaction in that."

"How would you know?"

"You said as much. If you go against what you implied, then you would be a liar as well as dishonorable. Then, again, you may be both, but I wouldn't hold that against you."

The slightest hint of color crossed the High Holder's face, and he took a step forward.

Ghretana stepped back slightly.

"You do not need to worry, dear one," oozed Fauxyn. "Not at present."

"You are a fool, Fauxyn, if you think that," she replied pleasantly, as if she were suggesting a walk on the verandah.

"I've been called many things, dear one, but there are none left who have called me that."

Quaeryt eased to the side as he heard footsteps so that he could watch both the archway and the parlor, but the only one who entered was Arion.

The major halted and handed the half-staff to Quaeryt. "Subcommander."

"A staff? You would face me with a staff?"

"I think you would be better served if we repaired to one of the entry halls," Quaeryt said. "After all, you would not wish to ruin this fine carpet with blood." He walked to the archway and turned. "Are you coming?"

"A staff? How did anyone ever allow you to become an officer?"

"Actually, that wasn't my choice. It was Lord Bhayar's. One refuses him at great risk, but you should know that about rulers . . . shouldn't you?" Again . . . that was a guess, based on what he'd seen so far.

Fauxyn's face tightened, just fractionally. "You do need to learn about your betters . . . even if your men decide to murder me once I've disposed of you."

Quaeryt glanced to Arion. "Major, if High Holder Fauxyn should happen to wound or kill me, he is not to be touched. Whatever his fate may be is to be left to Lord Bhayar. Is that clear?"

Arion's response was immediate. "Yes, sir."

"And the hold is to be left untouched—except for any supplies we may require."

"Yes, sir."

"You are so honorable." Fauxyn's words were mockingly ironic.

"My men will keep their word. So will I." Quaeryt walked back down the wide corridor to the receiving hall, where he turned and waited with Arion, who had accompanied him.

"Do not trust him," murmured the major.

"I will trust him to be what he is," replied Quaeryt, watching as Fauxyn stepped into the main entry hall with its goldenwood wainscoting and damask-covered walls.

"A staff . . . so awkward . . . so classless. But one must do what one must." Fauxyn eased his blade from the scabbard in a practiced and flowing motion.

"Let's call it a rod, Fauxyn. A rod for a spoiled child of a High Holder." Quaeryt smiled, taking the half-staff in a two-handed and balanced grip. He also raised full shields, but held them almost against his uniform. "Tell me . . . why didn't you leave Fauxheld? You must have heard we were advancing."

"That is another most impudent question." Fauxyn moved forward.

"Was it because you displeased your rex? Or because Lady Fauxyn would have greater freedom in Variana?"

"So impudent . . . and so foolish." Fauxyn's blade flickered toward Quaeryt.

Quaeryt moved the staff but slightly, deflecting the lighter weapon easily, his feet taking up a balanced stance. Even after all the recent battles where he had used the staff while mounted, he was far more comfortable with it on foot.

Fauxyn's blade was close to a blur, but Quaeryt had learned the half-staff on the pitching decks of a merchanter, and its greater length offset the speed of the lighter weapon.

The High Holder feinted, then danced to one side before dropping impossibly low, attempting an underthrust.

Quaeryt parried it, almost pinning the High Holder's blade to the polished marble floor before Fauxyn darted back.

"A rather accomplished blackguard . . . but when one deals with the lower classes, one must stoop to their level, must one not?" Abruptly Fauxyn stepped back and flipped the light blade to his left hand, and what looked to be a double-ended throwing knife appeared in his right. Before he finished speaking, the knife flew at Quaeryt.

Quaeryt twisted the staff, but missed . . . and the blade bounced off his tight-held shields just before it would have sliced into his shoulder. He moved forward immediately, twisting and turning the staff so that it was as close to a blur as he could manage.

"So fortunate, one time," said Fauxyn mockingly, retreating and producing another blade, which he hurled at Quaeryt's chest. The sharp-edged knife, deflected off shields and the staff, clattered to the marble. Fauxyn's eyes widened.

In that moment, Quaeryt struck, one end of the staff knocking Fauxyn's blade from his hand, and the other coming back and cracking the High Holder across the side of the jaw. As Fauxyn staggered, Quaeryt put as much force as he could into the next strike, right into the High Holder's right knee. The knee cracked, and Fauxyn went down, with a short scream that he could not quite choke off.

Lying on the marble and trying not to writhe, Fauxyn glared at Quaeryt. "Go ahead. Kill me. That's what you want." The words were almost garbled, most likely because Fauxyn's jaw was also broken.

Quaeryt shook his head. "No. That would be too easy. You need to understand that Lord Bhayar decides who lives and who does not, and that you need to obey. I will leave you to the tender care of your wife." He turned to Ghretana. "He should live. I expect him to live. Is that clear? Very clear?"

Lady Fauxyn tried to conceal her swallow. "It is indeed."

"Excellent. We will be back for what supplies we determine you can spare, most likely tomorrow. I expect nothing to be moved. Nothing at all."

She nodded, involuntarily, then said, "You are not just a subcommander. You are more than that." Ghretana looked to Arion. "Is he not, Major?"

"Yes, Lady. He is a lost one."

She frowned.

"A child of Erion, you would say."

"I meant . . . his position."

Arion smiled. "That is not my part to say, although he is well above me and his official rank."

Quaeryt looked to Ghretana. "Good day, Lady of Fauxyn."

"Good day, honored sir." There was not the slightest hint of mockery in the curtsey that followed her words.

Quaeryt turned to see the functionary with the scar glancing from Fauxyn to Ghretana before stiffening under Quaeryt's gaze. *What was all that about?*

While there was no point to asking about a glance, because the retainer would certainly deny anything, Quaeryt tried to fix the man's visage in his mind. Then he walked out of the damask-walled receiving hall, the unsmelled odor of corruption strong in his nostrils. Neither he nor Arion spoke as they reached their horses and mounted

25

Before leaving Fauxyn's holding, Quaeryt took the time and the precaution of inspecting the storehouses, where he discovered several hundred barrels of assorted provisions, including almost a hundred barrels of flour and ten of rice, not to mention other staples.

Once he'd completed the inspection and the companies were on the road back to Caernyn, he couldn't help thinking over the incident with Fauxyn. Fauxyn had been insolent, almost seeking a fight, creating a situation that no commander could have afforded to let stand, yet one that would most likely resulted in his own death. He couldn't have been so stupid as to think otherwise. Why had he behaved so? He'd been equally scornful and contemptuous of his wife . . . despite the fact that he'd gained title and lands because, under the laws of Bovaria Quaeryt had studied so many years before and which it was clear had not been changed, she'd been forced to marry him to keep the holding in her own bloodline.

At the same time, it bothered Quaeryt that he'd had to depend on his shields to avoid being wounded. *It was another form of battle, wasn't it? Fauxyn attempted to cheat as well, after all.* Still, the fact that he thought of shields as cheating bothered him.

"You are concerned about what happened?" asked Arion after they had ridden for several quints.

"More about why it happened," replied Quaeryt dryly. "Why were the holder and his wife still there?" He had his own ideas, but wanted to hear what Arion thought.

"He was ordered to remain," suggested the major. "Only Kharst could have done that."

"And?"

"You would know better than I, sir."

"He wanted to offend me enough that we would destroy the hold . . . and thus destroy his wife's heritage? And leave nothing for Kharst to claim if we'd executed the entire family?"

"I could not see any other reason for his acts."

Neither could Quaeryt.

"You have destroyed him," added Arion. "He will die or live as a shell of himself."

"Because his wife will make sure he survives as a cripple?"

Arion nodded.

"I thought that only fair. The lands were hers, and so long as he lives, she cannot be forced to marry someone else."

"If she has no children, he will live only long enough for her to find another High Holder suitable for her. If she has children . . . he will live only long enough for her to claim that he died of natural causes that came from his stupidity in attacking you."

Quaeryt nodded. Arion sounded as though he knew the Bovarian laws of succession better than did Quaeryt. "How do you know the laws of Bovaria?"

"I studied to become an advocate . . . until the time of the Red Death and the Bovarian invasion. Then there was greater need for skill with arms than with law."

"Isn't there a great deal of difference between the laws of Khel and those of Bovaria?"

"In many areas, they are similar. In the matter of property-holding and legal standing, women have more rights in Khel than they do in Bovaria . . . or Telaryn."

That scarcely surprised Quaeryt, not given what he had learned about Pharsi women, especially in the last year. "But why did you study the laws of Bovaria and Telaryn?"

"Not so much the laws of Telaryn. Because there was much trade between Bovaria and Khel, our factors needed to know what recourse they had under Bovarian law."

"Not much, I imagine," said Quaeryt dryly.

"More than the Bovarians wanted us to have. That was another reason for the invasion. Many Bovarian factors owed thousands of golds to Khellan factors and traders, and they did not wish to pay what they owed . . ."

As Arion explained, Quaeryt listened, discovering in greater depth yet another reason for the Bovarian invasion of Khel.

In the end, it wasn't much before the evening meal by the time the companies returned to Caernyn. Because Skarpa was tied up with his regimental quartermaster and requested that Meinyt and Quaeryt meet with him after the evening meal, Quaeryt checked with the other Fifth Battalion company commanders and the imagers, barely finishing before it was time to eat.

Afterward, Quaeryt and Meinyt waited until the public room of the River Inn emptied before joining Skarpa, as he had requested, in the corner farthest from the kitchen and the entry archway. Quaeryt brought a recently refilled mug of pale lager to the table. Meinyt's mug contained lager, Quaeryt suspected, while Skarpa's likely held ale.

Skarpa set down his mug and motioned for them to sit, then looked to Quaeryt. "How did your venture with the High Holder go?"

"Let's say that it didn't go exactly as planned, but he does have supplies that will be available to us. We also learned a few things . . . perhaps confirmed is a better word . . ." Quaeryt went on to explain what had happened.

When he had finished, Skarpa nodded. "That sounds like what I've heard about Rex Kharst. It's good to know about the supplies." He paused. "I'll need to report about your encounter."

"I had thought as much. I'll also note it in my observations of High Holders."

"Just say that this . . . Fauxyn was insolent and unwilling to be cooperative. He attacked you, and rather than killing him, you merely broke his knee and jaw. That should be sufficient, and that is what I will also report. His acts come from Bovarian law and customs, and Bhayar doesn't much care for them. So they shouldn't concern us or the campaign." Skarpa turned to Meinyt. "Do you have anything to add?"

"We've seen boats putting out from the north side of the river. They've had Bovarians in uniform watching us." Meinyt looked to Quaeryt. "You didn't see any sign of scouts, did you?"

"No tracks, no sign of them."

"Except for the river, neither have we," said the grizzled subcommander. "How long does Deucalon want us to sit here waiting?"

"He's decided to move," replied Skarpa. "This afternoon, just before supper, I received orders to advance to the town just east of Villerive. That's why I was talking to the quartermasters about supplies. We're to head west immediately and take up positions to be able to move within glasses to intercept any Bovarians using the bridge at Villerive. We're also to keep the bridge from being destroyed." Skarpa glanced at Quaeryt. "Or be prepared to rebuild it."

Quaeryt winced. "I think we need to be closer than that to the bridge."

"We'll see."

"Did the marshal say anything about how they're doing?"

"Only that they are advancing steadily without significant opposition." Skarpa snorted. "We'll likely run into that at Villerive."

"Or Nordeau," suggested Quaeryt.

"Why do you think they'll wait until Nordeau?" Skarpa's voice was level.

"If the maps are accurate, Nordeau is only a hundred milles from Variana. We're already two hundred milles into Bovaria. Villerive is close to eighty milles east of Nordeau. If they wait at Nordeau, rather than Villerive, Kharst will have more time to bring forces from the west and southwest. He has to know that he'll need every man and mount he can gather."

"You don't think they'll just let us take Villerive?"

"No. If I were Kharst, I'd try to bleed us as much as possible, using as few troopers as necessary, all the way from Villerive to Nordeau."

"They'll try and hold us until the fall rains come," said Meinyt. "Until winter, maybe. Said that Deucalon should have moved faster."

"It may be that Lord Bhayar has made that point," suggested Skarpa. "Regardless . . . we are where we are, and you need to have your men ready to move out at seventh glass in the morning, Subcommander Meinyt."

"Sixth glass for Fifth Battalion?" asked Quaeryt. "So we can pick up those supplies from Fauxheld?"

Skarpa nodded. "I'll have the quartermasters' wagons following you. You'll need to have all dispatches and reports ready just before sixth glass." He swallowed the last from his mug, then set it on the table and stood. "That's all."

Quaeryt and Meinyt rose as well, and then left to inform their officers.

It was more than a glass later before Quaeryt entered his room, and half a glass more before he finished his report to Bhayar. Only then did he turn to finishing his letter to Vaelora, beginning by recounting the events at Fauxheld before adding his own musings.

I cannot help but be amazed at the convolutions implied by their acts and attitudes toward each other. Fauxyn owes all that he enjoys to his wife, and attractive as she is, if not nearly so beautiful and charming as you, and certainly far colder within, neither she nor any other woman appeals to him, yet it appears as though he would deny her the pleasure of masculine company while pursuing his own interests . . . to the point that Kharst seems to have banished him to his own holding. Fauxyn even left her to face us as occupiers, and then intruded when it appeared that she might succeed in mollifying us and saving the holding. These events suggest much about

Bovaria, at least as it appears to me. A man must hold title to the lands of a High Holder, but a weak man or one who is overt in his interests in other men is banished to his lands, and not removed, yet a woman who is of the bloodline and competent cannot hold and direct those lands. Kharst has enough power to restrict that holder to his lands, but not enough to allow a woman to administer them in preference to an incompetent consort not of the bloodline. Or he is unwilling to do so for other reasons.

Such banishment suggests that Kharst holds enough power that he can compel, by force of arms, or other means, High Holders to his will to a far greater extent than can Lord Bhayar, and yet he is either unwilling or unable to impose justice upon them.

This, of course, raises questions for the future. How can a ruler have enough power to keep High Holders within limits and yet be limited in his use of power to the extent that he or his successors do not become the willful sort of tyrant that, from all reports, Kharst has become? I confess, at this moment, I have no answers, even in theory.

And now, my dearest, I must close, if I am to dispatch this tomorrow morning, and I know not when I will next be able to send what I write, far more often than it can be dispatched. My love to you and the child that is and will be.

Quaeryt swallowed as he signed the bottom of the last sheet, thinking about the fact that he and Vaelora would have a child, the Nameless willing. Then he smiled ironically in realizing he had once more called on a deity he did not even know existed.

26

Just as the sixth bell struck on Jeudi morning, Quaeryt lowered his arm, and Fifth Battalion rode out of Caernyn. When the remaining two regiments left a glass later, Skarpa would be leaving a company behind, but half of those were effectively riding wounded who would provide a continuing Telaryn presence while completing their recovery.

The early morning sky was filmed with a silver haze that suggested another hot day in harvest would follow. *Not that almost all days in harvest aren't hot, sticky, and dusty,* reflected Quaeryt. But then, Caernyn and the River Aluse, at least from Ferravyl to Variana, were only slightly north of Solis, and Solis had always been nearly unbearable to Quaeryt from midsummer to midharvest. At that recollection, Quaeryt thought of Vaelora, hoping that she would not suffer too much from the heat, although she did have the fountain garden at the palace, where he had first met her, and which was always much cooler.

Fifth Battalion reached Fauxheld somewhat after eighth glass. Two guards in peach livery awaited them and began to unlock the river road gates.

As they did, Quaeryt gathered the officers. "While the quartermasters are loading supplies, you can water the mounts down at the river, but the men are not to damage or remove anything. Once we're loaded, we'll be leaving."

"Yes, sir," came the reply.

"Imager undercaptains will water their mounts first and then return to where I am at the holding buildings."

The affirmation from the undercaptains was quick, but muted, and Quaeryt guided the mare to the side of the lane to let the undercaptains and Major Zhelan lead the battalion down to the river. Once they had passed, he led the wagons toward the hold house . . . and the storehouse beyond.

When he and the quartermasters and their supply wagons reached the paved area off the portico, he could see that Ghretana was waiting. She wore green trousers, a long-sleeved white shirt, and a sleeveless vest of a green that matched the trousers.

Quaeryt reined up short of her. "Good morning, Lady Fauxyn. We won't be long, and we'll leave enough for the holding, with supplies at least until the end of harvest, if not longer."

"I appreciate your consideration, Subcommander. We're not likely to receive such from Variana. Rex Kharst has announced that he will take the lands of any High Holder who supplies the enemies of Bovaria."

"Then we shall have to make certain that this part of Lydar remains Telaryn." Quaeryt smiled.

"It appears that we have little choice."

Quaeryt merely nodded, glancing toward the retainers. When he did not see the taller scarred man, he said, "There was a tall retainer . . . with a scar over his left eye?"

"Jaesyn . . . he took one of the boats and left soon after you did yesterday. That wasn't surprising. I always thought he was one of Kharst's men."

"And Fauxyn did nothing?"

"He wasn't in a position to complain about it, Subcommander."

Before Quaeryt could ask why, she continued quickly. "My men noticed an odd matter after you departed yesterday."

"Oh?"

"The gates were locked, and there was no sign of the locks having been severed or opened."

"Nonetheless, we did open the gates, Lady Fauxyn. How is High Holder Fauxyn?"

"He should survive. He remains in considerable pain. It will do him good, given all he has inflicted upon others."

"I take it that he was most successful with his blade in the past."

"He was most polite to those who might have bested him, or who were favorites of Rex Kharst, and most adept at discovering those who were neither his equal nor favorites of the rex."

"Then, if I might ask why . . ."

"He struck me when he thought no one was watching last spring in Variana. Kharst's spymaster discovered that." Ghretana shrugged. "I made certain, indirectly, that he would. Fauxyn was banished to Fauxheld as a result. He was also told that if I were touched, or if I died, so would he."

"This spymaster sounds rather accomplished. Who is he?"

"High Holder Ryel. He is obviously, not known widely as such. He is officially the minister of waterways."

"You do not trust this Ryel, or you have not told me the truth."

"Why would you say that?" She smiled winningly, the same smile that had chilled Quaeryt on the previous day.

"The information is too valuable to offer so freely."

She shook her head, and the smile vanished. Her eyes turned icy. "The price for having that information conveyed unimpeachably to Kharst was high. Too high, except that it was the only way to save my daughter."

"How old is she?"

"Nine. You will never find her. That I have made sure of."

"Lady Fauxyn, I am not looking for her. I am here only for supplies." Quaeryt decided to let the conversation take its course and see if it would reveal more of why Jaesyn had departed, not that Quaeryt didn't already have a good idea why.

She frowned. "Might I ask who you are . . . truly?"

"I am a scholar and a subcommander, who discovered little more than a year ago that he was also Pharsi by birth. Those define who I am, Lady."

"Chamyl—Fauxyn—says that you are not human, that you are a demon. His knives have never failed to strike an enemy."

"Lady . . . one thing I have learned is that there is always someone of greater skill and ability . . . or of greater stature and power." Quaeryt smiled wryly. "Even when there is not, there are enough curs to pull down the proudest stag. Perhaps . . . such as Jaesyn?"

"He is only the cur of a cur, and he will report that I have betrayed Kharst by not burning the hold to deny Lord Bhayar. So be it." She paused, looking directly at Quaeryt. "What is your role in dealing with Bovarian High Holders?"

"The same as that of any other subcommander—to report on what we have seen."

She nodded. "You are married, are you not?"

The shift in subject surprised Quaeryt for an instant, before he said, "I am, and far more fortunate in that than I ever dreamed."

Ghretana's eyes brightened, and they dropped for a moment, before she replied, "So, I imagine, is she."

"We're well matched for each other, especially for a marriage neither of us sought." Quaeryt smiled. "Good day, Lady. Take care of your lands, for they are indeed yours to care for." He turned the mare, then rode to the first supply wagon, gesturing for the teamsters to follow him to the warehouse he had inspected the day before. He could sense Ghretana's eyes on his back, but he did not glance behind him as he rode down the stone-paved lane toward the storehouses, the wagons following him.

He also knew it was no accident that she had revealed the name of Kharst's spymaster, and he concentrated on remembering the name— Ryel.

27

A quint or so past eighth glass on Vendrei morning, under gray clouds that did nothing to reduce the heat, Quaeryt and Fifth Battalion rode in the middle of the column, behind Fifth Regiment and in front of Third Regiment, although Skarpa rode at the front with Meinyt. The clouds were high enough that rain didn't appear likely, or not soon.

Roughly a mille ahead, the hedgerow ended, replaced by a few scattered trees with rough piles of rock between them. Even the ground that sloped generally upward from the road showed patches of dirt and clay, and little more than scraggly and sickly weeds. As Quaeryt rode closer, he could see that the hedgerow had not so much ended as had been hacked down, leaving dead brush, but no large sections of wood. With each yard he traveled, the picture of desolation grew more obvious, and more at odds with the verdant harvest landscapes of fields and forests, pastures and orchards they had recently passed, or even the grounds on the river side of the road.

All that remained of a long structure set on a rise in the fashion of many of the main dwellings of High Holders were the lower portions of the outside walls, all of them charred. Clumps of masonry and brick lay amid the dirt and weeds beneath the severely truncated walls. The same destruction had been wreaked on the outbuildings—or what remained of them.

Quaeryt frowned. The charring on the walls was still blackish, and not all that faded, and some of the trees, the few that had not been felled or were not leafless desiccated remnants, had leaves that were outlined in brown and broomlike twigs at the end of their branches.

"What do you think happened there?" asked one of the undercaptains riding behind Quaeryt and Major Zhelan.

Quaeryt smiled ironically, and asked, without glancing back, "What does it look like?"

"It burned, sir."

"Why might all of the buildings have burned?" asked Quaeryt.

"There was a high wind . . . ?"

Zhelan shook his head, ruefully.

"Sir?" asked Shaelyt.

"An accidental fire wouldn't have burned every building that completely, and fire wouldn't have knocked down the walls," replied Zhelan.

"A fire wouldn't have ruined the land, either. Places that have burned often have more growth," added Quaeryt.

"Someone did it all deliberately?" blurted the youngest undercaptain. "Destroyed the entire holding?"

"They even plowed salt into the ground, it would appear," added Quaeryt.

"I've heard of that," said Zhelan, "but to see it . . . What a waste!"

Quaeryt had another thought—just how many men and horses and how much salt had it taken to create that devastation? It had to have been done at Kharst's bidding. And for what? Why hadn't Kharst just turned the lands over to another favorite?

He studied the extent of the devastation, then nodded. The actual area reduced to uselessness, while not small, measured perhaps a half mille on a side, from what he could see, likely only a small fraction of the lands of a High Holder. Still . . . achieving that level of destruction had to have taken a significant amount of time and resources—just to punish a High Holder? And it would have increased the costs to whoever took over the lands.

It also suggests the men and golds available to Kharst.

Quaeryt had known the campaign would not be easy or quick. After what he had seen in the last few days, he had an idea that it would also be bloodier and more brutal than any of them had thought. After a moment he turned to Zhelan. "This is what Kharst will do on a whim, and that's what he'd do to Telaryn, given the chance. Pass it back."

"Yes, sir."

As Zhelan turned in the saddle to relay those words to Fifth Battalion, Quaeryt studied the road ahead, running straight for at least another two milles. Then he glanced to his right, but could not make out the River Aluse through the regularly planted trees that sloped down to the water.

Before that long, the road curved northward, following the river, as it generally did, but not precisely, because Quaeryt could see that it cut through a low swale in a ridge that continued northward and formed a point jutting into the river. He eased his map from his tunic and studied it as he rode. The point on the river was shown on the map, but not named. The map did show, if he squinted and looked closely, where the road cut across the base of the point. That made sense, he supposed, since a road following the point would be several milles longer and there appeared to be no towns there, although the map displayed an indentation on the west side of the point that might have been a cove or a bay, but no road to it that might have indicated a hamlet.

When the last companies of Fifth Regiment drew nearer to the cut in the ridge, one that had to date back generations, because there was no indication of an older road going around the point, Quaeryt could see where, beyond the narrow gap, the first companies in Fifth Regiment were slowing as they followed the road back to the south.

Some obstacle ahead in the road? he wondered.

Then he glanced at the brush-covered slope to the right of the road, almost but not quite too steep for a mount to climb, with scattered trees rising out of the undergrowth, one of the few places they had passed throughout the morning that showed no signs of ever having been cultivated, grazed, or logged or used as an orchard or woodlot. *Is that because the ground beneath that brush is too rugged or rocky?*

The air was heavy and almost oppressively still. Even though Quaeryt was a ways from entering the narrow cut, he could have sworn that some of the leaves on the bushes higher on the slope were moving, but he could feel no breeze. Nor could he see any other signs of even the lightest of winds.

Abruptly, more than a company of archers in the gray-blue uniforms of Bovaria appeared, rising out of the brush and from behind trees on the upper reaches of the north side of the cut, almost as if from nowhere. They immediately began loosing shafts down upon the last companies in Fifth Regiment.

Quaeryt immediately expanded his shields across the front of his own Fifth Battalion, but from the impact of at least one shaft on his shields before he did and from the yells behind him, he was too late to shield his battalion from the first volley.

"Imagers! Image on the archers!" he ordered. "Iron pieces to the head."

Quaeryt followed his own advice, as quickly as he could, forcing himself to ignore the troopers ahead of him, trapped in the cut. He cut down one archer, then another, and a third, and a fourth . . .

Close to a score of troopers in Fifth Regiment turned their mounts uphill, deciding to try to reach the archers, rather than remaining as near-passive targets. Two of the mounts went down immediately, their legs going out from under them on the unsteady dirt and rocks beneath the leafy brush.

More troopers went down, but Quaeryt could also see archers other than those he was targeting toppling, one after the other.

Two troopers, near the eastern end of the cut, had found a place where the ground was firmer, and others began to follow them, although several went down with arrows in their chest and shoulders.

Then, as quickly as the attack had begun, the archers disappeared into the brush and trees at the crest of the ridge, while the squad or so of pursuing troopers were joined by others scrambling, if slowly, after the fleeing archers.

Quaeryt had the feeling that the pursuing troopers weren't likely to have much success, not given the care behind the ambush. The archers had been placed on a slope that the Telaryn mounts could not climb, or not easily, and the shafts not loosed until the targeted troopers were effectively blocked in place by those in front of and behind them. There did not appear to have been any tracks in any place that scouts could have found them.

He turned in the saddle. "Good work, Undercaptains. Your efforts likely forced the archers to leave sooner than they would have, and that saved many troopers in Fifth Regiment."

"Sir . . ." began Shaelyt, who broke off his words. "Nothing, sir."

"Keep your eyes open. We'll see more of that." *Much more.*

"Yes, sir."

Once the rest of the Telaryn force had passed through the gap, now watched from the north side of the slope by two squads from Fifth Regiment that had reached the top of the cut, and casualties were taken care of, Skarpa called a halt in an open area another mille farther east, then summoned Meinyt and Quaeryt.

The three met under an oak that offered shade, but little other relief from the harvest heat and soggy still air . . . or the red flies that seemed to be everywhere. Quaeryt blotted his brow and waited for the commander to say what he would, absently shooing away the flies.

"We got too complacent," Skarpa said bluntly. "We can't afford losses like that. I mean, losses for no real purpose. They knew where we were and what we were doing."

"We haven't seen any scouts, and not even many boats on the river," said Meinyt.

"That doesn't mean there weren't any." Skarpa snorted. "It doesn't mean there were, either."

Quaeryt was afraid he knew exactly what the commander was suggesting, but decided to see if Skarpa would spell it out.

"They might have found it out from the other side of the river."

"Spies in the main body, you think?" said Meinyt.

"Where there are golds and armies, there are spies. Here or there, doesn't make much difference. From now on, we'll have to be doubly careful of places where we could be ambushed. Is that clear?"

"Yes, sir."

"How many casualties?" asked Skarpa, looking to Meinyt and then to Quaeryt.

"Thirty-two dead, a hundred and two wounded," replied the older subcommander, "and ten of those probably won't make it."

"Three wounded, one seriously," added Quaeryt.

"Your imagers killed thirty-one of the archers." Skarpa's voice was even. "Our best count was that there were two companies up there."

Quaeryt understood the unasked question. "Under those conditions, each imager has to concentrate on an individual archer. There are six imager undercaptains. That works out to more than five for each undercaptain in less than half a quint. The fact that they were killing archers is what prompted the Bovarians to withdraw when they did. Otherwise . . ."

". . . they would have kept shooting down at us far longer." Skarpa shook his head. "I'll need to brief the scouts. Just because a place looks impossible to get to doesn't mean that it is."

"How did they get there, sir?" asked Meinyt.

"They used flatboats, probably in the dark last night or the night before, and pulled up in a cove on the north side of the point. You can't even see it from the road because of the trees down there. Then they hiked up here and waited. The trail they took was too steep and narrow for the troopers to follow it down on horseback. By the time we had enough men to do that, they were on their flatboats heading across the river." Skarpa looked to Quaeryt. "With everyone jammed up, I couldn't get word to you quickly enough to get the imagers to where they could deal with the boats. That brings up another question. Could your imagers have set the upper slope afire? Could they do it again?"

Quaeryt considered before answering. "They might have been able to, but anything strong enough to fire green brush and kill archers might have been powerful enough to sweep down and kill some of our men." He smiled wryly. "I'd like to claim I'd thought of that at the time. I didn't. It just didn't seem right."

"You might keep that in mind in other places," said Skarpa. "Sticky as it is right now, doesn't mean we'll get rain you can freeze."

Quaeryt nodded.

"According to the scouts, there's another town some eight milles ahead. Road looks clear, and there aren't any more steep slopes or swamps along there, just fields and a bunch of orchards . . . and another holder's place that looks deserted, but I'll leave that to you and Fifth Battalion, Quaeryt."

"Do you want us to take the lead?"

"Might as well. That way, you can stop and look the place over, then bring up the rear when you're done. I'll have the supply types bring up a couple of empty wagons just in case."

"We can do that, but I'd wager it'll be cleaned out."

"I won't be taking that . . . but you never know with High Holders."

Quaeryt had known that for a long time, and the events of the last year had more than reinforced that lesson.

28

On Vendrei evening, the Telaryn forces occupied the small town of Fuenh eight milles west of the river point. Of the hundred or so dwellings, Skarpa had commandeered the large dwelling above the River Aluse that served as inn and public house. In the early evening, Quaeryt walked from the inn toward the stable that held the imager undercaptains.

Shaelyt and Akoryt were sitting astride a bench, playing plaques with a deck that appeared almost new. For a moment, Quaeryt wondered how that could be, then smiled and asked, "How many times have you imaged those plaques new, Shaelyt?"

The young undercaptain grinned. "These . . . not at all. They're Akoryt's. I do have a deck of fortune that's been renewed a few times."

"You didn't have a sideline before you became an undercaptain, did you?" Quaeryt asked Akoryt.

"No, sir. Not that kind." Akoryt offered a lopsided smile. "I did tell a few people that I could take their old plaque decks and trade them in for new ones cheaper than they could buy new ones. Mostly gamblers."

"You're from Estisle, right?"

"Yes, sir. Why do you ask?"

"It's one of the few places where you could get away with that. Enjoy your game." Quaeryt eased away, watching Baelthm, who leaned against the stable wall. The older man was watching . . . something. After several moments he could make out birds in a tree—a false olive with its silver gray leaves. He shook his head, remembering when, as a boy, he tried to eat one of the hard green false olives . . . and the bitter taste it had left in his mouth. He could see that the birds were young robins, trying to avoid the sharp thorns in getting to the fruit.

Baelthm looked from the tree to Quaeryt. "There's a place for everything in the world. The robins love the false olives and they'll risk the thorns to get to them."

Quaeryt nodded. "Sometimes, finding that place is hard."

"That's life, sir." The older undercaptain smiled.

Quaeryt moved on, toward the end of the stable, where Voltyr stood alone, looking through a gap between houses at the River Aluse. He turned as Quaeryt neared.

"Good evening, Voltyr."

"Good evening, sir."

"You have a pensive expression. What are you pondering on a night like this?"

"How you schemed to get Bhayar to send you to Tilbor, and how I am now an undercaptain in a war when I once thought that the greatest danger in life was scheming High Holders and jealous functionaries and scholars in Solis."

"You're suggesting a connection?"

"It's more than a suggestion." Voltyr looked directly at Quaeryt. "Sir . . . how many Bovarian archers did we kill?"

"You imagers, you mean? Twenty or so, I imagine."

"Ah . . . sir . . . I was talking to Undercaptain Jusaph. He heard that it was thirty-one. I wondered about that. I talked to the other undercaptains and counted up what each of us did. It came to eighteen, and none of the troopers killed any."

"And?" asked Quaeryt mildly.

"Others might also be able to count, sir, and come to certain conclusions."

"That's possible, but I'd like that to take as long as possible."

"Might I ask why, sir?"

"You may. Let me ask you a question or two in return. Haven't all of you undercaptains improved far more than you thought possible? Haven't many of you been able to image in ways you never thought possible?"

"Yes, sir."

"Would any of you have felt pressed, especially in the beginning, to improve had you felt that someone else, say . . . a more powerful imager . . . stood behind you if you failed?"

Voltyr said nothing for a long moment.

"In dealing with the flatboat attack on the bridge at Ferravyl, or the attack on Caernyn . . . could any one imager, no matter how powerful, have accomplished all that you did?"

Slowly . . . Voltyr nodded. "No."

"If we want imagers to have a better place in the world, or in Telaryn, there need to be more strong imagers. The only time to develop those abilities is when they are needed desperately. That is the only time those in power will allow matters to change—and even then only the best of rulers will allow that. Chayar would not have. Bhayar might not have except that he sees an opportunity." Before Voltyr could reply, Quaeryt asked, "Have you had any success with what we discussed in Caernyn?"

"Of a sort, sir. For a few moments, but it takes much effort."

"You might try letting the hooks be fewer or looser, and carrying the shield longer to build up your strength."

Voltyr nodded slowly.

"Have you talked with Shaelyt about it?"

"Yes, sir. I think he's better at it."

"Better . . . or working harder?"

After a moment Voltyr offered a crooked grin. "Perhaps both."

"What if one of those archers had targeted you today?"

"I thought about that, sir.'

"You might think about it more. You might also pass that along to Shaelyt quietly."

"Yes, sir. I will." After a pause Voltyr asked, "What do you plan, sir?"

"You're assuming a great deal," replied Quaeryt lightly.

"I think not. I thought you were a fool to get Bhayar to send you to Tilbor. But you had planned it all out, hadn't you?"

Quaeryt laughed. "I wish I could claim that. I just knew that I couldn't do any more than I had if I stayed in Solis, and the longer I stayed, the more enemies I'd make at the palace. Once I got to Tilbor, I didn't much like the plaques I'd been dealt, but you play what you get."

"To what end?" asked Voltyr quietly.

"Exactly what will depend on how the war turns out, but we need to develop the ability to support Lord Bhayar, so that he cannot do without imagers. There are too few imagers in the world for imagers to try to control or rule, but if we can find and train others, and we support him . . ."

"How do we know he will not turn on us?"

"Unlike some rulers, Lord Bhayar is very practical and thoughtful. He already frets and chafes about how the High Holders make his life difficult, and how his provincial governors rob him of his tariffs." Quaeryt paused. "It is most costly to maintain a large army, but imagers might well be able to use their skills in many ways to enhance his rule . . . and that would make it worth his while to protect them . . ."

"And worth the while of the High Holders to oppose us," suggested Voltyr.

"But not openly, not if the school or whatever it might be called were located near Bhayar and if the imagers were trained as you are . . . and as you should be."

"But secretly they still could."

"That might be difficult if most within the school and buildings were imagers."

Voltyr looked at Quaeryt. "How do you propose to bring that about?"

"By showing Bhayar, over time, that it is to his advantage."

"He's not even here."

"No, and it's better that he's not. He would expect too much too soon. Rulers always do, and others, who have their own goals, encourage them to do so, if only to distract the ruler from their own failures and short-comings."

Voltyr tilted his head to the side. "There is great risk to what you seek."

Quaeryt looked back. "Why not try? Could it be any worse than what . . . imagers have faced in the past?"

After another thoughtful pause, Voltyr shook his head.

"I'd appreciate it if you'd keep that between you and me . . . and Shae-lyt, if you wish."

"That might be best."

Quaeryt smiled. "Have a pleasant evening with your thoughts."

"You, too, sir."

Quaeryt turned and walked toward the false olive, then stopped, but the robins had flown away.

29

Before seventh glass on Samedi morning, as the two regiments and Fifth Battalion were forming up, Skarpa, Meinyt, and Quaeryt met on the narrow porch of the inn at Fuenh. As they stood there, Quaeryt shifted his weight off his bad left leg, and felt the planks underfoot sway ever so slightly.

"We've gotten back reports from the scouts. They've confirmed that the maps are mostly accurate," said Skarpa. "That's the good part. There are hamlets spaced almost every five milles apart from here all the way to Villerive. There's only one town of any size. That's Ralaes. It's some twenty-five milles from here, and a good ten from there to the outskirts of Villerive. Maybe fifteen."

"The bad part?" asked Meinyt.

"The roads aren't any better, and we've got company. The scouts haven't been able to discover where they are. There might be as much as a regiment out there. They're not riding together, either, but as separate companies."

"More of what happened at the river point yesterday, then?" asked Quaeryt.

"That's possible. Or hit-and-run attacks with archers or . . ." Skarpa shrugged. "Who knows? We haven't fought true Bovarian regulars yet." He paused. "Well . . . except at Ferravyl, but they didn't get much of a chance to show what they might do."

"Better that way, if you ask me," said Meinyt.

"What happened at Ferravyl might be why they've split up for now," added Skarpa. "Do you have any thoughts on what they're most likely to attempt?"

"More ambushes," said Meinyt. "Pits and fixed emplacements take too much time."

"An attack from the rear, the way the Tilborans did when we went to relieve Boralieu," suggested Quaeryt.

"I'd thought about that. We'll put the supply wagons in the middle of the column for now. That will allow whoever has rearguard duty to attack without worrying about supplies. Fifth Battalion will serve as vanguard today."

That alone told Quaeryt that Skarpa was worried. When the commander finished, Quaeryt left the inn and hurried to where Fifth Battalion was mustering. There he called for all the officers to join him. Once they all were present, he spoke, in Bovarian, because all officers were supposed to understand it, and because he wanted to make sure the Khellan officers did, in particular. "Yesterday, the Bovarians tried an ambush. This morning, Commander Skarpa told me that there are more Bovarian forces ahead. They'll try to inflict casualties on us and then withdraw so quickly that we either can't chase them or so that we'll follow them into another ambush. The best way to blunt them is to be ready. If you see anything strange—or anyone in a blue-gray uniform—have your men ready to fight and tell me or Major Zhelan immediately. We will be the vanguard. Now, for you imagers, if I'm not here, Undercaptain Voltyr is in charge, and you're to use your abilities to bring down the Bovarians as quickly as you can. Is that clear?"

There were nods, although Quaeryt suspected some of those from the imagers were perfunctory because several understood little Bovarian.

Major Calkoran immediately asked, "Can we not attack them?"

"You can, Major, but only if you can see clearly where your men will fight. You're not to move more than half a mille from the rest of the battalion without my approval. They'll try to draw us out and then cut off individual companies."

"They must have more than a few companies, then."

"Commander Skarpa believes they have almost a regiment nearby. That's not enough men to take us all on, but enough to wipe out individual companies."

Calkoran nodded. "Thank you, sir."

"Any other questions?" No one volunteered any, and Quaeryt had to wonder if he'd been too curt, although he certainly had attempted to be open to questions. "Then form up."

As the other officers began to return to their companies, Quaeryt beckoned to Zhelan.

"What do you think, Zhelan? Did I leave something out?"

A slow smile crossed the major's face. "No, sir. Not this time."

Quaeryt managed not to wince at the gentle reminder that he had before.

"The Khellans need to be reminded that they could be outnumbered. By including all the officers, you didn't offend their pride." Zhelan's smile became a grin. "They have a lot of pride."

Quaeryt grinned back, shaking his head. "We'd better get moving."

Even so, it was another two quints before Fifth Battalion began to move out at the head of the column, with Skarpa riding beside Quaeryt.

Once the troopers were settled into a good pace, Quaeryt turned to the commander. "You're worried. Did the scouts see something else?"

Skarpa shook his head. "Just a feeling. Always get into trouble when I don't trust that kind of feeling."

Unlike on previous days, which had been hazy, the sky was crystal clear, the morning already warm and promising to become a blistering harvest day. Even the River Aluse somehow looked to be flowing more slowly, as if struggling against the warmth.

Eighth glass came and went, and so did ninth glass, and there were no hints of any possible trouble. The huts and cots of the peasants and croppers were shuttered as the southern army passed, but the scouts reported no signs of Bovarians. That just made Quaeryt more certain that something would happen. A quint or so before noon, as Fifth Battalion began to ride up a gentle rise in the road toward higher ground, from somewhere behind the battalion came a faint trumpet call—the one that meant the some company was being attacked.

"Keep a watch here, Subcommander, but keep them moving unless I send word otherwise." With that, Skarpa galloped rearward along the shoulder of the river road.

Quaeryt immediately urged the mare to the shoulder of the road so that he could take a quick look back eastward, but he could see nothing for a good half mille, past the supply wagons. Beyond that, the road curved southward around a low rise. That the Bovarians would attack when the front of the column could not see the rear wasn't exactly surprising.

As he watched, a wave of riders in gray-blue uniforms charged from out of a woodlot set back a good two hundred yards south of the road, aimed straight at the supply wagons, set in the middle of Third Regiment. Almost as quickly, two companies from the regiment swung from the column to cut off the attackers.

"Imagers! Fifth Battalion!" Quaeryt turned in the saddle, looking at the six undercaptains. "Third Regiment is fighting off a hit-and-run attack on the supply wagons. Fifth Regiment is being attacked from the rear. Stand ready." He had the feeling that the Bovarians would wait for a time before attacking. He just had no idea how long, only that they'd seek a time and place to their advantage. "Major, pass it back!"

At that thought, Quaeryt glanced forward, only to see two large wagons, without a team before them, rolling down the road from the rise. The lead wagon was filled with large rocks, not quite boulders, and it was already less than a hundred yards from the outriders.

"Shaelyt! Threkhyl! Voltyr! Image the front wheels or axles off those wagons!"

Within moments, the front wheels of the lead wagon exploded away from the wagon bed, and the wagon nosed into the road. With the impact, the front end and empty seat gave way and round boulders began rolling downhill toward Fifth Battalion. The second wagon crashed into the wreckage of the first, and more boulders bounced and rolled downhill.

Because the grade was comparatively gentle, Quaeryt could see that most if not all of the large stones and small boulders would not reach Fifth Battalion, but all of the stones scattered on the road and the shoulder would certainly slow any massed charge by the Telaryn forces, unless they could get past the rubble quickly.

He glanced uphill, but saw no one, then turned to Zhelan. "Can we get past the stones quickly and re-form?"

"Yes, sir." Zhelan turned in the saddle. "First company! Forward and re-form!"

Quaeryt kept the mare close to the major as he threaded his way through the stones, but first company was barely in position above the stones when at least one company of Bovarians charged over the crest of the hill.

"Imagers! On me! Smoke and pepper across the front ranks! Now!" Quaeryt glanced to Zhelan. "First company forward!" Then he quickly guided the mare to the river side of the road, filled with brushy ground that sloped some two hundred yards down to the river.

"First company!" ordered Zhelan. "Charge! Second company! Forward past the rocks and re-form!"

Quaeryt watched as the mist of pepper and smoke spread across the first ranks of the Bovarian riders, who had angled to the south side of the road to avoid the rocks hurled from the broken wagons. The Bovarians did not move out of formation except slightly, but Quaeryt could see that many were rubbing their eyes and a number were sneezing.

He imaged more pepper and smoke, this time farther back in the ranks, then glanced up the slope on the river side of the road, feeling that more Bovarians were headed in their direction.

In moments, another company came charging over the low crest.

"Imagers! Smoke and pepper!"

Because the shoulder and area clear of brush on the river side of the road were narrower, the Bovarians were bunched much closer together.

Quaeryt waited until the second company was less than fifty yards away, then concentrated on creating an angled stone wall no more than five yards wide and a yard and a half high, just in front of the Bovarians.

The entire front line of riders went down, and those following plowed into the mass of men and mounts.

"Third company! On the river side!" ordered Quaeryt. "Imagers, clear the way! On me!"

Even before third company finished surging past the imagers and toward the attackers, the Bovarians on the north side of the road—those who could—were withdrawing. In moments, so were the trailing Bovarians on the south side. The others were quickly surrounded by Major Zhael's Khellans.

Quaeryt rode forward and eased his mount beside Zhael.

The major glanced at him. "They are like all Bovarians. When matters become difficult, they vanish."

"The problem is that when they vanish like that, they survive to try again," replied Quaeryt dryly.

"Some of these did not."

"No, but have the captives that are healthy start clearing those boulders off the road. If any try to run away, ride them down."

"We can do that, sir."

"The rocks first." Quaeryt nodded and rode back to rejoin the imagers.

"Where'd that wall come from?" demanded Threkhyl, even before Quaeryt had finished reining up.

Shaelyt glanced at Quaeryt, then at Voltyr. "Voltyr and I did it!"

"Excellent work!" added Quaeryt, although his words applied to the quick thought from the young undercaptain.

"We do what we can, Subcommander, sir," replied Shaelyt with a quick smile that vanished immediately.

"I could do that," announced Threkhyl.

"I'm sure you could," replied Quaeryt. "I saw what you did in Ferravyl after the battle, but it's also knowing when to do it."

"If you'd told me, I could have done it," Threkhyl reiterated.

Quaeryt held in a sigh and nodded. "I'll remember that." He was just glad Threkhyl hadn't seen Voltyr roll his eyes.

"Is there anything else you need from us now, sir?" asked Voltyr.

"See if you and the others can image those wagons back together. They might come in useful."

"Yes, sir."

As the undercaptains rode toward the ruined wagons, Quaeryt turned to Zhelan, who had returned from talking to Undercaptain Ghaelyn. "Send fourth company to hold the crest of the road up there while we clean up the mess here."

"Yes, sir."

A quint or so later Voltyr rode back to Quaeryt. "We got one wagon back together. The other one was . . . well . . . we made some mistakes, sir, but the one is sturdy."

"Good."

Quaeryt rode over to the image-repaired wagon, studying it carefully. From what he could tell, it looked sturdy. They'd had to use the wheels from the other wagon, possibly because none of them knew enough about wheelwrighting, but the bed and seats looked strong and smoothly fit together. "You all did a good job. Thank you."

He could see Skarpa riding up the road. He turned the mare. "I need to talk to the commander."

Shortly, Skarpa reined in beside Quaeryt, looked over the hillside, then asked, "How many attacked here?"

"Two companies, maybe three. They hit and when we surprised them, they immediately withdrew."

"They attacked, and you surprised them?"

"The imagers hit them with smoke and pepper and took apart the wagons they sent down the road . . ." Quaeryt summarized as quickly as he could, finishing up with the rebuilt wagon.

"I'm sure the quartermasters can use another wagon, especially since we got shorted leaving Ferravyl."

"What about the supply wagons and Fifth Regiment?" asked Quaeryt.

"The same sort of thing as here. The regiments had more casualties than you did, but so did the Bovarians." The commander glanced up the road to the top, where fourth company held the crest. "Have you seen any of the scouts?"

Quaeryt had no doubts that the scouts were captured, or dead, most likely the latter. "No. None of them returned. They were likely ambushed somewhere up ahead."

"Now we'll have to send out scouts in full squads," said Skarpa sourly. "Before long, they'll have to go in companies."

Quaeryt understood. That meant losing more men. "Won't they also lose more troopers?"

"They might."

Given Skarpa's tone of voice, Quaeryt didn't press.

More than a glass passed before the road was clear, and the casualties taken care of. Fifth Battalion's first and second company had suffered no deaths and only a handful of wounded, possibly because of the pepper and smoke, but the Bovarians had lost twenty men, and thirty six had been captured, half of them wounded, most severely.

A mille farther to the west, they found the bodies of five Telaryn scouts, thrown in a heap beside the road. Three had been hacked down and died fighting, it appeared. Two others had been wounded, but then had had their throats cut.

Skarpa looked from the dead scouts to Quaeryt. "Never thought much of Kharst before. Think even less of him now."

Quaeryt agreed. There was no reason the Bovarians just couldn't have left the wounded men behind . . . without cutting their throats. For a time, after Skarpa made quick arrangements for the dead scouts they rode without speaking.

A glass later, as they passed a marsh that looked to be drying out, Skarpa turned in the saddle and cleared his throat. "There's another matter we need to discuss."

"Yes?" replied Quaeryt warily.

"We've had quite a few weeks without proper services, Subcommander." Skarpa snorted. "Not even improper services. After everything today . . . well, tomorrow is Solayi . . ."

"I'd be happy to conduct services." Quaeryt wasn't about to argue, even though he had no idea what he might offer as a homily. Still . . . he had a day to think about it.

As the afternoon neared fourth glass, Quaeryt saw plumes of smoke ahead, at least two milles ahead, and possibly three. "I wonder if the Bovarians are burning more crops."

"Something's burning," replied Skarpa. "We'll know what when the scouts return."

Quaeryt nodded. So far, the tracks of the attackers had followed the river road westward. From all indications Skarpa and his forces were following close to a battalion of Bovarians toward Villerive. "You think they'll rejoin a larger force before we get to Ralaes?"

The commander shrugged. "They've got to have more troopers ahead. The ones that tried to surprise us are setting a good pace. That means they don't have to delay us."

"And they would if there weren't reinforcements waiting?"

"That's my guess." Skarpa laughed humorously. "But I've been wrong before."

Not often when it comes to battles and fighting, thought Quaeryt.

Less than a quint passed before Quaeryt could smell smoke, but the plumes had largely dissipated. What remained was an acrid miasma that did not rise much above the treetops, but created a spreading haze over fields and meadows. The few cots they passed looked vacant, with shutters tightly fastened, sheds closed, and no livestock visible anywhere.

Then two scouts from the squad sent out earlier rode back toward the head of the column, where they turned and rode along beside Skarpa.

"Sir . . . the Bovarians burned the hamlet ahead. Every last dwelling and shed. They drove out the livestock . . . and more."

"Do you see any Bovarians?"

"No, sir. They must have fired the place a while ago. It's mostly burned out now."

Skarpa nodded. "Report back to your squad leader. He's to make certain that no Bovarian troopers are within two milles of the hamlet."

"Yes, sir."

Once the two had galloped off back down the road and northwest around the bend, Quaeryt asked, "You intend to set up an encampment there?"

"It's too far to reach Ralaes. Be even a stretch tomorrow. We need an open area that's not swamp or muddy fields." Skarpa gestured toward the gray clouds to the north. "We'll likely get rain, and the hamlet's on higher ground."

Left unspoken was the fact that going significantly farther, to another hamlet, risked putting the regiments in unfamiliar territory in fading light.

Once around the bend, with the road less than a hundred yards from the river and once more heading west, Quaeryt's eyes burned more with smoke that was markedly stronger and more acrid. Ahead, on the left side of the road, was the blackened shell of a small cot, no more than five yards by four, with the burned-out remnants of a shed behind it. A hundred yards beyond the first ruined cot were two others, one on each side of the road. Before Quaeryt and Skarpa reached them, an outrider gestured to the left side of the road. A heap of bodies lay there, mostly men, able-bodied, but all at least partly gray-haired, and one white-haired woman. Quaeryt counted quickly—eleven bodies, most with blood across their heads.

"Looks like some of the villagers didn't like the idea of having everything burned," said Skarpa.

"They probably protested, and the Bovarians made an example of them," suggested Quaeryt. "That seems to be the way Kharst works . . . or the local commander decided that was the best way to slow us down and deny us supplies."

"Something like that." Skarpa's voice held a trace of skepticism.

Quaeryt glanced ahead toward a small stand of trees, an orchard in fact. The closer he rode the more puzzled he was. "That's an apple orchard, and most of the fruit is ripe, or close to it. Why wouldn't they burn it?"

"Ah . . . sir . . ." came a voice from behind Quaeryt. "You can torch a cot real quick. Takes a real fire to put a green tree to flame in spring, summer, or harvest. There's no wind, either, and those trees aren't that close together. That small shed, there, the one that's burned. It's not close enough to the trees. Might have had a cider press there. Lots of apples in the grass, though. They probably rode through and smashed what they could."

Quaeryt turned, realizing that Ghaelyn was the one who had spoken. "Thank you. They must have been in a hurry." But why? We weren't that close to them.

"Might have orders to fall back to Villerive." After a moment Skarpa raised his arm. "Column! Halt!"

The order echoed back along the long line of riders.

"Subcommander," Skarpa ordered Quaeryt, "have your companies patrol an area out to a mille in an arc around the hamlet. Have them check for tracks, any sign of the enemy."

"Yes, sir."

"We'll do the best we can here, for the night."

"Imagers, two undercaptains each with second, third, and fourth companies . . ." Quaeryt went on to organize the perimeter patrol.

Fifth Battalion settled into another apple orchard besides the one Quaeryt had first spied as a form of shelter. He slept uneasily on Samedi night, and not just because there was a brief shower a glass or so past sunset. The light rain barely wet the leaves or the ground, not even enough to dampen the dust, and no one attempted a night attack on Skarpa's force.

Quaeryt woke at the first hint of light, both stiff and puzzled. He pulled himself together and went to look for Zhelan, meeting him near the front of the orchard where a rutted lane ran from beside the trees and then joined the river road.

"Sir?"

"No problems last night?"

"No, sir. I thought there would be."

"So did I."

"Every company looks to be ready . . . or they will be shortly."

"What do you think about this?" Quaeryt gestured toward the nearest burned cot.

"I can't say I know what to make of it, sir. Unless it was to slow us down, but we wouldn't have pushed on last night anyway."

"They might not know that."

"If we're facing the less experienced Bovarians, they might not."

"You think the better Bovarian troopers are on the north side of the river?"

"Be my guess, sir. More of them, too."

"You might be right. But if we're not . . . however it's come about, it bothers me."

Zhelan offered a crooked smile. "Me, too, sir."

More than two glasses passed before the troopers were fed, gear was stowed, and the column rode out of the unnamed hamlet, with Fifth Battalion riding behind Third Regiment, the supply wagons following fourth company, and Fifth Regiment in the rear. While the day was overcast, the clouds were not dark, nor were they particularly low. That didn't matter, because they'd been riding for perhaps two quints when a gust of wind whipped over them, and rain began to patter down on the troopers, not enough to be considered a downpour, but enough that, if it continued, the road would turn to muddy slop.

Quaeryt was riding with Major Arion and fourth company, and since he couldn't do much about the rain, he turned to Arion, riding beside him. "You've fought against Bovarians, Major. Did you see anything like what we saw yesterday?"

Arion offered a bitter laugh. "Many times. They would burn any village that did not surrender. They would kill anyone who tried to stop their torches. In the end, when winter arrived, many froze. Most were women. The men had already died or were in the forces chased into the Montagnes D'Glace."

"They didn't treat their own people much better."

"Kharst trusts no one who does not obey his every word. That includes his subjects and his High Holders. His father before him was like that, and his grandsire before him."

"That's against the precepts of the Nameless," suggested Quaeryt.

"The Nameless is different in Bovaria." Arion's sarcastic tone would have curdled fresh cream. "As are many things. Why do you think every rex has needed so many troops?"

Quaeryt nodded, although he hadn't thought of using armsmen that way. Still . . . *to keep High Holders in line, a ruler has to have some leverage.* Bhayar and his sire had used rewards and prestige, and . . . occasional force. Kharst appeared to use terror, in one form or another.

After the briefest pause, Quaeryt asked, "Is the Nameless truly different in Bovaria, or are the ideas attributed to the Nameless just different?"

"So far as men are concerned, is there any difference?"

Quaeryt laughed, ironically. "Well taken, Major."

After another set of wind gusts, the rain subsided to less than intermittent, with drops occasionally striking Quaeryt, as if to remind him that it could resume at any time. For the next glass, the raindrops splattered down infrequently. Then the sky began to clear in the northeast, and by the second glass of the afternoon, only a few clouds remained and the afternoon became even more hot and steamy.

Skarpa called a halt slightly before third glass, and immediately thereafter came riding back along the side of the road. He eased his mount in beside Quaeryt's mare and dismounted, handing the reins to his mount to the ranker who held the mare's reins and walking to join Quaeryt and Zhelan.

"There's a high holding a bit more than a mille ahead on the left. I'd like you and your imagers to look into it and see what supplies—or anything else of value to the campaign—might be there . . . and if it would be suitable for sheltering the troops tonight." He looked to the northeast, where another set of clouds—far darker than those earlier in the day—had begun to mass and move slowly toward the River Aluse and the Telaryn forces.

"It looks empty?"

"It does. Whether that's so . . ." Skarpa shrugged.

"We'll look and see." Quaeryt glanced toward Zhelan, who had already mounted.

A half glass later Quaeryt, at the head of Fifth Battalion, had reined up before a pair of weathered and stained limestone gateposts. The iron gates themselves were secured with a rusted iron chain and a single lock. A wall of limestone, only two yards high, extended from the gateposts some twenty yards on each side, ending in earthen berms perhaps a yard and a half high, on the top of which were planted a form of spiky juniper. The berms stretched as far as the eye could see.

Through the iron bars of the gates, the holding looked to be far less opulent than Fauxheld, almost modest by comparison, with a good-sized hold house and several modest outbuildings. All were constructed of the same limestone as the gates, and all had weathered gray tile roofs. There was no sign of a single person or any livestock, nor did any of the chimneys show traces of smoke.

"I don't like this," muttered Zhelan. "They burned a hamlet, and they left an entire holding empty and untouched? It doesn't make sense."

Quaeryt was certain that it did, especially given that it wasn't the first time. He just didn't know in what way. Like Zhelan, he felt uneasy. He studied the gates, noting the deep wagon or coach ruts running from where the pavement ended onto the road itself. Those ruts had been softened by the rain that had fallen earlier that morning. Then his eyes went to the pavement. Outside the gate were tracks, but the pavement had been swept inside the gate—but only for a distance of fifteen yards or so. Yet there were no tracks or ruts in the uneven grass on each side of the swept portion of pavement.

"Look at the pavement inside the gate," Quaeryt said to Zhelan.

"It's some sort of trap."

"There may be a few." Quaeryt gestured to Desyrk. "Remove the lock, if you would."

"Yes, sir."

Desyrk studied the chain and lock. In moments, the lock was in two pieces, and one of the first company rankers stepped forward and unwound the old chain, then swung the gates open and outward.

"Undercaptain Threkhyl forward. Image something heavy onto the paving stone just inside the gate."

Despite a puzzled look, the ginger-haired undercaptain immediately replied, "Yes, sir."

Quaeryt thought he could hear a grinding sound. "Another boulder, if you would."

A second boulder appeared, next to the first, and abruptly the entire paved section of lane that had been swept collapsed, leaving a pit a yard deep.

Zhelan glanced to Quaeryt.

Quaeryt only nodded, then said, "Imagers forward."

Once the undercaptains were lined up facing the open gate, he added, "I'd like that pit filled in solidly and the paving stones replaced. Undercaptain Voltyr, you coordinate the effort."

"Yes, sir."

"Make certain it's firm. You six will be the first to ride across it."

Desyrk and Akoryt exchanged quick glances, but Voltyr only nodded, as if he'd expected nothing else. A faint smile flicked across Shaelyt's lips. Once again, Threkhyl looked puzzled, if but for a moment.

The undercaptains took almost a quint to fill and repair the pit. All were sweating from the combined effort of imaging and the mugginess of the day by the time they finished, mounted, and rode to the far side—which remained solid.

Baelthm was pale, Quaeryt noted, and he called out, "All of you eat something . . . and get a drink from your water bottles." He gestured to Zhelan. "Have the battalion follow . . . slowly."

"Yes, sir."

Quaeryt rode forward and joined the imagers, then motioned for them to follow him and the two outriders along the lane toward the hold house. As they neared the main dwelling, he called back to Zhelan. "Leave the main house alone for now. We'll start by looking for supplies."

The outbuilding nearest the hold house was the stable. The two strap handles of the main doors were not chained, but fastened with heavy rope tied into a simple knot. Quaeryt reined up and looked to Ghaelyn. "Have your men untie the knot. Then have them find something they can use to push the stable doors open. When they do, have them stand back."

"Yes, sir."

Quaeryt waited while the troopers followed his orders, then watched as they used weathered planks they'd found stacked in the rear of the stable to push open the doors. Nothing happened.

"Have them take the planks and wave them around inside the doors, and prod the ground there."

Ghaelyn conveyed that order to the troopers, and the men began to wave and prod.

Abruptly heavy sacks filled with something crashed down onto the packed clay just inside the stable doors, followed by what looked to be a small anvil.

"It might not hurt to prod some more," said Quaeryt.

More prodding resulted in no more objects falling.

"Now they can look inside . . . but carefully."

"Yes, sir." Ghaelyn raised his voice. "You heard the subcommander. Time to look for supplies, but watch where you put your heads, hands, and feet."

Quaeryt and the imagers waited, along with the remainder of first company, and the other companies of Fifth Battalion. He also listened to the low murmurs among the imagers.

". . . how does he know all that? . . . never been here . . ."

". . . doesn't trust anyone . . ."

"Would you, after what they did to that hamlet . . . ?"

". . . you think, Shaelyt . . . have that expression . . . again . . ."

". . . subcommander is a child of Erion . . . the hunter makes his own wary . . ."

Quaeryt wasn't so sure about that, or that he'd been wary enough in the past. He looked back to the stable doors as a squad leader walked out, dust on his sleeves, trousers, and boots.

"There's nothing at all in the stables, sir . . . except . . . a few barrels of oats, and I'd not trust 'em, not with a dead rat lying beside 'em."

"We'll make a more thorough search later," said Quaeryt.

The next outbuilding's entrance was trapped in a fashion similar to the stables. Once inside, Quaeryt could see that it had held various crafts, and held a smithy, a woodworking shop, a chamber used for carding and spinning. The third structure was a storehouse.

When Quaeryt reined up, Zhelan eased his mount alongside. "Do you think the entrance to every building is trapped?"

"Yes . . . but not terribly well. Enough to hurt the unwary, though."

"Why . . . ?"

"We'll talk about it later," Quaeryt said quietly. "I'd like to see more before I say much."

Unlike the other outbuildings, the storeroom doors were of heavy, ironbound oak, and were double-chained and double-locked. Voltyr and Shaelyt imaged away the locks. Once more, when the troopers probed the space behind the door, there was a reaction. Except this time, what dropped down behind the door were two huge timbers, either one enough to crush a man to a pulp. More probing released a third timber.

Yet when the area behind the doors was cleared, the troopers reported that the space inside was empty.

Quaeryt dismounted. "I think I need to take a look here."

Inside the stone-walled structure was a large open space, but on one side were several smaller rooms. All were empty. In the front west corner of the building Quaeryt found a trapdoor. Under it was a staircase. He had to wait another half quint for the troopers to find and light a torch before he could descend the stone ramp that lay beneath the door.

When he reached the lower level, it, too, appeared empty, except for the score or so of barrels stacked two high and deep against the rear wall of the lower level. He moved warily and held full shields, stopping short of the barrels.

"Pull out these barrels and stack them against the side wall."

Between two barrels in the second row, those against the rear wall, lay a dead rat. Quaeryt nodded. Then he studied the rear wall. There was some-thing about it. He looked up to the beams overhead. While the spacing was even, the braces for the long beams had been added later, and they did not look as if they actually were weight-bearing. *It's worth a try.* He turned and gestured. "Undercaptain Shaelyt . . . I believe this is a false wall. I'd like you to image an opening in it."

"Yes, sir." Shaelyt stepped forward without hesitation.

In moments a square opening appeared in the wall, revealing that it was of wood, faced with limestone to make it appear identical to the foun-dation walls.

Shaelyt wiped the sweat off his forehead.

"Good. Thank you." Quaeryt eased forward until he could see through

the opening. On the other side of the false wall, he could see more barrels, perhaps hundreds, stacked three high. He couldn't tell how deep.
"We've found our supplies."

Then he stepped back. "Desyrk and Akoryt, enlarge the opening so that
someone can get inside and open the real door so that we can roll out the
barrels."

After Quaeryt was satisfied that Major Arion and fourth company could
handle sorting and rolling the barrels from the lower level of the storehouse
up to the ground floor, he sent Voltyr, Akoryt, Desyrk, and Baelthm—and
third company—back to the stables to see if fodder or grain had been hidden somewhere behind false walls there. Then he inspected the last three
outbuildings, all of which were little more than empty livestock sheds and
barns. All held no traps, or none that he and the troopers could discover.

Finally, he rode back to the hold house with Threkhyl and first and
second company.

Once there, he studied the dwelling, not so large as Fauxheld or some of
the others, but clearly larger than Nordruil, if less appealing and more grim
in appearance. Every window was shuttered tight, and the shutter hinges
were attached to large, flat, and sturdy iron plates. He nodded, dismounted,
and walked up the wide stone steps of the receiving portico to the main
entrance. Threkhyl accompanied him. Above the doors, cut into the limestone, was the name "Laesheld." The outer ironwork doors themselves
showed no lock on the outside, but they would not open. Quaeryt studied
them for several moments, then pointed through the narrow crack where
the doors joined. "Undercaptain, there's an iron bar across the back there. If
you would remove a small section."

"Yes, sir."

A chunk of iron clanked somewhere, and Quaeryt pulled on the outer
doors. They opened, creaking slightly as they did, revealing a set of carved
and weathered goldenwood doors, with elaborate polished brasswork.
They also did not budge. He turned to the undercaptain and gestured.

Threkhyl concentrated, and the lock and lock plates vanished, but
when he tried to open the doors, they would move neither inward nor
outward. "Sir . . . I'll have to image away the doors."

"Go ahead." Quaeryt was getting irritated, especially since he'd tried
to be gentle to the High Holder's buildings and grounds.

With a puff of dust, and a brief flow of chill air over Quaeryt and
Threkhyl, the goldenwood doors vanished. Behind where they had stood

was a wall, its masonry fresh, the bricks certainly laid within the past few days.

"Undercaptain Threkhyl . . . if you would also remove this wall, preferably without destroying the archway."

"Yes, sir."

Quaeryt could see that Threkhyl was showing a certain tiredness, but that was fine. If he didn't push the undercaptain to his limits, Threkhyl's abilities wouldn't improve.

Just after Threkhyl had removed the wall, behind which was a dark entry hall, Zhelan called out, 'Sir, the commander is riding down the lane now.'

"Thank you." Quaeryt turned to wait for Skarpa.

In less than a fraction of a quint Skarpa rode to a point opposite the doors and reined up. He glanced back at the two companies and then at Quaeryt, clearly puzzled as to why Quaeryt was still at the entry of the hold house.

Before Skarpa could speak, Quaeryt did. "Commander, we've located supplies. Rather than start with the hold house, we began by going through the outbuildings. Fourth company is even now rolling barrels up from a hidden space in the main storeroom, and several imager undercaptains are searching the stables for possible hidden areas there that may contain fodder and grain. The main entry here was locked with iron doors, heavy wooden doors, and blocked with a masonry wall behind those. Undercaptain Threkhyl just finished removing the wall."

Skarpa snorted. "We should see what lies inside that is of such worth."

"Sir, most of the entries have held traps. I've had the troopers probe with planks and the like before entering."

"Don't let me stop you with what works," said Skarpa dryly.

There were no traps behind the main entry door, nor elsewhere in the hold house. Some paintings had been removed, but not all, and there were no small items of value remaining. The main parlor did hold a magnificent clavecin—with an elaborately inlaid keyboard cover—and many of the pieces of furniture and carpets were of considerable value, Quaeryt suspected.

Once the regiments and companies were fed and settled into various spaces, admittedly in very cramped circumstances, and hurriedly, to avoid the late afternoon rain, Skarpa, Quaeryt, and Meinyt met in the study of the hold house. There were gaps on the shelves that held books, where volumes of worth or personal meaning to the High Holder had likely been removed—hurriedly, because the adjoining volumes were angled, and in some instances, a few books lay where they had fallen on the polished dark oak flooring.

The three sat around a square table, lit by the light coming through the windows that Quaeryt had unshuttered. From what he could tell, the rain was letting up.

"Are your men settled in?" asked Skarpa cheerfully.

"As we can. I've already had men injured by little traps in the outbuildings," said Meinyt. "Wouldn't trouble me if we burned this place to the ground when we leave."

Skarpa smiled. "That would be a waste. We'll just report about all the traps, and if Lord Bhayar wills, let the good High Holder see his stead go to another. Odd that there were none here in the main house."

"Perhaps he didn't want the place torched . . . or didn't have time," replied Quaeryt. After a moment he added, "I have noticed one other thing. All of the traps and devices were designed and set in a way not to damage the buildings themselves much."

"Makes sense," rejoined Meinyt. "The holder wants to be able to claim to Kharst that he took many steps to harm us, while he can say to Bhayar that he only did what was necessary to keep Kharst from taking his lands."

Skarpa nodded. "Most of them will be like that. Those are the only kinds who'd prosper under a bastard like Kharst. Lord Bhayar's going to have his hands full. Wouldn't be surprised to have a battalion required to keep them in line. Likely for years." His eyes fixed on Quaeryt.

Quaeryt ignored the implication that he and the imagers might well be employed for that kind of duty, even though he had far earlier recognized that would be another means of strengthening the position of the imagers. "The way the buildings were trapped also suggests that the holder was told that Kharst has a plan for reclaiming the lands we've taken."

"That's possible. He'll certainly try to draw us in, and then cut us off and try to surround us. Deucalon stated that in his last dispatch. One of his scouting teams captured a dispatch rider. One of the dispatches stated that Kharst was summoning regiments from all over Bovaria, and that all growers and holders were to destroy stores and supplies rather than let them be captured. It also said that those who allowed Telaryn forces to take supplies would be guilty of treason and executed." Skarpa shook his head. "That's another reason why I've had you looking for supplies. Kharst will likely mount a solid defense, even a counterattack, when we near Villerive. He'll need to do that, if only to purchase time to allow more regiments to arrive with additional troops and arms."

"He didn't expect Bhayar to attack," suggested Quaeryt.

"He also didn't expect to lose more than eight regiments to the last man in Ferravyl. But he'll likely be counting on having greater numbers when we next meet."

"He's lost more than a regiment just to us since we've left Ferravyl," pointed out Meinyt.

"If he can find a way to do it he'll sacrifice every farmboy and laborer in all of Bovaria to stop us," replied Skarpa.

Quaeryt was afraid that was all too true—and that it meant that victory for Telaryn would likely be a bloody affair. *But then, when have wars ever been anything but bloody?*

"Regardless, we need to get on with our plans for the next few days," said Skarpa. "We're some eight milles from Ralaes, and that's where we'll stage and wait for the attack on Villerive. That's if the Bovarians haven't dug in and set up defenses this side of the town. So far the scouts haven't seen any sign of that kind of preparation." Skarpa spread out a map on the table. "Here's what I have in mind . . ."

Quaeryt listened intently, his eyes going from Skarpa to the map and back again, as he tried to visualize the positions and maneuvers the commander had in mind.

After two quints Skarpa rolled up the map and straightened up. "We'll go over this again in the morning, after you've had a chance to think about it." He looked at Quaeryt. "It's stopped raining, and you still have to conduct services, Subcommander. The men are beginning to gather already. I trust you'll be as inspirational as ever."

"I'll do my best."

Skarpa rose, and so did Quaeryt and Meinyt.

When Quaeryt reached the gently sloping lawn at the back of the hold house, he was surprised to see so many troopers and officers on the slope. There must have been close to a thousand waiting. There was also no way most of them would be able to hear him. *What about image-projecting your speaking voice? That way most of them will think your voice is barely reaching them.*

It was worth a try.

He walked to the circular paved area that surrounded a fountain that had been drained, moving to that part of the stone paving facing the base of the slope, then turned. Concentrating on image-projecting his voice, he began with the greeting. "We gather together in the spirit of the Nameless and to affirm the quest for goodness and mercy in all that we do."

Then came the opening hymn, and he began the only one he knew by heart—"Glory to the Nameless." At least some of the troopers knew it, and he did not project his singing after the first few words, knowing he'd get off-key sooner or later.

The confession, as always one of the hardest parts of the service for Quaeryt, came next. He felt fraudulent in leading a confession of error to a deity he wasn't certain existed, or that any deity existed, although he had no trouble confessing to error, just to the idea that he and those who followed his words would be forgiven by the Nameless, since he'd observed all too little forgiveness in the world.

"We name not You, for naming presumes, and we presume not upon the Creator of all that was, is, and will be. We pray not to You for ourselves, nor ask from You favor or recognition, for such asks You to favor us over others who are also Yours. We confess that we risk in all times the sins of presumptuous pride. We acknowledge that the very names we bear symbolize those sins, for we strive too often to raise our names and ourselves above others, to insist that our small achievements have meaning. Let us never forget that we are less than nothing against Your Nameless magnificence and that we must respect all others, in celebration and deference to You who cannot be named or known, only respected and worshipped."

Quaeryt did lead the chorus of "In Peace and Harmony."

In the silence that followed, he cleared his throat and began. "Good evening, and it is a good evening."

"Good evening," came the chorused reply.

"All evenings are good evenings under the Nameless. Some are good in and of themselves, and some are like this evening. They're good because most of us have survived to reach the evening, despite the best efforts of our enemies to the contrary . . ." Quaeryt paused briefly, looking upward to the higher part of the slope, but even up there several troopers had nodded, and that suggested his image-projection was working.

"Earlier today, I was talking to another officer, and I asked him if the Nameless was somehow different here in Bovaria—although I guess we're now still in Telaryn, according to Lord Bhayar . . ."

That brought a few smiles before Quaeryt went on.

". . . or was it that the ideas attributed to the Nameless were taken differently here. He just said wisely that so far as men were concerned, it made no difference. Why does it make no difference?"

Quaeryt paused, letting the silence draw out, before he went on. "It makes no difference because no matter what the precepts of the Nameless may be, we as men, and women as women, are the ones to interpret those precepts. The Nameless does not come thundering out of the sky—at least not very often from what I've seen—and strike down any man who lies, or cheats, or murders . . . or Names in some fashion. We are the ones who enforce, or fail to enforce, those precepts. We are the ones who lead by example . . . or fail to do so. The Nameless has not changed nature or precepts from one part of Lydar to another. In war, the Nameless does not tell Lord Bhayar to treat small growers with care and Rex Kharst to burn the lands of such small growers.

"How does this happen? It happens, it seems to me, when those with power become more interested how others view them—and they wish to make other men desire to be like them. They wish to create other men in their likeness. What is that but another form of Naming? Yet that is not the way of the Nameless. That is why the Nameless has no appellation. It is why there are no paintings or statues of the Nameless, because the Nameless gave us the freedom to be the best we could be, not to strive to be a copy of something.

"Look around at the world. Not all creatures are the same, nor are all the creatures of a given type all the same. The same is true of people. There are tall men and women and short ones, those with red hair, and those with black or blond hair. Across the world, the colors of people's skins differs. In these regiments, we have different men with different skills. If all of us were like each other, we could not accomplish nearly so much. We need troopers, and quartermasters, and scouts, and engineers, even imagers. There is not one likeness that fits all men—and yet rulers like Kharst would have it so . . . and that is one of the most evil forms of Naming of all, the vanity that one man, one ruler, would wish to have all people act in one manner, and in one likeness. And all of you have seen the evil that comes from this . . . and that is an evil we must firmly oppose while remaining true to what we are and can be—men with great differences striving toward a common goal, and that goal is to create a land where all can be the best that they can, and not pale likenesses of a ruler who has turned to the Namer in an effort at mindless conquest."

Quaeryt wished he could have come up with a better ending to the homily, but any words he had tried to make a rousing end had seemed false. So he concluded with a simple phrase: "The Nameless has told us to turn from false images, whether in our minds or in the minds of others . . . and so we should . . . today, tonight, and for all time."

He stood there silently for a moment after he finished, before beginning the closing hymn, the one he knew the best—"For the Glory."

> "For the glory, through all strife,
>   for the beauty of all life,
>   for all that is and will ever be,
>   all together, through forever,
>   in eternal Nameless glory . . ."

As in the past, when the voices of the men died away, he did not offer the standard benediction, but waited for silence, then simply said, "As we have come together to seek meaning and renewal, let us go forth this evening renewed in hope and in harmony with that which was, is, and ever shall be."

After the benediction, he just stepped back, and stood on the stone oblong, before the dry fountain, waiting for the men to disperse.

Skarpa walked over. "That was carefully worded."

"I hope so," replied Quaeryt.

"There was another thing . . ." The commander paused. "You didn't speak all that loudly, but all of the men seemed to hear and understand what you said."

"I'm glad they did." Quaeryt offered a grin. "At least, I think I am. I've done better."

"We all have, but you're still better than any chorister I've ever heard, and I've heard more than a few."

"Thank you."

"I'll see you and Meinyt right after breakfast."

"Yes, sir." Although Quaeryt had a chamber with a comfortable bed, he wouldn't be sleeping anytime soon.

He still had to write out notes for Bhayar about the High Holder of Laesheld, based on what he and Fifth Battalion had uncovered, and he hoped he'd have a chance to write a few lines to Vaelora as well . . . before he was too tired to think well enough to write.

After breakfast on Lundi, Quaeryt sought out Shaelyt and drew him aside into a dim parlor in the hold house.

"What is it, sir?"

"I had a chance to talk to Undercaptain Voltyr the other day, but not you. He said you had made some steps toward developing the ability to shield yourself. How much progress?"

"I can harden the air so that I cannot break through it. That tires me so much that I can only do it for perhaps a third of a quint."

Quaeryt nodded. "That's a good start. Can you make the air less hard, so that you can push a sabre through it, but only with great effort?"

"I have not attempted that, sir."

"You should. That should take less effort. That way you can hold the shield for longer."

"What good will that do, sir, if I might ask?"

"First, the longer you can hold shields, the stronger you will become. Second . . . have you seen what happens when an arrow or a blade strikes water? How far does either penetrate?"

Shaelyt frowned, then smiled abruptly. "Thank you, sir."

"You need to keep working every day, and you might pass that on to Voltyr."

"Yes, sir."

"That's all for now. You need to get ready to move out."

Once Shaelyt had hurried off, Quaeryt made his way out to the west courtyard for morning muster. After that, while the companies were readying to head out, he returned to the hold house study to meet with Skarpa and Meinyt.

The commander's first words were to the point. "The scouts I had out early this morning have discovered more Bovarians. Another regiment, half foot, is marching toward Villerive."

"Where did they come from if they're on this side of the river and marching away from us?" asked Meinyt.

"I'd guess they were stationed along the eastern end of the Bovarian border with Antiago. That dispatch indicated every regiment in Bovaria was being called in."

"They had to have left before the battle at Ferravyl," said Quaeryt. "If they came from there, they had to cover twice as much ground as we have to reach Villerive."

"That could be. It doesn't change anything. It's another regiment we'll have to fight. There's no telling when they might stop and take a stand, either."

"Not before Ralaes," offered Meinyt. "They'll need a day or longer to recover."

"That's only if they've traveled from the border," Skarpa pointed out. "For all we know, they could have been much closer. They could be waiting four milles west of here."

"What formation do you want this morning?" asked Quaeryt.

"The one with Fifth Battalion as the van."

After receiving quick status reports from the two subcommanders, Skarpa dismissed them to make ready for immediate departure. Quaeryt reclaimed his kit from the bedchamber he'd used and hurried out to meet with Zhelan and the company commanders to let them know that Fifth Battalion would again take the lead in departing Laesheld.

Two quints later, when Quaeryt rode out through the weathered limestone gates and onto the river road once more, he felt that the air was slightly cooler, most likely because of the scattered rains of the previous days, but the crystal clear skies suggested that the day might end up as hot, if not hotter, than the previous days. He glanced ahead where the second of the squads dispatched as scouting parties disappeared over the crest of one of the low rolling hills that flanked the River Aluse, although with each mille they rode westward, the hills had become less steep, and now resembled gentle rises.

From what Quaeryt recalled of geography studied years previously, the midlands of Bovaria, stretching from the hills that ran from Kephria to the western end of the Sud Swamp northward almost to the eastern end of the Montagnes D'Glace, were largely flat and fertile, and the River Aluse ran through the midsection of that fertile area.

Fifth Battalion had barely covered a mille when Skarpa rode forward and joined Quaeryt.

"Have you seen anything? Have the scouts reported?"

"No, sir."

"The Bovarians won't let us ride into Villerive."

"I'd think not, but who knows where they'll take a stand?"

Skarpa shook his head and said nothing more.

Quaeryt listened to the undercaptains riding behind them, trying to hear what they were saying. For a time, the talk was about the rain and the strangeness of Laesheld. Then the comments drifted more onto the campaign.

". . . seems like the Bovarians are letting us get too close to Variana . . ."

". . . want to draw us in . . ."

". . . commander and subcommander must know . . ."

". . . subcommander knows more than he says . . ."

"What's he done lately?"

That was Threkhyl's voice, louder than it should be, as always, Quaeryt reflected.

"Besides keeping a score of troopers from getting hurt with all those traps, you mean?" asked Voltyr cuttingly.

". . . not that special . ." muttered the ginger-haired undercaptain.

". . . and some imagers aren't that bright, either."

The last comment was murmured in such a low voice that Quaeryt barely heard it, but after that, for a time, none of the undercaptains spoke, not loudly enough for Quaeryt to overhear.

Another glass passed. While the day warmed, Quaeryt had to admit that so far it remained pleasant. Ahead, the road turned to the left, paralleling a narrow strip of water upstream of where it entered the River Aluse. Right after the turn, the dirt road was replaced by narrow stone paving, if ancient and worn. The waterway was so narrow that it had to be a canal, although it now appeared abandoned. The canal separated the river road from a wooded island or peninsula. Quaeryt couldn't tell which yet. There was only a narrow strip of brush in front of the line of shorter trees just ahead on the south side of the island. The land north of the canal and the ground where the river road ran once had to have been joined, Quaeryt felt, because they were almost the same level, and the first trees were less than a hundred yards from the right shoulder of the road. The slopes down to the almost stagnant water on each side of the ancient canal were steep, and Quaeryt could see the remaining riprap that still faced the slopes in places between the bushes and grass.

Why was there a canal here? With a paved road? He pulled out his map, but there was nothing that showed either the island or the canal.

"There's nothing on the map that shows this," he said to Skarpa, riding to his left. As he spoke, his eyes took in the area to the south on the map, and after a moment he nodded.

"What? The stream?"

"It looks like it was once a canal. It might be left from the time of Naedara. This part of the road, too." Quaeryt almost smiled because he'd been able to figure that out.

"You're the scholar. If they could build this, whatever happened to the Naedarans?"

"In some ways," replied Quaeryt, "we're their descendants. They were the first to worship the Nameless. There are still buildings in Ruile that they built, and supposedly they settled most of the larger towns south of here."

"So what happened to them?"

"No one really knows. Some think it was because the Red Death wiped out most of the people in their towns, and then the Bovarians finished them off. Others claim that . . ." Quaeryt paused, because he thought he heard hoofs moving more quickly, as if someone was riding quickly along the shoulder of the road. He looked back, then saw Major Calkoran riding toward them, almost at a gallop, on the river—or canal—side of the road.

"What is it?" asked Skarpa.

"Major Calkoran's riding hard to catch us."

In only a few moments, the Khellan officer pulled in beside Quaeryt, just as first company drew abreast of a stand of shorter trees that grew almost to the edge of the far side of the old canal. Quaeryt looked past Calkoran to the isle. Something about the trees . . .

"Subcommander!"

"Major . . ." Quaeryt wasn't certain what the Khellan officer had in mind.

"Subcommander, Commander! You must turn south, off the road. Now!"

"Why must we turn?" asked Skarpa.

Calkoran gestured toward the canal. "Those are not trees. They are—"

At that moment, a sound like rolling thunder swept across the column, and Quaeryt was rocked sideways in his saddle from impacts on his shields. Even as he struggled to right himself, he expanded the shields to cover those around him, hopefully the imager undercaptains as well.

"All companies! To the south! Off the road!" ordered Skarpa.

Quaeryt looked to the canal. Where there had been trees was a company of musketeers, each one with a heavy musket on a stand, with an assistant beside him.

Another volley followed, with smoke billowing up from the line of Bovarians.

"Imagers! Smoke and pepper into musketeers!" called Quaeryt. "Make it acrid and foul and thick!"

Quaeryt pulled the mare onto the canal side shoulder of the road, and began to image iron darts at the musketeers, one after the other.

"Threkhyl, Shaelyt, Voltyr! Image iron darts into the second line of musketeers!"

Another volley from the musketeers tore into Quaeryt's shields, and he had to grab the front of the saddle to stay on the mare. He could feel himself getting light-headed, and he paused for a moment from imaging darts and grabbed for his lager-filled water bottle. Several swallows later, after the impact of another volley of musketry, he thrust it back into the holder and looked around, discovering that he and the imager undercaptains remained alone on the road.

You should have thought about that.

"Keep imaging at the musketeers! Don't let a one survive!"

The fourth volley from the Bovarians was ragged, and Quaeryt could see a good half company of the remaining musketeers withdrawing into the taller trees. Others hurried forward, keeping low, to drag the musketeers wounded by the imagers iron darts back into the trees.

Quaeryt kept imaging his own iron darts at any musketeer he could see, trying to ignore the incipient light-headedness.

There was no fifth volley from the musketeers because there were none in sight. Quaeryt thought he might have killed or wounded close to thirty of the Bovarians, and the other imagers together might have accounted for almost as many.

Quaeryt watched for a moment, grabbing his water bottle and taking several swallows as he did, to make certain that the musketeers had indeed withdrawn. Then he turned in the saddle and looked toward the undercaptains.

"Sir! Akoryt took a musket ball!" Voltytr called. "There's blood everywhere."

Quaeryt rode over to where Voltyr had eased his mount in beside Akoryt. As Quaeryt moved his mount to the other side of the wounded undercaptain, he could see immediately that the musket ball had hit Akoryt in the upper right side of his chest. There was considerable blood, but it wasn't spurting. Akoryt's eyes were open, if glazed, and his breathing was labored.

What can you do?

Quaeryt swallowed, then leaned toward the injured man, concentrating on imaging out the ball, and immediately imaging into the gaping wound something like soft clean cotton. Then he glanced around. "Shaelyt. Get him to the surgeon. That way . . ." He gestured toward the south. "I got the musket ball out, and his wound is packed with clean cotton. Make sure the surgeon knows that."

"Yes, sir."

Quaeryt turned the mare and looked across the ancient canal, but there was no sign of the Bovarian musketeers. He urged the mare southward toward where the others were re-forming. In moments, he reined up beside Zhelan. "They've already cleared the isle, it appears. Every musket stand is gone. Do you know our casualties?"

"Thirteen men are dead, ten wounded," replied Zhelan, "most from first company."

"Make that eleven wounded. Undercaptain Akoryt took a musket ball in the chest."

Zhelan glanced at Quaeryt almost in disbelief.

"Imagers aren't invulnerable, especially less experienced ones," said Quaeryt.

"How badly is he hurt?"

"Badly. I don't know how severely, but he was having trouble breathing."

"That doesn't sound good."

Quaeryt finally caught sight of Skarpa. "I'll see what the commander wants, but keep them well back from the canal. The Bovarians might fire from the trees."

"Yes, sir." After a moment Zhelan began to issue orders to move the battalion farther south.

Quaeryt rode toward Skarpa and reined up.

"Fifth Battalion took most of the fire, Subcommander. How bad was it?"

"Thirteen dead, eleven wounded, including Undercaptain Akoryt. He looks to be in a bad way."

"I had a feeling about today."

Quaeryt forbore to mention that Skarpa had had a bad feeling for the last several days.

Skarpa shook his head. "Musketeers, no less."

"The imagers took out almost half a company of them," Quaeryt said.

"How did they do that?"

"Imaged iron darts into them."

"Ha! Good for your imagers. Might give them second thoughts. Except it won't. They'll still fear Kharst more than us."

Quaeryt had no doubts about that. *But isn't it somehow terrible that fear of one's leader is greater than the fear of death at the hands of the enemy?* That suggested, in another fashion, just how important it was for Bhayar and Telaryn to succeed.

"We'll see what the scouts discover, but I'd wager that the musketeers are withdrawing by boat already."

"You think so, sir?"

"Be most surprised if they weren't. Muskets and musketeers are too valuable to leave unguarded and outnumbered. They'll pull them back and use them against us again."

And again, thought Quaeryt.

"If that's so, we'll form up and keep moving."

"Yes, sir. I'll tell my officers." Quaeryt slowly rode back toward Fifth Battalion, but caught sight of the red banner that marked the surgeon, and turned his mount that way.

When he neared the banner, he saw Voltyr and Shaelyt. Both looked pale as he reined up beside where they stood holding the reins to their mounts.

"How is he?" asked Quaeryt.

Voltyr shook his head. "The surgeon—he's really a senior squad leader who's a field surgeon—said you'd stopped the bleeding, sir. Mostly . . . but that wasn't enough. Something with the lungs. He stopped breathing."

"He just gasped and gasped," said Shaelyt. "Then he didn't anymore."

Quaeryt didn't hide the wince. *Yet what else could you have done?* After a moment he said, "We'll need to form up again. The commander wants to keep moving."

"Yes, sir."

As Quaeryt turned the mare back toward Fifth Battalion, he couldn't help thinking, *Should you have started training all of them on shields earlier?* But that wouldn't have helped Akoryt, because he couldn't have developed enough strength as an imager to hold shields all the time, and the attack had come without warning. *Almost without warning.*

With that thought, he turned his mount toward second company and Major Calkoran.

The major was waiting for him.

"Subcommander, sir . . . your imagers . . . they kept us from greater casualties."

"They did. Undercaptain Akoryt took a musket ball. He died."

"I am sorry for him . . . and for us. He will be missed."

For a moment Quaeryt was stunned by Calkoran's coolness. He had to remind himself that the major had suffered incredible losses and seen far greater slaughter, and that the death of less than a score of men and a young officer could not compare to what Calkoran had experienced. "Major . . . how did you know they had musketeers on that island?"

"I saw those strange trees. Except they are not real trees. Each is a . . . screen . . . around the musket stand. The Bovarians used them to hide their musketeers in Khel," said Calkoran, adding, "Or something like them. The muskets . . . do not fire accurately, either uphill or downslope. They are terrible when they can be fired in mass across a level ground, and where they cannot be charged quickly."

Terrible . . . Quaeryt could see that. Four volleys into first and second company, and in a fraction of a quint, thirteen men were dead, and another eleven were wounded. *Fourteen dead, now, with Akoryt.*

Without the imagers—again—the results could have been much worse.

But the question of shields lingered in the back of his mind.

After he finished with Calkoran, Quaeryt rode to the front of first company, his eyes going to the trees on the north side of the road and the canal, not quite seeing either. *You tried to protect them . . . you just didn't think about muskets in a side volley.* He shook his head again.

No matter how much he told himself that in the few weeks he'd had the imagers he couldn't have taught them what it had taken him well over a year to learn and develop, he had the feeling that Akoryt's death . . . and perhaps those of others . . . would haunt him.

But he did need to give the others a better chance. *They might surprise you.*

One way or the other . . .

He glanced northward again, for a moment.

32

Just slightly after midday, Skarpa ordered resumption of the advance toward Ralaes, leaving Fifth Battalion as vanguard. He also sent out two squads of scouts and remained at the head of the column with Quaeryt as they rode alongside the ancient canal.

A mille or so past the spot where the Bovarians had attacked, the canal turned southward. Quaeryt couldn't help but study what the Naedarans had done. The far side of the canal was clearly a stone wall, backed by an earthen levee. On the far side of the levee was a marsh that extended northwest and joined the River Aluse. An ancient stone bridge—repaired in more recent times—crossed the canal, and on the far side of the bridge, the ancient stone road swung west to again parallel the river.

As he adjusted the visor cap and blotted the sweat off his forehead in the early afternoon heat, Quaeryt's eyes followed the canal. *Why isn't it swamp? There has to be water flowing from somewhere or it would have long since filled itself in.* Quickly taking out his map, he located where he thought they were. While the canal wasn't shown on the map, nor the bridge, the isle was. So was a large lake to the south, with a town called Chelaes located along the western side of the unnamed lake. *Chelaes must have been important for Naedara.*

"What are you thinking about? You've got that expression," said Skarpa.

"The canal and why it was built."

"It was built to get boats to the river. That was a long time back. Right now, the Bovarians used the canal wall to get off that isle. They have carts or wagons and they're moving west at a good clip."

"So they can set up another ambush or withdraw to meet their main body," suggested Quaeryt.

"Most likely both," replied Skarpa dryly.

Another glass passed before one of the scouts rode up beside the commander.

"What did you find?"

"The wagons that carried the musketeers and their muskets took another road just ahead. It's headed south. The millestones say that there's a place called Chelaes eleven milles south."

"It's on a lake, according to the map," added Quaeryt.

"They won't go that far. They need to get to Villerive." Skarpa shook his head. "We'll have to leave a company where the roads split . . . at least for a glass or so after we pass. I don't want them circling back and following us. Not too close, anyway."

"Maybe there's a back road that parallels the river road that will get them to Ralaes or Villerive sooner," suggested Quaeryt.

"That could be. The river swings north and then back south. Might be faster to cut across. But we don't know. Don't want to take any chances, though."

Quaeryt could understand that all too well.

"I'm going to ride back and talk to Meinyt. You see anything out of sorts . . . call a halt."

"Yes, sir." Quaeryt understood what Skarpa hadn't said—that he'd better be alert to something "out of sorts" early enough to avoid another ambush.

Skarpa looked to the scout. "You keep the reports coming to the subcommander."

"Yes, sir."

As the scout headed back westward and Skarpa rode toward the rear of the column, Quaeryt made an effort to study the terrain on both sides of the road—carefully, forcing his eyes to take in each area, from the scraggly weeds just beyond the shoulder of the road, to the sagging split rail fence of the small stead ahead and the lack of smoke from the chimney of the small cot.

Quaeryt kept watching.

Finally, a quint or so later, they reached the spot where the road to the south split off the river road, except it was a gentle turn, and the paved road was the one heading south, while the river road returned to being packed clay. Quaeryt studied the river road carefully, but there were no heavy wheel tracks and only a few hoofprints, likely those of the Telaryn scouts, heading west along the river. He could discern no attempts to blur prints or tracks on the river road, nor did he see any evidence of a concealed return to the river road as he and Fifth Battalion rode on.

Shortly, another scout rode back eastward and swung his mount in beside Quaeryt.

"There are tracks on the road ahead, sir, just past some fields that have been harvested. That'd be a mille or so ahead."

"What crop?"

"Looks to be hay, sir. They got those funny haystacks in the field, and the stubble's short."

"There's no one hiding behind those stacks, is there?"

"No, sir. Hardly big enough to hide a single man and mount."

Quaeryt recalled what Caltoran had said about muskets . . . and flat areas. "What's the ground like just ahead, between here and there?"

"You can see, sir. Pretty much the same as here."

That meant fields and small steads on the south, and a narrow strip of brush, bushes, and occasional trees between the river road and the River Aluse.

"Column! Halt! Third company! Forward! Pass it back!" Quaeryt couldn't quite have said why he had reacted so quickly, but there was something about the scout's report that bothered him, even if he couldn't have said what. He turned to Zhelan. "I don't like the scout's report. So I'm going to move ahead with third company. Keep Fifth Battalion at the ready."

"Yes, sir. Are you certain that you don't want the whole battalion?"

"If it's that bad, I'll let you know."

In less than half a quint, Major Zhael reined up, third company behind him on the shoulder of the road. "Sir?"

"We're going to look and see about something, Major." Quaeryt offered a smile. "I thought you and your men could keep me company." He eased his mount around to the south, so that Zhael would be riding on the river side of the road. Then he nodded to the scout. "Lead the way."

For the next half mille, Quaeryt could see nothing out of the ordinary. While the fields had been recently harvested, there were no haystacks or even enough grain or maize for gleaning. Then they rode past a cot set back some fifty yards from the road, with a weathered split rail fence some thirty yards to the west of the cot. Beyond the fence began another series of fields, beginning with a green plant that covered everything and stood a little over knee-high. Beyond that was the harvested grain field dotted with small haystacks.

As they rode past the fence, Quaeryt studied the green field, clearly something being raised for winter fodder for livestock, but he could see no sign that anyone had walked or ridden through the comparatively low plants. The haystacks beyond did indeed look strange, seemingly with hay bundled into pyramids and encircled with cord. But there was something about the haystacks.

There aren't any in the fifty yards closest to the road.

"Third company! To arms!" Even as he spoke, Quaeryt tried to extend his shields more and at an angle.

A thunderous roar swept across him, with multiple impacts on his shields nearly tearing him out of his saddle. As he struggled to regain his seat, his eyes went to the left of the road, from where the impacts had come. For a moment he saw nothing out of the ordinary, before he saw the slits in the "haystacks" that were nothing of the sort.

He didn't have much time to consider more, because a wave of riders charged out of the woods behind the recently harvested field—and past the haystacks that were screens covered with hay, concealing musketeers— toward Quaeryt and third company.

"Third company!" he commanded, in Bovarian. "On me! Charge!"

He wasn't certain he'd been heard, but then caught the words of Major Zhael, but not their meaning, as he turned the mare toward the oncoming riders, and narrowed his shields, if only slightly. Then he managed to ease the half-staff from its leathers and brace it across the front of the saddle as he guided the mare into the field.

Quaeryt sensed rather than heard another volley from the muskets, less thunderous than the first, but could feel no impacts on his shields.

"Zhael! Charge ahead! Not on me!" he ordered as he neared the first line of "haystacks." He could see musketeers and the loaders ducking behind the cloth- and hay-covered frames of their stands. Abruptly he turned the mare to the right at an angle and raced along the haystacks with his shields extended, using the shields as a weapon to flatten the Bovarians. By the time he'd reached the end of the musket screens, his head was splitting, and it was getting hard to see. Still . . .

You can't let them keep shooting troopers down . . .

Concentrating through the growing haze of blinding light and what felt like blows to his head, he wheeled the mare and started back along the second line. With each haystack he passed, the pain intensified.

Ahead of him and to his right, third company slashed into the Bovarians, shredding the ambushing company.

Quaeryt let the mare slow as he passed the last haystack/musket stand, so that by the time he rejoined the main body of the company, more than half the Bovarians were down, cut out of their saddles, and the remainder were fleeing back through the woods.

Then he reined up, gasping, trying to massage his forehead with one hand, leaving the staff across the front of the saddle.

Perhaps a quint later—Quaeryt wasn't sure—Zhael rode back and reined up beside Quaeryt.

"Sir . . . are you wounded?"

"I'll . . . be all right . . . in a while." Quaeryt fumbled out the water bottle and took a swallow, then another. "You and your men did well."

"You led us well."

Quaeryt wanted to laugh. "No, Major. I did my best to distract the musketeers. You led third company. I hope you didn't lose too many men." He had trouble focusing his eyes on Zhael.

"No, sir. Just two. Another eight might have small wounds."

Just ten casualties? That seemed terribly low. "What about the Bovarians?"

"More than fifty. They are not used to experiencing a charge when their muskets are not effective. We have eleven prisoners. Most will not live, I think."

"Are there any captive musketeers?"

"There are two, sir," answered Zhael, his voice subdued. "The others . . ."

"What happened to the others?"

"You killed them, sir. Their necks, their bones . . . Most of them. One or two ran into the woods. We did not chase them far . . . as you ordered."

"I just charged them with my staff so they wouldn't shoot any more of us."

"They will not do that." Zhael did not quite meet Quaeryt's eyes.

After a long moment Quaeryt said, "If you'd have some of your men collect the muskets and pile them by the side of the road for the wagons to pick up. I don't want the Bovarians to come back and collect them." Quaeryt massaged his forehead again. It didn't seem to help the throbbing in his skull. "Oh . . . and if you'd dispatch a trooper to tell Major Zhelan that Fifth Battalion can join us."

"Yes, sir." Zhael rode off.

Quaeryt didn't take in what happened, because his vision kept blurring with the pain in his eyes and head. He drank more water, then fumbled out several dry biscuits and methodically started chewing one. By the time he'd finished the second one, the pain had subsided from sheer agony to extreme discomfort, but he could see more clearly . . . for a few moments, if he squinted. He also realized that he was sore across his thighs and abdomen . . . and on his backside. Very sore.

He took another long swallow of the watered lager, then replaced the bottle in its holder, just as Zhael reined up beside him.

"You are wounded in another way, are you not, sir?"

"You might say that," Quaeryt admitted. "I'll recover." *If we aren't attacked again soon.*

"The Bovarians—the ones remaining—are long gone."

"For the moment I have to say I'm glad."

Zhael nodded.

Quaeryt reached up and massaged his forehead and neck again.

Almost two quints passed before Quaeryt and Zhael, waiting beside the pile of muskets, saw Fifth Battalion approach. Then Skarpa rode out along the shoulder of the road toward them. Major Zhael eased his mount away as Skarpa reined up.

"I understand you had a little action here." The commander glanced down at the muskets stacked on the shoulder of the road.

"Another musket attack."

"How many did you lose?"

"Two killed, eight wounded, not seriously, according to Major Zhael."

"What were their casualties? Do you know?"

"Some fifty dead, eleven captives, mostly wounded."

Skarpa's eyes narrowed. "You wouldn't have led the attack on them, would you?"

"They attacked us, sir."

Skarpa snorted. "I'll rephrase that. You wouldn't have led the counter-attack, would you?"

"Only against the musketeers. Major Zhael commanded the attack against the Bovarian cavalry."

"So you took out the musketeers . . . and they destroyed the Bovarians. Exactly how did that happen?"

"The major said the Bovarians weren't used to enemies who charged into musket fire."

"I suspect that the Bovarians weren't used to enemies who were able to charge through it."

Quaeryt managed a grin, but even that hurt. "We were fortunate."

"Didn't I tell you that I was already suspicious of that explanation?"

"What can I say, sir? We were."

"How many muskets are there in that pile?"

"Forty-one, sir."

"Did you kill all of the men who used them?"

"No, sir. I don't know how many I might have injured. I just charged their stands from the side, and they couldn't turn their weapons fast enough."

"Just?"

"Muskets are like pikes, in a way. They're awkward."

"Have you ever been attacked by muskets before this campaign, Subcommander?"

"No."

Skarpa nodded. "You can rejoin Fifth Battalion. We'll take a break here and bring Third Regiment forward. Fifth Battalion will take the middle of the column, before the wagons."

Quaeryt didn't protest. He just nodded.

33

Late on Lundi afternoon Skarpa received scout reports that the Bovarians
had invested the approach to Ralaes with revetments and trenches. He
called a halt to the advance at a small, nameless, and hastily abandoned
hamlet some four milles from the approach to the town. While the company officers and men of the regiments and Fifth Battalion were making
camp, setting up picket lines, and taking care of mounts, among other matters, and the cooks were preparing an evening meal, Skarpa called Quaeryt
and Meinyt to meet with him on the covered front porch of one of the
larger dwellings in the hamlet, and one with a view of the river and a
breeze off the water. For the breeze alone, Quaeryt was grateful. He'd made
the ride to the hamlet in a painful semidaze, not to mention being hot and
sweaty.

Skarpa had found a small table that he'd set in the middle of the narrow porch and some stools. He'd also spread a map on the table, weighted
on the corners with stones. As Quaeryt listened, he tried not to squirm too
much on the stool, but he was feeling more aches than he had thought he
would, and there were bruises in more than a few places he couldn't see.

". . . the ground to the south of the town is low and swampy, with thick
underbrush and mud holes and uneven ground. There are also extensive
false olive thickets on the higher ground. We'd have to ride more than
twenty milles to get around it . . ."

"What about that other road?" asked Meinyt. "The one the musketeers
took?"

"It joins the river road about a mille toward Raelaes from here," replied Skarpa.

"Too bad we didn't know that."

"You wouldn't have wanted to take it, not the part heading west from
the paved road." Skarpa cleared his throat. "The scouts found two abandoned wagons—both with broken axles."

"They just left them?" Meinyt frowned.

"Apparently they were worried about Quaeryt's third company catching them." Skarpa smiled.

"After the way Zhael's men ripped through their troopers," said Quae-ryt, "they were right to be worried."

Meinyt and Skarpa exchanged a quick glance, one that Quaeryt ignored.

"Anyway . . ." continued Skarpa, "there's about two milles of open ground east of the town, between that jungle and the river. They've thrown up revetments across most of the last mille, with ditches in other places. Most of the ditches are wide enough that a horse can't jump them, and they're filled with sharpened stakes and who knows what else . . ."

"Filthy water and mud, most likely," added Meinyt.

". . . it's hard to tell how many men they've got, but it looks like they've got at least three, maybe four, regiments of foot behind those earthworks."

"At least some muskets, too," said Quaeryt. "Where they've got a clear path of fire."

Skarpa continued using the map to point out what he'd learned from the scouts for another half quint before he finally said, "That's what we know now. I'm in no hurry to attack. Not for a day or so, anyway. The men could use some rest—and so could you and the imagers, Subcommander. We need to feel out where their strong points are and see if there's some-where we can break through and then wheel and pin them against their own earthworks." Skarpa looked at Quaeryt. "Tomorrow, when you're rested, I'd like you to ride closer and see what you think."

"Yes, sir."

"Get some food and sleep. Leave everything else to Zhelan. That's what he's there for."

Quaeryt nodded, not trying even to smile pleasantly.

Skarpa stood. "I'll see you both in the morning."

For all that Skarpa said, it would be a while before the cooks had ra-tions ready. While Quaeryt was sore and tired, he wasn't sleepy. So he made his way to the eastern end of the hamlet, where Fifth Battalion was settling in around cots abandoned by their owners or tenants.

Zhelan was the first to catch sight of him. "Sir . . . the first cot there . . . there's space for you and the imagers."

"Thank you. You've told them?"

"Yes, sir." Zhelan stood waiting.

Quaeryt knew Zhelan wanted to know what Skarpa had said, but wouldn't ask. So he said quietly, "The Bovarians have thrown up earthworks and trenches across all the approaches to Ralaes . . ." He went on to summarize Skarpa's words, then ended with, "We need to see that the men get rest, but that they're ready in case the Bovarians try another surprise attack."

"Do you think they will?"

"They very well might. We're getting close to Villerive, and they can retreat behind all those earthworks after they try a strike."

"A few extra sentries might be in order . . . posted farther out."

Quaeryt nodded, then added, "Perhaps mounts already saddled for a squad . . . or two?"

Zhelan offered a faint smile. "I'd thought that, sir."

After he talked over matters with the major, Quaeryt started toward the cot that Zhelan had pointed out. He was still some twenty yards away when Voltyr approached from where he had been standing under a small maple.

"Sir?"

"What is it, Voltyr?"

"I hoped I could talk over a few things with you."

Quaeryt nodded, wondering if he could evade the thrust of the undercaptain's inquiries, or if he should, for he had no doubt questions were on Voltyr's mind. *How could they not be after all that's happened in the last day or so?*

"There have been times when we should have suffered from arrows. Those around us did. This morning, those closest to you were not injured by the first musket attack, while many farther away were. This afternoon, those near you were not injured." The undercaptain paused. "You can extend shields some distance, can you not?"

What do you say to that? "Learning shielding, from what I know, is difficult, but I've tried to give all of you instruction in imaging . . . as best I could. It takes time to learn and strengthen abilities, and there's never been any imager who lived long enough or who worked with others enough to develop a way of teaching imagers. Not that I know."

"Until now," said Voltyr quietly. "That's what you have in mind, isn't it? You've been pushing us as fast as you thought we could learn."

"It wasn't fast enough for Akoryt," Quaeryt said quietly.

"He wasn't strong enough yet. Shaelyt and I can barely hold shields for a fraction of a quint." Voltyr stopped as Shaelyt walked around the end of the cot and then toward them.

"Good afternoon," offered Quaeryt.

"The same to you, sir." Shaelyt's eyes went to Voltyr.

The older undercaptain smiled. "I was telling the subcommander how it seemed more than fortuitous that anyone close to him suffered fewer, if any, wounds from arrows or musket balls, and that suggested shielding beyond just himself."

"Begging your pardon, sir," said Shaelyt, "but none of the undercaptains thinks it's fortune. Nor does most of Fifth Battalion. Wharyn told Shaelyt that you were not a lost one. He said you were the son of Erion. He said you rode down twenty-one musketeers, and their iron musket stands. Only two of those you struck survived. They counted twice."

"What do you two suggest I say, then?" Quaeryt kept his voice humorous. "No matter what Captain Wharyn says, I can't claim I'm a son of Erion. I'm not, and claiming such wouldn't be a good idea."

"It might not hurt to let the rest of the undercaptains know you're an imager, sir," suggested Voltyr. "Quietly, of course."

Quaeryt nodded. "You're probably right that the time for that has come. I'll let them know after morning muster. I'd like to let them have the day to think it over."

"I have another question, sir," ventured Shaelyt.

"Yes?"

"Many times when you have done what others would claim is not possible . . . you have been injured. Yet nothing has struck you. You are moving with great care even now . . ."

"I don't deny it. I'm a bit sore. You want to know why?"

Both undercaptains nodded.

"Beyond a certain point . . . I've learned from experience . . . when there are too many impacts on shields, the force of those impacts are born by the body." Quaeryt paused for a moment. "It's like a physical shield. If a sabre hits a shield that's properly held, the shield-holder doesn't feel much. If a horse rears and its hooves and a battle ax hit the shield, the man holding the shield is likely to have many broken bones, if he survives."

"You've survived worse than that with no bones broken," Shaelyt pointed out.

"At times that's been true. But not at other times. You saw what happened to me at Ferravyl. And I was bruised all over when I came to Ferravyl because I'd used shields against explosives in a wagon. The more you work on shields the stronger they get—but there's always a breaking point. I had shields, probably like yours, when I went to Tilbor. They weren't enough to protect me against a crossbow bolt fired at close range. They slowed the bolt enough that it didn't break my collarbone or go deep enough into my chest to kill me. But it was more than a month before I rode again. In the last battle in Tilbor, I wore myself out and was flattened by a heavy cavalryman. That broke my arm and tore up a few muscles."

The two exchanged glances again.

"So . . . you've continued to fight when you knew . . ." Voltyr let his words break off.

"When necessary," Quaeryt admitted. "Sometimes you have no choice. Just as sometimes troopers and their commanders have no choice." *No good choices . . . there are always choices . . .*

"Thank you, sir."

"I'll go over this with the others in the morning." Quaeryt nodded and turned.

As he walked back toward the central cot near where rations were being prepared, Quaeryt could feel their eyes on his back. *Did you say enough? Too much? Did you make it clear enough?*

He could only hope so.

34

Quaeryt woke in the darkness to an off-key trumpet and the insistent clangor of a bell, followed by shouted commands, and then by the muffled sounds of weapons. For a moment he had no idea where he was, not until the undercaptains around him began to stir. Then he sat up on the thin pallet he'd covered with his single blanket and yanked on his boots and put on the uniform shirt he'd folded and laid aside to sleep in the too-warm night.

"Imagers! Muster out front?" Quaeryt stood and hurried toward the door.

When he reached the narrow porch of the cot, he glanced around, but while he heard sounds, they did not come from the river road to the west, but more from the southwest. That made sense. The Bovarians wouldn't have attacked along the road if they wanted to surprise Skarpa's forces.

Both moons were but thin crescents. Neither shed much light, and in the near darkness, all he could see were the shadowy figures of troopers forming up.

What can you do that will be most effective? As soon as he asked himself the question, he realized how stupid it was, since he had only a general idea of from where the Bovarian attack was coming . . . and none about what Telaryn forces were responding and how.

When the imagers all appeared, after what seemed like a quint, but was closer to a few moments, he ordered, "On me! To the headquarters house." *At least we can protect Skarpa, if necessary.*

But by the time they had reached the large dwelling, it was clear that Skarpa and the other officers had already left.

"We'll move up the river road," Quaeryt stated firmly. "Be ready to image. Smoke first, then iron darts. Only on my command."

". . . can't see . . . friggin' thing . . ."

Quaeryt had no trouble recognizing Threkhyl's loud and surly voice.

". . . is night, you know?" replied Desyrk. "You expect the moons to shine for you?"

". . . be helpful . . ."

"Quiet," Quaeryt ordered firmly, but not loudly, image-projecting his voice back at the undercaptains. He strained to hear and to see any moving shadows, but the only sounds nearby were those of his men. Even the noise of fighting to the south had died away.

After walking another hundred yards or so, Quaeryt heard movements to his left, coming from the south, and he immediately extended shields. "Stand ready!"

At that moment a good squad of Telaryn troopers charged out from a small grove of trees on the left side of the river road toward the imagers.

The two troopers in the lead ran into Quaeryt's shields and rocked back. One stumbled, and the other fell at the edge of the road, then scrambled to his feet.

"Imagers! Halt!" snapped Quaeryt in Tellan. Then he image-projected his voice at the troopers. "As you were!"

The troopers stiffened, and a squad leader hurried forward, blade at the ready.

"Sir?"

"Subcommander Quaeryt. The imagers and I couldn't do much in the dark where every one is all mixed up. So I thought we'd cover the river road." Quaeryt hadn't thought it out quite that precisely. He'd gone more on instinct.

"Yes, sir. I'm sorry, sir. We didn't know."

"You wouldn't have. No damage done," said Quaeryt. *But there could have been. The last thing we need is to take out our own troops—or have them take out an unaware imager.* "We haven't seen any Bovarians. Have you?"

"Not here, sir. The ones who came from the south withdrew when we hit them. Well . . . after they hit us and we pushed them back. The captain sent us here to make sure they didn't circle us."

As the squad leader explained, Quaeryt could see more troopers gathering and forming up in the trees.

"It's just the imagers and Subcommander Quaeryt, sir!" the squad leader called.

A captain strode out of the trees. "Subcommander, sir, Subcommander Meinyt didn't tell us you'd be here." The accent suggested he was from one of the battalions from Piedryn.

"He didn't know. There wasn't time to inform him." Quaeryt gestured. "We can move west on the road together."

"Yes, sir. Appreciate it, sir."

As Quaeryt led the imagers along the road, flanked by the Telaryn company, his eyes searched the dimness ahead, barely illuminated by the stars and thin crescents of Artiema and Erion, but a portion of his thoughts were elsewhere.

Holding shields was the only imaging that was even halfway effective in deep darkness or where the imagers couldn't see, for one reason or another, and he was the only imager proficient in doing that. Yet . . . *Have you delayed too long in trying to start them in learning shields?*

He didn't think he could have started much sooner . . . but the question still nagged at him.

35

Quaeryt was up early on Mardi, dressed quickly despite muscles that were still sore, and saw to the imagers, telling them that they would meet again after breakfast. Then he met with Zhelan about Fifth Battalion before hurrying to the house that served as Skarpa's temporary headquarters. As he drew near, three tiny gray kittens darted under the front porch. He couldn't help but smile.

Meinyt arrived just as Quaeryt did.

"Good morning," said Quaeryt.

"Morning. Better than last night." Meinyt paused, then said, "Some of the Piedryn troopers said that they ran into you and the imagers last night." The older subcommander stepped up onto the covered porch.

"We went to cover the river road. We met up there. Never saw any Bovarians." Quaeryt moved toward the door, about to open it.

At that moment Skarpa stepped out and gestured to the stools and the table, still in place from the afternoon before. "We'll meet out here. Too hot inside already."

As soon as the three were seated, Skarpa began. "We lost close to fifty men last night, with another sixty wounded." His eyes focused on Quaeryt questioningly.

"It's hard to image when the imagers can't see where to image," replied Quaeryt. "It's also hard to figure out what sort of imaging will work."

"They imaged at night at Caernyn," Meinyt said.

"That worked because they knew where our troops were, and where the enemy was. Once our forces mixed with the Bovarians and Antiagons, we had to stop imaging."

Skarpa nodded slowly.

After a moment so did Meinyt.

"There's also the problem that none of them have ever been in combat, and some of them are limited as imagers. We have worked to improve that, but for example Undercaptain Baelthm will never be the strongest of imagers. He is, however, very precise."

"It's too bad we don't have more imagers," said Skarpa blandly. "I did suggest in one of my dispatches to the marshal that having more would be useful, particularly if you were in charge of training and deploying them."

"Deucalon doesn't like changes," said Meinyt with a snort. "That why you suggested they be assigned to you?"

"That had occurred to me" Skarpa grinned, but that expression faded quickly. "It also has occurred to me more than once that imagers reduce overall casualties. Unhappily, we're going to have to take Ralaes with what we have. That's why we're going to scout all the approaches very carefully."

"I'd like to accompany one of the companies or squads doing the scouting, with one of the imagers," requested Quaeryt.

"That would be for the best. They'll be departing in less than a glass. That's Captain Lhastyn's company—third company of First Battalion. They'll form up on the road here while I give the captain his orders. We didn't have enough sentries last night, and they were posted too far apart. The Bovarians may try again tonight . . . given their success last night . . ."

Quaeryt listened intently as Skarpa went on to outline his plans for the day and evening.

A quint later he was walking back to the smaller cot where the imagers were waiting for him. He said nothing until all of them had gathered on the narrow porch.

"First off, we most likely won't be attacking Ralaes today. Undercaptain Shaelyt and I will be accompanying one of Third Regiment's companies scouting the Bovarian defenses. Second, the rest of you are to work on your imaging under the direction of Undercaptain Voltyr. There is also a third matter." Quaeryt paused. "As some of you have already guessed, and quietly suggested, I am an imager . . ." He let the silence draw out before continuing. "There were reasons why I was asked not to make that known when first company and then Fifth Battalion were formed. I'm going to ask that, for now, you not speak of it except among yourselves. This is in your interest as much as in mine."

"Why is that?" demanded Threkhyl, quickly adding, "Sir?"

"Because the longer the rest of the battalion sees that I'm impartial and that the imagers help everyone, the more favorably you'll be regarded. The more favorably you're regarded, the better the position imagers and especially each of you will be in when the fighting is over."

Shaelyt nodded. So did Voltyt. After a moment Desyrk offered a faint smile. Baelthm looked skeptical, while Threkhyl's expression held puzzlement and doubt.

"That's if we live through it," Threkhyl finally said. "You'll do just fine."

Quaeryt would have liked to point out that he'd suffered more injuries than they had, which had been the case—until Akoryt's death. Instead, he replied, "I've been at the front all the time."

"You can protect yourself," countered Threkhyl. "We've all seen it."

"That's true. That's also why I've been in front, trying to protect as many of you as possible until you can learn how to protect yourselves."

"The subcommander's right about that," said Baelthm.

Quaeryt was surprised that the oldest imager was the one to speak up.

"You've not shown me one thing like that," insisted Threkhyl.

"Well . . . you can start working on that with Voltyr while I'm gone this morning. When I get back, I'll go over it with you."

"Now you—"

"Enough," snapped Quaeryt, image-projecting absolute authority into Threkhyl, enough that the big man stepped back. "It's not a matter of strength alone. It took me years to develop the abilities I have. I've been working with you barely more than a month, and every one of you can do far more than you could when I started. You'll be able to do more than that before long. I'm not trying to hold anyone back. If I were, why would I have worked so hard with all of you?" He looked hard at Threkhyl.

For once, the ginger-bearded undercaptain had no answer.

"We're all in this together. I've made mistakes. So have you, but the better all of you become, the greater the chances for all of us to come through this in a far better position than you ever thought possible." Quaeryt caught the slightest frown from Voltyr, but that vanished quickly.

"How's that?" demanded Threkhyl.

"It's simple, if you think about it. Together . . . we destroyed an entire Bovarian army. Alone . . . could any of us survive against that large a force? Even if we could, what power would we have to ask for and get better treatment once the war is over?" Quaeryt smiled wryly. "That is . . . if you all work and become better imagers." After just the slightest pause, he went on. "You all can think about it while Shaelyt and I are out with the recon company. You're in charge, Undercaptain Voltyr." Quaeryt motioned for Shaelyt to join him, then began to walk toward where their mounts were tethered.

Shaelyt had to hurry to catch up to Quaeryt. Once the undercaptain did, he took several more steps before he cleared his throat. Loudly.

"Yes?" asked Quaeryt.

"Sir . . . you most likely know this . . . but Threkhyl . . . he sees things . . . ah . . ."

"Directly. In terms of brute force and what happens right now? Is that what you meant?"

"Yes, sir. He only listens to you because you're stronger, and he knows he can't hurt you."

"He does have a way of showing that." Quaeryt managed to keep his voice mildly sardonic.

"If he learns more . . . sir?"

"I might be wrong, Shaelyt, but . . . he might have trouble learning what you and Voltyr do. He already thinks he knows all he needs to know."

"But . . . if he does?"

"You and Voltyr will just have to learn more, won't you?" Quaeryt turned his head directly toward the young undercaptain and grinned.

After a moment Shaelyt smiled back.

After they saddled their mounts, as they rode toward the river, Quaeryt glanced back and was glad to see the other three imagers were paying attention to Voltyr. Lhastyn was just leaving the headquarters house when Quaeryt and Shaelyt reined up at the front of third company.

The captain mounted, then rode over and joined Quaeryt and Shaelyt. "Sir, welcome to third company."

"Thank you, Captain. We're just here as observers. We need to see where the imagers might be of the greatest use in any attack on Ralaes."

"We're glad to have you. The things your men have done have made matters easier for us."

"That's the idea." *Even if sometimes they don't work out as they should.*

As Quaeryt rode beside Captain Lhastyn, within a few hundred yards of leaving the hamlet, he could see that the ground to the south of the river road was getting lower with each yard he rode so that after less than a mille the fields and tended groves had given way to a dense forest so thick that even in the bright morning sunlight, the shadows beneath the trees resembled twilight. The forest appeared to Quaeryt as a jungle with massive live oaks forming a high canopy over smaller trees between and beneath. Thorn vines and thick underbrush formed an intertwined barrier, totally unsuited to any form of mounted advance.

Quaeryt could hear various birdcalls, if muted, from the forest, suggesting a lack of human activity within the green walls, and neither he nor Lhastyn's scouts, riding along the edge of the forest, could see any footprints or hoofprints coming to or from the woods, although there were more than a few hoofprints on the road itself.

"They've had their scouts out," observed Lhastyn.

"Just as we have," replied Quaeryt.

Before long, one of the outriders turned his mount and rode back to report, easing his mount in beside Lhastyn. "Sir, once you get to the middle of the flat there, you can see pretty much the whole approach. They can see you as well, because there's no cover, except on the south side, real close to the trees."

Lhastyn looked to Quaeryt.

"Why don't you and I ride up on the south shoulder and take a look?" suggested Quaeryt. "Even if they see two riders, they likely won't send anyone out. If they do, they'll send fewer than if they saw an entire company."

Lhastyn nodded slowly, almost doubtfully.

"Undercaptain Shaelyt is most adept with smoke, pepper, and iron darts, if necessary," Quaeryt added, urging the mare forward, if gently.

Lhastyn turned in the saddle. "Heorot . . . you know what to do if you're attacked."

"Yes, sir."

Quaeryt didn't say anything more, but strengthened his shields as he edged the mare as close as he could to the woods while still leaving a clear path forward. He could sense the captain's unease and almost smiled. He did listen for the telltale rustle of leaves or branches, but heard none, only the breathing of the two horses, and the whisper of their legs swishing through the grass that grew between the road's shoulder and the trees. As soon as Quaeryt could make out the entire scope of the approach to the town, he reined up.

At first glance the Bovarian emplacements and revetments appeared almost randomly placed across the wide and low slope that led up to the town. On closer study, Quaeryt realized that they had been placed to block the more gradual approaches. Two of the larger revetments flanked the river road, leaving only the width of the road open.

The revetments had also been created hurriedly, since all were earthworks. That suggested that the Bovarians had decided recently to make a stand at Ralaes. *In order to slow or halt us so that they can deploy more troops against our northern forces?* He also couldn't tell whether the defenders had catapults for Antiagon Fire, but he had no doubts that there were archers behind at least some of those earthworks.

"They have enough trenches there to protect three or four regiments," observed Lhastyn, looking up from the paper on which he was sketching out the positions of the revetments.

"If all of them contain troopers," said Quaeryt, "then they might have even more, if they hold their reserves over the crest of the hill."

"They'll keep their mounted forces back."

"That's another question. How many mounted battalions do they have? According to what I've studied and what the marshal has conveyed to Commander Skarpa, the Bovarians have far more foot soldiers, as many as half their forces, if not more. I wouldn't be surprised if they lost a great portion of their cavalry at Ferravyl."

"All those foot types seem odd to me," murmured Lhastyn.

"We're the odd ones," replied Quaeryt. "Most rulers have armies with far greater proportions of foot troopers. It's less costly, and the logistics are simpler." He wasn't about to explain the circumstances of history and geography that had led to the Telaryn reliance on mounted troops.

For the next half quint, Lhastyn sketched and Quaeryt studied. Then, Quaeryt noted some flag waving, and before long a trooper hurried from a trench partway up the slope and began to run uphill across the grass that bore a myriad of recent gouges.

"I think we, or the company, have been noticed," said Quaeryt.

"We'll see if they send someone down to chase us off," said Lhastyn cheerfully.

"What are your orders in that event?" asked Quaeryt.

"To get as much information as possible and to avoid unnecessary losses."

"Have you finished sketching things out?"

"I'm close."

"As soon as you finish, it might be a good idea for us to withdraw." Quaeryt glanced at the Bovarian defenses again.

"I won't be that long." Lhastyn kept sketching. "I want to get this right."

Before that long, while Lhastyn was still sketching, Quaeryt heard a sound like drumming, but lower. "Horses! That sounds like more than a company."

"Time for us to go." Lhastyn folded his papers and slipped them inside his tunic, then turned his mount.

Quaeryt glanced back as they rode toward third company. So did Lhastyn. The column of riders pouring over the rise in the road above and to the north of the revetments looked to be far more than a company, possibly even a battalion.

"You lead the company back," said Quaeryt. "Undercaptain Shaelyt and I will ride with the rear."

"Sir?"

"We can create some delays."

"But, sir—"

"Go!" snapped Quaeryt. "Now!" As he neared Shaelyt, he angled the mare so that he was riding almost stirrup to stirrup with the undercaptain. "We have a job to do."

"Yes, sir."

"When we get just past the narrow part of the road up ahead at the end of the flat, when it starts to rise, we're going to stop for a moment. I want you to image smoke across the road where it's the narrowest. It doesn't have to be acrid, but make it as thick as you can."

"Yes, sir. Won't they ride through it?"

"I'm certain that they will."

After they passed the narrow point at the bottom of the slope heading eastward to the Telaryn encampment and had ridden another fifty yards or so, Quaeryt reined up and turned the mare. As he did so, he raised a concealment shield to cover just him and Shaelyt. "Wait. Don't image the smoke until I tell you to, and if you can, I'd like you to image it as if it were a fog drifting out of the forest."

"Yes, sir. I think I can do that."

Quaeryt continued to watch as the Bovarian column thundered toward them.

"They don't see us, do they?" asked Shaelyt.

"No. It's another kind of shield."

When the Bovarians were roughly a hundred yards from the narrow spot in the road, Quaeryt said, "Start imaging now."

Shaelyt's smoky fog appeared and began to drift quickly across the road, but the pursuing Bovarians did not slow down. Quaeryt hadn't thought they would, not when they could see third company riding up the long slope, with no other forces around.

Quaeryt waited until the Bovarians were almost upon the smoke, then concentrated, first on creating an image of the forest stretching across the road behind the thick smoke that Shaelyt had imaged across, and then building a solid shield across the road and the shoulder, from the edge of the forest on the south to the heavier chest-high undergrowth on the north side of the river road. He anchored the shields to the ground itself and waited.

In moments, he felt the impact on his shields, shivering him despite the anchoring. He watched as close to an entire squad piled into the unseen barrier, with horses screaming and men yelling. Flashes of light flared across his eyes, and he had to squint to see clearly.

"Time for us to go, Shaelyt." Quaeryt turned the mare, noting that the undercaptain did so immediately as well.

Still holding the shields and the forest image, Quaeryt glanced back over his shoulder, but the Bovarians were more concerned about their casualties than in further pursuit. He dropped the image and the shield barrier, but continued to hold the small concealment shield.

They rode for several moments before Shaelyt asked, "Sir . . . why didn't you image stone trees or something like that?"

"Because I not only wanted to stop them, I wanted them surprised and confused, and I'm hoping that when the survivors report back that will create doubts and concerns. If they found stone trees, they'd immediately suspect imagers. This way . . ." Quaeryt shrugged. "When someone can't explain something, that's always to our advantage."

"I hadn't thought of that."

Quaeryt glanced back again, but the Bovarians were still not pursuing. "We need to catch up to the company before Captain Lhastyn gets too worried that he's lost a subcommander."

As he looked ahead, he could see that fourth squad was waiting near the top of the next rise. He found himself swaying slightly in the saddle. Clearly, he hadn't recovered as fully as he thought he had from dealing with the musketeers. Or . . . *there wasn't a source of heat to defray the cost on you . . . Not one you wanted to use . . .*

"Sir . . ."

"I'll be all right . . ." In a while Quaeryt reached for the bottle of watered lager. That would help.

As he and Shaelyt continued to ride away from the confused mass of Bovarian men and mounts, something else nagged at him, something he'd noted, something that was so obvious, yet couldn't remember at the moment. Quaeryt shook his head, hoping it would come to him while it still mattered.

36

By the time Quaeryt and Shaelyt returned to the hamlet serving as their base, it was still slightly more than a glass before midday. Captain Lhastyn hadn't even asked about how they had halted the pursuing Bovarians . . . and that bothered Quaeryt in a different way.

The last thing we need is junior officers—or senior officers—expecting imagers to come up with near-impossible ways of dealing with the Bovarians. Except he realized that the more successful he and the imagers were and the more word passed through the companies, the greater the expectations would be.

Quaeryt reined up just short of the tie line that held the other imagers' mounts, then dismounted, rather gingerly, and unsaddled the mare. Then he turned to Shaelyt.

"If you'd give Voltyr a hand . . . I'm going to meet with Commander Skarpa."

"Yes, sir."

Quaeryt nodded, then walked back to the cot where Skarpa was talking to Captain Lhastyn and asking questions about the sketches the captain was explaining. He eased up the steps and onto the covered porch, but stood back and let the captain continue his explanations.

". . . could hold more than four regiments . . . sent a battalion of cavalry after us . . . Subcommander Quaeryt's imager was able to create a diversion that halted them . . . suggests that they also have a large number of cavalry companies . . ."

After a time Skarpa nodded. "Thank you, Captain. I'll keep those sketches. I do appreciate the detail you've provided." He rose from the table.

Lhastyn also rose and nodded. "If that will be all, sir . . . ?"

"For now. After I discuss matters with the subcommanders, I'll let you know what else we need to find out." As Lhastyn left the porch, Skarpa motioned for Quaeryt to take one of the two stools, then seated himself again.

Quaeryt sat, wishing the stool was neither so low nor so hard, given the bruises on his body and his general stiffness and soreness.

"I've gone over what Lhastyn saw and sketched." Skarpa raised his eyebrows questioningly. "You heard the last of it."

Quaeryt nodded. He really didn't know exactly what to say.

"Go on," prodded the commander.

"I'd guess that they have more troopers around Ralaes than we anticipated."

"Because they came after you so quickly?"

"Because they chased us so quickly and in such numbers."

"That would be my first guess." Skarpa smiled crookedly. "Then again,
that could be exactly what they want us to think. Lhastyn didn't see that
many troops in all those revetments. It was almost as though they didn't
want you to see that."

"They might have sent that battalion out to buy time."

"That's possible."

"Still . . . the musketeers were in a great hurry to return," mused
Quaeryt.

"Maybe we should keep testing them for a day or so. What do you
think?"

"Do you know where Marshal Deucalon's forces are?"

"Just about opposite Caernyn, I'd judge."

"Three days before they get to a point across the river from us?"

"More like four, unless Deucalon moves faster."

"It wouldn't hurt to spend this afternoon or tomorrow testing, then."

"We'll start early tomorrow. We'll have more sentries out tonight, and
several companies waiting." Skarpa paused. "What exactly did you and
the undercaptain do to stop that battalion?"

"Used the road, the forest, and imaging to block them and create a
mess . . ." Quaeryt went on to explain in more detail, although he was a
bit vague about who had done what.

"You still don't like to admit what you do," observed Skarpa when
Quaeryt finished.

"No . . . and I still think it's better that way."

The commander nodded. "Have to say you're probably right. We'll try
to test them tomorrow without imagers."

Quaeryt looked directly at Skarpa.

"You're still moving as if you hurt, and I'd rather have you in better
health when we actually have to take the town. Go deal with your imagers." Skarpa gestured.

Quaeryt couldn't argue with Skarpa's observation. He smiled and stood.

"See me early tomorrow."

"Yes, sir." Quaeryt turned and headed down the steps.

When he reached the cot where the imagers were staying, he saw Threkhyl sitting on the shaded side of the steps to the small cot. The undercaptain's face was pale, and his thinning ginger hair was soaked with sweat. Voltyr stood at the foot of the steps, a concerned expression on his face. Shaelyt, Desyrk, and Baelthm stood on the narrow porch.

"What happened?" asked Quaeryt.

"I was trying to give Threkhyl instructions on shields," explained Voltyr. "He created one . . . and then . . ."

"Better than anything you could do," muttered Threkhyl in a voice that might have been belligerent had it been louder, rather than low and raspy.

"Then what?" Quaeryt asked Voltyr.

"He started turning red, and then he fell over. We couldn't get to him until his eyes closed. His shield kept us away."

Quaeryt frowned. *That kind of strength and stubbornness could kill him.*

"Snotnose . . . didn't know what he was talking about," muttered Threkhyl.

Both Baelthm and Desyrk edged closer to Threkhyl, their eyes flicking from Voltyr to Quaeryt and back again. Shaelyt remained farther back on the porch, but Quaeryt thought he caught a hint of a smile.

"What did he tell you that you think he didn't know what he was talking about?" asked Quaeryt mildly, looking at Threkhyl.

"Doesn't know anything . . ."

"You didn't answer my question."

Threkhyl looked up at Quaeryt, but did not speak.

"If you're going to accuse another officer, you'd best have a reason."

"Idiot told me to think about holding the air together with little hooks. That didn't work. So I made it into a wall. Except it fell on me, and no one could see it."

Quaeryt nodded slowly. "What happened to you is exactly why Undercaptain Voltyr suggested the idea of hooks. It takes too much effort to make and hold a solid wall of air."

"I did it!" snapped Threkhyl.

"You certainly did," agreed Quaeryt. "With all your strength, you managed to hold that wall-like shield for only a fraction of a quint. I also would wager that you couldn't move two paces holding it. If you'd tied it to yourself, you might even have been badly injured." Quaeryt decided against mentioning death. That would only have made Threkhyl even angrier and less likely to listen. "How long does even a skirmish last?"

"I did it."

"Doing it isn't the question," replied Quaeryt more patiently than he felt. "You have to do it in a way that you can keep doing it for much, much longer. How long does a skirmish last? A glass . . . half a glass?"

"Something like that," Threkhyl admitted.

"A shield that you can't maintain and can't carry with you is useless. Voltyr was trying to give you an image of something that you can use right now and can build on and strengthen."

"Tried that . . . soft like cheese with holes."

"It's a start," Quaeryt said. "If you work on always holding lighter shields, you can carry them longer. Then you can strengthen them—"

"Weak stuff won't protect you."

"What happens when an archer looses a shaft through the leaves of a tree? Does the arrow have as much force?"

"No . . ."

"It just might lose enough strength that your tunic would stop it. Or keep you from being killed. My first shields were like that. They didn't stop a crossbow bolt, but they slowed it enough that it didn't kill me . . ." Quaeryt took a deep breath. Explaining to Threkhyl was going to be every bit as difficult as he'd feared. And if the ginger-bearded imager hadn't tried to do so much with his first attempt, it would have been even harder.

For that, Quaeryt silently thanked Voltyr.

He looked up to the other four imagers. "We need to go over shields in a slightly different way . . .'

37

Although Quaeryt saw several companies depart the hamlet on Mardi afternoon, and at least one return, Skarpa did not send for him or Zhelan. So he continued to work with the imagers. Even by the fourth glass of the afternoon, Threkhyl still could do little more than image solid shields or ones that were like cobwebs. Quaeryt couldn't understand why someone who had so much raw power as an imager could create shields at either extreme but nothing in between.

Is it because he sees the world in those terms . . . one way or the other?

Since all the imagers were close to exhaustion, Quaeryt dismissed them. Tired and sore as he was, he just retreated to the porch of the small cot and settled onto the sole stool remaining there, letting the faint breeze off the river to the north cool him. For a time, he just sat silently before he realized that Voltyr was sitting on the top of the steps, less than a few yards away.

"Threkhyl will get himself killed before long, you know?" offered Voltyr quietly.

Quaeryt had his own ideas on that, but wanted to hear what the other had to say. "How do you figure that?"

"He'll either try to do too much in the fighting, or he'll get so angry that he'll attack you. He might even do that in the middle of a battle so no one will think he did it."

That's been done before. Even as Quaeryt could see Threkhyl attempting such an attack, he didn't want to have that occur, ironic as it might be. "Do you have any idea why he's as angry as he is?"

"He was an imager for a High Holder in Estisle . . . Ghasphar or some such. He was dismissed. He won't say why."

Quaeryt frowned. When he'd talked to Threkhyl, the imager had mentioned working for a metal factor in Estisle, imaging special parts and shapes, but not anything about a High Holder. Quaeryt had heard of Ghasphar before, but he couldn't recall where. "Do you know anything about Ghasphar?"

"He's into shipping. Threkhyl did say that."

Quaeryt remembered. Ghasphar owned all the "diamond" ships, the ones with bronze long cannon that fired shells filled with Antiagon Fire. "And Threkhyl's never said anything about Antiagon Fire?"

An expression of confused puzzlement crossed Voltyr's face. "No. Why?"

"Because Ghasphar has imagers—or uses some—who can create Antiagon Fire. Didn't Threkhyl say he knew nothing about Antiagon Fire?"

Voltyr's brow furrowed, and he tilted his head, clearing trying to remember. "He said . . . I think . . . that he had no idea how it was made."

Quaeryt snorted. "That covers a multitude of various Namings."

"What . . . if I might ask . . . do you intend to do about it?"

"I'm inclined to believe him."

"Why?"

"Because . . . if he knew . . . Ghasphar would never have let him go . . . or let him live."

"But why . . . ?"

"If you had imagers with the secrets of Antiagon Fire, would you want Threkhyl working with it . . . or knowing the secrets."

"I see your point."

"Still . . . he bears watching." *As if you didn't already know that.*

"Closer watching," suggested Voltyr.

By the time cold rations were handed out for the evening meal, Quaeryt felt somewhat recovered, if still stiff and sore. That, he had discovered during the Tilboran revolt, was only normal. After eating he slipped away and tried to concentrate on what he recalled of the Bovarian emplacements guarding the approaches to Ralaes, thinking about what he and the imagers could do to make any attack easier for Fifth Battalion and the rest of Skarpa's forces.

. . . what about using shields to block the ends of trenches closest to the attackers . . .

Except, Quaeryt realized, he was the only one capable of doing that at a distance, and for any length of time. The more he considered the problems, the more apparent it became that, so far, the imaging techniques the undercaptains had already used remained the most practical for them . . . at least until their techniques and capabilities strengthened.

Quaeryt had no more than drifted off to sleep—or so it seemed—than he heard the alarm chimes and trumpets. When he bolted awake, it was pitch-dark . . . and before he more than had his boots on, another trumpet sounded the recall. The same thing happened twice more at intervals of several glasses, and Quaeryt woke in the early gray before dawn feeling sore and grouchy. He could understand the Bovarian tactics, but that understanding didn't leave him feeling any less uncharitable toward Kharst's troopers and their commanders.

Breakfast, such as it was, consisted of hard biscuits and harder cheese, with relatively fresh apples, and Quaeryt found himself alternating bites of each. After eating, Quaeryt went to find Skarpa, only to encounter Meinyt heading in the same direction.

"Long night for your men?" asked Quaeryt.

"For my second battalion. There weren't that many attackers. Just enough to require a response and to try to keep everyone from getting any rest." Meinyt laughed softly. "Didn't disturb most of the veterans that much."

By that token, you're still not a veteran, thought Quaeryt.

Skarpa was waiting and waved them to the stools around the table, then immediately spoke. "I think we ought to use the Bovarians' tactics against them. With a few twists."

"Such as?" Quaeryt inquired, since Skarpa was looking at him.

"What if we make sallies against them all day and into the night—except that the one that would be, say, two glasses before dawn wouldn't be just a sally?"

"What—just smash along the road to the top of the hill?" asked Meinyt. "Then hold the high ground and then move down as we can? Leave Third Regiment at the bottom and catch them in between?"

"Something like that." Skarpa turned back to Quaeryt. "Where do you think Fifth Battalion and the imagers might serve best?"

"With Fifth Regiment, I'd say. We can offer smoke and pepper and other things that will disconcert the defenders, and the undercaptains need to be closer to do that."

"I'd felt that, but I wanted your thoughts." Skarpa paused. "In the past, you've been able to get closer to the enemy than would seem possible . . ."

"We can try. What we've done in the past isn't as effective at night because sentries can't see as well and they're using their ears more."

"Anything you can do will help." Skarpa looked back to Meinyt. "Since your men were up much of the night, we'll use companies from Third Regiment for the early feints and sallies today."

After Skarpa dismissed them, Quaeryt and Meinyt walked away from the cot together. Once they were well clear, the older subcommander spoke. "What would help you with getting us closer before being seen?"

"At night . . . or before dawn, silent riding would be the most important. I'd guess that would require a slower approach, but the need to charge immediately once the Bovarians realize we're attacking."

"Quick response to a single command. We'll set it up that way."

"The imagers and I will need to be in the fore."

"Do you want to lead?"

"I'd say that the imagers and my first company should lead the approach until the charge, and then Fifth Battalion should follow your first battalion . . . if that's acceptable."

"You'd have to pull up below their first line of revetments . . ."

"We'll chance it. The undercaptains still would get scattered at the head of a charge, especially in the dark." Quaeryt thought he could shield them for a short time if necessary.

"Then that's what we'll do. I'll ride beside you with the trumpeter . . ."

Much as he hoped that matters would work out as they planned, Quaeryt had his doubts, since so often matters didn't go as planned.

Later on Meredi, Quaeryt took second squad from Fifth Battalion's first company and rode back toward Ralaes with Skarpa's second battalion. When the battalion began to ride forward, so did he, but he and the squad pulled off to the river side of the road. From there, Quaeryt studied the approach on the right side of the road more carefully than he had earlier.

When he returned he gathered all the officers in Fifth Battalion and went over the battle plan, using both Tellan and Bovarian, repeating himself several times. Then he dismissed the company officers and Zhelan and began to brief the imager undercaptains on what he expected of them in particular.

". . . and we'll be drawn up below the lowest revetment on the river side of the river road, waiting for Subcommander Meinyt's lead battalion to clear the way. Before they reach the revetment, you'll image smoke and pepper along the front lines of the earthworks . . ."

"Why are we doing this again, sir?" demanded Threkhyl.

"Because, Undercaptain, you won't be able to see much when we attack tomorrow, and I don't want you killed because you don't understand completely what we need to do. And if I have to give you spoken commands, that will reveal our presence earlier than necessary. That increases the chances that you or another imager might get killed or wounded." Quaeryt looked at Threkhyl. "Is that clear?"

"Uh . . . yes, sir."

Quaeryt *thought* he'd managed to make the stubborn undercaptain understand. "Once the lead battalion of Fifth Regiment passes, Fifth Battalion will follow, at my command . . ."

He had the feeling the day would be long, but he put that thought aside as he outlined the specific duties for each imager.

38

While Quaeryt was certain he wouldn't sleep at all on Meredi night, he did sleep, or at least he dozed, but he was awake even before he heard the voices outside the cot and then the steps on the cot porch in the darkness sometime after second glass after midnight. He had one boot on when the squad leader entered the main chamber of the small cot and spoke.

"Subcommander, sir . . . it's time."

"I thought so." Quaeryt pulled on the second boot, then stood. "Thank you."

"Yes, sir." The squad leader nodded, or Quaeryt thought he did, before leaving the cot.

Quaeryt finished dressing and readying himself, then mustered the imagers. Within another quint, Fifth Battalion was on the road, with first company in the van, followed by Fifth Regiment, the remainder of Fifth Battalion, and then Third Regiment. Meinyt rode beside Quaeryt with Ghaelyn immediately following. Skarpa rode at the head of Third Regiment.

"How did the attacks go earlier in the night?" asked Quaeryt.

"Too easy," replied Meinyt, "We could have reached the hilltop with a single company."

"Do you think they've pulled back to Villerive and left just a token force?"

"It's possible."

"You don't sound convinced."

"I'm not. Neither is Skarpa. Why would they abandon a strong defensive position?"

"To get us in a weaker one, I'd guess."

"How could they do that if we hold the high ground and have more troopers?"

How indeed? The obvious answer to Quaeryt was that the Bovarians had some sort of plan. "All those musketeers, maybe, lined up and waiting on the hilltop?"

"It would take more than that. We'd take losses, but we could still run them down."

"Hidden pits? Both? Heavy cavalry to the side?"

Meinyt shrugged. "We're guessing, but we'll need to be ready for any of that."

And more, likely. Especially since, once again, the woods—or jungle-like forest—precluded a circling attack from the south or southwest while the river protected the north side of the approach to Ralaes.

Almost a glass passed, and first company was heading down to the flat section of the river road that ended at the base of the fortified slope lead-ing to the town. While Quaeryt could see that Artiema, now almost a quarter full, hung well above the western horizon, it seemed that Erion had barely moved. *Not wonderful for a supposed son of Erion.* He smiled ironically. Somehow he doubted that Erion had been immobile in the sky or that the lesser moon's position in the sky would make much difference, not when neither moon was offering that much light.

As they came to the end of the flat section of the road, the sounds of horses breathing in the moist warm night air seemed preternaturally loud to Quaeryt, yet he knew that was his own sensitivity. He heard nothing at all from the revetments ahead. In one respect, that should be the case. If the Bovarian lookouts and sentries saw nothing and heard nothing, why would they say much of anything in the middle of the night?

Except that, after several attacks, they should be jumpy and saying things, shouldn't they? And why hadn't they had sentries posted farther out? Or had they . . . and had the sentries hurried back to warn the Bovarian commander?

First company continued forward as Quaeryt held concealment shields over the first ranks of first company. Nearly a quint passed as first company rode slowly up the slope toward the point where the two revetments nearly joined. Quaeryt could see lanterns, or torches, in a few places at the top of the hill, well above the defensive revetments on the slope, but not a glimmer of light from any of the revetments. For a moment he wondered why. Then, recalling his days as a quartermaster, he realized that the de-fenders could see better if their eyes were used to the darkness. It was the same reason as why ships that spread sails at night kept the open decks dark.

Or . . . it's because there aren't very many troopers down there.

He still felt that someone on the Bovarian side should have noticed something . . . or would before long.

"Attackers! On the road!" The words came from the revetment on the south side of the river road.

"Smoke and pepper in the revetments nearest the road. Now!" Quaeryt dropped the concealment shields and raised his own personal shields. "First company to the right!"

He edged the mare forward. While he could not see the smoke, first company was close enough to the earthworks that he could smell a hint of the acridity within instants.

"Column! Charge!" came the order from Meinyt, along with a trumpet call, and the first companies of Fifth Regiment galloped past Quaeryt and first company, with Meinyt joining the charge—but after the first company.

A metallic clanging issued from beyond the crest of the road, near the lanterns or torches that Quaeryt could barely see, given the slope of the road up toward the town beyond.

Half a battalion had ridden past before armsmen with bucklers strapped to their left forearms and blades longer than the Telaryn sabres swarmed toward the road, with some headed toward Quaeryt and the imagers. The first defenders from the revetments launched themselves toward the legs of first company's horses, holding their bucklers up as if to ward off down-cuts from the Telaryn sabres.

For just a moment Quaeryt expanded and extended his shields, knock-ing the Bovarians back. He didn't know what else he could do, not with Fifth Regiment thundering by them and filling the road. He hadn't ex-pected the defenders to ignore the regiments. *But you should have. You're sitting swans.*

"Imagers! First company! Forward with me and Fifth Regiment!" Quaeryt didn't see much point in holding longer. *You just hope this will work.*

He contracted his shields into a wedge extending perhaps a half yard on either side and urged the mare forward, riding past the edge of the revetment and inadvertently throwing several Bovarian defenders back into the trench behind the earthworks. He only could see the trench for an instant—and not much of it at that. But it appeared empty, as if the few handfuls of defenders were all that had held the position. He was past the first revetment too quickly to be sure, but that worried him. There should have been more defenders. Many more. And if the Bovarians had merely withdrawn . . . why would they have left any defenders at all?

Unless the Bovarian commanders didn't tell the poor bastards.

He tried to catch a glimpse of the revetments on the slope to the south side of the river road, but between the darkness and the troopers of Fifth Regiment to his left, he could make out nothing at all. There might have been thousands of Bovarians or none at all.

When, still on the shoulder of the road, he rode past the second revetment, some fifty yards farther uphill, and saw no troopers at all, he could only wonder what trap lay over the crest of the road . . . and what, if anything, he could do about it.

Quaeryt and first company were less than a hundred yards from the top of the rise when he heard the thunder of muskets—one volley, then a second, and a third. No defenders issued from the last line of revetments before the slope flattened out onto level ground.

In the dim light of a few lanterns hung on widely spaced posts and that of Artiema, Quaeryt could see that Meinyt had done exactly what he had said was necessary. He'd thrown his first battalion right at the musketeers— arrayed behind earthworks midway between waist-high and chest-high. The first troopers to actually reach the earthworks had tried to jump them, and some had succeeded. Others had left their mounts, or perhaps their mounts had been shot from under them, and climbed or vaulted over the earthen revetments.

Then the Bovarian heavy cavalry had smashed into Meinyt's right flank. In turn, from what Quaeryt could see, Fifth Regiment's second battalion had hit the Bovarians on the flank and rear, and the Bovarians were being hacked down—but by the sheer numbers of Fifth Regiment, and the two Telaryn battalions were taking heavy casualties in the process.

"Desyrk! Baelthm! Voltyr! Into the middle—just the middle—of the Bovarian armor, smoke and pepper! Hold here and do what you can!"

Quaeryt turned in the saddle, trying to make sense out of the confusion in the dimness, looking from the north end of the hilltop ridge to the south.

Another roll of thunder shook the hilltop, and Quaeryt rocked in his saddle as musket balls slammed into his shields—from the south. He struggled to widen his shields slightly, enough to cover the imagers. A flicker of red-orangish lights appeared some hundred yards away, but before he could say or do more, another volley ran out, and his shields again shivered, sending jolts of pain into his body, or so it seemed.

He turned the mare. "Shaelyt! Threkhyl! After me, behind me!"

How long it took him to get near to the second musket emplacement he couldn't have said. But as he neared it, he could see a dark space between the musketeers and the mare. *A pit moat, for the Namer's sake. Frig!*

"Threkhyl! Image a bridge across this pit moat wide enough for a mount, and stay behind me!"

Quaeryt half wondered if Threkhyl could—and would—do so, and was ready to turn the mare, but just before he started to do so, a flat white stone ramp appeared before Quaeryt, and he urged the mare forward onto the stone, hoping it would hold. The stone didn't even shiver, and the next volley from the musketeers didn't even strike his shields.

Because you're too close?

Abruptly he realized he needed his staff and struggled to get it free of the leathers, barely getting it into position before he was at the end of the stone. He almost flew over the mare's neck, but managed, somehow, to keep his seat as she jumped from the low rampart to which Threkhyl had linked the stone bridge. He came down among the second row of musketeers, staggered, to afford them a clean line of fire. His shields threw one musketeer and his stand to the side before Quaeryt managed to turn the mare back east and start down the line of Bovarians. Several saw him coming and tried to scramble out of the way.

As he had done with the musketeers hidden behind false haystacks, he braced the staff against the front of the saddle and linked the shields to the saddle, trusting the girths held. He could only hope that Threkhyl and Shaelyt could use their sabres effectively, or follow him. He didn't look back. There was no point whatsoever in doing that.

But when he neared the end of the second line of musketeers, he slowed the mare enough to turn her back to where she was just behind the front line. From there he could see that Threkhyl had gone the other way and was applying his sabre to the musketeers he could reach. While some clearly managed to scramble away, the effect was the same, in that by the time Quaeryt neared the far end of the first line he had to ease the mare to the side to avoid plowing into Threkhyl.

"Hold up! They're all gone!"

"So they are!" Threkhyl offered a booming laugh. "Stopped those bastards, we did."

Quaeryt looked around again, but was relieved to see Shaelyt coming up to join them, his sabre also at the ready. Quaeryt looked back to the north, where more Telaryn horsemen poured onto the hilltop, but re-formed almost immediately.

Quaeryt realized that no one was left fighting near him and that most of the sounds issued from wounded men and mounts. He looked back at Threkhyl's bridge, knowing he didn't want to have the mare jump up on it again, but from what he could see, the dry moat completely surrounded what had been the musketeers' position.

"All right," he muttered under his breath, bringing the mare around in a circle to the back of the redoubt, where he heard moans from the moat. He ignored them and urged the mare forward.

The mare had far less a problem with the low jump onto the bridge than did Quaeryt, who found himself, again, slightly off balance, but righted himself in the saddle and then reined her up a good ten yards beyond the dry moat. He looked around, but the only fighting going on was at the north end of the ridge, where Meinyt's Fifth Regiment had surrounded the remaining Bovarian heavy cavalry, and there was little he or the imagers or Fifth Battalion could do.

So Quaeryt waited for the other two imagers, taking a quick breath of relief as Threkhyl and Shaelyt joined him. They continued to wait perhaps half a quint, Quaeryt holding personal shields around all three, hoping he could keep doing so until the fighting was clearly over.

Finally, Ghaelyn and a squad from first company rode toward him. The three imagers with the undercaptain looked unharmed.

Quaeryt could feel some of the tightness within loosen. *Thank the Nameless you didn't lose any more imagers.*

"You all right, sir?" asked Ghaelyn, looking at Quaeryt's shoulder.

Quaeryt glanced down at the dark stain, not that he could tell what color it was in the dimness lit but faintly by Artiema and a few remaining lanterns to the west. He flexed his shoulder. "I'm fine." *You think.* "How about first company?"

"Not near so bad as it looked—"

Before Ghaelyn could say more, a trumpet blared out, followed by a powerful voice—Skarpa's.

"Subcommanders! Report!"

Quaeryt had no idea what to report and looked to Ghaelyn.

"Two dead, five wounded, none seriously."

Only two dead . . . in this mess?

"Fifth Regiment took the worst of it, sir."

Zhelan reined up beside Ghaelyn. "No casualties in second, third, and fourth companies." He offered a crooked smile. "I think the Khellans were almost disappointed."

Quaeryt suspected that Meinyt would be happy to have had the "disappointed" Khellan officers and their men in the position of his first battalion, but said nothing except, "Thank you, Major, Undercaptain."

Then he rode toward where he had heard Skarpa's voice.

As he reined up, he heard Meinyt reporting.

"About eighty dead in First Battalion. No count on the casualties. Thirty dead in Second Battalion." After a pause he added, "Rather not take the lead in going after the others . . . sir."

Quaeryt winced silently at those words. For Meinyt to say that suggested the total of his wounded was even greater than those killed.

"There aren't any others," Skarpa said. "There's no sign of any other Bovarians."

"They just left a company or so of foot, those Namer-cursed musketeers, and two companies of heavy cavalry?"

"It looks that way. While you were finishing them off, I sent a company into Ralaes. The locals we rousted out say everyone else pulled out right after dark."

As Quaeryt looked past Skarpa and back toward the center of the hilltop . . . and the carnage there, Quaeryt could see that, in a sense, all his fears had been realized. The Bovarians had indeed planned—and executed, if not as well as they had hoped—a trap with cavalry and muskets. They'd also effectively sacrificed several companies of their own foot to bait, or at least disguise, the trap.

He wasn't looking forward—at all—toward the battle for Villerive.

As he thought that, he found an ironic smile on his face. *No intelligent officer looks forward to these kinds of battles.*

39

Dawn was already breaking before all the Telaryn companies, battalions, and regiments were re-formed, the wounded tended to, and the comparatively few Bovarian captives confined. Only then did Skarpa, Meinyt, and Quaeryt finally leave the battlefield southeast of Ralaes, but by then Zhelan and several other majors had commandeered the necessary quarters for the Telaryn forces. Even so, it was well past eighth glass on that cloudy Jeudi morning when the commander and two subcommanders met in a corner of the public room of the South River Inn, the largest of the three inns in the once-quiet town.

Skarpa sat down heavily and rubbed his forehead. Under his eyes were dark circles. Meinyt's eyes were bloodshot, possibly from the imagers' smoke and pepper, and his face was generally haggard. Quaeryt doubted that he looked any better.

"We lost nearly two hundred," said Skarpa slowly, "and there might be another fifty that don't make it. They lost more than four hundred, all told. It could have been better. It also could have been much worse."

Quaeryt had to agree, much as he had worried about how things had gone the night before . . . and his own failure to realize that he'd trapped first company. As he considered that, his eyes scanned the public room, a space some eight yards wide and possibly twelve long, with four narrow windows across the front and four high windows across the back. All were open, but the room was still close because, even outside, there wasn't the faintest trace of a breeze.

A round-faced woman with black hair in a bun and narrow-set eyes watched from the archway into the kitchen at the far side of the chamber. Two troopers guarded the front entrance to the public room, and Quaeryt had seen a squad stationed in the courtyard beyond the kitchen, as well as one on the front porch of the inn.

"It would have been if the imagers hadn't taken out that second company of musketeers," averred Meinyt, "the ones across that moat to the south. We'd have lost another hundred or so troopers, maybe more."

"I'm glad we could, but . . " Quaeryt paused. "We should have been nearer the front on the charge."

"You'll go mad if you keep guessing on what you could have done," said Skarpa. "I planned the attack, and you both carried it out. We took the town, and they had more than twice the casualties we did. We've done better, but Namer-few others have done as well as we did last night against an entrenched position."

"Why do you think they sacrificed two companies, maybe more, of musketeers?" asked Quaeryt. "I can see them losing the foot, but heavy cavalry and musketeers?"

"I don't know," replied Skarpa. "They had to know we'd capture at least some of the muskets. So far we've counted over two hundred. You two and your men killed over a hundred musketeers, and we captured some thirty, all wounded."

"What about powder and ball?" demanded Meinyt.

"Half a dozen kegs of powder, and four hundred rounds."

"Someone knew it was a sacrifice," suggested Quaeryt.

"I don't think the foot or the musketeers were told," replied Skarpa. "There were wagons waiting on the west side of the hill. The ones who escaped took them."

"How many wagons?" asked Meinyt skeptically.

"There was one left. The driver must have run off or been killed. The scouts said there were tracks left by five others."

"So their commanders told the poor bastards to hold as long as they could and then to withdraw to the wagons. Just six wagons for close to seven or eight hundred men?" Meinyt snorted.

"The cavalry didn't need wagons," said Skarpa dryly.

"If they'd risk that many muskets, they must have more muskets and musketeers than Bhayar and Deucalon thought," said Meinyt.

"Or someone realized that the musketeers aren't as effective against us during the day," suggested Skarpa.

"They aren't that bright," countered Meinyt.

"They were bright enough to slow us down."

"Deucalon already did that," said Meinyt. "Besides, you already said we'd need to stay here for several days until the northern army gets closer to Villerive."

"The men need a day or so of rest at the least. I sent out patrols early. All the Bovarians have pulled back to Villerive. The defenses there make the earthworks here look like a bowling green. They also have large cata-pults."

At a scraping—or scuffling—sound from across the public room, or perhaps beyond, Quaeryt looked away from Skarpa and toward the kitchen archway. The dark-haired woman no longer stood there.

Then four men appeared, moving quickly, each with a small crossbow aimed toward the three Telaryn officers. All four wore blue-gray Bovarian uniforms.

Quaeryt sprang to his feet, expanding his shields to cover the other two officers, then imaged iron darts into the chests of the attackers. Even so, all four loosed their bolts, all of which slammed into Quaeryt's shields, driving him backward against his chair and the wall. He staggered, then finally managed to catch his balance and stand up.

"What . . . !?" Meinyt glanced from Quaeryt to the four figures on the floor by the archway, then at the two troopers who had sprinted across the room.

Quaeryt contracted his shields and hurried toward the archway.

"Sir?" protested one of the troopers.

Quaeryt ignored the man—as well as the throbbing headache that had arrived with his imaging—and dashed into the kitchen, where two other men held knives at the throats of the black-haired woman and a blond woman scarcely more than a girl.

"Stop right there!"

Quaeryt stopped, imaged the knives out of the hands of the two Bovari-ans, and then imaged them through the men's boots and feet, pinning them to the floor.

The women jumped free, but the older woman shuddered as she looked at Quaeryt.

"Namer's spawn!" swore the taller Bovarian.

"Pharsi bastard!"

No one had time to say anything else before a squad of Telaryn troop-ers burst into the kitchen.

The squad leader glanced to Quaeryt. "Are you all right, sir?"

"I'm fine." *What else can you say?*

"Tie them up!" snapped the squad leader.

Quaeryt waited until the two were restrained before walking toward the taller Bovarian. "How did you get in?"

"Wouldn't you like to know?"

Quaeryt smiled, then image-wrapped a shield around the man's head,

"There's another question," offered Meinyt. "How did they know we'd be here? They had to have been there since sometime last night."

Skarpa laughed. "We've been predictable. All they had to do is ask what we did in any town we've taken. We haven't commandeered houses in the larger towns, and this is the best inn. Where else would we be?"

"So they sent scouts back?"

"Spies. They couldn't have gone in uniform. They probably just left people behind, men who were from the area and posing as deserters who didn't want to get caught by either us or Kharst. People would certainly believe that. They know how brutal Kharst can be. Then those men would pass on the information. Right now, there's not much we can do about it— except check the cellars and closets of every public house we go into first."

"But . . ." Meinyt shook his head. "I suppose they're everywhere."

"I'd be very surprised if they weren't," replied Skarpa. "We'll never know. If we hold this part of Bovaria, and we will, they'll become deserters in truth, and we won't know the difference. Even if we discover some of them, we certainly can't hang them unless they break laws in some other way, because we'll never know if they were truly deserters or truly spies."

Just another aspect of war you hadn't considered. But Quaeryt understood exactly what Skarpa meant. To most people, deserters were those who didn't want to fight or who opposed Kharst. While some might think them cowards, and while desertion was a hanging offense, for Bhayar to have ordered them executed for effectively supporting Telaryn would have seemed cruel and hypocritical. *Besides, most people would likely be wary of them for the rest of their lives.*

He took another swallow of lager, better than most he'd had since leaving Nordruil more than a month before. He thought his headache was easing.

After Skarpa dismissed Quaeryt and Meinyt, Quaeryt put his gear in a small room in the inn, as had Meinyt, in order to leave the larger chambers for majors and company officers to share, and washed and shaved. It was well after ninth glass when he began the four-block-long walk to the smaller Black Pot Inn, where Fifth Battalion and its company officers were based, to meet with Zhelan. He already told the imager undercaptains to be ready to meet with him at second glass in the side courtyard at the South River Inn.

A light misty rain sprinkled down intermittently from light gray clouds, but died away as Quaeryt neared the blocklike two-story inn, with wooden walls stained almost the gray of the clouds. Zhelan was standing and waiting on the side porch, empty of anyone but the major himself. Quaeryt took the sagging wooden steps carefully, because he found himself limping again, a sign that he was more tired than he realized.

"How are you feeling, Subcommander?" Zhelan glanced to the pair of chairs.

Quaeryt needed no reminders and seated himself. So did the major.

"About the same as everyone else, I imagine. Tired and sore." Quaeryt cleared his throat. "A little hoarse, too." After another pause, he went on. "We'll be here for another day, possibly longer. I don't know if word has reached you from other officers, but the morning scouting patrols reported that the Bovarians have pulled back to Villerive, and it's fortified all the way around . . ." From there Quaeryt passed on the rest of the information that Skarpa had divulged about the general disposition of the Bovarian troops and the likelihood that the northern forces might be several days in arriving.

"None of that's exactly a surprise, sir."

"No," replied Quaeryt with a slight laugh.

"Sir . . . might I ask . . . but it seemed that some of the undercaptains are . . . ?"

"Getting more accomplished as imagers? I certainly hope so. We'll need everything that they can do at Villerive and later." *And especially at Variana.*

"Sir . . . it's also been said . . . ah . . . that you . . ."

Quaeryt nodded. "It has been said." He paused. "Imaging is very diffi-cult, and it takes a great amount of strength. By the end of a battle or skir-mish, even at the beginning if an imager tries to do too much, imagers can be very vulnerable. At times, improper imaging can kill an imager." Quae-ryt smiled sardonically. "And yes, I was an imager from the first battles in Tilbor. I've learned a great deal from that, and I'm trying to see that the undercaptains don't make as many mistakes as I did. They'll probably make as many, though; they'll just be different ones."

Quaeryt could still see the hint of a question in Zhelan's expression. "Being an imager is a bit like being an armored heavy cavalryman. You have better weapons and protection, but it takes more strength to use both, and if you're in the wrong place or make the wrong decision, all your weapons and armor may not be enough to help you survive. They may even weigh you down more. That's why it's better that too many people don't know who's an imager and who isn't. Especially since we have so few."

After a moment Zhelan nodded. "I hadn't thought about it that way. Thank you, sir."

"You're more than welcome. Without first company, I doubt any of us would have made it this far."

"You would have, sir."

"Perhaps . . . but the others wouldn't have, and we'll need them more and more."

"I can see that, sir."

"Now . . ." said Quaeryt, "you need to tell me about how the rest of Fifth Battalion is doing, and if there's anything you or they need."

"Yes, sir. We've got maybe a hundred mounts could stand reshoeing . . ."

Quaeryt listened for a good two quints before rising and heading back toward the South River Inn. As he strode back through the warm damp air, he decided that before he started working with the imagers, he needed to make arrangements for one of the farriers attached to either Fifth Regiment or Third Regiment to work on the battalion's mounts, since Fifth Battalion hadn't been assigned a farrier.

That took almost a glass, before he ran down Skarpa's farrier in the stable beside yet another inn, The Overflowing Bowl, and extracted a firm com-mitment from the trooper, officially a senior squad leader, to report to Zhelan first thing on Vendrei morning. As he crossed the courtyard, he saw a brown dog lying on a heap of straw beside the stable door.

"Hello there," he said warmly.

The dog lifted its head slightly, and its tail gave a single thump.

"You're right," replied Quaeryt. "It has been one of those days."

"Careful, sir." A stable boy stepped out of the stable. "He can bite. That's why the chain."

"Thank you." Quaeryt hadn't noticed the chain. He decided against trying to give the dog a pat, mournful as the canine looked.

By the time he neared the South River Inn, it was nearly second glass . . . and he had to retrieve his staff from his room before working with the imagers. The two bells of the afternoon chimed out as he hurried down the steps with his staff in hand. Not only was he later than he would have liked getting back to undercaptains who he expected would be both tired and restless, but he was also late, and he hated that, even if it happened to be by only a few moments.

The five of them were indeed in the east courtyard, beside the roofed porch holding neither stools nor chairs. Quaeryt did not bother with much of an introduction to what he had in mind. "You have all been working to see if you can learn another imaging skill. This afternoon we'll see how well you're coming. I'll be testing your shielding skills."

He took in the resigned expressions and grinned. "I've told you before. You only improve when you're required to do more when you're already tired. That makes this afternoon a perfect time to try to improve."

He gestured toward Shaelyt. "Step forward."

The youngest undercaptain did so.

"I'm going to try to hit you with my staff. It won't be that hard. Try to block the blow with an imaging shield. Ready?"

"Yes, sir."

Quaeryt took the staff in the two-handed grip of a seaman, feinted, and then came forward with the lower end of the staff. He could feel some resistance slowing the staff, but the end struck Shaelyt's thigh. Quaeryt stepped back. "Try to tighten the hooks or whatever image you're using. Ready?"

"Yes, sir."

The second time Shaelyt managed to stop the staff, although Quaeryt thought he could have pushed through if he'd used more strength. "Better. I'm going to use more force this time. Ready?"

Shaelyt nodded.

Quaeryt struck, but from the other side. Shaelyt's shield stopped the staff, but the force knocked him back half a yard, and the Pharsi almost fell. "Much better." Quaeryt lowered his staff. "What happened there is something else you all need to understand. Imaging shields spread the force of a blow across the whole shield. If you're not balanced, you can stop a blow and still end up pushed from your mount and trampled or worse. Still"—Quaeryt nodded to Shaelyt—"you have the idea, and you need to build up your strength."

"How do we do that, sir?" asked Desyrk. "Are we supposed to beat each other bruised?"

"No. You can build up strength by holding the shields as long as you can, then taking a brief rest, and doing it again and again. It's even better if you do it while walking or riding." Quaeryt motioned to Voltyr, ignoring the slight wince. "You're next."

Voltyr's shields were more like unseen soft cheese, slowing but not completely stopping the staff. Desyrk's effort slowed the staff, then collapsed. Baelthm was unable to mount any sort of shield. On the other hand, Threkhyl could block anything—for a few moments—but was so exhausted after three tries by Quaeryt that he was shaking and almost collapsed.

Quaeryt lowered the staff and looked at the ginger-bearded imager. "When you can raise a shield, it will likely stop almost anything, but you can't keep doing what you're doing and have any strength left. I'd like to suggest something else for now. What about creating momentary shields, solid ones—when you see or feel something headed in your direction— but holding them just long enough to block something. Perhaps, if you start that way, you can do it more quickly and more often without exhausting yourself."

Threkhyl frowned, then nodded slowly. "I can do that."

"There's one other thing," offered Quaeryt.

"Yes, sir?" Threkhyl's words were cautious, his eyes wary.

"I'd like to commend you, again, on creating that stone span across the dry moat. You reacted quickly. You made taking out those musketeers much easier and allowed us to do it much more quickly. Subcommander Meinyt said it likely saved a good hundred of his troopers. I thought you ought to know." Quaeryt smiled as warmly as he could.

Surprise flickered in Threkhyl's eyes for an instant before he spoke. "Thank you, sir."

"You did a good job. You should know it." Quaeryt stepped back and surveyed the undercaptains. After his testing, he had the feeling that none of the imagers really understood how shields could and should work, and that even Shaelyt and Voltyr had little more than a vague idea. *And that's your fault, not theirs.*

He cleared his throat. "It's clear that all of you think about shielding in a slightly different way. I'm going to offer some thoughts and observations that I trust will be helpful. The first is going to sound strange, but I'd like you to consider it." He turned to Voltyr. "Undercaptain, can you walk as quickly through waist-deep water as you can out of the water?"

Voltyr looked appropriately surprised. "No, sir."

"Why not?"

"The water gets in the way."

"It's thicker than air, isn't it?"

Voltyr nodded.

"But what if you made the air—somehow—as thick as water? Then wouldn't you have as much trouble walking right here?"

"Well . . . yes . . . I suppose."

"That's another way to look at shielding yourself. You're trying to make a thin skin, if you will, of air thicker, stronger . . . strong enough to stop things like staffs or shafts or quarrels. Each of you may have to find your own way of doing that. For me, I've thought about tiny unseen hooks linking pieces of air together like armor. That may or may not work for you, but you all can see that you can create shields to protect yourselves . . ."

As he finished his talk, Quaeryt saw that Skarpa had been standing on the porch watching. He didn't know how long, but it was clear the commander had seen at least some of the shield instruction and practice.

"Undercaptains." Quaeryt waited until the five were looking at him. "That's all the formal instruction for today. You need to practice for another half glass. After that, you're free until the evening meal. If you leave the inn, you're to go in pairs at least, and with your sabres. I'd also suggest you practice shields as long as you can everywhere you go." He turned and climbed the steps to the porch.

"We should go inside," suggested Skarpa.

Quaeryt followed the commander back to a corner of the empty public room, where the two sat.

Skarpa looked at Quaeryt. "Falossn didn't get that much out of the assassins. That was because they didn't know that much. There are several Bovarian companies that specialize in assassinating enemy commanders. That's why the small crossbows. They infiltrate towns and wait. Their orders were specific. They were ordered to target those who are subcommanders and higher. Preferably higher, much higher." Skarpa shook his head. "Another thing we'll have to keep an eye out for."

"They were after you because you've been more effective?"

"Who knows?" Skarpa smiled sardonically. "Falossn asked if they had other duties . . . such as dealing with those who gave Rex Kharst . . . difficulty. They do . . . but only High Holders."

Quaeryt nodded.

"You don't look that surprised."

"It makes sense. You can't train assassins in a few weeks. They knew what they were doing. It also explains the actions of some of the High Holders we've encountered."

"They would have been effective here, except for you. After what happened this morning, I've been thinking. Then I saw your drill outside." Skarpa gestured in the direction of the east courtyard. "You were working on something like that with your imagers, weren't you?"

"We've just started on that in the last week or so. Right now . . . none of them can do it for long or even with enough strength to protect themselves except briefly. As I mentioned earlier today, doing that takes great strength, not to mention skill. Second, it doesn't always work. If the imager is tired, he can't do it. Second, most imagers can't hold even weak shields. Some can't at all. It's basically a skill that might allow some of them greater personal protection so that they can do what else they need to do."

"If they get stronger, they could protect others . . ."

"Then they become almost useless," said Quaeryt. "If they even can do shielding, they can't do things like image iron darts into musketeers. And their shields are small. If they try a larger shield, it's good only for moments, a faction of a quint at best. If they had been far enough along to raise shields against musket attacks, you'd have lost two or three times as many troopers as you did because they wouldn't have been able to attack the musketeers or image smoke and pepper."

"I still don't see why they can't do both . . ."

"Why don't your troopers carry large iron shields?" asked Quaeryt. "Large shields would certainly protect them . . . wouldn't they?"

Skarpa frowned, then smiled and shook his head. "I think I see." Then he frowned again. "But why teach them that at all?"

"So that they can survive long enough to do what is most useful for you." *Should you hint at more?* "If they can protect even themselves, then they can image smoke, pepper, iron darts. Holding a shield for a quint—and that's something none of them can do yet—would render them useless for the rest of a skirmish or battle. There are reasons why I've kept them close to me or away from the worst of battles, but I cannot be everywhere. I would like to send imagers out with other companies. Without being able to shield themselves, they risk dying—like Akoryt did. And there are too few of them to risk them unnecessarily. I wish we had more." *For more than one reason.*

"You can do that for longer."

Quaeryt nodded. "I have my limits, too. You've seen that."

"I've seen you go beyond them."

"And there I've been most fortunate. Twice, at least, I could have died."

Skarpa grinned. "More like four or five times." The grin faded. "I understand. Try not to risk that much again. I'll talk to Meinyt about it as well." He rose from the table.

"Thank you." Quaeryt stifled a yawn as he stood. It had been a long day, indeed.

"You look like you need some sleep."

"Don't we all?" replied Quaeryt wryly.

Skarpa chuckled, then turned and strode out of the public room.

Quaeryt had thought to go to bed early on Jeudi evening, after supper, and making a final round of the battalion and checking once more with the imager undercaptains and with Zhelan. That didn't happen, because he ended up working out patrol schedules for the town with Meinyt and Skarpa, so that it was after eighth glass when he collapsed on the bed in his room at the South River Inn.

41

Quaeryt jolted awake with sheets of warm rain gusting through the gaps in the inn shutters, plastering his underclothes to his skin. Outside was pitch-dark except for the rolling thunder and an occasional flash of lightning so close that the entire inn seemed to shudder under the force of the storm.

He sat up, then, at the creaking of his door, turned to see it swing open.

Didn't you bar it?

Two thumps followed and, ridiculously, sitting in the doorway was a black rabbit, staring fixedly at Quaeryt. But before he could even stand, a musketeer filled the doorway, leveling a dark musket directly at him. Quaeryt immediately raised full shields, but as the musket ball struck the barrier, ice formed everywhere.

Because of the warm rain?

The cold was so intense that he immediately began to shiver . . . and then the ice that coated everything shattered, and chill rivulets covered Quaeryt. His head felt as though it would burst.

His skin was like ice . . .

. . . and he found himself lying on his back in bed, once more, covered in shards of ice that were melting into his underdrawers and undershirt.

Slowly he sat up in the darkness, his eyes traveling to the door, still barred, to the window, its shutters still fastened, and to the floor, covered, as was the bed, with slivers and shards of clear ice. His breath steamed in the cold air of the small chamber.

He stood, wincing as one bare foot came down on a fragment of ice, and then made his way to the windows, where he opened the shutters and let the moist warm night air flow into the room. Where the breeze from the window met the frigid air of the chamber, droplets of water pattered to the plank floor for several moments as he stood there.

What was that all about?

He'd imaged in his sleep. That was clear enough from the ice shards around the small chamber and the throbbing in his skull. But what did the black rabbit and the musketeer have to do with anything? The dream of the musketeer, that he could understand after having been fired upon so often in recent weeks, but the black rabbit? The idea that black rabbits were a harbinger of doom was strictly a belief of people who lived in the southern parts of Lydar.

They're not even your myths or superstitions.

He pulled off his undershirt and hung it on a wall peg, then bent and brushed the remaining fragments of ice off the bed. After a moment he concentrated on imaging away water droplets. At least that small imaging didn't worsen his headache, although it did leave the sheets chill. But then, warm as the air from outside was, that wasn't exactly a problem.

Finally, he closed the shutters again and lay back down on the bed, hoping he could drop off to sleep again. While he did drift off into an uneasy slumber, he woke slightly before dawn, sore and groggy, but not feeling as tired as he might have. After cleaning up and dressing he made his way down to the public room, where he found Skarpa and Meinyt eating breakfast.

He'd no sooner seated himself than the blond serving girl hurried over with a mug of lager and plate of eggs and half a loaf of dark bread for him.

"Thank you," he said warmly.

"It's nothing, sir," she replied, avoiding his eyes and slipping away.

"You seem to have made an impression," said Skarpa.

"Not necessarily a good one." Quaeryt took a sip of the lager, then a swallow. He said nothing more until he'd had several mouthfuls of the cheese-scrambled eggs and a chunk of the moist dark bread. "What is the plan for today?"

"Have breakfast first," said Skarpa jovially.

"We've taken Ralaes," said Meinyt. "When do we move on to Villerive?"

"We haven't heard," said Skarpa. "I'm expecting dispatches before long. Then, I thought we'd hear something yesterday. The scouts can't find any sign that the Bovarians are venturing beyond their perimeter defenses around Villerive. That tells me that Deucalon is on the move."

"Slowly, as usual." Meinyt snorted. "So it's rest the horses, check and sharpen blades, and wait?"

"You don't think the men and their mounts couldn't use the rest?" countered Skarpa.

"They need it, but Deucalon's likely to demand we do something to sacrifice them so it doesn't cost him—and he'll order it at the last moment."

Quaeryt almost nodded, then realized that, much as he felt the same, he really had no evidence that Deucalon would do that. *Or did he?* The marshal had ordered Third Regiment into the most dangerous fighting in the battles around Ferravyl. But had there been any other reasonable choice? Quaeryt didn't honestly know.

"Deucalon will do what he thinks is necessary," replied Skarpa. "That's true of all marshals, all that are worth anything."

Meinyt nodded, although his mouth looked as if he'd swallowed a spoiled lemon.

Quaeryt decided to concentrate on finishing his meal.

After breakfast and the morning muster of Fifth Battalion, Quaeryt again summoned the imager undercaptains to the east courtyard of the South River Inn. There he worked with them for two glasses, before giving them two glasses to recover, and then worked with them for another glass, until a squad leader summoned him for a meeting with Skarpa.

"You're dismissed," Quaeryt said, "but you're to remain near the inn. We may have orders from the marshal."

"Yes, sir."

Quaeryt ignored the expressions suggesting that none of them were that happy with his restriction. He didn't care. They had far more freedom, better quarters, and better food than the rankers . . . and he didn't want them going off until he knew what Skarpa had planned. "I'll let you know after I meet with the commander."

Skarpa was waiting in a small room off the front hall, a plaque room with a circular table and six chairs, and a sideboard that had likely held mugs and pitchers for local plaque players. The commander gestured to one of the chairs.

"Thank you."

"We'll wait for Meinyt. He won't be long," said Skarpa. "I saw that you were working the imagers hard. How are they coming?"

"They're able to do much more than before. I worry that it won't be enough."

"From the way you looked, I thought as much."

The door opened, and Meinyt entered. "I came as quickly as I could."

"We have some time," said Skarpa dryly as the older subcommander seated himself. "The northern regiments are about ten milles east of Ralaes on the north side of the river. There are only small hamlets between where they are and Villerive."

"So the marshal will need another day or two to establish a position and base from which to mount the attack on Villerive?" asked Meinyt.

"He will inform us in due course."

"Four days, at least," predicted the older subcommander.

"He might surprise us," suggested Skarpa.

"Oh . . . a week, then."

"I doubt that. Lord Bhayar is not likely to be that patient," said Skarpa, looking to Quaeryt. "That is my thought, but you know him better than any of us."

Quaeryt shrugged. "He can be very deliberate, but he gets impatient when there is little reason for delay."

Skarpa nodded. "I'd wager it will be far less than a week. Make sure your men get plenty of rest. There will be little of that after we advance on Villerive." The commander reached into the dispatch case and extracted two envelopes, passing them to Quaeryt. "These arrived with Deucalon's message."

"Thank you." As he took the envelopes, Quaeryt immediately recognized Vaelora's script on one. The other was addressed to "Scholar Quaeryt Rytersyn, Aide to Lord Bhayar" in a hand Quaeryt did not recognize.

"That's all for now." Skarpa glanced around the chamber as he stood. "Very modest for a plaque room. Must not be too many gamblers here." He started for the door.

"Or this is where the modest gamblers meet," replied Quaeryt.

"More likely those who don't gamble well," said Meinyt, following Skarpa.

He's probably right about that, thought Quaeryt.

After leaving Skarpa, Quaeryt returned to the courtyard, where he told the imagers that while they would be at evening mess, they were free to walk the town, but only in pairs. Then he retreated to his room on the second floor of the inn, a space scarcely large enough to hold a bed and a table and chair. He smiled wryly as he closed the door and sat on the narrow straight-backed chair. The narrow space reminded him of the inn at Nacliano, a place whose name momentarily eluded him as he struggled to remember it.

The Tankard . . . that was it. For some reason, that recalled the patroller who'd destroyed the innkeeper's priceless Cloisonyt vase just to prove he could, and that brought a comparison to mind. Was there really any difference between the patroller and Kharst, each destroying things of value to show power? *Aren't there better ways to show power?*

He shook his head, then looked at the two envelopes, deciding to open the mysterious one and save Vaelora's letter until he had dealt with the other—one that was far thicker, as if it contained more than a few sheets of paper. *Who would be addressing me that way and as an aide to Bhayar?* Shaking his head, he used his belt knife to slit the large envelope, finding inside a single sheet of paper—and another envelope, addressed to Governor Quaeryt Rytersyn, Extela, Montagne Province.

The single sheet was thick high quality paper. He began to read.

Scholar Quaeryt—

Upon arriving in Extela, I received the letter from you that awaited me, as well as your summary of the situation facing me as governor. I must state that I was greatly impressed with the scope of your accomplishments in the short length of time in which you served as governor, and I can see why Lord Bhayar would require your abilities in dealing with the Bovarians. Your direct approach, while possibly not practical for governing over an extended period of time, will doubtless make my tenure as governor far more pleasant than it might otherwise have been. I will consider your recommendations most carefully in the months ahead and wish you the very best in your present capacity.

I have also enclosed a letter which arrived shortly after I did and trust it will reach you in good stead.

My felicitations and best wishes for you in the campaign ahead.

At the bottom were a signature and title—Markyl Quintussyn, Governor, Montagne Province, by the grace of Lord Bhayar of Telaryn.

Who is writing you as governor? He realized that it was likely someone from Tilbora, since word might not have reached Tilbor that he'd been replaced. *Straesyr, Nalakyn?* Those were the two most likely. Curious, he immediately slit the enclosed envelope and extracted the sheet within.

Dear Governor Quaeryt:

I trust this missive finds you and your lady well and prosperous.

I find myself writing in search of guidance, for there are none here for whose advice I can ask. All come to a chorister for such . . .

Quaeryt glanced to the bottom of the missive, taking in the signature—"Gauswn Holussyn, Chorister, Scholarium of Tilbora." He smiled faintly, realizing that he'd never known Gauswn's patronymic, then resumed reading.

. . . and my experience in matters other than being an armsman and a junior officer is most limited. Master Scholar Nalakyn has improved the course of studies considerably, but in all other matters he is reluctant to reach decisions. Instead of following his own mind or deferring to the princeps, he inquires about every matter from the least to the greatest with every scholar. Long and lengthy discussions follow. In the end, the scholar princeps decides, but not until many faces are red and flushed. I understand that all the scholars will make their wishes known as to who will be master scholar in another nine months, but matters may be most unruly by then. As a young chorister who is not a scholar, I believe there is little I can or should do, yet for all the efforts you made to save the scholarium, I felt I would be remiss in not informing you.

There is another matter that gnaws at me. Before you departed, you arranged for two young imagers to become student scholars. You drafted rules and procedures for them. At present, those appear to suffice, but Chartyn and Doalak often come to talk to me because the other students and the scholars will have little to do with them, save as necessary in instruction and other scholarium matters and duties. They are good youths, but I have some doubts as to whether either would wish to be a chorister, and their isolation is pushing them away from wishing to be scholars, despite their talents. If you have any suggestions or advice, I would be most grateful.

May the Nameless continue to watch over and protect you.

With a sigh, Quaeryt lowered the letter. He had worried about Nalakyn from the beginning, but there hadn't been many choices open to him . . . and less time. If Bhayar had let him remain in Tilbor as princeps for longer, he could have done something. But then . . . he couldn't do what he was doing now, and that might yield greater results. Yet, what could he tell Gauswn?

Counsel him to be patient? Quaeryt shook his head. Patience would serve Gauswn well personally, but it wouldn't help the Tilboran scholarium.

As for the two young imagers . . . the reactions that they faced were exactly why he wanted to create a place that would be both a school and more for imagers—but that couldn't happen unless and until Bhayar was successful and Bhayar realized that the imagers had been instrumental in that success . . . and both aspects of that were anything but certain at the moment.

Because he'd need to think over a response, he set aside Gauswn's letter and picked up the one from Vaelora, noting that the seal had been lifted and replaced. He shook his head. That didn't surprise him.

My dearest,
We have traveled quickly and today arrived in Tresrives at the third glass of the afternoon. The quarters here are even more deserted than when we were here together . . .

Just from Tresrives . . . not Solis? Quaeryt stopped reading and looked at the date at the bottom of the letter—the twenty-fourth of Juyn, nearly a month? Then he looked at the date on the letter from Governor Markyl—the third of Agostas.

Markyl's letter had taken roughly two weeks less time to reach him from a destination almost twice as far away, even though Vaelora's missive had been sent on the most frequently traveled dispatch route. Why had her correspondence taken so much longer?

The most logical reason was that Vaelora's letter had languished somewhere along the way.

The discrepancy bothered Quaeryt. *Is that just because you'd far rather hear from Vaelora and wanted to know she was doing well?* That was certainly one reason, but her correspondence hadn't been delayed before. *It's probably one of those onetime foul-ups,* he told himself. *Besides, who would care about a personal letter of that nature?* He lifted her letter again, then stopped. He still didn't like the time the letter had taken in reaching him, especially when she had used official dispatch riders. *But who would delay it?* Bhayar might read it, but he certainly wouldn't have held on to it for weeks.

Finally, he continued reading.

> . . . *and they felt deserted. We did not eat away from the mess. Without you, I would not have felt secure, although my dreams have not been disturbed.*

Quaeryt nodded at that intimation that she'd had no more farsight flashes.

> *So much has changed, it seems to me, but as a mere woman, I cannot say whether my feelings are a result of my lack of experience in the wider world or because we are living in a time that foreshadows great change. From the little I have seen, I do believe that those with power are reluctant to relinquish it, and more so when their power derives from another than from their own position or ability. There is none so vindictive as a vengeful assistant who believes one of greater ability has attained position through familial ties, and who will not believe that those in power who have great ability demand more of those with whom they share family than those who are less familiar . . .*

Deucalon, Myskyl? Too many men fit the description of a vengeful assistant, but perhaps another letter would reveal more.

He kept reading through the more cheerful observations about the pleasant weather and her desire to see her brother's wife, and at the end, he realized that she had mentioned no one related to her by name, nor did her letter bear any identification except a single "V" at the bottom, below the words "all my love."

Abruptly he realized that it was almost fifth glass and that the officers' mess was about to begin below in the public room of the inn. He folded up the three letters and slipped them into his personal dispatch case, the one that had accompanied him all the way from Solis, through shipwreck and worse. He could barely fit them in, given Vaelora's other letters and that the case was far from large. He eased the case back into his kit and then hurried from his chamber down the steps to the main level.

42

Vendrei came and went, leaving a cloud-covered sky that promised a down-pour on Samedi, but ended up only offering scattered showers. Quaeryt found a waterproof and took a squad from Major Arion's company and rode west to inspect and study the Bovarian defenses surrounding Villerive. Un-like the other river towns, there were neither swamps, marshes, nor forests blocking the approaches to the city on the south side of the River Aluse. In fact, the southern section of Villerive, located on largely flat and slightly raised ground, did not appear that much larger than Caernyn. It was encir-cled by a recently constructed set of earthworks that extended little more than a mille from one end to the other. Still, an earthen berm nearly two yards high suggested considerable effort, and several score catapults behind it implied the strong possibility of Antiagon Fire. The level ground made the danger from muskets, and possible hidden pits, greater as well. Yet the sheer openness of the approach made Quaeryt question why Kharst had chosen Villerive as a position to hold. When he returned to Ralaes, he and Meinyt discussed the defenses with Skarpa, but none of them had been able to discern what else lay behind that recently constructed berm.

The intermittent rain stopped sometime on Samedi night so that by the time Quaeryt finished breakfast on Solayi and headed to the onetime plaques room in the inn to meet with Skarpa and Meinyt, the clear sky and warmth promised a steamy day.

Meinyt was already in the plaques room. Skarpa was not.

The older subcommander looked to Quaeryt. "Wager we'll attack Vil-lerive tomorrow. The commander looks worried, and that ass-saving bas-tard Deucalon will want things as easy as possible for his troopers."

"So we attack first, and Deucalon holds back. The Bovarians move more reinforcements across the bridge to stop us, and then Deucalon at-tacks?"

"Something like that." Meinyt fingered his chin. "Hope your imagers can do what they've done before."

Quaeryt smiled wryly. "We'll need to do more." *Not that you know exactly what more to do, since the Bovarians have remained holed up behind their earthworks.*

"You will indeed," said Skarpa, closing the door behind himself and motioning to the chairs around the battered dark oak table. "We're to attack tomorrow. Marshal Deucalon has not ordered or suggested a specific plan for us. He has ordered us to make a strong enough push to fully occupy the Bovarians."

Meinyt glanced sideways at Quaeryt, with an "I told you so" look.

"You both have studied the maps and the defenses. Does either of you have any other thoughts? Any concerns?"

Who wouldn't have concerns? Still, there was nothing he could do about them. Quaeryt shook his head.

Meinyt frowned. "They've only got earthworks, so far as I can see."

"You're wondering why they're picking a city that's not walled?" asked Skarpa.

"It had occurred to me, sir."

"When was the last time anyone managed to make an attack more than two hundred milles inside Bovaria? For that matter, are there any walled cities in Telaryn except Ferravyl?"

Quaeryt did not mention that some of the older towns, such as Cloisonyt and Montagne, had vestiges of ancient walls remaining.

"Kharst didn't ever anticipate an attack this far inside Bovaria," said Skarpa. "And you can't build stone walls overnight . . . not even with imagers. Anything else?"

Both subcommanders shook their heads.

"Then we'll proceed as planned, with each regiment and Fifth Battalion assaulting a different stretch of earthworks so that the defenders can't concentrate their forces. I've already sent a dispatch. Deucalon's just a few milles east of us on the other side of the river. We've got courier boats to cross now." Skarpa glanced at Quaeryt. "I imagine there will be space for a few private dispatches."

"Thank you."

"There is one other matter."

Quaeryt caught the twinkle in the commander's eyes. "Yes, sir?"

"I'd appreciate it if you would consider . . ."

". . . conducting services this evening?" finished Quaeryt.

Skarpa nodded.

"I'll do what I can."

"You always do. Still say you're the best chorister I've ever heard."

After leaving Skarpa, Quaeryt returned to his small chamber in the inn, where he quickly read over the letter he had written the night before, especially one section . . .

> After we took Ralaes, we discovered once more the methods by which Rex Kharst enforces control over his High Holders. Commander Skarpa summoned a meeting of senior officers, and as we began, assassins with small crossbows attacked the officers. Through sheer chance . . . none of our commanders or subcommanders were injured, and we captured two of the assassins. We discovered from them that Kharst maintains several companies of such assassins and that one of their duties is to deal with recalcitrant High Holders. While it is clear that any successful ruler must find a way to maintain order and control over High Holders, it would strike me that a quieter and more subtle form of control might be better suited to a ruler, and that perhaps one that incorporated knowledge and persuasion, leaving a quiet but completely effective force as a last resort . . . Those problems, if they should exist at all, are in the future. Before long we will be facing the Bovarian forces at Villerive . . .

He nodded. That would have to do. He added a few sentences of affection and concern, then sealed it and tucked it inside his uniform before heading downstairs. After locating the dispatch orderly, he handed over the letter and a silver, then went to meet with Zhelan.

First he went over the plans for the assault on south Villerive with Zhelan and the company officers, emphasizing the key points in Bovarian to the Khellan majors, then accompanied Zhelan and each officer on an inspection of his company. After that, several glasses later, he returned to the South River Inn and briefed the imager undercaptains, then sent them off to practice another skill that he hoped would prove useful with the earthworks.

Finally, he retired to his chamber to try to come up with yet another homily for the evening services. For a time, he just stood and looked out the window. Finally, he pulled out the small thin book about Rholan and began to page through it, reading phrases and sections until one section finally caught his attention and interest.

> The problem with justice is that it is always defined with regard to who offers the definition. Rholan avoided this problem simply by refusing to address it and by defining it as what men and women should do. The definition of justice by a High Holder, however, is

likely to differ greatly from what a grower or a peasant regards as justice. A peasant regards it as just that he and his family have enough to eat; the High Holder insists that it is just that sustenance be grown or paid for by those who consume it, while the factor feels that it is only just that he retain a portion of whatever food is traded because he facilitated the exchange. Yet is it just that a man and his family starve because of flood or drought? Is it just that all the effort a High Holder puts into maintaining order and providing seed and storage go for naught because others are hungry? What portion of a harvest is a just portion for a factor to take in return for finding a buyer where the grower cannot? Those scholars who study the exchange of goods claim that justice can only be found in what terms a fair seller and a fair buyer agree upon. But in a time of famine, those who have golds will have food, and those who do not will starve. Is that justice? In a time of war, those who have blades and the skill to wield them best will have golds and food. Is that justice? Yet without the order provided by those with arms, all will suffer, and there will certainly be no justice.

So far as I know, Rholan seldom, if ever, addressed such a question, except in generalities, and with humor, and that may be why he will be remembered, and why I have chosen to remain, if you will, nameless.

Quaeryt couldn't help but ask, *Who was the writer who knew and understood Rholan so well?* So far as he could tell, the book didn't offer any clues, not in all the times he'd read it and leafed through the pages. Even at the end of all the text, in the lower left-hand corner of the page there was only a jumble of letters, "T(N)of D." Had that meant, "The End" or did it signify something else?

Nor was justice an apt subject for troopers about to attack a town, where, as Rholan had said, the only "justice" was provided by the edge of a sabre.

He finally came to yet another section that offered a certain . . . possibility.

Rholan traveled much, although his journeys were seldom that long, and most, if not all, of his travels remained within Tela. He often commented, both in conversation and in his public utterances, upon roads, using them both factually and metaphorically.

Upon one occasion at table he observed that all too many wide and smooth roads leading from towns or holdings soon deteriorated into the meanest of ways once the traveler was beyond the eyeshot of those in power. As he so often did, however, he reversed that observation by declaring that a traveler need be most cautious when the meanest of ways turned within a few hundred yards to a splendid road. That proclaimed more clearly than anything that those in power were self-centered and egotistical because only the road they could see mattered to them, and not the roads they could not see and would never travel.

Quaeryt closed the book and sat down at the small table, trying to turn what he read into a semblance of a homily. Two glasses later, he was still struggling, but he finally had something workable, if not ideal, just before he had to join the other officers in the public room.

That evening, after dinner, at slightly before half past sixth glass, Quaeryt approached the door in the South River Inn leading out onto the courtyard porch.

Skarpa stood beside the door, with a slight smile on his face. "Both courtyards are filled. I hope your voice is in good fettle."

"So do I." That meant image-projecting his voice, but that wasn't tiring, and he would have a night's sleep before they advanced on Villerive.

He stepped out onto the porch, and the conversations died away. He let the silence draw out for a bit, then image-projected his voice. "We gather together in the spirit of the Nameless and to affirm the quest for goodness and mercy in all that we do."

Then came the opening hymn, again the only one he knew by heart— "Glory to the Nameless"—followed by the confession beginning with, "We name not You, for naming presumes, and we presume not upon the Creator of all that was, is, and will be . . ."

As always the confessional words that followed were difficult for Quaeryt, but he did lead the response that followed, "In peace and harmony."

He waited for a long moment, and then spoke. "Good evening, and all evenings are good evenings under the Nameless, but we say that so often that, for many, it is like saying a day is a day, an evening an evening, and all roads lead somewhere. When I thought that, I wondered what Rholan had thought about roads, since he walked and rode many in his time. Then I recalled what he had said. He claimed that whether a road was good or not so good depended on how you looked at it. Were you considering where a road stopped as its end or its beginning? Now . . . if we're walking a road, and it stops, we think we've come to the end. But what of the man who steps out of the woods and sees where we thought the road ended? He sees it as a beginning. In that way, whether a road is an end or a beginning depends on where you're going. That's true of every man here.

"Before long, we will be heading west, toward Villerive and then toward Nordeau and Variana. If we are to be successful, we must consider the road we travel, the road we must fight to travel, as a beginning, and not as an end. It must be the beginning of a better time for all of Lydar . . .

"Why do I say this? Some of you may know that Rex Kharst sent out his own men to burn the crops of his own holders for fear that we might benefit from them. His own holders, and his men burned crops we could not have used. Some others of you may know that he has sent assassins with crossbows to kill our officers, but these assassins were not trained to kill Telaryn officers. They were trained to kill anyone in Bovaria—not in Telaryn, but Bovaria—from High Holders to important factors who uttered a word against the rex. Rex Kharst does not have a few assassins; he has companies of them.

"We did not start to travel this road. In order to attack us, Rex Kharst sent his troopers down the very road we travel in the opposite direction. If we do not travel this road all the way to Variana, and beyond, then you, and your children, and your children's children will live in fear that, at some time, another rex will burn your crops and worse. For as Rholan said many years ago, a road is measured by its quality and the goodness of not only those who create it, but those who must travel it . . . and we are traveling it to return goodness to Lydar . . ."

As he went on to finish the service, Quaeryt realized that he had twisted Rholan's words, although, from what he'd read of the Unnamer, he doubted that Rholan would have found too much fault.

Still . . . it bothered him, for all of Skarpa's nod when Quaeryt spoke the last words of his final words that followed the closing hymn.

"As we have come together to seek meaning and renewal, let us go forth this evening renewed in hope and in harmony with that which was, is, and ever shall be."

43

When the sun cleared the eastern horizon on Lundi morning, Quaeryt and Fifth Battalion were riding westward on a narrow lane that circled a series of fields and would turn northward, less than a mille ahead, back toward the river and the western end of the earthworks around the southern part of Villerive. Because Fifth Battalion had the farthest to travel, Quaeryt and first company had been the first to leave Ralaes, shortly after daybreak.

Quaeryt studied the fields to his right, most holding some sort of bean plants that were near harvesting and stood waist-high. He would have preferred maize, because the taller plants would have concealed their movements, but then he doubted that his force would have gained much advantage from not being seen until later. The Bovarians had to know they were coming.

"Have the scouts reported anything more about where the defenders might be located?" asked Zhelan. "Or any areas where there might be fewer?"

"All they have reported is that the Bovarians have enough archers to keep them from getting too close to the earthworks. They could discover no pits or traps beyond two hundred yards, and there appeared to be few or none between one and two hundred yards."

Zhelan glanced back at the undercaptains, then looked straight ahead. "In how many places will the imagers be able to weaken the defenses?"

"Three, at least."

Although Skarpa was in favor of what Quaeryt would have called a measured and inexorable attack on Villerive, he had suggested that Meinyt and Quaeryt proceed as their men, their opposition, and circumstance allowed. Quaeryt intended to use imaging to change those circumstances.

He studied the lane ahead, where it curved northward toward the western end of the earthworks, and the fields of more beans that ran almost to the hurriedly built revetments. With the haze hanging over the fields and the woods farther east, Quaeryt couldn't even feel the heat of the sun on his back.

He turned in the saddle as Threkhyl eased his mount forward.

"Sir . . . a question, if you would?"

"Go ahead."

"You don't care how we do this, sir?" asked Threkhyl. "In dealing with the earthworks? So long as we flatten them?"

"Whatever takes the least effort for you," replied Quaeryt, his thoughts more on what lay behind the earthworks. "That way, you can open a wider gap. That will leave less cover for the defenders and more space for the troopers."

"Yes, sir. I think we can do the same thing if we image the earth back, especially if they have trenches behind."

"You can try it, but it's got to be low enough for the troopers to go through without being slowed."

"Yes, sir. We can do that." Threkhyl let his mount drop back.

Another quint passed, and Fifth Battalion left the narrow way that had already dwindled to little more than a path and began to form up some 250 yards away from the earthworks, companies abreast with a five-man front. The area Quaeryt had picked was located just before the earthworks turned sharply north toward the low bluff that marked the edge of the river. The section of earthworks that ran north was less than fifty yards long, while the target area for Fifth Battalion ran roughly from east-southeast to west-northwest, so that the troopers would not be attacking into the morning sun. The earthworks before Quaeryt showed only two catapults rising above the defenses, not that there might not be smaller ones as well. He could see a few defenders here and there, but try as he might, he could make out no sign of muskets, or any sort of variation in the front of the earthworks that might conceal musketeers.

He heard bells or chimes clanging and thought he saw a few heads bobbing behind the earthworks, suggesting that the far side of the revetments were likely stepped, so that the defenders had some height, with trenches behind the space for supplies and others manning the earthen walls.

Zhelan and Quaeryt had decided on literally walking the mounts toward the earthworks, at least until the defenders reacted, whether with volleys by archers or a musket barrage or an attack from behind the earthworks. The longer the battalion could maintain a slow approach, the more likely the troopers could avoid stakes and hidden ditches or other pitfalls. That also meant that the imagers could get closer before having to image, and that would save their strength.

Of course, the Bovarians could put an immediate stop to that by attacking first.

"Sir . . . look at the bean plants," said Zhelan.

Quaeryt looked, but all he saw was greenery. "What should I be see-ing?"

"Some of them are like beans should be. Others are sagging and wilt-ing."

Frig! You should have seen that. "That's where there are pits and they've tried to conceal them with nets and plants?"

"I can't be certain, sir, but I'd wager a gold on it."

"I won't take that wager. You'd better pass that to the company offi-cers now. We can wait until you do."

Another half quint passed before a squad leader returned. "All compa-nies informed, sirs!"

"Fifth Battalion! Forward! Measured pace!"

As the companies moved forward, heads popped up from behind the revetments, but no defenders left the cover of the earthworks. Not until Quaeryt's troopers were about a hundred yards away did the first volley of arrows arch out over the earthworks and sleet down toward the battalion.

Quaeryt briefly extended an angled shield that diverted the first fall of arrows into the plants before the advancing battalion. "Imagers! Smoke and pepper! Now!"

As the haze of acrid smoke and pepper covered the rear side of the earthworks, he watched to see if the undercaptains had followed their briefing, and so far as he could tell, the smoke and pepper blanketed the two-hundred-yard stretch that was Fifth Battalion's target.

"Imagers! Breach the earthworks! Now!" Quaeryt did not immedi-ately attempt to personally image gaps in the earthworks before Fifth Bat-talion, although he was ready to do so, if necessary.

His mouth opened. Directly before Fifth Battalion was a break in the defenses close to fifty yards wide. Moreover, the area behind it was flat, as if the defenses had been leveled and used to fill any trenches behind the walls. Two smaller breaches, slightly over ten yards wide and some fifty yards on either side from the main breach, had also appeared.

"Second company! Into the center breach!" ordered Zhelan.

Major Calkoran repeated the order in Pharsi, and second company swept toward the opening in the earthworks in a curved path around a stand of wilted beans. Even so, one rider and his mount went down.

"Third company! The right breach! Fourth company! The left breach!" commanded Zhelan.

"First company! On me!" ordered Quaeryt, keeping the mare moving at a fast walk while trying to study the charging companies and the defenders.

Not a single defender even appeared in the open space where the center breach was until the riders were within a handful of yards of the openings.

The movement of one of the catapults caught Quaeryt's eye, and he tried what he'd suggested to Threkhyl—a quick shield in front of the basket being swung forward.

Fire—Antiagon Fire—flared up and around the basket, then cascaded down into the trench holding the catapult.

A few yells and screams pierced the morning, then died away.

Quaeryt kept riding, looking at the second catapult, then toward the cleared spaces in the earthworks ahead, and back to the catapult.

Around the middle breach, from both sides, scores of defenders rushed forward, a few handfuls with pikes or long spears. Most could not set their pikes firmly before the Khellans were upon them, at least in part because the gap in the earthworks was so wide.

The second catapult moved—or Quaeryt thought it did—and he realized he didn't have time to keep watching it. So he imaged away one of the main timber supports and watched a moment longer, to make sure the frame sagged. He just hoped there weren't too many catapults with Antiagon Fire on the east side of Villerive, where Skarpa and Meinyt were attacking. *You can only do so much.*

He shifted his attention to the other two breaches, where a number of defenders were already trying to fill the gap. *Why so few defenders in the middle?* He didn't have an answer, or time to worry about that, but guided first company behind second company, since it appeared that the wider breach would offer less opposition. He wanted to keep the imagers clear of hand-to-hand fighting as long as possible in order to use them as necessary to reach the bridge over the River Aluse.

Thinking about hand-to-hand combat, he belatedly eased his staff from the leathers and continued riding forward. Second company had pushed back the defenders, many of whom had thrown down arms and were running toward the houses to the north of the earthworks. Another group of defenders had formed into a circle with pikes pointing out.

Should you use your shields to break the pikes? Guiding the mare to the right slightly, in the direction of the pikemen, Quaeryt glanced down as he rode through the wide breach in the earthworks, catching sight of the soles of a pair of boots, and then the backside of a figure in blue-gray. He swallowed, fully understanding what Threkhyl had meant by his question earlier. The ginger-bearded imager—and likely the others—had "simply" flattened the earthworks back into the trenches behind the raised clay and dirt, and that imaging had instantly buried any and all defenders standing on the stepped rear surface of the earthworks or in the trenches below.

No wonder there weren't any defenders left standing behind the gaps.

At that moment Quaeryt heard the rumble of hoofs, and a company or more of horsemen charged along a narrow road from Villerive toward Calkoran's troopers. The old major clearly expected something like that, because second company had already re-formed and rode toward the defenders.

Quaeryt didn't want to see second company forced back into the pikemen.

"First company! On me!" He urged the mare forward, keeping his personal shields close to him and his mount—until the last moment before they reached the sharpened ends of the pikes, when he spread them like a wedge as he plunged into the tightly packed mass of men, linking the shields to the nearest first company mounts as well.

Weapons and pikemen sprayed everywhere, and Quaeryt immediately shrank and unlinked his shields, trying to save his imaging strength as much as possible. Behind him, Ghaelyn's men began to cut down the defenders. Before him, defenders on the far side of the roughly circular formation dropped their pikes and ran, unable to turn the long and unwieldy weapons in time to face a charge from the rear.

Quaeryt turned gradually, leading first company toward the mounted forces of the defenders, only to find that few of them remained, as second company had been joined by third and fourth companies, and all three were riding toward the town along the road that appeared to lead to the bridge over the River Aluse.

As he led first company after the three companies, letting the Khellans take the lead, from what Quaeryt could see, the streets and sidewalks of the town were empty, the windows largely shuttered, and not even a stray dog ran into or out of the narrow alleyways. He eased back his cap and blotted his forehead and his temples to keep the sweat from running into his eyes, aware once more of just how hot and damp Villerive was in midharvest.

Should we attack the defenders to the east from the rear? Or try to take the bridge? The first made more immediate sense . . . except that if the Bovarians rushed reinforcements from the north, he'd rather fight them in the narrow confines coming off the bridge than chance having them evade Fifth Battalion and join the defenders. Failing to stop forces coming from the bridge would only increase the number of defenders arrayed against Skarpa and Meinyt.

He kept riding, glancing to one side and the other as well as ahead, where the remnants of the Bovarian cavalry fled the Khellans, making for the bridge that was less than a half mille away.

Quaeryt glanced toward the bridge over the River Aluse. The road they had followed had turned and angled into the main avenue that, in turn, ran straight into the bridge approachway. At a point just beyond the end of the approach and the beginning of the bridge proper, there was a stone wall three yards in height. Two heavy iron-bound gates, now open, afforded the only break in that gray stone barrier.

The fleeing Bovarians, both those mounted and those on foot, sprinted toward the gates, clearly hoping to get behind them and close them, in order to deny the Telaryn forces access to the bridge and the main part of Villerive.

You need to get to them before they can close the gates and escape—and block you from being able to reinforce the Telaryn forces when they attack.

Calkoran understood that, because the Khellans pressed their mounts up the approach to the bridge, cutting down Bovarian stragglers . . . but the gates were beginning to close as the Bovarians on the bridge obviously decided to leave the last of the fleeing defenders to the Khellan blades.

Quaeryt turned. "Voltyr! Image something to break the gates or keep them from closing!"

"Yes, sir!"

For a long moment the gates continued to close. Then, the gate on the right sagged and crashed forward onto the paving stones of the approach.

The Bovarians behind the gates abandoned their efforts to close the gates and tried to flee, but the Khellans were through the gates in moments, their blades flashing.

Quaeryt signaled first company to a halt. Adding another company to the melee on an already narrow bridge wouldn't help matters. He watched in not quite dispassionate awe as the Khellans destroyed the few handfuls of Bovarians remaining. While a Khellan occasionally fell, that was seldom indeed, Quaeryt could see.

After the last of the Bovarians went down under the Khellan sabres, or jumped or dived off the side of the bridge into the dark waters below, the three companies re-formed, one—fourth company, Quaeryt could tell—remaining beyond the gate. Major Calkoran led the other two back through the gates and toward Quaeryt.

"Sir?" asked the older major.

"Hold the approach to the bridge against any Bovarians."

"Yes, sir."

"First company! Hold here!" Quaeryt rode back toward the gates and through them along the east side of the bridge, wide enough for three wagons abreast, with an iron railing about a yard and a half high on each side. As he passed Major Arion, Quaeryt glanced to the other side of the bridge, taking in the second set of iron gates there, gates that were now closed.

Yet, in the distance, both in front of him and behind him to the southeast, Quaeryt heard horns and bells, both imbued with a frantic urgency, and that spoke to Skarpa's success—and that the Bovarian defenders were calling for reinforcements.

Quaeryt looked back, but saw—besides first, second, and third companies—no other riders or troopers on the approachway or the main avenue to the south. Fifth Battalion was alone. When he looked to the north end of the bridge, he saw that the gates there, gates that had been closed, were now opening.

You had to have Voltyr destroy the gate on this end. Idiot! Unfortunately, what was done was done.

Even through that narrow, if widening aperture, he could see hundreds, if not thousands, of armed Bovarians lined up as far as his eyes could see, ready to storm across the bridge. Quaeryt had no idea where Skarpa and Meinyt were, but he doubted, fierce as the Khellans were, and comparatively narrow as the bridge was, that less than four hundred troopers could hold off thousands, not without severe losses, and not for that long.

"Imagers! On me!" Except he didn't have time to wait on them.

He rode forward until he was less than fifty yards from the oncoming Bovarian foot, led, of course, by three rows of pikes. There, he reined up and concentrated on linking to the river below—there had to be warmth there, after such a long hot summer and harvest! He also concentrated on linking and drawing from the advancing mass of blue-gray clad Bovarian soldiers, all of them.

Then he pictured a stone wall to the north of the one holding the gates that had just opened to the flood of Bovarian troopers, a solid gray stone wall at the edge of the bluff to the west of the bridge, across the bridge and then at the edge of the east bluff.

A blinding flash of light seared across him, followed by a chill that cut through his body like a thousand knives. Then came thunder, and hail that slammed into his body, no longer protected by his personal shields,

shields that had somehow vanished. His muscles felt like watery jelly, yet he could see, surprisingly, if barely, through a splitting headache and searing flashes of light that stabbed into his eyes like daggers.

When he could finally straighten up, hail and ice flowed off him and his uniform and down off the mare's coat. The roadway of the bridge was also white with ice and hail. Slowly, he looked toward the north end of the bridge.

Beginning less than twenty yards from him, at least two hundred ice-covered troopers lay scattered and frozen on the bridge between him and the open gates. Beyond the gates were more ice-covered bodies, frozen where they stood, wedged and welded together in ice. Farther to the north was a featureless gray stone wall running along the river bluff and across the point where the approach ended and the bridge proper began. Quaeryt wondered yet how many more ice-covered bodies lay sprawled beyond the wall he had imaged.

Then he shook his head—and was rewarded with an even more intense flash of pain, so much so that he couldn't see for a moment. He turned in the saddle . . . slowly. "Arion! Get your men to that gate, and get it closed." He looked at Shaelyt and Voltyr who were riding slowly toward him. "You two need to image beams and bars in place on this side once they get those gates there closed. Follow Arion's men!"

"Yes, sir."

Quaeryt just watched, squinting and massaging his forehead with one hand, while the fourth company rankers moved bodies and forced the gates shut and while the two imagers created brackets and beams to keep them shut.

Then he turned to Arion, whose eyes remained wide. "Major?"

"Yes, sir?"

"You and your men are to make sure that no one gets past those gates."

"Yes, sir." Although Arion's voice was firm, his eyes flicked to the bodies and the walls.

"Once the bodies aren't frozen, you'll need to have them cleared from the bridge." Quaeryt paused. "I'd appreciate it if they weren't thrown in the river. Thank you."

Arion nodded.

Slowly, Quaeryt rode back across the bridge, followed by Shaelyt and Voltyr. When he reached first company, he saw that Threkhyl was in the saddle, but pale as ice, as were Desyrk and Baelthm.

"All imagers . . . please eat and drink something." After a moment he reached for his own water bottle and began to sip the watered lager, hoping that his guts would settle down. He doubted he would even have been in the saddle if he hadn't had the presence of mind to link his imaging to the warmth of the river.

Almost a glass passed before riders appeared coming from the south on the main avenue to the bridge. They wore the green of Telaryn.

Quaeryt continued to wait, slowly eating the hard biscuits he'd taken from the inn that morning.

In time, Skarpa rode forward and reined up. "Even from here I can see there's another wall on the north side of the bridge, and ice formed around the bridge piers . . . and probably on the river earlier." Skarpa's voice was half sardonic and half dry.

"There was some ice," Quaeryt admitted.

"Why the wall?"

"Fifth Battalion wasn't ready to face two regiments or more of Bovarians." Quaeryt paused. "I suppose there are fewer than that now."

"They're frozen?" Skarpa's voice held little surprise.

Quaeryt nodded.

Skarpa glanced beyond Quaeryt to where fourth company rankers were piling corpses on a wagon that they'd found somewhere. "Two regiments less, I'd wager . . . or close enough. The marshal won't be pleased, especially since the bridge is blocked."

"When Threkhyl and the other imagers have recovered and the northern army holds Villerive, the imagers can create an opening in the wall."

Skarpa chuckled.

"You hold all the southern part now?" asked Quaeryt.

"After you cut through the west part, the Bovarians lost heart. They didn't expect you to just wipe out chunks of their earthworks and ride through them. Or to take out their catapults and spill their own Antiagon Fire on them. We tried to avoid the catapults, but we lost a good hundred troopers to the fire . . ."

Catapults . . . there was something about catapults, but Quaeryt couldn't think of what it might be.

". . . The Bovarians also didn't expect you to wipe out so many defenders so quickly. Or turn their reinforcements into icy corpses. You keep this up, Subcommander, and . . ." Skarpa shook his head.

"What?"

"No matter what they've said about Kharst, before long, they'll fear Bhayar more than they ever did their rex."

"I don't see why. Over the years he's slaughtered more than we ever could."

"The numbers of dead matter less than the manner of their death."

Quaeryt was all too afraid that Skarpa was right. Yet, again, what else could he and the imagers have done?

"I'll be sending a boat with a courier to the marshal informing him that we hold the south side and the bridge."

"Do you think the Bovarians will withdraw now?" asked Quaeryt.

"Do you?"

Quaeryt shook his head. "Not from what we've learned about Kharst."

"I don't think so, either. I need to get that courier off. I'll leave it to you and Fifth Battalion to hold the bridge for now. Third and Fifth Regiments will finish up with the defenders and take positions just south of the bridge."

"Yes, sir."

Skarpa turned and rode off the bridge, his mount's hooves clicking dully on the gray paving stones.

Quaeryt looked back to the north. The ice had vanished. Most of the bodies remained.

44

More than two glasses had passed, and Quaeryt had moved the undercaptains—and himself—to the Bluff Point, an old inn just west of the approach to the bridge—where he'd made sure that everyone was fed and resting. At close to the second glass of the afternoon, the supply wagons arrived, with gear. Shortly afterward, Skarpa returned, and he and Quaeryt met in the plaque room of the inn. Quaeryt had decided that the closer they came to Variana, the more likely inns were to have plaque rooms, although the innkeeper couldn't tell him why.

"Have the Bovarians tried to climb that wall you put up?" asked Skarpa.

"Arion reported that one or two looked over, but no one has tried to climb it or reclaim the bodies." Quaeryt took a deep breath, then used his right hand to massage his forehead, trying to ease the pain and pressure there. Even the creaking of the old stairs outside the room seemed to worsen the headache. "When it gets later in the day, we'll unbar the old gate at that end and pull out the bodies. We'll need to do that before we're ready to do whatever the marshal wants."

"He wants us to attack this afternoon. Then he'll move against the city."

Quaeryt laughed, roughly and not humorously, but broke it off as light knives flashed across his vision. "He'll have to wait until tomorrow if he wants any imaging. Two glasses ago, I had two imagers who couldn't see, one who kept puking his guts out and the other three of us who couldn't have imaged a false copper right now."

"And now?" asked Skarpa.

"I have five imagers who might manage a false copper and one who might be able to image a single silver." Quaeryt took another swallow of the too-bitter lager from the mug he'd brought with him, hoping that would help him regain some strength.

"He won't like hearing that."

"I'm sure he won't. How many regiments did the Bovarians have here on the south side? Not on the bridge. On the south side?"

"The Bovarian officers who survived claim they had four regiments. I'd say three and a half at most. We've got half a regiment in captives, mostly wounded, and maybe another five or six hundred escaped." Skarpa paused. "I know where you're going. We've taken out another four and a half regiments, and lost almost a battalion in casualties. The marshal won't see it that way. He wants to hit them now."

"After dawdling up the river for a month?" Quaeryt shook his head. "I won't send Fifth Battalion into battle without imagers, not when we're not threatened."

Skarpa smiled wryly. "I guess I'd better wait a while and then send a message saying that because the effort of destroying two regiments left the imagers unconscious or otherwise incapacitated, you moved them to safety, and it took a while to determine the status of Fifth Battalion and the regiments. By then, hopefully, he'll decide on an attack tomorrow."

"Your way is better," said Quaeryt. "Maybe I'm just too tired to be tactful."

"He'll know what we think," replied Skarpa. "This way he just won't be able to prove it. He'll be just as unhappy."

"His men weren't the ones dying."

"No . . . but he's lost more troopers than we have. More than two regiments worth in dead and wounded. That's what I heard from the dispatch couriers."

Quaeryt frowned. "There are more and larger towns on the north side of the river. That's why he needed a bigger force."

"He's losing a greater proportion than we are. That's because . . . he says . . . he doesn't have Fifth Battalion."

"He didn't want us. Even without Fifth Battalion, you wouldn't be losing as great a proportion as he is."

"Doesn't matter." Skarpa sighed. "He thinks if a trooper can move, he can fight. He doesn't understand. Not sure I would if I hadn't seen what happened to you."

"Tell him imagers are like blades. When they're pushed too hard, they break. Rest can reforge them. Trying to make them fight when they're broken destroys them beyond hope of reforging." Quaeryt massaged his forehead again.

"He might understand that."

Quaeryt saw Skarpa had his doubts. "They're like muskets when the powder's gone."

"I'll think of something." Skarpa paused. "Where are they?"

"Sleeping . . . or lying on a bed so tired they can't move."

"Your head is pounding, and you have trouble seeing, don't you?"

"Something like that," Quaeryt admitted.

"Might not be a bad idea if you turned things over to Zhelan and got some sleep."

"I mostly have, but I thought I'd better wait to see what you had to say."

"You've heard. Go get some rest." Skarpa stood.

So did Quaeryt, not quite so quickly or vigorously.

45

Quaeryt slept for two glasses Lundi afternoon, woke and checked with Zhelan, made certain all the battalion was quartered and fed, ate what he could, and went back to his chamber and collapsed. He woke before dawn on Mardi morning, with only a trace of a headache and clear vision. Relieved at discovering that, he hurried into his uniform and went to find Zhelan.

He did not have far to go, since the major was standing in the doorway between the narrow public room and the kitchen.

Zhelan turned. "Good morning, sir."

"Have the Bovarians tried anything with the bridge or the wall?"

"No, sir. I had squads on the bridge last night and companies on standby just in case—two glasses for each one. That was so all the men would get at least six glasses of sleep. In case they had to fight today."

"Good. I appreciate your taking care of that. I wasn't thinking too clearly last night."

"Sir . . . what you and the undercaptains do keeps men from getting killed. By now, they all understand that. They also know that imagers can be killed just as they can."

That might be the only good thing about poor Akoryt's death. Quaeryt nodded. "Is the kitchen here feeding the troopers?"

"I took the liberty of getting that done early, sir. Some of our cooks are working with the inn's cook. We've got the first two companies fed, and the others will be getting fed in a quint. They have to eat in the courtyard, but for hot food they don't mind, so long as it's not raining."

Once more, Quaeryt was more than grateful for Zhelan's competence and experience. "That was a good thought. I have the feeling we may have to move over the bridge and into north Villerive fairly soon."

"I had thought so. The sentries heard horns and chimes late in the day yesterday. Someone was attacking someone on the other side of the river. Have you heard, sir?"

"Not yet. The marshal wanted us to use the bridge to attack the

Bovarians yesterday afternoon. I told Commander Skarpa that if the marshal wanted our forces to attack, it would be without Fifth Battalion."

"Sir?"

"You and the troopers protect the imagers. The imagers have done their best to protect the troopers. Not a single imager was capable of even imaging smoke after we took the bridge. I would not hazard Fifth Battalion without the support of the imagers."

"You told . . ."

"I told Commander Skarpa. I believe he found a way to convey that in more appropriate terms."

"That is a battle I could not have fought, sir."

"Isn't that what subcommanders are for, Major?" Quaeryt smiled wryly.

"Better you than me, sir."

"And better you than me in handling many other things, for both of us, I suspect."

"Yes, sir." Zhelan smiled. "Now that you're here, we could feed the officers."

"You didn't have to wait . . .'

"It wouldn't have been ready sooner. The imagers . . . I did send a squad leader . . ."

"Good."

In less than a fraction of a quint, the company officers and the imager undercaptains were seated in the public room and eating.

Quaeryt was halfway through the overcooked cheesed eggs and chopped mutton on the slightly chipped brown crockery platter when a squad leader hurried into the public room. He looked around, then headed for Quaeryt. "Sir . . . Commander Skarpa and Subcommander Meinyt . . . will be here shortly. Their regiments are also on the way. The commander wants to meet here with you and Subcommander Meinyt."

"How soon will they arrive?"

"Less than half a quint, sir."

"I'll be ready."

As the squad leader hurried off, Zhelan looked across the table at Quaeryt. "I'd best get the companies formed up."

Less than the half quint the squad leader had promised passed before Skarpa marched into the inn, followed by Meinyt. Quaeryt said nothing, just gestured to the open door, and followed the other two officers inside, closing the door behind himself.

Skarpa turned. He did not take one of the chairs around the polished but battered dark oak table. "The Bovarians tried to break out last night. It was bloody. They lost close to two thousand men. Deucalon lost a thousand. He's furious."

"How can you tell?" asked Meinyt. "He's always angry about something."

"Because of the way he wrote his latest dispatch. He wanted to know if I would inform him when Fifth Battalion and Third and Fifth Regiments deigned to resume fighting."

Quaeryt winced. "We couldn't have done any more yesterday."

"How about today?"

"Not as much as yesterday . . . but the undercaptains can fight now. Some of them could barely even ride at the end of the fighting yesterday."

"You weren't much better," noted Skarpa. "I didn't put that in the dispatch."

"What do you want us to do?" asked Quaeryt.

"Fifth Regiment is mustering on the bridge approach, ready to attack. They took fewer casualties yesterday." Skarpa offered a crooked smile. "That might have been because your efforts flung some Antiagon Fire into the trenches near where Fifth Regiment attacked. That caused some confusion and disorganization. Subcommander Meinyt used that to his advantage. You and the imagers will need to create an opening in the wall you built. It should be as wide as the roadway . . . if that is possible."

"We will make it as wide as we can. Then what?"

"You will support Third Regiment, as necessary."

In other words, be close enough to deal with unexpected problems, but don't lead and get your imagers into trouble unless there's no alternative. "We can do that, sir. When?"

"You have two quints. Form up Fifth Battalion on the approachway with Third Regiment. You and the imager undercaptains will be on the bridge where you can open the wall. Once that's done, rejoin Fifth Battalion."

"Yes, sir." After the slightest pause, Quaeryt went on. "Where are we headed once we cross the river?"

"The marshal sent maps . . . and directions. Besides whatever forces are guarding the bridge, the largest numbers appear to be stationed behind and near the revetments to the north of the city. Our task is to strike from behind and not to allow them to escape."

Quaeryt just nodded.

"The main avenue from the bridge splits into two roads at a square a half mille from the river. Fifth Regiment will take the eastern road, Third the western. Fifth Battalion will accompany Third Regiment . . ."

Skarpa finished outlining the plan of attack in less than a third of a quint, then departed with Meinyt, leaving Quaeryt to ready his own battalion. That was not difficult, since when Quaeryt left the inn, with the first low golden-white light of dawn spreading across the sky, he found Zhelan had already issued the orders and the battalion was largely ready to move out.

"Have the battalion form up with Third Regiment, wherever the commander orders. The imagers and I will rejoin you after we open the bridge wall."

"Yes, sir."

Quaeryt nodded acknowledgment and crossed the courtyard of the Bluff Point to where the imager undercaptains waited. Once there, he studied each with care. Threkhyl, unsurprisingly, looked hale and healthy, as did Voltyr and Shaelyt. Desyrk looked tired and slightly wan. Baelthm had deep circles under his eyes, and his face was grayish.

"Late yesterday," Quaeryt began, "the northern army encircled north Villerive. The Bovarians attempted to break out. Casualties were very heavy on both sides. In order to prevent more heavy losses to our forces, Marshal Deucalon has ordered Commander Skarpa to attack the Bovarians from the rear by using the bridge. Fifth Regiment will lead the attack, followed by Third Regiment and Fifth Battalion. The first evolution of the attack will require us to clear the wall from the far end of bridge. That means removing the section now blocking access to the north. After that has been accomplished, we will rejoin the battalion in support of Third Regiment." Quaeryt paused. "Any questions?"

Head shakes were the only replies.

"Mount up, then."

When Quaeryt rode out of the courtyard and down the side street to the main avenue, the imagers behind him, Fifth Regiment was riding onto the bridge, but there was enough space for Quaeryt to guide the undercaptains along the railing, until they moved ahead of Meinyt and his vanguard, then through the gates on the south side and across the span to the north gates on the far side, still guarded by a squad from Fifth Battalion.

The squad leader rode over to meet Quaeryt. "Sir."

"Are there any Bovarians on the bridge between these gates and the wall?"

"No, sir. Leastwise, there weren't just a bit ago, less than a third of a quint ago."

"Good. Once Fifth Regiment is in position, you can return to the battalion. Major Zhelan has it formed up with Third Regiment behind Fifth Regiment."

"Yes, sir."

In just a few moments, Meinyt rode up with his vanguard, then eased his mount up beside Quaeryt's. "How do you suggest we handle this?"

"According to the squad leader who's been guarding this gate, there aren't any Bovarians on the bridge between the wall and the gate. I'd venture that any forces they have will be beyond the wall. So . . . we'll have one of your men ride up to the gates, climb up, and make sure. If it's still clear, they open the gates, and we ride to the wall. We do the same thing there to see what's beyond. Then the imagers remove that section of the wall. If there are pikemen beyond the wall and waiting, I'll lead the charge far enough to break the pikes, and then . . ." Quaeryt looked to Meinyt.

"We'll take over from there. If there aren't any pikes, we'll lead."

"They might have a pike emplacement at the foot of the approach, instead," said Quaeryt. "We'll stay with the van until we know."

Meinyt nodded, then motioned.

In moments, a trooper mounted the gates and peered to the north. "The bridge is clear to the wall, sir."

"Open the gates!"

Once the gates were open, Quaeryt and the imagers rode through them and forward the thirty yards to the gray stone wall. Quaeryt couldn't be certain, but he thought he heard footsteps beyond the wall.

Once again, a trooper scaled the wall, but it took three men to help him because of the height and the smooth stone face. From the top, after looking northward, he reported, "There's no one right near on the other side of the wall, sir, but looks like they've built a barrier of stones and stuff at the foot of the approach to the bridge. It's got spears and spikes and pikes pointed our way in it, and pikemen waiting behind that."

"How far away is the barrier?"

"Fifty yards, I'd say."

"How many troopers can you see beyond the pikemen?"

"Hard to say, sir, but looks like a battalion or so. Might be more. Still a lot of shadows there."

Meinyt motioned for the scout to descend, then looked at Quaeryt.

"We'll take out the wall. Have at least a squad move forward, to shield the imagers once it's down. Then we'll do what we can to destroy the barrier with the spears and spikes After that . . . we'll still do what we can, but I don't yet know how much that will be."

"Do what you can." Meinyt turned in the saddle. "Once the wall's gone, first squad escorts the imagers forward on the right, the rest move forward into a five-man front, measured pace. Pass it back."

Quaeryt waited until the orders echoed back, then looked to the undercaptains. "Threkhyl, I'd like you to remove the wall from one side of the road to the other. If you can't do that, then take out as much as you can from the center of the roadbed outward. Is that clear?"

"Yes, sir."

"Then image, now!"

For a moment nothing happened. Then there was a flash of light, and a gust of chill air. The wall vanished, but a cascade of ice droplets clattered to the paving stones.

Quaeryt was impressed, in spite of himself. "Excellent!" He looked at Threkhyl, who swayed slightly in the saddle and who appeared pale. "Drink something, and eat a biscuit or bread. Right now "

The ginger-bearded imager reached for his water bottle, lifted it, and slowly drank.

"First squad! Forward!"

The first ranks of the vanguard rode through the wide gap in the wall.

"Shaelyt, Voltyr . . ." Quaeryt motioned for the two to ride behind him as he eased the mare to the right side of the roadbed and moved forward. Then he looked forward, noting that two lines of pikemen, perhaps three or more, had angled the long weapons toward the Telaryn riders, the tips of the forward-most pikes even with the spears and sharpened poles protruding from the rubble barrier at the end of the approach to the bridge.

The good thing is that they can't easily charge us with that barrier and the pikemen. Once through the gap and against the railing on the right side, with enough room for the other imagers behind them, Quaeryt reined up and turned in the saddle. "Can you two remove that rubble barrier?"

Voltyr and Shaelyt exchanged glances.

"Yes, sir."

"Then, when I give the command, do so . . . but wait until I do."

Meinyt eased his mount beside Quaeryt. "We don't have much room here."

"We can take out the barrier, and maybe some of the pikes. If we can't do that, I can still break part of the center. Are you ready?"

"We're ready."

Quaeryt eased his staff from the leathers and laid it across his thighs, evenly balanced. "Don't give the order to charge until I tell you."

Meinyt nodded.

"Voltyr, Shaelyt! Image now!"

The flash of light was momentary, and not quite all the rubble barrier vanished—leaving some spears and rubble about a half yard into the approach road on each side.

"Imagers! Remain with first squad!" Quaeryt lowered his voice and said to Meinyt, "I'll have to lead this charge through the pikes, but your men will have to be close behind."

"They'll be on your heels."

Quaeryt urged the mare forward, strengthening his shields. Even as he rode forward, the lead company of Fifth Regiment close behind, he could see more pikemen moving toward the center of the road.

Abruptly smoke and pepper sprayed into the arrayed pikes, and some of the unwieldly weapons wavered.

Quaeryt formed his shields into an unseen wedge, linking them to the mass of mounts behind him. As the shields impacted the first pikes, he could feel pressure everywhere, as if he were being fed into an olive press or a grape press. Then suddenly the constriction vanished, and pikes and pikemen sprayed aside from the shields. For a moment Quaeryt felt as though he were burning up, but that was followed by a chill like ice water cascading over him.

Ahead was open pavement. To the right, he corrected himself, but to the left were more Bovarians who moved toward the attacking troopers.

He contracted his shields to cover just himself and the mare and eased her to the side of the square he was riding across—away from the Bovarians. Looking around, he could find no one before him, just the empty square, but as he turned the mare, he saw the Bovarian reinforcements meet the oncoming troopers.

For several moments, and then for longer, perhaps half a quint, the Bovarians gave ground, slowly at first, and then more quickly. Then, the remaining Bovarian pikemen and footmen dropped their heavy square shields and began to run.

In less than another quint, the square below the bridge held only Telaryn troopers and the long shadows cast by a sun that had barely risen. *All this so early? With a long day yet ahead?*

Shaking his head, Quaeryt rode back to rejoin the imager undercaptains, all of whom looked to be unhurt, although Threkhyl's eyes were twitching, and his face was pale. Baelthm's countenance remained grayish. "Undercaptain Threkhyl Undercaptain Baelthm, no more imaging today unless your own life is threatened. Is that clear?"

"Yes, sir . . ." came the low rejoinder.

"I want you healthy for the rest of the campaign, and you won't be if you do too much on any one day. Second, I'd like to say I very much appreciated the smoke and pepper. It made what I had to do much easier."

"Sir . . ." murmured Voltyr, gesturing.

Quaeryt followed the gesture with his eyes to see Skarpa riding up at the head of Third Regiment.

"If you and the undercaptains would join us . . . We do have more to do."

"Yes, sir." After gesturing to the undercaptains, Quaeryt turned the mare and rode in behind the commander, who followed a single company of his first battalion, the remainder of Third Regiment closing up behind the imagers who had taken station on Quaeryt.

"With me, Subcommander" said Skarpa, looking back.

Quaeryt eased his mount forward.

"How are your imagers?"

"Two are likely finished for the day. Three can do smoke and pepper, possibly some small barrier removal. One can do more than that."

Skarpa nodded. "I just received another dispatch. The Bovarians are massing on the west road. They've abandoned their position on the east road. We're to strike them from behind as hard as we can and as soon as we can."

"How far ahead is that?" Quaeryt glanced around as they rode out of the bridge square. As in other towns and cities they had entered, all doors were closed, all shuttered fastened tight, and no one appeared anywhere on the streets or in the alleys. The shops on the main avenue were largely built of a yellowish brick, with pale red tile roofs in most cases. A few were of wood, and one or two had been constructed of a red stone. All looked well kept.

"Not quite two milles."

Alert as he tried to be, Quaeryt could detect no sign of other Bovarians. After riding perhaps a half mille, or a bit longer, the column came to another square, this one with a center pedestal bearing a statue of a man on horseback. Around the pedestal was a low redstone wall, topped with an iron railing.

Definitely Naming there, thought Quaeryt as he studied the square, vacant except for the Telaryn troopers, and the raised stone platform on which the statue had been set.

After another hundred yards or so, farther ahead, Quaeryt caught a glimpse of light on metal, and then the sight of armored cavalry charging from a side avenue into one of the companies of Fifth Regiment. Meinyt's troopers appeared to be prepared, moving out of the way and then attacking mounts or men from the rear while another company rode in behind the armored riders.

As Skarpa slowed Third Regiment, Quaeryt kept his head and eyes moving, wondering when and if another force would charge out of a side street or boulevard. He saw nothing, and before long the column was moving again, past fallen men and mounts moved out of the road, with perhaps a squad tending to Telaryn wounded.

The dwellings along the avenue increased in size with each block they traveled, and the space between the houses increased as well. Many of the dwellings had walls encircling them, and stables and outbuildings. Then, ahead, Quaeryt caught sight of two large stone gateposts, one on each side of the avenue. As he rode closer, he saw that there were no gates, nor were there any houses immediately beyond the gates, but an expanse of fields, whose plants or grasses had largely been trampled flat. Overlooking the fields on the west side of the avenue that had become a narrower but still stone-paved road was a low ridge.

Abruptly Quaeryt realized that the eastern side of that ridge held masses of men and mounts, and it appeared that, under the press of the larger Telaryn forces, the Bovarians had withdrawn onto what looked to be the hillside estate of a High Holder. Small catapults flung dark objects into the Telaryn forces, objects that exploded into crimson-greenish-yellow fire, clinging to whatever they hit.

Fifth Regiment had already turned westward to reinforce the Telaryn forces pressing the Bovarians, but the Bovarian line, roughly halfway up the gentle slope, appeared to be holding their own, possibly because of the effects of the Antiagon Fire grenades.

"Antiagon Fire! We need to get closer," Quaeryt yelled to Skarpa.

"Second company, escort the imagers forward! Captain, you're under the subcommander's orders!"

"Sir!" called a muscularly rotund captain. "Over here!"

"Shaelyt, Voltyr, Desyrk! With me."

The second company edged onto the left flank of Fifth Regiment, increasing the pace until the riders were moving past the column at what Quaeryt thought might be a canter. Even so, close to a quint passed before they reached the rear of the Telaryn forces.

"To the left, there!" called Quaeryt, gesturing toward what looked to be a gap between the advancing Telaryn troopers.

That "gap" was an irrigation ditch, empty but somewhat muddy. Quaeryt didn't care about the mud, but he did slow the mare. Taking the ditch was still faster than trying to force his way through Deucalon's troopers, although the troopers did give way slightly as they saw the troopers leading officers along the ditch.

Quaeryt did overhear a few muttered remarks.

". . . officers wanting to get into battle . . . friggin' idiots . . ."

". . . let 'em . . ."

Idiots? With what you want, is there any choice? He didn't answer his own question, but concentrated on getting to where he could do something.

In the end, Quaeryt and the imagers could only reach the base of the ridge. He reined up and gestured for the others to halt as well. He was still a good two hundred yards from the catapults near the top of the ridgelike rise. *No help for that now.*

He concentrated on the nearest catapult, almost directly uphill from him, and as the dark object that had to be a fire grenade soared free, he imaged it back, back onto the group of officers higher on the slope. The crimson-greenish-yellow that burst from the grenade enveloped the center of the group. Quaeryt immediately looked toward the second catapult, waiting, waiting . . . and the second fire grenade soared . . and then vanished—reappearing as it smashed into the remnants of the command group. When the third catapult began to move, Quaeryt returned the grenade to the base of the catapult, and the structure and those operating it flared into ugly flame. Then he returned his attention to the first catapult.

Quaeryt's skull was splitting by the time all three catapults were flaming masses.

But by then the Bovarian lines had totally crumbled, and what had been a static melee was turning into a rout.

Quaeryt, the imagers, and the company detailed to protect them just held their position as the Telaryn forces surged past them and into the hand-to-hand fighting. Quaeryt could still maintain his personal shields, although he doubted that he could have done much more than that, and in the growing confusion he decided against trying to find Fifth Battalion. *Skarpa and Fifth Battalion can come to us.*

In less than half a glass, the Bovarians had fragmented into small clusters surrounded by Telaryn forces. A glass later the hillside and the lower grounds of the estate were littered with bodies in bluish gray, and hundreds, if not more than a thousand Bovarians, had fled away from Villerive and the River Aluse, heading north and west.

The one Bovarian force he had not seen had been musketeers. Had they attacked earlier and been dispersed? Or did they take so much time to set up that they had never been in position? Even from what he'd seen, that appeared to be the strongest possibility . . . but it was only a half-informed guess on his part. *But aren't too many conclusions you're making just that these days?*

As the fighting dwindled away, Quaeryt watched as Deucalon dispatched patrols from the northern army to ride down every lane and road, as much as to fragment the survivors and chase them away from ever regrouping as to cut them down, Quaeryt suspected.

Not that some probably weren't cut down, he thought, massaging his forehead.

This time, he could still see, and that amazed him, even as it strengthened his belief that continually stretching himself to his limits seemed to extend those limits once he recovered. *But for how long? Is there a point when your body can do no more?*

What Skarpa called follow-up operations took most of the rest of Mardi,
and early on Fifth Battalion was dispatched to occupy and guard a large
manor house a half mille west, beyond the estate and ridge on which the
morning's battle had taken place. The Khellan companies patrolled the area
around the near-palatial dwelling with great diligence, a diligence, Quaeryt suspected, that assured that no Bovarian troopers would have dared
even to approach the grounds and well-tended gardens. He'd posted troopers at the front and rear entrances to the house, more to create a certain
respect than because he thought anyone would likely try to break in or
attack anyone inside.

Once he and Zhelan had worked out the details of quartering and patrolling, Quaeryt found himself at a loss, walking the first floor of the
dwelling and the terraces from which he could observe the Khellan patrols,
and in the distance the gathering of some regiments around the High
Holder estate that had seen too much blood and fire.

The bells had just struck third glass when the house assistant steward,
the steward having fled with the family, cautiously eased up to Quaeryt,
who stood in the shade of the east porch, again studying the hold house
below which all too much, if necessary, carnage had occurred.

"Sir . . . ?" The man, a few years older than Quaeryt, and balding,
looked nervously up to the taller subcommander, his eyes seemingly focusing on the silver crescent moon insignia on Quaeryt's collars rather
than meeting his eyes.

Quaeryt half turned. "Yes?"

"Will . . . we . . . I mean . . . you have men to feed . . ."

"Yes, they will need to be fed. Is there a problem, Chaefur?"

"The head cook, the second cook . . . they went with the family. Just
two assistant cooks . . ."

Chaefur's Bovarian held the trace of a regional accent, but whether that
was local or not, Quaeryt had no idea.

"The troopers and officers don't expect meals for a High Holder. If
your cooks . . ." Quaeryt paused. "The battalion has several cooks. They'll

be in the kitchen as well." *That way they can make certain nothing untoward gets into the food.*

"Yes, sir . . ." Chaefur paused. "Might I ask how long . . . ?"

"That's up to Lord Bhayar."

"Lord Bhayar? Not . . . Is Lord Bhayar here? Here in Villerive?"

"I haven't seen him lately, but I think I'd know if he weren't."

"Oh . . . oh, dear . . . what shall we do if he comes here?"

"He might summon me," Quaeryt said, "but he won't come here. Why do you worry about that?" *There should be more of concern to you and the staff than whether Bhayar appears.*

"Master Saarcoyn . . . he always wants everything to be proper . . . whoever might arrive . . ."

"Master Saarcoyn, of what is he a master?"

"He's a master factor, sir. A grain and timber and metals factor. He's got three factorages, sir . . . and some mines to the north."

Quaeryt glanced at the stone pillars that ran up three stories, supporting the porch roof, then out over the iron filigree of the railing bordering the porch and down to the precisely trimmed hedges of the formal garden on the terrace below the porch. "He obviously does well."

"That he does, sir. But now . . ."

"We'll do our best to leave his house undamaged. That is, if we have no trouble."

"No, sir . . . you'll have no trouble. No, sir."

At the sound of hooves, Quaeryt turned to see a squad of Telaryn troopers riding up the narrow limestone-paved drive to the front entrance. One of the mounts, led by a ranker, held an empty saddle. *That doesn't look good.* "You'll have to excuse me, Chaefur. If I'm not here, direct any questions you have to Major Zhelan."

"But . . . sir . . . dinner?"

"Plan on fifth glass. Set up serving tables for the troopers in the courtyard off the kitchen. The servers can dish the food into the troopers' mess kits. They'll serve me and the officers in the dining room *after* the men are all fed." Quaeryt turned and followed the porch that circled the entire dwelling back to the front.

Chaefur did not follow. Quaeryt only had to wait a few moments under the roof of the entry portico before a squad leader dismounted and hurried up the four wide limestone steps, halting and inclining his head politely before he addressed Quaeryt.

"Subcommander, sir, Lord Bhayar would like to see you. We have a spare mount."

"One moment, Squad Leader." Quaeryt turned to the pair of troopers flanking the front door. "Troopers . . . if one of you would immediately convey to Major Zhelan that Lord Bhayar has summoned me."

"Yes, sir."

"Thank you." Quaeryt nodded to the troopers, then followed the squad leader to the mount, a chestnut gelding far larger than Quaeryt's mare. The fact that he had no trouble mounting, or riding down the drive, was another indication of how much had changed for a scholar who had seldom ridden until a year earlier.

The squad leader headed almost due east, back to the hold house that Quaeryt had been observing less than a quint earlier. When Quaeryt dismounted under a portico easily three times the size of the one at Master Saarcoyn's manor-like dwelling, he noted a good squad of troopers stationed there, half on each side of the double doors.

"We'll be waiting for you, Subcommander."

"Thank you." Quaeryt turned and walked toward the doors.

One of the troopers opened the left door.

Once Quaeryt stepped into the large marble-floored circular entry hall, a young captain moved forward. "Subcommander Quaeryt . . . sir. It will be a few moments, sir. Would you like a cool lager while you wait?"

Quaeryt had to admire how the captain eased him toward what had to be a receiving parlor. "I would thank you." He took a seat in the velvet-upholstered armchair, rather than the matching green settee.

Almost immediately, the captain returned, extending a crystal beaker containing a lager so light that it was barely golden.

"Thank you."

"My pleasure, sir." The captain slipped away, leaving Quaeryt with the lager.

Quaeryt took a sip. The lager was good. Not excellent, but good, and Quaeryt didn't hurry in drinking it. He'd often had to wait on Bhayar.

Even so, he'd almost finished the beaker when a tall and squarish figure in Telaryn officers' greens strode past the receiving parlor toward the entry hall. The older officer's face was impassive, and his jaw clenched. Quaeryt recognized Deucalon, but the marshal did not even glance in Quaeryt's direction. More likely he doesn't want to.

Several moments later the captain returned. "Subcommander . . ."

Quaeryt took a last swallow of the lager and placed the crystal beaker on the side table, then stood and followed the young officer down the hallway to the second door.

"The subcommander, sir."

"Have him come in."

Quaeryt eased off the visor cap, slipped it under his arm, and stepped through the white oak door that the captain had opened for him. As soon as he stood in the study, its paneling matching the white oak of the door, with a wall of shelves to his right, the door closed.

Bhayar sat alone at a circular conference table of polished white oak, but rimmed with inlaid green stone, most likely malachite, reflected Quaeryt. The Lord of Telaryn gestured to a chair across the table. "Please sit down. I hear you've had several hard days."

Quaeryt sat. "I've had harder, but not many."

"I thought as much." His dark blue eyes intent, Bhayar looked directly at Quaeryt. "Deucalon is furious at what you did, you know? Or didn't do, more precisely."

"He didn't look particularly happy when he left you." Although Quaeryt had a good idea why, he wanted to be sure. "With what is he displeased?"

"You know as well as I do. Your imagers created that wall on the north side of the bridge. That kept the Bovarians from retreating to the south side of the river."

"We had orders to take and hold the south side and to keep the bridge from being destroyed. We did that, sir."

Bhayar smiled. "You did indeed."

"Did Marshal Deucalon wish us to take heavier casualties to spare the northern army when we have a much smaller force?"

"I don't believe he mentioned that to me. He is most careful with his words." Bhayar's smile turned into a grin, and then faded. "He does not forget, Quaeryt."

Neither do I. Ever. "I will keep that in mind." Quaeryt paused. "By the way, there is one other small matter of which you might wish to be aware. Just two days ago I received a letter from Vaelora. It was dated the twenty-fourth of Juyn . . ." Quaeryt went on to explain about Governor Markyl's letter and the dates.

Bhayar's face darkened and stiffened, if but for a moment. "I can do nothing until I know more, but that is good to learn." He shook his head. "At times I fear I am fighting my own officers and their schemes more than Rex Kharst. Were you more experienced as a commander, I would that I could name you marshal."

"I can serve you far better in lesser capacities."

"Less obvious," countered Bhayar. "Not lesser."

How much does he suspect about your plans and ambitions? Unlike many, Quaeryt knew well enough not to underestimate Bhayar, young though he might be for a ruler. Quaeryt nodded. "I would hope so, but that is your choice."

"Always so cautious . . . except in battle, I understand."

"The marshal thought I was too cautious," Quaeryt pointed out.

"I met with Commander Skarpa earlier. He confirmed that neither you nor the undercaptains could have done more than you did yesterday. He also noted that you accounted for more than two regiments of dead Bovarians yesterday and made possible the destruction and scattering of two more this morning. That did not include the destruction of the Antiagon Fire catapults later."

"Which, I suspect, Marshal Deucalon felt should have been destroyed earlier? Even though we could not have reached them any sooner."

"Commander Skarpa noted that you moved ahead of all his forces to reach them as soon as you could." Bhayar held up a hand. "No more about Deucalon. He will never accept that a scholar could be an effective officer. He could accept even less that an imager should hold such a position. One way or another, in time, that will not matter, but for now it is best to let your actions, and those of Fifth Battalion, speak for you."

"I'm here, I take it, so that you can tell the marshal that you conveyed his concerns to me directly and personally?"

Bhayar laughed, if softly. "You understand, sometimes too well—as does Vaelora."

"And Aelina," added Quaeryt.

"Of course."

"What do you need from me?"

"To keep on doing what you are. We should be receiving reinforcements, for your battalion as well."

"Ah . . . sir. For first company, I don't see a problem . . ."

Bhayar smiled. "There are over a hundred Khellans. Some of them were with those you already have, but they needed to recover from injuries and wounds. They won't make up all the losses, but they'll help. There will be enough replacements to fill your complement and add an extra squad for your first company. With them will be a number of other regiments, at least four, I'm told. I expect them all within the next few days. One of those regiments will be assigned to the southern army. Skarpa will remain in command in the south." Bhayar smiled. "There will also be certain . . . reinforcements for Fifth Battalion, a few additional undercaptains."

More imagers to train?

"You look surprised."

"I had not expected that."

"I understand they will not be so effective. Not until you have had some time with them. Skarpa was truly amazed at how far you have come in improving the imagers." Bhayar paused. "Once this is . . . all over . . . we should talk about their future."

"I have some thoughts about how they might best serve you."

"Good . . . but they must serve . . . in, as I said earlier, a less obvious manner."

"I understand that also."

"I have no doubts of that. Both you and my sister understand me too well. That is why you have each other . . . and children, in time."

Quaeryt understood that as well.

"You have done well, better than I could have expected, and I do not forget, my friend." Bhayar smiled, a warm expression, with face and eyes, then stood. "I will not keep you long. That would not be wise, for either of us."

Quaeryt stood, then nodded respectfully.

"Take care . . . Quaeryt."

"As I can, sir." Quaeryt turned and left the study.

47

Quaeryt had barely dismounted and walked up to the entry doors to Master Saarcoyn's dwelling when Zhelan appeared.

"Good afternoon, sir."

"Good afternoon, Zhelan. Why don't you join me in the study?" Quaeryt turned and led the way to the study, the first chamber beyond the modest square entry hall.

Saarcoyn's study was far less prepossessing than any High Holders' studies Quaeryt had seen, but with well-polished golden oak wainscoting and bookshelves, along with a matching desk and circular table that looked to have been used for plaques, it reflected more than the prosperity of an average factor. Quaeryt took a seat at the table and waited for the major to sit.

"How are matters with the battalion?"

"As before, sir, since we suffered no casualties today. Only Fifth Regiment actually fought . . . from our forces, that is."

"Did the Khellan officers complain about that?" asked Quaeryt dryly.

"No, sir. They did seem pleased at the number of Bovarian casualties."

"I can't imagine why." Quaeryt let the silence draw out.

"If I might ask, sir . . . what did Lord Bhayar wish of you?"

"A number of things." Quaeryt smiled. "He said that we would be receiving some reinforcements, enough for first company to be at full strength and add an additional squad. There will also be some . . . undercaptain trainee imagers. He expects more regiments to arrive in the next few days as well. One of those will be attached to the southern army under Skarpa's command."

"What about the Khellan companies?"

"There are somewhat over a hundred Khellan troopers coming."

"Is there anything else I should know, sir?"

"We're most fortunate to be in the southern force under Commander Skarpa."

"Will we be transferred?"

"There was no mention of that. Since Lord Bhayar made certain to tell me that Commander Skarpa would remain in command, I suspect that

Fifth Battalion will remain with him at least through whatever is our next engagement."

"That would look to be Nordeau, would it not, sir?"

"Do you think we'll face any opposition before that, Major, if we take the south river road?"

"I'd be surprised, sir. They've taken far heavier losses than we have. All their unwounded survivors can't number much more than two, maybe three regiments. Marshal Deucalon lost maybe a regiment or two, but that still leaves him with twelve."

That did surprise Quaeryt. He'd seen the massive numbers of Telaryn mounted and foot, but he hadn't exactly had time or space in which to count, and he hadn't asked Bhayar. *And you should have.* He wanted to shake his head. There were still so many aspects of commanding that he didn't know, or know well enough. For Zhelan, and Skarpa, and Meinyt, he was truly grateful.

"And with four additional regiments," added Quaeryt, "he'll have sixteen."

"I don't see the Bovarians trying to stop almost twenty regiments for some little town."

"No . . . not when we've got another eighty milles to Nordeau." Quaeryt offered a sardonic smile. "But then, they might just decide to do that, and try to catch us by surprise."

"More likely us than the marshal, too."

"If you don't mind, Major, I think I'd like to be the one to tell the officers about this at the mess tonight. I haven't seen the company officers as a group in several days . . ." *And that's less than two glasses from now . . . and not much will change between now and then.*

"That might be best, sir." Zhelan nodded thoughtfully.

"If I leave out anything, of course, you can make sure they know that, as well." Quaeryt smiled. "As you have done more than once, and for which I am grateful."

"You do what I cannot, sir."

After Zhelan left, Quaeryt thought about telling the undercaptains before mess, then decided against that, since if it got out, and everything eventually did, it would appear he was favoring the most junior officers over the company officers, and that was certainly something he didn't want to do, especially since there was no urgent necessity.

Absently, he walked over to the single wall of built-in bookshelves, and studied the volumes there, opening one book after another, most of which appeared to have been unread, and in some cases not even opened. The one slim volume that had definitely been opened and read, often, was entitled, unsurprisingly, Factors and Factoring.

The most surprising volume, to him, was a thicker tome—The End of Naedara. While he knew he shouldn't spend too much time reading, he couldn't resist opening the book and paging through it, occasionally reading a paragraph or two. As always seemed to be the case when he read something one section stood out . . . and he reread it again

> . . . while Chelaes was the largest and most important city in Naedara, stories told by the descendants of those who lived there suggest that the Naedaran interpretation of the precepts of the Nameless required that no town or city grow to be too large. Yet Chelaes was clearly larger, until the end, when the other Naedaran towns and cities, according to the stories, turned upon Chelaes, tearing down buildings and carting off goods . . .

The vanity of size—a form of Naming—and they destroyed their capital city . . . because of the precepts of the Nameless? Or were those precepts just a convenient excuse?

Reluctantly Quaeryt closed the history and replaced it in the bookcase.

When are precepts good guidelines for action and when are they merely a rationale for doing what one wishes to do?

Still pondering that, he left the study, heading out to make his way through the grounds in order to casually inspect every squad and company in Fifth Battalion. Although he expected no surprises, he checked his shields before he stepped out the rear door of the factor's residence onto the rear terrace, since Villerive wasn't exactly friendly territory.

Voltyr was standing in the shade of one of the massive pillars, talking with Desyrk, but both stopped immediately when they saw him.

Quaeryt walked toward the pair. "Are you feeling better Desyrk?"

The undercaptain's mouth almost dropped open, but he caught himself. "Sir?"

"You looked like you weren't yourself when we started at the bridge this morning. I was hoping you felt better."

"Ah . . . yes, sir."

"Good." Quaeryt looked to Voltyr. "How about you?"

"Yes, sir."

"You both, as you're able, need to practice shielding as much as you can. Things won't get any easier as we near Nordeau and Variana."

"Yes, sir."

Quaeryt nodded and turned, heading toward the stable, far too small to accommodate the battalion's mounts, although a combination of using a riding arena, and tie-lines and temporary corrals, seemed to be suffi-cient for the time being. As he walked down the steps from the terrace, he caught a few words.

". . . how did he know . . ."

". . . never underestimate him . . . sees more than you'd ever believe . . ."

Quaeryt smiled wryly. *If you only did . . .*

After circling the area where the mounts were kept, Quaeryt approached a captain who was inspecting a horse. He waited until the officer stepped back, then said cheerfully in Bovarian, "Good afternoon, Stensted."

Arion's second in command turned, inclining his head. "Good after-noon, Subcommander."

"How are your mounts holding up?"

"Well enough, sir. The reshoeing helped." Stensted smiled. "We cap-tured almost fifty Bovarian horses this morning. They will also help."

Quaeryt laughed softly. "I imagine they will."

"They need care, some of them. The Bovarians, they do not know horses."

"I've heard that those of Khel are known for that."

"All know that." Stensted smiled broadly. "It is in the blood. They say that you rode little until the last year, but you ride like one of Khel."

"Thank you, but I fear I don't ride like you do."

The undercaptain shook his head. "None could tell the difference. I cannot. My men cannot." He offered a sheepish grin. "The imager under-captains, though . . ."

"They've gotten better, don't you think?"

"They have . . . but they could not have been more awkward."

"We all have to learn things we don't do well."

"Yes, sir. We all do." After a pause the captain ventured, "Do you know what Lord Bhayar will do . . . after he takes Variana?"

"That has yet to happen," Quaeryt replied mildly.

"It will happen, sir . . . and we wonder . . ."

"If Khel will be free once more?"

Stensted nodded. "One cannot but hope."

"Captain . . . I do not know what Lord Bhayar plans. I do know that he believes all Lydar must be one land or there will always be war. But I . . . like you . . . would like Khel to be more like it once was. From what I have heard from Lord Bhayar. I would think he would feel in a similar fashion. But I do not know, and he has not spoken of it directly. He has only spoken that the cruelty of Rex Kharst must be ended.' Even that was a bit of a stretch Quaeryt knew, and yet he felt it was true.

Stensted nodded slowly. "You offer hope, but you do not promise what cannot be. Will you speak for us . . . as you can?"

"I will." That, Quaeryt could promise. He didn't see why some form of the Khellan councils couldn't report to a governor of the province of Khel, so long as tariffs were gathered and order was maintained. He doubted they would be any more trouble than High Holders . . . and they might be less.

"Thank you, sir." Stensted inclined his head politely.

Quaeryt nodded in return and then resumed his informal inspection.

By the time it neared fifth glass, he had not finished what he had intended, and he had to hurry back to the residence . . . and then wait in the study.

Quaeryt had to remind himself that since he was the senior officer, he couldn't enter the dining room—or mess—until the last bell was struck, by the trooper serving as mess orderly.

When he stepped into the dining room, all thirteen officers rose. Quaeryt noted that all were seated by rank, although he hadn't specified that. To the right of his place at the head of the long table stood Zhelan, by virtue of his position as assistant subcommander of Fifth Battalion, and to the left was Major Calkoran, as the most senior of the company officers.

"Please be seated," Quaeryt began in Bovarian. "I will stand for a moment, so that you all can hear what I have to say." He paused. "First, I haven't had a chance to tell all of you how well you've performed over the last week, and how much both Lord Bhayar and I, in particular, appreciate your efforts and accomplishments. Without the courage and skill of every trooper and every officer, we would not be dining here . . . and many of us would not be here at all. You all may know that, but too often what is known is not acknowledged." After another brief pause, he went on. "As some of you know, I met earlier this afternoon with Lord Bhayar, and he conveyed his appreciation to me personally, as well as some information . . ." Quaeryt continued with a brief description of what he had told Zhelan earlier, ending with, ". . . we will have greater challenges ahead, but I am confident that we will be able to meet them through your skill and that of your troopers." Then he looked to the end of the table and switched to Tellan. "I've been telling the company officers that it took the efforts of all officers and men to accomplish what we have, and what you all did was vital. I'll tell you the rest after we eat."

With that he seated himself.

Once the porcelain mugs—Quaeryt decided that the factor's crystal was not to be used—had been filled with ale or lager, he raised his mug. "To Fifth Battalion, officers and men."

"To Fifth Battalion."

Surprisingly, after the first toast, Major Calkoran stood. "I do not make toasts. This one I must. I have seen many commanders and subcommanders. Never before have I seen one who would share all the risks faced by company officers and troopers, and other risks as well." Calkoran stopped and looked to Zhelan.

The hard-faced major smiled and added, "We all know that the subcommander can avoid some risks because of his abilities. What some don't know is that he has fought at the front time and time again when he had no special abilities left. He has fought when he could barely see and when most of his body was covered with bruises. He has been wounded more than any living man in first company."

That's because you've done stupid things and aren't that good at hand-to-hand fighting, thought Quaeryt, although he did not say it, injecting quickly, "No more than any other trooper."

"To the subcommander," concluded Zhelan.

After the mugs were lowered, Quaeryt said, in a dryly cheerful tone, "And now it's past time to enjoy some food."

He'd judged correctly, because there were smiles around the table.

48

Mardi night, rain began to come down sometime after midnight. The heavier rainfall had dwindled to a drizzle by dawn on Meredi morning, light enough that the men could be fed on the roofed terrace-like porch that encircled Factor Saarcoyn's dwelling. After breakfast, Quaeryt again met in the study with Zhelan.

"You think this rain will let up before long?" offered Quaeryt conversationally.

"It looks like it might, sir, but this is Bovaria."

"Not everything is different here."

"I'd be having some doubts about that, sir."

Quaeryt waited, wanting to see what Zhelan might add.

"The assistant steward . . . well . . . all of them . . . they act like any moment we'd cut down any of them or the men would take liberties with the serving girls without so much as a by your leave. They can't believe we're . . . well . . . mannered."

Quaeryt nodded. "After the way some of the High Holders behaved, would you expect otherwise?"

"High Holders . . . they're different. This is a factor's household."

"Factors in Telaryn are better behaved, it appears. So are many High Holders."

"Might not be so hard as I thought for Lord Bhayar to govern this part of Bovaria."

"Yes and no, I suspect," mused Quaeryt. "The people might like him better. The High Holders and wealthy factors won't." He offered a short laugh. "That's something we can worry about later. Is there anything else?"

"The Khellan officers appreciated your telling them about what was happening in Bovarian, sir . . . but I noticed some of the imager under-captains . . ."

"I met with them later last evening and spelled it out in Tellan." Quaeryt smiled crookedly. "I also suggested that anyone who wants to be useful to Lord Bhayar in the years ahead had best know both Tellan and Bovarian."

"Some of them weren't too pleased with that, I'd think, not that they'd dare say a word."

"Pleased or not, it's likely to be that way."

"I can see that, sir."

"What else about the battalion?"

"We've got a good fifty mounts lame or nursing injuries . . . the ones captured will help . . . still looking for good spares . . ."

Quaeryt listened for another quint, asking occasional questions.

After Zhelan left, Quaeryt walked to the window and looked out into the misty grayness, wondering how often Bovaria was so dismal, and if the winters were damp and gray.

"Sir?" Behind him, the study door opened.

Quaeryt turned.

"Commander Skarpa and Subcommander Meinyt are riding up the drive," offered one of the troopers from the front entrance.

"Thank you." Quaeryt hurried from the study, down the hall, then out onto the covered portico, where he waited as the other two officers dismounted.

"Good morning, Quaeryt," offered Skarpa as he climbed the steps to the front entry level. He removed his visor cap for a moment and shook off the rain, then replaced it on his head.

Meinyt did the same.

"Good morning, I didn't know whether to expect you or not. Would you like to meet in the study?"

"That would be good."

Quaeryt led the way. None of them spoke until Quaeryt closed the study door and gestured toward the plaques table.

"It was easier to come here after Deucalon's regimental commanders' general meeting than to arrange to meet elsewhere." Skarpa's voice was even as he seated himself at the table.

"Regimental commanders' meeting?" Quaeryt sat down across from Skarpa. "Not senior officers' meeting."

"Interesting that no one raised that point."

"No one," agreed Meinyt, settling into the seat facing the window.

"Was Lord Bhayar there?"

"No. He was touring Villerive. I believe the marshal did not call the meeting until after Lord Bhayar had made plans. I understand that he told him that it was a routine staff meeting."

Quaeryt smiled and shook his head.

"When you get that look, Quaeryt," said Skarpa, "it worries me."

"Do you think Bhayar doesn't know what Deucalon and Myskyl are doing? People are always underestimating him."

"Do you want to explain?"

"You know as well as I do," replied Quaeryt with a laugh.

"I think I do. I don't think Meinyt here does, and he should."

"It's fairly simple as politics go. By announcing a routine regimental commanders' meeting at a time when Lord Bhayar is otherwise occupied, Deucalon is making a declaration."

"That you're not really a subcommander . . . and not to be considered as such." Skarpa nodded. "That you're only one because you're a favorite of Bhayar's. And since none of them have ever seen you fight and lead men, they'll have no reason to dispute that."

"Exactly," agreed Quaeryt. "And if Bhayar changes his plans and appears at the meeting, he's either in the position of not saying anything and tacitly accepting Deucalon and Myskyl's unspoken declaration . . . or having to say something and effectively proving that I'm a favorite who needs to be protected."

"Where does Myskyl fit in?" asked Meinyt. "I can't see why Myskyl would do this. He's given every indication that he doesn't want to cross you in any way."

"Exactly. He hasn't. He's setting up Deucalon for later . . ."

Skarpa's mouth opened momentarily, then shut.

"This sort of maneuvering was one reason why I persuaded Bhayar to send me to Tilbor last year." Quaeryt shrugged. "But wherever there are people seeking power and influence, it goes on."

"You're not going to raise this with Bhayar?" asked Skarpa.

"Not now, and never as such. If he hasn't seen what Deucalon—Myskyl, really—is doing, and I bring it up, I seem petty. If he does see, and I suspect he does—he's very good at seeing that sort of thing—then I don't have to, and I don't place him in a difficult position. Rulers don't like being placed in difficult positions. So don't you bring it up either."

"But . . ." Meinyt broke off what he might have said.

"It doesn't matter right now. Bhayar needs us. He knows he needs us, and Deucalon knows he needs us. Bhayar will need us for a long time." *Longer than either Deucalon and Myskyl have any idea.*

Skarpa shook his head. "Are they that stupid?"

"No. They just don't know. Bhayar is willing to put up with this sort of petty scheming in Solis when the land is at peace because there's no cost to it. Or not too much cost. Both he and his father never let scheming cost them golds or men. I doubt if Bhayar will now." *You hope he won't, and that he sees what you think he does.* "Also, I doubt that either Deucalon or Myskyl has seen what the imagers have learned to do. It's one thing to get reports; it's another to see. Frankly, right now, I'd just as soon they didn't see."

"But they saw the catapults . . ." said Meinyt.

"What did they really see? Just that the catapults ended up in flames. Sheer good fortune, that's all. The imagers took credit for it." At that moment, Quaeryt recalled what he had been trying to remember about catapults, except it was why the Bovarians were using catapults and muskets, but not cannon. "There's another matter. We've seen musketeers and catapults, but no cannon. I can see why Kharst wouldn't want to try to get cannon to smaller towns, but Villerive isn't tiny."

"Would you want to drag those monsters along these roads?" asked Skarpa. "How long would it take to get cannon from Variana?"

"Likely they couldn't have gotten them this far, anyway," added Meinyt.

Quaeryt nodded. He'd been thinking of the roads in Telaryn. "Now . . . what else should I know?"

"Our reinforcements are still two days away, and Deucalon carefully avoided mentioning any 'special' officers or reinforcements for Fifth Battalion. In fact, he didn't mention Fifth Battalion at all. It will be at least a day and probably two after their arrival before we move out. If we have heavy rains . . ." Skarpa shrugged.

"What kind of regiments . . . mounted, foot, mixed?"

"Foot and mounted. We'll be assigned one of the mounted regiments. He did make that clear. Wouldn't make any sense to give us a foot regiment."

"Did he say how many regiments would be arriving?" asked Quaeryt.

"He said he hadn't had word as to how many had been sent."

"He's marshal, and he doesn't know?"

"He didn't say, and if you'll pardon me, I didn't feel like questioning him in front of everyone. I asked Pulaskyr afterward, but he hadn't heard, either."

That lack of information gave Quaeryt a most uneasy feeling, but he understood why Skarpa hadn't pressed.

"Myskyl isn't happy that we don't have more archers," volunteered Meinyt. "There are only six companies in the entire force."

More than a regiment of archers, and he's unhappy? But then, Quaeryt recalled that Myskyl had never appeared to be cheerful about much of anything.

"And he's asked quietly why we don't have musketeers," Meinyt continued, looking to Quaeryt.

"I know Bhayar was looking into forging muskets some time ago, but I don't know what he decided or why."

"Would have helped if he'd done more."

There were always hindsights like that, Quaeryt knew, but forbore pointing it out.

Skarpa had little else new to offer, and that confirmed to Quaeryt that the real purpose of the meeting had been to inform him about the scheming of the marshal and submarshal.

After Skarpa and Meinyt departed, Quaeryt sought out Zhelan and informed him of what the commander had reported about reinforcements and the possible departure westward. Once he finished with Zhelan, Quaeryt then sent word for the imagers to meet in the study. They all arrived together a quint later.

Quaeryt did not sit, but stood before the desk and addressed them. "Commander Skarpa has informed me that Fifth Battalion will be receiving reinforcements, most likely in two days. We are to receive some new imager undercaptains. How many and what their abilities are, I do not know. Once I have assessed those abilities, if they are not up to yours, and I doubt that they are, in one way or another all of you will assist me in training them, because we will have very little time before we will be heading toward Nordeau and then to Variana. If Rex Kharst has any imagers, we are likely to encounter them before long. Likewise, we are likely no longer to be ignored and will probably encounter greater efforts aimed at us. I can't say what those will be because so far as I am aware, never before has any army used more than one or two imagers." What he was not about to point out was that almost none of those imagers employed in past battles had survived the conflicts in which they had been engaged.

"Sir," asked Desyrk, "do you know how many others will be coming?"

"I don't. From what I can gather, Lord Bhayar gave instructions that imagers of the proper age in good health were to be conscripted and dispatched here." Again, Quaeryt was guessing, but since that was what had been done with the undercaptains before him, it was more than likely that the same process had been used. "Are there any other questions?"

After several moments of silence, Quaeryt went on. "While we are waiting, you are to practice your skills, especially strengthening your personal shields. I expect you to work with each other, using staffs or poles to test your shields. At the same time, I'd prefer that you do not maim each other. At third glass, you're all to meet on the terrace outside the study here, with staffs, and I'll be going over shielding with you." He paused. "That's all."

As they filed out of the study, Quaeryt could only hope that their working with less skilled imagers would also lead them to improve their own imaging skills. In the meantime, he needed to think about what other imaging skills might be useful—and unexpected by the Bovarians.

49

Even into Jeudi, drizzle cozed from the low gray clouds, but in not enough volume to prevent the imagers from working on various skills and for Quaeryt to test them. Threkhy had become more and more proficient in creating almost-instant heavy shields and moving them around. So long as he alternated shields, he could maintain that form of shielding for a good quint. Yet, for some reason, he seemed unable to find a way to create and hold a continuous shield for more than a tenth of a quint, and doing that left him totally exhausted.

On the other hand, Voltyr and Shaelyt could hold and maintain light to moderate shields for more than a quint, and heavier shields for up to a third of a quint. Quaeryt took them aside and tried to explain the idea of "triggering" heavier shields. Both understood the idea, but neither seemed able to do so . . . no matter how Quaeryt tried to explain or demonstrate. In the end, he told them both to just build up their shields and keep the idea in mind.

Desyrk could hold moderate shields for a few moments, but not a lighter shield, and a heavier shield exhausted him in moments . . . but Quaeryt could sense that his abilities were improving. Baelthm was unable to master shields, but surprisingly, Quaeryt discovered, he had become able to image much larger iron and metal darts up to a hundred yards.

Late on Jeudi, Quaeryt received a brief message from Skarpa that the reinforcements would arrive on Vendrei around midday, and that the southern army would be riding out on Solayi morning. Since the roads on the south side of the Aluse were poorer, the marshal was allowing additional time for them to reach Nordeau to be in position to fully support an attack there, should it be necessary.

As he stood alone in the absent factor's study, Quaeryt shook his head. *Is Deucalon that unaware, or is he fully aware and playing along with Myskyl until he can undercut him in a way that will totally discredit him?*

Quaeryt knew that, at the moment, he had no way of determining which, if either, might be the case. He also knew that he was seeing only the beginning of political maneuvering that would get deadlier as the battles against Kharst's forces intensified.

He set down Skarpa's message, then looked at his notes, scattered fragments and thoughts about better ways to employ the talents of the imagers. Finally, he reached for the slim leather-bound volume, opening it and paging through it. Reading about Rholan wouldn't solve his problems, but it might take his thoughts out of the ruts he'd worn in his mind by going back and forth over the problems he faced.

Rholan stated on more than one occasion that many faiths declared that man was made in the image of his deity. He went further than that, declaring that this was false, because, in fact, man created the deities he worshipped in his own image, or at least in the images in his mind, and that was why it was all-important that the Nameless not only not ever be named, but never described or depicted, because to do so would prove that the Nameless was merely a creation of men . . .

That angered few because those who declared such largely lived far from Lydar. Such observations would not have, in themselves, led to the events that likely forced his death or disappearance. Nor would the observations that followed, when he declared that those who rule best are those who accept each man or woman for who each is, and that seldom are such rulers remembered in the chronicles of the great, for it seems that little has happened during their reigns. Even when they are successful at conquest, that success is attributed to others, to their marshals, to the times, to the weakness of the enemy. What angered many was his observation that those who are remembered are those least worthy of such veneration, because they were the rulers who have attempted to mold others in their image, either through fear or flattery, because they had not the strength to recognize different strengths in others . . .

Quaeryt set down the small book, turning it over on the plaques table to keep his place. *Is that the difference between Kharst and Bhayar?* He frowned. *Or are you creating that difference in your own mind?*

50

Immediately after the morning muster of Fifth Battalion on Vendrei, Quaeryt met with Voltyr and Shaelyt. The three of them decided on a sheltered courtyard behind the stable to test the arriving undercaptains, then gathered the necessary materials. Although Quaeryt had not yet received word as to when the reinforcements would arrive, he knew he would need every moment he had to assess them and to begin instructing them in the basic imaging in combat. He left Voltyr in charge of setting up the barrels and stands for testing.

While the imagers were so occupied, Quaeryt and Zhelan reviewed the supply situation in turn with each of the company officers. Quaeryt was relieved to learn that Zhelan had been successful in dealing with the local factors and Skarpa's supply major and that enough provisions had been obtained to fill all the wagons.

After he and Zhelan left Major Arion, Quaeryt looked at Zhelan. "I didn't wish to ask around the company officers how you managed all that. But you've worked wonders. How?"

Zhelan tried to smother a grin, then shook his head. "I was most polite, sir. I just kept asking the factors and the supply types in the other regiments for what we needed. If they weren't as helpful as they might have been, I just said that you'd be disappointed if you couldn't support the battalion and the imagers after all the work Lord Bhayar had done to create the battalion. I didn't ask for too much from any of them."

"You're a rogue, Zhelan." Quaeryt shook his head.

"The locals are scared to death of imagers, more so than in Telaryn. Don't know why, sir, but they are, and the supply types in the other regiments know that Fifth Battalion has saved a lot of their men. The ones who are smart want to help. Those who aren't don't want you upset."

That worried Quaeryt, after a fashion, because it suggested that someone, most likely Myskyl, was depicting Quaeryt as vengeful and possibly petty.

Once he and Zhelan finished, Quaeryt returned to the study to go over the maps he had, trying to learn as much as he could from them about what the battalion might expect on the ride to Nordeau. He wasn't certain, but he thought he saw what might have been a part of another old Naedaran canal branching off from the River Aluse just east of Nordeau. At least there was something that looked like a too-straight section of river that paralleled the River Aluse in a general way and ran almost to Nordeau. He couldn't help but wonder how many other canals there had been running to the Aluse or from the lake on which Chelaes was located.

At slightly past first glass, one of the troopers acting as guards rapped on the study door. "Sir . . . there's close to two companies riding up here."

"Summon Major Zhelan and have him join me on the front portico."

"Yes, sir." The trooper hurried off.

Quaeryt made his way out to the front portico. There, as he waited for the riders—and Zhelan—to reach him, he stood and looked out to the west at the scattered clouds that were slowly breaking up. Despite there only having been partial sunlight that morning, the day was warm and humid, and he had to take off his visor cap and blot away sweat before replacing it. The oncoming riders were still some fifty yards away when Zhelan hurried around from the south porch to stand beside Quaeryt.

"Has to be our replacements and reinforcements," offered the major.

Quaeryt looked to Zhelan.

"Uniforms have more color."

Quaeryt smiled. *Something else you hadn't thought of.*

Leading the riders was a captain Quaeryt didn't recognize, scarcely surprising since there were at least fifty captains and undercaptains in Deucalon's forces, most of whom he'd never even seen, let alone met. The captain called the column to a halt, then rode forward, his eyes taking in the two on the portico.

"Subcommander, Major, Marshal Deucalon is transferring these officers and troopers to your command." He dismounted, handing his mount's reins to one of the guard troopers who had hurried down, and climbed the steps. He extended a dispatch pouch. "There is a dispatch there. It confirms the transfer, and the number of officers and men involved." His formal expression softened slightly. "There are also several other communications there."

"Thank you, Captain. We accept the transfer of the officers and men, as described in the dispatch."

"Yes, sir. Thank you, sir." The captain nodded sharply, stepped back, and turned. "You are all now assigned to Fifth Battalion, and Subcommander Quaeryt." Then he walked down the steps and remounted his horse.

"If you'd handle the trooper replacements and reinforcements," Quaeryt said to Zhelan, "and have the undercaptains remain here with me."

"Yes, sir." A faint amused smile appeared on Zhelan's face. "Undercaptains! Forward!"

After a brief hesitation, four men in undress green officers' uniforms, without collar insignia, rode forward and reined up. They appeared passably comfortable in the saddle, but they should have been, reflected Quaeryt, given the days and possibly weeks they had been riding.

"Undercaptains, remain here. Troopers! Follow me." Zhelan hurried down from the steps and walked quickly down the lane toward the stables and outbuildings.

As the troopers slowly rode after the battalion major, Quaeryt studied the undercaptains. Two, from their dark hair and eyes and light-honeyed skin, were most likely Pharsi, and probably younger than Shaelyt. The third undercaptain was sandy-blond, suggesting he was a norther. The last was a man close to forty, with a grizzled gray beard, recently trimmed, Quaeryt suspected, and a narrow lined face that had spent most days out in hard weather.

"Undercaptains . . . welcome to Fifth Battalion. I trust that you're all imagers." Quaeryt paused and scanned the faces, catching the hints of nods. "You're now part of the largest group of imagers assembled as part of a fighting force. You're going to learn how to apply your talents in support of Lord Bhayar. If you're like most imager undercaptains, you'll be asking why you should put yourselves out for Lord Bhayar when you're likely been dragged from wherever you were and whatever you were doing. The answer to that is simple. It's better than the alternatives, and you're being paid reasonably well for your service. More important, it's the only way that you, and all imagers, can obtain a place where you'll be respected and appreciated. If Lord Bhayar succeeds in subduing Bovaria, we'll have a better life and future. That will be true of all imagers. If he fails, we'll all likely have neither life nor future. I don't expect any of you to accept this until you've been with Fifth Battalion for a while. I do expect you to act as officers and to obey orders." He paused.

"And what if we don't?" asked the older man, his tone verging on the insolent.

"That wouldn't be terribly wise, for a number of reasons," replied Quaeryt mildly. "Why are you here?"

"Governor threatened to kill my family."

Quaeryt nodded. "Do you really want to be unable to see them again, to be in hiding the rest of your life, not knowing when someone might recognize and kill you? That's another reason why you're here, isn't it?"

The undercaptain glared at Quaeryt, then nodded grudgingly.

"So . . . doesn't it make sense to do the best you can do here, get your pay, and earn Bhayar's gratitude, rather than run for the rest of your life?"

"Life won't be long here, anyway."

"You'd be surprised," replied Quaeryt with a laugh. "Commander Skarpa's done well at keeping casualties low, far lower than in the northern army."

"You didn't tell me why I should obey you or anyone else."

"Because it's a good idea. Besides, if you disobey, you'll be punished. If you disobey in combat, you could be executed." Quaeryt tried to image-project friendly reasonableness.

"I'm likely to die anyway. Might just be better to off you and stop this nonsense."

"That wouldn't be a very good idea." *What can you say or do to convince this idiot? In a way that won't terrify the others and start them off with the wrong impression . . . if you haven't already?*

"Why don't you let me decide what's a good idea?"

"Because you don't know enough to make a good decision," said Quaeryt. "None of you do . . . yet. Now . . . it's time for you to follow me down to meet the other undercaptains. After that, we'll assign you quarters, and you can stow your gear."

"No. Not until we know more."

Idiot! Quaeryt looked at the graybeard and instantly clamped shields around him, so tightly that the man could not breathe. "You are in Fifth Battalion. You will obey orders, either mine or those of other senior officers, and if necessary, I or the senior undercaptains will take any steps necessary to assure that you do. Or you will no longer have to worry about anything at all." He waited until the older man was turning red before he released the shields, then waited until the undercaptain stopped gasping. "I'd prefer not to have to do anything like that again."

"You can't do that all the time. I've dealt with things larger and tougher than you."

Quaeryt image-projected absolute force and cold authority at the older man, and the absolute certainty that Quaeryt could shred him into bits smaller than grains of sand.

The older imager's face paled.

So did the faces of the other three. The two Pharsi undercaptains exchanged a knowing glance.

"Who . . . what . . . ?" murmured the graybeard.

"Subcommander Quaeryt Rytersyn. I'm a scholar, and the former governor of Montagne, former princeps of Tilbor, and I've survived more than a few battles along the way. Oh . . . and my wife is Lord Bhayar's sister. Do you require any more explanations, Undercaptain?"

"No . . ."

"No, sir, if you please, and I don't wish to correct you again. Ever."

"Yes, sir."

"Let me make this very clear once again. You are all undercaptains in the forces of Telaryn. Provisional undercaptains assigned to the first company of Fifth Battalion. That means you will obey not only my commands, but those of either Major Zhelan or Undercaptain Ghaelyn. Because it is very much in our personal interests not to have you killed, we will not give you orders that are foolish or unnecessary. At times, there will be risks, but all officers have the same risks as the troopers. Now . . . follow me." Quaeryt walked down the steps, making certain his shields were fully in place.

As the four followed him, Quaeryt listened for murmurs, but none of the four said a word. *You tried to be persuasive and rational. But you couldn't let the quibbling and arguing go on. Why do some people only listen to force?*

51

After introducing the new imagers to the other undercaptains, while Voltyr and Shaelyt arranged quarters in the upper levels of the house for the four new undercaptains and took care of other details, Quaeryt returned to the study. He wondered about the regiment likely to be assigned to Skarpa's forces, but the commander would be the one to tell him—if and when Skarpa found out, and Quaeryt suspected that Deucalon would take his time.

Once Quaeryt settled at the plaques table, he set aside the letter from Vaelora, as well as one for Shaelyt, and another for Baelthm, and opened the dispatch from Marshal Deucalon.

> Subcommander Quaeryt Rytersyn
> Fifth Battalion
>   Attached is a listing of four undercaptains (provisional) and 182 troopers
> assigned to Fifth Battalion in order to bring the battalion up to full fighting strength.

Beneath the words was a seal, not even a signature. The second sheet held four names:

> Horan Horotsyn, Undercaptain
> Khalis Mhaersyn, Undercaptain
> Lhandor Lohansyn, Undercaptain
> Smaethyl Rytersyn, Undercaptain

Quaeryt nodded. The names did match those the officers had given, not that he'd doubted it, but sometimes you never knew, Quaeryt reflected. The next five sheets held the names of the troopers. Quaeryt returned his attention to the second sheet, looking at the names and mentally connecting them to the undercaptains. Horan was the mountain steader and trapper who'd given him trouble and who would likely be less difficult as time went by. *You hope.* Khalis and Lhandor were Pharsi, but

Khalis was from Estisle, while Lhandor was from Lucayl. Smaethyl was from a small town in Montagne that Quaeryt had never heard of—Taelyrd.

He laid the dispatch on the table and studied Vaelora's letter. Again, the seal had been carefully removed and then replaced. With a nod, he opened it and began to read.

> My dearest,
> The summer here in Solis has been long and hot. The first two days of harvest have
> been no cooler, and we have had no rain to cool the nights.
>   You cautioned me that this war would be long and bloody. Lord Bhayar must
> feel the same way, as new regiments are being formed and trained every other week.
> At least, it seems that way, and Aelina told me that another ten regiments will be
> dispatched to join the northern forces early next week.

Ten regiments? Had ten regiments arrived? Certainly Bhayar had given the impression that there were far fewer. He'd actually mentioned four. Why hadn't he known there were ten? And if there weren't ten, where had the others gone? Or had someone drawn the golds to supply ten and sent four or seven or whatever number less than that and pocketed the "extra" golds. Or were Myskyl and Deucalon keeping the exact number from Bhayar as long as possible—or at least until Skarpa and his command had left Villerive—so that more regiments weren't assigned to Skarpa?

> . . . There are also some undercaptains being sent to assist you. I understand that
> most of them come from smaller towns. In the weeks and months ahead, there will
> likely be others found with talents that you can use, since local governors have been
> promised a bonus for those found, and since such discoveries may also suit both
> High Holders and larger factors.

In short, they want to remove imagers. Quaeryt smiled. They should be careful in making such wishes. After a moment he thought, So should you.

When he finished the letter, he studied the date—2 Agostas. Almost four weeks—and it had arrived with the reinforcements that had been dispatched a week later. Again, it appeared as though her letter had been opened and delayed. So you wouldn't know the number of reinforcement regiments?

He certainly had no proof of that, but the pattern was suggestive.

Vaelora's letter reminded him that he needed to send what he had already written to her, and what he would write later that evening—and that he had never replied to Gauswn.

He stood and slipped her letter into his personal dispatch case, leaving it on the table, then picked up the two letters and the five sheets that held the names of the new troopers to give to Zhelan. Then he headed back down to the stable courtyard to evaluate the new imagers.

Two quints later, Quaeryt stood fifty yards back from the stable wall, against which were two barrels set on their ends, the closed butt end up. A thick plank ran from one barrel to the other, set on its edge with each end propped in place with bricks. The four most recent imager undercaptains stood in a line even with Quaeryt. Voltyr and Shaelyt watched from the side.

"Undercaptain Khalis," said Quaeryt, "image an iron dart into the plank."

"Yes, sir." The Pharsi undercaptain, a gawky young man, barely more than a youth, who looked to be two or three years younger than Shaelyt, concentrated. An iron dart, more like a knife that was made of iron, appeared in the heavy plank fifty yards way, its tip barely sticking into the wood before it wobbled and dropped to the dirt.

"Less iron in the dart and more force into the plank next time," commented Quaeryt before turning to Smaethyl. "Undercaptain Smaethyl, an iron dart into the plank."

Smaethyl's dart was half the size of the previous one and buried half its length in the wood as it carried the plank to the back ends of the barrel butt, and then over, so that the plank dropped until it was wedged between the barrel and the stable wall, the iron dart still protruding.

"Good," declared Quaeryt. "Barbed blade?"

"Yes, sir." Smaethyl's face showed momentary puzzlement.

"You look like a hunter, and the blade didn't move." Quaeryt nodded to Voltyr. "If you'd image away the dart and re-set the plank."

The dart vanished from the plank and reappeared at Voltyr's feet. He picked it up and handed it to Quaeryt. Then he and Shaelyt walked forward to the barrel and replaced the plank, then returned to their position behind Quaeryt.

Quaeryt kept his smile within his face after watching Horan's face as Voltyr imaged away the knife. The older imager had clearly been surprised. *Good. After a few more surprises, he might not be so arrogant.* "Undercaptain Lhandor, your turn."

Lhandor's dart was more elegantly shaped, but buried itself in the plank as deeply as had that of Smaethyl.

"Your turn, Undercaptain Horan."

Horan didn't image a dart but something more like an ax that splintered the top of the plank.

Quaeryt looked at the perspiration and the redness suffusing the older imager's face. "If you would do that again."

Horan opened his mouth, then shut it, and turned to face the plank. A second ax dart wedged itself into the plank, but not nearly so deeply. Horan staggered, then lowered his head for several moments.

"Undercaptain Horan," said Quaeryt firmly but not angrily. "We're training for war, not for hunting. If you use all your strength in the first effort, the least experienced trooper will be able to knock you out of the saddle in moments. The idea is to be able to repeat the effort, quickly time after time."

Horan straightened.

Quaeryt could almost read the other's thoughts. He concentrated.

One after the other, five iron darts buried themselves in the plank, with such force that they went through the wood and pinned the plank to the stable wall, so quickly that the plank was not slanted in the slightest.

"Do you see?" asked Quaeryt, smiling.

Horan swallowed. "Yes, sir."

"Now . . . one of the tactics that has been most useful in dealing with the Bovarians is imaging thick and acrid smoke mixed with the finest grains of pepper. For some reason," continued Quaeryt, "they find it hard to concentrate on trying to kill us when they have trouble seeing and they are sneezing violently. Undercaptain Shaelyt will demonstrate . . ."

Quaeryt, Voltyr, and Shaelyt worked with the newest undercaptains until two quints past fourth glass, when Quaeryt dismissed them all in time to wash up before mess. He returned to the factor's house and washed as well, for although he had not been exhausted from imaging, the afternoon had still been hot and damp, and his face was damp and coated in dust and sweat.

After he cleaned up, he went down to the study, where he sat down at the plaques table and considered what he had seen of the four imagers. All of them were as accomplished, if not slightly more so, than Shaelyt had initially been. That made sense, because accomplished imagers who were either more isolated or more accomplished might not have been so easily discovered.

Then, a good quint before the evening mess, Quaeryt raised a concealment shield and slipped out of the study when no one was looking and eased down the hallway to a point near the archway into the main dining chamber where the officers were beginning to gather.

Smaethyl was talking to Desyrk, and Quaeryt could only catch some of the words.

". . . always . . . work that hard . . . so quick . . ."

". . . had us out working and seeing what we could do the morning after he showed up."

". . . always wants us to do more," murmured Baelthm. ". . . find you can . . ."

Horan looked at Threkhyl and lowered his voice. "The officers in the other army never said the subcommander was a master imager. They said he was a scholar."

"More than a master imager," said Threkhyl curtly.

"He is both," replied Shaelyt, "and more."

The other two Pharsi undercaptains, who flanked Shaelyt, both nodded.

"How do you two know that?" asked Horan. "You never saw him before."

"We saw him today," replied Lhandor. "It is worth your life to cross one such as he."

"He is a lost one," added Khalis. "Or . . . as you easterners might say, a Namer-cursed spawn of Erion."

You easterners? thought Quaeryt. *Where is Khalis from? Another Khellan refugee? But he speaks Tellan without an accent.*

"Except the lost ones are doomed to do good, no matter what it costs them," added Shaelyt. "That's why so many curse them."

Shaelyt didn't quite let you know that, either.

"True what he said about being a governor and all?"

"Every word of it," interjected Voltyr. "He didn't tell you, but he's known Lord Bhayar since they were students as youths."

"Then . . . why . . . ?"

"Why is he only a subcommander?" answered Voltyr. "Because that is what Lord Bhayar wants and because Subcommander Quaeryt knows his limits and seldom presses beyond his capabilities—except sometimes— when he truly astounds anyone who has eyes to see."

"You make him sound like . . . a god . . ."

Voltyr shook his head. "He is very human. He listens to what others say and thinks about it. He tries hard to be a good man and a good commander, and he's better than most in those . . . but I would not cross him for anything."

"When we might have died if we had fought, he refused to take the battalion into battle," added Shaelyt. "He defied the marshal for us."

I had Skarpa's help and support, thank the Nameless . . . and Braylar's. After a moment another thought came to Quaeryt. *How did Shaelyt find that out? From Zhelan? You'd best be more careful in what you reveal.*

". . . pay's not bad, either," added Threkhyl.

Quaeryt did not want to move, for fear of making sounds that would reveal him. So he listened as the talk turned to what had happened on the way to Villerive. Finally the chimes sounded fifth glass, and the officers filed into the dining chamber. When everyone had entered, and he saw no one around, Quaeryt released the concealment and stepped into the dining chamber. As usual, all the officers stood.

"As you were." Quaeryt stepped to the head of the table. "No long talks tonight. I'd like to welcome Undercaptains Horan, Khais, Lhandor, and Smaethyl. They're solid imagers, and they'll strengthen our ability to deal with the Bovarians." With that, he seated himself.

After everyone had been served, and lager and ale filled every mug, Zhelan asked, "Do we know when we'll be setting out on Solayi, sir?"

"Commander Skarpa hasn't said, but if he's the one to decide, and not the marshal, we'll be on the road two quints past dawn on Solayi. I should know tomorrow."

From that point on, the conversation turned on speculations as to what they would face on the south side of the River Aluse on the way to Nordeau.

After dinner, Quaeryt returned to the study, imaged one of the lamps into light, and settled at the table to deal with his correspondence. First, he needed to write Gauswn, even though the letter would offer no solution. He'd have to send the letter through Straesyr, since regular dispatch riders would only go to Solis and then to Tilbora, but he had no doubts that the governor would have it delivered to the chorister—although it was likely it would take weeks, if not a month or more, to reach its destination. So the first letter was to his former superior.

Dear Governor Straesyr—

I would appreciate it greatly if you would see that the enclosed letter to Chorister Gauswn reaches him, since he took great pains to request my advice regarding

imagers and the scholarium in Tilbora. I regret that I cannot provide any solutions
for his difficulty and only advice, but I would suggest to you, if news of great
difficulty at the scholarium comes to you, that you replace the master scholar with
the princeps for the rest of the master scholar's year, and return the master scholar
to his previous position. Of course, if you have a better solution, and well you may
have, since it has been some time since I was in Tilbora, I would certainly
recommend you implement it . . .

The remainder of the letter was a quick summary of what had occurred to Quaeryt himself since he had left Tilbor, followed by good
wishes and pleasantries.

After that, it took several attempts before he could write the letter to
Gauswn.

Dear Gauswn—
Your letter just recently reached me, since Lord Bhayar requested I leave my position
in Extela and join the campaign against the Bovarians. I am currently a
subcommander in command of Fifth Battalion somewhere in Bovaria . . .

    I understand and appreciate your concerns about both the scholarium and the
young imagers who find themselves with you as their only true friend. I commend
you for your concern and compassion for them, and I cannot tell you how much I
appreciate that. While there is little I can do at this very moment, I can assure you
that I am working toward a goal that may help resolve the problems you brought to
my attention. I have also made a suggestion to Governor Straesyr as to one possible
course of action, should matters at the scholarium worsen. If you, in your best
judgment, feel that the existence of the scholarium is threatened, do not hesitate to
seek him out. He is a good man and governor, and just as well as fair.

    In the meantime, I wish you well and trust that sometime in the year ahead I
can offer more than advice . . .

He concluded with a few more pleasantries, then reread Vaelora's letter before attempting a reply.

My dear one,
Your second letter has just reached me, and I have little time in which to respond
before we again set out. The battle for south Villerive was difficult and exhausting,
so much so that my undercaptains and Fifth Battalion required some rest before
joining in the battle for the north side of the city, an unfortunate situation whose

necessity Commander Skarpa was able to convey to the marshal with far greater skill and diplomacy than I possess. In the end, we were able to assist the marshal's valiant troops to some degree, and to help in enabling his forces to rout and destroy a great proportion of the Bovarians arrayed against us.

Quaeryt paused and set down the pen. Why hadn't there been more resistance? Admittedly, the defenders had certainly fought, but shouldn't there have been more of them? In fact, there should have been more all along. *Was it because Kharst had only intended to try to seize Ferravyl, and then withdraw if matters turned unfavorable?* That was certainly possible. The history of war in Lydar had a common thread—no ruler had ever successfully conquered a strong and prepared neighbor, only ones with internal weaknesses or problems. Had the Bovarian attack on Ferravyl been more an attempt to probe for Telaryn weakness, a weakness suggested to Kharst by the revolt of the Tilboran hill holders? Had the Bovarian rex assumed that Bhayar was a weak heir to his father and that most Telaryn forces remained in Tilbor? Given that, had the attack on Ferravyl been designed, at most, as the beginning of a campaign of piecemeal acquisition, as Bhayar had told Quaeryt?

Then, when Quaeryt had destroyed the majority of the Bovarian forces, Kharst had not been prepared for a Telaryn counterattack in force, and had been using the troopers who remained in the east to slow the Telaryn advance, giving up territory while he mustered troops from across all Bovaria. To Quaeryt, that was the only thing that made sense. After several moments, he picked up the pen again.

I did not receive your latest correspondence until after the reinforcements arrived, and that was several days after the battle, but I was delighted to learn that all was well with you, even if Solis has been hot and damp. The newest undercaptains should prove most helpful, and their training is already well under way . . .

I also heard from Chorister Gauswn, since he wrote me for advice on dealing with the students for whom you helped me draft rules of conduct, and while I could not offer him an immediate solution, I am hopeful that once matters in Bovaria are settled, we may be able to resolve the problems he faces as well by setting up another scholarium, but one designed more for students such as those.

The weather here remains as hot as if it were still late summer or early harvest, rather than mid to late harvest, but warm as it is here or in Solis, I would that we were together . . .

When he finished the letter, he sat back, then reread it again. Assuming that Vaelora actually received it, he thought she would be able to read beyond what he had written. He could only hope that she and Aelina were handling the responsibilities with which Bhayar had left them, and that those surrounding them were not surreptitiously lining their wallets in too excessive a fashion.

52

On Samedi, all of Fifth Battalion was up early. Quaeryt set the companies to working drills immediately after muster, conducting maneuvers and drills to familiarize their replacements with their officers, tactics and squad leaders. He worked with all the imagers on both the tactics that had become basics, such as imaging smoke and pepper, and targeting enemies with iron darts, but also trying to at least familiarize the new undercaptains with the idea of shields and shielding.

During the first break in training, at around eighth glass, a brief message arrived from Skarpa, noting that the southern forces had been assigned Eleventh Regiment, led by Subcommander Khaern, and that Skarpa and the other subcommanders would join Quaeryt sometime after third glass to discuss Solayi's evolutions. Since Quaeryt really wanted to talk to Skarpa before all the subcommanders met, he sent a messenger to locate Skarpa, but a glass later the trooper reported back that the commander had been summoned by Marshal Deucalon early that morning, and that none of the Third Regiment battalion majors knew exactly where Skarpa was or when he was expected to return. The trooper checked with Fifth Regiment, but Subcommander Meinyt had no idea, either, beyond the fact that Skarpa had to be doing something Deucalon desired.

Although Quaeryt suspected he knew where Skarpa was likely to be, he wasn't about to charge over to Deucalon's headquarters and burst in and demand to see Skarpa. Such an act wouldn't change anything, but it would prove to everyone that Quaeryt thought he was above his rank and cast doubt on Bhayar's appointment of him as a subcommander. So he went back to working with the imagers, until slightly after third glass, when he dismissed them.

At roughly fourth glass, Skarpa rode up to Saarcoyn's dwelling, with a half squad of troopers as an escort. Quaeryt barely managed to get out onto the portico before Skarpa reined up.

"Meinyt will be here shortly. So will Khaern," the commander announced as he dismounted "I sent a messenger to them both. This is

midway between all three regiments, and we need to go over our departure tomorrow."

"We can wait in the study, and I'll send for some lager."

"That would be welcome."

"I thought it might." Quaeryt gestured toward the entry, then followed Skarpa inside, after sending one of the troopers to have three mugs
of lager brought to the study.

Once the lagers arrived, and the study door was closed, Quaeryt sat
down across the plaques table from Skarpa. "I need to talk to you before
the others arrive. I sent a messenger to you this morning. I'd hoped to
talk to you, and I hadn't realized that you'd be tied up all day. I'm sorry I
didn't seek you out last night, but . . ." He shrugged. "I should have
known better."

"About what?"

"I received a letter from Vaelora yesterday afternoon, but I didn't read
it until later, when I thought I'd have a moment to enjoy it. In it she mentioned that I would be getting some more undercaptains and that ten
regiments were being sent to reinforce us—"

"Ten regiments?"

"That's what she wrote. What's also odd is that the letter was sent a
week before the regiments were due to depart from Solis. Yet it arrived
with the marshal's dispatch accompanying the Fifth Battalion reinforcements. Oh . . . and the seal had been removed and replaced"—Quaeryt
quickly explained about the altered seal and the unusual delay of Vaelora's
first letter—"so when I read about ten regiments of reinforcements . . ."

"That frigging bastard Deucalon . . . calling Khaern's regiment the
Eleventh! I should have guessed . . . I saw an awful lot of troopers, and I
asked Deucalon about the number of reinforcements. He never really answered me."

"You couldn't very well demand an answer," Quaeryt pointed out.

"But you could have asked Bhayar. That's why Deucalon summoned me
early. I'd wager you weren't supposed to get that letter until later . . . except
someone saw it who might report that to him. I had the feeling they were
up to something. What they said they wanted was a waste of time after the
first glass. When I'd say I needed to get back to the regiment, Myskyl or
Deucalon had one request after another. 'If you wouldn't mind telling Commander Crecytt about the musketeers . . . Commander Dafaul about . . .
Bovarian scouts . . .'"

"But if I went to Bhayar, around you and Myskyl and Deucalon . . ."

Skarpa nodded slowly. "You'd have undermined me, and hurt yourself, and you wouldn't have gotten us any more troopers. If Bhayar had overruled Deucalon, then he'd have pissed off every senior officer in Telaryn, except us, and Deucalon would have resigned." After a moment he mused, "Actually, it's not a bad plot on Myskyl's part. He puts you in a poor position no matter what, and even if you got us more troopers, then he's got a shot at becoming marshal."

"Or Deucalon throws the blame on Myskyl and demotes him, and we still aren't much better off," replied Quaeryt.

"Don't you just love being a senior officer, Quaeryt?"

"You've got no one but yourself to blame," countered Quaeryt with a smile. "You're the one who insisted I'd be good at it."

"You are. I'd rather have you than two full regiments. The problem is that Deucalon and Myskyl know it, and they'll try to get a victory over the Bovarians by putting you and the imagers in a situation where even if you win, you'll lose."

"That thought had occurred to me." Quaeryt took a swallow of the lager, then set the mug down on the table. "We just have to figure out a way to play our plaques so that everyone wins and it becomes obvious that Deucalon and Myskyl didn't want it to happen that way."

"You have that figured out?"

"Not yet." Quaeryt offered a grin. "I've got until we take Variana, maybe even longer."

"You make that sound easy. You really think . . ."

"No . . . it will either be long and bloody, or short and horribly brutal. That all depends on what Kharst does."

"What's your wager?"

Quaeryt shook his head, even as he thought, *Horribly brutal, no matter how it turns out, but especially if Kharst can gather all his troops.*

"Oh . . . I should tell you about Khaern. He was posted here from Lucayl. He commanded a battalion there that was charged with rooting out the pirates. Won't say he got all of them, but the number of merchanters lost dropped by more than two-thirds in the two years he was there." Skarpa snorted. "Rumor is that was one reason why he was promoted and his battalion became the core of Eleventh Regiment."

"Oh . . . ?"

"Several of the High Holders southeast of Rule have holdings and wealth far more than might be expected from their lands."

Quaeryt didn't bother to sigh. He could believe it.

"Anyway, he seems like a solid type. Most likely why we got him."

"And because he's junior to you," suggested Quaeryt.

"Of course." Skarpa lifted the mug and took a swallow.

For a short time, neither officer spoke.

"Don't look forward to the month ahead—"

At that moment, a trooper rapped on the study door. "Subcommander Meinyt and Subcommander Khaern are here, sirs."

"Show them in."

Meinyt opened the door, ushered in a short and wiry subcommander with red hair shot liberally with gray, and stepped into the study, closing the door behind him before the trooper standing there could. "We got here as soon as we could."

Both Skarpa and Quaeryt stood.

Skarpa looked to Khaern. "Subcommander, this is Subcommander Quaeryt." After the slightest pause, he added, "I've told each of you about the other."

"I'm pleased to meet you," offered Quaeryt.

"The same." Khaern grinned warmly. "You don't look like the deadliest officer Commander Skarpa has ever seen . . . but he said you wouldn't."

Quaeryt shrugged helplessly. "I just do what's necessary to support the commander."

"Sometimes that's whether I've ordered him to or not."

"Have I ever done anything that wasn't to support you and in our interest?"

"No"—Skarpa laughed—"but at times you've done it before anyone realized what happened."

Quaeryt decided to put an end to that line of bantering and gestured to the plaques table, saying cheerfully, "Your lagers are waiting for you."

"We could use those." Meinyt dropped into the chair across from Skarpa, who had seated himself.

Khaern eased into the one opposite Quaeryt, waiting momentarily for Quaeryt to sit.

After taking a swallow from his mug, Meinyt asked, "Have you two decided how to take Nordeau before the marshal orders another stupid attack that will cost too many troops?"

"We were getting to that," said Skarpa.

"If he'd just have let the Bovarians withdraw to that hill and let the imagers deal with the Antiagon Fire first, we'd have lost less than a battalion, instead of a regiment. But no . . . he wants to attack when he wants to attack." With a snort, Meinyt lifted his mug again.

After setting down his mug, Khaern gave the slightest of nods, but said nothing.

"How are your replacements?" asked Skarpa.

"They're replacements. Some of them barely know one end of a sabre from the other. A few even have to hang on to the saddle if they move faster than a trot." Meinyt took another healthy swallow of lager.

"And your new battalions?" Skarpa asked Khaern.

"I had to raise them out of Lucayl and around there. We trained them for a few weeks there, and then on the road. We joined the others at Ferravyl."

"That explains the Eleventh Regiment," said Quaeryt to Skarpa.

For an instant Skarpa looked as though he would swear, but he only nodded.

"What are you talking about?" asked Meinyt.

"The marshal decided that when he received eleven regiments of reinforcements, the southern army should get one." Skarpa nodded to Khaern. "Not that I'm not very glad to have you, but another regiment in addition to yours would have been helpful."

A puzzled expression appeared on Khaern's face. "How many regiments are there in the northern army, then?"

"Twenty-two, from what we can figure," replied Skarpa.

Meinyt almost choked on his lager. "That—" He stopped as he caught the look from the commander.

Skarpa said to Quaeryt calmly, "I haven't heard about your new under-captains."

"They're not bad," Quaeryt admitted. "Two Pharsi youths who still could be students, but they're decent imagers. Two hill types. One wanted to kill me, but decided trying wouldn't do much for his future. The other I don't know, but he can image a lot of iron darts."

"Sounds like you did better than I did," said Meinyt.

"Zhelan had the same complaint as you did about the replacements for first company," said Quaeryt. "The Khellan officers didn't get enough to reach full complement, but all the ones they got were Khellan Pharsi types who'd been injured and had recovered. They got replacements for about nine of every ten they've lost."

"Why do you think you got better imagers?" asked Skarpa.

"A lot of the factors and High Holders don't like imagers. Second, the four I got don't look that good—two almost still schoolboys, a wild imager trapper, and an independent norther."

"Still less than half a squad . . . well, half a squad counting you," said Meinyt.

"Let Deucalon and the Bovarians think that," declared Skarpa. "We need to talk about what we're going to be doing tomorrow and on the way to Nordeau . . ."

Quaeryt nodded and squared himself in the chair.

53

Skarpa insisted that Fifth Battalion lead the way back through Villerive and over the bridge—and that he ride with Quaeryt. Third Regiment followed Fifth Battalion, then Eleventh, the engineers and support wagons, and finally Fifth Regiment. The column moved out from Saackon's grounds just as the sun cleared the tops of the ridge to the east. Shaelyt and the two young Pharsi undercaptains rode immediately behind Quaeryt and Skarpa, while Voltyr rode beside Horan, with the other undercaptains behind them.

"Don't see many of the marshal's troops up this morning," observed Skarpa as they rode past the estate quartering senior officers under Deucalon and some of the northern regiments.

"Ours wouldn't be moving this early, either, if we weren't headed out," replied Quaeryt with a smile "It is Solayi." That was why he'd been up later than he would have liked on Samedi night arranging his letters to be dispatched through one of Bhayar's personal aides. They still might be read, but they would be sent

"Speaking of that . . ." Skarpa drew out the words

"Yes?"

"You know very well what I'm about to say, Subcommander and Master Chorister."

"I fear that I do. What choice do I have?" Quaeryt paused. "But only if it does not take away from what is necessary for a proper encampment."

"We won't hold services if we cannot do so safely and properly," agreed Skarpa.

As they rode past the abandoned earthworks and into Villerive proper, Quaeryt noted that few if any windows were shuttered, and that, early as it was on Solayi, people were on the streets, and taking only passing notice of the Telaryn troopers. *What does that mean? That they expect we'll come and go? Or that it matters little who rules, so long as their lives are not disrupted?*

Quaeryt suspected that indifference to who ruled combined with a recognition that Bhayar had not allowed and did not intend to allow his troopers to molest the locals was the most likely reason for the near-casual acceptance of the troopers. Even with the apparent calm in Villerive, he maintained full shields, rather than triggered shields, as much to try to build up his imaging strength as because he expected a sudden attack. *Those will come once we're nearing Nordeau.*

When the outriders and scouts reached the approach to the bridge over the River Aluse, Quaeryt noted that all traces of the barricades that the Bovarians had erected had vanished, as had any traces of the battle—except for the fact that the stonework and pavement were far, far cleaner than was usual in any city he'd visited.

Behind him, he could hear Shaelyt's quiet explanation to Khalis and Lhandor as they rode through the gap in the wall he'd imaged to block the Bovarians.

"Subcommander imaged that wall in place, except it was all the way across the bridge, until Threkhyl removed the middle part . . . Subcommander led the charge that broke their pikemen, and then rode three milles and took out the Bovarian catapults and their Antiagon Fire . . ."

Quaeryt winced, noticeably enough that Skarpa chuckled and said, in a voice that barely carried to Quaeryt, "You can't keep what you've done that quiet."

"Except among Deucalon's senior officers," Quaeryt murmured back.

"They don't care much for scholars who are good commanders."

"Or those officers who are the best commanders."

"Too many marshals and submarshals are like ministers that swarm around a ruler. They toady up to him. Worried more that a better commander might replace them than about the best way to win. Might be why we got Khaern. He might show up some of Deucalon's favorites."

Quaeryt certainly hoped so. He'd been impressed by Khaern's quiet assurance when they had met the afternoon before.

Once they were over the bridge and through south Villerive, Quaeryt couldn't help but notice that locals had been digging where the imagers had buried defenders under the flattened earthworks. *Scavengers . . . but how can you blame them with the way Kharst treats his own people?*

While Quaeryt had anticipated that the road to Nordeau would quickly deteriorate once they left the more populated area, it did not. Less than a mille west of what remained of the earthworks, the south river road ended at a road that had come from the south—one that was narrower than the compacted clay and gravel way that had led out of Villerive, but constructed of a solid, if somewhat worn, gray stone, wide enough, if barely, for two wagons side by side. It was also far more level than the river road had been heretofore—except for the one stretch near the old canal.

Quaeryt looked south, but the road angled to the southwest, its course not following the valleys but low ridges and even cut into the gentle hillsides in places. The dust over the stone indicated it was seldom traveled to the south.

He turned to Skarpa. "This is a better road than the one out of Villerive. The maps don't give an indication how good it is."

"Could be that it won't last. Might just be a stretch leading to a High Holder's place."

At Skarpa's remark, Quaeryt realized that for the last thirty milles or so leading into Villerive, they'd seen no trace of a High Holder. *Was that another reason why the Bovarians drove off the locals? Or aren't there many High Holders around on this side of the river?* There was so much he didn't know and not enough time to find it out.

His eyes went back to the road, and then to a low retaining wall on the side of the road away from the river. He frowned. *Where did you last see stonework like this?* After a moment he remembered. *The Naedaran canal!*

Quaeryt wondered just how long the paving would last, but after five milles it showed no sign of vanishing. Although the map showed it as just the south river road, and did not depict the section running southeast from outside Villerive, Quaeryt had the feeling that the road might have once run all the way to Chelaes, not that he had any way of proving that at the moment. If so, it suggested that Villerive wasn't nearly so old as it appeared, or that it had been little other than a village until recently because if a city of any size had existed at the time the Naedarans had controlled the area, the road from Chelaes would likely have gone more directly to Villerive.

When they stopped to water the mounts and give the men a break just after noon, Quaeryt couldn't resist saying to Skarpa, 'Quite a stretch for a High Holder's drive."

Skarpa smiled back. "He must have wanted it badly."

As Quaeryt considered the road, that gave him an idea for a homily—one that would be appropriate whether he had to conduct services that night or sometime in the future.

By late afternoon there was still no sign that the ancient stone road would disappear, but the scouts rode back and reported. "Sirs, about a mille ahead there's a holding. Looks like a High Holder's place. Gates are locked, but we can see the hold house, and it's shuttered. Couldn't see anyone around."

"Might be a good place to stop," Skarpa said to Quaeryt. "Why don't you see?"

"Shaelyt, Khalis, join me. Undercaptain Ghaelyn . . . if you'd assign a squad to accompany us?"

"Yes, sir. First squad on the subcommander!"

A quint later Quaeryt reined up before the entry lane on the south side of the stone-paved road that continued westward into the distance. The iron gates to the holding were attached to pillars a yard square, each faced with dark red brick and topped with a square flat gray capstone. A low wall, less than two yards high, extended for thirty yards on each side of the gates before merging with ancient hedgerows. A large single lock held the chains that secured the gates.

Quaeryt turned to Shaelyt. "If you would remove the lock, Undercaptain."

"Yes, sir." Shaelyt dismounted, handed his mount's reins to Khalis, and walked over to the gates. After a moment the lock hasp separated from the body, and Shaelyt caught the lock, then extracted the hasp from the chains.

"Squad Leader, if you'd have troopers open the gates," ordered Quaeryt.

In moments Shaelyt had set the lock and hasp on the stone paving by the gate pillar and remounted, while two troopers were unwinding the chain and then opening the gates.

Once the gates were open, Quaeryt eased the mare forward and led the way. The lane to the hold house was paved in the same gray stone as the ancient road and ran straight back less than two hundred yards to the top of a rise so low that the incline was barely perceptible.

When Quaeryt reached the square paved area before the hold house, he reined up. The hold house itself was modest, at least for a High Holder's dwelling, built of a dark reddish brick with a rose-colored tile roof and perhaps only a third again as large as Factor Saarcoyn's dwelling. The main entry had a small roofed porch, not even a portico, behind which was the main section of the dwelling, large and square, from which extended two wings. The shutters, tightly closed, were of dark stained wood, while the wooden trim was painted an off-white. The wide single front door was of oiled oak and ironbound.

Quaeryt dismounted, handing the mare's reins to Shaelyt, and walked to the door, carrying full shields. He pounded on the door, not expecting any response . . . and after a time was convinced that he would receive none.

He studied the door for a moment, then concentrated, trying to image away the door hinges. Nothing seemed to happen. He stepped forward and pressed on the door. It shivered, but did not move. Then he pulled on the door lever—and jumped to the side as the door leaned toward him and then crashed down on the stone paved entryway. In the archway behind the door was an iron gratework. Quaeryt could see the bolts holding it in place and imaged them away. The gratework fell inward and struck the polished stone floor of the narrow entry hall with a dull dung.

With three troopers leading the way, Quaeryt made a quick inspection of the dwelling. Some of the larger and more common furnishings remained, but only those that were worn, at least what would have been considered worn for a High Holder. Everything smaller and of value had been removed—and relatively recently, from the lack of dust. After checking the hold house, Quaeryt returned to the front, mounted, and rode to the courtyard on the west side between the dwelling and the three outbuildings.

None of the three had been constructed recently, but all had rose-colored tile roofs that appeared comparatively newer than the buildings. The smallest and oldest-looking structure was of one story, square, and built of gray stones that looked to be similar, if not identical, to the paving stones in the ancient road, while the long stable and what seemed to be a warehouse were built of the same dark reddish brick as the hold house. *Do the road, the lane, and the oldest building actually date back to Naedarar times?*

Inspections of the stables and the two storehouses revealed that all stores had been emptied and all livestock driven away. While Quaeryt doubted that such quantities could have been moved far, it would have taken days, if not longer, to track it down. Still, all the buildings made the hold a good point for stopping, especially since the map showed no towns or hamlets that close and since the scouts had discovered nothing better. The stone-paved road had also meant they had covered far more distance than either Skarpa or Quaeryt had thought possible.

With those thoughts in mind he rode back and met Skarpa, who had halted the column at the gates.

"Well?" asked the commander.

"It's largely empty. No stores and no supplies, but there's fresh water, and it would be a good place to stop."

"Hoped it might be." Skarpa grinned. "And there's time to have evening services."

"I didn't think you'd forget that."

Fifth Battalion led the way up the narrow lane. It was more than a glass later before all the troopers and wagons had been drawn up around the hold house, and another glass after that before men and mounts were settled. The troopers did get warm food, if hastily prepared, half a glass before sunset, and it was twilight before Skarpa announced services would begin in a quint.

Even so, more than a thousand troopers and officers were waiting when Quaeryt stepped onto the porch overlooking the west courtyard where they were gathered.

More voice image-projecting, he thought as he moved forward to the wooden railing that ran from the end brick pillars over a line of half pillars. "We gather together in the spirit of the Nameless and to affirm the quest for goodness and mercy in all that we do."

Once more he led them in the opening hymn, and then the confession.

"All evenings are good evenings under the Nameless." He paused slightly after beginning the homily. "Even those spent riding along a stone-paved road that appears unchanging and endless while squad leaders and officers insist that it does lead somewhere, and that you really want to get there."

At least a few chuckles murmured up from the men.

"But the more I looked at that road, and if you're riding in front, you can occasionally see it, the more I wondered about it, because that road has been there not for years, but for hundreds of years, and it was so well built that it still rides better than most roads built since then. Who built it? Why did they build it so well? As a scholar, I can answer the first question. The Naedarans built it. Who were they? No one, including scholars, knows much about them, except that they were the first people to declare the Nameless as the creator of all and that they ruled this part of Lydar from Solis almost to Variana and as far south as the Lohan Hills that form the border with Antiago . . . and that they built buildings, canals, and roads that still endure.

"What does this have to do with us? More than you might think. Once they were the greatest people in Lydar and possibly in all Terahnar. Today we know little of them and none of their names. Only their works survive . . . Can you think of a greater testament to the futility of trying to make your name last forever? Doesn't this suggest that the works we do will long outlast who we are and who will remember us?

"All of us are engaged together in a great work. We are working—and fighting—to unite all Lydar under the most just ruler. Is Lord Bhayar perfect? Of course not. But he is a lord who seeks justice and who does not burn his own people's crops and send assassins after any lord or factor who has the slightest unkind word for him. He has applied the same laws to Tilborans, Piedrans, Pharsi. and imagers." After the slightest pause, he added, self-deprecatingly, "Oh . . . and scholars as well."

That brought a brief laugh.

"In a generation, even in a few years, no one will remember heroics on the battlefield, but when we succeed in building a land where the laws apply equally to all, that will be a greater legacy than any name . . . any reputation . . . for names fade, no matter what the disciples of the Namer may claim, but deeds and good works do not."

After the closing hymn, he concluded with the simple words that approximated a benediction. "As we have come together to seek meaning and renewal, let us go forth this evening renewed in hope and in harmony with that which was, is, and ever shall be."

Then he stepped back into the west parlor of the hold house.

Skarpa, who was waiting, shook his head. "Your words are good, but you hold them even beyond that "

"I try not to say anything I don't believe," Quaeryt replied.

"That shows through."

"That's why I can't say what I don't believe." Quaeryt smiled wryly.

54

As they rode westward on the narrow ancient stone-paved road on Lundi morning, Quaeryt noted that the road had been constructed to stay as flat as possible over long stretches and well above the flood level of the River Aluse, even when that meant detouring several milles from the river. Also, the scouts had been unable to detect any sign of Bovarian troopers. Was that because most of the Bovarians at Villerive had been on the north side of the river? There had still been hundreds on the south side who had fled and could not have crossed the river to the north. Had they all simply deserted?

Quaeryt had also initially wondered why the Bovarians had not at least tried to remove or damage the few places where there were bridges, but after studying the solid and massive ancient stone construction of the bridges, he'd smiled. It would have taken a team of engineers with dray horses and who knew what else to remove the span of even one bridge.

When Skarpa called a halt just before noon, Quaeryt mustered the imager undercaptains and put them through various drills, then drew each of them aside and gave each a specific set of imaging drills to practice on the afternoon ride—while riding.

Shaelyt was the last one, and Quaeryt gave him close to the same set of instructions he'd conveyed to Voltyr. "I want you to hold the heaviest shields you can until you can't. Then rest for as long as you could hold the shields and start all over. When you can't do any more, rest for a glass and start once more."

Rather than asking for the rationale for the exercise, as Voltyr had, Shaelyt looked at Quaeryt. "Might I ask, sir, what the Bovarians might have waiting for us at Nordeau?"

Quaeryt eased back the visor cap and blotted his forehead before finally replying. "That could be anything we faced before or more, but I have to say that I'm more worried about what lies beyond Nordeau. Bovaria is a large land, and I'm guessing that all these battles are more to delay us so that Rex Kharst can gather a massive army to defend Variana—so that

he can crush us there, and then march back down the Aluse and take Solis . . ."

"Do you think Lord Bhayar expects that?"

"Lord Bhayar has not volunteered that information, and I have not asked
him. We have received almost twenty thousand troopers as reinforcements.
Most have gone to northern army. He has also sent us another regiment and
more imagers. It is clear that he understands we will face much more nu-
merous Bovarian forces as we near Variana." Quaeryt paused. "Now . . . I
have a question for you. Exactly what did you tell Khalis and Lhandor about
me and Fifth Battalion?"

"Sir . . . ?"

Quaeryt grinned. "Undercaptain Shaelyt . . . I need to know what I'm
supposed to live up to or live down, and what harm you may have done
to their minds."

"Sir . . . I told them that you were the son of Erion who had returned
to Terahnar to right all wrongs and to serve the cause of justice. I said that
you were particularly hard on young Pharsi men who thought too highly
of themselves . . ."

Quaeryt managed not to laugh. He just looked at Shaelyt. "Besides telling them that I was a lost one doomed to serve others . . . what else?"

"That all the hopes of the Pharsi in Lydar likely rested on your shoulders and that we should support you as best we could.'

The absolute directness of Shaelyt's last words cut through Quaeryt
with the pain of a blunt blade. After a moment he said dryly, "You don't
expect much, do you?"

"No more than you expect of yourself, sir."

Quaeryt nodded. "Then you'd better work your ass off on those
shields, because I'll need all the help you and the undercaptains can provide." *And more than that, most likely.* "And remember to keep eating biscuits
and drinking when you're working on those shields."

With a smile, Quaeryt turned and walked to where Zhelan was
waiting.

"How is the fifth squad doing?" asked Quaeryt.

"Better than Ghaelyn or I hoped. Not as well as they need to be. We'll
work in extra drills when we can."

"What about the replacements for the Khellan companies?"

Zhelan smiled. "They're good. A few . . . they're still riding wounded,
but they want to be here. You're part of that."

"All three companies have good troopers and officers. We're fortunate to have them . . . and you."

Zhelan looked slightly embarrassed, but was saved from having to say anything by the command that echoed back along the column. "Mount up! Move out!"

"Time to get going." Quaeryt nodded to Zhelan, walked to the mare, and mounted.

The rest of Lundi and Mardi morning were uneventful, with no signs of Bovarians, and by fourth glass on Mardi afternoon, Skarpa's forces had reached a village barely larger than a hamlet, set beside a creek that emptied into the River Aluse. The locals had fled, but not long before the Telaryn forces had crossed the gray stone bridge over the creek, because the cook fires in hearths were still burning.

Even before the regiments and Fifth Battalion had begun to set up the encampment, while Quaeryt and Zhelan were discussing where to put which companies, a half squad of Telaryn troopers, escorting a dispatch rider, came down the road at a fast trot. Both officers looked at the dispatch rider, who had reined up before Skarpa.

"We've barely stopped, and here come more orders, I'd wager." Zhelan gestured to the southeast, where thickening gray clouds were massing and moving northwest, slowly covering the sky. "With rain coming. Might be here before we're set up."

"More than likely," agreed Quaeryt. "That's why the commander stopped here."

"Better get on with it, then," said Zhelan. "The undercaptains in the first cot here, and first company with that shed . . . and the others—"

"The way we talked about," said Quaeryt, still watching Skarpa.

No sooner had Skarpa received the dispatch and read it than he gestured and three troopers from Third Regiment immediately departed—one heading for Quaeryt.

"Best of fortune to us all, sir," said Zhelan before turning and striding toward the nearest cot. "First company!"

In moments, a ranker hurried up to Quaeryt. "Sir . . . ?"

"Commander Skarpa would like my presence?"

"Yes, sir."

"Thank you." Quaeryt walked swiftly along the shoulder of the dirt path that would likely become mud with the slightest rain. He was the first of the senior officers to reach Skarpa.

"Good or bad?" he asked.

"About what you'd expect. Let me tell you all at once."

As soon as Khaern and Meinyt joined them, Skarpa held up a single sheet of paper, at the bottom of which was a large crimson and green seal, then folded it and tucked it inside his uniform shirt. "I've just received an urgent dispatch from Marshal Deucalon. He's ordered us to take that part of Nordeau on the south side of the river. We are to hold it until the northern forces reach the northern part. When that happens, we are to mount an attack on the remaining Bovarians in the north. We are not to destroy the bridge over the River Aluse. We are not even to block it unless required to hold the southern part of the city." Skarpa paused. "Right now, they're already two days behind us, and they don't travel as fast."

None of the three subordinate commanders said a word.

"I'm not one to stall. You all know that. I'm also in no hurry to fight if we'll have to wait days for the marshal to arrive. Once this rain comes and goes, we'll send out scouts to see why he's so eager for us to move quickly. Do any of you know anything about Nordeau?" Skarpa looked at Quaeryt.

"I've only read a few things about it. It's old. It might date back to the Naedarans."

Skarpa raised his eyebrows.

"The road, sir. It was built to last, and the only place it can go is Nordeau, because the Naedarans never controlled Variana. That likely means Nordeau was a border city, and it will either have lots of stone walls and fortifications . . . or none."

"Depending on whether some later rex kept them or tore them down?" asked Skarpa. "I'd wager the walls are still there and that's why the Bovarians will make a stand there and why Deucalon wants us to attack first." He looked to Khaern. "Any thoughts?"

"Not that I'd be wishing to guess what I don't know, sir, but there are some old walls in Ruile and elsewhere. They'd be difficult to take without siege engines and more. If there are such walls in Nordeau . . ." Khaern shrugged.

"I'd like to hear what the scouts find out," said Meinyt. "Rather not worry about things I don't have to."

Quaeryt couldn't help but smile at the grizzled subcommander's pragmatism.

"We'll see," agreed Skarpa. "In the meantime, keep your men and provisions dry."

As Quaeryt looked to the sky on his way back to tell Zhelan and the company officers about Deucalon's orders, he had his doubts about how dry anything might remain.

55

Mardi night the rain began. By Meredi morning it was still coming down. Skarpa decided against moving on in the downpour, and by midday, the creek had risen by almost a yard, pouring a torrent of yellowish brown water into the dark gray-blue expanse of the Aluse. Shortly after the first glass of the afternoon, the deluge subsided to a gentle rain, and by midafternoon, the skies had cleared, and although the creek did not go down, it did not rise farther, either.

Once the rain ceased, Quaeryt went to work with the imagers, pressing Voltyr, Shaelyt, Desyrk, and Threkhyl on strengthening and improving their shields. What surprised Quaeryt the most was that Threkhyl could stop anything with his momentary shields from hundreds of yards, but could not maintain any continuous shield, something that even Desyrk could do, if only with very light shields so far. Yet Desyrk was limited in how far he could image, being unable to image anything except substances as light as smoke and pepper much more than a hundred yards or so. That underscored for Quaeryt the variability of maging talents.

Perhaps because Shaelyt had taken an interest in the two younger Pharsi undercaptains, both Khalis and Lhandor had already begun to grasp the basics of shielding, although their attempts at holding shields were weak and flimsy indeed. Horan's abilities seemed more like those of Threkhyl, in that he was strongest at imaging familiar objects, or those similar to them, while Smaethyl's progress seemed like it would mirror Desyrk's, although Quaeryt had the feeling that the norther had stronger innate imaging capabilities.

By Meredi evening, Quaeryt had exhausted them all, as well as himself, and he slept soundly, even on the uneven plank floor of the small cot.

Jeudi morning saw Fifth Battalion and the three regiments on the old stone road once more. Skarpa alternated riding with his senior officers, beginning with Khaern, since Eleventh Regiment led the column, and then Quaeryt, because Fifth Battalion was next.

"What have the scouts found?" asked Quaeryt as soon as Skarpa joined him.

"So far, there's still no sign of any Bovarian forces nearby. No tracks at all."

"They could have come downriver by boat."

"They could scout that way, but you can't see much from the river, and once they set foot on shore, they'll leave tracks. How are your new imagers coming?"

"They're solid, but they need training and experience. I did get in some extra training yesterday. That was helpful, even if I suspect the marshal didn't like the delay."

"He might not, but one of the old armsmen's sayings is 'Don't fight two enemies at once.'" Skarpa offered a short barked laugh. "I'm not about to try to fight the weather and the Bovarians at the same time. I'd wager he didn't, either."

No, but Deucalon's the type to claim you could because you've got fewer men to lead.

"If the maps and the millestones are accurate, we're about fifteen milles short of the outskirts of Nordeau," Skarpa went on. "I have the scouts looking for places to stay tonight . . . or longer. That depends on what the defenses look like. And whether we get more rain. Sky's clear now, but you never can tell once you get past midharvest."

Quaeryt adjusted his cap and blotted his forehead. The clear sky and blazing sun suggested to him that Vendrei would also be hot and without rain.

"If they've got stone walls, can your imagers pull them down or put gaps in them?"

"A few might be able to create gaps. With stone, they'd be narrow. It might be easier to destroy the gates or build earth ramps up the lower walls. I'd have to see the walls before I could say."

"What about Antiagon Fire?"

"We've been working on dealing with that in a number of ways."

"You're sounding more and more like Meinyt. You don't talk the same, but you're like every other experienced commander. You don't like to promise anything."

"That's because I have the feeling that the Bovarians are going to spring some surprises, probably some here, and then a lot more as we near Variana. Don't you?"

"I've been expecting more than we've seen," Skarpa admitted. "Why do you think they haven't shown more?"

"Because Rex Kharst underestimated Lord Bhayar. I have the feeling he thought Bhayar was a weak successor to his father, and that the revolt in Tilbor proved that. Kharst may have thought he could take Ferravyl and then slowly carve out chunks of western Telaryn. When he lost most of his army in eastern Bovaria and Bhayar attacked, all he could do was withdraw slowly while he called in troops from everywhere else. At some point, we're going to encounter more troops than we have." *A whole lot more.*

"I've thought something like that myself."

"Has Deucalon?"

"I hinted at it. He dismissed what I said, but he thinks the same thing."

"You think that's because he doesn't want to admit that a junior commander came up with the same thought?" *Or because he wonders if I came up with it?*

"Might be. Also might be because he doesn't have any proof."

"If we're right," said Quaeryt dryly, "we'll get the proof when we find forty Bovarian regiments facing us at Variana."

"I've had a similar thought about that, too."

Quaeryt just nodded.

After discussing possible tactics for another quint Skarpa eased his mount off the road and onto the shoulder, riding back to talk to Meinyt.

At a quint or so past the first glass of the afternoon, with the sun beating down as if it were still midsummer, as Quaeryt rode around a sweeping turn to the northwest, to his right he caught sight of a shimmering straight line running westward from the River Aluse, roughly paralleling it, bounded by darker gray, and then by trees on the northern side. The road turned due west just south of where the canal entered the River Aluse, with stone walls rising from the river. The ancient road continued beside the canal as far as Quaeryt could see. Unlike the first canal Quaeryt had encountered, though, the water in the canal was shallow and stagnant, and in less than a half mile from where the canal ended at the river, the shallow water became a marsh. After another half mille, the marsh turned to swampy grassland between the gray stone walls.

Ahead to the left was a small hamlet of a score or so small dwellings and outbuildings, with fields and woods alternating in an irregular pattern, much as had been the case for most of the ride that day. Narrow paths wound in and around both fields and woods, and the fields were marked off by sagging split-rail fencing. Once again, Quaeryt realized that they had seen no high holdings. *That doesn't mean there aren't any around, just that they're not along the river road.* Given that the road was excellent, he couldn't help but wonder why High Holders had not positioned themselves close to it.

Another two glasses passed, with one short break. The road and the dry grassy canal continued westward together. Quaeryt checked his map, and then had Zhelan, now riding beside him, check as well, thinking that they must be within ten milles of Nordeau and wondering when and where Skarpa would call a halt for the evening.

Less than a quint later, a squad leader came riding back along the shoulder, then eased in beside Quaeryt. "Subcommander, sir, Commander Skarpa has requested that you and Fifth Battalion make your encampment in the second hamlet ahead. The first one is larger, and that will be for Fifth Regiment. The smaller one is about a mille ahead."

"What about the other regiments? Do you know?"

"There's a village not quite a mille south of the hamlet where Fifth Battalion will be, and another just to the west of you. If you'll excuse me, sir, I need to tell Subcommander Meinyt."

"Don't let me keep you." Quaeryt gestured for the squad leader to depart.

With a nod, the trooper pulled out and headed down the shoulder.

Quaeryt turned to Zhelan. "If you'd pass word to the company officers?"

"Yes, sir."

Before long, Fifth Battalion neared the first hamlet mentioned by the squad leader, a gathering of close to forty dwellings and more than a few outbuildings, one or two of which looked to be large and solid. All the dwellings and buildings were of timber, much of it unpainted or stained so long ago that the wood had grayed to the shade of untreated and weathered wood. A few wisps of smoke rose from some of the chimneys, but it was clear the villagers had fled.

Zhelan, again riding beside Quaeryt, shook his head. "Poor folks. Don't even know what it's all about. Just hope that we leave them something."

"We've left more than Kharst's men have."

"Just hope we haven't ended up leaving it for them."

So did Quaeryt.

Another quint brought Quaeryt and Fifth Battalion to the smallest hamlet—the one assigned to Fifth Battalion. It looked to be far older than

the hamlet Meinyt's regiment was doubtless already occupying. As Zhelan
directed the companies, Quaeryt remained mounted, half watching as
Third Regiment rode by on the old stone road. When they had passed,
Quaeryt took a moment and crossed the road to take a look at the narrow,
grass-filled canal that still seemed to him that it once had led to Nordeau.
He frowned. The stone walls ended less than half a mille west of the
hamlet. Beyond that point, a low swale continued westward in a straight
line, but there was no sign of stonework.

Someone must have mined the canal for stone. But who? And why?

With that thought in mind, he rode back across the road and toward
the large center cot, where Zhelan had positioned himself. "What do
you think?"

"Most of them will want to sleep outside. The cots . . . they . . . well,
they stink."

That didn't surprise Quaeryt. Still . . . he wondered. Most cots, hum-
ble as they might be, didn't. So he dismounted and tied the mare to a tree
beside the cot, then walked to the dwelling.

The roof was barely level with his eyes. *Why would anyone build a house with
such a low ceiling?* Then he looked at the entry and realized, belatedly, that
the steps led down to the doorway, and that the lower section of the walls
were constructed of finely fitted gray stone, while the upper walls consisted of rough planks, with a reed-thatched roof above that. *They used the
foundations of an older building for the lower wall.*

The door was open, and a trooper stepped out and looked to Quaeryt.
"Sir . . . no one's here. Banked the hearth and ran, it looks like. There's
even food." He wrinkled his nose. "Doesn't smell inside, but it sure does
here."

Quaeryt could sense a faint odor, but it eased as he moved to the steps.
When he moved back along the side of the cot, the odor was greater, almost as if wastes had been dumped around the cot. He shook his head and
walked to the next cot, a smaller dwelling, and then around it. The lower
side walls were of the well-fitted gray stone, but the lower rear wall, while
of the gray stone, showed almost crude workmanship, as did the lower
walls flanking the front door and, again, steps led down to the door, offering entry to the cot a yard or so below ground level.

He walked through the center of the hamlet, looking at the cots and
their small wooden outbuildings. When he finished, he nodded. At some
time in the past, there had been a complex of well-crafted gray stone

buildings. Had they been the Naedaran equivalent of a high holding, a fort or the like, or something else? With the closeness to the road and to the canal, it made sense, but why had it all been abandoned?

In less than a glass, under Zhelan's direction, the battalion was mostly settled into the hamlet, at least as settled as they were likely to be, reflected Quaeryt as he stood outside the largest cot, waiting for the imagers to join him, still puzzling why the stones had been removed from just the section of canal closest to Nordeau. Had the stones been used in building dwellings farther west? He'd just have to see.

He wasn't looking forward to drills with the undercaptains. He suspected that they weren't, either, since none of them had yet appeared, but he'd scheduled the drill before the evening meal, because Skarpa had sent word he would brief the subcommanders at sixth glass.

Quaeryt glanced around again, then nodded as he saw Khalis and Lhandor walking toward him. Lhandor was carrying what looked to be an oblong grayish stone, and Khalis held something in his hands. When the two reached Quaeryt, Khalis nodded and then stepped forward.

"What is it, Khalis?"

"I'm not sure, sir, but when the cooks were digging one of the firepits . . . they found these . . . this, I mean." The young imager opened his hands to show fragments of a stone statue of some sort. "Well . . . actually they found the stone Lhandor has and then these."

Quaeryt looked closely, but the darkness of the stone—most likely black marble—made discerning what the fragments had comprised difficult. "What is it?"

"That's what I wanted to know, sir. So I pieced it together." A smile crossed the young man's face. "It's a coney, sir . . . a black one. Well, it was before someone smashed it. It was buried under the stone."

Lhandor handed the stone to Quaeryt, a heavy oblong some nine digits wide and perhaps fifteen long. Quaeryt lifted it and studied the brief inscription that had been chiseled—shallowly but cleanly, as if by a trained stone carver—into the grayed white marble. While the letters were largely the same as those used in Bovarian and Tellan, there were several that were unfamiliar, and the words looked like nothing he'd ever seen. *Naedaran?*

Why had someone gone to the trouble of crafting the figure, and then smashing it, but burying it under a stone with a carved inscription?

"Where did you find this? Near which cookpit?"

Khalis turned and pointed. "That one. The cooks were going to dig more to the right, but there are stones there, almost like a floor."

More evidence of a far larger holding or base or fort?

"It's not like any coney I ever saw, sir. If you'll come over here, sir?" Khalis moved over to the side of the cot beside a window that had a narrow ledge.

"Might I ask why you think that?" Quaeryt followed the young undercaptain.

"It . . . well . . . sir, it feels different. It looks different, and it scared the cooks." Khalis laid the pieces out on the ledge, arranging them with care until he had them together.

Quaeryt leaned forward and studied the pieced-together figure. The head of the rabbit was in only two sections. Abruptly Quaeryt realized that the stone was black marble and that it had been shattered with care. *Black marble? We haven't seen anything like that in any of the dwellings, not even in the few High Holdings.*

He reached forward and touched the stone with his fingertips. Despite the warmth of the late afternoon, the stone was cold, seeming far colder than it should have been. He wondered, then looked at the fragmented shape and concentrated. Light flickered around the sections of black stone . . . and the black coney was whole.

As a whole statue, the coney, upright and balanced on its hindquarters, was no more than eight digits tall, but looked much taller. It was also a skillfully done representation, with the stone's texture giving the impression of realistic black fur. Even the toenails were carved in place. And the face . . .

"It looks . . . spiteful," observed Khalis.

"It does." Abruptly Quaeryt laughed.

"Sir?"

"I'm just guessing, Undercaptain, but I'd wager that to whoever buried this hundreds of years ago, the black rabbit symbolized bad luck, and when they smashed it and buried it, that was to bury black luck."

"You put it back together, sir." Khalis's voice contained a note of worry.

"It was their bad fortune, not ours. And their ill fortune might well be our good fortune."

"The rabbit, sir?" Khalis picked it up and extended it to Quaeryt. "You repaired it."

"Don't break it, but find a safe place to bury it." Quaeryt certainly didn't want to carry around a spiteful-looking black marble rabbit. *And if it is bad luck, it needs to stay here.* "Bury it deep enough that the locals won't find it."

Khalis frowned. "It doesn't feel cold anymore."

That surprised Quaeryt. The statuette should have felt colder, if anything, after being imaged back together. "Just bury it, with the oblong stone over it, but put the inscription side down." Why he'd said that, he didn't know, but it felt right.

"Yes, sir."

The two hurried away from the cot and toward the cooks, where Lhandor asked for and received a small spade, before the two continued toward a small woodlot to the rear of the cot.

Quaeryt turned to watch as Shaelyt and Desyrk approached.

Shaelyt's eyes followed the younger Pharsi imagers.

"They'll be back. I gave them a task." *The Nameless only knows what they'll tell Shaelyt.* "No one gets out of exercises and imaging drills."

Quaeryt had to wait another half quint before all the undercaptains gathered. He ended up working with them slightly less than a glass before dismissing them to eat. He grabbed a few rations himself, gulped them down, and then went to find Zhelan.

After checking with the major, Quaeryt walked to where the mare was tethered, outside one of the outbuildings, untied her, and mounted. As he rode westward to the largest hamlet to meet with Skarpa and the other subcommanders, he found his thoughts going back to the hamlet that had been something far more imposing . . . and the Naedarans.

What happened to make a great land collapse, or any land? Some ended up being conquered and absorbed by other lands, as had happened with Tilbor and Tela. Some were conquered from outside, in the fashion that the Yaran warlords who had been Bhayar's forebears had conquered Telaryn and made it their own. From what he'd read of Naedara, though, the land had been strong and prosperous. Then it had not, and by the time the Bovarians began to expand, the cities of Naedara were shadows of their former greatness, offering little or no resistance.

Even in his brief time as a provincial governor, Quaeryt had seen the underlying problems facing Bhayar, especially the difficulty of holding both governors and High Holders accountable without requiring a large force of troopers. And as he'd seen with Rescalyn, whoever was in command of an army also posed a threat. Could a force of imagers be somehow trained and organized to support Bhayar? Would they provide the force necessary to keep the governors and High Holders in line? *And keep Bhayar and his successors from becoming tyrants like Kharst?*

Quaeryt laughed softly at the arrogance of the idea, even as he considered how it might be possible.

As he neared the larger village, he saw a squad of riders formed up at the road that led south toward the center to the houses and buildings.

"Subcommander, sir, the commander is waiting at the large dwelling off the square. It's maybe four hundred yards on the right side."

"Has Subcommander Meinyt arrived?"

"Not by this road, sir."

"Thank you." Quaeryt guided the mare onto the rutted side road, past two small fields that separated the first cots from the old road. *Why aren't they located directly off the road?* In bad weather, access would be so much easier.

Around every cot, everywhere he looked as he rode into the center of the village, there were troopers and those were only the men of Third Regiment. The other thing that struck him was that none of the cots were built of the gray stone that had lined the ancient canal. So where had all those well-cut stones gone?

In less than a fraction of a quint, Quaeryt reached the square. It was literally just that, a square expanse of gray stone, but the stones were, surprisingly, not the same size as the evenly cut and sized stones of the canal, but much larger. On the west side was a chandlery, while shops dotted the north and south sides. Quaeryt turned the mare toward the two-story dwelling on the east, a weathered wooden structure that would have been considered modestly large in most Telaryn cities, but which towered over the other dwellings. Khaern and Skarpa stood on the narrow porch. Neither spoke as Quaeryt reined up and tied the mare to one of the hitching rings beside the gravel path.

"Good evening," offered Quaeryt as he stepped onto the porch, his words punctuated by the creaking of worn planks beneath his boots.

Khaern smiled and nodded pleasantly.

"Evening," replied Skarpa. "Porch is like everything else around here. Barely held together. Didn't see Meinyt, did you?"

"He wasn't close behind me, and the watch squad hadn't seen him."

"Not like him. Must have run into a problem. How is that hamlet you're in?"

"Old," replied Quaeryt. "A number of the cots are half built out of

Naedaran foundations, and there are gray stones everywhere just below the ground around the cots."

"Everything around here is old," observed Khaern. "It's old and worn-out."

"That doesn't make much sense," said Skarpa. "Farther east, it isn't like that. It's almost like the Namer cursed this part of Bovaria."

Quaeryt couldn't help but think about the black coney, and the superstitions surrounding it. Had the area always been worn-out and tired? Not if the Naedarans built that canal and had buildings all along the old road.

"What are you thinking?" asked Skarpa. "You've got a funny look."

"Just that the Naedarans had a canal that looks to go twenty milles or more with large estates and buildings along it. It's been unused for years, centuries, probably, but it couldn't always have been worn-out and tired."

"Maybe the Namer cursed the Bovarians who drove out the Naedar-ans," suggested Khaern almost laughingly.

"Who knows? Who cares?" said Skarpa, turning and pointing. "Here comes Meinyt."

The three waited as the last subcommander rode up, dismounted, and tied his mount beside Quaeryt's mare.

"I'm sorry I'm late," said Meinyt as he hurried up onto the porch. "My mount came up lame just after I left the camp. Had to walk him back and saddle a spare."

"Those things happen. Better now than in a fight," replied Skarpa. "I'd have you sit down, but it's a lot cooler out here, and this shouldn't take too long." He cleared his throat. "I have the first reports from the scouts." Skarpa glanced to Quaeryt. "You were right. The entire south side of Nor-deau is walled. The walls are not high, about three yards, but they're solid stone. There are only two sets of gates. Both are heavily fortified, with much taller gate towers. The gates are ironbound. There may even be a portcullis in the gate towers behind each set of gates."

"What about the north side?" asked Quaeryt.

"The north side is walled as well, at least the older part of the city. Both walled cities are connected by a stone bridge which is anchored to an isle in the middle of the river. The isle is also walled on all sides. On the north side, dwellings, shops, and other buildings have been built well beyond the old walls. The walls are well maintained on the south side. They appear that way on the north. There's no way to tell how many men are behind the walls, but if they've got even what we have, it's going to be cramped."

Quaeryt could see that the other three officers were all looking at him.

After a moment he spoke. "Until I can study those walls and gates myself, I can't offer you any idea of how we can take the city." *Or if we can without losing thousands of men.*

"Thought as much," replied Skarpa. "Won't hurt the men to have a day or so of rest."

Quaeryt could sense what the commander hadn't said—that he didn't want to wait any longer than necessary. Neither did Quaeryt, if possibly for very different reasons.

56

Quaeryt and first company set out early on Vendrei because he hadn't slept
that long and because the days along the River Aluse got warmer and wetter
as the day progressed, and he was tired of feeling hot and miserable when
he didn't have to. He had left all the imagers, with Voltyr in charge of working with Threkhyl, Desyrk, and Baelthm, and Shaelyt in charge of the newer
undercaptains.

He kept looking to his right, but the road and what remained of the
ancient canal continued westward in a straight line along flat land that
rose or fell by no more than a yard or two at most. After a mille, the fields
ended, and to the right of the road and canal swale rose woods, not thick
forests, but well-tended trees, spaced well apart. By then, even with the
cool morning air, Quaeryt was blotting his forehead and readjusting his
cap. Ahead, the woods ended, giving way to meadows or pasture, because
the ground was green, and most crops, except beans and a few others,
would have turned or shriveled by the last month in harvest.

When first company reached the end of the woods and Quaeryt was
surprised to see that they were roughly two milles from Nordeau, and
that there were no trees at all between where he rode and the walls. Nor
were there any structures at all—not a one.

"Company! Halt!" Before proceeding, he wanted to take in what he
saw.

The River Aluse curved back southwest, so that the low grassy swale
that had once been a canal ended in a hillock at the river's edge less than
a half mille south of the gray stone walls of Nordeau. Quaeryt couldn't
help but believe that the low hill covered some sort of ruin. He'd studied
the map again before setting out, and where the river curved, northeast of
Nordeau, it also narrowed, suggesting a difficult passage for boats or barges.
The fact that the Naedarans had built a canal more than twenty milles
long indicated to Quaeryt that they'd had a reason for it, and that reason
had to be trade. That raised questions that he needed to put aside while he
concentrated on the problem at hand—how to get Skarpa's forces inside
the walls.

He saw no one on the road that ran straight toward the walls, and finally he gestured for the company to proceed.

The closer they drew to Nordeau, the more obvious it was that south Nordeau was a fortress that had been built to last. While Quaeryt looked in every direction as they moved toward the walls, no one emerged from the one set of gates he saw, the ones to which the ancient road led, as straight as a quarrel.

"Do you see anyone, Ghaelyn?"

"No, sir. Scouts haven't signaled, either."

At slightly more than a half mille from the closed ironbound gates, Quaeryt reined up. He could see another road, also gray and apparently paved, that led from the western side of the walls that arced around the city, but because of the curvature of the walls, he could not see the other set of gates. The walls held no banners, and he saw no defenders, but since there were embrasures at regular intervals in the walls, defenders could have been watching him and first company, and probably were. He did see wisps of smoke rising from chimneys beyond the walls, enough so that it was clear that Nordeau was not deserted.

But why aren't there sentries on the walls? Why hasn't anyone come out to challenge us?

After several moments, he shifted his weight in the saddle and turned to Ghaelyn. "Undercaptain . . . we're going to ride closer, but I'm going to try something, and I want silent riding. Not a word. Tell the men to be ready to turn and ride back at a moment's notice."

"Yes, sir."

While Ghaelyn rode back and conveyed the orders to all the squad leaders, Quaeryt slowly raised a concealment shield, trying to do so in a way that might give the impression that he and first company had slowly withdrawn.

The undercaptain returned and said, "Ready, sir." His voice was low.

Quaeryt raised his arm, then lowered it, and urged the mare forward. He'd ridden several hundred yards when he realized that holding the concealment, even over the entire company, was scarcely noticeable. He concentrated on the low gray stone walls, which had to have been built by the Naedarans, because the workmanship was similar and because the stone matched so closely that of the ancient road. Yet the stones had not come from the canal, because they were larger and cut in an interlocking pattern that made them less susceptible to siege engines—or cannon.

When they were only a few hundred yards from the gate, Quaeryt raised his arm and reined up. From here, he could see some figures on the upper level of the wall, and guards watching the road from the slits in the guard towers flanking the gates. With the interlocking stones of the walls, at first glance, Quaeryt thought imaging away the gates looked more likely, but when he studied them closely, he could see that they had iron bands at top and bottom as well as a series of heavy diagonal bands. He'd never seen walls or gates like those. Yet the walls weren't all that high, and siege engines could easily have been built to overtop the walls.

Except Antiagon Fire would make short work of siege towers.

But what about the walls . . .

They're designed to resist imagers!

It also meant that the walls had stone foundations all the way down to bedrock, and that Nordeau had been built in a place where there was bedrock near the surface. All of that indicated strongly that the only ways for Telaryn forces to enter Nordeau were either over the walls with some sort of ramps or through the gates—assuming the Bovarians didn't have their own imagers.

Quaeryt didn't like the idea of using the gates, because the towers surrounded the gates, and in such confined spaces it would be difficult, if not impossible, to shield troopers from boiling oil or Antiagon Fire.

After a time of studying the walls, Quaeryt turned his mount to the southwest, toward a narrow path that seemed to circle the walls, gesturing for the rest of first company to follow him. He kept looking toward the gates, but they did not open, and no Bovarian troopers appeared.

After riding another half mille, Quaeryt could see the second gate and the road leading from it. The southwest gate was closed and guarded in the same fashion as the southeast gate. The road from the southwest gate was stone paved and indeed wider than the ancient way that led to the southeast gate, but Quaeryt could see that it was not nearly so level as the older road, although it did parallel in a general way the River Aluse.

The newer road had to have been built by the Bovarians, but why had they built a road from Nordeau to Variana on the south side of the river when they had not done so anywhere else along the River Aluse, and when Villerive was larger than Nordeau with presumably more trade and commerce? Was there a similar road on the north side of the river?

He shook his head. From where he was there was no way to tell.

After more study, he turned the mare and the company and rode along a path that gradually carried them both away from the stone walls and back to the ancient road—though browning high grass and some low bushes, but not a single tree. The fact that he saw no trees—and no sign of any having been cut down—also concerned him. Was the entire plain that stretched away from the walls somehow paved under the dirt so that trees would not grow? But he'd seen trees grow through the tiniest gaps in stone.

Everything he saw raised more questions.

As he rode back toward the village to report to Skarpa, he thought over his earlier conclusions and decided he'd been too hasty. Defenses and walls usually reflected what the builders knew, not what they faced. Most likely, the Naedarans had built the way that they had because they had had trained imagers, not because they were defending against them. *That also might explain their decline . . . if they lost too many imagers or didn't continue to train and support them.*

In turn, that raised more questions about what he planned . . . and how he needed to approach Bhayar about his thoughts and plans.

On Samedi morning just before seventh glass, the three regiments and Fifth Battalion drew up facing the walls of Nordeau. The sun hung barely above the trees to the east of the plain extending out from the gray walls, and the browning knee-high grass was heavy with dew under a crystal clear sky. The air was neither cool nor warm, but felt thick to Quaeryt as he watched Ghaelyn ride forward toward the southeast gate under the blue-bordered white parley flag.

Skarpa hadn't been especially pleased with Quaeryt's report on the defenses of Nordeau on Vendrei afternoon, but he'd agreed to the plan of attack Quaeryt proposed. After that agreement, Quaeryt had briefed the imager undercaptains, and then Zhelan and the company officers on what each company was to do.

On Samedi, the first step was simple enough, to send forward Ghaelyn to request the surrender of Nordeau. Neither Skarpa nor Quaeryt expected that the Bovarians would even consider surrender, but Quaeryt had insisted that Skarpa make the offer.

"Why?" Skarpa had asked. "They won't consider it. You know that."

"I do."

"Then . . . ?"

"Because I want to be able to try to soothe my conscience," replied Quaeryt.

Skarpa had merely nodded sadly.

Skarpa and Quaeryt were right. The Bovarians refused to surrender. But they didn't try to kill poor Ghaelyn, for which Quaeryt was most thankful, recalling as he did how the hill holders of Tilbor had dealt with troopers carrying the request for their surrender. The Bovarians had just laughed and, from the gate towers, showered the undercaptain with ridicule.

Once Ghaelyn had returned, the Telaryn forces moved forward, slowly. Fifth Battalion, led by Quaeryt with Baelthm beside him, took the old road toward the southeast gate. Eleventh Regiment, positioned some six hundred yards to the south and west of Fifth Battalion, rode through the knee-high browning grass toward a point on the walls some four hundred yards southwest of the southeast gate towers. Near the front ranks rode Voltyr and Smaethyl.

Due south of the curved walls of Nordeau, Third Regiment rode toward the southernmost point of the wall, and close to Skarpa rode Threkhyl, Desyrk, and Horan. Farther to the west, aiming at a point on the walls equidistant between the target of Third Regiment and the southwestern gate, was Fifth Regiment, without any imager undercaptains. Taking the newer road toward the southwest gate was a battalion detached from Fifth Regiment, with the major in command accompanied by Shaelyt, Lhandor, and Khalis.

Quaeryt would have liked to have had imagers with each attack formation, but he didn't have enough for that, and he was asking a great deal of them. At the same time, they needed to see what it was like when their lives and those of others depended on themselves, and not on Quaeryt. Some of them, he suspected, hadn't even realized how much he had shielded them.

Even when the Telaryn formations had reached a point two hundred yards from the walls, the defenders had made no moves and launched neither arrows nor Antiagon Fire.

Then . . . dark shafts rose from behind the walls and angled down toward the attackers. There weren't that many shafts targeted at each regiment and battalion, one of the reasons why Skarpa and Quaeryt had decided on the spread approach that they had adopted.

Quaeryt only had to raise and expand his shields for an instant so that the shafts dropped into the grass and road ahead of Fifth Battalion. From what he could tell, the other imagers had shielded most of the troops, with Lhandor, Khalis, and Shaelyt providing some coverage for Fifth Regiment as well as for the battalion they accompanied.

As the arrows were shunted away, a horn signal sounded from Third Regiment, and all the riders urged their mounts forward at a quick trot—because Skarpa had determined that the archers were behind the walls and not firing from the scattered slits and embrasures. That meant that the closer the attacking troopers were to the walls, the harder it would be for the archers to target the Telaryn forces, all the better for the attacker since the imagers couldn't provide shielding and do what else they needed to accomplish next.

Because Quaeryt had studied the gates, he thought he could bring down those in front of him without too much strain, not that he intended to lead Fifth Battalion through them unless absolutely necessary. He'd also gone over the details of the gates with Shaelyt, suggesting the points of attack for the southwest gate.

As he rode forward on the ancient road, Quaeryt contracted his shields, to cover just the front of the column, then concentrated on removing a line of wood and metal from the outer edge of the gates. A flash of fire-pain lanced through his eyes, then dissipated so quickly that his eyes watered but for a moment. When he blinked again, he saw that the gates had dropped perhaps a third of a yard. There was the thinnest sliver of light on the left side, between what remained of the edge of the gate and the recessed stone that had held the ironbound wood in place. He concentrated once more, this time across the bottom, trying to angle what he imaged away.

The fire-pain lasted longer, and for another moment or two he could not see, but he did hear a muffled crash, and when his eyes cleared, the gates lay almost flat on the gray stone. As Skarpa's scouts had reported, though, behind the gate was an iron portcullis, already lowered into place.

Quaeryt grabbed for his water bottle, then took a long swallow of the lager before recorking the bottle and slipping it back into the leather holder. Another attempt at image-cutting the iron of the portcullis followed, based on what he'd studied of such construction.

The third flash of fire-pain was no greater than the second, suggesting that the gates themselves had contained far more iron that he'd thought, and the portcullis crashed forward.

Quaeryt's eyes flicked from the seemingly open southeast gate toward Eleventh Regiment and then toward the walls before them, drawn by a flash of light.

A narrow stone ramp, barely wide enough for two mounts stirrup-to-stirrup, stretched some fifteen yards from the ground to the top of the wall, and the troopers of Eleventh Regiment were riding straight toward it. Quaeryt could only hope that Voltyr and Smaethyl had been as successful at creating a ramp on the far side.

An even brighter flash of light flared from the south, but Quaeryt could only see the base of the ramp imaged by Threkhyl and Horan, and it appeared far wider and lower than the one imaged by Voltyr and Smaethyl. Quaeryt could not see anything near the southwest gate, and could only hope that the Pharsi imagers were able to create another entry to Nordeau. What he also did not see were defenders near the fallen gate or on or near the ramp up to the walls that was closest to Fifth Battalion.

One or even two ramps wouldn't be enough to force an entry, especially once the defenders regrouped. Quaeryt looked at the fallen gate and took a deep breath.

"Fifth Battalion! On me! To the gate!"

As he neared the gate, and could feel the dull impact of arrow shafts on his shields coming through the opening where the gate had been, the thought crossed his mind, not that he could remember where he had heard the words, that even the best battle plan didn't survive after the first moments. Abruptly the impacts of the arrow shafts stopped just before the mare's hooves clattered on the wood and metal of the fallen gate.

Because Quaeryt had to slow the mare slightly in order to allow her to pick her way over the flat iron of the fallen portcullis, at any moment he expected either Antiagon Fire or burning or boiling oil. There was neither, but once he passed through the gate towers, the morning warmth of harvest was replaced with the chill of winter, and his breath and that of the mare steamed in the frigid air.

Quaeryt glanced around, seeing frost-shrouded figures sprawled everywhere within some fifty yards of the gates. His eyes went to his left, down the wide paved courtyard or street behind the foot of the walls to the south, where he saw horsemen pouring off a ramp.

"There!"

At that command from somewhere ahead, Quaeryt's eyes flicked back forward along the street that connected to the gate, but which curved gradually past stone buildings until it headed northward to the bridge.

Archers scattered and ran down a side street as a company of pikemen marched toward Fifth Battalion, pikes angled toward first company. Quaeryt calculated. There might be seven or eight abreast. "First company! On me! Charge!"

Even as he issued the command, the pikemen stopped, and the first rank knelt, likely bracing their pikes against joins in the stone paving of the street.

Quaeryt extended his shields to a point, almost like the prow of a vessel where the stem rose just above the water, then linked them to the mounts that followed him. Even so, the impact when his extended shields struck the pikes jolted through him, pummeling him on his chest, forearms, and thighs. Pikes and pikemen and their armor clattered as they were hurled against the stone walls of the dwellings lining the narrow street. Beyond the pikemen, the company of lightly armored foot scattered, fleeing into alleyways and side streets. Quaeryt kept the mare and the company moving, following the street as it turned toward the bridge, joining another stone-paved street that most likely curved northward from the southwestern gate.

Quaeryt glanced back down the other street, but could make out neither Bovarian nor Telaryn troopers for the hundred yards he could take in

before he turned his eyes forward toward the bridge. A few people actually stood on the narrow raised sidewalks, staring at the oncoming troopers, before fleeing into shops and dwellings, or other buildings.

From somewhere to the north came the clangor of bells and then a
mournful sounding series of horn blasts. Ahead of him, a line of armored
footmen sprinted up the gently angled stone approach to the bridge itself.

Where the approach to the bridge ended, so did the stone railings,
replaced by comparatively narrow wooden handrails. Quaeryt blinked—
the trailing armored footmen were jumping, as if over something, and
the handrails were moving and flattening, leaving a gap between the
stone walls and those very same rails.

Frig! A Namer-built retracting bridge!

Quaeryt reined up, barely coming to a halt before reaching the open
space. A handful of armored footmen jumped, missing the retracting
bridge and tumbling into the river below. The timbered section of the
bridge continued to recede toward the small fortified garrison whose
walls seemingly rose from the River Aluse itself. Given the efforts he'd
already made, Quaeryt wasn't about to try to image the bridge into place
or create another span. He was surprised to see that the handrails on each
side of the timbered section had dropped so that they lay flat against the
roadbed, as if each railing support had been mounted on something like
an axle.

Quaeryt slowly turned the mare and looked down the bridge approach into the southern part of Nordeau. While first company held the
top of the approach, the remaining three companies were involved in
dealing with the surviving Bovarian footmen and pikemen. Given the
narrowness of the streets, there was little first company could do without
getting in the way of the rest of Fifth Battalion.

Quaeryt's eyes were watering, his head aching, and he didn't want to
do any more imaging unless it was absolutely necessary. He looked to
Baelthm. "Are you all right?"

The older undercaptain looked back at Quaeryt. "Better question might
be, sir, whether you are."

"So far . . ." Quaeryt paused as more Telaryn troopers rode up the
curved street that had to have come from the southwest gate, but they
halted where the two streets merged, then reversed position and held. On
the other street, the Khellan companies had largely stopped fighting, having either destroyed or routed the Bovarians they had encountered.

Quaeryt turned to Zhelan, who had eased his mount closer. "I need to see how the imager undercaptains are doing. I'm going to ride down to Fifth Regiment."

"If you plan to go farther, sir, I'd recommend a squad going with you."

"If I do, I'll send for one, or take one from their companies." Quaeryt edged his mount down along the side of the stone wall of the bridge approach until he reached the more open space near the last squad of first company. From there he could see Shaelyt and the two younger Pharsi undercaptains, one of whom was leaning over in his saddle and retching. Shaelyt was bent forward, his head almost resting on the neck of his mount.

"Undercaptain Shaelyt," called Quaeryt.

Shaelyt straightened and turned in Quaeryt's general direction, but it was clear that he did not see his subcommander. "Sir?"

Quaeryt rode closer. "I'm here. You're having trouble seeing?"

That brought a nod, and a swallow, as if Shaelyt were trying not to retch. Both Khalis and Lhandor stiffened, but did not speak. Khalis was pale, but he'd been the one retching, Quaeryt realized. Lhandor was slightly wan, but looked composed, as if exhausted, but not nauseated.

"Did you get the gates down? Any luck with the ramp?"

"The gates . . . yes. We couldn't manage a ramp, but . . . Fifth Regiment didn't have a problem following us through the gates. There was . . . were . . . two companies . . . frozen . . . but another company of pikemen . . . we managed to hold shields enough to scatter the front lines . . . After that the troopers took over . . ." Shaelyt swallowed again.

"You're not doing any more imaging today," said Quaeryt.

"No, sir . . . can't see, except in flashes . . ."

"And your head throbs like someone's beating it like an anvil or jabbing it with spears?"

"Yes, sir."

"What about you two?" Quaeryt looked to Lhandor.

"I don't think I could image a copper, sir."

"What did you image on the attack?"

"I can't do shields, not properly. I imaged iron darts into some archers who were taking aim on us and Captain Kharaf. So did Khalis."

"Are you feeling better, Khalis?" asked Quaeryt.

"Some, sir . . ." The young undercaptain swallowed.

"All of you, sip from your water bottles until you can swallow. Then eat some of those biscuits I insisted you bring. Yes . . . I know they're like bricks, but gnaw on them as you can. It will help."

"Yes, sir."

Quaeryt stood in the stirrups, trying to look farther south to see Meinyt and the rest of Fifth Regiment. While he could discern troopers who
were likely from Fifth Regiment, he couldn't make out Meinyt. He dropped
back down into the saddle. "Undercaptains, we'll return to first company."
He turned the mare and rode up the gradual stone-paved approach to the
bridge, reining up at the rear of the troopers and turning the mare so that
he could see whoever might be approaching.

The other undercaptains were supposed to rejoin Fifth Battalion as they
could, but so far there was no sign of those who'd been with Eleventh
Regiment and Third Regiment. Quaeryt blotted the sweat off his forehead,
sweat he hadn't even realized was there until it oozed into the corner of his
eyes and delivered a salty sting.

To the south he saw the Fifth Regiment troopers ease to one side of
the street and allow the Khellan companies to ride to rejoin first company.
As Major Calkoran neared, Quaeryt didn't see any empty saddles, and second company looked to be close to full strength. Quaeryt did see blood
splatters and streaks on the sleeves of many of the troopers.

Zhelan rode forward and spoke to Calkoran, then continued onward
to get reports from Zhael and then Arion before he rode back to Quaeryt.

"Sir, reporting on Fifth Battalion."

"Go ahead, Major."

"First company, two dead, fifteen wounded. Second company, four
dead, five wounded. Third company, three dead, six wounded. Fourth
company, three wounded. That does not count the undercaptains assigned
to other regiments."

"Thank you." *Only nine dead, and twenty-nine wounded.* Unfortunately, Quaeryt had no doubt that the casualties were far higher among the regiments.

A squad leader wearing a green and red armband edged his mount
along the side of the bridge approach toward Quaeryt and finally reined
up facing him. "Subcommander, sir, the commander asks that Fifth Battalion continue to hold the bridge and prepare for an attack on the isle fort
and beyond."

"Tell Commander Skarpa that we hold the bridge but that an immediate attack on the isle fort is not physically possible. The Bovarians retracted
the bridge before we could reach it." Quaeryt gestured toward the open
space beyond the bridge approach.

"Yes, sir." The squad leader nodded, then turned his mount and rode
back down the bridge approach and then onto the street that led to the
southeastern gate.

Quaeryt eased out the water bottle and took a longer swallow, before fumbling out a biscuit and slowly chewing on it. *You're a little late in taking your own advice.* He glanced back south, then northward toward the isle. He could see nothing behind the walls of the small fort in the middle of the river.

Before all that long, the troopers now in formation on the streets and the approach to the bridge made way for Skarpa, flanked by Khaern and Meinyt. Behind them rode the remaining imager undercaptains—Threkhyl, Horan, Desyrk, Voltyr, and Smaethyl. All five were sweat-drenched and pale.

Quaeryt eased the mare forward to meet the senior officers, then halted, as did the other three.

The imagers made their way past, and Quaeryt could see that Voltyr's eyes were twitching. Horan was almost leaning on his mount's neck. Quaeryt looked at Skarpa.

"I got your message, Subcommander. How did that happen?"

"We broke through the gates, and I led first company straight to the bridge. We didn't hesitate at all. They were retracting the bridge before we were even close to it. They left some of their own men on this side rather than letting us even get close."

"Figures." Skarpa snorted.

"How did the imager undercaptains do?" asked Quaeryt.

Skarpa nodded to Khaern.

"They got us a narrow ramp, and one most of the way down inside the walls. We got some cover from the arrows, but we were on our own inside the walls. Not too bad. We lost maybe fifty troopers, and another hundred wounded."

Meinyt cleared his throat. "They kept the arrows off us, but we had to follow them through the gates. They couldn't do much once we were inside. Didn't have to, though. They killed a good company of defenders near the gates. Froze some and got a bunch with iron darts."

"The two you sent with me did the ramp all right," said Skarpa. "Broad and wide. Even cut away a yard of the top of the walls and some buildings on the other side."

"But?" asked Quaeryt, sensing Skarpa wasn't totally pleased.

"They couldn't do anything after that. The newer one could barely ride. We lost almost a hundred troopers to archers."

"I was afraid of that. I gave you the ones I knew could give you the best access, but they're not that good with stopping arrows."

Skarpa laughed roughly. "Better than I thought. Anytime you can take

L. E. MODESITT, JR.

a walled city without siege gear and only lose a few hundred men . . . Have to say I was worried, but we took most of the casualties on the ride to and up the ramp. Almost nothing after that."

Most likely because any defender close to the walls and ramp was frozen solid, and the archers fled. Quaeryt nodded. "I haven't seen much of the city. We've been holding the bridge. I didn't want to leave it and have them attack again."

"No one was living in the dwellings directly behind the walls. Most were either sealed up or used to store goods," said Khaern.

"There weren't that many people living here on the south side of the river, except for the troopers in the barracks and garrison," added Skarpa. "None of the locals we saw looked that prosperous, either."

"There were more people on the avenue leading to the bridge," Quaeryt pointed out. "There are shops there."

"Still the poor side of town," said Meinyt.

"It's almost like it was all a garrison," mused Skarpa. "This side of the river, anyway."

Quaeryt stopped and looked back south. Everywhere he looked the walls were stone, the windows narrow, with inside shutters. The streets were all of gray stone. The roofs were primarily of grayish tile, although there were replacement tiles of yellowish rose, and on some roofs there were far more replacement tiles than gray ones. "I think it was. I think . . . it was a Naedaran garrison."

"But . . ." Khaern protested, "they've been dead and gone for hundreds of years."

"Good stonework lasts almost forever," said Skarpa.

"Or longer," said Quaeryt dryly. *Especially if it's imaged in place.* He wasn't about to point that out.

Meinyt frowned. "There's something else. There aren't any marks on the stone. No names or initials cut or scratched into it. Not anywhere. If this part of Nordeau is that old . . ."

"Why aren't there any marks?" asked Skarpa. "Because the frigging stone is hard. One of the troopers tried to cut down a Bovarian. He didn't realize just how close he was to a dwelling, and his sabre hit the stone and shattered. Didn't leave a mark on that gray stone. If a blade wielded by a strong man doesn't leave a mark, there won't be many. Enough of that. We've got another problem." His eyes went to Quaeryt. "How wide is that gap to the isle fortress?"

"Not that wide. Ten yards, perhaps a bit farther."

"Can your imagers build a stone span across it?" asked Skarpa.

"We likely can," replied Quaeryt, massaging his forehead. "But not to-day. Perhaps not tomorrow. From what I've heard and seen, none of them could now, and probably not today."

Meinyt and Skarpa nodded. A look of puzzlement crossed Khaern's face.

"It's a matter of strength," Quaeryt explained. "Imaging takes great effort. If an imager tries to do too much when he's exhausted, it can kill him. I don't see any point in killing people when there's not that much to be gained, especially if it means Commander Skarpa won't have imagers when we get to Variana."

"No one ever mentioned that," replied Khaern.

"That's because no one's ever studied imaging before," said Quaeryt.

Khaern looked more closely at Quaeryt's greenish brown shirt. "Oh . . . that's why . . ."

"One of the reasons," Quaeryt agreed.

"I'll send a dispatch to the marshal, telling him that we can probably take the isle fort . . ." Skarpa paused. "I'd wager they've got another pull-away bridge on the other side."

"We can likely do two spans," said Quaeryt.

"I'll let him know and see what he has in mind."

Quaeryt doubted that Deucalon would be all that pleased, no matter what.

58

The south side of Nordeau was quiet by the first glass of the afternoon, with patrols riding the stone streets, the sound of hooves clattering off the stone buildings, the echoes reverberating with a hollow sound that offered at least one hint why the old section of the city was a less favored place for domicile and business. Two companies, rotated every two glasses, were guarding the bridge, with a battalion ready to reinforce them at a moment's notice, should the Bovarians start to extend the bridge from the isle fort.

Quaeryt had arranged for the imager undercaptains and company officers to be billeted in one of the handful of inns—Stone's Rest—and quartered the rest of the battalion in both the inn and various buildings nearby. He determined that all the inns and taverns south of the River Aluse catered almost entirely to travelers and traders. Once again, he'd also discovered that the locals didn't seen to care who was in charge, so long as they weren't hurt and they received some recompense, not that they'd get all that much.

Then, he slipped into the public room of the Stone's Rest, with a concealment shield, to see what he could overhear from the imagers who were seated or half slumped around a long table. The rest of the chamber was empty, except for a serving girl.

Horan held his head in his hands, massaging his forehead.

"It's not that bad," muttered Smaethyl.

". . . speak for yourself . . ." replied the older imager. "Head like to split."

"What did you do? Threkhyl did the ramp."

"Who'd you think was imaging iron darts when we went down over the wall? All that iron hurts. Don't see how the subcommander does it . . ." Horan raised his head and looked at Lhandor. "Not another word about his being a son of Erion . . ."

Lhandor and Khalis exchanged glances, but neither spoke.

"Not so easy, is it?" offered Baelthm.

"You didn't have to do anything, just stick with the subcommander," said Threkhyl, nursing an ale.

"Keepin' up with him isn't easy . . . Took down those gates like they were rotten wood, kept the battalion casualties real low . . ."

"How low?" asked Voltyr.

"Maybe ten dead, thirty wounded, and he took 'em through a whole two companies of pikemen, scattered 'em like leaves before the wind . . . not counting the archers and the foot."

"How the frig does he do it?" asked Smaethyl. "Never heard of an imager that powerful."

"You wouldn't except in war," answered Voltyr. "That's because he's married to Lord Bhayar's sister. He's serious about trying to make things better for imagers. That's why, every battle, he does everything he can. He didn't have to do it. He was a scholar assistant to Bhayar in Solis. No one even knew he was an imager. He could have stayed there safe and out of danger."

"He just wants power," said Threkhyl.

Shaelyt shook his head. "He might be made a commander. He'll never hold a rank higher than that. He knows that. Rulers and their ministers don't trust imagers."

"Why's he do it, then?" asked Horan.

"He told you," said Desyrk tiredly. "Bhayar's the only ruler in the frigging world who'll give imagers even half a break. That's because some of his family was Pharsi, they say."

"Doesn't make sense," declared Threkhyl.

"Sure it does," retorted Desyrk. "He's married. If he doesn't make things better for us, and all imagers, what will happen to his children and his children's children once he's gone?"

"Sounds like you like him." Threkhyl snorted.

"You'd be a fool to like him. But you'd be an idiot not to respect him and support him. He's the only hope we've got. You don't think so, talk to the Khellans."

"Didn't know you talked Pharsi."

"I don't. The officers talk Bovarian, and my ma did. He's their only hope, too."

None of the undercaptains replied, as if Desyrk's words had quieted everyone.

Only hope? Quaeryt winced. Then he slipped away and went back to the stable. From there, with a squad from third company, he rode back to the bridge approach, where he took his time studying the isle fort. The fort had been placed, as had the city, at a point where the river was narrower and deeper and where it had cut through higher ground so that both sides of the city rested on low bluffs. As Quaeryt had thought, the fort's walls merged a yard or two above the water with the gray mass of stone that was the isle. As he looked to the north side of the river, he noted that the area below and to both sides of the north span was walled in the ubiquitous gray stone, but beyond the walls, both to the east and west, the low bluff was composed of a reddish stone. Quaeryt moved to where the stone wall on the west side of the bridge approach ended and looked west and down. On the south side as well, beyond the gray stone facing below and to the sides of the stonework supporting the approach, the rock of the bluff was red.

While there was certainly no way to tell, Quaeryt had a definite feeling that the isle was not at all natural and that it had been imaged in place, just to support the fort.

For the next two glasses he rode through the streets, looking at everything with great care. Skarpa had been right about the general absence of marks on the stone walls. Even the pavement had only the faintest of grooves worn by wagon wheels. Finally, he returned to the Stone's Rest, where he stabled the mare, and then searched out the proprietor and found him just outside the kitchen that served the public room.

"Yes, sir, and what might I do for you?" replied the innkeeper, a youngish man for owning or running an inn, since he was not too many years older than Quaeryt.

"Answer a few questions. That's all for now."

The innkeeper frowned slightly. "As I can."

Quaeryt glimpsed a narrow-faced woman with strawberry-blond hair pulled into a bun watching before she slipped into the kitchen. "Why are there so many empty buildings here?"

"This is the old trading quarter, sir. The larger traders have their warehouses on the north side. Once there was more trade on both sides, but that was afore Lord Bhayar started tariffing the river traders going beyond Ferravyl. Leastwise, that's what my father says."

"Is he an innkeeper, too?"

"That'd be the family trade. He runs the Black Goose north of the river."

"It's the more prosperous inn?"

"More so than here, but . . . we do well enough."

"This part of Nordeau seems very old, yet the stones seem new . . ."

"Always been like that, sir."

"Who built it?"

The innkeeper shrugged. "I wouldn't know, sir. Some say the old ones did, years and years back."

"The old ones?"

"The ones who came before . . . from Chelaes or thereabouts. I wouldn't know. My great-great-grandsire came here came from Tuuryl. This was his first inn. Grandsire built the Black Goose before I was born."

While the man was polite, Quaeryt realized that he avoided looking quite directly at him. "Did the troopers from the barracks frequent your public room?"

The innkeeper chuckled. "Hadn't a been for them, might have closed down years ago." He paused. "You did say we could charge your men for the second ale or lager, didn't you? And all after that?"

"I did indeed. Or for any ale or lager they want when you're not serving them breakfast or dinner. No more than two coppers for the ordinary. Three for the special."

"Fair enough, sir."

Quaeryt suspected that what the man meant was that it was fair enough under the circumstances. "Have there been any more or any fewer troopers here in the last weeks?"

"I couldn't say, one way or another, sir. Looked to be the same to me."

"Did anyone tell you that we were marching on the city?"

"No one said anything . . . except . . . well, a few days ago, one of the traders I knew took everything he could and headed north . . . told me Rex Kharst's forces were losing and pulling back . . . said we'd be wise to do as he was."

"Why didn't you?"

"The inns are all we have. Besides, my sire . . . he said that you'd let the inns be, leastwise those in Villerive."

Quaeryt asked more questions, but it was clear that the innkeeper knew little beyond what he had already said. Finally, Quaeryt smiled and said, "Thank you. I appreciate your time."

The innkeeper nodded. "Pleased to have been of help, sir. If you would excuse me . . ."

"Of course."

Quaeryt waited until the innkeeper turned. After glancing around for a moment and seeing no one near, he raised a concealment shield and slipped after the man. Quaeryt stopped just outside the archway to the kitchen, because the innkeeper was on the other side talking to the woman Quaeryt had observed earlier.

". . . .did he want, Shajan?"

". . . asked questions about the old quarter here and the Bovarian troops . . . lots of them . . ."

". . . why would he? He looks like one of them . . ."

". . . can't be. He's a Telaryn officer . . . maybe more than that . . . what I've overheard . . ."

"Still looks like an old one . . . yellow-white hair . . . those eyes . . ."

Old one . . . is that the same as a lost one?

". . . how would you know? . . . no paintings of them . . ."

". . . I've heard tell . . ."

". . . don't upset him . . . the way things are . . . we'll survive . . ."

". . . won't . . . but you deal with him . . ."

Quaeryt shook his head and moved away, still holding the conceal-ment. He needed to check with Zhelan about the billeting and feeding for Fifth Battalion.

A glass or so later, after he'd finished with the major, as Quaeryt was waiting to enter the public room of the inn, a squad leader hurried up to him. "Subcommander . . . Commander Skarpa has called a meeting of all the subcommanders at sixth glass at the Traders' Bowl."

"Thank you. I'll be there."

"Yes, sir. Thank you, sir."

Once the squad leader had left the small front hall of the inn, Quaeryt permitted himself a sardonic smile, wondering what Deucalon's reaction to Skarpa's dispatch had been.

After he finished eating with the company officers and the undercap-tains—a subdued affair, possibly because the imagers had little to say, and because Quaeryt could only tell the company officers that he'd heard nothing yet—he headed out for the Traders' Bowl, the larger inn where Skarpa had made his headquarters.

As Quaeryt walked along the stone-paved way, carrying shields, de-spite a certain strain, he made a point of taking in every building and dis-covered that every one was built of gray stone, giving the quarter a cold and forboding appearance despite the warm damp air of harvest.

The Traders' Bowl looked as though it might have once housed a wealthy family because the stone window frames were far larger than most of those he'd seen in Nordeau so far. When Quaeryt stepped inside, he saw a Telaryn ranker standing in the entry hall, a large foyer with niches in the walls, possibly designed for statues or the like, but devoid of ornamentation, pos-sibly most recently removed, thought Quaeryt.

"Sir, the others are here, the first door back on the left," said the ranker.

"Thank you." Quaeryt walked swiftly to the door, opened it, stepped inside, and closed it behind himself.

Skarpa, Meinyt, and Khaern sat around a table in a small chamber across a wide hallway from the public room, but one that did not strike Quaeryt as originally intended as a plaques room, not given the arched ceiling with carved moldings that had later been whitewashed, although the circular table and the worn round-backed chairs proclaimed that plaques gaming had been its latest use. Skarpa motioned to the chair across from him.

Quaeryt took it and waited.

"Earlier this afternoon, I got a dispatch from the marshal. He had no problems with our not being able to cross the river today. In fact, he does not wish us to attack the isle fort and cross into the northern part of Nordeau until early on Lundi."

"You mean he's still a day away?" asked Meinyt sardonically.

"He did not convey when he and his forces would arrive."

"Mardi, most likely."

Skarpa looked sharply at Meinyt.

"He's right, you know?" Khaern said.

"That may be," replied Skarpa, "but he is the marshal, and it's best to stick to the facts in officers' meetings." He went on. "Otherwise, we might be too free with our opinions in meetings with other commanders, and I do believe that you three are the most junior subcommanders, and I know I'm the most junior commander." He softened his words with a faint smile.

Quaeryt had his doubts about whether he'd ever be included in such a meeting, at least voluntarily, by Deucalon.

"The isle fort isn't that big," Skarpa went on, looking at Quaeryt. "Once your imagers put a span over to it, I'd wager the Bovarians abandon it."

"They might slip out of it tonight," suggested Meinyt.

"That's possible. If they don't know it yet, they'll find out soon that we've got imagers that can create a span," added Skarpa.

"Why didn't they know before?" asked Khaern.

"They likely knew we had some imagers, but the only time they built a bridge was at Ferravyl," replied Skarpa, "and none of the Bovarian troopers or officers who saw it survived."

"Still . . ." pressed Khaern.

"If you hadn't seen it," asked Meinyt, "would you have believed it?"

Khaern laughed softly. "Probably not."

"Getting across a narrow span to the far side . . . that could be a problem," said Skarpa.

"We might be able to image a wider span, maybe even two," suggested Quaeryt. "The undercaptains will get another day to rest up. That will help." He didn't mention that there would likely be more than a few Bovarian casualties if the Bovarians massed troopers on and around the northern bridge approach.

"Good. If they have more pikemen in those narrow streets, that could be a problem . . ."

Quaeryt listened and gave the best answers and suggestions he could. By the time the meeting was over, less than two quints later, his head was aching even more and his eyes burning, and he was ready to walk back to the Stone's Rest and get some sleep.

59

The chamber Quaeryt had taken in the Stone's Rest was at the top of the building, in fact the only room on the third floor, perhaps four yards by five with not only a wide bed, and a night table, but a writing desk with a matching chair, and a doorless armoire for hanging garments. Quaeryt picked up his kit from the floor and set it on the chair, while he took out the pouch with soap and personals, noting that the writing desk, once a decent piece of oak furniture, was battered and the surface of the wood worn and scratched, as was that of the desk chair.

There was an adjoining washroom, with a chamber pot, but not a jakes, reminding Quaeryt, again, of the age of the building. The outer walls were stone, of course, as were the floors, and the wall plaster held an uneven off-white shade that was not the result of design, but age and less than enthusiastic cleaning.

After he hung up his spare uniform to at least air out, and taken off his shirt and hung that up as well, then washed up, he walked back into the main chamber and looked at the desk. He thought about writing Vaelora, but decided against it, since he really only wanted to write about taking Nordeau once. He wasn't sleepy, tired as he felt, and the walk back from the Traders' Bowl had cleared his headache and eyes somewhat.

He pulled the small leather volume from his kit, although he hoped, given the tight quarters in Nordeau and the lack of open space, that Skarpa would not insist on services on Solayi evening. Still . . . just in case . . .

In the dim light from the single lamp, he began to page through the book, hoping for something that would provide inspiration. One passage that he'd noted before struck him in a different light in view of what he'd surmised about the Naedarans.

Before Rholan, the Nameless was more a deity of battles and of rough justice, justice administered at the edge of a blade or under an ax.

Was that really so, or did Rholan . . . or the writer . . . just assume that?

Again, Quaeryt had no way of knowing.

Another passage caused Quaeryt to smile, as it had every time he'd seen the words.

Contrary to the legends that are already springing up about Rholan, he was never a proper chorister, or even an improper one. More than one chorister, especially the noted Basilyn of Cheva, berated his congregants for following a man who was "neither a proper scholar, nor a chorister, nor much of anything but a believer in his own rectitude." To his credit, Rholan never claimed to be a chorister, but only that he attempted to follow the way of the Nameless as best he could. On more than one occasion, he was denied entry to an anomen to speak, the most well-known instance, of course, being when Chorister Tharyn Arysyn barred him from the north anomen in Montagne, not far from Rholan's own home. Tharyn declared that all were welcome to worship in the anomen, but only those who had studied the Nameless could speak.

It is said that Rholan smiled and declared, "How can any man, even a chorister, study the mightiness of the Nameless when none can describe the Nameless? I only claim to study the precepts of the Nameless, for those are what must guide men." Those were not quite his words. What he said was, "Tharyn, you cannot even describe the Nameless. Nor can you explain His way. Yet you would bar one who can for fear that you will be found out as the fraud you are." Shortly after Rholan's disappearance and presumed death, Tharyn also vanished and was never seen again. Many of the faithful swore that they would never name a son Tharyn and that the Nameless would turn any with that appellation to the Namer. While there are reports of such, I cannot speak to them, for any malefactor named Tharyn would call up that story in the minds of followers, and none would note those who bore the name who were not evil.

In the end, Quaeryt put down the volume because his eyes were twitching and because nothing he had read gave ready inspiration for a homily, especially when he did not even know whether he would be conducting services. After blowing out the lamp, he walked to the window and opened the shutters wide, hoping for a cool evening breeze, then returned to the bed. For a time he just lay there, but his thoughts turned images of the Bovarians, frozen behind and around the gates he had taken down with his imaging.

Troopers and armsmen die in war. After a moment came the second thought. *But you've killed more than your share . . . except . . . is there such a thing as a fair share? Does it matter whether you've killed one man or a thousand? Or is that just a rationalization? But then, in a battle, if you don't fight to win . . .*

Lying there in the darkness on the bed, he couldn't help but think about Vaelora's point that, so often, thousands would die, and his actions only determined which thousands.

He wasn't sure how much that thought helped as he tried to ignore the soreness in his chest, arms, and thighs, and then . . . he didn't even notice his eyes closing.

Somewhere in the night, the warm breeze turned cool, and Quaeryt fumbled for a blanket, but he couldn't find it in the darkness. Then the sky rumbled, and the air got colder still. He sat up in the bed and swung his feet onto the stone floor, but the floor was so cold that his feet froze to the stone. Across the room from him was a shadowy figure. Then he realized that the figure was not shadowed, but coated in ice, and a bitter chill extended from that icy shape.

Warmth! He needed warmth, but his teeth were chattering so much that he could not even reach for a striker to light a lamp or a candle. In desperation, he tried to image a hearth and a fire, and flames roared up before him, so fierce and so quickly that he could soon free his feet.

But with those flames came smoke, acrid bitter smoke, and he began to cough, retchingly, time and time again.

Then . . . Quaeryt found himself back lying in his bed, with black and gray smoke all around him

Idiot! You imaged in your sleep . . .

Through the smoke he could see that the desk and chair were in flames. Still coughing, his eyes burning from the smoke, he struggled to image a film of water over them both. The flames began to vanish, but there was even more smoke. He imaged a bit more water, then staggered, barely able to see, to the window.

From there, he stood and imaged in fresh air from somewhere until he could stop coughing.

Then there was a pounding on the door.

"Subcommander! Sir! Are you all right!"

Quaeryt recognized Zhelan's voice and slowly walked to the door, removing the bar. "I'm fine now." *Should you open the door? If you don't, he and everyone else will think the worst.* With a sigh that turned into a cough, he slowly opened the door. "You might as well come in, Major."

Zhelan stepped inside, his eyes widening. "I smelled smoke. It came drifting down the steps. What . . . happened?"

Quaeryt closed the door. "One of the dangers of imaging. Every so often, just like everyone else, imagers have nightmares. I had one where I was freezing. In my nightmare, I tried to start a fire . . . I got more than I wanted." Quaeryt started to laugh, then began to cough from the little bit of smoke still in his chest.

"Sir . . . can I do anything?" Zhelan glanced at the soot on the walls and the charred table. Then his eyes went to the bruises on Quaeryt's thighs and arms, widening slightly.

"No. I can probably remove most of the damage. Just tell anyone who asks that smoke drifted in through my open window."

"Yes, sir." Zhelan looked dubious.

"I can. If not tonight, tomorrow. I'd appreciate your not mentioning this to any of the company commanders or the imagers. The majors are uneasy enough, and this sort of thing won't hurt anyone but me. As for the undercaptains, they're not experienced enough to worry about it." *Yet.*

"I can do that, sir."

"Thank you."

After Zhelan left, and Quaeryt closed the door, he thought about his last words. *How soon before that sort of thing happened to some of them?* And how could he prevent it or deal with it? Clearly, when imaging nightmares happened, it wasn't exactly safe for anyone sleeping nearby . . .

At that moment he recalled the small stone-walled sleeping chamber in the dwelling in Gahenyara, the one occupied by Vaelora's great-great-grandmere. *She wasn't only Pharsi; she was an imager! That's why she slept alone . . . because of imaging nightmares.*

That raised other questions . . . such as how much Bhayar knew about his family's past. Was that why he wasn't unsettled about Quaeryt and Vaelora marrying? Or did he have plans for Quaeryt, just as Quaeryt had plans for him?

How could he not? But were they instinctive, as Vaelora believed, or were they more focused? Quaeryt suspected the instinctive and opportunistic, but he'd have to be very careful in laying the groundwork for his own plans.

He still had a slight headache, but he needed to do something about the sooty mess his nightmares had created . . . and working on that might well tire him enough so that he didn't have any more unsettling dreams . . . or feelings of guilt and concern about what he had done. *And what you might yet have to do?*

He looked at the charred desk and chair . . . and then at the soot streaks and smudges on the white plaster walls and ceiling . . . and the puddles of water on the floor.

60

Solayi was the first of Erntyn, the second and supposedly cooler month of harvest. It didn't feel any cooler when Quaeryt woke. He had only a trace of a headache, but he felt tired and drained. When he looked around the room, he didn't see any obvious sign of damage. Unfortunately, there were problems. The chair that he'd repaired with imaging had a smooth, if aged, golden oak finish. The same was true of the writing desk. He hadn't been about to try to duplicate the battered and scratched finishes. Likewise, the plaster walls and ceiling were a clean off-white, rather than showing the uneven patina of age and dirt, but the innkeeper might not notice that.

Quaeryt washed up and shaved, a necessity for him in hot weather, because his skin developed rashes if he let a beard grow out, then began to dress when there was a rap on the door. He pulled on the least soiled of the uniform shirts and walked to the door. "Yes?"

"Sir . . . it's Shajan . . . the innkeeper, I would hate to disturb you, but there is the odor of smoke . . . I wished to know if you were all right . . ."

And if you've damaged my family's inn. Quaeryt wiped a wry smile off his face and opened the door, standing in such a way that the innkeeper could see everything, but not pass Quaeryt. "I smelled smoke last night as well . . . but I'm fine."

The innkeeper tried to study the room without looking too obvious. "I'm sorry to disturb you, but . . ."

"I understand. You would not want a guest to suffer or the premises to be damaged. As you can see, I am fine, and so are the premises." Quaeryt paused. "Could you wash some uniforms for me—for whatever the normal charges are—and have them ready by this evening?"

"Why . . . yes, sir."

"Good. I'll get them for you." Quaeryt walked to the armoire and took the two sets of soiled uniforms and carried them back to Shajan, who had stepped into the room, his eyes studying everything, a puzzled expression on his face. "Here you are. My thanks."

"Yes, sir." The innkeeper took the uniforms, glancing around the chamber a last time before stepping back into the narrow landing at the top of the stairs.

Once Shajan departed, Quaeryt finished dressing before heading down to the public room for breakfast and the officers' meeting to follow, in lieu of a formal muster.

What the Stone's Rest offered for breakfast was related to a domchana, Quaeryt thought, consisting of two pieces of egg toast dipped in batter a second time and fried around a slice of ham and topped with a drizzle of an apple-berry syrup. Each officer—and trooper—got two and an ale or lager.

At the officers' meeting, Quaeryt began, in Bovarian, "As I told Major Zhelan last night, unless the Bovarians mount an assault of some sort, we will not be undertaking any attacks today, but the bridge will remain guarded. We are to be ready to attack the north of Nordeau by early tomorrow." He looked across the faces of the officers. "Major Calkoran, you have a question?"

"Your imagers will create stone bridges for us?"

"They will."

"If they reach from that tiny fort to one point on the far shore, the Bovarians may be able to blunt the attack. Unless you lead the charge."

"Thank you. We'll be sure to spread out the attack in one or more ways so that your troopers are not crammed together and unable to fight their best. How we do that will depend on how the Bovarians are assembled to defend the north shore."

"Thank you, sir."

Quaeryt turned to Zhelan. "I had forgotten to ask you. The horses have been ridden a great deal on stone lately. Have we had more trouble with shoes or lameness?"

"Some, sir, but so far we've had enough spare mounts. Wouldn't hurt to gather more if we could after tomorrow."

Quaeryt nodded. "If you'd see what can be done when the time comes. What about grain?"

"That's in short supply, sir, but I have suggested that some of the factors would be well advised to see if they can find some."

Quaeryt wasn't about to ask what Zhelan's suggestions entailed, but he wouldn't have been surprised if they mentioned the relation of a subcommander to a certain ruler. "And?"

Zhelan smiled. "They thought we might have some by this afternoon."

"Good!"

After a few more items, and a report on the state of the troopers wounded in the assault, Quaeryt dismissed all the company officers, which left him alone in the public room with the imager undercaptains.

He let the silence draw out before speaking. "Tomorrow you'll have to image a stone span from the end of the approach to the isle. After we take the isle, you'll have to do the same to the north shore. If they have troops arrayed there we'll need at least two wide spans that aren't too close together. I'll be scouting that out later this morning, and I'll let you know either tonight or in the morning what will be necessary."

"Will they have archers, sir?" asked Horan.

"They have archers. They also have musketeers. We've seen the archers here, but we haven't seen the musketeers. Yet."

"Why might that be?" asked Voltyr politely, in a tone that suggested he knew the answer and that Quaeryt should tell the others.

"From what I understand from Major Calkoran, who has faced the Bovarian musketeers far more than any of the rest of us, the muskets are far more effective on open level fields or in places where they have a clear field of fire. The south quarter of Nordeau is not suited to that. Neither are the approaches to the bridge. It may be that there is a level square beyond the approach to the north side of the bridge. If so, that would be where we would be most likely to encounter musketeers."

"Thank you, sir." Voltyr nodded.

Quaeryt scanned the faces of the undercaptains. "How many of you still have headaches? This isn't a time for bravery or bearing pain without saying so."

After a moment, Horan raised a hand, then so did Smaethyl, followed by Khalis, then Desyrk.

"Is there anyone who has trouble seeing?"

Every head shook "no."

"Good. For those of you with headaches, it will help if you drink watered ale or lager. Not enough to get tipsy. That will only give you a second kind of headache, and you don't need two right now."

His words brought several smiles.

"Some walking and fresh air will help, but walk in groups of three if you do. If you can, take a nap this afternoon. You may need all the rest you can get before tomorrow . . ." He went on with a few more suggestions, then dismissed them.

When he finished with the imagers, Quaeryt reclaimed the mare from the inn stable, saddled and mounted, and rode up to the bridge to the isle fort under a sun that was already sweltering. It might be past the middle of harvest, but so far he hadn't noticed any decrease in either the heat or the dampness of the air.

A full company was guarding the bridge approach, but three of the squads were engaged in sabre drills on foot, while the fourth squad was drawn up in loose formation just short of the gap between the approach and the isle fort. Quaeryt rode up the eastern edge of the roadway and reined up short of the formed-up squad.

A captain stepped forward. "Good morning, Subcommander."

"And to you, Captain. Have you seen anyone in the fort today?"

"No, sir. The companies watching last night saw lots of lamps and lanterns. Nothing so far today. Not a soul. I'd not be surprised if they've left. That, or they want us to think so."

Either wouldn't have surprised Quaeryt, although he had the feeling that the Bovarians had left the small fort. "Just don't let them surprise us."

"No, sir."

Quaeryt turned and eased the mare a bit closer to the end of the approach where he studied the fort. The foundation rising from the isle was not all that large, perhaps running thirty yards upstream to downstream, and although it was hard to tell from where he looked, about two-thirds of that from north to south. The fort proper was set on the western end, so that, were the bridge spans in place, riders or wagons would move straight across the span from one side of the river to the other. The stone roadway across the eastern end fort was bordered by a low stone wall a yard and a half high. The wooden span between the fort and the north shore had also been retracted so that the fort was truly an isle at the moment.

Quaeryt guided the mare down the approach and then westward on the narrow street bordering the bluff. Unlike in many towns and cities, there were no buildings or dwellings perched on the edge of the bluff, just the street, with a chest-high gray stone wall at the edge of the stone sidewalk.

Once he had ridden close to two hundred yards, he turned the mare and reined up so that he could see the isle. The span to the north approach had definitely been retracted. He squinted and looked again. He'd originally thought that the isle fort was in the middle of the river, but from the southern side and as far west as he'd ridden, it was clear that the gap between the fort and the northern shore was at least twice as far as between the fort and the southern shore.

That suggested that the Naedarans feared more from the north than from the south, not surprisingly, since the bulk of the Bovarian heartlands lay to the north and west of Nordeau. Still . . . with all the skill embodied in the stonework, Quaeryt couldn't help but wonder how and why Naedara had declined without any record of a great war or conquest, with not even a story or a tale, except muttered references to "the old ones."

While he had no doubts that Skarpa already knew what he'd just discovered, he turned the mare toward the Traders' Bowl. There, after turning the mare over to a trooper, he found Skarpa where he expected to find him—in the plaques room of the Traders' Bowl, seated at the table.

"Good morning, sir. I assume you've received reports that both bridge spans to the isle fort have been retracted, possibly removed."

"Captain Faurot reported that early this morning." Skarpa did not stand, nor did he gesture for Quaeryt to seat himself. "You think the Bovarians know we have imagers and that the fort offers little protection?"

"That's possible," Quaeryt agreed. "It's also possible they've set a trap on the other side."

"Musketeers again? Set to rake the entire approach from the bridge?"

"That thought had occurred to me."

"It occurred to me as well. What can you do about it?"

"There are some possibilities . . ." Quaeryt went on to lay out what the imagers and he could do, although he did not differentiate his capabilities from those of the undercaptains, ending up with, ". . . about all that I can come up with, sir."

"More than most. Prepare for that, and if they haven't thought it out that well, we'll count ourselves fortunate."

That we will. "I've already gone over the possibilities with the officers."

"Good. Plan for assembling on the bridge approach beginning at sixth glass." Skarpa stood. "Sorry I can't talk longer. Deucalon wants an immediate response. Friggin' idiocy!"

Quaeryt nodded. "Tomorrow."

Once he departed the Traders' Bowl, he rode back to the bridge and the street fronting the river where he spent some three glasses studying the river, the fort, and what he could see of the north side of the river.

When he returned to the Stone's Rest somewhat past midafternoon, he'd no sooner stepped into the small front hallway than Shajan stepped forward, bowing slightly. "Subcommander, sir, I hope that I did not trouble you unduly this morning."

Quaeryt smiled politely. "No . . . I understand your concern. The inn is your livelihood, and you would not be diligent if you did not look to see that all was well. You have a responsibility to your wife and to your family."

"Thank you, sir." Shajan added, "I just returned your uniforms to your chamber."

"Thank you. I do appreciate it. Is the usual fee two coppers for each?"

"Sir . . . you do not owe us."

Quaeryt smiled again. "I cannot change what Lord Bhayar requires of you, but I can insist on paying for what I require of you." He extended four coppers.

"Sir . . ."

"Please. Take them, if you will not for your services, as a favor to me."

For a moment Shajan froze. Then he swallowed and took the coppers, as if he had no choice.

Quaeryt feared he'd used a phrase with a second meaning to those in Nordeau, and one he'd certainly not intended. He image-projected warmth and concern. "Shajan . . . I am not an old one. I am Pharsi, though I did not know it until I was well grown, and that is why I command a battalion that is largely Pharsi, but most are from Khel."

Some, but not all, of the fear left the innkeeper's face. "Thank you, sir."

"It's my pleasure, and I do appreciate having clean uniforms."

As he walked up the steps to the third level to his chamber, where he wanted to wash up and rest before the evening meal, he wondered, once again, just what the old ones of Naedara had done that was so awful that folklore and legends could terrify a grown man after so many years.

61

By half past sixth glass on Lundi morning, Skarpa's forces had assembled on the south side of the River Aluse, with Fifth Battalion taking up the bridge approach and Third Regiment directly behind. Quaeryt absently patted the mare's neck, then straightened himself in the saddle and looked to the early morning sky—absolutely clear with only the faintest hint of a breeze— then across to the bridge approach on the north shore. Not a single figure was visible there, although there could have been Bovarians hidden behind the low bluff wall. Still . . . seeing no one only meant the Bovarians were out of sight. He couldn't imagine they'd abandoned the city, yet it did seem as though they had not put a tremendous effort into holding it. Was that part of their plan to bleed Bhayar's forces and draw them farther and farther into Bovaria. *Quite possibly, but as soon as you believe that, you'll find yourself outnumbered and in severe difficulty.*

He looked to Voltyr, mounted and waiting beside him. "You can image a span twice as wide as the old wooden one? Just to the fort."

"Yes, sir."

"Do it now, then."

"Now? It's not seventh glass."

"The Bovarians couldn't extend the bridge in time to get to us even if they were standing there on the other shore, and they're not. This way, it will be longer before you have to do anything else."

Voltyr nodded, then looked straight ahead.

A quick flash of light flared and vanished, followed by a gust of cool air. A gray stone span stretched from where the bridge approach ended to the roadway on the narrow isle fort. The side walls even matched and joined the narrow section on the east side of the fort.

Quaeryt studied the far approach, but no Bovarians appeared. Still, he had no doubts that there were sentries or observers watching and relaying what they saw to the Bovarian commander or commanders. "Undercaptains! Forward! Fifth Battalion, after the undercaptains!"

Holding full personal shields, Quaeryt urged the mare forward, relieved as he heard the solid sound of her hooves on the stone and as he could feel no vibration beneath them. No one emerged from the isle fort, even as he and Voltyr approached, followed by Threkhyl, Horan, and Smaethyl and the other undercaptains and first company, with the remainder of Fifth Battalion moving forward as quickly as the troopers could.

Quaeryt turned. "Undercaptain Ghaelyn! A detail to check the fort before we proceed!"

"Yes, sir. First squad! Dismount and inspect the fort!"

As the troopers hurried through an unsecured door—a good sign that the fort was empty, Quaeryt thought, he eased the mare forward until he was less than a yard from the gap between the fort and the north shore. He still could detect no movement on or around the north approach to the bridge. There was a large open space to both sides of the bridge approach on the north shore of the river, but because of the wall along the northern bluff, he could not see whether it was a square or a park or even a lake. He suspected it was a square of some sort, and from the buildings behind it—the upper part of the first floors he could see—there did not appear to be any mounted forces or catapults or the like. But then, there might well be thousands of troopers below his line of sight and behind low barricades, or pikemen, or musketeers . . . or all three.

Almost half a quint passed before the troopers from first squad emerged from the gray stone walls of the narrow isle fort.

"Not a soul here, sir! Nothing at all."

"Thank you." Quaeryt looked back. Fifth Battalion was ready to move. "Undercaptains Threkhyl, Horan, and Smaethyl! Forward!"

When the three undercaptains were in position, Quaeryt ordered, "Image now!"

Almost instantly, two wide spans angled from the north side of the roadbed section of the isle fort. The right-hand one merged with the north bridge approach. The left span merged with the bluff wall and then angled down into what Quaeryt thought had to be a square.

Quaeryt gave the three undercaptains a quick look, but all three were still in the saddle, then glanced down and to his right. On the surface of the River Aluse, the thin film of ice caused by their imaging was already moving east of the bridge with the water, while fragmenting into shimmering pieces, already melting in the orangish white light of the early morning sun.

"Undercaptains Shaelyt Desyrk, Lhandor, and Khalis forward!"

"Ready, Undercaptains?"

"Ready, sir."

"Fifth Battalion! Forward!"

Ghaelyn and Zhelan echoed the orders as Quaeryt urged the mare forward onto the gray stone of the new span. Khalis rode beside Quaeryt on the right-hand span while Shaelyt, Desyrk, and Lhandor led the way on the left. Baelthm was farther back behind Quaeryt, who could only hope that Shaelyt's shields were up to what was likely to strike them.

Even before Quaeryt reached the point where the newly imaged stone span met the roadway of the old bridge, he was scanning what lay ahead—a gray stone square roughly two hundred yards on a side, surrounded on three sides by gray stone buildings of two and three stories that could have been identical to the structures on the south side of the river. Quaeryt extended his shields to cover the front of the column he led, looking for Bovarian defenders.

Why a square on this side of the river and not on the other? Quaeryt pushed that thought aside. A second glance revealed that in the center of the far side of the square was a low stone barricade no more than fifty yards long, behind which crouched troopers. What looked to be a low brown earthen berm crossed the square some ten yards in front of the stone barricade.

Then from the two streets leading from the square arched hundreds of arrows, some directed at Quaeryt's column, the remainder toward the western column where Shaelyt led the riders into the far side of the square. Quaeryt barely felt the shafts impact on his shields. He kept riding forward, down into the square. Behind him Fifth Battalion's first and second companies began to spread out. He glanced to his left, where third and fourth companies were already doing the same behind Shaelyt, forming up side by side with a five-man front.

There have to be more defenders! Where are they?

He looked beyond the low barricade at the featureless gray stone front of the line of buildings.

Featureless? How could the buildings have no windows or doors?

Just as that thought crossed his mind, the far side of the square exploded, and Quaeryt felt as though his shields had been compressed into an iron jacket that instantly slammed thousands of spear-points into his chest, upper body, forehead, and face. He contracted his personal shield to cover just himself as he struggled to stay upright in the saddle. He did manage to see hundreds of musketeers revealed from behind gray drapes just in front of the buildings at the end of the square.

A quick horn triplet followed, and what Quaeryt had thought was a berm turned out to be pikemen huddled under brown cloth as they struggled to throw off the cloth and take their positions, trying to raise pikes against the oncoming Telaryn troopers.

"Fifth Battalion! Charge!" ordered Zhelan.

Quaeryt let the troopers surge past him, knowing that there was little he could do at the moment . . . or perhaps for some time. Again, he was grateful for Zhelan. He did manage to pull to the side, out of the way of troopers coming off the bridge and to order, "Undercaptains On me!"

While he was anything but content to let others charge while he remained stationary behind what remained of his shields, he doubted that he could even have lifted his staff, let alone used it in any meaningful way.

Should you have tried?

He almost snorted. His shields wouldn't have held, and with his stiffness and inability to move or ride well, he'd likely have lost his staff at the first contact and become more of a liability than a help. Again he was lucky that he had Zhelan as a second in command, and even more fortunate that Skarpa understood that.

In what seemed moments, Fifth Battalion was reinforced by the lead companies of Third Regiment, then by the rest of Skarpa's regiment, and by Eleventh Regiment. From what Quaeryt could see, Fifth Regiment poured into the square from the western span.

In less than two quints, Quaeryt, the undercaptains, and a squad from first company detailed to protect them were almost alone in the square, except for the dying and the wounded of both Telaryn and Bovaria. Quaeryt had taken some time to drink a little lager from his water bottle, but reaching for it had been painful.

Desyrk had guided Shaelyt and Lhandor over to join the group. Shaelyt was slumped in the saddle, and Quaeryt could see red marks across his face and neck. He had no doubts that they were everywhere, as they likely were on his own body.

Quaeryt swallowed, then asked Desyrk, "Did Shaelyt's shields take the brunt of the muskets?"

"I . . . think so, sir. No one seemed wounded by the volley, but he nearlike fell out of the saddle. I . . . we.. caught him. He's hurt . . . maybe . . . bad . . ."

"He's bruised all over," Quaeryt said.

Desyrk looked at Quaeryt. "Like you, sir?"

"The same reason. I'm a little stronger than he is."

"You took much more fire," said Khalis from beside Quaeryt. "I saw it. You saved hundreds."

"Some. Probably not hundreds." Quaeryt looked out over the fallen lying across the square, but most of those wore blue-gray, rather than the faded green of Telaryn, and there were pikes lying everywhere.

The shields must have helped. He hoped so, because every one of his ribs hurt, and sharp pains stabbed across his chest with every movement he made. But what had also helped the Telaryn forces was that the musketeers hadn't been able to fire a second volley without doing in their own pikemen, and the pikemen hadn't been able to properly form up and set their pikes before Zhelan had charged them. The defense had been too complex, but it had revealed the weakness in Quaeryt's plan. *Too complicated, and too much reliance on imagers doing too many things.*

He looked over at Shaelyt again. The Pharsi undercaptain was no longer slumped, but he was pale, and clearly in great pain. Quaeryt eased his mount over beside Shaelyt. "Are you feeling any better?"

"Not . . . much." After a long pause, Shaelyt said slowly, "Your shields . . . hurt like this?"

"They hurt," Quaeryt admitted. "It's hard to move."

Shaelyt looked as if he wanted to shake his head, but decided against it.

"That's why I don't want any of us getting into the habit of shielding troopers. You and I just covered the front. What would have happened if you'd tried to shield them all?"

"I . . . wouldn't be . . . here?"

"No. You'd be dead. So would I, if I'd tried that." Quaeryt winced. He'd spoken too forcefully, and his body had let him know. "Drink some lager or ale, whatever's in your bottle. It will help."

"Yes, sir." Shaelyt moved slowly, reaching for his water bottle.

Quaeryt understood all too well how the undercaptain felt.

After a glass or so had passed, Major Arion returned to the square with fourth company, reining up before Quaeryt. "Subcommander, sir . . . You're wounded!"

"In a way. Bruised all over. So is Undercaptain Shaelyt."

"You . . . stopped the musket balls?"

"We did . . . many of them, anyway. We weren't able to follow the charge. What happened?"

"They did not expect us to charge so quickly. They are all fleeing. There were not that many. Two or three regiments at most . . . and the musketeers. Already, there are no more in Nordeau . . . except those who are hiding. We killed many of them. Commander Skarpa says that as many as a regiment may have escaped. Marshal Deucalon—his forces are nowhere near." Arion's face screwed up into an expression of disgust.

Deucalon's absence did not surprise Quaeryt.

"When it is certain that all are vanquished, Fifth Battalion is to return to the south shore and hold it. Eleventh Regiment will join us."

"Do you know if Subcommander Khaern has a surgeon?"

"Sir?"

"If he does, I'd like him to look at Undercaptain Shaelyt."

"I do not know. If he does, he should look at you as well, sir."

Quaeryt surveyed the square, trying to ignore some of the moans from the fallen men. He gestured. "Some of them need help more than we do. We'll survive." For now. "We'll wait here for Fifth Battalion to finish up. Then we'll join them for the return to the south shore."

"Yes, sir. I will be leaving another squad with you. It is best that way."

Quaeryt managed a smile. "I won't argue with you over that, Major."

He watched as Arion and fourth company headed out again, this time taking the eastern avenue from the square.

For the next two glasses, the imager undercaptains and the two squads guarded the square. Two of the troopers, who had some knowledge of wounds, did what they could for the fallen. At least, Quaeryt reflected, they kept the locals from scavenging and doing worse to the wounded who still might survive.

It was well after second glass when Zhelan returned with Fifth Battalion, and news that Eleventh Regiment would follow later. From what Quaeryt could see, the battalion's casualties had not been heavy.

As he rode back over the rebuilt stone bridge and past the abandoned isle fort, Quaeryt could not help thinking, You can't do this again. That, he knew, because the next time they faced the Bovarians, he had no doubt that there would be even more musketeers. Especially if someone noticed what happened here and escaped.

He also wondered who might be the greater enemy for him—Myskyl and Deucalon or Rex Kharst?

62

When Quaeryt finally reached the Stone's Rest, he could barely dismount, and he had to request that someone else unsaddle and stable the mare. He hated asking for that, but he knew he wouldn't be able to handle the saddle. He almost tripped twice climbing the stairs to the third floor, and he was uncomfortable sitting in the desk chair and worried that he wouldn't be able to move if he lay down.

He did anyway, but he hurt too much to sleep, and he kept thinking about what had happened at the square. He'd been prepared for muskets. He just hadn't been prepared for hundreds of them all firing at him—or the front of the column. Had the Bovarians known that Skarpa would have the imagers near the front? Or had the attack in the square just been designed to catch the Telaryn forces off guard?

After thinking it over, Quaeryt still didn't know. The comparatively small number of Bovarian defenders suggested that they'd been told to deliver enough of an attack to slow the Telaryn advance and then withdraw. Yet the defenders' battle plan had been well thought out, and especially effective at minimizing the impact that the imagers otherwise might have had. Had it been an inspired plan designed by a junior commander who knew something about imagers and who'd seen their effect in the battle for the southern part of Nordeau? Or had it been planned by a senior commander who knew too much about Bhayar's forces?

But even if any of those possibilities were so, why had the Bovarians risked—and lost—so many musketeers? Especially when there had been comparatively so few foot or cavalry to support them?

To Quaeryt that made little sense, and yet the planning of the defenders' tactics showed considerable thought—although the sloppy execution had made matters less disastrous for Skarpa's forces than otherwise might have been the case.

Quaeryt lay on the bed for several glasses, thinking, semidozing . . . and failing to come up with answers that satisfied him, only yet another question that he should have considered earlier. Why hadn't he seen any cannon? The Bovarians had powder; the exploding barges had proved that. They had muskets, and plenty of those, and they had used those for years. Cannon had been used at sea for several decades, but nowhere had the Telaryn forces faced cannon.

Because they're heavy and hard to move quickly, and Kharst didn't expect to use them inside Bovaria?

He could think of no other answer, but the fact he couldn't satisfied him not at all, because that suggested he hadn't considered all the possibilities.

In time, he rose and struggled down to the public room to eat with the other officers, all of whom were polite enough—or tired enough—not to comment on his appearance and stiffness. He did indulge in having two mugs of lager, and that seemed to make the climb back up the stairs somewhat less painful.

Khaern's combat surgeon, a squad leader, did not return to the south side of Nordeau until after seventh glass, and there were deep circles under his eyes and blood splatters all over his sleeves. Even so, he winced as he looked at the welts and incipient bruises across Quaeryt's body . . . and the slight black eyes that were also forming.

"You've got a lot of bruises here, Subcommander, and I'd say you came as close as possible to fracturing at least one of your ribs, maybe all of them. Your whole chest is going to hurt for weeks, maybe longer. Your eyes might even swell shut. You shouldn't be doing much."

"I still need to ride before long."

"We can wrap your chest with some stays, but if you get hit again like you did here, you could break a rib or two. If it's a bad break . . ." He shook his head. "That doesn't even count your eyes . . ."

Quaeryt understood all too well. He also understood that Myskyl or Deucalon would likely want to put him in that position again. *And you can't let them.* "Wrap me up. I'll have a few days to recover. After that, I'll try to avoid getting hit." He paused. "How about Undercaptain Shaelyt?"

"He's better off than you. Not much." The squad leader and field surgeon paused. "If I might ask, sir . . ."

"We were leading the charge. We . . . got pounded pretty hard."

"You'd better let someone else lead for a while, Subcommander, or you won't be leading again." He paused. "I'll bring by some canvas tomorrow, and we'll figure out the best way to brace you and the undercaptain."

"Thank you."

After the combat surgeon left, Quaeryt eased out of the rest of his uniform and returned to the bed. He had absolutely no doubt that he faced a long and painful night.

63

When the first gray light of Mardi morning oozed through the shutters of
his room at the Stone's Rest, Quaeryt tried to turn away from the window, except his neck was so stiff that his head barely moved. Eventually,
he did manage to sit up. After an even longer time, he stood and tottered
to the washroom where he viewed himself in the mirror.

Most of his forehead was turning bluish, as was the skin and flesh
over his cheekbones, and he definitely had two bloodshot and black eyes.
About the only parts of his body that didn't ache were his legs below the
knees and his feet. Washing up was painful and time-consuming.

Getting downstairs to eat felt as though it took more than a quint for
the two flights of stone steps. Fortunately, the field surgeon did return
with canvas and some bone stays, and the wrapping helped immobilize
his ribs and chest, but even so, taking a deep breath shot pains through
his entire chest.

Quaeryt was sitting in the public room, sipping on a lager, not wishing to climb steps or anything else, debating whether to try to make his
way to see Skarpa when the commander arrived at the Stone's Rest and
slipped into the chair opposite Quaeryt, who had made no move to rise,
although he would have, had he felt more able to move easily.

"I'd heard you'd been injured," began Skarpa, "but how . . . like this?"

"Undercaptain Shaelyt and I were shielding the front of the columns
as they came off the spans into the square. The Bovarians fired too many
muskets . . ."

Skarpa frowned. "We recovered over four hundred muskets, but . . .
you've faced them before."

"Not five hundred all fired at once."

"They fired all at once? That's not . . ."

"That's not the way they're supposed to fire. They're supposed to alter-
nate volleys so that they can't be rushed while reloading."

"Why did they change? I'm not sure I understand . . ."

"Someone had an idea about how much protection an imager can provide. We can create shields, but if there's too much . . . force . . . the

shields give and crush in on our bodies." That was an oversimplification, but Quaeryt wasn't about to try to explain it all.

"You were able to do more than they thought, weren't you? Was that why, even with so many muskets, there was so little damage to the troopers?"

Quaeryt gave a very small nod.

"That's why Zhelan could get to the pikemen and muskets before they could do worse," added Skarpa. "He thought you'd done something."

"I think we helped," Quaeryt admitted.

"More than helped. Made all the difference. Said you were a good officer. Too friggin' brave, but good."

Brave? I don't think so. "Have you heard from the marshal?"

"Got a dispatch this morning. He wrote that they were slowed by logistical difficulties." Skarpa snorted. "Logistical difficulties, my ass."

"He wants to save his forces for the assault on Variana," suggested Quaeryt.

"That's where the glory is," said Skarpa. "If he wins."

"That's just the beginning of the problems. You know that. How long did it take to bring Tilbor under control?"

"Ten years . . . and it's less than a third the size of Bovaria."

"If we defeat Kharst and his forces—decisively—at Variana," said Quaeryt, "Bhayar could probably work out something with the people of Khel. That would leave the western part of old Bovaria. Pacifying that could take over a year and use all the forces Deucalon has."

"He'll stay in Variana and have Myskyl do it."

Not if either of us has anything to say about it. "Lord Bhayar will have to decide about that, based on what happens at Variana and how."

"You have something in mind, Quaeryt? When we get to Variana?"

"Only the general idea that I can't do what I did yesterday again."

"What else?"

"We need to make sure that Kharst masses his forces."

"After what we've done to smaller forces along the way, that might not be a problem."

Unless Kharst or his commanders understand what actually happened at Ferravyl. "I hope not. When will Deucalon arrive?"

"Not before tomorrow sometime."

"Good and bad," Quaeryt said.

"That will give you and the imagers more time to recover," agreed Skarpa. "It will also give my men too much time to get in trouble."

Quaeryt frowned.

"They said Villerive was a bawdy city." Skarpa snorted. "The north side of Nordeau is far worse. You and Khaern are fortunate to have your men here."

"They won't think so once they've heard from the others."

"They won't hear until we've left for Variana."

"And if we wait too long, that will give Kharst more time to amass forces there."

"You seem convinced that he'll have a huge army there."

"Aren't you?" countered Quaeryt.

"You almost convince me. I still have trouble seeing why, if he does, he hasn't used it before now.'

"Because he has the same problem in Khel that Bhayar had in Tilbor, and getting troopers back from the west takes even longer. He also doesn't care that much about the cost to his people so long as it costs us more. What he doesn't understand is that the people know that as well, which is why we've not had too much difficulty with them. Even the High Holders have avoided us when they could. Kharst wants us weakened as much as possible and as far into Bovaria as possible before he attacks . . . but he can't afford to give up Variana. So that's where he and his forces will be."

"Have you told Bhayar this?" asked Skarpa.

"When have I had a chance? I'd suggest," Quaeryt went on, "that you not mention all that to Deucalon or Myskyl. If they've thought of it, they'll think you're trying to take credit for the idea. If they haven't, they will take credit."

Skarpa nodded slowly. "You are feeling better, aren't you?"

"Not much, but I'm not feeling worse, and that means I'm likely getting better."

"Good."

After Skarpa departed, Quaeryt remained in the public room, nursing his lager, then saw Shaelyt standing in the archway. "Shaelyt!"

At Quaeryt's gesture, the undercaptain moved gingerly into the public room and eased himself into the chair across from the subcommander. His face bore the same kinds of bruises as did Quaeryt's. "Sir?"

"How are you feeling?"

"Not too bad, sir."

"And I'm Lord Bhayar's grandsire," replied Quaeryt sardonically. "Is there anything that doesn't ache or hurt?"

Shaelyt smiled sheepishly. "My feet and calves."

"Mine, too." Quaeryt paused, then asked, "Has your family always lived in Fuara?"

"I don't know about always, sir. My grandfather was born there. So was my grandmere. Their parents, I don't know. No one ever talked about it. You know how families can be."

Quaeryt chuckled. "That's one thing I don't know."

"Oh . . . sir . . . I'm sorry. I forgot."

"You don't have to be sorry. I just don't know. If families are anything like scholars, there are many things they don't talk about. Are both your parents Pharsi? Are there many Pharsi in Fuara?"

"Not that many. My father said that Mother was the only Pharsi woman he could wed because she was the only one in town who wasn't at least a first cousin."

"Are there any other imagers?"

Shaelyt pursed his lips. "No one talks about my aunt. My mother's older sister. She was always a little different. That's what Mother said. It was about all she said. She took a position as governess with a wealthy family in Bhorael."

"That's a fair ways from Cloisonyt and Fuara," observed Quaeryt.

"Two weeks on horse in good weather back then." Shaelyt took a swallow of lager from the mug before him. "I don't think she had much choice. She might have been with child."

"Do you think she could image?"

"I don't know. Ma—Mother said she could sometimes tell when things were going to happen. Usually they were terrible things. She dragged everyone out of Grandpere's house when she was barely twelve. It was in the middle of a rainstorm. The house was buried in mud when the stock pond dam gave way. Mother didn't tell me that. Grandmere did."

"You got along well with your grandmere, then?"

"Better with her than my parents." Shaelyt smiled crookedly. "She once said I was more like my aunt."

"How did you get conscripted . . . or found out as an imager?"

"Greed." Shaelyt grinned. "I'd figured out how to image coppers. You make them dirty. I'd done that for years. You spend a copper here and there. People don't notice."

Quaeryt kept his smile to himself. "That's true."

Shaelyt's grin vanished. "They ask questions when you have silvers. Too many questions, especially if your family are weavers."

"But if a coin is pure silver . . ."

"That makes them even less happy. My father didn't know what to do with me, and he was afraid someone would try to kill me. So when he heard Lord Bhayar was offering a gold for imagers to become undercaptains, he put me on a mule, and we rode to Cloisonyt." Shaelyt shrugged. "He was right. Sooner or later, things would have gotten worse in Fuara, and I'd have had to flee or worse." He looked to Quaeryt. 'Voltyr said no one knew you were an imager. Why did you let it be known?"

Quaeryt laughed. "Partly to survive, and partly because of love. Bhayar suspected for years, but it wasn't in his interest to pursue it, since I'd never caused anyone any trouble. But when his sister became interested in me, he decided having an imager married to his sister might be in his and her interest. Then, when we fell in love . . . there weren't many choices. I didn't want any of you knowing it to begin with because I wanted you to rely more on yourselves. Maybe that was a good idea. Maybe it wasn't."

"You protected us, didn't you?"

"As I could . . . until Akoryt died. Then I decided that I couldn't keep doing it. There were too many things I couldn't control."

"You've still done it."

"So have you," Quaeryt pointed out. "That's why you're all bruised and sore." He took another swallow of the lager, then raised a hand to the serving girl who peered out from the kitchen. "Another lager here." He pointed to Shaelyt.

"Yes, sir." The serving girl hurried back into the kitchen, returning almost immediately with a mug she set before Shaelyt.

Quaeryt put three coppers on the table.

They vanished into her calloused hand. "Thank you, sir." Then she was gone.

"You didn't have to do that, sir."

"It's little enough. If you hadn't held shields yesterday, scores of men would have died. They may not know that, but I do."

Shaelyt lifted the mug and sipped, finally setting it down. "Sir, what will happen . . . afterward?"

"I'm working on that. I'd like to keep the imagers together in a way that would allow us to work under Lord Bhayar's protection. That way everyone could have families and a more . . . customary . . . life."

"It still wouldn't be customary."

"No . . . but wouldn't it be a great improvement?" Quaeryt raised his eyebrows.

Shaelyt smiled. "Might I ask how . . . ?"

"You might, but I'm not ready to answer that. We have to make sure Lord Bhayar triumphs and that he knows he owes us. After that . . ."

"If anyone can do that, you can."

That might well be true, Quaeryt reflected, but that didn't mean it was possible. He lifted his mug and took another swallow of lager, trying to ignore the aches all over his body.

On Meredi, Quaeryt felt worse than he had on Mardi, but in a way that told him he would recover. The good news, if it could be called that, was that Deucalon's forces were not expected to reach Nordeau until late in the day. Quaeryt wondered what was taking the marshal so long, since he doubted that Deucalon was encountering any armed Bovarian opposition . . . or that any Bovarian forces remained anywhere close to Nordeau.

Pacifying or placating the High Holders? Or merely extracting supplies and equipment? Both? Quaeryt doubted that he'd learn anything about that from Skarpa, because neither Myskyl nor Deucalon would inform the commander.

By Meredi afternoon, he did force himself to direct imager drills for all the undercaptains except Shaelyt, although he had Shaelyt watch and offer advice to the newer undercaptains. A squad leader dropped by with a message from Skarpa to the effect that he and Khaern were to "hold the south city and keep the peace" and wait for further instructions.

Those instructions came early on Jeudi morning, when an undercaptain who was an aide to Bhayar arrived with a request that Quaeryt accompany the undercaptain to meet with Bhayar at his temporary quarters north of Nordeau. Quaeryt asked Calkoran to supply an escort squad and waited until the troopers were ready.

When Quaeryt did walk toward the front door of the inn, Shajan appeared.

"Subcommander, sir . . . ?"

"Yes?"

"I must beg your pardon, sir."

"For what?" asked Quaeryt gently, as always, in Bovarian.

"It is said . . . you suffered all your wounds . . . so your men would not . . ."

"So did Undercaptain Shaelyt."

"The young Pharsi officer?"

Quaeryt nodded. "The same."

"I must beg you to forgive me for thinking you an old one. No old one

would ever have risked his life for another, and not for those he commanded." The innkeeper bowed deeply. "I most humbly apologize."

"I accept your apology," replied Quaeryt, "but I must also apologize for
not understanding your concerns. Despite your concerns and worries, you
have been most helpful to me and to my men, and I do appreciate that."

Shajan bowed again. "You are most kind."

"Not always, I fear, although I try." Quaeryt smiled and image-projected
a certain slight warmth, not wishing to raise yet other concerns.

The squad from Calkoran's fourth company was waiting outside the
stable, along with Undercaptain Yaffon and Quaeryt's mare. Mounting
was still an effort, but Quaeryt managed it without falling or appearing
too awkward.

Yaffon did not say much until they reached the bridge over the River
Aluse. "Your imagers . . . created the newer stone spans, sir?"

"They did."

"It's said that your Fifth Battalion led the attacks on both the south city
and the north city, yet did not suffer extraordinary casualties, yet you
obviously have been injured."

"So have others, and Fifth Battalion has suffered more than enough on
this campaign, Undercaptain," Quaeryt replied pleasantly.

"I did not mean . . ."

"I'm sure you did not . . ." *I just don't like probing and insinuations when the
main force with almost ten times as many troopers is letting us do all the work . . . and I
can't say a Namer-frigged thing about it . . . except generalities.* ". . . but Fifth Battalion
has taken more than its share of attacks and casualties." Quaeryt smiled,
but did not volunteer more.

For the first mille beyond the square where the massed musketeer fire
had come all too close to killing him—and Shaelyt—the buildings of Nordeau were essentially the same as those south of the river. Quaeryt could
see why the Bovarians wouldn't have risked cannon in the center of the
town, especially since they would have been of limited usefulness anyway.
And he understood the difficulties of moving the heavy cannon. *Or is it that
Kharst doesn't have that many cannon because there's no way to transport them easily?* That
seemed more reasonable . . . and it meant that they'd be more likely to face
cannon the nearer they came to Variana—something he needed to keep in
mind.

The wall enclosing what might have been called "the old city" on the
north side was similar to the one on the south side, but the gates to the wall
had clearly been removed years before. Outside the old walls, the build-

ings were set more widely apart, with far larger windows and many of
the larger dwellings had their outer walls constructed of blocks of gray
stone, each block of exactly the same size. That told Quaeryt what had
happened to the stone blocks in the walls of the last five milles or so of
the ancient canal.

As he expected, the majority of the houses were shuttered, and none
appeared to have been ransacked or damaged, but the only living things
he saw on the streets were Telaryn armsmen and stray dogs. When he
reached the walls around the much newer section of Nordeau, he could
see they were lower, barely more than two yards and almost perfunctory.

Deucalon had to know this. Despite realizing that, and what it meant, Quaeryt managed to keep a pleasant expression on his face, but he did shift his
weight in the saddle, because riding was less than comfortable.

"It's another two milles," Undercaptain Yaffon said apologetically.
"On a little hill west of the side road."

Side road? Quaeryt wondered. That became clear in less than two hundred yards, when the paved main road swung westward, presumably to
parallel the river, and Yaffon gestured for them to continue along a much
narrower, if paved way that appeared more like a lane.

Quaeryt could see that troopers had followed the lane because the graveled shoulders and even the grass beyond the shoulder had been trampled
flat by hooves. The lane began to angle up a low rise, then came to a set of
gates guarded by a full company of troopers. The lane split at the gate, an
unpaved way continuing north, while the paved lane ran through the gray
stone gates, constructed of a different stone than that of the canal and not
cut or finished so well, and up the gentle slope to an imposing building
that could have served as a palace.

A captain rode forward, took in Quaeryt's face and collar insignia, and
nodded. "Sir, Lord Bhayar is in the study in the main building."

"Thank you, Captain."

Quaeryt couldn't help but notice the withering glance the guard captain bestowed on Undercaptain Yaffon, who seemed oblivious to it, as
they rode past him and through the gates.

Quaeryt led the squad to the front portico of the palatial hold house, a
covered portico extending upward more than two stories, supported by
massive square gray stone pillars. There he dismounted and handed the
mare's reins to one of the Khellan troopers who, unbidden, rode forward
to take them.

"We'll be waiting, Subcommander," announced the squad leader.

"Thank you." Quaeryt nodded and walked up to the entry door.

Yaffon had to scramble to catch up.

One of the troopers guarding the doors opened them for Quaeryt, who nodded his thanks and stepped into an arched entry hall with a black marble floor and shimmering white walls.

A captain hurried forward. "Subcommander, Lord Bhayar is still meeting with Marshal Deucalon. Submarshal Myskyl would like a moment with you."

"Of course," replied Quaeryt politely.

"This way, if you would, sir."

Quaeryt followed the visibly nervous captain from the outsized entry hall down a side corridor into a small study—likely a lady's study, given the delicate curves of the desk from which Myskyl rose.

"Greetings, Quaeryt."

"And to you, Submarshal." Quaeryt inclined his head just a touch more than would have been considered slighting.

"You do look like you encountered the Namer or one of his demons," observed Myskyl, still standing.

"It sometimes happens when you get involved in the thick of things."

"Really, Subcommander, you should delegate some of these matters—or have your undercaptains not attained . . . your capabilities?"

"They have done rather well, considering that I've only been able to work with them two months or so. There's now a solid permanent bridge across the Aluse rather than those rickety wooden spans. But you should ask Commander Skarpa. The question isn't how I feel they have performed, but whether he believes they have been useful and instrumental in accomplishing the tasks you have set him."

"He professes to be most satisfied. But what else would he say?" Myskyl's smile was cold, calculating.

"The commander has always been known to speak his mind, if perhaps more politely than I have upon occasion."

"You do yourself an injustice, Quaeryt. Your speech has always been above reproach and as indirect as necessary without ever committing a falsehood. Most masterful, I've always thought."

"I've only followed the examples with which you and Rescalyn provided me."

Myskyl nodded, as if thoughtfully, then asked, "What do you believe lies before us?"

"Exactly what, I have no idea, except that Rex Kharst is unlikely to allow Variana to fall to Lord Bhayar without doing all in his power to prevent it. I am certain that this is not a new thought to you, given your far greater experience than mine."

"Do you believe he has imagers?"

"I have no idea. If he does, no doubt we will learn of them outside Variana."

"Have your Khellan officers mentioned imagers?"

"They have not. They have mentioned greed, treachery, and total brutality on the part of the Bovarians, but not imagers."

Although Myskyl again nodded, Quaeryt had the feeling that, somehow, his response had disturbed the submarshal.

"Well . . . I should not keep you. Lord Bhayar did summon you, no doubt to be able to assure his sister that her husband was well."

"That is indeed possible, but I have learned over the years that to guess at Lord Bhayar's reasons is to be avoided if at all possible."

"Ah, yes, I forgot that you were students together."

Quaeryt doubted that Myskyl had forgotten any information that could be used in one way or another. Instead, he inclined his head. "A pleasure to see you again, Submarshal." Then he turned and slipped out the study door, walking back to the main entry hall, where he waited for less than half a quint before another captain appeared.

"Subcommander . . . this way, sir, if you would."

Bhayar was pacing back and forth in front of a set of long windows overlooking a formal flowering garden when Quaeryt stepped into the long white-goldenwood paneled study.

"Greetings . . ." Bhayar stopped and looked at Quaeryt. "What in the Nameless happened to you?"

Quaeryt quickly scanned the room. Bhayar was alone. "Several hundred muskets discharged at my battalion all at once."

"Did you know that was likely?"

"I knew that there might be pikemen and musketeers. I didn't expect hundreds. There might have been five hundred or more. Skarpa recovered over four hundred muskets. They all fired at once."

"Then they know we have imagers."

"They know we had imagers. We didn't do any imaging after that."

Bhayar fingered his chin. "You think they might be uncertain?"

"I don't know. I'd like to think they'd be at least uncertain. What I think you should do is to tell Deucalon and Myskyl that the key imagers were badly injured, and you don't know what they'll be able to do at Variana, and that you'll need to approach the city with care—"

"I'm not about to tell Deucalon that." Bhayar's words were low, but almost snapped out. "He's already too Namer-cursed careful."

"Has he said when he would plan to leave Nordeau?"

"He suggested a week. I told him two days. He offered excuses. I told him they were excuses." Bhayar paused. "Do you think someone's passing information to the Bovarians?"

Quaeryt shrugged, and wished he hadn't as pains shot across his chest. "I don't know. It won't hurt to act as if someone might be."

"That's true enough. What other recommendations do you have?" Bhayar's voice was both tired and dry.

"You need more imagers, sir."

Bhayar frowned. "I meant about strategies."

"So do I."

"Have I not found you a number sufficient for our needs."

"Imagers have made a difference in a number of battles so far, but there are only nine imager undercaptains. I've trained them so that they are much more capable, but nine is a small number, and Bovaria is a large land . . . and together Telaryn and Bovaria are very large."

"I can see that . . . but . . . the marshal and others will certainly worry about what will happen . . . in the future . . ."

"You need to worry, if I might say so, sir, about your needs and not their desires. What most people, indeed, most rulers do not understand is that there are too few imagers born in any land to be a threat to the people as a whole. They can only be a threat to individuals, and that threat exists because most imagers live in fear. What you can do is to bring those few imagers together to help deal with not only defeating Bovaria, but with keeping it under control. You keep the imagers in Variana, far from Solis."

"Solis is the capital of Telaryn," protested Bhayar. "The last thing I want is a group of trained imagers in Variana when I'm back in Solis."

"How long can you rule Bovaria and Telaryn from Solis?"

"You are assuming . . ."

"Am I? Besides . . . do you really want to keep living in Solis?"

Bhayar laughed softly. "Go on."

"You need a force large enough to be effective and small enough for you to control and strong enough to keep the High Holders in line, but one not requiring a large standing army."

"You think your imagers could be that force?"

"Only as a quiet last resort, sir. What I would suggest is that you point out, as necessary, after you take Variana, and only then, is that by putting the imagers in one place, you reduce the danger to the people and you train the imagers to be useful to the ruler and the people. In return for safety and a good education, they will serve Telaryn . . . much as the scholars assured that I would serve you." Quaeryt smiled wryly. "Even if they did not know it."

"You are a dangerous man, Quaeryt." Bhayar paused. "Assuming . . . just assuming . . . that I agree to all of this . . . what happens when Clayar succeeds me and you are gone?"

"That's why you set up the school and the grounds and the training now . . . after you take control of Bovaria. You train all the young imagers in their roles as a pillar of the ruler, and you make sure they all know what happened to imagers in the past, and how they are treated in other lands across the world . . . Perhaps you even give a gold or silvers to parents who send their imager children to the school . . . you've already set a precedent similar to that."

"How long have you been thinking about this?"

"Some of it for years, and some only for months," Quaeryt admitted.

"What if we must leave Bovaria? While we are winning now . . . who knows?"

"Then send Vaelora and me and the imagers back to Extela, and we'll set up the school and training there. That will still increase your power."

Bhayar smiled, an expression both warm and calculating. "You have thought this through in great detail."

"I've tried," Quaeryt admitted. "Also, if we incorporate a scholarly element, with a school and a large library, it will seem more familiar to many."

"It might also give me greater control over the scholars."

"In a way that would not seem so."

"Well . . . I have to say I'm intrigued, and I like the idea. It would also keep Vaelora busy. But you'd have to be the head of it. It wouldn't work any other way."

"For the next years," Quaeryt said, "but it needs to be set up in a way that it doesn't depend on who succeeds in power among the imagers."

"That . . . that will take some doing."

"Yes, sir."

"Now . . . what do you think awaits us in Variana?"

"The largest army ever assembled in Lydar," Quaeryt said bluntly. "Kharst will try to crush us so thoroughly that he can do what he will. You must destroy him in a way he does not see coming."

"How do you propose I do that?"

"You will have to merge both the northern and southern forces so that Kharst faces a united force. That way, he will believe that if he destroys that army, he can march down the River Aluse all the way to Solis."

"Deucalon won't like that. He is the marshal."

"Insist on putting Fifth Battalion in front, backed and flanked by the rest of Commander Skarpa's forces. That way, you can tell Deucalon that he can maneuver as he pleases *after* the Bovarians attack. You can also point out, by letting the imagers take the brunt of the attack first, that will assure fewer casualties among his troops."

"Should we join forces together on the way to Variana?"

"No, sir. We should join somewhere south of Variana, so that Kharst will not know where we might strike."

"Where would that be, Subcommander Marshal?" asked Bhayar ironically.

"Wherever necessary to make him attack us in full force."

Bhayar laughed.

When Bhayar's laugh died away, Quaeryt added, "I'd also suggest not telling Deucalon about massing forces until as late as possible and not before we're close enough to know where Kharst's forces are. Suggest that the marshal's strategy of keeping the southern army small and mobile has worked so far and that you see no reason to alter it until circumstances change."

"You don't trust him much."

"I have far more to gain if you win and everything to lose if you do. Whom would your father have trusted?"

Bhayar nodded.

Quaeryt wasn't quite so sure what that nod meant.

"Vaelora said I should trust you above all others. Did you tell her to say that?"

"Nameless, no. I'd never tell her what to say to you . . . or anyone else."

"You and anyone who knows her well." Bhayar shook his head. "Is there anything else?"

"Nothing that you don't already know, if you think about it."

"You sound like my father, rather than my friend."

"I only met him that one time, you know?"

Bhayar gave a short barked laugh. "You know what he said?"

"No. I have no idea."

"He said you were the kind of man to keep as a friend, and never make an enemy. He was right, I've learned." Bhayar smiled. "I almost forgot." He reached down and picked up an envelope, extending it. "From Vaelora. It was enclosed in a letter to me. She mentioned fearing that her missives to you were experiencing 'undue delay.'" His eyebrows lifted. "I assume you wrote her about it? Was that necessary? You did mention that to me earlier."

Quaeryt took the missive. "I did write and tell her that the letter forwarded to me by the new governor of Montagne arrived with her last missive to me, even though the governor's letter had been dispatched almost two weeks later."

"I don't need reminding from both of you, Quaeryt."

Sometimes you do. "Yes, sir."

"Keep that in mind." Bhayar gestured toward the study door. "I need to think, and you need to write a letter."

Quaeryt smiled, nodded, and bowed slightly, then turned and slipped from the study.

As he walked out from the vaulted entry hall into the hot harvest noon, Quaeryt wondered if another undercaptain would be waiting to accompany him back to the Stone's Rest.

There wasn't.

The squad from fourth company formed up, and a ranker rode forward leading the mare.

Although Quaeryt desperately wanted to read Vaelora's letter, trying to do so while riding wasn't the best idea, especially given how sore he was. He had to content himself with knowing that it was tucked inside his uniform and that he would have more than enough time to read it once he returned to the Stone's Rest. As he rode across the bridge to the old southern section of the city, he realized the letter would have to wait.

He turned to the squad leader. "We'll need to stop at the Traders' Bowl first."

"Yes, sir."

While Quaeryt did stop, Skarpa wasn't there, and the duty squad leader could only say that the commander was meeting with the marshal. Quaeryt left word that he would like to talk to Skarpa when he returned.

Zhelan was waiting in the modest foyer when Quaeryt stepped out of a sun that felt entirely too hot for harvest and into the coolness of the Stone's Rest. Quaeryt gestured toward the public room. "I've had a hot ride, and you could use something while we talk."

"I'll not complain about that, sir."

Once they were seated in a corner away from the archways, with a mug in front of each of them, Quaeryt looked to the major. "You had a question?"

"I was hoping, seeing as you were headed to see Lord Bhayar, that you might have some idea as to when we'd be packing out."

Quaeryt took a swallow of the lager, a trace more bitter than he liked, before he spoke. "At least two days, and not more than a week. I'd wager on two days, but I don't think anyone's been told. You should tell the men to plan on no more than two days, but that it could be longer. We may know when Commander Skarpa returns. How are you coming with getting grain?"

"We should have enough for a week . . ."

For almost a glass, Quaeryt went over matters concerning Fifth Battalion before he and Zhelan finished. Only then did Quaeryt retreat to the third floor, almost falling down the stairs between the second and third level when he caught the boot heel of his bad left leg on a stair riser. When he finally reached his chamber, he settled onto the chair and slit open the letter. The seal had been tampered with, most likely by Bhayar. After looking at the dates, he began to read.

Dearest!
Finally, a letter from you, one that I so looked forward to and enjoyed reading, although I must say that it appears my correspondence must have been misaddressed for it to have taken so long to reach you. I am responding as swiftly as I can. I have been more careful in addressing this and trust it will arrive more quickly. I was glad to hear that you remain well and trust and pray that you will continue so.

Your observations about how Rex Eharst maintains control over his High Holders were most disturbing. I share your belief that a ruler who wishes to remain both respected and loved should adopt methods more effective and yet less cruel and less obvious. I will be most interested in discussing such with you once we are reunited, though I fear that time will not be soon. Matters here in Solis have developed in much the way one might have guessed. They are not as good as one would like, nor as difficult as might be . . .

In short, Quaeryt thought, the ministers are quibbling about finances and making matters hard, but not defying you and Aelina outright.

My digestion has improved. That is good, because it has been a very hot summer. I have had to retreat to the coolness of the fountains more than in past summers, and there is no sign of the heat becoming any less. There is also little rain, and the harvest may be scant if more does not bless the lands of Piedryn.

In past letters we discussed to what extent those in power could trust those who provide them with counsel and advice. While at times, I have little else to do besides advise the lady who is as much my sister as if we share the same blood, interesting though that may be at times, some further thoughts have occurred to me in regard to who may be trusted and why and who may not. The man whose future can only improve if others fail or die is one who must be watched most closely, unless he is one who would prefer to serve than to lead. Yet there is an exception even to that, for there are those who would wish matters a certain way and would advise those they serve, who in turn directly serve a ruler, in such a way as to bring about such ends. Such men are seldom scrutinized for the effect of their advice by rulers because the *ruler assumes that his direct subordinate is acting in either that subordinate's interest or the ruler's . . .*

Quaeryt nodded. *Has she heard about Myskyl's actions from some other source?*

. . . This is most common, or so I have heard, having no experience at all in such, where men go to war. I can but assume that such self-oriented advice is less common among those who bear arms and risk their lives, and more common among those who are farther from dangers of personal injury . . .

A smile spread across Quaeryt's face. She wanted her brother to read those words. He shook his head in amusement.

When he set down her letter, he wondered what he should write. How much and how directly? After more than a glass of struggling with his own words, he looked down at the page on the desk.

My dearest,

Your latest letter arrived in far greater haste than those earlier, and it was with great pleasure that I read it, especially to hear that you are again enjoying your food. Here, of course, our food ranges at best from that prepared indifferently to hard rations or biscuits, or very occasionally less than that.

We are now recuperating from our efforts in the ancient town of Nordeau, which we now hold, the Bovarians, those who survived, having fled. Through some form of miscommunication, Commander Skarpa's forces first took the southern part, and then two days later, the northern part. Marshal Deucalon's forces arrived almost two days later. My undercaptains all survived, but several of us are rather bruised, still, and sore, but will certainly recover before we press on . . . whenever that may be.

As in Solis, harvest here has been especially hot and damp, and there is no sign of the weather becoming cooler, although we have had more rain here than has apparently fallen on Piedryn. It would be for the best, I fear, if the weather remains warm, but the Nameless will have things as they will be . . .

As for your thoughts on the trustworthiness of advice, in the end, the trust must rest in the character of the man or the woman, and not in the position that either may hold. You suggested that there is a greater risk of untrustworthiness among those of higher position, and I fear, alas, that such is indeed so, particularly when the ambitions of a man exceed his true abilities, especially of those men who have not been tested, always having been in secondary positions. Yet who of us can accurately judge what we may accomplish and what we may not . . .

Another glass passed before Quaeryt finished the letter and went to find a courier to dispatch it . . . and that took more than a glass before he finally entrusted the missive to one of Skarpa's majors, with a silver for the dispatch rider.

On Vendrei, Quaeryt mustered the imager undercaptains and put them through imaging drills, both morning and afternoon, allowing several glasses rest in between. He did not press Shaelyt excessively, but Shaelyt did seem to be recovering somewhat more quickly than had Quaeryt, possibly because he was younger . . . or because he had not taken the brunt of the musket fire. By the end of the afternoon session, it was clear that both young Pharsi undercaptains had greatly improved. Quaeryt had to smile at the thought that they were now the "young" imagers, and Shaelyt, who he had thought was young, was now no longer so, at least comparatively.

But then, battles and death age us all, in mind if not in body. He paused, then had a second thought. Except for those not wise enough to age.

He went to bed on Vendrei evening having heard nothing from Skarpa, not that the lack of information surprised him. He was certain Skarpa had heard nothing, either.

On Samedi morning, after returning from arranging for the undercaptains to work with the best of Zhelan's squad leaders on improving their use of the sabre, he was sitting alone in the public room of the Stone's Rest, looking at a mug of lager that a serving girl had just brought him, when a trooper hurried in.

"Sir! Lord Bhayar is looking for you."

"I'll need to saddle the mare." Quaeryt thought he was up to that, finally. He took a swallow of the lager that he had not even sipped and then stood. "That won't take but a fraction of a quint, and then I'll be on my way."

"No, sir. He just reined up outside. He's coming inside."

Quaeryt barely managed not to choke on the lager. "Tell him I'll be right there." He glanced around, then headed for the kitchen. He'd no more than reached the archway when the woman he thought was the innkeeper's wife appeared.

"Sir?"

"Do you have a small private room, like a plaques room?"

"Why . . . yes, sir. It's the door right across from the entrance to the public room. Not used much these days." She gave him a quizzical glance, as if to inquire why he hadn't asked earlier.

"I just discovered Lord Bhayar is here, outside, and wants to meet with me. Is the room presentable?"

"Lord Bhayar?" The woman's mouth opened. "The . . . Lord Bhayar?"

My thoughts exactly. "The same. Is the room fit to be used?" Quaeryt pressed again.

"Oh, yes, sir. We keep it clean all the time." She hurried past Quaeryt, and he followed her to the door to the plaques room.

"I'll be opening the shutters, sir."

Quaeryt turned and headed for the front entry, meeting Bhayar outside. "Welcome, sir."

Bhayar scanned Quaeryt. "You're looking better. Not much, but better. We need to talk before I resume my tour."

"There's a small room just inside. Would you like a lager?"

"Not now. It's early yet, and I'll have to drink something when I see Commander Skarpa." Bhayar turned to the major who had followed him. "Just wait out here, Major. I won't be that long." His eyes went to Quaeryt.

Quaeryt turned and led the way inside and through the small entry foyer, where the innkeeper's wife stood to the side, bowing, and then to the open door. He gestured for Bhayar to enter the plaques chamber that could hold comfortably the round table and five chairs, then closed the door quietly but firmly, and turned to Bhayar. "I didn't expect to see you again so soon."

"I do try to inspect the areas we have acquired," Bhayar said dryly, looking toward the high narrow window with its recently opened shutters. "I learn something about the towns and the people, and more about my commanders. Both are useful." He settled himself at the table and gestured for Quaeryt to sit.

Quaeryt did so, across the table from Bhayar. He forbore asking what Bhayar had learned in touring the south of Nordeau.

"You and the imagers did a rather remarkable job in reducing a walled city without siege engines. Those stone ramps are quite something." His voice turned wry. "We'd best not have to defend Nordeau in the future, though."

"It did take all of us," Quaeryt said.

"Given the distances between the imaged efforts, I gained that impression." Bhayar leaned forward. "Since our last meeting, I've thought some more."

"You've always kept thinking," Quaeryt said cautiously.

"I know you've wondered how much I know about you, Quaeryt. I've always had suspicions that you were more than you represented yourself as. Vaelora loves you so much, and she would not, were you not more than you seem. That has created problems, as we both know. I am pleased that you are considering ways to extend your usefulness while solving a problem that has vexed every ruler in Lydar, if not across all Terahnar."

"The imagers?"

Bhayar nodded, then went on. "About many things we agree. Do you know why?"

"Not exactly, except that you've always known a great deal and taken care not to reveal nearly so much as you've learned."

"As have you. In that regard we are similar. I'm going to read you something that came from a very old book of my grandmere. She wouldn't tell me from where it came, except that it had been in the family for a very long time."

Quaeryt waited.

Bhayar extracted a single sheet of paper from his belt pouch, unfolded it, and smoothed it out. Then he cleared his throat.

> The older ones, how did they build so much
> to leave no quarries, tools, or plans and such?
> Ah, by image, wrenched from servant dreams,
> they built the roads and bridges over streams,
> with perfect stone no tool can mar or tame
> so they did dream and live the Namer's Name.
> But when the dreamers dreamed full awake,
> their masters found the Namer's fate and take . . .
> Who'er would seize the image and the dream
> know now that imaging holds more than seem.

Bhayar looked directly across the table at Quaeryt. "When I saw the outer walls of Nordeau, for the first time I understood fully from where those verses came."

"The Naedarans," said Quaeryt. "After I saw the canals—"

"Canals?"

"There are two ancient canals on this side of the river. The stonework is the same. The stones used to built the last five milles or so were removed and used to build many of the dwellings in the newer part of Nordeau."

"Was that why you proposed using the imagers the way you did?"

"No, sir. That reinforced my feelings, but if you wish, you can ask Vaelora. This is something I have considered for some time." Quaeryt paused just briefly. "Do you recall the bedchamber of the old chateau at Gahenyara?"

Bhayar frowned for a moment. "The one with the storeroom that had shutters?"

"It wasn't a storeroom. It was a separate bedchamber for your great-grandmere. That's where the book your grandmere gave you came from."

"There's always been farsight in the family. That's from the Pharsi."

"There are ten imagers in Fifth Battalion. At least four come from Pharsi stock." *Should you tell him?* After a moment, Quaeryt went on. "Vaelora's with child."

"I got that impression."

From reading her letters, no doubt. " There's a very good chance the child will be an imager." Quaeryt hadn't realized it, but he knew that was so

Abruptly Bhayar laughed, a warm and amused sound, not the cold laugh that meant the worst. "So we both have every reason to create what you have in mind."

"I would hope so," replied Quaeryt. "It's in Vaelora's and my interest, and it's certainly in yours."

"There are others who will oppose that."

"We can face that when the time comes. They may see that their worth and abilities are not threatened. If we are careful, they will, at least in time."

"Oh?"

"It will take some time to . . . stabilize Bovaria—but you'll need to come up with a new name for the land. And Autarch Aliaro will present certain problems."

"Quaeryt . . . first we need to defeat Kharst and capture Variana."

"True . . . but you need to think beyond that so that you are prepared. Not that you doubtless are not already."

"That's also what you're here for." Bhayar stood. "You've done well. I would that all were both so capable and loyal. Too many who are capable are not loyal, and too many who are loyal are not capable."

Quaeryt rose, trying to do so smoothly, despite his aches and stiffness. "That is why you need to set up matters so that the capable must be loyal."

"After . . . Variana, we will talk of such." Bhayar smiled broadly. "We will leave Nordeau tomorrow, but let your commander tell you so."

"I will." With a nod, Quaeryt followed Bhayar out through the door that the Lord of Telaryn opened for himself.

In leaving Nordeau on Solayi morning, Skarpa rode with Fifth Battalion, once more in the van, along the wide and well-paved river road that led from the southwest gate of the old southern section of the city westward and, according to the maps, to Variana. For one of the few times in months, there was a trace of coolness in the air, but the sky was clear.

Are we going to get a foretaste of fall? Quaeryt had his doubts, especially as the day quickly warmed as mille after mille passed. As it did, Quaeryt began to sweat, if less than on previous days, and he thought more and more about the road. Why, after hundreds of milles of generally poor roads, except for the stretches created by the ancient Naedarans, had Kharst or his predecessors built such a superb road on the south side of the river?

The roadbed itself was wide and solid, but he did notice that it rose and fell more than the Naedaran road, which had maintained more of a level path, and the Bovarian road was, for the most part, closer to the river.

He asked Skarpa, riding beside him, "Why do you think they built this road so well?"

"I haven't the faintest idea. Maybe they knew we were headed to Variana." The commander offered a low laugh.

"Or maybe there are more High Holdings on the south side from here to Variana," countered Quaeryt, "and Kharst wanted to reach them more easily."

"Them or the holders' ladies?"

"Both, most likely."

The only problem with the idea of High Holdings was that Quaeryt didn't see a trace of one for the first two glasses of the ride. He also realized, belatedly, that he really hadn't talked to many of the undercaptains in days, except for Voltyr and Shaelyt, beyond instructing them or drilling them. So, when Skarpa rode back to check on Third Regiment Quaeryt motioned for Baelthm to ride with him on his right, since the road was wide enough that Zhelan was already riding on his left.

"Sir . . . have I done something . . ."

"No. We have a long ride, and it's been a while since I've really talked to any of you. You told me you'd agreed to be an imager undercaptain when Lord Bhayar's men came for you. Was that forced . . . or was it a better choice?"

"Some of both, sir, I suppose. It wasn't like I had that much choice. Fewer and fewer of the local tradespeople wanted me to image things for them, except maybe the masons, and in that part of Cheva, none were building houses that needed scrollwork or metal trim. The gold for going to join you, excepting that I didn't know it was you, sir, would pay for food and more, enough that Rashyl could feed and clothe the boys. With her lacework, that is."

"Have you sent script for coin back to her?"

"Most of my pay, sir. One of the dispatch riders brought me a note, a mere scrap. He didn't take her coin. He said that taking notes to tell a man his pay scripts made it to his wife would have been a crime against the Nameless." Baelthm chuckled in his deep voice. "Long as I live, they'll be doing fairly well, and if I don't . . . well . . . there's the death golds. What is it, four golds for an undercaptain?"

Quaeryt knew the death gold payment was two golds for a ranker, if he had a wife, none otherwise, but for an officer, he'd never asked, but Baelthm's comment reminded him that he needed to check to see that the proper payment request had been lodged for Akoryt. Rather than answer Baelthm directly, he only said, "It could happen, but it's best not to dwell on it."

"You'd be right about that, sir."

"Have there been any other imagers in your family?"

"None that I know of. I wonder at times if my youngest might not be growing in that direction."

"How old is he?"

"He's but four." Baelthm added immediately, "I did not wed young. Few women in Cheva would willingly wed an imager, especially one with a Pharsi grandmother. But Rashyl . . . her sweetness was a boon and well worth waiting for."

"What sort of lacework does she do?"

Baelthm beamed. "Any kind that needs doing." The broad smile faded. "At times, the ladies wanted more from her than the masons did from me."

"Was your father an imager?"

"Who could say? I don't remember much of him. He was a boatman on the river. He died when I could barely walk. Drowned, my mother said. She never spoke much of him, and the way she didn't, I didn't ask much. Not after she said that he was a boatman and that was all I needed to know."

Quaeryt nodded and waited.

"Not that it'd be good to dwell on it, sir, but you did say something about how things might be better for us after the campaign . . ."

"After the war is settled, one way or another," Quaeryt affirmed. "Lord Bhayar has agreed not to forget the imagers, and he has always kept his word on such matters."

"And you being an imager, then, and wed to his sister . . ." Baelthm raised his eyebrows.

Quaeryt nodded.

"What about families, sir?"

"I'd like them to be able to join you." *You can't promise that. Not now.*

"Be good to think that I might not have to return to Cheva. The whole province . . ." The oldest undercaptain shook his head.

"The folk of Piedryn haven't been as charitable as they might have been to imagers . . ."

"Those words, sir, are all too charitable for the folk of Piedryn."

Quaeryt wasn't about to point out that those words applied to all too many people in Lydar and that was one reason why he was risking so much for Bhayar. "That may be, but we do what we can do."

Quaeryt talked for another quint before he felt he'd spent enough time with the older imager and sent Baelthm back to the undercaptains. But before summoning another undercaptain to talk with, Quaeryt turned to Zhelan. "I know it's late, and I should have realized it earlier, but the death payments for Akoryt?"

"You had much to do, sir. I took care of it when we had time in Ralaes, then sent it off after we took Villerive. Be a few weeks before his wife receives those golds, and she'll grieve again." Zhelan added quietly. "It's five golds for an undercaptain."

"Thank you."

Desyrk was the next undercaptain. Quaeryt gestured to ride beside him. The blond undercaptain looked quizzically at Quaeryt. "Sir?"

"You'd told me you were a potter before you became an undercaptain. You avoided talking much about it, and I didn't press . . . then. Why didn't you want to say more?"

"Just didn't."

"I need to know more now." Quaeryt image-projected a hint of warmth and curiosity.

"Might I ask why, sir?"

"The more I know about you, now that your imaging has improved, the more I can try to put you where you're the most effective," replied Quaeryt. "Did you like being a potter?"

"Well enough."

"How much imaging did you do to help in forming or throwing pots?"

"Couldn't have been any kind of potter without it." Desyrk paused, then went on. "My pots'd sag. Didn't have my brother's touch. He was even better than our da."

"Your father was a master potter, then?"

"Hardly! We made pots and jugs for the poorer folk north of Thuyl. They were strong and solid, and they didn't leak. Other than that . . ." He shook his head.

"Was anyone else in your family an imager?"

"Not that I know. Until my brother caught me imaging a pot, even my folks didn't know. He was the one who told Bhayar's men. Even kept the gold, the miserable whelp."

"Why did he turn you in?"

"He didn't know how come I could form pots as good as they were. He'd see 'em sagging and lumpy, and I'd image 'em better before we put them in the kiln . . . when no one was looking. But he kept watching closer and closer, and he caught me. Said I wasn't doing it right. Said a potter had to work the clay, not just image it. I told him it was work one way or the other. He didn't want to hear it. Da didn't believe it, and Jorj went and told the local constable or whatever, and they put me on an old mule and sent me to Solis and then to Ferravyl." Desyrk shrugged. "You know the rest."

"You never married."

"Couldn't raise the bride price. Pots don't bring a lot."

"What do you think about being an imager?"

"It's not great, sir. A lot better than being a potter in Thuyla, though."

Quaeryt continued to ask questions and listen as they rode westward along the well-paved road that led to Variana.

68

Over the remainder of Solayi and all of Lundi, there were absolutely no signs of any Bovarian forces, reinforcing Quaeryt's—and Skarpa's—belief that Rex Kharst was amassing forces near Variana. Yet Quaeryt couldn't dismiss the possibility that the Bovarians might attack at any point. While he rode and waited for that possibility, he spent time talking to each of the imager undercaptains. From some of them, such as Threkhyl and Horan, he learned little unexpected, only more detail about what they had initially told him. Quaeryt had already known that Threkhyl had been a small holder outside a small village northeast of Piedryn, far enough from the larger towns that no one noticed that he almost never bought tools or plows or saws or spades or that in even the worst of times his family somehow had enough to eat—until a local cooper tried to woo and marry his daughter. Threkhyl had turned the fellow down, and in weeks, Threkhyl had been rounded up by Bhayar's men, with a pair of golds going to the cooper and the daughter who was likely now his wife.

Quaeryt could see how that had happened, or that a trapping rival had turned in Horan, since neither undercaptain was versed in subtlety.

Smaethyl was the essential loner, in some ways the closest to Quaeryt and in others totally foreign, as when he had observed, "I'd say that the Nameless doesn't want anyone to have any glory, and most lords and High Holders don't want anyone else to have many golds. That doesn't leave much for most folks."

It wasn't that Quaeryt disagreed with Smaethyl's observation, but the almost fatalistic attitude behind the words chilled him.

The three Pharsi undercaptains came from different towns, yet shared many similarities, all from their Pharsi heritage, the most notable being their quiet pragmatism.

Shaelyt, his words capturing the spirit of that practicality, had simply said, "Erion and the Nameless watch, but do not interfere often enough for any man to count on it. Stupid men end up dead. Dead men do not see the next dawn, and with the next dawn there is always hope."

Quaeryt hadn't been able to refrain from asking, "Doesn't that open a man up to seizing the opportunities of the moment?"

"My mother told me that a man who cannot see beyond tomorrow is also a stupid man. I have not seen that she was wrong."

Quaeryt had laughed.

As he rode beside Zhelan on Mardi morning, under high gray clouds that made the day both cooler and the air a bit damper, a quint before ninth glass, he couldn't help reflecting on what more he'd learned—or hadn't—about the imager undercaptains over the previous two days.

Shouldn't you have done more of that earlier? Except that he'd been far too absorbed in teaching them what they needed to know. *And to further your goals for them, perhaps?* He couldn't deny that, but there was also the problem that he didn't have the experience to be a subcommander and that he'd been trying to learn how to be more effective as both an imager commander and a troop subcommander. *There are always excuses.* And there were, he acknowledged, and all he could do was learn from the experience of being sidetracked by excuses and move on as best he could. His ruminations were cut short as a scout rode back eastward along the road toward Fifth Battalion, once more in the van.

Quaeryt waited as the scout eased in beside him.

"Sir . . . there's a High Holding two milles ahead, sir. The gates are chained, but it looks deserted. There are tracks on the road and on the shoulder heading west."

"Go and let the commander know. He'll decide who will look into it." The scout would anyway, but reinforcing Skarpa's precedence never hurt.

"Yes, sir."

While he was waiting for Skarpa to receive the report, Quaeryt studied the road ahead, as well as the small shuttered cots and dwellings they passed, as well as the absence of livestock, noting what the scouts had kept reporting—that there were no signs of any Bovarian forces.

In less than half a quint, Skarpa was riding up the shoulder of the road. By then, Quaeryt had sent a ranker to notify Major Zhael that third company might be required to accompany him and several undercaptains on a reconnaissance mission.

"You have a company ready to ride out and see?" Skarpa was wasting no time.

"Third company, with Desyrk and Lhandor."

Skarpa nodded. "Make it quick. If there are supplies, let me know as soon as you can. If not, just leave the place . . . unless you think there are weapons or other useful items."

"I'd be surprised if there were either."

"So would I," replied Skarpa. 'Do what you can. I'll call a halt by the gates."

Quaeryt and third company moved out from the vanguard, and little more than a quint later, they reined up in front of the gates on the north side of the road. Quaeryt could scarcely miss the hold house, situated as it was on a rise overlooking the river, and so large that even from the chained gates, the structure still loomed impressively above the extensive formal gardens and forest park that surrounded it.

Yet, once they opened the gates and went through the buildings, that inspection revealed that the entire hold house and outbuildings had been recently and completely emptied.

But who could have done that so quickly? Kharst? The holding was certainly large enough and well appointed enough to be his. Still, there was little point in spending time there, not when there were neither supplies nor weapons, and Quaeryt had the gates rechained.

For the rest of Mardi and for the first glasses on Meredi, Skarpa and his forces saw only traces of the withdrawing Bovarians, or perhaps they were tracks of retainers hurrying Kharst's goods from the holding back to Variana, mused Quaeryt—if the hold had been Kharst's at all.

A quint or two after ninth glass on Meredi, the scouts came riding back with the report that the span over the fair-sized river three miles ahead had been destroyed, most likely with explosives. Once more, Fifth Battalion was in the van, as it had been for most of the ride west from Nordeau.

Skarpa didn't have to glance at his map, but responded immediately. "That has to be the River Sommeil."

"Whatever it is, Commander," replied the squad leader of the scouts, "it looks to be too wide and too deep to ford."

Of course it is. They wouldn't destroy it if it weren't. Quaeryt merely smiled.

Skarpa turned in the saddle and looked at Quaeryt without saying a word.

"We'll see what we can do. I'll take first company and the undercaptains."

"Take the entire battalion, Subcommander."

"Yes, sir."

Shortly, Fifth Battalion moved ahead of the main column at a moderately quick trot. After riding about two milles Quaeryt glanced to the north and noted that the paving stones of the river road were only perhaps ten or fifteen yards higher than the River Aluse, if that. Ahead was a slight rise, and when Quaeryt came to the crest and looked ahead, he could see that the Bovarians had indeed chosen well.

The River Sommeil meandered through a swampy flood plain a good three milles wide, and the only raised ground was a tongue of land that led to the bridge. The structure itself had been a solid-looking stone span connecting two tongues of more solid land, although for a good hundred yards on each side of the bridge the road had been constructed on a causeway that was more like a levee. What the scouts had not mentioned was that, some hundred yards short of the east end of the bridge was a large gap in the road . . . and the causeway that had supported it.

While the terrain suggested it was unlikely that Fifth Battalion would face Bovarian forces, at least on the east side of the bridge, the gap in the road and the missing spans of the bridge indicated more work for the imagers. Since the bridge itself blocked a clear view of the road on the far side, there might also be other gaps.

Quaeryt kept studying the causeway and the terrain on the far side of the bridge, but could see no sign of Bovarians. If they waited, they were concealed in the trees that flanked the open ground on each side of the road.

Once he had reached the missing section of the causeway, he reined up and studied the damage in the road. While the gap wasn't that wide, no more than five or six yards, the material that comprised the levee and roadbed had been blasted away to the point that whatever base remained was below the water level of the swamp surrounding the levee. He turned the mare sideways. "Undercaptain Horan, forward!"

"Yes, sir."

"You're to start imaging rock into that gap. Not dirt because the water will turn it to mud."

"Any kind of rock, sir?"

"Any kind that's solid. Not sandstone or pumice. Do it in smaller amounts at a time, rather than trying it all at once."

"Yes, sir."

Quaeryt watched as the slightly grizzled imager concentrated. The water in the gap swelled as though a current pushed it upward, but Quaeryt did not see anything but more muddy water. A second swell of water followed, and when the current subsided, he could see grayish stones being washed by the swamp water. He glanced to Horan, whose forehead was glistening with sweat. "Wait a moment. Take a swallow of ale or whatever's in your bottle."

Horan needed little urging to reach for the water bottle.

Quaeryt once more surveyed the lands beyond the swamp to the west, thickly forested with trees and undergrowth that could hide regiments. He had his doubts that there were regiments concealed, but the flatness of the causeway on the far side concerned him, since it was a perfect situation to use musketeers. The road would only allow three riders abreast at any speed, and it would take time to cover the mille or so beyond the bridge.

But then, they wouldn't be all that accurate at that distance, and they'd wait until we were closer to the woods. That was another worry.

He waited for a time, then looked to Horan. "Ready for another imaging?"

"Yes, sir."

In between periods of imaging and resting, it took Horan more than four quints to replace and raise the causeway to within two handspans of the stone paving on each side.

"That's enough, Undercaptain," said Quaeryt.

"I can do more, sir."

"You're getting pale. You need to drink some more and rest. Otherwise you'll collapse, and we may well need you again if the Bovarians have done the same thing on the far side."

"Oh . . . yes, sir."

Quaeryt got the impression that Horan had not thought about that.

"Undercaptain Smaethyl, forward!" Quaeryt waited until the former hunter, not quite so angular as he had been when he'd first joined the battalion, rode up and joined him. "I'd like a layer of gravel, small pebbles, to cover the stones smoothly."

Smaethyl managed that quickly, and without sweating.

Quaeryt then had Zhelan summon a squad of troopers to walk back and forth on the gravel, even jumping on it, until the gravel and pebbles would no longer sift downward. Then Smaethyl imaged finer gravel, followed by paving stones.

Finally, he rode across the stones of the repaired road and causeway, but sensed no give in the road. You can only hope that it holds. Still the stones Horan had imaged looked solid, and while they might settle some, Quaeryt doubted that they would totally give way, at least not in the next few days.

"Fifth Battalion! Forward!" As he urged the mare forward, he glanced back. The van of Third Regiment had reached the crest of the rise that marked the edge of the swampy valley holding the River Sommeil and the bridge. *They'll likely catch us before we finish image-repairing things, especially if there's another hole blown in the causeway on the other side.* There was no help for that. Imaging took time, just not as much time as having rankers and engineers repair the gaps.

When they reached the base of the bridge and Quaeryt reined up, he smiled. The Bovarians had blown out most of the middle of the stone spans, but had left the center pier. While imaging the spans back in place would take a strong imager, it wouldn't take the piecemeal effort that repairing the causeway had. He glanced down, past the ragged ending of the approach where some stones remained and others did not, to the water of the River Sommeil less than four yards below, where he could barely see the current. That suggested that the river was deeper than it looked. Then he straightened. "Undercaptain Threkhyl, forward."

Threkhyl rode forward.

"Just the span from here to the pier. Without the side walls."

A frown of puzzlement crossed the face of the ginger-bearded imager.

"I want the others to get some practice, but I need the basic span to be strong. I also want to make sure the pier is sound with weight on it before you expend the energy for the second span."

At that, Threkhyl nodded and concentrated. In moments a gently arching stone span connected the approach to the center pier. The undercaptain turned to Quaeryt. "Sir."

"Thank you. Undercaptain Lhandor, forward."

"Sir," said Lhandor as he eased his mount around Threkhyl's big gelding.

"I'd like stone retaining walls a yard and a half high, no more that two handspans in width, their outside edges even with the edge of the span."

Lhandor managed the walls on the south side, then had to rest, drink, and eat a biscuit before he could image the second set of walls.

Quaeryt, with some trepidation, urged the mare onto the span. He could feel no give, and there was no echo from his mount's hooves. He kept riding, then turned back. "Imagers, forward! Just imagers."

Quaeryt reined up on the new span several yards short of where it met and seamlessly joined the center pier. From there he studied the open water and the bridge approach. Once again, he had Threkhyl do the main span, but this time he called on Khalis to handle the side walls.

Quaeryt waited for Khalis to recover, then urged the mare onto the second span. The undercaptains followed, and then the rest of Fifth Battalion, behind Zhelan, followed over the spans. As Quaeryt's mare stepped off the second span, Threkhyl moved forward, until his mount was close behind Quaeryt's.

"You know I could have done all that . . . sir," pressed Threkhyl. "I know you said they need practice. But I could have done it."

Quaeryt refrained from sighing. "You might recall it took more than one or two imagers for us to take Nordeau, did it not?"

"It did."

"What do you think will happen when we get to Variana? Can you and I and Shaelyt and Voltyr do it all?"

"We can, sir. I know we can."

Because Quaeryt could sense that there was something Threkhyl wasn't saying, he pressed on. "That's all well and good to say, but what happens if we can't?"

"We haven't seen any other imagers, sir."

What does that have to do with anything? Quaeryt was about to reply, then saw a darkness in the causeway ahead. He took a deep breath and pointed at another, even wider gap in the causeway. "Look ahead, there. I think you'll need to help Horan with this one." He smiled. "Remember, there's always something unexpected in warfare." *Always . . . and sometimes even more unexpected than you think possible.*

In the end, Quaeryt assigned Horan, Threkhyl, and Shaelyt to fill and pave the second gap in the causeway. While they worked, taking long breaks between imaging, at Quaeryt's insistence, he continued to study the remainder of the causeway and then the space cut for the road through the forest and heavy undergrowth beyond the end of the causeway. The forest growth between the river road and the River Aluse appeared to be close to a half mille wide, but given the path of the road, the tree-filled area narrowed so that, most likely, several milles farther along, the road was much closer to the river. From where he was, Quaeryt could make out a brown line to the left of the river road, mostly straight, running roughly parallel to the road and equidistant between the road and the woods on the south side of the road. It was some sort of drainage ditch several yards wide.

Once the repairs were complete, Quaeryt had the three rest for another half quint before he had Fifth Battalion resume riding. As he rode along the causeway arcing gently northward to meet a tongue of land that the road followed through a narrow gap in a forest that might well be swamp forest at times of the year, Quaeryt tried to catch murmurs from the imagers.

". . . not too bad . . ."

". . . didn't image himself . . ."

". . . has . . . reasons . . ."

Quaeryt did indeed, and he hoped that his suspicions were unfounded.

Once they left the causeway and rode on the slightly raised road flanked mainly by knee-high and browning grasses—and red flies and mosquitoes—Quaeryt kept studying the trees, looking for anything that appeared less—or more—than it should have been. Then . . . he stiffened in the saddle, immediately turning. "Imagers! Mark the brown stump ahead and to the left. Stand ready to image iron darts into any Bovarians who appear! At my command."

Quaeryt was partly guessing, but there were far more wilting and yellow leaves ahead to the left. He concentrated on removing all the leaves—or what seemed to be leaves—across a space some hundred yards wide.

Instantly, he heard screams and saw wooden frames, with musketeers and their loaders.

"Image darts! At the musketeers!" Then he extended his own shields at an angle just before a ragged volley discharged.

He reeled back in the saddle, but the impact was nothing compared to what he'd experienced in Nordeau. He contracted the shields to protect a smaller area, basically the imagers, and imaged iron darts at three musketeers.

Another volley, smaller than the first, ripped in the direction of Fifth Battalion. Quaeryt felt no impacts on his shields. He kept imaging darts. So did the other imagers, especially Voltyr, but that was one reason why Quaeryt had kept one of the stronger imagers fresh.

There were only a few musketeers who fired a third volley, and there was no fourth volley. Quaeryt saw some Bovarians crawling or scuttling back into the thick forest.

"Shaelyt! Image pepper and smoke across the whole area where the musketeers were."

"Yes, sir."

"Major Zhelan, forward!"

Zhelan moved up beside Quaeryt. "Sir?"

"We need to send a message back to the commander, telling him what happened and warning him that there might be a musketeer or two left."

"You don't want to send troopers in to clean them out?" Zhelan's voice was level.

"I think we've put them to rout, and I'm not inclined to send troopers across uneven ground, maybe even with swampy spots, not to mention a wide ditch just to have them try to catch a few Bovarians in a thick forest that doesn't look friendly to horses." Quaeryt looked at Zhelan. "If I'm wrong, please tell me. I value your judgment."

"Sir . . . you have to make the decision . . . but you wouldn't catch many." Zhelan paused. "You were busy, sir, but whatever you did at the beginning killed about half of them, ripped off arms and the like."

Quaeryt winced. He had heard screams, but he'd only meant to remove the musketeers' camouflage. "I didn't realize."

"That's why any troopers might not find much."

"We'll leave it that way, but the commander needs to know."

"Yes, sir. I'll take care of it . . . and we can send out the scouts now."

That was another thing Quaeryt had forgotten.

As he looked southward at the gash in the trees, Quaeryt swallowed again. He hadn't done that kind of imaging before . . . and with any new imaging . . . there were often costs. *That one . . . you just didn't expect.*

He kept riding, looking for other ambush spots, although he doubted there would be another too close. Still . . .

69

That evening, after the three regiments and Fifth Battalion were settled in for the night in a small town that the locals called Byun, and the map showed as Reyks, Quaeryt had just finished a short session with the new imagers when Skarpa rode up. Quaeryt and the commander ended up on a small porch of a dwelling less than fifty yards from the south bank of the River Aluse.

"How are your imagers coming?" asked Skarpa.

"Each day, most of them are getting stronger, even Baelthm, not that he'll ever have much strength. Some of the younger ones show great promise . . ." After reporting on the rest of Fifth Battalion, Quaeryt asked, "Is there anything else I should know?"

"We haven't heard from the marshal since this morning's dispatch. He was still about a half day behind us on Lundi. His scouts reported a regiment moving westward toward Variana. The Bovarians spurred their mounts and even made their foot trot to avoid Myskyl's vanguard."

"Have they experienced any musketeers?"

Skarpa frowned. "Come to think of it, I don't think they've encountered any musket fire."

"Doesn't that strike you as strange?"

"It tells me that the Bovarians are targeting you and the imagers."

"How did they know early enough to get the musketeers into position? Moving all those stands, the camouflage, the powder, the muskets—that's not nearly so easy as moving a mounted company."

"They must have spies."

"Of some sort," said Quaeryt blandly.

"You'd best leave it at that, right now, unless there's proof," cautioned Skarpa.

"I intend to, but I'll keep it in mind." Quaeryt paused. "There's one other thing . . . cannon."

"You mean that we haven't seen any? We might at Variana or closer to it."

"Why not now?"

"I'd guess that they don't have that many, and most were probably around Ephra. They're Namer-fired heavy. Muskets are easier to move, and you can get a more rapid fire from them." Skarpa shrugged. "Those'd be my thoughts."

Quaeryt still wondered. "Is there anything you have in mind for us tomorrow?"

"I still want Fifth Battalion in the van." Skarpa stretched, then glanced toward his horse, tied to a sturdy, if slightly angled post just beside the path to the cot.

"We'll be there."

"Good." The commander turned and made his way off the narrow porch, pausing beside the post, his eyes going to the River Aluse. "Don't see why they build so close to the water."

"They don't have to drag a boat too far or carry water for hundreds of yards," replied Quaeryt. "That gets tiring after a while. Besides, the land's so flat here that they'd likely get flooded even if they were hundreds of yards away."

Skarpa looked toward into the rapidly purpling eastern sky, where the three-quarters-full disc of Erion rung well above the trees in the distance. The smaller moon's shade was more like amber, but would turn its usual reddish tint once the sky darkened. "Might just be full when we reach Variana." Then he looked to Quaeryt. "How did you know the musketeers were there?"

"I didn't," Quaeryt admitted. "I just knew that every time that there's been a perfect place for an ambush by musketeers in the past few weeks . . . there has been. So when I saw all those trees and all that flat land and, most likely, a place where we couldn't charge them without scores of horses breaking their legs, I thought it was more than likely."

Skarpa nodded. "Said you'd make a good commander."

"Only because I'm an imager."

The commander shook his head. "Every man has his strengths. The best know how to use them. The worst don't know what they are. It's the ability to use your strengths that makes you a good officer."

Quaeryt couldn't help but think about all the small details he hadn't known. "Is that why you assigned Zhelan?"

Skarpa laughed. "I didn't assign him. Myskyl did. He's feared you ever since Rescalyn's death. So he gave you a senior junior officer who knew squad-level combat, procedures, and discipline and not much more. He hoped the two of you would bungle things. He didn't understand that

Zhelan knew what you didn't. You've both learned from each other, and he could command a battalion now."

"He already does," said Quaeryt dryly. *Some of the time, if not more.*

Skarpa shook his head. "You command. You delegate, but you still command. Don't forget it."

Although the last words were spoken as evenly as those which preceded them, Quaeryt recognized them as a command, not a suggestion. "I won't."

"We're little more than sixty milles from Variana. How much opposition do you think we'll face tomorrow or the next day?"

"Who knows? They're not defending the way I would or you would. After today, I'd be a bit surprised, but not astonished, if we faced more than delaying attacks tomorrow. I wouldn't be at all surprised if we faced a stronger attack on Vendrei." Quaeryt laughed softly. "And that probably means we'll get a heavy attack tomorrow and delaying harassment on Vendrei."

Skarpa smiled. "I still think you're right about Kharst wanting to draw us in and crush us. The question is where . . . and how—in one blow or two."

"And how the marshal will attempt to have us take the brunt of it," added Quaeryt.

"How can you believe that of our most illustrious leader?"

"Ignorance, I suppose," said Quaeryt dryly. "I must not know him well enough."

"I won't comment on that, but I will observe that he doesn't know you well enough, and it's best that way." Skarpa untied his mount.

After the commander mounted and departed, Quaeryt walked around the section of Byun that held Fifth Battalion, checking with each company commander. He didn't discover anything he didn't already know, but as he was about to leave Arion, the major said quietly, in Bovarian, as always, "Had you been with us in Khel, the Bovarians would not have defeated us, outnumbered as we were. Their musketeers made the difference."

"You didn't mention this before."

Arion offered a slightly embarrassed smile. "We have found that none who have not seen what the muskets could do would believe their power."

"Lord Bhayar has worried about the muskets for some time. How many more do you think they have . . . waiting for us at Variana?"

Arion shrugged. "I cannot say. They had more than a thousand at Khelgror. You have destroyed almost half that many."

But it's been more than a few years since the battle of Khelgror, and Kharst has to have forged more muskets and trained more musketeers.

Quaeryt frowned, remembering the meeting he'd had in Solis with Bhayar more than a year before when Bhayar had been asking about whether imagers would be able to image musket parts with enough precision. Had he known about Quaeryt's abilities then . . . and been probing?

Unless you ask, you'll never know. He smiled. Even if he did, he'd likely not get a conclusive answer, and it made little difference now . . . although the Bovarian muskets well might, especially if Kharst had more than a regiment and used the musketeers as a massed unit.

Still . . . from what he knew, muskets could not be cast, not yet, at least, but had to be forged, and that took time and trained armorer-smiths.

"Could we use the muskets you captured?" asked Arion.

"We have several hundred captured muskets, but we don't have much of the proper powder nor musket balls . . ." Quaeryt shrugged. "I believe Lord Bhayar had men working on this, but he did not expect war with Bovaria to come quite so quickly."

"Then it will come to whether you and your imagers or Kharst's musketeers will triumph."

"And how badly we are outnumbered," suggested Quaeryt.

"So long as you stand, we are not outnumbered."

"No . . ." replied Quaeryt, with a slight smile, "so long as the imagers stand." *Because either most of us will stand, or none of us will survive either Kharst or Myskyl, if not both.*

"Some of the others are now more powerful. That I can see. But are they strong enough without you?"

"The young Pharsi imagers could be very strong. They're already able to do more than I could do two years ago." *Even if that was partly because you feared trying until you had no choice.*

"They will support you. They will never surpass you."

Quaeryt laughed, if softly. "You never know."

Arion shook his head. "I do not know, but Erion does, and I can see his words."

Quaeryt wasn't about to argue about that. "I'll leave it to him, then."

Arion nodded. "As you should, sir."

After Quaeryt left Arion and began to walk back toward the dwelling that held the imager undercaptains, he glanced at the eastern sky, where Erion was definitely taking on a clear reddish cast. Then he shook his head and laughed softly. For all the superstitions, in the end it came down to who accomplished what and how, not which moon hung overhead. *Didn't it?*

70

Despite Quaeryt's worries, none of Skarpa's forces encountered any opposition or even caught sight of any Bovarian forces on Meredi, nor on Jeudi morning . . . until ninth glass when the scouts rode back to report that a vast shallow lake covered the road ahead. Skarpa immediately called a halt, and Quaeryt and Fifth Battalion rode forward another two milles. There Quaeryt reined up and studied what lay before him.

Muddy water covered the road and the lower ground on each side, extending a half mille ahead and two hundred yards north to the raised bank of the River Aluse, but more than a mille to the south. Immediately before Quaeryt, the water was barely a few fingers deep, and he doubted that in the middle of the shallow lake created by the Bovarians the water was more than a yard or so deep, although it was difficult to tell under the high but comparatively thick gray clouds that had not reduced the harvest heat and only made the air seem stickier and damper.

There were no cots or buildings rising out of the muddy water, although Quaeryt could see wooden fences and a low hedgerow to the south, suggesting that the area might well have flooded often. *But you don't know really how deep it is, not for certain, and you don't know what else the water conceals.* After a moment a second thought occurred to him. *That couldn't have happened with a Naedaran road. They kept their roads on higher ground.*

There was something about the newly formed lake. He glanced to the north, then realized that the land covered by water was higher than the river itself. The water couldn't have come directly from the river. He looked westward again, noting the gradual slope of the land upward in the distance.

He turned in the saddle. "Undercaptain Ghaelyn, if you'd send a request for Major Calkoran to join me."

"Yes, sir."

"Undercaptain Voltyr, forward. Undercaptains Horan and Smaethyl as well."

When all three faced him, he looked to Voltyr. "It's likely that this lake was formed by some sort of breach in a stream or ditch to the south or west. I'm sending you with fourth company and Horan and Smaethyl to find and repair whatever was breached."

"Yes, sir."

Shortly, Calkoran rode up, and Quaeryt repeated his instructions in Bovarian, adding, "If you do encounter any large Bovarian forces, I'd appreciate prudence, Major, considering you have three regiments and a battalion behind you. I'd like to have you and your men have the satisfaction of helping take Variana."

"Yes, sir."

Once Calkoran and the three imager undercaptains had ridden back to second company, Threkhyl moved his mount forward, pushing Khalis's mount to the side, in order to reach Quaeryt. "Sir? Why didn't you send me?"

"Because I need you here to do a bigger job."

The expression of puzzlement that was beginning to irritate Quaeryt more and more appeared on the older undercaptain's face.

"Undercaptain . . . even once Undercaptain Voltyr and the others repair whatever caused this . . . overgrown puddle, the water isn't going to vanish. It's filled a big depression. Maybe it was once a lake. You and the others need to image a stone-paved top to the existing road, and you need to do it carefully and slowly, bit by bit. If you do it all at once, you'll freeze the water, and you may well create ice between the old roadbed and what you create. By the time three regiments ride over it, the stone might crumble or break."

Threkhyl still looked puzzled.

"Take my word for it, Undercaptain." Quaeryt didn't want to get into the fact that great imaging might freeze the lake solid, because it would still melt fairly quickly, leaving the same muddy water that now faced them. "Imager Undercaptains, forward!"

Quaeryt had Desyrk begin the work, and a stretch of stone running some five yards appeared. Then came Baelthm, who could only add a few yards. It had been clear to Quaeryt that the process would take some time . . . and the imagers were proving that. Still . . . after a glass, the raised section of the road extended some three hundred yards.

A little more than a glass later, Voltyr returned with second company, then rode forward to report to Quaeryt.

"Sir. As you suspected, there was extensive damage to an irrigation ditch to the south. We repaired it and strengthened it. But the ground is so flat here that there's no way to drain the water away. If we had created a breach all the way through the ditch, it just would have flooded the other side, and then the water would have kept rising on both sides of the ditch."

"Thank you. Somehow . . . that doesn't surprise me. Now we'll need what help you can give to raise the roadbed here."

With all the imagers alternating, and with generous rest breaks, it took until the second glass of the afternoon before the work to raise the roadbed a third of a yard or so above the water was completed. Immediately, Skarpa's scouts rode out once more.

Fifth Battalion moved forward behind them, beyond the lake onto the section of the road beyond the water where the land sloped gently, barely noticeably, upward, but it was almost a half mille farther to the west before there were any cots or outbuildings near the road.

Skarpa rode forward and eased in beside Quaeryt. Zhelan dropped back, deferentially.

"Took you a while to fix that," offered the commander. "Good job, though."

"Building up a half mille of road takes time and effort, even for imagers. I also wanted to rest them as I could, just in case we ran into more Bovarians."

"Good thought, but the scouts haven't returned. So they're not likely to be too close."

"I'd hope not. Some of the undercaptains won't be able to do much imaging until tomorrow."

"I'd thought as much, but we don't have to press that hard. We'll stop earlier tonight. We've made good progress."

Quaeryt nodded, waiting.

"We'd better hang on to all the lands we've taken," said Skarpa sardonically. "Be a shame to let Kharst benefit from all the improvements you and the imagers have made."

"I'm beginning to think more and more like that. They were his lands, and people, and he's destroying things, and we're supposedly conquering them, and we're rebuilding and improving things." After a brief pause Quaeryt added, "Except for the gates at Nordeau."

"They were old," rejoined Skarpa. "Besides, we need to leave reminders here and there."

Besides thousands and thousands of dead Bovarians?

Skarpa said nothing else, and neither did Quaeryt for the moment as they continued westward toward Variana.

By midday on Vendrei, Skarpa's forces were within a few milles of Caluse, which appeared to be a moderate-sized town. Skarpa had summoned all the subcommanders, and he and Quaeryt waited for Meinyt and Khaern under a large oak tree that provided some relief from another day of blazing sun.

It may be harvest, but it's more like midsummer . . . Does summer ever end here? Or is this just an unusual year? Quaeryt noted that even Skarpa had pushed back his visor cap and wiped his brow with the back of his sleeve.

"Almost as hot as Solis," muttered the commander.

"Hotter, it seems to me."

"Could be. Like to think it's why they're not fighting." Skarpa broke off as Meinyt and Khaern rode up, then dismounted, and turned their horses over to waiting rankers.

Once the two joined Quaeryt and Skarpa in the shade, all four standing well back from the shoulder of the wide but dusty gray stone road, Skarpa blotted his forehead again, cleared his throat, and spoke. "The town ahead is Caluse. Scouts can't find traces of any Bovarian forces, and the place looks deserted. Everything's shuttered, and there's no one on the streets." Skarpa shook his head. "Don't know as I believe that, but I've sent out two squads and one even rode partway into town. What's stranger is that there's a three-span bridge across the Aluse, and they left it standing. Why'd they do that? Variana's only twenty milles to the west . . . if we can believe the maps."

"They didn't expect us to get this far," suggested Khaern. "Or this quickly, and they didn't have time to destroy the bridge."

"They want us to settle in here, comfortable-like, before they attack us while we're sleeping," suggested Meinyt. "Or not expecting them."

"We have another problem," Skarpa pointed out. "Or maybe it's an opportunity. We're a day ahead of the marshal's forces. If we hold up here, we can join his forces, or he can join us."

Not if Myskyl and Deucalon get their way, thought Quaeryt.

"Either way," continued Skarpa, "it's easy with the bridge not being damaged. That might be why the Bovarians left it intact."

"As a trap to entice us to join up?" asked Khaern.

"What other reason could there be?" demanded Meinyt

"You haven't said anything, Quaeryt," noted Skarpa.

"You've all suggested any of the possibilities I could think of." *Except total Bovarian incompetence, and I don't believe that.* "Most of the town is on the south side of the river. This is the first town with a bridge over the Aluse where most of the dwellings are on the south side. All the other towns have much smaller southern quarters." He paused. "Except the old quarter of Nordeau on the north side was smaller than the old quarter on the south. But all the Bovarian-built towns, except this one, are larger on the north side of the river."

"That's so," said Skarpa, "but there had to be one."

But why this one? Quaeryt didn't voice the question. He had no answer and had no doubt that none of the others did, either.

"Well . . ." drawled Skarpa, "it seems to me that we might as well spend the night here. The Bovarians can't get us all right now, because we're not all here, and it will be more than a day before the marshal reaches the north side of the bridge. We'll set out extra sentries and keep more troopers on standby. I'll send off a dispatch to the marshal declaring our intent to stay here until his forces can arrive to take over protecting the bridge and requesting his instructions. Then we'll see." After a pause he added, "We'll enter the town with all arms ready, using the three different roads, with space between units to allow different points of attack."

Khaern nodded, if skeptically, followed by Meinyt.

Skarpa took less than a quint to outline the plan of approach or attack, with Third Regiment leading the way, and Fifth Battalion moving out to cover the road from Variana.

By the first glass of the afternoon, despite all Quaeryt's concerns, Fifth Battalion occupied the Agile Coney, one of the close to a score of inns that the town boasted, as well as two nearby inns and their outbuildings and stables. Once he was convinced that all the companies were not only settled, but ready to respond to any sort of immediate attack, with imager undercaptains assigned to each company, since their shields, limited as they were, would be of far greater advantage within a town, Quaeryt returned to the Agile Coney.

As he walked up onto the wide porch, empty of anything but a single

plain wooden bench, his eyes took in the signboard that depicted a muscular rabbit leaping over a stone wall. Both the signboard and the name suggested to Quaeryt that Caluse had never been an integral part of Naedara. *At
least, the rabbit's not black.* He still wondered about why the black marble statuette of the coney had been smashed and buried under the stone with a chiseled inscription . . . and who had done it for what purpose.

Quaeryt located the innkeeper with whom he and Zhelan had dealt
earlier. The slightly stooped but clean-shaven Culum was arranging tables
in the public room.

"This is your inn?" Remembering to speak Bovarian, Quaeryt noticed, for the first time, that the man's right arm was shorter than his left
and his left hand was twisted slightly.

"Ah . . . it is my grandsire's, sir, if he remains alive."

"So far, we haven't killed anyone. We told you that before. If we're not
attacked, we won't. They left you here to see if you could manage? Or
because they felt we wouldn't slaughter a man who was crippled?"

"Might be both, Commander."

"Subcommander. The insignia are gold for commanders. How long
has your family owned the inn?"

"Since my great-grandsire, sir. That was when Rex Hrensol built the
grand road on the south side of the river from Variana, and the first bridge."

"Why did he build the road? There's only a good road from Nordeau
west. Farther east, the south road is little more than a trail in places."

"I'm certain I wouldn't be knowing that, sir. It was well before my
time."

"That may be, but an innkeeper—or an innkeeper's son or grandson
hears stories . . ." Quaeryt image-projected friendliness and curiosity.

"It's only a story . . . but . . . well . . . some say that it was after the
good rex built his white palace on the hill south of the River Aluse, and he
wanted travelers to approach it along the great avenue beside the river."
Culum shrugged. "Others say it was because Hrensol wanted traders to
avoid Kurmitag. That was the town where High Holder Kurm had his timber and woolen mills. Can't say as which story might be true. Might be
neither is."

"Where did the name of the inn come from?"

"That'd be a strange question, sir."

"Not so strange. Some of the folks to the east don't seem too fond of
coneys."

Culum laughed. "Old aunt's tales. My great-grandsire's wife's father raised rabbits . . . big fat juicy ones. He said that you had to be an agile co-ney to get around the old man, but he did, and he wed my great-grandmom. My grandsire laughs when he talks about it." He paused "Your men'll be careful of the kitchen?"

"As best we can."

"You'll keep 'em from breaking the chairs and benches?"

"We haven't broken any in other inns." After a moment Quaeryt asked, "You have problems with Rex Kharst's troopers?"

"It'd not be my place to say, sir."

Quaeryt understood. He smiled. "You'll find that Lord Bhayar's troop-ers are far more careful." *And they'd Namer-well better be.* "That's something Lord Bhayar expects."

Culum opened his mouth, then shut it, before finally speaking. "Be most appreciated, Commander."

Quaeryt didn't correct him.

72

By the time all the officers and troopers had been fed and settled once more into quarters on Vendrei night, Quaeryt had taken one squad or another through Caluse at least three times, as well as once a good three milles west on the river road. He'd seen nothing, and neither had any of the sentries or the scouts, but he continued to worry about what the Bovarians had planned.

Skarpa had received no messages, orders, or dispatches back from Deucalon, although neither he nor Quaeryt had expected such a dispatch until Samedi. Quaeryt had to trust that Bhayar would accept his suggestions, but if Bhayar did, that might mean that Myskyl, and possibly Deucalon, would realize the extent of Quaeryt's influence. In turn, that would doubtless result in another attempt by the submarshal and the marshal to place Quaeryt and Fifth Battalion in a position of maximum danger—and that would also place the imager undercaptains in great danger . . . when every imager lost would make Quaeryt's goals harder to reach, especially against the opposition of Myskyl and Deucalon, not to mention those senior officers beholden to them.

Even after all his patrols, when he retired to his room in the Agile Coney, Quaeryt was restless and could not sleep.

Although he had written Vaelora a week before, and had not yet received another letter from her, after tomorrow or perhaps Solayi, he doubted he would have time to write . . . unless, for some reason, Kharst avoided battle, but how long that might be, especially if Bhayar followed Deucalon's counsel, Quaeryt had no idea. With those thoughts in mind, he took out a sheet of paper and began to write, painstakingly, since he did not wish to redraft his thoughts.

> My dearest,
> We are now in the rather large town of Caluse, some twenty-odd milles east of
> Variana. It is a pleasant enough place, although it seems strange that the Bovarian
> forces have withdrawn without destroying the bridge over the River Aluse . . .

He went on to describe the town and what had happened since his previous letter, then turned to other thoughts.

I cannot but think often of you and of our child to come, and the world into which she will be born, especially since I realized, by way of comparison to a cool morning in Nordruil, the meaning of the separate bedchamber in the chateau of your great-grandmere. Much as I know, if we are successful, that life in Variana will be unsettled, and possibly dangerous, I would wish that you join me as soon as practical and possible, since, for many of the reasons we have discussed, I think it highly unlikely that, given my future duties and goals, I will be able to return to Solis in the foreseeable future . . .

How do you close a letter like this? Quaeryt shook his head.

As I can, I will dispatch this, with all my desires and affection, and my hopes for our future together . . .

After he finished, he snuffed out the lamp.

Almost a glass later, he was still lying there. Finally, he relit the lamp and opened *Rholan and the Nameless* and began to page through it before a section caught his eye.

Even before his disappearance and presumed death, Rholan had come to take on the appellation of "Rholan the Unnamer." Certainly, he spoke against the sin of Naming, and he spoke well against it in its many manifestations, from boasting and bragging, to vanity—although his strongest words there were reserved for women, as I have noted earlier—and especially to the exultation of titles, and that did little to endear him to young Hengyst, especially when Rholan proclaimed that young rulers too often confuse titles with deeds and then are forced to shed the blood of others to justify the titles they inherited or assumed . . .

"The exultation of titles . . ." mused Quaeryt, closing the small volume and setting it on the small night table.

Assuming that Bhayar did defeat Kharst and managed to rule Bovaria, he couldn't for very long style himself Lord of Telaryn and Rex Bhayar of Bovaria. That would just perpetuate the idea that they're separate lands. Besides, sooner or later, Antiago would be a problem, if only because Bhayar held Autarch Aliaro responsible for the death of his sister . . . and Bhayar had been close to Chaerila. According to some rumors, Bhayar had opposed his father's efforts to wed Chaerila to Aliaro. Because Bhayar had refused to talk about it, Quaeryt had never pressed Bhayar into talking about how the marriage had come about, but having seen Bhayar's stony grief, Quaeryt could well believe the rumors.

For that reason alone, he doubted that if Bhayar had his way, Antiago would long remain independent—regardless of the cost. And that was yet another reason why Quaeryt needed to keep training and building a corps of imagers, because the Antiagons would certainly have Antiagon Fire to spare for any Telaryn invaders, and given their expertise with cannon onboard their merchanters and warships, cannon as well.

After sitting there for a long time, thinking, he finally snuffed out the lamp and lay down, hoping that he would at last be able to drift into some sort of sleep.

When Quaeryt woke abruptly in the grayness of dawn on Samedi morning, he was still trying to puzzle through the situation facing them. Was Kharst a ruler who simply could not believe that his land could be invaded and his capital threatened? Or was it all part of a strategy, as Quaeryt had believed all along, to suck all of Bhayar's forces deep into Bovaria and then annihilate them?

All you can do is prepare for the worst . . . and don't even hope for the best.

He washed, shaved, and dressed, then made his way down to eat, where he fended off questions from Zhelan and the company officers with the truth—that he hadn't yet heard from the commander because, in all likelihood, the commander hadn't heard from the marshal. As he finished eating, he overheard, more than once, words suggesting that there was all too much hurrying up to get places, only to sit and wait.

"You want to hurry on into something worst than Villerive or all those musket attacks?" asked Desyrk. "Go ahead. I'd rather wait."

Overhearing those words, Quaeryt couldn't help but smile.

A good glass after Quaeryt mustered men and officers, then sent out his own patrols through the town, he was standing on the porch of the Agile Coney, waiting, when Skarpa rode up, accompanied by a squad from Third Regiment. The commander reined up, vaulted off his mount, handed the reins to the nearest ranker, and jumped over the two steps to the porch. He walked over to Quaeryt and handed him a single sheet of paper.

In the same spirit, Quaeryt said nothing, but began to read, his eyes going quickly to the key phrases of the dispatch.

. . . You and your regiments as well as Fifth Battalion, are to remain at Caluse until the bulk of Lord Bhayar's forces have invested the town. At that point, once you receive orders, you are to begin the advance on Variana, using your regiments and the capabilities of Fifth Battalion, to remove all possible distractions and delays so that, after rest and resupply, the northern forces may proceed as then directed by Lord Bhayar . . .

Quaeryt managed to keep his face expressionless.

"Now you've read it. What do you think?"

Quaeryt knew very well what he thought. Bhayar had indicated he wanted to proceed behind Skarpa's forces, but Deucalon didn't want to. So he was reserving his options by not directly contradicting his lord, while he hoped to spend the next day changing Bhayar's mind.

"Well?" pressed Skarpa.

"It reads as if the marshal is of two minds and has not decided whether to attack Variana with all forces united or to proceed separately. That is why he wishes to preserve control of the bridge."

Skarpa snorted. "Something like that . . . except it smells worse than week-old fish in summer . . . or harvest here in Bovaria."

"Land of endless summer," added Quaeryt, keeping his voice light.

"Until we get cold rain and sleet out of nowhere when we least expect it."

"Right about the time we face endless Bovarian hordes," countered Quaeryt.

"Something like that."

"Do you know where the marshal is?"

"Two glasses south of Caluse on the north bank."

"You want Fifth Battalion ready to move out at noon?"

"That's my thought, but don't have anyone mount up until you get word."

Because we both know Deucalon doesn't always move his forces with any haste. Quaeryt only nodded. "Is there anything else?"

"I hope not." Skarpa flashed a sardonic smile, then walked back off the porch.

Quaeryt watched until the commander had ridden down the street, then turned and headed to find Zhelan. He also needed to find a way to dispatch his letter to Vaelora.

The town bells had already struck the first glass of the afternoon before Fifth Battalion actually mounted up and rode out of Caluse, once more in the vanguard.

Less than three milles west of Caluse, the River Aluse began a wide and sweeping curve that, over three milles, resulted in its course running almost due north, a course that would remain generally northward until well beyond Variana. Although Skarpa rode beside Quaeryt, the commander remained tight-lipped, even more self-contained than usual, for close to two glasses. Quaeryt did not press him, knowing that he would offer what he would when he would, although Quaeryt suspected that what Skarpa might say would be less than pleasant.

While he waited for Skarpa to speak, Quaeryt studied the road, the river, and the surrounding terrain, as well as listened intently to the scouts as they reported periodically to Skarpa.

Just after the vanguard rode onto the first few hundred yards where the river and the road both headed north, Quaeryt caught sight of a deep wagon wheel rut on the shoulder of the road, as if the wagon had been pulled over to allow something or someone else to pass. Yet he saw no disturbance, tracks, or gouges in the paving stones . . . nor any sign the stones had been removed or replaced. Yet the shoulder was of firm ground. There had been little rain, and the depth of the rut and the width of the wheel indicated a heavy load indeed.

Quaeryt couldn't help but think that the wagon carried something like explosives, cannon shells, or worse . . . but that was only speculation.

The road itself had come more to resemble the Naedaran road since Caluse, in that it followed higher ground, and there were also few trees between the road and the river, and a cleared space of at least fifty yards to the west of the road before either fields or woods began, mostly fields, with low stone walls marking the edge of the lands. The cots, as usual, were tightly shuttered, and no traces of smoke rose from their chimneys. And there was no sign of any high holdings.

Several hundred yards farther along, Quaeryt saw another deep rut at the edge of the road, but where the wagon had moved back onto the paved area, the wheel had fractured the edge of one of the paving stones.

Definitely heavy.

"You were right, you know," Skarpa finally said.

"About what?" replied Quaeryt cautiously.

"Deucalon summoned me personally. That was one reason we were later than I told you we would be. It did allow me to hand your letter to a courier. That was the easy part." Skarpa readjusted his visor cap, still not quite looking at Quaeryt. "Deucalon was less than direct . . . in that way that he could deny what he conveyed. There was also no one else present."

Quaeryt nodded.

"He said that we had an important task. That was to remove all Bovarian devices, tactics, and unusual forces that might have a disproportionate impact on the main body. I was to spare none of my forces in such efforts. In fact, if any such Bovarian units remained, especially if my forces appeared to have resorted to positional tactics to temporarily isolate, rather than remove, such Bovarian units, he would regard that as a lack of enthusiasm in carrying out my orders."

"In other words, you're to keep Fifth Battalion in the van and order us to destroy anything and everything that may pose a threat, regardless of whether better tactics or even accepting prisoners would accomplish the result of defeating those Bovarian units?"

"That was his point, without ever stating it." Skarpa snorted. "He did ask if I understood what he expected. Twice. And he was careful not to ask or allow me to comment on what I thought of those orders."

Some commanders never do. Even as he thought that, Quaeryt recognized that he'd been one of them more than once. "What do you suggest?"

"Whatever tactics will get the task accomplished without you and your battalion taking major casualties while never seeming to be out of the fight."

"Yes, sir." Quaeryt understood exactly what Skarpa was saying. Accomplishing that was likely to be far more difficult than it sounded, and it didn't sound easy to begin with.

For another mille, neither officer said anything.

"Trouble ahead," said Skarpa, turning in the saddle and ordering, "Column! Halt!"

Quaeryt had already reached the same conclusion, as soon as he'd seen the scout riding swiftly toward them and leading a riderless mount.

"Sirs!" called the scout, who reined up before Skarpa. "They've got musketeers ahead. Over that rise."

"How far beyond the rise?" demanded Skarpa.

"Four hundred yards or so, sir."

"How did the other scout get shot, then?"

"There were two of them and a squad hidden by bushes . . . much closer. Soon as we saw them, we turned. They got Vaern before we could get away."

Quaeryt estimated the distance to the top of the rise as perhaps three hundred yards. "I'd like to take a look."

"I don't need a subcommander being shot," said Skarpa.

"They won't see me. There's something not right about this."

"That's new?" rejoined Skarpa dryly.

"I want to see if the ground will allow us to spread out, or if we need to just move around the Bovarians and attack from the south or even the north."

"It won't. They wouldn't have taken a position if we could."

Quaeryt was afraid Skarpa was right, but he still wanted to see.

"Go ahead. Be careful."

Quaeryt eased the mare forward, slowly, taking his time, and raising a concealment shield before him, as well as his personal full shields. When he neared the top of the rise in the road, as he passed a narrow lane that ran westward, he guided his mount onto the left shoulder of the river road, just in case someone might see dust or something and target the middle of the main road.

He was a good twenty yards from the crest when he could see the Bovarian position, and he reined up immediately. The musketeers were lined up across the road and a good fifty yards on either side, if not more, protected by a chest-high earthen berm. As the scout had reported, they looked to be a fifth of a mille to the north. There looked to be another battalion of foot dug in behind the musketeers, keeping low in shallow trenches behind the earth excavated from the trenches, and several other berms farther back, although he couldn't see what kind of troops they sheltered. There were even berms between the lines of trenches, at the west end, as if the Bovarians expected a flanking maneuver of some sort.

The squad on the right side of the road had retreated and was more than a hundred yards north of the hill crest.

Quaeryt felt cold inside, even if he couldn't have said why.

He kept studying the Bovarian position, then the ground to the west of the road, mostly consisting of fields and small holdings, with cots and out-buildings scattered here and there. The side lane that he had just crossed was little more than a path, as were most of those many they'd passed over the last few glasses, and ran due west from the river road. After perhaps a half mille, it split, or joined another narrower road running north parallel to the river road. Farther back was a long narrow lake that stretched for a mille or more to the north, confirming Skarpa's skepticism about avoiding the Bovarians, although there was an area several hundred yards wide without defensive emplacements. Quaeryt shook his head. Getting there would still expose the Telaryn forces to musket fire.

Finally, he nodded. If he took Fifth Battalion along the side road, under a concealment shield, and then they followed the side roads, they could flank the musketeers. He'd have to be careful though because the land flattened some to the west of the road, and after some fifty yards whoever rode on the side road would be exposed to the Bovarians, not that such would be a great problem if he and the other imagers could maintain concealment shields. He kept studying the land, but the cots were shuttered, and no smoke rose anywhere.

Finally, he turned the mare and rode back to rejoin Skarpa. He began, "I think we can flank them . . ." and then went on to describe the terrain, the positions, and what he proposed.

"You'll need the entire battalion."

"I intend to take all the companies."

"We'll move up to just below the crest of the road and re-form into a wide front. We'll wait until you begin your attack. Then we'll follow up as quickly as we can . . ."

When Skarpa finished, Quaeryt moved back and gathered all the Fifth Battalion officers. Once they were all present, he cleared his throat. "We have Bovarian forces with musketeers in position directly over that low rise before us. Our task is to swing out to the west and then flank them. Lhandor, Khalis, you'll ride with me. Voltyr and Threkhyl, you'll accompany Major Calkoran. Shaelyt and Horan, you'll be with third company, and Desyrk, Smaethyl, and Baelthm will protect fourth company. Our first objective is to flank and then attack the musketeers. We'll move out under concealment shields . . ." Quaeryt went on to explain, then repeated his orders in Bovarian to make sure the Kellan officers fully understood, then added, in both languages, one after the other, "Because we don't know what else may be out there, I may have to take first company with me. If I move away from the attack on the musketeers, do not follow me. I repeat. Do not follow me. Your task is to take down the musketeers so that the regiments can advance without getting shot to pieces."

Thankfully, no one mentioned the possibility that Fifth Battalion also risked getting shot to pieces if matters went ill.

Another quint passed before Fifth Battalion, moving slowly so as not to raise dust that would linger after the riders and their concealment shields passed, moved westward on the side road, first on the section hidden from the Bovarians and then on the more exposed part of the narrow clay and dirt road. After Quaeryt had ridden several hundred yards, he realized that the road was not nearly so rutted as most of the side roads, and, in places, the locals had filled in areas and packed the dirt.

That bothered him, and he glanced to the north to determine whether the musketeers were moving or tracking the battalion, not that they should have been able to see through the concealment shield. He saw no movement there. Then he glanced back over his shoulder to check the battalion's progress. He'd hoped that the concealment shield would cover the battalion, but the road was so dry that Arion's last squads were trailed by the faintest signs of dust.

Let's just hope that the Bovarians don't see that.

Thwump! Thwump!

The entire road shook, and Quaeryt swallowed as he saw men and mounts from the middle of third company hurled southward.

Cannon! Frigging cannon. Those repairs in the road weren't from wear! They ranged the cannon and then concealed the impacts.

"Fifth Battalion! Off the road! Into the fields! On me!" Quaeryt image-projected the command back at the battalion, still holding the conceal-ment shields between the battalion and the Bovarians.

Thwump! Thwump! Cannon balls exploded everywhere, as Quaeryt rode north, aiming the mare between the rows of harvested crop stubble to-ward a point to the west of the berm that sheltered the Bovarian muske-teers facing the remainder of Skarpa's forces.

More cannon shots tore into the dirt road, now empty of Fifth Battal-ion troopers—except for those already dead, dying, or wounded. Unable to see who lay there because of the smoke and dust, Quaeryt could only hope that his failure to anticipate the cannon fire had not caused too many deaths.

Quaeryt turned the mare toward the first line of musketeers some of whom, he could see, were already trying to swivel their cumbersome weapons to the west, as if they knew that they faced an attack, while oth-ers were aiming at the oncoming troopers of Third Regiment. A moment later he saw that the westward-facing berms also had musketeers, and they were trying to sight their muskets, most likely based on the dust raised from the Telaryn mounts as they charged through the fields.

Namer-frigged mess!

He yanked his staff from the leathers and braced it against the front of the saddle, then at the last moment dropped the concealment and ex-panded his shields into an angled wedge, anchored to the mounts behind him, hoping that not too many of the musketeers behind the west-facing berms fired at once.

A muted roar sounded, and while he could feel impacts on his shields, they barely rocked him in the saddle as he leaned forward and extended his shields to the side as the mare jumped the berm. From the corners of his eyes, he saw musketeers and cadders crumple, and he turned north-ward again, angling toward the foot behind the second line of lower berms, not that he was that interested in them, but only because they protected the cannon emplacements farther back.

He had no doubts that Voltyr and Calkoran would continue against the musketeers, and that Shaelyt and Major Zhael—and what was left of third company—would as well.

The rearmost berms had to be those sheltering the cannon, but Quaeryt wasn't about to charge them directly. Instead he urged the mare toward the Bovarian foot berms, where, since he saw no pikes, he hoped to demoralize the foot and push them back.

Except . . . the space behind the berms was empty . . . or mostly so, with just a few foot troopers sprinting away from Quaeryt and first company.

Had the Bovarians dug trenches to create the impression of a larger force just to get at the imagers?

He still wasn't about to ride into the cannon. Instead . . . he imaged hundreds of tiny pieces of white-hot iron into the space behind each of the berms he could see. *Surely . . . some of them . . .*

That was as far as his thoughts went before thunder roared up around him and his shields shredded and squeezed him into darkness.

74

Quaeryt woke with someone sponging his face with a damp cloth. Where was he? He could smell dust, and blood, and sweat, but his eyes burned so much he could see almost nothing except a grayish haze. Then . . . a young face swam into view, leaning over him.

"Sir?"

Khalis . . . that's who it was.

Quaeryt tried to speak, but only a croak issued forth. Somehow, he managed to swallow, and then say, "I'm here . . . I think." His entire body felt sore, but . . . he slowly tried to move toes, fingers, hands . . . Everything felt as though it were still attached to him. He realized he was lying on something hard, the ground, most likely, except that there was a blanket under his head.

"Did I . . . get blown off . . . my horse?"

"Ah . . . yes, sir."

"How is she?"

"Better than you, I fear, sir."

That doesn't sound good at all.

His expression must have alarmed the young imager undercaptain, because Khalis quickly added, "I don't think you broke any bones. Your shields must have held until you and the mare hit the ground. You rolled clear. But . . . you have scrapes and gashes. You will have more bruises, I fear, sir."

Quaeryt struggled into a sitting position, but Khalis had to help him before he could drink any of the lager from his water bottle. That helped some, although he still found it hard to see, given the painful flashes across his eyes. "What time is it?"

"After fourth glass, sir."

"We prevailed?" *You hope.*

"Yes, sir."

How that had happened, Quaeryt had no idea. The Bovarians had set up the whole situation as a trap, a trap for imagers. The one thing none of the imagers could have withstood, even Quaeryt, was a cannonball against his shields. And there was no doubt that Kharst, or his commanders, knew that Skarpa's forces were protected by imagers who rode near the front. *No doubt at all.* The only question Quaeryt had was how the Bovarians knew. He also had an answer to the question of where the Bovarian cannon were—at least some of them.

"Sir?"

Quaeryt looked up at the second voice, one he recognized, belatedly, as that of Zhelan, who stood behind Khalis.

"I'm here. How bad was it?" Quaeryt had to squint to see Zhelan because his eyes were still mostly blinded by the darts of light that stabbed into them.

"Third company was hit the hardest," replied the major. "Most of Zhael's third squad was killed, and a few in fourth squad. Sixteen dead, five wounded. The wounded only got shallow cuts from rocks and pebbles blasted at them. The first and second squads weren't touched. Second company lost the last three men in fourth squad to cannon. All the others were killed or hurt once we attacked the musketeers. Thirty-one dead, twenty-three wounded, over the whole battalion."

Quaeryt shook his head slowly. Only fifty-four casualties out of that mess?

"Sir . . . we took most of the casualties for the entire force. The regiments only had forty men wounded, and not a single death."

Exactly what that bastard Deucalon wanted . . . and you obliged him.

Rather than say anything, Quaeryt nodded, then took another swallow of lager from the water bottle. Finally, he said, "We were very fortunate. I'm glad it wasn't worse."

"You were why it wasn't worse. You got everyone off the road quickly."

Not quickly enough. "I did what I could."

Zhelan straightened. "Here comes Commander Skarpa."

Just what you need now. Quaeryt did not try to stand, but waited as Skarpa dismounted and walked toward him.

"I see you're in one piece," offered the commander.

So far. But how long can you keep pressing your abilities as an imager? "How many cannon did they have?" Quaeryt asked before Skarpa could ask him more.

"Ten. We found pieces of ten, anyway."

"Just ten cannon . . . ten frigging cannon," Quaeryt muttered.

"It could have been much worse," replied Skarpa. "I don't see how you managed to incur so few casualties. After the first two shots, that entire lane went up almost at once."

"At the first shot . . . I realized how stupid I'd been."

"Stupid?"

"Stupid," said Quaeryt. "The road wasn't rutted enough. There were places where it had been repaired and packed down. The cannoneers had been practicing. They'd ranged the entire frigging road . . . They knew we were imagers and that they'd be firing blind."

Skarpa shook his head. "Do you know how many officers could have reacted that fast?"

"A really good officer would have seen those patches in the lane and known instantly," said Quaeryt

"How? We haven't seen any cannon at all . . . until now."

"No . . . but we've talked about it, wondered why there weren't any . . ."

"Stop second-guessing yourself. None of your officers even knew what was happening. You've trained them well enough that they didn't even hesitate, and they carried out your orders after you were out of the battle."

At least you did something right. But will you next time . . . or the time after that?

"How many Bovarians did you capture?" Quaeryt asked, almost as an afterthought.

"Maybe thirty."

"They must have had at least a battalion supporting the musketeers. Did the rest escape?"

"No. When they saw you and Fifth Battalion smash through, most of them dropped their weapons and fled. They were running past the cannon emplacements . . ."

"Oh . . ."

Skarpa nodded. "It was bloody. Your men saw you go down. They weren't exactly gentle with the survivors."

Quaeryt didn't know what to say.

"Undercaptain Lhandor told me that your shields saved most of first company, but they weren't happy about what it did to you. Neither were the Khellan officers and men."

For some reason, this time that didn't bother Quaeryt. It didn't even bother him that it didn't, although he suspected he'd feel guilty later. "Do you know how many Bovarians there were in position before . . . ?"

"Two battalions."

"Only two battalions. They were sent out just for us "

"That's likely. I don't like it either."

"We'll have to be more careful." Quaeryt paused. "We've stopped here for the night?"

"Maybe longer. I've sent a dispatch to the marshal. I reported that Fifth Battalion faced cannon fire and took the heaviest casualties of all my units. Then I asked if he wanted us to press on tomorrow."

"He will."

"That may be, but I'd wager we won't get a response until sometime in the morning."

Quaeryt nodded, but he had his doubts about that. Deucalon might lag with his forces, but he'd have no qualms about pushing Skarpa and Fifth Battalion.

"You need some food and rest."

That, Quaeryt didn't doubt.

75

Quaeryt was standing outside one of the temporarily abandoned cots west of the battle site before seventh glass on Solayi morning still thinking about the results of the cannon. *You've worried about trying to do too much with your imaging, but somehow it's always worked out. Can you count on that?*

He was still pondering that when Skarpa rode up and dismounted.

"How are you feeling this morning?" asked the commander.

"Sore. What else would you expect?" Sore was an understatement, since every movement hurt to some degree, and his chest which had almost felt healed, ached once more.

"A dispatch rider showed up about a quint ago. I thought you'd like to see what the marshal's orders are." Skarpa extended the sheet of heavy paper.

Quaeryt took it and began to read, skipping past the salutation and flowery first words.

> . . . Given the likelihood that favorable weather will not last, you are to press on with deliberate haste until you reach a favorable staging position for a final attack on Variana. Such a position should be no farther than a half day's travel from the city's edge unless you earlier encounter any defensive works too great for your forces to surmount without exorbitant cost . . .

Quaeryt handed the sheet back to Skarpa. "What cost is exorbitant? When you don't have enough troopers left to hold off the Bovarians before Deucalon can arrive?"

"Something like that."

"When should we be ready to ride out?"

"Well . . ." drawled Skarpa, "the orders say deliberate haste Say around ninth glass. By then I should have good scouting reports for the river road over the next ten milles. That's almost to the outskirts of Variana." He offered a crooked smile. "I told the scouts to look for places on the side roads with recent smoothing or repairs. Also for really deep ruts anywhere."

"Do you think we'll see more cannon before we reach Variana?"

"I'd not be surprised if there might be one or two that try to loft a shot or two into the front of the column." Skarpa shrugged. "Also wouldn't be surprised if there were none, and all that Kharst has could be waiting for us outside Variana."

"The maps don't show any bridges over the Aluse between Caluse and Variana."

"Might be because there aren't any. That also might be why Deucalon didn't have much choice in crossing the Aluse."

"Because Kharst wouldn't want us to take his chateau?"

"That . . . and most of the city is east of the River Aluse. So Deucalon would have to take the city first just to get to the bridges in order to reach the chateau. Also . . . once we take the chateau and defeat Kharst, the folk in the city will give Lord Bhayar less trouble. Makes sense."

"It also makes sense for us to soften things up for the marshal."

"That's what junior commanders and subcommanders do. Even when they're not imagers."

Quaeryt smiled wryly, accepting the modest rebuke. "We'll be ready by ninth glass."

"We likely won't see any Bovarians for a bit, but you never know." Skarpa nodded, slipped the order sheet back into his uniform, then returned to his horse and mounted.

As the commander rode off, Zhelan appeared. "Sir?"

"We're to be ready to ride by ninth glass."

"With all due respect, sir . . ."

"It's not the commander's decision, but the marshal's."

"Yes, sir."

The way in which Zhelan agreed suggested the major was less than impressed by Deucalon's orders.

By ninth glass, Quaeryt was still sore, but not quite so stiff when he mounted the mare, who seemed wholly untroubled or bruised. "You're hardier than I am."

"Sir?" asked Khalis, who'd had a tendency to hover around Quaeryt, and who was already mounted and waiting.

"Just telling my mare she was tougher than I am."

Khalis shook his head.

"She's fine. I'm the one who's sore."

"That's because you shielded her, sir. She knows that."

Quaeryt had his doubts about that, but only said, "She's been good to me." He wasn't looking forward to the day's ride, and he had the feeling many of the troopers likely weren't, either, especially those in third company.

Fifth Battalion led the column, and Skarpa rode beside Quaeryt under a hazy sky. Again, they saw no High Holdings anywhere near, and only two that might have been, in the distance to the west, down narrow lanes. Quaeryt couldn't help but wonder why there were so few. He would have thought there would be more nearer to Variana. Then again, maybe it was just that there weren't that many High Holdings. Even a thousand High Holders spread over a land the size of Bovaria would mean not that many all that close together.

So why were there so many more closer to Ferravyl? Because of the Naedaran influence and affluence in the past? Trade on the river? Quaeryt had no idea, only possibilities.

As the time neared third glass, Quaeryt noted that the sky had turned slightly darker with thin high gray clouds.

"It's a bit cooler," observed Skarpa in the early afternoon. "Might get more so."

"I'll take the heat if it means we don't get cold rain," replied Quaeryt.

At a quint past first glass, a scout galloped back toward Quaeryt and Skarpa and pulled in beside the commander. "Sir! There are repaired holes on the side of the road ahead, and it looks like some of the paving stones have been replaced."

Skarpa turned in the saddle. "Column! Halt!" Then he turned his attention to the scout. "How far ahead?"

"You see that pair of lowland pines on the right side of the road up there? Maybe a hundred yards past that . . . where that big lake and swamp begin, right west of the road. There are foot troopers on the flat farther along, but they're not dug in. Didn't see anything like cannon."

"What about repairs?" asked Skarpa. "Are they longwise, running the length of the road, or sideways?"

"More like an angle, sir."

Skarpa and Quaeryt studied the terrain. Farther west was a thickly forested area that seemed to stretch for milles, with but a single narrow dirt road angling south and then west from the small hamlet north of the swamp-fringed lake. The forest came to within a few hundred yards of the lake at the south end, and within a mille or so farther north, the trees were practically on the shore.

Quaeryt could also see that the narrow strip of land between the road and the river was low and open as well.

"What do you think?" asked Skarpa.

"The cannon have to be somewhere in front of the woods on the other side of south end of the lake," suggested Quaeryt. "Maybe just inside the trees."

"That would account for the angle of the gouges in the road that they repaired." The commander paused. "We couldn't ride through the road ahead or the land flanking it without taking a lot of casualties . . . if they have cannon."

"Then we'll have to see if they do and take their cannon. Once they're gone, dealing with whatever forces are waiting beyond the low rise there shouldn't be too great a problem."

Skarpa motioned the scout away, waited, then turned to Quaeryt. "Subcommander, I don't do this often, but I'm ordering you not to lead or participate in this mission. You need to recover. Lord Bhayar and I will need you even more when we reach Variana. You are to send whatever imager undercaptains necessary, but you are not to be anywhere near those cannon. Fifth Battalion will bring up the rear when we attack the Bovarian forces ahead. Is that clear?"

"Yes, sir."

"I will leave the details of how you plan and staff the imager operation to you. While you do, I'm going to inform the other subcommanders."

As Skarpa rode back along the column, Quaeryt considered, then sent for Major Arion and Shaelyt and Threkhyl.

Once the three officers arrived, Quaeryt explained, in Bovarian. "The Bovarians appear to have set up another cannon trap, and from what we can tell, they've ranged the guns to the road and the land on this side of the lake. The woods there are too extensive to send all the regiments that way."

"What do you need from us, sir?" asked Arion.

"I need fourth company to escort Undercaptain Shaelyt and Undercaptain Threkhyl close enough to where we believe the cannon are so that they can remove them. If the cannon aren't there, of course, you'll just return the way you came."

"We stand ready, sir," replied Arion.

"Good. Once I brief the undercaptains, they'll join you."

"Yes, sir."

After the major rode away, Quaeryt addressed the two undercaptains in Tellan. "Shaelyt, your duty is to shield the company with a concealment from the time you leave the river road until you can get close enough for Threkhyl to take out the cannon."

"Yes, sir."

"How am I supposed to do that?" demanded Threkhyl.

"The same way I did yesterday. You image hundreds of tiny pieces of white-hot iron into the area where the cannon are. You keep doing it until one of them hits the powder and everything starts to explode. You're a very strong imager, Undercaptain Threkhyl, and I have no doubts that you can do that."

"Yes, sir. Who's in command?"

"You're both under Major Arion's command, but Shaelyt is in charge of concealment, and you decide when and where to image against the cannon. Just don't get any closer than necessary. That's for your own protection. Now . . . go join Major Arion and fourth company."

Quaeryt watched as the two rode back past first company, then second. Skarpa returned shortly, and saw Quaeryt watching as fourth company prepared. "You have to send them out on their own."

"I've sent them out before."

"Not on anything like this, I'd wager."

Quaeryt knew the wager was rhetorical, but he didn't have to like it, much as he knew sending the undercaptains out without him near was something he'd have to do more and more—even if the battle for Variana happened the next day and Bhayar won. That would be part of what imagers supporting Bhayar would have to do. *You can't do everything yourself.*

"Subcommander, if you'd order your battalion off the road so the others can move up . . ."

"Yes, sir."

Once Fifth Battalion cleared the road, Quaeryt watched as fourth company vanished from sight. Then he waited . . . and waited.

Nothing seemed to happen. Shaelyt held the concealment. The Telaryn forces remaining in formation on the river road did not move, and neither did the Bovarians, suggesting that the defenders had far too few troopers to attack . . . and were there only to force the issue by not allowing the Telaryn troopers to gallop through the gap between the lake and the river single file and widely spaced.

Close to a glass passed. That worried Quaeryt. Shaelyt had never had to hold a concealment that long, but the young undercaptain apparently was managing, because neither Quaeryt nor Zhelan could catch sight of fourth company.

"There!" said Zhelan, even as Quaeryt saw a small flare of light in one spot before the forest, much farther north than Quaeryt had estimated.

The first point of light was followed by several others, and then by explosions and a roar like muted thunder as a section of forest some hundred yards wide disintegrated into broken trees and saplings, with smoke billowing up. Even as Quaeryt watched, flames began to lick what were likely dead trees or limbs.

From the front of the column came a horn signal, and Third Regiment moved out at a quick trot. In time, the last squad of Fifth Regiment began to ride northward.

A section of the forest was in full flames by the time Quaeryt nodded to Zhelan, and the major ordered, "Battalion! Forward!"

Quaeryt kept glancing across the lake, but he saw nothing except smoke everywhere.

Before that long, even Fifth Battalion had ridden north of the area that the cannon had ranged . . . and never fired at again. Quaeryt kept looking across the lake and to the south, but between the almost imperceptible slope and the smoke, he could make out nothing.

When they reached a point near the north end of the lake, east of where the Bovarian foot had been formed up, there were few signs of the Bovarians, only the troops of Third and Eleventh Regiments. Peering at the fields farther to the west, just at the edge of the forest, Quaeryt could see a handful of Bovarians sprinting toward the woods, pursued by Telaryn troopers. Those who reached the trees survived, because the Telaryn forces obeyed the orders not to break formation and did not enter the forest.

Since there was little either Fifth Regiment or Fifth Battalion could accomplish by entering an already one-sided fight that was almost over, Meinyt and Quaeryt held their men in the five-front formation on the road, ready to move as necessary.

Later, as Third and Eleventh Regiments re-formed, Quaeryt began to look for Arion and fourth company. Finally he saw riders appear on the river road behind them, riding slowly toward them. He realized that fourth company had likely had little choice, given the swampy ground around the lake, but to retrace their path back to the river road.

"Major," called Quaeryt, "I'm riding to the end of the battalion to meet fourth company. You're in charge if the commander has any orders." *Not that it's likely at the moment.*

When he reached the rear of Fifth Battalion, fourth company was still a good half mille away. Quaeryt forced himself to wait, although he eased the mare onto the west shoulder of the road, so that he could see what was happening to the west, what Zhelan might be doing, and still watch fourth company.

It was well past fifth glass when the riders were close enough for Quaeryt to see them clearly. Arion and a squad leader were at the front of the column. Behind the major rode two rankers, stirrup to stirrup with Threkhyl, his visor cap gone, the rankers clearly supporting him. Behind them was another ranker leading a mount with a body strapped across it. The body bore a green undress officer's shirt.

Quaeryt swallowed, then rode forward as Arion signaled for a halt.

"The mission was successful, sir," Arion reported, his voice somber.

Quaeryt glanced back along the company. He only saw a few empty saddles. "Thank you, Major." After a silence, he asked, "What happened to the imagers?"

Arion offered a sad smile. "I fear they were too successful, sir. There was more powder than we expected. After he fired the powder, Undercaptain Threkhyl created smoke to stop the few musketeers remaining. Then he collapsed, but he looks to recover. Your young undercaptain shielded us from the great explosion . . . until he could take no more. We tried to revive him. His body . . . it is red all over"

So much for setting an example or protecting others. "He was skilled and brave to the end." Too skilled and brave. Quaeryt's eyes were burning.

"Yes, sir."

"Thank you, Major." He paused. "The fighting here is almost over. We're awaiting orders." Then he turned the mare. It was best that no one saw the tears.

76

In the end, Skarpa ordered the regiments and Fifth Battalion to set up an encampment that took in the small hamlet near the battle, if it could even have been called that. Quaeryt did not seek out Skarpa, but made certain that Zhelan had Fifth Battalion well in hand . . . and that Threkhyl was only exhausted.

". . . be fine," mumbled the burly older ginger-beard before collapsing into a sleep that was as much unconsciousness as slumber.

After settling Threkhyl, Quaeryt gathered the remaining imager undercaptains and briefed them, quietly and quickly. All of them were somber, as if it had taken Shaelyt's death to make the point that even shielded imagers could die. Then Quaeryt walked out into the gathering twilight, standing alone, his eyes looking vaguely south in the direction of the lake he could not see because of a slight slope.

Khalis followed, saying nothing, standing well back.

Finally, Quaeryt turned. "Yes?"

"Sir . . . you would have gone, wouldn't you? Except the commander ordered you not to."

Quaeryt nodded.

"With all due respect, sir . . ."

Quaeryt almost grinned at the phrase usually used by squad leaders coming from the youngest Pharsi undercaptain, but just waited.

". . . he was right, sir. We can do much of what you can, but there isn't anyone to replace you."

"The commander made that point. He was right. I don't have to like it."

"Sir . . . there's something else. Something Shaelyt told me."

Again, Quaeryt waited.

"He . . . he said . . . that . . . if anything happened to you . . . there wouldn't be another lost one . . . not for generations . . . maybe not ever . . ."

"He told you that?"

"He told me and Lhandor. He made us promise . . . well . . . to do what we could, sir."

Wonderful . . . not only do you have to find a way to have Bhayar win against cannon and muskets . . . but you're being told that the hopes of the Pharsi ride on your shoulders. What in the Nameless's sake do you say to that?

"Shaelyt was a good man, a very good officer and imager, especially for one with so little experience. He may have thought I'm more than I am." *More than any man could possibly be.*

"Sir . . ."

"We all do what we can and what we must. I will do that, and I appreciate your loyalty and support. But . . . do not make me into more than I am. I've made mistakes, and I'll doubtless make them again, as will you and every other officer. We can only learn from our failures and strive to do better."

"Yes, sir." After a pause, Khalis added, "Thank you, sir. I think I'll check on Threkhyl."

In the late twilight, Quaeryt slowly walked back to the cot that held the battered imager, thinking. *Another handful or two of cannon . . . and one less imager . . . a good solid young man . . . and a bit more powder and Threkhyl might not have survived, either. You could have been killed the last time.* He shook his head. There had to be another, better way to deal with muskets and cannon. *And then there was also the risk associated with trying to gain even greater imaging abilities. At some point, will you just attempt too much?*

He had too few imagers, and cannon had been more of an encumbrance than useful in all the fighting in Telaryn's history. There might be a hundred cannon in all of Telaryn, and none of them particularly mobile or suited for land wars.

He was still pondering when Skarpa arrived. In fact, he only realized the commander was there when Skarpa spoke.

"I heard you lost Undercaptain Shaelyt. I'm sorry."

"Thank you." Quaeryt nodded. He didn't really want to say what he felt. "Undercaptain Threkhyl looks to recover, but he'll not be at any strength for a few days." *If not longer.*

"I had the engineers check things after the fires died down. There were more than twenty cannon there. They had enough of those explosive cannonballs to take out several regiments."

"They didn't have that many foot troops."

"No. Three battalions at most. You know what that suggests, don't you?"

"That they have plenty of cannon and that they're saving their troops for the invasion of Telaryn after they smash us at Variana?"

"I don't know it's that bad. It is a matter of concern. I'll be sending a dispatch to the marshal shortly. Is there anything you'd like to add?"

"You might make sure that your report mentions the death in action of imager Undercaptain Shaelyt, and the near-death of Undercaptain Threkhyl. I'm certain that the marshal and submarshal would wish to know that."

Skarpa stiffened, just slightly, for a moment before speaking in a softer voice. "I'm sorry, Quaeryt, but it could have been you, especially since you've not fully recovered. We need you more than we needed the under-captain, and there are times when good officers die, no matter how well we plan."

But there are so few imagers . . . so few . . . "You're right, sir, but he was one of the best and most talented."

"Only because you trained him and pushed him. Remember that." Skarpa turned. "Now get some rest. We'll be at the edge of Variana tomorrow . . . or fighting another skirmish to get there. There will likely be more cannon."

Is there any doubt? "We'll do what we can, sir."

"I know. You always do."

After Skarpa rode off, Quaeryt looked into the night sky, where Erion was nearly overhead, seeming redder than usual, although that might have been his state of mind. *So much for Erion favoring the lost ones of the Pharsi.*

He took a long slow deep breath, still looking in the direction of the lake he could not see, with the acrid scents of exploded powder and wood smoke burning his nostrils and his eyes. He wouldn't be able to sleep, not yet, not after brooding about Shaelyt. The young imager had shown such dedication, such promise, and then . . . he was gone, and not even in a major battle.

77

Even by seventh glass on Lundi morning, Skarpa had issued no orders to break camp and to proceed, and for a time Quaeryt wondered why . . . until he realized that they were most likely far less than ten milles from the outskirts of Variana. That was confirmed when he overheard one of the scouts saying that once over the rise to the north, there were cots and small holdings stretching to the north and west as far as the eye could see.

So he and Zhelan wrote up the papers dealing with the death of Shaelyt and the few others from fourth company who'd been killed. When Quaeryt finished signing them, he went outside the cot he'd taken and looked northward. The sky was still hazy with a few high thin clouds, and the faintest hint of a breeze out of the northeast.

He'd been standing there, thinking about Shaelyt, when a squad leader rode up and halted his mount.

"Subcommander, sir, the commander requests that all subcommanders join him outside the large cot with the hedge on the south side," said the squad leader, pointing. "That way, sir. It's about a hundred yards."

"Thank you."

"My pleasure, sir."

Once the trooper had ridden off, Quaeryt began to walk in the direction he had indicated. As he neared the next cot, he caught sight, if but for a moment, of a small gray cat in the calf-high grass at the side of the cot. Then it was gone, possibly under the dwelling.

Even the cats are wary of us.

As he neared the only cot with a hedge, Quaeryt saw Skarpa standing on the small square side porch, talking to his four battalion commanders and punctuating his words with quick sharp gestures. Rather than interrupt or distract Skarpa, Quaeryt stopped and eased close to a bush, one that he belatedly recognized as a black raspberry, although most of the berries had been long since picked.

He didn't have to wait long before the majors departed and he could approach Skarpa.

"Good morning, sir," offered Quaeryt as he walked up to the side porch.

"Good morning. I've just received the marshal's latest orders, but something else came with them. It's for you." Skarpa handed an envelope to Quaeryt as he stepped onto the porch.

"Thank you." Quaeryt took the envelope. Only his name was written on it, in a hand he didn't recognize, but he thought he felt another envelope inside. He thought about opening it, but then paused as he saw Khaern and Meinyt riding up. Instead, he tucked it inside his jacket.

Skarpa waited until the last two officers arrived. "We won't be riding out today, but I do want full-squad patrols sent out in all directions, even back along the river road. We're so close to Variana that the Bovarians could attack from any direction. The marshal has decided that we are to remain where we are for today, and perhaps tomorrow, when the main body will rejoin us. Then we will lead the advance on Variana. As some of you already know, we are less than five milles from the earthworks the Bovarians have thrown up just south of the city . . ."

"Aren't there any city walls?" asked Khaern.

"Why would there be? No one's ever attacked Variana. Until now."

"What about cannon?" asked Meinyt.

"There are emplacements that could hold cannon. Quite a number, but the scouts weren't able to approach close enough to determine the numbers. The earthworks run more than a mille, and there are two lines of them with the cannon emplacements on higher ground behind the second line."

"Could we flank them?"

Skarpa laughed. "Anything's possible, but the earthworks form an arc around Kharst's personal grounds and his chateau. The ground is hillier to the north, especially along the river, and there are earthworks there as well. There are also at least thirty regiments, from the regimental banners. I'd wager there will be more once Kharst confirms that all our forces are on this side of the river. Now, we need to talk about patrol schedules . . ."

Since Fifth Battalion wasn't included in the patrols, for which Quaeryt was grateful, he just listened as the other three discussed the schedule, which took another quint.

"That's all," concluded Skarpa. "I'll let you all know when I hear more from the scouts or from the marshal."

Once he had left Skarpa and had walked enough to be alone, Quaeryt opened the outer envelope to reveal a second one, addressed to him in Vaelora's handwriting. While Quaeryt could not tell, he suspected the outer envelope had most likely come from Bhayar, although there were no markings indicating that. Before he returned to Fifth Battalion to relay Skarpa's orders to Zhelan, the company officers, and the imager under-captains, Quaeryt quickly read through Vaelora's missive.

> My dearest,
> I have another letter from you, but it takes so long for them to reach me that I have no idea where you are or what has happened to you recently. I can but guess that you must be nearing Variana . . .

Good guess . . . or farsight? Either way, she was right.

> . . . and making ready for that which will change the present and the future of all Lydar, one way or the other, although I pray most fervently that the outcome is the one for which you have striven.
>
> I know nothing of matters military, nothing of arms, and who should attack what and how. Nor do I know about the glory of victory or the pain and suffering of defeat, although it seems to me that either engenders great suffering for both the one who is hailed as victor and the one who is derided and disgraced as the vanquished. I have also read and heard tales of those battles in which the outcome balanced on the blade of a knife, and for years thereafter resentments and rebellions simmered, much as what you witnessed in Tilbor. As in Tilbor, it would seem to me, frail woman that I am . . .

Frail? Hardly. Quaeryt almost snorted.

> . . . conquests that never end bleed both the victor and the vanquished until neither prospers, and that all would be better for a victory so absolute that none would dispute it for years. Such a victory, alas, is usually beyond the power of those who contend . . .

In short, if you have the opportunity don't hesitate to repeat what you did at Ferravyl.

> . . . Even when such a victory is within the victor's power, often he will offer ill-considered mercy before it is clear that the defeated is truly vanquished . . .

That might well have been the problem in Tilbor.

Quaeryt smiled bitterly. It was well that a battle did not appear likely at the moment. In the mood that possessed him, he scarcely felt anywhere close to merciful, but the warmer lines with which Vaelora concluded the letter did lift his spirits somewhat.

As Quaeryt neared the cot that had sheltered the imagers the night before, he slipped the letter into his jacket, then saw Khalis beside the door. "How's Threkhyl? Do you know?"

"He ate some this morning, sir. He has bruises. Not so bad as the worse you had, sir, I'd wager. I made some willow-bark tea for him. He complained, but it helped."

"Were you a healer or apprenticed to one?"

"My grandmere is. She taught me some things. The willow-bark tea is easy. I've set bones. That's harder. I wouldn't want to try that unless no one else could."

"Let's hope you don't have to." Quaeryt offered a smile, then stepped into the cot and the main room.

Threkhyl sat on an old straight-backed chair. He looked to Quaeryt but did not speak.

"I hear you're a bit sore," Quaeryt said.

"Don't think there's anything doesn't hurt . . ." mumbled the ginger-bearded undercaptain. "Tell me you've been bruised worse." The words were almost a challenge.

"I likely was, but I didn't feel anything for days. That was after what happened in Ferravyl."

"Oh . . . leastwise you weren't awake."

"No, but everything was yellow and purple when I did. Hopefully, it won't be that bad for you."

"Hope so." After a moment Threkhyl asked, "When do we have to ride out?"

"Not today. Probably not tomorrow. After that . . . it's up to the marshal."

"The Bovarians got more cannon at Variana?"

"Hundreds, it looks like."

"Frig," muttered Threkhyl.

Quaeryt agreed. "We'll just have to see what we can do."

"Rather not do that again. Wager you wouldn't, either, sir."

"No, I wouldn't, but we'll have to do what's necessary if we don't want Rex Kharst as our ruler."

"That bad?" asked Horan from where he stood at the side of the room.

"I'd expect he'll have forty regiments, if not more, and at least a thousand musketeers." Those were guesses, but Quaeryt would have wagered they were, if anything, low, given what he'd seen so far and what the scouts had reported. "That doesn't count the cannon."

"What if we just stand back away from the cannon?' asked Smaethyl. "They can't feed all those troopers forever."

"Neither can we," said Lhandor. "Can we, sir?"

"Food will be a problem for both sides, but if a stalemate lasts until late fall or winter, we'll likely fare worse."

"So we imagers have to find a way to defeat the Bovarians . . . is that it?" asked Threkhyl. "Even after all we've done already?"

Unless Deucalon or Skarpa can come up with a better plan.

"We'll just have to see." Quaeryt forced a grin he didn't feel. "We haven't done too badly so far."

Horan and Threkhyl exchanged looks, expressions that were more than slightly dubious.

Rather than say more, Quaeryt turned to Lhandor. "Would you see if you could find Major Zhelan?"

"Yes, sir."

"Thank you." Quaeryt nodded and slipped back outside the cot behind Lhandor.

He needed to think. Threkhyl was right, in a way. What he'd been doing with his imaging wasn't likely to be enough. At Ferravyl . . . and even at Extela, he'd been able to use some source of heat—hot rain and hot lava—to increase the power of his imaging.

Could you have used the heat of exploding powder? He shook his head. By the time there was enough heat, his shields had already taken too much punishment. *What about water?* Even cold water had to have some heat because it got even colder when it froze . . . and the battle site wasn't that far from the River Aluse.

He nodded slowly. He'd have to try things out, but he could walk to the lake south of the encampment and see what might be possible.

"Sir!"

Quaeryt looked up to see Lhandor hurrying back.

"The major will be right with you."

"Thank you." First, he'd have to brief Zhelan and then finish letting the imager captains know. Then . . . maybe after that he could find time to work on a more reliable way of putting greater strength into his imaging.

He shook his head, thinking about the Naedarans and their "old ones." More power was dangerous to everyone. *Is that why you've been leery of trying greater and greater imaging? Or just a certain amount of fear that it might be that extra effort that kills you?*

Yet . . . what choice did he have but to try?

78

Lundi came and went with no word from the marshal. That gave Quaeryt time to walk to the lake to try new imaging techniques, but his progress was slow, especially with the time spent trying to improve techniques among all the imagers.

Finally, on Mardi, late in the day, well after the fourth glass of the afternoon, Skarpa received a dispatch announcing that Lord Bhayar and the marshal's forces would arrive by midday on Meredi. Even so it was more like the first glass of Meredi afternoon when the vanguard neared the encampment. By third glass, troopers and horses were everywhere, and the hamlet had been transformed into a welter of tents, wagons, and men that seemed to stretch for a mille to the north and from the forest to the river road.

All commanders and subcommanders were summoned to a briefing at sixth glass, on a knoll on the lake's east side. Quaeryt had assumed that the briefing would be outside because there were no cots or outbuildings in the hamlet that could hold the more than thirty senior officers summoned by the marshal. When he and Skarpa arrived, followed by Meinyt and Khaern, all four having walked close to half a mille, Quaeryt discovered a tent some ten yards by ten had been erected. Once inside, Quaeryt saw a low platform at one end, and ten commanders and a few subcommanders waiting before the platform. The only officer who looked in their direction was Commander Pulaskyr, but he'd known Skarpa and Quaeryt in Tilbor.

"They didn't provide you with a tent like this," murmured Quaeryt to Skarpa.

"No tent at all," said Meinyt.

"Wouldn't know what to do with it," said Skarpa, with a short laugh.

Another group of commanders entered the tent through a flap beside the platform. With them was Submarshal Myskyl. He did not so much as glance in Quaeryt's direction.

A burly major stepped onto the platform and announced, "Marshal Deucalon!"

The officers had barely stiffened when Deucalon appeared on the raised platform and said, "As you were," his voice filling the tent, seemingly without effort on his part. "Good evening. You've traveled hundreds of milles. You've fought and won battles all along the way. None of those victories will mean anything if we don't defeat the Bovarians here. We can do this, but it won't be easy. Not at all." Deucalon surveyed the officers in the dim light of the tent.

"The Bovarians have assembled the largest army in the history of Lydar. The largest, but not the best. You're the best. Commander Skarpa's scouts have provided very thorough reports. So have the scouts we have dispatched to reconnoiter Bovarian positions on both sides of the river. We believe that by tomorrow and certainly by Vendrei, Kharst's commanders will have more than forty regiments in position between us and Kharst's chateau. Half are foot . . ."

While we have maybe five regiments of foot troopers, thought Quaeryt, *and who knows how good they are?*

"We cannot determine with certainty the exact number of musketeers," the marshal continued, "but it appears that there are the equivalent of two regiments. These are in addition to the more than two regiments of musketeers already destroyed by Commander Skarpa's forces. The number of cannon is unknown, but the emplacements the scouts have seen could hold between fifty and a hundred . . ."

Enough to destroy all of our imagers, thought Quaeryt.

". . . Kharst has left at least three regiments, if not more, guarding the east river road into Variana. It is possible that more Bovarian regiments will arrive, but that appears unlikely for a number of reasons I will not address at the moment. At the very least, our arrival has forced Rex Kharst to tear up his rather large hunting park and private grounds to dig trenches and throw up earthworks . . ." Deucalon smiled, and murmurs of low laughter ran through the tent.

It also suggests that he's confident enough that he believes he can defeat us easily and wants to be able to chase down survivors, reflected Quaeryt, *which he couldn't do if his troops were actually inside the city or even within his chateau.*

". . . the comparative openness of the terrain will allow us greater opportunity to maneuver at will and to concentrate our forces as necessary as well as to move quickly enough that we do not suffer significant casualties from cannon fire . . ."

Deucalon continued to talk in generalities for almost another quint before he finally said, "Please convey this to your battalion and company officers. Unless matters change suddenly, there will be another briefing for all of you, here, tomorrow evening at the same time." Deucalon stepped back, and a major Quaeryt did not recognize stepped forward.

"That is all, sirs."

By the time the major had delivered those few words, the marshal had vanished from the tent. In moments, Myskyl and the commanders around him were also gone.

Skarpa said nothing until he and his three subcommanders were well away from the briefing tent. Then he looked to Quaeryt. "What do you think?"

"He didn't mention who will lead the attack."

"He didn't, did he?" Skarpa smiled sardonically. "What do you think that means?"

"That we will," growled Meinyt from behind Quaeryt. "He's not saying because he doesn't want anyone to notice that we keep getting thrown into the fire."

"Or that he doesn't want the Bovarians to know," suggested Quaeryt.

"How would that . . ." Meinyt stopped abruptly. "You don't think . . . ?"

"I don't know what to think, except it's more than a little unusual that our forces are much smaller and yet the only musket and cannon attacks have been against us."

"Even Myskyl wouldn't do that," Meinyt admitted.

"Exactly," said Skarpa. "I count any of the senior officers would, either, but with over a hundred majors . . . the marshal might not want to say anything yet. He didn't tell us anything that the Bovarians wouldn't already know."

"I didn't see Lord Bhayar," said Khaern.

"He doesn't usually attend briefings," said Skarpa. "He gets briefed first."

"Why is Lord Bhayar even here?" asked Khaern abruptly. "If the marshal is making the decisions . . . ?"

Skarpa looked to Quaeryt and smiled. "You might explain that best."

"It was his decision to attack Bovaria when we did. He'll be the one executed if Kharst wins. His family will be destroyed. And . . . he was trained by his father to make those kinds of decisions. He can and will override the marshal if he thinks it necessary."

"And . . . if you think so . . . ?" pressed Khaern.

"I can occasionally tell him what I think. He still decides," replied Quaeryt dryly. "That's why I'm a subcommander and not on his staff or the marshal's."

"It's also why you're married to his sister," said Skarpa. "He didn't give you any choice there, either."

"You're . . . married to Lord Bhayar's sister?" asked Khaern. "And he put you where you'd be leading charges?"

Belatedly, Quaeryt realized that he'd never mentioned Vaelora to anyone outside Fifth Battalion except Skarpa and Meinyt, and it was clear that neither of them had told Khaern. "Why not? He'll be where he can be killed when we meet the Bovarians." That wasn't quite true, because Bhayar would be farther from the action than Quaeryt would be, but Quaeryt had no doubts that Bhayar would not survive if the Telaryn forces were routed. "His father sent him as a ranker to Tilbor during the fighting there, and his grandsire sent his father into battle as well."

"No other rulers in Lydar do that," Khaern said.

"No other rulers are descended from Yaran warlords." Quaeryt's words were dry.

"Do you think we'll attack on Vendrei?" asked Meinyt.

"It won't be tomorrow," replied Skarpa. "That's about all we know."

With Deucalon advising Bhayar, Skarpa was absolutely right, Quaeryt reflected.

The four kept walking, with Erion slowly rising in the east behind them, Artiema almost ready to set in the west, even before the sun.

79

Almost exactly at the second glass of the afternoon on Jeudi, Quaeryt was standing at the north end of the lake that formed the southern end of the Telaryn encampment, still trying to improve his imaging by trying to draw heat from the lake water or, later, from a river, rather than from the rain that wasn't likely to arrive when he needed it.

The first step had been easy enough. He'd managed that two days earlier. He'd just imaged a tiny stone tower, no more than the length of his middle finger, into being at the edge of the water, drawing heat from the surrounding water. A thin film of ice extended little more than two fingertips from the stone tower. The second step was to image the little tower out of existence while drawing heat from the water. That had taken him almost two days of intermittent effort to work out. Destroying the tiny tower hadn't been hard at all, but finding a way to obtain the strength to do the imaging from the water had been the hard part. Once he'd mastered the technique, it was actually less tiring, he could tell, even on that small a scale, than imaging without seeking sources of heat.

Of course, it wouldn't work all that well in the winter. Or if there isn't a lake or a big river nearby.

"Subcommander, sir!"

He turned to see Lhandor riding toward him, leading Quaeryt's mare. Riding beside the young Pharsi officer was another undercaptain Quaeryt did not recognize.

"Sir, Lord Bhayar would like to see you," said the undercaptain. "I'm to escort you, but Undercaptain Lhandor may certainly accompany you."

"Good," said Quaeryt, taking the mare's reins from Lhandor and mounting.

The undercaptain led the way around the northeast side of the lake, past the large briefing tent and then into an encampment surrounding a second tent barely smaller than the briefing tent. He reined up before the squad of troopers stationed in front of and around the tent.

A major, another officer Quaeryt had not met, stepped forward as Quaeryt dismounted. "Lord Bhayar awaits you, Subcommander."

"Thank you."

One of the troopers lifted the tent flap for Quaeryt, then dropped it behind him.

Inside, the tent was partitioned into two sections, one containing a camp bed and a chest, and no one. Quaeryt pushed aside the flap to the other side. Bhayar rose from a small desk, the kind that could be folded into a flat oblong to fit in a wagon. The wooden stool on which he had been seated had a thin cushion that fell to the plain gray carpet that covered the ground as Bhayar rose. Hangings ran from the tent ridge poles to the carpet, enclosing the area around Bhayar and the desk. A small noisy burbling fountain, clearly fed from a tank set on stakes, stood in one corner. The space felt confining, close, and Quaeryt couldn't help but frown when his eyes lighted on the fountain.

Bhayar laughed. "The hangings and the fountain make it hard to overhear what is said here . . . if one speaks quietly and not at a great distance from me."

"What might I do for you?" asked Quaeryt.

"Kharst has twice the troops we do, not to mention muskets and cannon," said Bhayar mildly, adding, "And while there are high clouds, there do not appear to be any heavy rainstorms in sight. I understand you also lost one of your imager undercaptains."

"Undercaptain Shaelyt. He was one of the most promising."

"How did that come about?"

"I was injured in the first cannon attack last Samedi, and we ran into evidence of another cannon emplacement on Solayi . . ." Quaeryt went on to explain what happened.

"Skarpa was right," said Bhayar. "You are not indestructible, Quaeryt."

"I know that."

"There are times when you have to let others die, and you will again."

Quaeryt knew that as well, but he only nodded.

"You have lost two out of ten, or eleven if you count yourself. You must find a way to prevail, Quaeryt, one that preserves most of our forces and few of theirs."

"And if I do?"

"Then I can claim that the valiant efforts of the imagers who sacrificed much made it possible . . . and you will have what you want for imagers."

"If my plans meet your approval. And if you prevail . . . as a result of our efforts, but—"

"Do not mention such." Bhayar paused, then added, "A debt is still a debt." After yet another pause, he asked, "Do you have any plan that might work? Better than charging cannon and exploding the powder?"

"There is one possibility," Quaeryt conceded, "but it can succeed only if you do not reveal all of it. And if Kharst has no imagers to counter us."

"It appears he has few, or so we have been led to believe, and they remain far from him and close to his commanders. He distrusts them."

That's not exactly surprising, given what we've seen of how he handles High Holders. "You might think about this, sir. So far as I can determine, cannon and muskets are by far the most effective weapons against imagers. All imagers were on the south side of the River Aluse. So were all cannon and musket attacks, even though the forces on the north side of the river, until you reached Caluse, far outnumbered those on the south side."

Bhayar frowned. "I had not heard that."

"It is true, so far as Commander Skarpa has been able to ascertain. That is why I would ask that you not tell anyone all of what we are about to discuss."

"I must be the judge of that."

"Of course. But our lives and what we can do are then in your hands."

"Tell me."

Quaeryt did, beginning with those strengths and limitations of imaging that might apply to the attack on Kharst's forces.

When he had finished, Bhayar asked, "Will this work? How much will it harm our forces?"

"I believe it is workable. It is also dangerous. Any great imaging is, even when it goes exactly as planned. *And you have no idea whether this will.*"

"I fear we must risk it."

"Are you certain that most of Kharst's troops are surrounding his chateau or near the defensive earthworks?"

"They appear to be, but one can be certain of nothing in war. You should have learned that by now."

"I have, but it is best to start from what is known."

Bhayar began to point out positions on the map that lay on the small writing desk.

A quint later, Quaeryt left the tent.

Lhandor was still waiting.

Neither spoke until they had left Bhayar's encampment.

"Can you tell me anything of what Lord Bhayar said?" asked Lhandor, riding closely beside Quaeryt.

"Very little," replied Quaeryt. "He wants us to be careful that we do not waste our abilities on matters that will not count in affecting the result of the battle . . . and the war."

"He told you not to hesitate in sacrificing us if it would preserve you, did he not?"

"No. He said that none of us were to waste ourselves."

"I fear I did not say what I meant. I meant that you must be preserved to do what only you can."

"Have you been talking to Khalis, Lhandor?" Quaeryt's tone was skeptically sardonic.

"About what, sir? We often talk."

"Never mind." Quaeryt shook his head. "When we get back to the encampment, you need to gather the imager undercaptains and Major Zhelan."

"Yes, sir!"

Don't be so frigging enthusiastic, for the Nameless's sake. Quaeryt was all too aware that what he planned could kill all of them if he didn't do it perfectly . . . and might well, anyway.

80

Interestingly enough, at least to Quaeryt, was the fact Deucalon canceled without explanation the Jeudi evening briefing for senior officers, which had been scheduled for sixth glass. Even more interesting was the order waking the entire combined armies at fifth glass on Vendrei morning and ordering the advance on Variana to begin at sixth glass. Most interesting of all was the envelope sealed with Bhayar's personal signet that the unnamed undercaptain delivered to Quaeryt at a quint past fifth glass Vendrei morning.

"You're to open this, sir, read it, but not to tell me what it says, and then acknowledge that you have read it and will comply."

Quaeryt studied the seal, then broke it, opened the envelope, and extracted the single sheet of heavy paper. The message was simple enough.

> Proceed as we discussed. Use your own judgment as to timing and positioning after the assault begins. Fifth Battalion will be initially placed to the east of the center of the attack, directly behind another regiment of Commander Skarpa's choosing. You are not to lead any charges.

Behind another regiment of Skarpa's choosing?
Beneath the words was the single initial "B."

Quaeryt folded the sheet and replaced it in the envelope, then looked up. "You can convey that I've read the message, that I understand it, and will comply." *To the best of my ability and that of the imagers.*

"Thank you, sir."

Once he'd seen the undercaptain off, Quaeryt gathered the imagers inside the cot. "It appears we'll be attacking Variana today. It also appears that we will not be in the van, but slightly back. Once we move into position, we will assume a five-front formation, with Undercaptains Voltyr, Threkhyl, Lhandor, and Khalis flanking me, and Horan, Smaethyl, Baelthm, and Desyrk in the line behind us. First company will be directly behind us, and if necessary the other battalion companies may flank us . . ."

After finishing his briefing and ordering the imagers to make ready to mount up, Quaeryt then summoned and addressed the company officers. "We're being ordered to attack Kharst's defenses and his chateau at Variana. It's called Chateau Regis, if anyone cares to know. Fifth Battalion will initially follow whatever regiment Commander Skarpa chooses, and we will be to the right of the center of the main thrust. First company will lead . . . with all imagers flanking or directly behind me . . . I have direct orders from Lord Bhayar to take independent action at any time I see fit . . ." When he finished, he asked, "Are there any questions?"

"Begging your pardon, sir," offered Zhelan, "but we're going to ride straight into the muskets and cannon of the Bovarians?"

"We likely won't, but some of the marshal's regiments will."

"Sir . . . ? Behind another regiment?"

"The Bovarians have muskets and cannon, as you've just pointed out. They know we've almost always led. If we're in front, the imagers will spend all their imaging shielding, and none will be able to do any damage to the Bovarians. Whatever regiment leads us is Commander Skarpa's decision. That's up to him. We need to get as many of the Bovarians as close together as possible. Picking off isolated units doesn't work very well when there are likely to be more troops in any of their isolated units than we have in three regiments."

"That's so you can do something with the imagers?"

"That's the idea." *Whether it will work that way is another question.* It should, Quaeryt thought. He'd tested all the aspects of it on a small scale. *A much smaller scale.* "Remember, keep your men from doing anything stupid. Even after this battle there are bound to be other battles, and we'll need every man until this war is over."

"Yes, sir."

Then Quaeryt left the company officers to Zhelan and went to see to his own preparations. As he mentally reviewed what he planned, another thought came to him. *You should have written one more letter to Vaelora.*

He shook his head with a rueful smile. *That's too fatalistic.* And yet, while he knew that thought might nag him, all he could do was push it away as he continued with his preparations.

Less than a quint later, as the regiments were forming, before Quaeryt had mounted, Skarpa rode up, not dismounting, but motioning for Quaeryt to join him well away from the others.

In the gray light before dawn, Quaeryt did so. "Yes, sir?"

"Once we assemble for the attack on Kharst's defenses, we'll form the second prong of the attack to the right of the main thrust—which the submarshal will direct. I've been ordered to place Fifth Battalion behind another regiment, and I've chosen Eleventh Regiment, but to allow you full freedom of movement. No one mentioned Fifth Battalion in the order of movement, and I was told not to tell anyone. Fifth Battalion is not even in the written orders of battle. That was your doing?"

"Yes, sir. Well . . . it was my request. That was to keep—"

"I know. It won't keep them from finding out. It will just take longer."

"That was the idea." *And it will also likely mean that some of the regiments in front will get pounded by cannon fire.* Unhappily Quaeryt knew why Skarpa had chosen Eleventh Regiment, and Skarpa knew that Quaeryt knew or would figure it out.

"Will whatever you plan work?"

"Yes, sir. I just don't know if it will work well enough."

"And if it doesn't work, it will be an even bloodier day?'

"Yes, sir." *As it will if it does.*

Skarpa nodded. "You've got less than three quints to have Fifth Battalion in formation, ready to ride."

"We'll be there."

Fifth Battalion was mounted in formation, if only half a quint before the glass. Quaeryt and Zhelan weren't about to rush matters on what would be a too-long day.

At what was likely sixth glass, from well ahead of Fifth Battalion came the horn signals, but almost a quint passed before the last company in Eleventh Regiment began to move, and Fifth Battalion followed those troopers across the fields and onto the gray stone road toward Variana.

Quaeryt listened, almost absently, as he rode northward on the gray stone road.

". . . subcommander hasn't said much . . ."

". . . never does before a fight . . ."

". . . good . . . waste of breath . . . what will be will be . . ."

Unless you can change it, reflected Quaeryt.

As they passed more shuttered and abandoned cots along the river road, spaced ever more closely together as they neared the south of Variana, the already few comments died away, possibly because of Quaeryt's palpable reserve.

The sun, struggling to break through the thin gray clouds that had been almost constant for the past several days, was barely visible above the rooftops of Variana on the east side of the River Aluse by the time the Telaryn forces were in position, almost a mille back from the first line of earth-works. The air was cool, but not chill, and still, without the slightest breeze.

Quaeryt surveyed the terrain as best he could, from the grass that had not so long before been cut, to the few perfectly placed trees and the lack of tenant cots that showed the fact that the area had indeed been a hunt-ing park. Then he studied the Bovarian positions. While it was obvious that the defensive emplacements were fully manned, and primarily by men with pikes behind the first line of earthworks, Quaeryt noted that the top of the second line of earthworks was all exactly the same height, as if it had been measured with a spirit level.

Why would that be? Then he nodded. That was where the muskets were, high enough to fire over the first defenders, and low enough to rake the attackers on the level ground before the earthworks—as well as whatever imagers were riding in the fore. He could also see that Deucalon had rec-ognized that also, because, behind the first line of regiments, the other regiments were being moved slightly, enough so that they could charge to the sides once the attack began in earnest.

Even so, Quaeryt could also see that huge numbers of Bovarian troops remained farther up the slope, presumably so that they could move down to wherever the lines were threatened, or to take the offensive in any place where the Telaryn attack showed vulnerability. In one place, their gray-blue uniforms almost seemed to blend into the light gray stone of the top of the Chateau Regis, a good mille to the north.

What he had planned would likely not work, or not work well, unless more of the Bovarians could be drawn farther downhill, nearer the initial fray. Quaeryt didn't like what that would cost in Telaryn casualties, but it might be that he could use some targeted imaging to make the Bovarian commanders commit more troopers earlier.

In one respect, the entire battle was almost senseless, since neither side actually had to fight at the present time and place. Certainly losing Kharst's chateau would not have been that great a loss for the rex, and Bhayar could have moved his troops around the massed Bovarians to take lands and wait for greater advantage. In another respect, it was absolutely necessary. Kharst couldn't afford to leave more than twenty Telaryn regiments intact and op-erational in the middle of Bovaria, while Bhayar needed a decisive and ab-solute victory well before mid-fall in order to consolidate his position and gain control of the midsection of Bovaria—at the very least—before the onset of late fall and winter.

But then, Quaeryt reflected, *similar rationales have been the reason for most large* battles in history. He glanced to one side, then the other. The two Pharsi undercaptains were on his right, with Voltyr and Threkhyl on his left.

". . . when they going to do something?" muttered Threkhyl under his breath.

"Soon enough," replied Voltyr curtly, if in a low voice.

Quaeryt forced himself to wait. Doing anything too early would ruin his plans. *And so would doing what was necessary too late.*

Another quint passed . . . and still none of the Telaryn forces moved.

The horns sounded again, and the first Telaryn regiments began to move forward, slowly, giving themselves the chance to move quickly when necessary or to mitigate the effect of musket fire.

Quaeryt expected some cannon fire from the Bovarians almost immediately, but the morning was quiet, with only the sound of the horns and the drumming of hooves.

No cannon yet? Or muskets? Caution over powder? Or premeasured and ranged target points?

Quaeryt looked northward once more. The whitish gray walls of the Chateau Regis rose above everything, unsurprisingly, since it was a tall oblong structure with its longest sides running north and south located on the highest hill west of the River Aluse . . . more than a mille from the river and directly west of the single isle in the middle of the river, an isle used mainly by factors for warehouses, and piers for barges and flatboats, at least by its appearance and the weathered look of the structures.

Waste of a perfectly good isle, thought Quaeryt absently. Then he concentrated on what was beginning to happen before him . . . and what was not. The first line of defenders extended pikes, or more likely braced them against the rear of the narrow trenches in which they waited so that the first earthworks bristled.

Then Quaeryt watched as the last ranks of Eleventh Regiment's fourth company began to move forward.

He could only estimate how far the leading squads of Eleventh Regiment had gone when the initial volley of musket shots ripped into the troopers of Khaern's first company. A second volley did not follow immediately, but Quaeryt could see that one of the spindly catapults behind the musketeers composing the second line of defenders began to arch, as if being winched back to release something. With no doubts as to what that might be, Quaeryt imaged away the smallest chunk of ropelike cable.

The catapult buckled, and whatever was in the sling or bucket tumbled backward and dropped just behind the catapult frame. The Antiagon Fire flared up from the earthworks that held the catapult. Quaeryt could not hear, but could imagine, the screams of men being consumed by living fire of crimson-green and yellow.

He looked to the Bovarian reinforcements, but unsurprisingly none of them had moved from their reserve positions higher on the low slope.

The sound of another volley of musket shots echoed back toward Quaeryt, but the smoke indicated that it had been aimed from defenders well away from Eleventh Regiment and opposite the western side of the Telaryn forces, at some of the marshal's regiments who were advancing more slowly than was Eleventh Regiment. *Everything he does is slower . . . but it won't help him that much today.*

Quaeryt looked to a second catapult, but it wasn't moving. He concentrated on imaging several tiny pieces of white iron into a space where he thought the Antiagon Fire canisters might be . . . but nothing happened. He decided against trying again, because trying to replicate his success with the first catapult through blind imaging could easily wear him out before the Bovarians reacted in the way he needed. And then he would need all the strength he could muster . . . and more.

He didn't want to think about the "more" part yet.

Another volley of musket fire ripped into Eleventh Regiment, and troopers went down, and horses screamed.

Then a rolling rumble echoed out of the north. For a moment Quaeryt thought it must have been thunder, but a quick glance skyward confirmed that the moderately high gray clouds were not that dark, and that there were no lightning flashes.

Gouts of dirt, turf, stones, and who knew what else erupted into the air less than a hundred yards in front of Eleventh Regiment's first company.

As he kept riding, Quaeryt tried to judge the distance between the first riders of Eleventh Regiment and the earthworks ahead. "Imager Horan, forward! Beside me."

Horan rode forward. "Sir?"

"Do you see the earthworks directly before Eleventh Regiment?"

"Yes, sir."

"I need you to image them flat, as wide a section as you can without exhausting yourself. Just push the dirt and fill back over the defenders." Quaeryt lurched in the saddle as the mare rode over something uneven, then caught himself.

"Now, sir?"

"Now. That's so that Eleventh Regiment can gallop through and put a break in the defenses." *And so that the cannoneers won't be able to fire there without hitting the defenders who will rush to fill the breach.* "Threkhyl! Can you do the same for the earthworks directly behind the one Horan is targeting?"

"Yes, sir!"

In moments, there was a space some fifty yards wide where there had been an earthen barrier, and some fifty yards behind that and several yards higher was an even wider area of flattened earth.

Quaeryt glanced at Horan, whose face had paled, and at Threkhyl, whose face had not, then back at the Bovarians. For a moment all action seemed to stop on the low slope that held the Bovarians.

Then Khaern reacted immediately, putting Eleventh Regiment into a full gallop toward the gap in the Bovarian lines.

Unfortunately, within several moments, the Bovarian cannoneers reacted as well, and cannonballs tore into the midst of the charging troopers.

Quaeryt began to smell the acrid odor of powder, as well as the dryness of dust thrown into the air by the impacts of the cannonballs. Ignoring the bitterness in his nostrils, he turned to his left. "Voltyr . . . can you image a spray of white-hot iron fragments into the cannon emplacement directly up the slope from us?"

"Yes, sir."

In moments a series of small explosions crescendced into a large roar, and the ground shook. Then white and black smoke rose from the emplacement and began to drift slowly downhill and then across the Bovarian earthworks.

"I can do another, sir!" called Voltyr.

"Do it, then! But just one more."

A second cannon emplacement went up in a roar

Quaeryt glanced across to the west side of the battlefield, finally standing in the stirrups before he saw another series of musket volleys rip into Deucalon's forces, this time at the middle of the assault. Still standing in the stirrups and knowing that he was making himself a target, he scanned the earthworks and the slope, trying to see the damage and the gaps in the defenses.

There were a few gaps here and there, but what were a few hundred yards at most across a mille of defenders?

Yet the Bovarian reserves remained planted on the upper slope.

"Voltyr! Can you take out a cannon emplacement to the left of the last one?" Quaeryt hoped that the smoke from such an explosion would create an impression among the Bovarian commanders of more damage to the defenses than was actually the case.

"Yes, sir!"

Quaeryt caught sight of a third catapult being winched back. "Smaethyl! The catapult to the right of the breach ahead! Take it down! Now!"

"Yes, sir!"

Quaeryt could barely hear the response, but he did, and he watched as the catapult bent forward in its release—and the cable snapped and released the canister almost straight up. The dark object went upward end over end and then came down forward of the emplacement, spewing Antiagon Fire largely in front of the earthworks.

At least it didn't land in the middle of eleventh company.

"Subcommander! Down, sir!" That was Zhelan's voice.

Quaeryt dropped back into his saddle. Instants later he heard and half felt a volley of musket balls pass overhead.

More cannonballs ripped into the rear of Eleventh Regiment, less than twenty yards ahead of Fifth Battalion, with more acrid smoke drifting toward Quaeryt and Fifth Battalion, but the first companies of the regiment had reached the gap in the defenses and were cutting down the defenders who were trying to fill the gap.

As more of Eleventh Regiment surged forward into the gap, finally a mass of Bovarian reinforcements began to hurry down from their reserve positions toward the attacking Telaryn troopers.

Despite heavy musket fire from the west side of the defensive emplacements, one of Deucalon's regiments had broken through as well.

Yet more and more troops, mostly foot, poured over the hill and down toward the advancing Telaryn forces, a mass that had to outnumber the attackers by twice . . . if not three times—and Quaeryt had no idea how many more might be held in reserve.

Not only that, but he could see that he and Fifth Battalion, despite his efforts to keep some space, were so hemmed in by the other regiments that they had nowhere to go except continuing forward into the cannon fire.

Another gout of soil, grasses, and far worse erupted just ahead and to Quaeryt's left.

Like it or not . . .

You can't wait any longer. You can't!

Quaeryt did not even attempt to draw in the other imagers . . . but instead reached out to the River Aluse, and then across the entire hillside before him, seeking any source of heat possible . . .

Lines of heat and cold crisscrossed over him and through him, but he continued to concentrate on three things—seeking heat, flattening and destroying everything in front of the Telaryn forces, and, just to be sure, imaging a coating of impenetrable white alabaster across every exterior surface of the Chateau Regis—the last, because he wasn't quite certain that what he was doing would work without at least some constructive imaging. At the same time, he concentrated on holding links to the river, and to the warmth of thousands of bodies of poor hapless Bovarian troopers and officers, and even to all those within the Chateau Regis, for they too would pay . . . as would Quaeryt.

Of that, he had no doubt, even before the last links of his imaging all came together, and he felt himself frozen in place in the saddle, both moving and motionless, as if time itself had solidified into a solid block of ice around him, yet from nowhere he could feel the needles of ice being jabbed into him by winds that, using those ice needles, were scouring everything before them, leaving nothing standing anywhere, no trees, no bushes, no cannon, no catapults, no Bovarians, no earthworks . . . nothing . . .

Nothing except the wailing and pleading of those whose warmth he had seized, whose voiceless voices screamed in the white darkness . . .

And blinding bitter white wrapped itself around him and the block of ice that held him, locked to him and to his shields, shields that seemingly had done little or nothing to protect him from the devastation he had unleashed onto the Bovarians—and Eleventh Regiment and those Telaryn troopers brave and determined enough to have breached the Bovarian defenses.

With the white chill came a soaring roaring cyclone of ice needles that felt as though they had shredded Quaeryt's uniform, all he wore, and flensed even the very flesh from his skin.

And then the flames of the Namer burned him even while he found himself in frozen agony . . . unable to speak or move . . . unable to close his eyes, unable to escape into unconsciousness . . .

. . . unable to escape the tens of thousands of wailing voices . . .

No matter where he seemed to be, or where he looked, there was first the chill, and the whiteness that never ended, even in darkness, but worse were the wailings, oh so many of them, voices . . . cries . . . so many of them, all pleading, questioning . . . as if . . . as if . . .

He could not go there, not after what he had done, and did not resist as the swirling storm of tiny white ice needles and lacy flakes swirled around him, then enfolded him even as it sliced away who and what he was, carrying him off in bits of whiteness until he was no more . . .

Then . . . as if in the eye of that storm, all was quiet, and he opened his eyes and beheld . . . whiteness, more whiteness everywhere. He looked down . . . what he wore was white. His arms were white . . . as were his hands . . . and even his fingernails . . . but before he could think about what that meant, or even where he was . . . the howling blizzard of white ice knives carved him into chips of ice and flakes of snow and swirled his being back into the storm.

Yet when the tempest subsided into intermittent flakes, burning flakes that buried him in chill, somewhere beyond the whiteness, he heard words, sounds carried on the howling storm that buffeted his ears, blinded his vision . . .

". . . he'll eat . . . drink . . . but . . . not hear . . ."

". . . and at night . . ."

". . . as always . . ."

". . . the doors hold?"

". . . so far . . ."

He winced as the storm grasped him again . . . and the blinding white turned to darkness out of which hurled white spears of ice that crashed against his shields, shields that were so difficult to hold, so tiring . . . but so necessary to keep out the worst of the wailing that assailed him . . .

". . . Bhayar insists . . ."

". . . how could he not . . ."

Bhayar . . . Bhayar? The name . . . it should have meant something, as once it had, but the meaning disintegrated under the assault of the ice and the white flakes that should have been soft and cold, but were not, as they cut and then burned his skin wherever they touched, they burrowed into his flesh and turned it to ice.

And . . . again . . . the voices, so close and yet so far.

". . . Subcommander, sir . . ."

". . . did what you had to . . ."

Did what you had to? Done under the sun, under the clouds, done for the crowds . . . to the crowds . . .

His eyes clinched shut, as he recalled the voices, the thousands of voices . . . and their pleas . . . or had they even had a chance to plead?

He let the storm carry him away, bearing the burning cold so much more easily than those voices he could not help but hear across the devastation of whiteness that stretched in all directions away from and around him.

". . . here but not here . . ."

". . . weeks now . . . Quaeryt . . ."

Quaeryt? Another name he should recall . . . so familiar, but did he want to remember it? Had there not been . . .

Once more he surrendered to the swirling storm before those forlorn wails surged over him.

Amid the swirls of ice and the endless snowflakes, there was a voice . . . a gentle voice, a voice pleading . . . and the words tore at him, yet did not burn or cut as did the snowflakes or the ice knives that flensed him into the ice mist where he did not have to think . . . before he once again stood in the tempest, to be cut apart once more.

He peered through the storm . . . but how could he, a man who had become nothing but swirling bits of ice and snow, even peer?

The voice faded as the storm rose once more, drowning out both the insistent wailings and the gentle voice.

But when it subsided into a mere flurry of white, that voice, a voice he should recognize, returned, and there was something . . . something beyond the wailing and the pleading of the other voices. He tried to look beyond the storm and whiteness that swirled in and around him, and then for a moment, he saw a figure seated beside him. "Who . . . ?"

"Are you here, dearest, really here?" Warm arms wrapped around him. "Please be here. Please stay here this time."

This time? Had he gone somewhere?

Then his eyes, eyes that had been open and seen nothing, saw her—saw Vaelora. Icy tears oozed down his cheeks. "You're . . . here."

"I've been here for days, dearest. You've so worried everyone. I'm here. I'm with you."

He looked around the room, a chamber whose walls were shimmering white stone, where even the single chair on which Vaelora sat was white, as was the one where he was seated. Even the bed and the coverlets were white, as was the ceiling, the stone floor, the square rug . . . everything . . .

"Where . . . ?" His voice was rusty.

"In a tower chamber of a High Holder's summer residence," replied Vaelora. "It's three milles north of the Chateau Regis."

"But . . . it's all white . . ."

"It is," she said, gently clasping his left hand.

As her warm grip tightened, he could feel something strange, wrong about his hand, as if he had but a thumb and two fingers. He looked down.

All his fingers were there, but when he tried to tighten his own fingers around hers, the little finger and the one beside it, the ring finger, for all that he had never worn a ring, did not move.

"My fingers . . ."

"That's all, dearest," Vaelora said warmly, squeezing his hand tightly. "Everything else is fine. And they may yet recover."

"But . . . ?" He looked down at his forearms, bare below the elbows. Every single hair was white, brilliant snow-white, not the blond-white of his hair, not brown or black. Snow-white, white against his honey-gold-colored skin.

"Your hair is white, too, but it looks good on you," Vaelora said quickly.

Quaeryt looked at his right hand. His fingernails were white as well. Someone had trimmed them, but they were solid white. Snow-white. Not painted in the Antiagon fashion. Just . . . white. He didn't want to think about that. Not when considering it might call back the storm. "How . . . how did you get here so quickly?"

"It . . . wasn't so quick. I had a farsight vision. You were surrounded by sheets of white rain. That was what it looked like, but I found out when I got here that it was ice. Then I had to persuade Aelina—and some of Bhayar's officers—to let me go. They feared a squad would not be sufficient protection, but I dared not take more."

Quaeryt had a sinking feeling. "Are matters that bad in Solis?"

"Not any longer. That's because of you and the imagers. Once word came about you . . ."

"Me?"

"Bhayar could explain that better than I."

Quaeryt could see she didn't want to talk about that, and as long as whatever difficulty had eased in Solis . . . but that raised a more urgent question. "What date is it?"

"The nineteenth of Feuillyt."

"Almost a month . . . a month?"

"Yes, dearest."

"When did you arrive?"

"A week ago Lundi."

"You've been here more than a week?"

She nodded. "At first you didn't hear me, but the last few days, something was different, and I kept hoping. Then you would stop listening and murmur about the wailing and the pleading . . ."

"What happened? Why can't I remember?"

"That's because you didn't see what happened," she said. "Khalis told me that when the ice flakes fell from everywhere you sat in the saddle and never moved. They had to pry the reins from your hand, and three of them had to lift you out of the saddle."

"You haven't told me what happened."

"You secured a great victory for Bhayar." Her words were even.

"How great a victory?" Even as he asked, he feared that he already knew. Still . . . he had to know. He disengaged his hand from hers and stood, twinges running through his bad left leg, then slowly walked, his legs shaking under him, even with Vaelora supporting him, toward the window, its interior trim white, the glass set in small panes suggesting that the frame was old and belonged to someone of wealth. *But then, High Holders seldom lacked for golds.*

"Dearest . . ." Vaelora stopped him before he could reach the window.

"What?" He looked into her warm brown eyes and saw only love and concern.

"Remember it is now fall, not harvest."

Why would she say that? Then, as he turned back to the small tower window, his eyes took in the seemingly endless brown and gray, the trees without leaves, and the few evergreens that he could see from the height of the tower even looking beaten down, he understood . . . and swallowed. "How much . . . ?"

Vaelora was silent.

"How much?" he repeated.

"A great area around the Chateau Regis, all the way from the isle of piers to a mille west of the chateau, nothing north of your battle lines within a mille survived. That is what Khalis said. All was ice for days. Even the river froze solid."

The river he understood, but so much else? "You saw this?"

"Most of the ice had melted when I arrived."

Quaeryt did not have to ask how many had died. "What about Rex Kharst?"

"He and all his family were in the Chateau Regis."

"Where is Bhayar?"

"Somewhere below, waiting, doing what he must, and hoping that you will be yourself again. I told him you would be."

"You saw?"

She smiled. "I know what I know."

As he turned from the window, he caught sight of an image in the wall mirror—a man with light honey-gold skin and snow-white hair, and white eyebrows, yet the face was yet that of a man young and in his prime, if haggard, except for the darkness in the black eyes, a darkness that went beyond mere black. For a moment, if only a moment, he wondered who that man might be, that man of winter.

Who indeed, to have done what has been done?

"Dearest . . . you have me . . . and you have our daughter."

Quaeryt stopped, then turned back to her, forcing a smile, sad as he knew it to be. "Yes, I do." *And I will need you both . . . more than even you know.*

"And we have our dreams . . ."

Ah, yes, the dreams of what will be . . . He kept smiling, hard as it was. "For them, for our daughter . . . there is tomorrow." *When all will change, change utterly.*